PENGUIN BOOKS

# BEAT DOWN TO YOUR SOUL
## What Was
## the Beat Generation?

Ann Charters has had a thirty-year involvement in reading, collecting, teaching, and writing about Beat literature.
She began collecting books written by Beat writers while
still a graduate student at Columbia University, and after
completing her doctorate she worked directly with Jack
Kerouac to compile a bibliography of his work. After his
death, she wrote the first Kerouac biography and edited the
posthumous collection of his *Scattered Poems*. She was the
general editor for the two-volume encyclopedia *The Beats:
Literary Bohemians in Postwar America,* as well as *The
Portable Beat Reader,* and she published a collection of her
photographic portraits in a book called *Beats & Company*.
More recently she edited two volumes of Kerouac's *Selected Letters* and *The Portable Jack Kerouac Reader*.

# BEAT

# DOWN

# TO YOUR SOUL

## What Was

## the Beat Generation?

*Edited with an Introduction by*

# Ann Charters

PENGUIN BOOKS

PENGUIN BOOKS

Published by the Penguin Group
Penguin Putnam Inc., 375 Hudson Street,
New York, New York 10014, U.S.A.
Penguin Books Ltd, 27 Wrights Lane,
London W8 5TZ, England
Penguin Books Australia Ltd, Ringwood,
Victoria, Australia
Penguin Books Canada Ltd, 10 Alcorn Avenue,
Toronto, Ontario, Canada M4V 3B2
Penguin Books (N.Z.) Ltd, 182–190 Wairau Road,
Auckland 10, New Zealand

Penguin Books Ltd, Registered Offices:
Harmondsworth, Middlesex, England

First published in Penguin Books 2001

1 3 5 7 9 10 8 6 4 2

Pages 659–663 constitute an extension of this copyright page.

CIP data available

ISBN 0 14 10.0151 8

Printed in the United States of America
Set in Fairfield
Designed by Cathryn S. Aison

Again, to Nora Lili and Mallay—

and to the next generation:

Andy and Timmy Charters,

Naomi, Leo, and Zoë Stoll,

Jordan and Gabriel Colyer,

William Hadd and Kelsey Brandon.


Here's some of what I inherited in 1936, described by Edward Sanders in *America,* volume I:


"Djuna Barnes *Nightwood*
John Dos Passos *The Big Money* (completing the trilogy *USA*)
Faulkner *Absalom, Absalom!*

"Robert Frost *A Further Range*
Dylan Thomas *Twenty-Five Poems*
George Orwell *Keep the Aspidistra Flying*

"The *Partisan Review* was reborn as an anti-Stalinist
    journal of the left
    It had begun in '34 sponsored by the NY John Reed club
    but, with the Popular Front,
    it began walking the path of the independent left
    publishing some of the best of American writing
                                        till the War.
"Allen Lane in England founded Penguin Books
    & what they called the Paperback Revolution began."


Here's some of what happened next, what I lived through. . . .

# CONTENTS

# PREFACE

*Beat Down to Your Soul: What Was the Beat Generation?* was conceived as a companion to *The Portable Beat Reader* to suggest the diversity of voices involved with this literary movement as it developed in post–World War II America. Originally the idea for the anthology occured to me a few years back, when I began to think about what the writers and critics themselves had said about the word "Beat" and the topic of the Beat Generation. In this new collection I have included all the material I considered important for which I could obtain reprint permission. I have tried not to duplicate commentaries included in the earlier anthologies that I have compiled for Penguin Books. For example, readers will find the two essays by Jack Kerouac on the Beat Generation that I discuss at length in the introduction to this volume in *The Portable Beat Reader* and *The Portable Jack Kerouac Reader*.

I decided to organize the selections in this anthology alphabetically, to make the presentation as different as possible from these two earlier volumes. This organization also seemed to suit the subject matter. Without being placed in arbitrary categories, the essays, reviews, poems, letters, and sketches are introduced by headnotes suggesting each author's connection to the Beat Generation. The volume also includes the transcript of a panel of several women writers of the Beat Generation, discussing (among other subjects) their responses to traditional gender roles in the 1950s. Finally, a chronology of selected books, magazines, films, and recordings relating to Beat Generation authors of 1950–2000 concludes the anthology, followed by the Selected Bibliography, which gives the sources for the material I have woven into my introduction and headnotes.

Many people have been of inestimable help to me in completing this project. As always, my husband, Samuel Charters, has been encouraging at every step of the way. He suggested the title of the anthology and wrote a tribute to the original hipster Lord Buckley for the book. At Viking Penguin, Paul Slovak and David Stanford enthusiastically supported my ideas; my editor, Michael Millman, was an untiring and steady source of good will and practical advice; and Bruce Giffords guided the book through copyediting and proofreading with exemplary care and insight. Compiling the anthology, I am thankful for the generosity of Brenda Frazer, Jeffrey Weinberg, Sandy Broyard, Carolyn Cassady, Gregory Corso, Diane di Prima, Ann Douglas, Lawrence Ferlinghetti, Nancy Peters, Bill Morgan, Bob Rosenthal, Joyce Johnson, Hettie Jones, Eileen Kaufman, Ken Kesey, Joanne Kyger, A. Robert Lee, Norman Mailer, Joanna McClure, Michael McClure, Fred McDarrah, David Meltzer, Peter Orlovsky, Ariel Parkinson, Edward Sanders, Gary Snyder, and Anne Waldman, who helped me make selections and sometimes wrote new material. Fred Courtright gave good advice about obtaining permissions. I am also grateful to Bob Chatain for reading a draft of my introduction, Jack Foley for supplying the Herbert Huncke quotation that begins the introduction, and John Tytell for sending me the *American Book Review* issue on the Beats. I thank Robert Hawley for providing a much appreciated clipping service to keep me up to date over the past quarter century about important events in the East Bay poetry scene. In San Francisco, Janice Belmont and Bill Belmont offered welcome rest and recreation while I was working on the anthology. In London, Faith Evans and John Stokes were good listeners when I described the project to them in its infancy. They told me, "Keep it personal!" Well, this is as personal as I get on the subject of the Beat Generation.

Finally, I wish to thank my friends Doreen Bell, Rose Kovarovics, and Helen Azevedo-Smith in the English Department office at the University of Connecticut in Storrs for their cheerful company and technical assistance during my hours at the Xerox machine. The students in my Beat Writers graduate seminar at UConn during the Spring 2000 term—including Justin Short, Jennifer Ridder, Michael

O'Neill, Daniel Kos, Thomas Higgins, and Miranda Green—gave intelligent feedback when I showed them various texts; their responses helped me to shape the anthology's contents. Sharon Fisher and Anita Hellstrom came up with several gems from articles about women in the 1950s in the collection of small-press periodicals housed in the Thomas J. Dodd Center at the Homer Babbidge Library. Philip Deslippe researched the early stages of the chronology of material related to the Beats, before he was called off to greener summer pastures in Scotland. To all of them, my heartfelt gratitude and thanks. I am responsible for the errors and omissions in this book, but as always, my students have helped immeasurably to clarify my ideas about my subject.

# INTRODUCTION

## What Was the Beat Generation?

When I said I was *beat* I was *beat,* man,
I was tired, exhausted, worn out. That's
what *I* meant.

—Herbert Huncke

Gary Snyder once told me, half seriously, that there was no Beat Generation—it consisted of only three or four people, and four people don't make up a generation. He was thinking about the group of friends in New York City—among them Herbert Huncke, Allen Ginsberg, William S. Burroughs, and Jack Kerouac—who met in 1944 and were the nucleus of the so-called generation. As the story goes, the idea that they all belonged to something called a "Beat Generation" occurred to Kerouac one evening in November 1948, during a long conversation with John Clellon Holmes, a new friend who was also an aspiring novelist. A decade later, in an article published in *Playboy* titled "The Origins of the Beat Generation," Kerouac remembered that he and Holmes "were sitting around trying to think up the meaning of the Lost Generation and the subsequent Existentialism and I said, 'You know, this is really a Beat Generation,' and he leapt up and said, 'That's it, that's right!' "

But who and what *was* the Beat Generation? In the article Kerouac defined it as "a swinging group of new American men" in the late 1940s who were "intent on joy" because they had survived World War II and possessed "wild selfbelieving individuality." The earlier term "Lost Generation," which Kerouac and Holmes were trying to define for each other, was equally hard to pin down. Representing an important period of cultural activity between the two world wars, it had also originated in a casual context. Apparently the term had been invented by Gertrude Stein shortly after World War I, during an encounter with a young French garage mechanic who was having difficulty repairing her car. As she waited for him to finish, Stein tried to find words to describe what she saw as the predicament of the young Frenchmen devastated by the carnage of the war who had to readjust to civilian life. Probably at the moments when the words "Lost Generation" spontaneously occured to Stein, and "Beat Generation" occurred to Kerouac, they reflected a personal vision of the world as much as any larger social reality. Later, when other people picked up the terms, the words unfolded like umbrellas that could expand to cover almost everything.

Kerouac himself shrugged off a precise definition of "Beat Generation" and used the word "beat" in different contexts as he struggled to make sense of his life. But the Beat label stuck long after the passing of the postwar era, all the while meaning different things to different people. For Snyder, who met Ginsberg and Kerouac in 1955, "beat" had nothing to do with the late 1940s. In Snyder's vision, it described "a particular state of mind" that occurred within "a definable time frame," from "sometime in the early fifties up until the mid-sixties when jazz was replaced by rock and roll and marijuana by LSD and a whole new generation of youth jumped on board and the name beatnik changed to hippie."

As Snyder's definition makes clear, there is no doubt that the "particular state of mind" went on for a considerable length of time. And of course more than four people were part of the Beat Generation. The writer Hettie Jones complained that in 1959, when she and her then-husband, LeRoi Jones, were putting out issues of *Yugen* magazine with the help of their friends in their New York apartment, the Beat Generation was "really a misnomer because at one point everyone identified with it could fit into my livingroom, and I didn't think that a whole generation could fit into my livingroom." Actually, by the end of the 1950s, many thousands of us throughout the United States felt that we belonged to the Beat Generation, even if we all didn't go on the road with Kerouac or take off our clothes with Ginsberg or get stoned with Huncke.

I first became aware in May 1956 that I was part of a community of disaffected Americans who would later be identified as members of the Beat Generation. As a nineteen-year-old college student, I attended a poetry reading in Berkeley with a blind date named Peter

Orlovsky, who thought he wanted a girlfriend and took me to hear his lover Allen Ginsberg read a newly completed poem, "Howl for Carl Solomon." Neither Peter nor Allen referred to himself as a Beat, nor did the five other poets on stage, nor the hundred people who crowded into the small theater along with us.The label surfaced eighteen months later, when the writers became news.

The reading I saw was the second performance of a reading in San Francisco that had been so powerful it was repeated by popular demand seven months later in Berkeley. Writing an essay with Gregory Corso about the 6 Gallery reading, which originally took place in San Francisco on October 7, 1955, Ginsberg described (in *Deliberate Prose*, 1957, pp. 239–40) the circumstances behind what was destined to become one of the most famous American poetry readings of the century:

> In the fall of 1955, a group of six unknown poets in San Francisco, in a moment of drunken enthusiasm, decided to defy the system of academic poetry, official reviews, New York publishing machinery, national sobriety and generally accepted standards of good taste, by giving a free reading of their poetry in a run down second rate experimental art gallery in the Negro section of San Francisco. They sent out a hundred postcards, put up signs in North Beach (Latin Quarter) bars, bought a lot of wine to get the audience drunk, and invited the well known Frisco Anarchist resident poet to act as Master of Ceremonies. Their approach was purely amateur and goofy, but it should be noted that they represented a remarkable lineup of experience and character—it was an assemblage of really good poets who knew what they were writing and didn't care about anything else. They got drunk, the audience got drunk, all that was missing was the orgy. This was no ordinary poetry reading. Indeed, it resembled anything but a poetry reading. The reading was such a violent and beautiful expression of their revolutionary individuality (a quality bypassed in American poetry since the formulations of Whitman), conducted with such surprising abandon and delight by the poets themselves, and presenting such a high mass of beautiful unanticipated poetry, that the audience, ex-

pecting some Bohemian stupidity, was left stunned, and the poets were left with the realization that they were fated to make a permanent change in the literary firmament of the States.

Twenty-nine-year-old Ginsberg had worked as a journalist and market researcher before he stunned his audience with his reading of "Howl for Carl Solomon" at the 6 Gallery. In addition to his genius for poetry, he also possessed a great talent for promoting himself and his friends. In his account of the 6 Gallery reading, he described the four other poets who read with him as if he were their press agent: Philip Lamantia was "a surrealist blood poet"; Michael McClure was the creator of "relatively sober mystical poetry"; Philip Whalen was "a strange fat young man from Oregon," author of "learned mystical-anarchic poems"; and Gary Snyder was "now occupied in the study of Chinese and Japanese preparatory for the drunken silence of a Zen monastery in Japan." Ginsberg's closest friend, Jack Kerouac, who was also present at the 6 Gallery reading and who would include an exuberant description of it in his novel *The Dharma Bums* (1958), got a paragraph of his own:

Perhaps the most strange poet in the room was not on the platform—he sat on the edge of it, back to the poets, eyes closed, nodding at good lines, swigging a bottle of California red wine—at times shouting encouragement or responding with spontaneous images—jazz style—to the long zig-zag rhythms chanted in *Howl*. This was Jack Kerouac, then unknown also, now perhaps the most celebrated novelist in America. Mr. Kerouac is also a superb poet, his poems are automatic, pure, brilliant, awesome, gentle, and unpublished as of yet.

Ginsberg was his own best interpreter, explaining in "The 6 Gallery Reading" that "*Howl* is built like a pyramid, in three parts, and ends in fantastic merciful tears—the protest against the dehumanizing mechanization of American culture, and an affirmation of individual particular compassion in the midst of a great chant." He wrote about himself in the third person:

The reading was delivered by the poet, rather surprised at his own power, drunk on the platform, becoming increasingly sober as he read, driving forward with a strange ecstatic intensity, delivering a spiritual confession to an astounded audience—ending in tears which restored to American poetry the prophetic consciousness it had lost since the conclusion of Hart Crane's *The Bridge,* another celebrated mystical work.

The 6 Gallery reading in the fall of 1955 precipitated Ginsberg's discovery of his vocation. His ecstatic experience reading "Howl for Carl Solomon" before an appreciative audience in the "run down second rate experimental art gallery in the Negro section of San Francisco" confirmed how he saw himself as a visionary moral poet. He never suffered from self-doubt again, either about his own genius or the existence of a Beat Generation.

Ginsberg didn't use the term "Beat Generation writers" in his account of the 6 Gallery reading. The term wasn't widely associated with a specific group of poets and novelists until the fall of 1957, after the publication of Kerouac's best-selling novel *On the Road* and the conclusion of the obscenity trial in San Francisco against Lawrence Ferlinghetti for publishing Ginsberg's *Howl and Other Poems* as number four in the City Lights Pocket Poets series. After the trial, in which Judge Clayton Horn concluded for the defendant that "Howl" had what he called "redeeming social content," the Beats became the first members of a bohemian literary movement in the United States to be tirelessly promoted by its leading poet while also being exploited by commercial interests, hounded by the national press, and ridiculed on television and in the movies.

The times were ripe for change. By the end of the 1950s, the country was experiencing the rumblings of widespread radical dissent, partly as a response to the tumultuous historical events of the Cold War, with the United States' bloody efforts to curtail the global expansion of Communism, and partly as a reaction against self-complacent conformity at home. Among other important events, Senator Joseph R. McCarthy had led a devastating Senate investigation of what he called "un-American activities" in the government and in the private sector; both the United States, under President Dwight Eisenhower, and the Soviet Union, under Premier Nikita Khrushchev, had built and tested hydrogen bombs; an armistice was negotiated in Korea after three years of fighting and the death of more than 25,000 men and women in the American armed services; Communist China observed its tenth birthday; and the Cuban rebel leader Fidel Castro waged a successful guerrilla war against the repressive regime of President Fulgencio Batista. Many Americans sensed that their country lacked a clear moral direction, even if—as Kerouac understood—no word existed in the English language to describe the feeling of alienation so brilliantly captured in the literature by French philosophers a decade before with the term "existentialism."

While Jean-Paul Sartre had in mind a prevailing human condition of anguish, abandonment, and despair, the word "beat" was less prescriptive. As slang, it sounded fresh, somehow more upbeat. It suggested the arrival of something unconventional and different from the mainstream, marginalized yet possessing potential force and authority. The term caught on because it could mean anything. It could even be exploited in the affluent wake of the decade's extraordinary technological innovations. Almost immediately, for example, advertisements by "hip" record companies in New York used the idea of the Beat Generation to sell their new long-playing vinyl records. In an issue of *The Village Voice* in November 1957, less than two months after the publication of *On the Road,* Atlantic Records took a whole column of advertising space in the newspaper, linking the Beat writers to the musical "beat" of its best-selling jazz records. This may have been the first advertisement to cash in on the Beats:

> Charles Mingus' **The Clown** (Atlantic LP 1260), with its improvised narration by Jean Shepherd in a jazz setting, unpremeditatedly has played right into the jazz-cum-poetry movement out in San Francisco ("heaping fresh fuel on the fire" according to the *Examiner*). This development helps to explain in just what way ours is a beat generation. Use the word "beat" as a noun rather than an adjective, and then it makes sense. This is the generation-of-the-beat and it is inspiring a new literature and a new music.
>
> If there is anything that the beat generation wants, it is to get back to fundamentals, to honest emotional responses—and that is why "funky" jazz has come to be their music above

all. Gratifyingly, this has made phenomenal sales successes of **The Great Ray Charles** (Atlantic LP 1259) and Milt Jackson's **Plenty Plenty Soul** (1269). John S. Wilson explained in a recent article how these men fashion the kind of jazz "that sticks to the ribs" out of the deep resources of the blues and the gospel song.

In talking about beat, we always come back to the Modern Jazz Quartet, who are now in Europe on an extended tour. In their absence, we'll turn many times to **The Modern Jazz Quartet,** their latest LP (1265), the swingin-est disc of them all.

*Atlantic is the label in tune with the BEAT generation. We produce the music with the BEAT for you. Write for free catalogue.*

In "The Origins of the Beat Generation," Kerouac had heralded "a revolution in manners in America." After the publication of *On the Road* and "Howl," the media leapt on the bandwagon, and by attacking the books that he and Ginsberg wrote, they helped to spread the word. During the late 1950s and early 1960s, numerous anthologies and books of poetry and fiction by Beat writers established the literary movement, but the term was so elusive, the writers themselves were so different, and the commercial fanfare was so excessive, with the "Beat" label used to sell everything from long-playing jazz records to black berets to bongos to television "road" programs such as *Route 66,* that readers and critics gave up trying to find a common aesthetic. To add to the confusion, "beat" was not only a literary movement that described a generation of writers (whether the writers liked it or not), but also a new lifestyle. "Beat" was literary. "Beatnik" was lifestyle. There might have been something called a Lost Generation, but there were no "Lost writers" or "Lostniks." Clearly there was something about the word "beat" that resonated for many Americans at mid-twentieth century.

Ginsberg didn't originate the term "Beat Generation," but he was the champion "beat" explainer of all time. As Ed Sanders described in his introduction to Ginsberg's volume of essays *Deliberate Prose* (2000), Ginsberg loved to teach: "If he opened his refrigerator door, he gave a lecture on the rice milk and organic food on the shelves." So with "Beat Generation." Like rice milk and organic food, the word "beat" was one of the poet's favorite foods for thought. Ginsberg's explanations always told you as much about him as about his subject, just as Kerouac's and Holmes's visions of "beat" essentially revealed much about themselves. The problem with "beat" was that when the writers first adopted it as an adjective to describe their generation, the word primarily had negative connotations. It was a hard scramble to make it stand for something good.

Ever the promoter, Ginsberg usually began by crediting his friend Herbert Huncke for passing on the word "beat" to his New York friends in the 1940s. At the time Huncke was a young hustler and drug addict from Chicago who introduced William Burroughs and Jack Kerouac to what was then known as "hip language," a slang vocabulary used by hipsters—streetwise drug users, jazz musicians, and others—in which the word "beat" (as in "Man, I'm beat . . .") meant being "without money, without a place to stay, without drugs for withdrawal symptoms." This street usage, according to Ginsberg, "meant exhausted, at the bottom of the world looking up or out, sleepless, wide-eyed, perceptive, rejected by society."

Ginsberg gave his own positive spin to the word "beat" when he added the qualities of "wide-eyed, perceptive" to its implications, insinuating that someone who was "beat" automatically possessed a private, mystic insight into the real nature of things, an essential quality now more frequently associated with the words "hip" and "cool." As a slang term, "beat" was widely used long before Huncke came to New York. In earlier usage, as for example by Zora Neal Hurston in her "Story in Harlem Slang," first published in *The American Mercury* in July 1942, the word "beat" was an unflattering adjective describing the lowest of the low. In the story Hurston included a conversation between two zoot-suited pimps who live off women. Meeting on 132nd Street, one of the pimps tries to bring the other one down: "Last night when I left you, you was beating up your gums and broadcasting about how hot you was. . . . Didn't I see you last night with dat beat chick, scoffing a hot dog? Dat chick you had was beat to de heels. Boy, you ain't no good for what you live." The word "beat" was so commonplace that Hurston saw no need to define it in her "Glossary of Harlem Slang" following the story, where she explained that "beating up your gums" meant "talking to no purpose."

In fact, the word "beat" has been traced back to the Civil War, according to John D. Billings's book *Hardtack and Coffee* (Boston, 1888). Originally it meant "a lazy man or a shirk who would by hook or by crook get rid of all military or fatigue duty that he could," but the term grew to have broader significance. As used by people in the world of circuses and traveling shows, "beat" metamorphosed into a word that meant to be in straitened circumstances or to have no place to stay. A half century later, the use of "beat" began to appear specifically in a drug context. In *The Man with the Golden Arm*, written in 1947 and published in 1949, Nelson Algren used the word "beat" as an adjective describing the appearance of a Chicago heroin addict in acute physical distress: "This guy got somethin' eatin' on him, he got that beat look them Safari junkies got." This is the context of the word as Huncke used it when he explained it to Burroughs and Kerouac. In the drug world, "beat" was also used as a verb meaning to be cheated or robbed. When Burroughs added a glossary of terms after his preface to *Junky* (1953), his first published novel, he had in mind this negative connotation of "beat." There Burroughs defined it as "to take someone's money. For example, addict A says he will buy junk for addict B but keeps the money instead. Addict A has 'beat' addict B for the money."

Ginsberg emphasized a different interpretation of "beat" in an effort to deflect its negative connotations, insisting that the word had spiritual implications beyond its use as a slang term by junkies, pimps, and jazz musicians. To Ginsberg, being "beat" implied being "wide-eyed" and "open" in a sense explored by the earlier poets William Blake and Walt Whitman, that is, "receptive to a vision." In "The Origins of the Beat Generation," Kerouac said that he discovered the religious implications of "beat" in 1954, when he took a trip back to his hometown in Lowell, Massachusetts. Visiting Ste. Jeanne d'Arc, one of the Catholic churches of his childhood, Kerouac heard "the holy silence in the church" and made a connection between the words "beat" and "beatific." As defined by *Webster's Collegiate Dictionary*, "beatific" means "possessing or imparting beatitude; having a blissful or benign appearance: saintly, angelic." This usage of "beatific" is much older than the slang term "beat." "Beatific" was first used in print in 1639, in the sense of a "beatific vision," or the "direct knowledge of God enjoyed by the blessed in heaven."

In the introduction to *The Beat Book* (1996), an anthology of writings edited by Anne Waldman, Ginsberg tried to put the conversation about the Beat Generation between Kerouac and Holmes in 1948 into a broader perspective. Ginsberg added a historical context, saying that his friends were trying to characterize the specific quality of their own time after the nuclear holocaust that ended World War II. In contrast to Hemingway's dramatization of the psychological distress of the Lost Generation survivors of World War I in *In Our Time* and *The Sun Also Rises*, Kerouac and Holmes were fascinated by physical decay and the aimlessness of the down-and-out characters they saw hanging out around the cafeterias and cheap amusement centers in Times Square. As a Columbia undergraduate, Ginsberg interpreted this urban decay as a sign of widespread nuclear fallout after atomic bombs destroyed Hiroshima and Nagasaki. In their novels, his friends had their own interpretations of the midtown scene.

In 1948–49, in the process of writing *The Town and the City* (1950), Kerouac included a description of what he called the Times Square "riff-raff" or "drifters" in Part Four of the novel. In *The Town and the City* Kerouac didn't use the term "Beat Generation" to describe the people he saw hanging out in Times Square. In Part Five of the novel, however, he wrote that one of his characters wanders " 'beat' around the city in search of some other job or benefactor or 'loot' or 'gold.' When you were loaded with loot and having your kicks, that was living; but when you were hung up without gold and left beyond the reach of kicks, that was a drag." Kerouac was using Huncke's interpretation of the word, the idea that beat "meant beaten. The world against me." It was only in conversation with Holmes, making an effort to characterize the quality of his time in a single phrase, that Kerouac made his inspired reach and said, "Ah, this is nothing but a Beat Generation." He had in mind the soft, flat, yet oddly musical and resonant sound of the word "beat" as Huncke had said it hunched over a cup of coffee in a Times Square cafeteria. The sound apparently suggested to Kerouac a new language expressing a darkly mysterious force out of which a new art could be fashioned, the powerfully transformative condition of being not only "down and out" but also "full of intense conviction."

In 1951, after his whirlwind cross-country trips with his Denver friend Neal Cassady, an adept at "bumming and hitchhiking" across

America, Kerouac portrayed Cassady as the epitome of "beat" when he completed the draft of a novel later published as *On the Road.* This was written shortly after Burroughs had finished *Junky,* his first book about his drug addiction, and Holmes had completed his first successful novel, *Go,* in which he dramatized the lives of his friends Kerouac, Ginsberg, Cassady, and others in their circle, whom he also regarded as members of a new generation. Unlike Burroughs, Holmes was an old-fashioned Romantic. In the last pages of his autobiographical novel, Holmes idealized his friends as "children of the night: everywhere wild, everywhere lost, everywhere loveless, faithless, homeless." In *Go,* Holmes, who named himself "Hobbes," asks himself, "But why did I dignify their madness? And why does everything else seem spiritually impoverished?"

Holmes and Kerouac romanticized the lives of drifters and jazz musicians much as Norman Mailer was to idealize the figure of the hipster a few years later in his essay "The White Negro" (1957). In "The Black Boy Looks at the White Boy" in *Nobody Knows My Name* (1961), James Baldwin understood that these contemporary white writers were appropriating what they imagined as the specially soulful quality of black experience to empower themselves. "I had tried to convey something of what it felt like to be a Negro and no one had been able to listen; they wanted their romance." Later Holmes wrote me a letter trying to explain the fascination that the Times Square drifters held for him and Kerouac in the years shortly after the end of World War II.

Why did "Hobbes" yearn to know every aspect of the Times Square world? Undifferentiated reality. That is, life lived moment to moment as it unfolds. Cerebral young men (and women, too, I'm sure) are attracted to the spontaneous, the improvised, the random, thus the wondrous. Also, to everything beyond the pale, outside the firelight, everything that has escaped the circumscribed. To "Hobbes," the Times Square world was a gigantic anteroom, off which myriad other worlds opened—hustlers, thieves, whores, pimps, lost kids, musicians, etc. A variation on a tag-line for a radio show of those days: "There are three million stories in the NAKED CITY. This is one of them." I was hungry to know everything then. It was a thrill to be young, energetic, imaginative, curious and selfless in the New York of those days. One could entertain the notion that a long, rich, varied shelf of books lay ahead that might start to do for one's New York what Balzac had done so profligately for his Paris. And we were unafraid in those days—alike of such audacious dreams *and* the chancy areas of experience into which we were venturing. (Holmes to Ann Charters, June 23, 1987)

*Go* was published in October 1952. It appeared after two other novels had come out that year also exploring similar subjects summarized by the *San Francisco Chronicle* as "dope, bebop, and bohemia." Set in Greenwich Village, George Mandel's *Flee the Angry Strangers,* in which a troubled white teenage girl "drops out" of her middle-class family to become a runaway and a drug addict, was indebted to Nelson Algren's *The Man with the Golden Arm,* published three years before, about an ex-GI heroin addict in the Chicago slums. But Mandel's book had none of the grit and despair of Algren's naturalist fiction, nor Algren's passion for exposing what he called "the disease of isolation" in American society.

Chandler Brossard's *Who Walk in Darkness,* about a young man suffering in Greenwich Village from a bad case of writer's block, was praised by the San Francisco critic Kenneth Rexroth as being the first novel to explore a "beat" consciousness, but New York critics were less impressed. On June 22, 1952, Gilbert Millstein (who five years later was to praise Kerouac's *On the Road* so highly that it rocketed to the best-seller list), wrote in *The New York Times* that Brossard's hipster characters "talk a kind of jargon—and the author has rendered it with chilling accuracy—compounded of bop terms, the intellectual leavings of little magazines and big books, and any psychoanalysis they happen to have borne away from the couch." Brossard later explained that he had taken Albert Camus as his literary mentor, trying to write what he described as "the first Existentialist novel in America." Kerouac dismissed the novel as completely unimportant. He thought Brossard would have done better to leave Greenwich Village and hang out uptown in Times Square, where he would have met real hipsters, not the downtown literary pretenders.

Published after *Flee the Angry Strangers* and *Who Walk in Dark-*

*ness, Go* was recognized by many critics as a novel of what seemed to them to be more troubling substance. They were intrigued by Holmes's insistence that there was an entire generation of disaffiliated Americans, some doing drugs and digging bebop and Existentialism, others searching desperately for new values. Frederick Morton in the New York *Herald Tribune Book Review* concluded his remarks about the novel: " 'A beat generation,' philosophizes Paul Hobbes toward the end. We hope he is not right. But the adjective seems useful. This is a beat novel." Shortly after *Go* was published, Gilbert Millstein contacted Holmes and suggested that he write an article for *The New York Times* defining what he meant by the term "Beat Generation." Holmes told me, "I sat down, discovered I didn't really know what I meant by 'the beat generation,' thought about it and wrote the piece in four days. It created a stir."

Holmes's article appeared on November 16, 1952, while *Go* was in the bookstores. In "This Is the Beat Generation," Holmes defined "beat" as a particularly American brand of Existentialism, involving "a sort of nakedness, of mind, and, ultimately, of soul . . . a feeling of being reduced to the bedrock of consciousness." Rather than accepting the conventional view that Americans comprised a complacently prosperous, homogeneous population, Holmes focused on the young, middle-class rebels whose behavior had begun to challenge mainstream society in the United States. He wrote, "The absence of personal and social values is to them, not a revelation shaking the ground beneath them, but a problem demanding a day-to-day solution. *How* to live seems to them much more crucial than *why.*"

Holmes's article was ahead of its time and didn't reach a national audience. I read it in 1967, when it was reprinted in his collection *Nothing More to Declare.* By then I caught a glimpse of my own rebellious spirit in Holmes's description of the teenage members of the Beat Generation. As early as 1950, when I was thirteen, the media had given me evidence that I didn't fit in, when *Life* magazine surveyed its teenage readers and published a list of their most popular idols: Louisa May Alcott, Joe DiMaggio, Roy Rogers, General Douglas MacArthur, Clara Barton, Doris Day, Florence Nightingale, and Abraham Lincoln. In 1955 I found myself sympathizing with the frustrated, angry high school characters alienated from their parents and their peers played by James Dean, Natalie Wood, and Sal Mineo in the film

*Rebel Without a Cause.* Watching the movie after I had left home for college, I identified with the so-called rebel's confusion. I shared his sense of a yawning gulf between his stark view as a teenager of the hypocrisy of American social codes and his parents' nervous protestations that everything was just fine. In 1956, when J. D. Salinger published his novel *The Catcher in the Rye,* as well as his later stories in *The New Yorker,* which I read avidly, I felt that I had found the first contemporary writer who seemed to speak directly to my sense of disaffection with the narrow conformity of American life.

In February 1958, Holmes published his second article on the Beats, "The Philosophy of the Beat Generation," in *Esquire.* By this time the Beat Generation was a fiercely debated topic. The occasion of Holmes's article was not the publication of one of his novels, but the success of *On the Road* after its publication in September 1957. Holmes began his article with a reference to Kerouac's novel, quoting the review in *The New York Times* by Gilbert Millstein calling it "the most beautifully executed, the clearest and most important utterance" yet made by an American writer. Holmes insisted that the quality that made the characters in the novel "beat," and not just "slum-bred petty criminals and icon-smashing Bohemians," was that they were on a spiritual quest. He quoted Kerouac as saying, "The Beat Generation is basically a religious generation."

As in Holmes's earlier article, he suggested that the Beat Generation was a harbinger of momentous social change without specifying what these changes would be, but he didn't write from his own personal experience. Instead he referred to statistics to establish the antisocial, rebellious behavior of the members of the group, noting "more delinquency, more excess, more social irresponsibility in it than in any generation in recent years . . ." Kerouac disliked the article because he felt that Holmes emphasized criminality, so Jack dug out an essay he had written during the summer of 1957 at the request of a Viking Press publicist, Patricia MacManus, who had asked him to explain what he meant by the Beat Generation, for a publicity release being prepared for the then-forthcoming *On the Road.* In March 1958, *Esquire* published Kerouac's essay, which the magazine titled "Aftermath: The Philosophy of the Beat Generation."

Kerouac told Ginsberg that he wrote the article, originally called "About the Beat Generation" (as in *The Portable Jack Kerouac*), to show MacManus that Beat was a religious movement prophesied in

Oswald Spengler's *Decline of the West.* The *Esquire* version of Kerouac's essay dropped a long paragraph in which he described the different visions "all inspired and fervent and free of Bourgeois-Bohemian Materialism" of his friends who were what Kerouac called "the early hipsters" in the original group of Beats: Herbert Huncke, Allen Ginsberg, William Burroughs, Neal Cassady, Gregory Corso, Gary Snyder, Philip Whalen, Philip Lamantia, and Alene Lee, the only woman in the crowd. Kerouac's love affair with her was his subject in *The Subterraneans,* the novel published at the time that his *Esquire* article was on the newsstands.

Kerouac opened this essay with his most eloquent definition of the term:

> THE BEAT GENERATION, that was a vision that we had, John Clellon Holmes and I, and Allen Ginsberg, in an even wilder way, in the late Forties, of a generation of crazy, illuminated hipsters suddenly rising and roaming America, serious, curious, bumming and hitchhiking everywhere, ragged, beatific, beautiful in an ugly graceful new way—a vision gleaned from the way we had heard the word "beat" spoken on streetcorners on Times Square and in the Village, in other cities in the downtown city night of postwar America—beat, meaning down and out but full of intense conviction. . . .

Kerouac insisted that Beat "never meant juvenile delinquents, it meant characters of a special spirituality who didn't gang up but were solitary Bartlebies staring out the dead wall window of our civilization." Members of the generation took drugs, listened to bop music, "talking strange, being poor and glad, prophesying a new style for American culture, a new style (we thought) completely free from European influences (unlike the Lost Generation), a new incantation." In this essay, Kerouac's contribution to the evolution of the meaning of "beat" was to blur the distinction between a person who was "beat" and the "hipster," an earlier slang term for people outside the mainstream. After listing the hipsters' and the Beats' bebop heroes—Wardell Gray, Lester Young, Dexter Gordon, Willie Jackson, Lennie Tristano—Kerouac admitted that "as to the actual existence of a Beat Generation, chances are it was really just an idea in our minds."

In this early essay, Kerouac explained that the Beat Generation originally had few members and was short lived, disappearing only a few years after its emergence. During the Korean War in the early 1950s, its original members "vanished into jails and madhouses, or were shamed into silent conformity." Ginsberg had chronicled their wasted lives in the first part of "Howl for Carl Solomon." Then, Kerouac continued, in the mid-1950s, "by some miracle of metamorphosis, suddenly, the Korean post-war youth emerged cool and beat, had picked up the gestures and the style, soon it was everywhere." Bop was played on the radio alongside commercial popular music, terms like "go" and "crazy" in hipster language became common usage, drugs were available everywhere (including tranquilizers such as Valium), and "even the clothes style of the beat hipsters carried over to the new Rock'n'Roll youth via Montgomery Clift (leather jacket), Marlon Brando (T-shirt), and Elvis Presley (long sideburns). . . ."

Shrugging off a formal definition of "Beat," Kerouac attempted to analyze "what it means," answering, "who knows?" He acknowledged that "even in this late stage of civilization when money is the only thing that really matters to everybody, I think perhaps it is the Second Religiousness that Oswald Spengler prophesied for the West." Then Kerouac went on to describe the "stoned-out visions" of his Beat friends (this passage was cut in the magazine article):

Strange talk we'd heard among the early hipsters, of "the end of the world" at the "second coming," of "stoned-out visions" and even visitations, all believing, all inspired and fervent and free of Bourgeois-Bohemian Materialism such as Philip Lamantia's being knocked off his chair by the Angel and his vision of the books of the Fathers of the Church and of Christ crashing through Time, Gregory Corso's visions of the devil and celestial Heralds, Allen Ginsberg's visions in Harlem and elsewhere of the tearful Divine Love, William S. Burroughs' reception of the word that he is the One Prophet, Gary Snyder's Buddhist visions of the vow of salvation, peotl visions of all the myths being true, Philip Whalen's visions of malific flashes and forms and the roof flying off the house, Jack Kerouac's numerous visions of Heaven, the "Golden Eternity," bright light in the night woods, Herbert Huncke's geekish visions of Armaggedon (experienced in Sing Sing), Neal Cas-

sady's visions of reincarnation under God's will . . . Alene
Lee's vision of everything as mysterious electricity. . . .

Kerouac concluded that in "the sunset of our culture," the effect of
the Beat Generation "has taken root," but "what difference does it
make?"

Like Holmes, Kerouac romanticized the alienation of the founding members of the Beat Generation, but by blurring the distinction
between hipster and beat, he made the term sound much more attractive. He attempted a more definitive essay on the subject, "The Origins of the Beat Generation," published in *Playboy* in June 1959.
Kerouac had written it the previous November, when he had been invited to speak at a symposium at Hunter College on the topic "Is
There a Beat Generation?" Showing up on stage drunk to hide his self-
consciousness, he read his essay before a panel of "literary lions" including the British novelist Kingsley Amis, the Princeton University
anthropologist Ashley Montagu, and the *New York Post* editor James
Wechsler. In the debacle that followed, when (as Kerouac told his
friend John Montgomery) he "generally acted like a mad drunken fool
just off a freight train," Kerouac became the leading representative of
the lifestyle he and Ginsberg had popularized.

"The Origins of the Beat Generation" was Kerouac's fullest account of "his" generation, and like all his writing, it was intensely personal. This time he said that he traced the beginnings of the Beat
Generation back to the 1880s, in the antics of his fun-loving immigrant
French-Canadian family in the backwoods of New England. The
emergence of bop music in the early 1940s, and the city-smart hipsters
who hung around the New York City jazz clubs and "kept talking about
the same things" Kerouac liked, were the next phase of what he saw as
the evolution of the Beat Generation, "the slogan or label for a revolution of manners in America."

In the *Playboy* essay, Kerouac divided what he called "the hipsters,
or beatsters," into two groups, "cool and hot," and tried to differentiate
between their styles, describing himself as "a hot hipster" who "finally
cooled it in Buddhist meditation." He thought that "cool hipsters"
such as the jazz musicians Lennie Tristano and Miles Davis were
Beat. Beat progenitors also included the film noir actors Peter Lorre,
John Garfield, and Humphrey Bogart, as well as (among many others)

Joan Crawford, Clark Gable, W. C. Fields, the Three Stooges, the Marx Brothers, Laurel and Hardy, and "the inky ditties of old cartoons (Krazy Kat with the irrational brick)."

By the time Kerouac published "The Origins of the Beat Generation," his readers probably thought that the term had been defined more coherently by its critics than by its originators. The confusion was there to stay. The invention of the word "beatnik" by the journalist Herb Caen in his *San Francisco Chronicle* column on April 2, 1958, adding the "-nik" suffix as in the Soviet Union's recent space launch *Sputnik,* even suggested that it was vaguely subversive to be "Beat" during the Cold War.

Some confusion also existed about who actually were the members of the Beat Generation. Kerouac and Ginsberg described New York City and the Bay Area in Northern California as the locations attracting disaffiliated writers, musicians, and artists in the postwar years, but people who identified with "Howl for Carl Solomon" and *On the Road* inhabited cities and towns throughout the United States, as witnessed by the proliferation of the little magazines that they spun off on electric typewriters and mimeograph machines in the early 1960s. Forty years earlier, little magazines published by small presses had begun a tradition of supporting avant-garde writers in the United States. To establish a new literary movement, Ginsberg understood that he needed to get his poetry and the writing of his friends Kerouac and Burroughs into important little magazines such as the *Chicago Review* and the *Black Mountain Review.* This would help him wrest control from the academic poets who he thought were stifling American literature. Ginsberg was right. As Thomas Pynchon later wrote in his introduction to *Slow Learner* (1984),

The conflict in those days [the late '50s and early '60s] was, like most everything else, muted. In its literary version it shaped up as traditional vs. Beat fiction. Although far away, one of the theatres of action we kept hearing about was at the University of Chicago. There was a "Chicago School" of literary criticism, for example, which had a lot of people's attention and respect. At the same time, there had been a shakeup at the *Chicago Review* which resulted in the Beat-oriented *Big Table* magazine. "What happened at Chicago" became shorthand for some unimaginable subversive threat.

As a young writer, Pynchon found the Beats' linguistic freedom in the fiction and poetry that he read in the *Evergreen Review* "an eye-opener." After the successful *Howl* trial, outspoken and subversive literary magazines sprung up like wild mushrooms throughout the United States. Not all of the writers creating them considered themselves members of Kerouac and Ginsberg's Beat Generation, but taken together, they formed a roiling "underground" literary movement in rebellion against the mainstream. The poet Carol Bergé recognized that "in storefronts and walkups in Cleveland, Wichita, New York, Chicago, and San Francisco, a related generation, who came alive simultaneously with the Beats, was producing literary small-press magazines that published the early poems, plays, first books, and interesting adventures into multimedia of the era from 1956–1980." For example, in Taos, New Mexico, *Suck-Egg Mule—A Recalcitrant Beast* (1961), on sale for fifteen cents an issue, announced that "Contemporary poetry as such is a vast amorphous dung heap" and urged its readers to fight the censorship of the U.S. Postal authorities: "They will actually go so far as to disregard the purpose and intent of the artist and to read into it misconceptions that arise only out of their own sick subconscious."

*Olé,* published in Bensenville, Illinois, in 1965, proclaimed itself "A magazine for all those unacknowledged legislators of the world, especially those who are *really* unacknowledged." *Mother,* "a Journal of New Literature" published at first at Carleton College, Northfield, Minnesota, then in Galesburg, Illinois, New York City, and Dallas, Texas, featured work by the unknown poets Ted Berrigan, Ed Sanders, Ron Padgett, Tom Clark, Lewis MacAdams, John Wieners, James Schuyler, and Bobbie Creeley, the then-wife of Robert Creeley. Throughout the United States, little magazines declared their editorial independence and challenged the mainstream, or as *Yowl'*s co-editors George Montgomery and Erik Kiviat put it in 1963:

This is YOWL #2, still swinging to you thru the grasping tendrils of censorship & puritanism. We are alive; a living organism. We are here to challenge the essence of Death taking root in our culture: we fling our omnipotent words to the ground at the feet of the world and YOWL for freedom of expression. Join us in our crusade, Poets & People: LIVE & GROOVE IT!

In the creative tumult of the burgeoning literary underground of the 1950s and 1960s, the writers didn't cohere in any absolute lines of allegiance to "schools" of influence. The categories came later, particularly after the editor Donald M. Allen organized the poets in his influential anthology *The New American Poetry* (1960) into five groups: poets associated with *Black Mountain Review* and *Origin* magazine, poets associated with the San Francisco Renaissance, the Beat Generation poets (Kerouac, Ginsberg, Corso, and Orlovsky), the New York poets, and the "younger poets." The actual situation was much more fluid. For readers of *The Dharma Bums*, for example, Gary Snyder belonged to both the San Francisco Renaissance and the Beat Generation groups. For some reviewers, the poetry of Denise Levertov in the 1950s was considered "Beat," but her later work was not. Categories were made by the editors, critics, and historians, not the poets themselves. What was clear was that by the end of the 1950s, a radical change was occurring in what Ferlinghetti called "the world of poetry," when "the center of gravity left the hallowed precincts of the East Coast establishment" and became "raunchier, wilder, and woollier."

Determining who belongs and who does not belong to the Beat Generation is a challenging exercise, because while Kerouac, Holmes, and Ginsberg named and promoted it, many disaffected writers and artists throughout the United States were beginning to recognize themselves as belonging to a far-flung underground community celebrating "wild selfbelieving individuality" by the time that Ginsberg had moved to San Francisco and written "Howl for Carl Solomon." Ginsberg's letter to his Bay Area friend John Allan Ryan on September 9, 1955, gave a sense of this community of what Ginsberg called "angelheaded hipsters" in the opening lines of "Howl." Ginsberg described the forthcoming 6 Gallery reading and his pleasure in his new friendships with the "Berkeley characters" such as Gary Snyder whom Allen was meeting after he had moved from San Francisco to his cottage on Milvia Street. In a postscript at the end of the letter, he told Ryan that he was enclosing "a piece" of a poem ["Howl for Carl Solomon"] whose lines "read a little more crudely than they will with a little work clearing up syntax, etc. There's a whole section about cocksuckers & madhouses & police & jazz. City Lights will put it out as a pocket pamphlet next year—they have a Series now." A short time later, after the *Howl* trial in San Francisco and the success of *On the Road,* the

Beat Generation had become news. Ginsberg's letter to Richard Eberhart and his essay on "Poetry, Violence, and the Trembling Lambs" defended his practice of poetry for a general audience and argued that "Howl" was not a "negative howl of protest," but rather "an act of sympathy."

By the end of the 1950s, books by Ginsberg, Kerouac, Burroughs, Ferlinghetti, and others had made such a strong impact on thousands of readers that their authors were widely perceived as belonging to a different generation, and controversy about the Beats waged hot and furious. As historians Douglas T. Miller and Marion Nowak understood in *The Fifties: The Way We Really Were* (1975):

> The Beats made the establishment afraid because they were a genuine bunch of dissenters; they were humanitarian, attractively hedonistic, very vaguely left wing, and most of all, popular. That gave them a dangerous power. That is why virtually every established commentator overreacted so strongly against the Beats. The mass media, since it served the mainstream, had slightly different attitudes toward the Beat revolt than did the literary establishment. But their motivation was the same: a perceived need to smash this appealing movement by belittling it.
>
> The innumerable articles such publications as *Time, Life,* and *Look* printed on the Beat Generation inevitably referred to the public's fascination with these figures. That fascination was also reflected in the many ways kids imitated Beats—in the proliferation of coffeehouses, poetry readings, jazz listening, and hip slang later in the decade. They were seemingly superficial things. But they were the most visible part of the disaffection young Americans were channeling in new directions. This disaffection, of course, had been reflected already by most of the modern novelists of alienation [Norman Mailer, Saul Bellow, Ralph Ellison, Kurt Vonnegut, Richard Yates, among others]. But in the late fifties some few people understood it was time to do more than be cynical and disaffected. The Beats were among these people, and they were the first in the postwar years to use literature as one of their tools. They attracted so many young people because, through

the mass media, they flamboyantly spoke of the possibilities of choice and change. Such ideas repelled the conservative forces in America, which needed abdication, acquiescence, or at least apathy to survive. Attacking the Beats was first of all a recognition that this statistically tiny group disproportionately countered such acquiescence.

In the late 1950s the belittling responses of academic critics such as Robert Brustein in *Horizon* ("The Cult of Unthink") or mainstream critics such as Paul O'Neil in *Life* magazine ("The Only Rebellion Around") suggest the intolerance of most of their contemporaries toward the Beat writers' mission to confront and transform their world. During the postwar years in the United States, a narrowly conservative literary establishment dominated criticism in journals such as the *Hudson, Kenyon,* and *Partisan* reviews. Cautious in the wake of McCarthyism, most American intellectuals believed that Bohemianism was no longer possible after the glorious years in London and Paris during the 1920s, with the extraordinary experimental work of avant-garde Modernists such as T. S. Eliot, Gertrude Stein, and Ernest Hemingway. As William Phillips wrote in a 1952 *Partisan Review* article, "The most serious artists are now concerned with sales, markets, publicity, and public response."

Kerouac, Holmes, Ginsberg, and their friends thought differently, and their commitment to "choice and change" was timely. On September 25, 1957, less than three weeks after the publication of *On the Road,* the United States Supreme Court ruled that racial segregation in the schools was unconstitutional. In Little Rock, Arkansas, nine black teenagers defied white mobs and a hostile governor and marched into Central High School, supported by federal marshals. In the decades of the Cold War, the Beat Generation writers inspired other generations of writers throughout Eastern and Western Europe as the United States and the Soviet Union fought a quietly murderous tug-of-war for nuclear arms supremacy, while the social fabric of this country unraveled during the civil rights era, protest against the Vietnam War, and the reemergence of the Feminist movement, among the many momentous changes at home.

In the wake of the social changes that they had, in part, helped to call forth and encourage, the Beat writers continued to publish and attract oncoming generations of appreciative readers. In recent years, a new spirit has evolved, expressed by both a wider acceptance by academic critics and an affectionate self-parody by the writers themselves. The phenomenon known as the Beat Generation has become part of the fabric of cultural life in the United States, and the weave seems enduringly strong.

# PART ONE

---

## Writers on the Beat Generation

## (1948–2000)

People keep seeing destruction or rebellion in Jack's writing, and *Howl,* but that is a very minor element, actually; it only seems to be so to people who have accepted standard American values as permanent. What we are saying is that these values are not really standard nor permanent, and we are in a sense I think ahead of the times. . . . When you have a whole economy involved in some version of moneymaking—this just is no standard of values. That it seems to offer a temporary security may be enough to keep people slaving for it. But meanwhile it destroys real value. And it ultimately breaks down. Whitman long ago complained that unless the material power of America were leavened by some kind of spiritual infusion we would wind up among the "fabled damned." It seems we're approaching that state as far as I can see. Only way out is individuals taking responsibility and saying what they actually feel—which is an enormous human achievement in any society. That's just what we as a "group" have been trying to do. To class that as some form of "rebellion" in the kind of college-bred social worker doubletalk . . . misses the huge awful point.

—Allen Ginsberg to Louis Ginsberg,
November 30, 1957

# GEORGE BARKER

GEORGE BARKER (1913–1991) was one of the contemporaries of the Beat writers who could neither admire nor ignore them. Born in Essex, England, Barker lived in New York and California in his twenties. Then after more than a decade in England, Italy, and Spain, he returned to the United States in 1957 and stayed for two years, reading his poetry at a dozen American colleges, before he went back to live permanently in Europe. In the poem "Circular from America," Barker attacked with the playful guns of comic doggerel what he considered the pretentiousness of some early Beat writers and their followers. The poem first appeared in the English little magazine X (1959) and was included in Barker's collection *The View from a Blind I* (1962). Impressed almost despite himself by Ginsberg's "Howl for Carl Solomon," Barker acknowledged in one of his "IX Beatitudes to Denver," a later poem in *The View from a Blind I,* that

> To Ginsberg reality has, for a longwinded moment,
> Broken down, howled, and shown her disconsolate heart.
> It is much to his honor that he has not attempted
> To edit her real hysteria. Or his own.

---

## *Circular from America*

> Against the eagled
> Hemisphere
> I lean my eager
> Editorial ear
> And what the devil
> You think I hear?
> I hear the Beat
> No not of the heart
> But the dull pulpitation
> Of the New Art

As, on the dead tread
Mill of no mind,
It follows its leaders
Unbeaten behind.
O Kerouac Kerouac
What on earth shall we do
If a single Idea
Ever gets through?
The English have seventy
Gods and no sauce
(The French have Voltaire
And Two Maggots of course)
But $1/2$ an idea
To a hundred pages
Now Jack, dear Jack,
That ain't fair wages
For laboring through
Prose that takes ages
Just to announce
That Gods and Men
Ought all to study
The Book of Zen.
If you really think
So low of the soul
Why don't you write
On a toilet roll?
And as for Rexroth
That angry king
He'd court anyone
Or any thing.
If you pick your judgments
Up in the street
Why be so bloody
Indiscreet
As to display 'em
Like a dirty sheet?
O pen is alive
I beg you tell 'em
What wouldn't we give

For some cerebellum?
Whole chapters and verses
Of bric-à-brac
Will bring Carlos Williams
And not a dove back.
"I first met Dean
Not long after my wife
And I split up."*
Gawd, what a life.
I'm a Dharma Bum.
Gawd, I'm a toad.
I'm wide. I'm out.
I'm off the Road.

But on Third Avenue
(Like Rome only more so
A street as gregarious
As any Corso)†
The shady bars
Open at morning
Like nenuphars
And the Beats yawn in
From their motor cars.
O it's early to bed
You story tellers
If you're not on Fulbrights
Or Rockefellers.
And only the blondes
In their skin tight jeans
Are living on private
Or pubic means.
Whaddya want?
A spade?‡ A fink?§
Don't goof, cripple.
Man, I stink.

---

* The opening of *On the Road*. [All footnotes are by George Barker.]
† Gregory Corso, author of *Gasoline*.
‡ Negro.
§ Homosexual.

And the silver towers
Of vanity sink
Into the golden
Seas of drink,
And round and round
At the fiery brink
Fly those who do every
Thing but think.
And all the while
From Maine to Utah
The virgins arrive
On foot and scooter
With bags that will never
Again be neuter.
Yes, far away
On the other side
Of the Middle Worst
And the Great Divide
There, there on the gilded
Coasts of the West
The Great I Am's
Are the happiest
For somewhere in Yonkers
They're shocking amoeba
With a cyclotron
Or the Queen of Sheba.
O beautiful
America
I have a feeling
I've come too far—
Did the plane put down
On the right star?
O tell me where the Statue
Of Libertines is
In the middle of Erewhon
Or Atlantis?
And the dead whores glitter
In Central Park
Just before every

Thing goes dark.
Down in the Village
The parvenu
Dreams of Madison
Avenue
And on Madison
The copywriters
Dream of the calm
Nights of St. Vitus
As in the arms
Of their advertisers
They gollop down
Their tranquilizers;
And the workmen burrowing
Into the sidewalk
("Dig we must
For growing New York")*
Chaw ten-inch cigars
As they work,
And dogs and children
On long lists
Attend their psycho
Analysts.
The automobiles
As large as whales
Sweep up and down
Like hearses. Tales
Of Offmen softly
Echo over
Streets choked up with
Four leafed clover,
Yet oh us lucky
Eleven million
Would give it all
To be one simple
Nice Sicilian.

* Stenciled on all roadmenders' trestles.

And, every week,
Like a public crime
We sit in our toilets
Glued to the slime
Of the last issue
Of a loose Time.
And high on their pinnacles
The Committees sit
Denouncing all sanity
In the name of God
And unanimity.
And the ghost of a great
Democratic conception
Shrieks out: "I confess
To a little deception
But I meant well
Make me an exception."
O Gawd once again
I hear the beat
Of the rock and rolling
Paraclete:
Man, you know
Our attitude
Ain't a defeat,
It's a beatitude.
We all mean well,
Yeah, we all mean well
Like the Esso pipeline
That goes to hell.
For brother, brother,
The Am Express
Has illegalized
Human distress
And in the end
All our ills
Succumb to a bottle
Of vitamin pills
And the logic of
The formal mind

Acknowledge it's super
Annuated
By IBM
Incorporated.
Till the voice of the Turtle
Or the New Yorker
Intones the verses
Of Garcia Lorca:
"The jungle of To-morrow.
Ah, that's it, man
All caught up in
The beard of Whitman."
And "Enough!" enunciates
The Specter of James
"Don't spare the horses.
Throw out the dames.
Just drive like mad
Straight through the flames
And we'll all take tea
At the Court of St. James.
The pyrotechnics
Of shall I say Hell
Have reached Minneapolis
And St. Paul as well:
So lower the curtain
At all the borders
And close my books
Until further orders."

# AL BENDICH

AL BENDICH found himself defending the legal rights of the Beat writers shortly after he graduated from the University of California's Boalt Hall School of Law. In September 1957, as Staff Counsel of the American Civil Liberties Union of Northern California, he argued his trial brief in Judge Clayton Horn's courtroom in San Francisco, defending Lawrence Ferlinghetti against the charge of obscenity for printing and selling Allen Ginsberg's paperback volume *Howl and Other Poems* at City Lights Bookstore. After Bendich gave the closing arguments, the legal team, which included co-counsel Jack Ehrlich and Lawrence Speiser, won a ruling that the ACLU *News* characterized as "a sharp and staggering blow to the chops of prurience and censorship." Bendich later joined the faculty of the Speech Department at U.C. Berkeley. Currently he is vicepresident and general counsel of Fantasy Records and the Saul Zaentz Company in Berkeley. On December 12, 1999, at the American Civil Liberties Union of Northern California's Bill of Rights Celebration at the Argent Hotel in San Francisco, Bendich presented the Earl Warren Civil Liberties Award to Lawrence Ferlinghetti.

## Award to Lawrence Ferlinghetti

It is my great privilege to present the ACLU of Northern California's annual Earl Warren Civil Liberties Award to Lawrence Ferlinghetti. This is the twenty-seventh annual award, but the first to a poet. Poetry, as F. R. Leavis said, is "humanly central," it deals with the profoundest of basic questions; it undertakes to define for thought, and vindicate, humanity's sense of the real and its relation to it. It requires "honesty"—percipience, intelligence, and self-knowledge. But, as T. S. Eliot has pointed out, the processes of society which constitute our ordinary education "consist largely in the acquisition of impersonal ideas which obscure what we really are and feel, what we really want and what really excites our interest." If poets reveal the deepest truths of ourselves to us, they also reveal what prevents us from realizing our humanity. And so poets must be free to think and feel and express themselves; and we must be free to hear them. The First Amendment guarantees us that freedom against governmental intervention. But, it can only be kept alive by constant attention and application. As Frederick Douglass said, "without struggle, there is no progress" or freedom. Lawrence Ferlinghetti has helped keep the First Amendment alive and well through constant struggle.

Of his early childhood, Ferlinghetti has written in his poem *Autobiography*:

> I am an American.
> I was an American boy.
> I read the American Boy Magazine
> and became a boy scout
> in the suburbs.
> I thought I was Tom Sawyer
> catching crayfish in the Bronx River
> and imagining the Mississippi.
> I had a baseball mitt
> and an American Flyer bike.
> I delivered the Woman's Home Companion
> at five in the afternoon
> or the Herald Trib
> at five in the morning.
> I still can hear the paper thump
> on lost porches.
> I had an unhappy childhood.
>
> I got caught stealing pencils
> from the Five and Ten Cent Store
> the same month I made Eagle Scout.

After high school, he enlisted in the Navy in 1941 and served as a captain of a sub-chaser in the Atlantic, including the Normandy landing. After VE day he shifted to a Navy freighter in the Pacific, delivering supplies to Midway, the Philippines, and other Pacific Islands, landing

in Japan on the first day of occupation. Six weeks after it had been "A"
bombed, he visited Nagasaki. Deeply affected, he wrote: "you'd see
hands sticking out of the mud . . . broken tea cups . . . hair sticking
out of the road . . . total destruction . . ."

Using the GI Bill, he took a Master's at Columbia with a thesis on
the relation between Ruskin and Turner. Then he went to Paris, pursuing a Ph.D. at the Sorbonne while he learned French, studied painting, wrote a novel and a series of poems. When he was defending his
thesis, written in French, on the City as a Symbol of Modern Poetry, a
professor challenged as inaccurate a translation of a line of Eliot's
"Wasteland." Ferlinghetti replied: "I'd like to quote an old French
adage: When the woman is beautiful, she is not faithful. When she is
faithful, she is not beautiful." He got his Ph.D.

He returned to America, married, and settled in San Francisco.
He worked on translating the French poet Jacques Prévert; he worked
on a novel titled *Her,* he wrote art criticism for the *Art Digest,* and he
painted. He taught a Shakespeare sonnets class at USF in 1952 and
lectured on the theme of homosexuality in the poems. He was not re-
hired. He wrote book reviews for the *San Francisco Chronicle* and also
about readings by poets like Dylan Thomas and Kenneth Patchen. At
Rexroth's open house nights he met other poets and painters who
would soon be known as the creators of the San Francisco Renaissance. In 1953 he opened a paperback book shop called City Lights
with Peter Martin. He wanted also to publish books, particularly poetry. Martin disagreed and Ferlinghetti bought him out in 1955. In that
year there was a revival of an attempt to remove the Anton Refregier
Murals from the Rincon Annex Post Office—a congressional resolution accused him of Communist associations. Ferlinghetti, defending
the murals, wrote that they had become the latest battleground of intellectual and artistic censorship. As you know, the murals are still
there.

Lawrence Ferlinghetti has been struggling consistently against the
forces of ignorance and censorship, against war and exploitation, au-
thoritarianism and prejudice.

One such struggle, with which I had the honor to be associated,
was precipitated by his publication of Allen Ginsberg's poem "Howl."

In October 1955, there was a poetry reading at the 6 Gallery in San
Francisco, including work by Ginsberg, Philip Lamantia, Michael

McClure, Gary Snyder, and Philip Whalen. They were introduced by Kenneth Rexroth. Ginsberg electrified the audience with his reading of "Howl." Michael McClure reported that "Allen began in a small and intensely lucid voice. At some point Jack Kerouac began shouting 'Go' in cadence. . . . In all of our memories no one had been so outspoken in poetry before. . . ." Ferlinghetti had gone to the reading with Ginsberg. When he got home that night he typed and sent a telegram to Ginsberg echoing Emerson's salute to Whitman on *Leaves of Grass:* "I greet you at the beginning of a great career," he wrote. And he concluded: "When do I get the manuscript?"

Ferlinghetti arranged to have the poem published in the Pocket Poets series being issued under his City Lights imprint. Before he sent it to the printer in England, he submitted it to the ACLU "to see," as he wrote to Ginsberg, "if they would defend us if the book was busted . . . since without the ACLU, City Lights would no doubt have gone broke and out of business."

Assured of the ACLU's support, Ferlinghetti had the poem printed. Chester McPhee, collector of customs, stopped a second printing from reaching City Lights on March 25, 1957, confiscating 520 copies as obscene.

The ACLU informed McPhee it would contest the seizure. Ferlinghetti then printed a new edition in the United States, thus removing it from Customs jurisdiction.

Ferlinghetti wrote in the *Chronicle* of May 19, 1957, that McPhee deserved thanks and perhaps a medal for making "Howl" famous. He wrote: "I consider 'Howl' to be the most significant long poem to be published in this country since World War II, perhaps since Eliot's 'Four Quartets.' In some sense it's the greatest and archetypical configuration of the mass culture which produced it.

"The results are a condemnation of our culture. If it is an obscene voice of dissent, perhaps this is really why officials object to it. Condemning it, however, they are condemning our world, for it is what he observes that is the great voice of 'Howl'. . . ."

The U.S. Attorney refused to institute condemnation proceedings, causing Customs, on May 29, to release the books they had seized.

The San Francisco police then took over, arresting Ferlinghetti and Shigeyoshi Murao, the City Lights manager, for selling *Howl*, an obscene book, as they charged.

"Thus during the first week in June," Ferlinghetti wrote, "I found myself being booked and fingerprinted in San Francisco's Hall of Justice. The city jail occupies the upper floor of it, and a charming sight it is, a picturesque return to the early middle ages. And my enforced tour of it was a dandy way for the city officially to recognize the flowering of poetry in San Francisco. As one paper reported: 'The Cops Don't Allow No Renaissance Here.'"

The ACLU posted bail and the prisoners were released.

At this time I was practicing labor law. A. L. Wirin of the Southern California ACLU told me ACLU Northern California staff counsel Lawrence Speiser was planning to leave. I applied for the job and was hired in September 1957. I was immediately assigned to assist in the preparation for the *Howl* trial, which Larry Speiser and Jake Ehrlich had been working on that summer. Thrilled with the opportunity to defend poetry and freedom of speech against the censors, I took on the task of preparing a trial brief, laying out the law we hoped would guide and govern the judge in the case.

Captain William Hanrahan, chief of the police department's juvenile bureau, announced, "We will await the outcome of this case before we go ahead with other books." In the face of this threat he was asked what standards he used to judge a book. He replied: "When I say filthy I don't mean suggestive, I mean filthy words that are very vulgar." He was asked whether he'd have his men confiscate the Bible, which he vehemently denied, adding: "Let me tell you, though, what King Solomon was doing with all those women wouldn't be tolerated in San Francisco."

At the trial, our major argument was that before a literary work could be tested by the application of such obscenity formulas as whether its dominant theme appealed to the prurient interests of the average member of the community, it had to be determined to be utterly without social importance.

This allowed us to introduce evidence of the literary values of the work rather than on whatever prurience it might stimulate.

The defense produced nine expert witnesses, all eminent in their field of literature. The first witness, Mark Schorer, professor of English at UC Berkeley, author of novels and poetry and the definitive biography of Sinclair Lewis, testified that "Howl," like any work of literature, "attempts and intends to make a significant comment on or interpretation of human experience as the author knows it."

Thus the battle was joined. Though deeply serious, it was in a sense also shamefully farcical. Ralph McIntosh, the assistant DA prosecuting the case, cross-examined Schorer, trying to get him to provide literal prose translations of various lines of the poem.

"Sir," Schorer responded, "you can't translate poetry into prose. That's why it's poetry."

McIntosh kept trying to seize on individual words out of context and revealed his lack of understanding of the poem. "I presume you understand the whole thing, is that right?" he asked. Schorer responded: "I hope so. It's not always easy to know that one understands exactly what a contemporary poet is saying, but I think I do." "In other words," McIntosh pursued, "you don't have to understand the words?" Patiently Schorer replied, "You don't understand the individual words taken out of their context. You can no more translate it back into logical prose English than you can say what a surrealistic painting means in words, because it's not prose."

Walter Van Tilburg Clark, author of *The Ox Bow Incident*, testified that "Howl" was the "work of a thoroughly honest poet, who is also a highly competent technician."

"Do you classify yourself as a liberal?" McIntosh asked him. Judge Horn promptly disallowed the question.

The defense witnesses all testified to the honesty and literary and cultural importance of the work. Kenneth Rexroth said "Howl's" "merit is extraordinarily high. It is probably the most remarkable single poem published by a young man since the Second World War."

McIntosh had been unable to deal with these witnesses in any effective way. He then called two experts of his own to prove the poem had no merit. The first, an assistant professor of English at USF, gave it as his opinion that the poem belonged to "a long dead movement called Dadaism" and that it was a "weak imitation of a form used eighty or ninety years ago by Walt Whitman." Thus, he concluded, "the opportunity is long past for any significant literary contribution . . ."

McIntosh's second and last witness had been handing out brochures announcing her qualifications and offering private lessons in diction. She testified that she had rewritten *Faust,* among other creations. Her opinion of "Howl" was expressed this way: "You feel like you are going through the gutter when you have to read this stuff . . . I didn't linger on it too long, I assure you . . ."

Farcical and pathetic as the prosecution's case was, it nevertheless was evidence of the grave danger posed to civil liberty by ignorance, arrogance, and governmental censors great or small.

Books are easier to burn than to write; the new and creative is easier to attack than defend; it is easier to express conformist thought than to dig for the ore of truth.

The trial, in its way, illustrated what "Howl" was howling about.

As we had the first amendment on our side, we had, theoretically, the legal advantage. We had also the advantage of the support of the community of culture in the Bay Area.

Judge Horn took the case under submission. He took two weeks to decide it. He took James Joyce's *Ulysses* to Yosemite, where he read it carefully. He was still smarting from the public criticism he had suffered when he sentenced five women shoplifters to attend Cecil B. DeMille's *The Ten Commandments* and write essays on its moral lessons. He was determined to regain public confidence.

When he announced his decision, that "Howl" was not obscene, he supported it in the following ways.

He said "Howl" was written in three parts, with a footnote. Then he analyzed each part: "The first part of 'Howl' presents a picture of a nightmare world; the second part is an indictment of those elements in modern society destructive to the best qualities of human nature; such elements are predominantly identified as materialism, conformity and mechanization leading toward war. The third part presents a picture of an individual who is a specific representation of what the author conceives of as a general condition. 'Footnote to Howl' seems to be a declaration that everything in the world is holy, including parts of the body by name. It ends in a plea for a holy living . . ."

He then laid out rules governing obscenity prosecutions and added some general observations as follows: "The people owe a duty to themselves and to each other to preserve and protect their constitutional freedoms from any encroachment by government unless it appears that the allowable limits have been breached, and then to take only such action as will heal the breach. I agree with Mr. Justice Douglas: I have the same confidence in the ability of our people to reject noxious literature as I have in their capacity to sort out the true from the false in theology, economics, politics or any other field."

Ferlinghetti was pronounced not guilty. Shig Murao had earlier had the case against him dismissed as there was no evidence that he was acquainted with the contents of the books sold at City Lights and could therefore not have the requisite intent to sell an obscene book.

Were it not for Ferlinghetti's commitment to art, to culture, to freedom of expression, were it not for his courage in standing up to the censors, there may well have been no trial, no opportunity for the ACLU to defend the first amendment, no celebration of the triumph of poetry, no education of a judge and a public.

Some four years later, the *Howl* trial was still powerfully affecting our cultural freedom as Judge Horn presided over the prosecution of Lenny Bruce for obscenity. Consistent with his ruling in *Howl*, he instructed the jury concerning first amendment standards and protections, and Bruce was perforce acquitted. Unfortunately, it was the only trial in which he was acquitted, being convicted in a series of other trials around the country and eventually silenced.

Ferlinghetti has continued to stand courageously for human values. He was arrested in 1967 at the Oakland Army Base with sixty-seven others, including Joan Baez, the recipient of this award in 1979, in a protest against the Vietnam War.

In 1970, he succeeded in preventing the postmaster from blocking receipt of a paper from Beijing, *The Crusader,* sought to be suppressed because of its content regarding black soldiers in Vietnam and their relation to whites. The list of his struggles on behalf of international solidarity, freedom of expression, and against war and destruction is too long for the time I have. I'd like to close with a quote from his poem *Autobiography:*

> . . . I have read somewhere
> the meaning of existence,
> yet have forgotten
> just exactly where.
> But I am the man
> And I'll be there.
> And I may cause the lips
> of those who are asleep
> to speak.

Lawrence, thank you for being the man, and for being there— for us.

# BONNIE BREMSER

BONNIE BREMSER is one of the many women who have written about how their lives were changed after they fell in love with a Beat writer. It is the name under which Brenda Frazer has published her poetry and her book about her travels in Mexico with the poet Ray Bremser, *Troia: Mexican Memoirs* (Tompkins Square Press, 1969). "Poets and Odd Fellows" and "The Village Scene" are chapters from an earlier, unpublished section of this memoir, describing how she met Ray Bremser in Washington, D.C., and lived with him in Greenwich Village from 1959 to 1960.

## *Poets and Odd Fellows*

First there was me. Then there was Ray and me. It happened like this. I had dropped out of college and Ray was fresh out of jail, practically at the same time. I was living at 19th and F near Pennsylvania Avenue, just two blocks from the White House in D.C., my first apartment. It was 1959 and I was nineteen years old. Ray was twenty-five and came down to D.C. with a bunch of New York poets.

I met him at a poetry reading at the Odd Fellows Hall. I had seen the poster in the window of a little lunch counter near GW University. I thought it was a student event but it wasn't. I remember how I got ready for this evening, more important than I knew. Bathed and girdled up, didn't know this was the last time I would put on a girdle or a bra in my life, never again. Even as I looked in the mirror and lifted my arm for deodorant didn't know that someone, someone like him, would prefer my natural smell.

I just thought I was getting ready for a poetry reading. Maybe it would even be a little dull, too intellectual. Art and ideology all together in a bookish atmosphere, a roundtable where poets wore glasses and droned monotonously, something like that. My own image, Bohemian. I put on my black stockings and a skirt, a black sweater too, loafers and a camel hair coat. My hair was very short like François Sagan on the cover of *Bonjour Tristesse*.

And there would be music too the poster had said. I was curious and even more because of the name Odd Fellows. What was that about? Anyway it was a reason to go out. My social life was nil, more and more withdrawn lately. I'd stayed in bed with my copy of Balzac the last few weeks before I'd left college. Now I read Shakespeare every chance I got, home from work for lunch sitting on the trunk that held my belongings, the only piece of furniture besides a bed and a kitchen table, both there when I moved in. My apartment was near the Federal Office Building where I worked as a clerk-typist. Lunch was Campbell's vegetable soup with chili powder. I was dieting again.

Anyway that night it was dark and raining and I didn't know where the Odd Fellows Hall was. I'd take a cab. "Do you know where the Odd Fellows Hall is?" I asked the cabdriver, and felt silly just saying it. "The one at Ninth and T Northwest?" he asks. "They're having a poetry reading, I guess that's it." Was there more than one Odd Fellows Hall?

February was cold in D.C., the bare trees, wet with the winter rain, were close around the entrance of the Odd Fellows Hall as I got out of the cab. Kind of a surprise. The big glass doors, though pointed obliquely into the winter wind, were brightly lit, and winter stayed outside.

The lonely day fell away from me as I entered. The atmosphere was warm and I felt my face relax as I looked around to see if people were staring at me as I was them, amazed at the differences. But no one noticed me, for the poetry reading had already started. I was free to study the interesting faces there. What beautiful long hair and gentle expressions of countenance. Soft smiles, a little ecstatic. But even more, a sense of excitement, perhaps it was hope, shining from eyes. Maybe the poetry was doing it, opening emotions, lifting the spirit. Maybe it was communication making them all understand as one mind. It felt good to be there and yet the familiar discomfort in my own skin made me an outsider. Had I experienced any of that communication? Would someone teach me? I took a deep breath, trying to be ready for whatever came.

The crowd more than filled the hall and I leaned against the wall on the nearest side where many people were sitting on the floor. I could see well there and yet was somewhat removed. Down front was a stage on which were a grand piano and a small table with one chair. All of the lights were on in the hall, illuminating the audience as well as the stage. No artificial barrier between the crowd and the poets except the elevation of the stage. The poets stood around the stage. This small Negro guy apparently was in charge making introductions. He introduced the next poet, Peter Orlovsky, very blond and good-looking. I thought I would like to know someone like that. He laughed at himself while reading a very short poem. Then another poet stood and read in an excited voice about a lion in his bedroom closet. "Yeah, a lion, wow!" I thought, laughing with the people around me, catching the excitement of his reading. Who? Allen Ginsberg? But he was funny. "There goes my image of an English professor," I thought, glad that I had come.

The crowd was noisy and excited. "Thanks to the education of the New Jersey penal system, a jailhouse poet, Ray Bremser!" I heard the announcer say something about Poems of Madness. And then there was this tall guy with an army fatigue jacket and red sweatshirt underneath, the hood drooping down his back. He looked like a monk. He sat at the little table looking down at the audience, reading with a strong accent. A black binder full of poems was on his lap. The poem was about how his father always bet on the horses. The words came fast in a barrage and I couldn't catch it all. But the rhythm carried it and I found I could understand anyway.

Here one of my shy moods overtook me. What if someone spoke to me, or asked my opinion? Suppose I were expected to be friendly, spontaneous and free like these other people. I'd have to come out of my aloof, stuck-up shell, even admit that I was painfully scared of people. What if I had to turn my head and look directly at the person next to me? I was uncomfortable that way. I felt suddenly confused and wanted to get outside again, back to my apartment, and yet at the same time I wanted more than anything to be a part of this crowd for once, to fit in. I moved to the back of the hall on an impulse to leave. OK, so maybe I am a phony, so what, I swung my ass a little, in defiance of the human race.

"Hey, wait a minute! You can't leave like that! Don't you like the poetry?" This tall black guy accosted me just when I was about to escape. I mumbled something inarticulate, thinking that would get rid of him, but no, apparently it didn't matter that I made no reply. He told me stay and wait to the end. There was going to be a party and he'd take me. He told me that the reading had been set up by him and some other students at Howard University. "The poets read at Howard last night too. Where were you?" he said, facetiously. I knew he wanted to impress me with the fact he was the organizer, and I was, but still said nothing. "My name is Brick," he said.

The poets were reading again, another round. They acted as though they were trying each to come up with a better one than the other. It was exciting. Brick told me their names as they appeared. The reading was in full swing now. Gregory Corso came to the edge of the stage, shouting out into the air with a large gesture. "BE A STAR SCREWER!" And then the announcer, LeRoi Jones, read his own poem about music.

Then the piano player Cecil Taylor comes on and Brick asks me, "Do you like jazz?" and I have to say yes because I like this large music being played now. And I like very much the intense face of the piano player with his round and intellectual eyeglasses. "They are almost done," Brick says to me. "You wait for me here, OK?"

When Brick came back he took me up to the stage and introduced me to some of the poets. Then a bunch of us got in a station wagon with a guy named Dave driving. I was in the front seat while Brick and A. B. Spellman, another student from Howard University, were in the back. Also the poet Allen Ginsberg rode with us. Brick told me, "Dave drove the van with the poets in it down from New York." Then Dave said, "Yeah, I had to take over the driving from Peter O. because he used to be an ambulance driver and he never drives slow." "Besides he was too high," said Allen G. in the back seat, and "Who's the pretty girl up front?" and so I was introduced to him too. We were passing through Northwest D.C. The special feeling that black neighborhoods have, people still on the street. Where's the party? When we arrived the others were already there and gave a shout of greeting. Allen was obviously the favorite.

Brick got me a beer and left me alone. Allen sat right down on a big hassock in the middle of the room with a fat black guy. They got into an intense conversation that made their faces shine with sweat and happiness. I wandered to the kitchen where Peter O. was. I found him almost as shy as I was and we only talked for a few minutes. I was disappointed and retreated to the bathroom. Looked at myself in the mirror in a negative way, and asked myself what was I doing there? The excitement and cold air and maybe the beer had made my cheeks flushed. I went and sat down on a couch in the other room by myself.

Almost immediately Ray Bremser came and asked if he could sit next to me, which he did for about five minutes without saying anything. Somehow I was entirely reassured by his quietness. Then finally he said to me, "Do you like this party?" and I said, "No," and he said, "Well, why don't we get out of here then?" I said, "OK."

Driving around in another taxicab and Ray was trying to figure out a place to go. Now I knew where we were. We had just passed the Greyhound bus station. Across the street was an art movie theater. A week before I'd gone there to see the new film sensation, Brigitte Bardot. She danced on the screen, bigger than life and more or less nude. With tropical skin and long loose hair, she was soft and sexy as sand between bare toes. I wanted to be like her.

We were just passing Pancake Heaven, all lit up like an oasis in the night. "Do you like pancakes?" I suddenly craved butter and syrup, comfort. "I love pancakes!" The bright lights in the pancake house were like a spotlight on us. I could see Ray's handsome face, pock-marked and angular, savage and gentle at once. His curly hair fell over his forehead, not quite a pompadour. I was nervous about the conversation and we didn't get very far. We talked about my leaving school and he told me, "I never got beyond the seventh grade. I didn't like school. But when I was in jail I was the librarian and could order books from anywhere, read what I wanted, things you can't find in the store." I was strangely reassured by the fact that he'd been in jail. Perhaps it was immediately proof that he was different, like me.

Even when we lapsed into silence it was not so painful. He was gentle with me and instead of pushing questions he said, "I like quiet people. It shows they have thoughts they've never expressed. Most of the women I know talk endlessly about nothing." I liked being seen as different from other women. He pulled a wad of bills from his pocket saying, "I just got paid for the reading." He gave me a sense that everything was OK and only today mattered.

"What now?" I wondered. He simply asked, "Would you like to come with me?" And I simply said, "Yes." It was Saturday night; no worries and no work tomorrow, no virginity after all. I trusted him without thought. We got into another cab and drove to the address where they were staying. We entered down some stairs that went directly to a room with two beds. It was a basement apartment with several rooms. "We'll kick them out if they try to get in," he said, turning on the bare lightbulb over the bed. I was standing shyly, not knowing what to do. He noticed and turned the light off again. "I hate bare bulbs," he said, and I could hear him taking off his clothes. I undressed in the dim light from the street window, balancing on one foot as I peeled the girdle off.

As I got into bed he handed me one of two lit cigarettes, twin burning coals in the darkness. We were strangely relaxed and quiet, smoking, perhaps wondering what to do and how to do it. Then he said, "Are you tired?" And almost disappointed I said, "Yes." But it was a lie and he knew it. Maybe I thought we could spend the night just pretending to sleep. He reached over, putting his arm lightly around me, and said in a surprised voice, "Jesus! You're naked!" And we laughed together at the silliness of shy preliminaries. "Well, what did you expect?"

His body was long and sinewy. His kisses were chaste and gentle. He used his lips to delicately touch my face, my neck, and my mouth. His fingers brushed lightly over my skin as he said, "So smooth." And I felt his skin a little prickly with hairs rising. "Was it a good ball?" he asked afterwards as I touched his face tenderly. And without answering I thought that between my legs he was a perfect fit. Large enough to seem completely new, as if the first love.

We rested in each other's arms smoking again and there were voices of people arriving in the next room. Ray sighed, "The party must be over, here they come." A voice came through the wall, "I'll bet that Bremser is in there getting laid. Bet he's with that chick from the party." "That's Gregory," Ray whispered. "Weighed, Laid, and Parlayed, as they say in New Jersey," he imitated Ray's accent, which he could do almost without trying since his own New York accent was heavy. "Look out for Gregory, he's a rabbit fucker." Ray laughed in my ear and called out, "YEAH, GREG, IT'S ME!" "Oh, man you're so cool the way you bird-dogged that chick from Brick," Gregory again. "No man, I ain't cool. I'm hot!" And we heard other voices laughing as Ray pulled me to him. "Leave them alone," someone said. "That Ray's a Romeo," said Gregory.

This time as we balled, oblivious of the voices in the next room,

there was a loud thump and we rolled off onto the floor as the bed collapsed. A voice from the other room, "What happened, man?" And Ray
answered, "THE FUCKING BED BROKE!" And we laughed hilari-
ously.

The sky was getting light through the basement apartment windows. Already up, so we dressed and left the broken bed behind. Satisfied anyway for the moment and full of joy from the feeling. "Where
will we go to breakfast?" he said as we stepped up to the sidewalk.
"Why don't we go to my place?" I suggested. "Well, why didn't you say
so before?" and we got into another cab and went there.

Remember my place was barely furnished. Although a nice old
brownstone house, my apartment, on the top floor, had been painted
over too many times. The thick pink covered the boarded front and
mantel of an old fireplace. A chocolate cake on the kitchen table had
been left open to the air. I liked it stale. Kidney stew in a small skillet
on the stove, which I'd made the night before. Ray said, "What the
fuck is this?" and threw it out so he could use the pan for eggs. He
told about cooking in the jail over a roll of toilet paper. "The skillet has
to be hot for eggs." He was standing on the step up to the stove and
fridge in the corner of the kitchen. Kind of like on a stage and I
watched him perform.

My first apartment seemed even cozier now that I had a lover. The
welcome sunshine came in the window through shutters in the little
bedroom. In the diffused sunlight we could see each other. His long
body looked like a naked Jesus, stretched out in undershorts. We
stayed awake only long enough to make love one more time. And to
talk about my sexual history, the four or five men that I'd been to bed
with. And he'd been with at least that many in the past two months. "I
was a virgin until I was twenty-five. Angel, the dancer, took my cherry.
It's all here in my address book." He showed me his system of letters
and dots by women's names. He marked the tally of our lovemaking on
the pink paint of the bedroom wall, four lines and a diagonal across.
"Keep that there now."

He was modest though and put his underwear on again as soon as
we made love. He was self-conscious of the acne on his shoulders. "In
the jail we always had to wear short-sleeved shirts and I hated it. After
I became a trustee I was allowed to wear long sleeves and to keep my
collar up."

While we were falling asleep the pigeons cooed on the little balcony outside, which overlooked the park across the street. Ray spoke of how they had arrived in town on Thursday and immediately went to see the White House and the statue in Lafayette Square, which was covered with pigeon droppings. "Gregory hates the government buildings. He says they make him feel guilty for something, anything, for just being alive. He practically grew up in jail, you know. He says the pigeon shit everywhere is poetic justice."

In the afternoon when we woke Ray called Dave, who said they were all meeting for lunch in a restaurant, which was only two blocks away from my place. I knew that they were planning to leave soon and I began to feel frightened and insecure. As we walked down the steps of the brownstone house I wondered what was going to become of me. At the restaurant we ate hamburgers while Gregory told us about the milk bath he'd had at Elizabeth Arden's. Afterwards we went out on the street and Gregory came up behind us and said, "Hey, Ray! Did you tell her about your wife and kids?"

His words were like a shot to my heart and it collapsed noiselessly within me. Maybe, could it have been all a lie between us? What a fool I'd been. I barely knew his name! "Aw, Gregory, shut the fuck up," I heard Ray say. And we walked back to my pad where the others would pick him up later when it was time to leave. As we turned the corner I said, just barely able to get out the words, unrehearsed. "What does he mean, your wife and kids!" Angry tears of frustration, I felt the shadow of doom. Never that angry at anyone before. Stupid me to trust? No! It wasn't my fault! So what does it mean? Obviously he would have to leave his wife. At that moment I realized I was in love.

"Aw, you don't really believe that, do you? Gregory's just jealous because he sees we've got something going." (Something going. Does that mean that he feels the same way?) I stopped crying, but only after I made him say the words. "No," he said, "I'm not married. And I told you before, I was a virgin till two months ago, so how could I have kids? Gregory's a troublemaker. I told you that too. Now who're you going to listen to?" He put his arm around my shoulder, holding me to him as we walked.

## The Village Scene

It was pretty obvious who was who among the crowded throngs of the Greenwich Village streets on Saturday night. The straights were painfully normal, women in high heels and stockings and men in dress shirts. The "villagers" were conspicuous for their hair, sandals, and predominantly black or dark blue clothing, dressed up to fit their philosophy. As inside or hip residents of the village scene Ray and I were irritated by the stares of the tourists who came there just for that, to stare. Heavy black makeup, cygnet eyes, sunglasses at night could relieve some of the exposure.

There were the kids who came to the village from New Jersey, Brooklyn, or the Bronx looking for a good time, hoping to swing, and some of them stayed for good. Two teenagers from Hackensack, Janine and Barbara. We met them, Ray and I were introduced to them the first day they showed up. They both had strong Jersey accents, like Ray. There was some grass and beer and we were sitting around in the dark, somewhere in the East Village. Barbara said, "I gotta pee so bad my back teeth are floating." It was really funny and square with the background we all remembered from the fifties and Ray put it in a poem sometime later. Janine and Barbara stayed with Allen for while and they made sexual scenes with whoever showed up. Sometimes it was Kerouac, Peter and Allen too even though they were homosexual. I heard about it from Ray, not gossip though. I myself was curious about the expansion of sexual activities in such a group. But Ray and I were a married couple and didn't experiment.

The only job I could get was at the Café Bizarre. I was very unhappy about it but I was coerced. "How are we going to eat?" And I couldn't argue with that. The Café Bizarre was a coffee shop right across from Washington Square Park. Everything about it was gross, intentionally grotesque and designed to hustle tourists. It was a firetrap, the walls were painted black and everything kind of Halloween-like, but not funny, flying bats and black drapery from the ceiling.

I couldn't remember the names of the drinks, ice cream concoctions with weird names like Witches' Brew. The customers were curious about everything. "What does the Tahitian Fantasy have in it?" they asked. "I think grenadine, I'm not sure," I said, just wishing they would leave me alone. Some of them asked personal questions—some were drunk. We had to wear black leotards, which didn't bother me because I'd always been inclined to the dance, even studied on Fifty-seventh Street in my own early days when I lived in New Jersey. But this was different, the leotards were so that the customers could ogle the waitresses. The other waitresses didn't mind and some of them made a lot of money. The place was always packed and very hot. Every night I dreaded it. Then one day I quit and went and sat by the fountain in the Square and cried.

I went back to Allen's apartment on Sixth Street, which we were watching for him while he was traveling, only it was hot and I dangled my bare legs out the street window fire escape and the neighbors complained bitterly to Allen about it when he came back. Months later a picture of me appeared in a Swedish magazine, an article about the Beats, and it was me in my black leotard with legs hanging out the fire escape window. Everybody was mad at me it seemed. Allen's cats were shitting in the bathtub. Ray was mad because I quit the job and then Allen yelled at us when he got back for messing things up and not getting along with the neighbors. I felt defensive at the criticism but the only thing I could say was "There's never anything in the refrigerator but borscht."

Dark streets in the village. Lampposts and atmosphere. Tenements above the coffee shops. In the Gaslight Café where Ray often read, I was always there; he would make comments at me from his place on the little stage, about me, gentle and admiring. I could have anything I wanted there, but it wasn't the same as if I had a dollar or fifty cents of my own to go sit at my own table with a cup of coffee in Rienzi's or the other authentic coffee shops where the real villagers spent time.

The Gaslight was a place for bad poetry although sometimes a young person would show up and Ray would be impressed. I was learning to distinguish the legitimate from the bad. Ray was a very impressive poet and a great performer too. It made me cringe to hear some of the other poets—pure sentimentality and yet not sincere, and totally disconnected from any meaning. Ray used the word pretentious. The contrast with Ray's work was a lesson in itself. Ray treated them all as friends, only condescending to the degree that was obviously required, and that allowed him to ask them for money when necessary. Because the quality of poetry did not determine how much money you made. Many of the poets did regular sets every hour or so, and it didn't really matter that most of them read the same two or three poems, because the influx of tourists was great and originality was not a requirement.

But when Ray read it was different. Even the owner would sit down and people in the kitchen would listen too. The sound of his New Jersey accent, with Shakespearean inflections, was enough to impress. The poetry itself linked words, music, rhythm, and meaning in a way that perfectly matched his voice. Even if you didn't immediately understand the intent of the poem, the sound of it persuaded you with its artistic impact.

A few dollars, some food, enough for cigarettes. We wander in the night, down MacDougal, across Washington Square, under the Fifth Avenue arch in the lights, looking for a place to stay. We end up in Hugh Romney's basement apartment on Bleecker Street. Hugh was one of the Gaslight poets. Ray said he had a good heart. He wore a beret and clipped his beard in a goatee. I didn't like the idea of being obligated to Hugh. I wasn't as chummy with these Gaslight poets as Ray was. But Ray got respect from them, and also got most of what he needed, whether through loans or marijuana deals. Ray's gentle philosophy was that many people would give up their money just because they had it, that they felt guilty about their affluence and it made them feel good about themselves to lose money even if there were a burn involved. Ray was doing them a favor, validating their worth. So we stayed at Hugh's that night, and maybe for a few nights. It was very damp and the bedroom was tiny, just big enough to hold the bed, and a mouse came and sat up on its haunches on the bedcovers. I could see its little eyes looking at me intently, and I was intimidated, couldn't sleep. But Ray could. He'd had plenty of experience with mice in jail and wasn't afraid of them.

My family ring went next to pawn, pay for necessities. Some of these things might have been romantic if one had a good night's sleep in between, woke up rested, had regular meals for a while and hygienic conditions. My gums were getting unhealthy from not having a toothbrush. However, I told myself that I didn't miss the things of normal life, because after all I'd gotten the better part of the deal in being Ray's wife.

It was not a comfortable time. I was still getting used to New York. Ray often left me alone, or had me meet him somewhere. I had to trust in his way of doing things and it was difficult because he didn't like to explain. The streets were threatening, and it was extremely hot. The impact of so many strangers, and so much hot concrete, the sense of no home, no place to hide, no rest except for nights when we had an invitation to someone's apartment had an impact on my sense of security, which depended on our relationship. Sometimes we stayed in Hoboken at John Rapponick's, the owner of the 7 Arts Gallery, and sometimes we'd hang out with a new friend, Irving R., who had just come in from Chicago, an editor who had just been through an obscenity trial for his magazine *Big Table,* the first to publish William Burroughs. He had come to New York City to be closer to the Beat scene. But even when friends helped us there was no job, no money, always having to move fast and arrange to get through the day or night.

Even if there was a place to sleep, sometimes sleep didn't happen, and not because of lovemaking. I got puzzled. Ray was uneasy. Was it the heat, was it worry? I didn't know what to do, how to act. I was completely helpless when he didn't give me all of his attention. I needed him. One such day we took the subway up to Central Park in the early morning and waited for the Museum of Natural History to open. He explained to me about Cleopatra's obelisk, which was in the gardens to the south of the museum. We spent long hours looking at the exhibits, especially the ones about ancient Egypt. It was cool and pleasant in the museum and we had smoked a joint in the early morning. Things took on a great imaginative depth. Ray was excited. We were having a good time and felt as though our marriage was somehow being reconsecrated in this mythological setting. On the way home we walked by the East River, looking deep at the water that lapped against the concrete of the breakwater, peering over the railing where a condom swelled and shrank like a jellyfish, loose and misshapen.

That night Ray was completely distant. What was the matter, what had I done? I couldn't tell if he was asleep or not, lying on his stomach, the toes overhanging the bed tapping gently to the beat of the music on the phonograph. Was he doing that in his sleep? I had a sense that he didn't want to touch. How else to communicate? Maybe he didn't want to communicate. As soon as I dozed off he got up and left, went for a walk alone, and I awoke more anxious than ever. No explanations at all, what about the greatness of our earlier outing, what about the things we'd seen with the same eyes, the same expansive consciousness?

He came back at dawn, in the few moments of respite from the heat before the sun came up again. We happened to be in a place where there was a typewriter. He started writing and stayed at it for two hours. When he was done he showed me the poem, called "Follow the East River," about the experience the day before, mythologizing it, suggesting the reincarnation of ancient Egypt in us, a married couple, the king and queen, the cycles of life and death.

There was still a sense of uneasiness, although he was back to me, arm around me while I slept. Later that day, the sun went down and the sound of the city changed from humdrum of business to soothing dark corners, streets and shops, awake and ready to go, it was the night life again and even though the Gaslight was a place of some jealousies for me, tonight it was the place to go.

I began to understand our life in a larger sense as Ray read the new poem, as if reporting on the day, our outing at the museum. Only of course it came out as poetry, the outlet of poetry, the shape of our lives' daily happenings. However, was I the only one he identified with Hatshepsut and Nefertiti? Or could there still be some other woman in his life? And the sound of him against the world was still there as if he were mankind going through a penitent stage. I did adore him for his role as Everyman but it made me even more insecure. Where did I fit in? I began to read things into this poem, which had so profoundly upset him. His reading of the poem was a release, the rhythm and cadence of it carrying to the climax where he raised a pedantic finger as I'd seen Allen Ginsberg do. He announced our high discoveries of Egypt as if an accomplishment and enacted its performance as if relived theatrically but actually in poetry. The poem carried all of the despair, the discomfort, connected with the larger consciousness, and then resolved it. Calm. OK.

I felt like I was the only one able to fully respond to his reading. But as a poet he belonged not only to me, and perhaps the poem had something to do with that too. Imprisonment in a larger sense, imprisonment in relationships, imprisonment in layers of history. His voice was sepulchral as he described the sound of the tunnel stone closing, so deep and hollow like the resonance of his cheeks where all of the back teeth were missing. His voice smoked out of his mouth heavy with nicotine and I thought it perfumed with poetry. People had responded to him, fascinated, as the narrative grew with intensity, hieroglyphic with metaphor, speaking with its own meaning, in sound, in the definition of words.

"This is what we are about," I was thinking, "and I am a part of it, in a large sense, a part of the poem. Not only the poet's wife now, not just the 'old lady' to show off, not only as a woman but that we are solid, a reality, not just for thrills. This is our experience together." And as he read I was moved in another way. I was proud of him, proud of myself for being a part of his fame.

The crowds moved through. The moment of authenticity vanished. I could have been anyone, anonymous, browsing in the way the tourists did—how strong the impulse to separate from that. In the very yellow incandescence of the Gaslight Café the crowds arrived with carnival regularity. We were as much a part of the show as any. But Ray made the connection, made us human through the poetry, and also through the way he felt about people. Out for a buck, sure! But the touch, when he put the touch on them, it was a touch that they wanted. It was a hustle and redemption all at once. "You see, Bonnie?" he explained. "It all works. It's all OK." He made it OK. His voice, mesmerizing. The poetry imaginative, yet embellished with his experience of the courts of law, justice, life, civilization. And the understanding of it. Our love made it expansive and human palpitating with heart, the sharing of our life. The security I'd been missing was there in the poem, along with the reshaped understanding. All in one imaginary ride on a barge in the East River, the Nile of our dawn. The clutter of days before and after was just more artifacts, our heritage was in poetry.

But don't forget that Ray was humorous too, in fact he mastered the humor of words taking their proper place with perfect timing, the poetry coming round on itself. After the dramatic poem, then he read "I Hate Grapes," which had to do with my boyish body and small breasts and how we liked to ball each other as we said then. The poem began "There is a grape dribbling over my wife's bosom/more flute in her muted pouting than a Lateef record." Something to do with compulsion and satiation, the suggestion of orgy in a bunch of grapes. I left there satisfied with my life as a poet's muse.

A few days later, another late afternoon, hot as hell. We'd been hanging out with Irving a lot, and he was in and out of John Fles's apartment too. Were they lovers? Irving was very discreet, almost reclusive, and not yet ready to commit to the day-to-day indiscretions which we took in stride. Maybe we turned Irving on to pot the first time and we had jazzy zany conversations where I'd be very quiet while everyone else was bopping around, especially Ray, and they were all in awe of him but scared too. I would size up people, size up the situation, quiet, and then noticing a vulnerability come in for the put down. It was funny, no one minded we were all so high and silly. Irving would shout, "Bonnie! You're TOO MUCH!"

John was also from Chicago and somehow had got some peyote and left it for us while he was away for a day or so. Ray and I chewed it up in the late afternoon. What would happen? The stories had grown legendary, about the American Indian Church, legalized peyote ritual, part of their religious ceremony. Wow!

Incredible heat and the sunset was a sizzler. John's top floor apartment windows had been taken out of their casements, leaving a full view of red sky in the northwest, above the streets and brick tenements of humanity. As it turned dark we lit a candle. Kind of spooky at first, the drug not only tasted like the ultimate alkaloid with extreme vegetable bitterness, but when it hit my stomach there was an uneasiness like nausea, something green and indigestible residing, palpable in the stomach. I couldn't tell if I was high and asked Ray again, "What's it supposed to be like?" but just then my focus was drawn to the flame of the candle as if it were the teacher. "Look, Ray, there's a man in the candle," I whisper. And we watched the little man who stood with head bowed and arms folded, that was the wick you see. The flame was like a halo or a hood on the man's head and it made me think of Ray in his red sweatshirt when I first met him. I was afraid and half wanted to switch on the light or shout out loud. But Ray was beside me and I knew he loved my high experiences so of course I couldn't stop. We went through it together. "The wick is one with the flame, the wax feeding it." By that time I was crying. "That's what it is, oneness. Everything fits tight together, the material and the energy. The wax, the wick, and the flame consuming!" It was joy—a vision as well as an answer, a cleansing sight! Then there were changes, just like a key or tempo shift though we were for once not listening to music. Ray took the candle and wrote on the white ceiling, low enough for him to reach standing. The flame smoking, the black letters THERE IS SALVATION.

John was a little pissed about that, or maybe there was a money issue going down between him and Ray. I didn't know. But I was beginning to understand that Ray usually came out on top. It had to do with being a poet, as opposed to just an editor or a literary person. "You still don't have any money, what are you going to do?" John asked. It was apparent that he was worried about his privacy. "Money's not the issue, John, not even a question," Ray said. And I thought, "John surely won't admit that he needs security, that would be too normal." "Yeah, sure, it's not an issue until something comes up, like hunger, or a party." I knew that he was trying to allude to the many times that Ray had coerced him, perhaps on the most whimsical pretext. "It's not! Period! Just only love, just poetry and being together, making the scene, going places and seeing people," Ray said, and knew that these were things that some villagers actually would pay money for.

So John had to swallow his annoyance, which was not unusual. When Ray got imperious and used words like love and poetry there just wasn't any way to argue. No one ever wanted to refute him. Probably to save face John said, "I'm going to Ohio to get married. You could ride along with me if you want." Ray was excited. "That's halfway to the West Coast! We could go and see Wally Berman and Lamantia!" Berman and Lamantia were persons on the West Coast scene it was necessary for every fine poet to know. "It'll be like getting high on poetry just to meet them!" It did seem like a good idea, even if we didn't have any money. Somehow it was decided that we would go in spite of situations that stood in the way. "All the reason more!" Ray would say. New York was too hot, too crowded. And Allen and Peter had just taken off to Tangiers. It was as if the tide had gone out, leaving the scene in the city dry.

It was my turn to feel insecure. Could I have taken a more active part in this decision making? Did I even want to? Maybe I was content to just be Ray's old lady and tag along? But it was scary, no money, never been on the road to California. But we were living the life, things were happening fast. I had to believe when he said it was OK. Something about the awe other people felt for Ray was rubbing off on me, oblit-

erating independent thought. It was part of the closeness to let him
say, "It'll be OK." At every turn the philosophy of our love, of our beatness, or even smoking pot and the whole rebellion. "It's our identity,
Babe!" I could hear him say, challenging me to believe. "Have trust
and faith in the goodness of what is happening!"

But the West Coast scene was a whole other situation and I was still
hurting from some of the experiences in New York, even wondering if
Ray's brief involvement with that woman Marlene might mean he
didn't love me. "What about the parole officer?" I asked, even knowing
as I said it that it was useless to insist on New Jersey's right to his freedom. "We'd be back within the month easily and I'll make sure to stop
in just before we go. When we get back I'll go in there as if nothing
has happened. He'll never know."

Kind of risky, but there it was. Opportunity arose, an idea formed and it
was suddenly a reality. Maybe it was the peyote experience, everything
was so intense, the emotions were so exciting that there was no way to
consider it otherwise. I had to trust him and I did. So it was decided.

So what was going on? Was this the new face of America? What
was happening to us, to everyone? Didn't know, but it was. Changing. Was it the drugs? We all talked about it the next day in Irving's
apartment. John told us, "It's going on everywhere. The universities
are being funded to experiment with the psychological effects of hallucinogens. They think that they can remedy mental illness within the
drug-induced psychic state."

"Perhaps we are more interested in experiencing those psychic
levels," I thought to myself. "John and Irving are staying on the edges
where it's safe, John with his observations, Irving with his discipline."
Irving was in fact worrying that the joint we were now smoking would
interfere with him getting to work the next morning. "What will they
think if I come in with my mind expanded?" And he chuckled in spite
of himself. "And now. AND NOW . . . !" he said, just to make sure we
were paying attention, "You expect ME to experiment with peyote?"
Ray said, "You can't be natural, can you? Just sit down anywhere, it
doesn't matter, gulp down the fear of the unknown, gulp down some

buttons. Like us, we were wondering if we did it right, and suddenly there the experience was! Visionary! Less talk!"

We all smoked pot together in spite of our differences and ignoring the necessities of Irving's disciplined day. The brave and the irresponsible sucking up the smoke right along with the rational, the job and house holders. All gone off to another level of awareness together, laughing and high.

# RAY BREMSER

RAY BREMSER (1934–1998) was born in Jersey City, New Jersey. In the Bordentown Reformatory he began writing poetry, which found its way into Hettie and LeRoi Jones's little magazine *Yugen* in Manhattan. In 1959 and 1960, while Ray lived with Bonnie Bremser in Greenwich Village, he wrote the poems "Follow the East River" and "Blues for Bonnie—Take 1, January 1960." They were included in Bremser's first collection, *Poems of Madness,* published by the Paper Book Gallery in New York City in 1965.

## *Follow the East River*

Aquarius carried plague & water
Germans hepatitis & the crud
from over Europe,
carried the westerlies of queen Hat Shepsut
squatting the dismal width of the delta of Nile . . .

we couldn't find Memphis knowing it always was there,
thoroughly withered, neither did we reach the proper time,
period that is,
& the gears propell, repell, repeal the gloom of those tombs
we visted there.

shot out of ageless temporary america
into the middle Nile & upper regions, lower valley of Kings,
somewhere at Thebes
cataracts make their oracular presence known . . .

Amun destroy us!
shepherd annul your sheep standing on banks
& impossible ever to locate river of hell,
difficult into the Nile the Gods do wreck us
earthbound wed to the book of the dead
listening & witching
bitching the scent of an offering up to the scarab,
deathly idolon I do not assimilate prayer
& do scepters of horror instead.

we had come up the river of East on the morning of soon
or maybe yesterday, conducting a great apothogem with us,
expedition to Rome put off for the sake of the mummy
whose wrappings are there in the power that lies upon heads
which have fallen, heads which are bound & to fall
to fall is the only glory of Egypt
glory of Nefertiti wallowing there in the wine.

my dandelions gleam
wondering why the safari,
I hover the sky hover the clover blowing across the waste . . .
sphynx who are sentient yet, watching the Nile
& the fending of mad pterodactyls never in Egypt
whistle my why.

knowing the strength that is there
we ascended the hill, 61st street & hired a cab
for the graces of gods & the journey continued over the
plains of the park.

we found the museum then.
ignored the bright armor
entered the valley of pottery, mosque of the silly carpenter
burrowed amongst the pages of edible books ascribed up to

Hathor, that diligent smuggler, baker of bread for the poor
& immediately eating . . .

saw Anubis & terror
saw motion of witchery there,
saw bone of the filthy embalmer
saw seven league boots on the feat of those birds
more soarey than Bela Lugosi

It was always the mythical bird,
the Phoenix or Griffin,
Basilisk burning with eyes,
murdering mere epileptical end of the man.

those birds, those finite horrors,
birds with eagle claws & lion's breast,
gone heartless
& lacking a soul
birds who do dealings with eyes
& do evil with wings.

It was always the myth of the bird,
if we sometime could fly . . .
if we woke in the morning after next
finding wings or the power of flight by ourselves
all the birdkind of mankind would take second place for a
change.
take your museums, marijuana!!!
stick them in high & go haywire . . .

onward into the trussed up reason of myth,
we entered the hall of the barges & yachting did go . . .
I passed out at this point & awoke again amidst rowers,
rowing powerfully up the rush of the Nile.
it was midday & oceans were far in the back,
the sand of the banks grew red
& the girl in the center smiled to my wakening head.

I wanted to know this woman
—most biblical, this—the wanting of knowledge

but carnal!
I would like this of all the known women
in every known time, to possess the full snatch of the Earth,
& then maybe the visions of ultimate visual cunt
would congeal into wombus etc.
this difficult phrase to suppose.
this difficult trick, too,
fuck 'em all & continue the rest of antiquity all by myself.

this is ambition, O, dribbling jackal of art
O, fender of years in my heart's place resume of fear . . .
I pretend into pure dislocation & end in the palace of a
great queen whose bath has been drawn against logic,
for rending me there.

the funeral dirges begin.
table of maybe marble.
simmering flames, burning,
wrappings flopped in a great heap,
the vat of the end waiting, bubbling off in a corner,
doctor arose & examined the sound of my blood bleeding behind my
heart.

I am given the leave to die
in the cellar of ancient embalmers,
given the honor of dying
& suddenly thrown on the slab which is table,
slit at the throat & bleeded carefully
but quick,
damn, these Egyptians are deft & efficient!
no blotching of blood, I wonder what they do—
no spilling of fluid rushing into the veins,
but the blood which is hidden,
the blood which is mine, mine
what do they do what do they do!!!

later, forgetting the snores of all those masses of people,
forgetting the smell of formaldehyde only unknown,
I am entering pyramid slowly,
getting orisons offered & food for my travels in space,
wife to envelop my scepter with hubris of womb

& vagina utters the last gasping asking of mercy
who faltered & fell to the idiot idea we needs have of our history.
thus history kills me
history murders & offers no other appeal
in its court of museum of wax and museum of horror
the courts of our drags
our tapestry flowing down mighty
rocks of injustice, these courts in these middle dynastical
times only sentence not listen,
but murder & bury & sift out the pebble of sod
so that I might not have even the slightest of tools,
only Hathor, ammun, Hat Shepsut—& ibis
wickers about his wings gleefully over my mummified stopping of
                                                                    speed.


we return to museum,
I suffer the vision of all former life,
incarnation,
O listen you blunt cogs of humanity, reason this out for yourselves . . .


incarnation,
carnation, calling
reducing down to
the fifth only
sound of the
gods who
are new
who
are


through with it!

I have only to walk & forget to return.
my psychologist stutters,
alone in the world,
I embronzen the book of the dead in my fantastic library,
peel off the dusty umbilical cord of the dead
& paper my rooms with the odor of mold
& of tomb.

this droning of eon begging my voice to give note
only recons too slow,
that I creep into alcoves
a woman to screw & begin it again,
& again, & again,
ah, Hat Shepsut, Morgana, Elizabeth,
harpies of there
& here everywhere, harpies of lewd lack of clothing.
I rupture myself for your favor,
your hover of bower of snatch
for the ending of life
only my life.

If I dont cop no queens,
screw no queens,
I might never cop
anywhere ever.

So goes my disarmament plans
down the drain
into void
outer realm
& beyond
into ball
with a mummy or
ball with a bundle of flesh or of cloth
or of ball's very essence,
I dont know
I dont care
I am out of museum & go,
quickly frightened to home & ball wife
in defiance of the gods,
who are watching the course of my mankind,—
how history does repeat,
how it comes & comes on again & again
& tomorrow, tomorrow we visit King Arthur's Halls,
imagine . . . . . . . . . . . . .

## Blues for Bonnie—Take 1, January 1960

"these blues broke out in a gallery,
   on 9th street . . ."

"no."

"9th avenue . . . 43rd street."
   "hell—it's hell's kitchen again."

funny blues . . .
                  bonnie in washington
                  waiting for march and
                  cummings coming
                  bringing glad tidings.

                     "of 9th avenue?"

zoo.

      a dam-giraff.

                  whallop, a
                  lalapalooza floozie
                  on via flamina piazza
                  masticating a ruddy pizza
                                    pie—
                                    pie-pie.

      bye-bye, baby.

                  off to Riker a foodery . . .
                  (i dig food—soup.)

                  (if i dont get straight quick
                  the fuzz'll bust me sure as
                  i reek o reefer.
                  Rio Rita—that's as far as i'm
                  taking it.)

. . . i would eat the food
instead, oney this stud
along side me pounces eyeball
gawks as if to say,
"high as rat-shit."
and 2 fried eggs in my plate
the same thing.

how do you eat
the accuser?
and which one first?

Rio Rita.

# ANATOLE BROYARD

ANATOLE BROYARD (1920–1990) was a book critic, columnist, and editor for *The New York Times* for eighteen years. Born into an African-American family in New Orleans, he grew up in Brooklyn and attended Brooklyn College. After serving in the U.S. Army during World War II, he opened a bookstore on Cornelia Street in Greenwich Village and began to pass as a white man. Broyard later wrote in a *Times* column, "My mother and father were too folksy for me, too colorful. . . . Eventually I ran away to Greenwich Village, where no one had been born of a mother and father, where the people I met had sprung from their own brows, or from the pages of a bad novel. . . ." In 1948, describing himself as "alienated from alienation, an insider among outsiders," Broyard began publishing essays on black culture in mainstream intellectual journals such as *Commentary* and *Partisan Review.* "A Portrait of the Hipster" (*Partisan Review,* 1948) is one of these early works. It is an important if puzzling essay because, as Henry Louis Gates, Jr., later understood in his *New Yorker* profile, Broyard had "privileged access" to blacks and black culture. "But was he merely an anthropologist or was he a native informant?" In Broyard's posthumously published memoir, *Kafka Was the Rage: A Greenwich Village Memoir* (1993), he chronicled his life in Greenwich Village at a time when he felt that "American life was changing and we rode those changes. The changes were social, sexual, exciting— all the more so because we were young."

---

## A Portrait of the Hipster

As he was the illegitimate son of the Lost Generation, the hipster was really *nowhere*. And, just as amputees often seem to localize their strongest sensations in the *missing* limb, so the hipster longed, from the very beginning, to be *somewhere*. He was like a beetle on its back; his life was a struggle to get *straight*. But the law of human gravity kept him overthrown, because he was always of the minority—opposed in race or feeling to those who owned the machinery of recognition.

The hipster began his inevitable quest for self-definition by sulking in a kind of inchoate delinquency. But this delinquency was merely a negative expression of his needs, and, since it led only into the waiting arms of the ubiquitous law, he was finally forced to *formalize* his resentment and express it *symbolically*. This was the birth of a philosophy—a philosophy of *somewhereness* called *jive*, from *jibe*: to agree, or harmonize. By discharging his would-be aggressions *symbolically*, the hipster harmonized or reconciled himself with his society.

At the natural stage in its growth, jive began to talk. It had been content at first with merely making sounds—physiognomic talk—but then it developed language. And, appropriately enough, this language described the world as seen through the hipster's eyes. In fact, that was its function: to re-edit the world with new definitions . . . jive definitions.

Since articulateness is a condition for, if not actually a cause of, anxiety, the hipster relieved his anxiety by disarticulating himself. He cut the world down to size—reduced it to a small stage with a few props and a curtain of jive. In a vocabulary of a dozen verbs, adjectives, and nouns he could describe everything that happened in it. It was poker with no joker, nothing wild.

There were no neutral words in this vocabulary; it was put up or shut up, a purely polemical language in which every word had a job of *evaluation* as well as designation. These evaluations were absolute; the hipster banished all comparatives, qualifiers, and other syntactical uncertainties. Everything was dichotomously *solid, gone, out of this world,* or *nowhere, sad, beat,* a *drag.*

*In there* was, of course, somewhereness. *Nowhere,* the hipster's favorite pejorative, was an *abracadabra* to make things disappear. *Solid* connoted the stuff, the reality, of existence; it meant concreteness in a bewilderingly abstract world. A *drag* was something which "dragged" implications along with it, something which was embedded in an inseparable, complex, ambiguous—and thus, possibly threatening—context.

Because of its polemical character, the language of jive was rich in aggressiveness, much of it couched in sexual metaphors. Since the hipster never did anything as an end in itself, and since he only gave of himself in aggression of one kind or another, sex was subsumed under aggression, and it supplied a vocabulary for the mechanics of aggression. The use of the sexual metaphor was also a form of irony, like certain primitive peoples' habit of parodying civilized modes of intercourse. The person on the tail end of a sexual metaphor was conceived of as lugubriously victimized; i.e., expecting but not receiving.

One of the basic ingredients of jive language was a priorism. The a priori assumption was a short cut to somewhereness. It arose out of a desperate, unquenchable need to know the score; it was a great projection, a primary, self-preserving postulate. It meant "it is given to us to understand." The indefinable authority it provided was like a powerful primordial or instinctual orientation in a threatening chaos of complex interrelations. The hipster's frequent use of metonymy and metonymous gestures (e.g., brushing palms for handshaking, extending an index finger, without raising the arm, as a form of greeting, etc.) also connoted prior understanding, there is no need to elaborate, I dig you, man, etc.


Carrying his language and his new philosophy like concealed weapons, the hipster set out to conquer the world. He took his stand on the corner and began to direct human traffic. His significance was unmistakable. His face—"the cross-section of a motion"—was frozen in the "physiognomy of astuteness." Eyes shrewdly narrowed, mouth slackened in the extremity of perspicuous sentience, he kept tabs, like a suspicious proprietor, on his environment. He stood always a little apart from the group. His feet solidly planted, his shoulders drawn up, his elbows in, hands pressed to sides, he was a pylon around whose implacability the world obsequiously careered.

Occasionally he brandished his padded shoulders, warning humanity to clear him a space. He flourished his thirty-one-inch pegs like banners. His two- and seven-eighths-inch brim was snapped with absolute symmetry. Its exactness was a symbol of his control, his domination of contingency. From time to time he turned to the candy store window, and with an esoteric gesture, reshaped his roll collar, which came up very high on his neck. He was, indeed, up to the neck in somewhereness.

He affected a white streak, made with powder, in his hair. This was the outer sign of a significant, prophetic mutation. And he always wore dark glasses, because normal light offended his eyes. He was an underground man, requiring especial adjustment to ordinary conditions; he was a lucifugous creature of the darkness, where sex, gambling, crime, and other bold acts of consequence occurred.

At intervals he made an inspection tour of the neighborhood to see that everything was in order. The importance of this round was implicit in the portentous trochees of his stride, which, being unnaturally accentual, or discontinuous, expressed his particularity, lifted him, so to speak, out of the ordinary rhythm of normal cosmic pulsation. He was a discrete entity—separate, critical, and defining.


Jive music and tea were the two most important components of the hipster's life. Music was not, as has often been supposed, a stimulus to dancing. For the hipster rarely danced; he was beyond the reach of stimuli. If he did dance, it was half parody—"second removism"—and he danced only to the off-beat, in a morganatic one to two ratio with the music.

Actually, jive music was the hipster's autobiography, a score to which his life was the text. The first intimations of jive could be heard in the Blues. Jive's Blue Period was very much like Picasso's: it dealt with lives that were sad, stark, and isolated. It represented a relatively realistic or naturalistic stage of development.

Blues turned to jazz. In jazz, as in early, analytical cubism, things were sharpened and accentuated, thrown into bolder relief. Words were used somewhat less frequently than in Blues; the instruments talked instead. The solo instrument became the narrator. Sometimes (e.g., Cootie Williams) it came very close to literally talking. Usually it spoke passionately, violently, complainingly, against a background of excitedly pulsating drums and guitar, ruminating bass, and assenting orchestration. But, in spite of its passion, jazz was almost always co herent and its intent clear and unequivocal.

Bebop, the third stage in jive music, was analogous in some respects to synthetic cubism. Specific situations, or referents, had largely disappeared; only their "essences" remained. By this time the hipster was no longer willing to be regarded as a primitive; bebop, therefore, was "cerebral" music, expressing the hipster's pretensions, his desire for an imposing, fulldress body of doctrine.

Surprise, "second-removism" and extended virtuosity were the chief characteristics of the bebopper's style. He often achieved surprise by using a tried and true tactic of his favorite comic strip heroes:

> The "enemy" is waiting in a room with drawn gun. The hero kicks open the door and bursts in—*not upright, in the line of fire*—but cleverly lying on the floor, from which position he triumphantly blasts away, while the enemy still aims, ineffectually, at his own expectations.

Borrowing this stratagem, the bebop soloist often entered at an unexpected altitude, came in on an unexpected note, thereby catching the listener off guard and conquering him before he recovered from his surprise.

"Second-removism"—*capping* the *squares*—was the dogma of initiation. It established the hipster as keeper of enigmas, ironical pedagogue, a self-appointed exegete. Using his *shrewd* Socratic method, he discovered the world to the naive, who still tilted with the windmills of one-level meaning. That which you heard in bebop was always *something else, not* the thing you expected; it was always negatively derived, abstraction *from,* not *to.*

The virtuosity of the bebopper resembled that of the street-corner evangelist who revels in his unbroken delivery. The remarkable run-on quality of bebop solos suggested the infinite resources of the hipster, who could improvise indefinitely, whose invention knew no end, who was, in fact, omniscient.

All the best qualities of jazz—tension, élan, sincerity, violence, immediacy—were toned down in bebop. Bebop's style seemed to consist, to a great extent, in *evading* tension, in connecting, by extreme dexterity, each phrase with another, so that nothing remained, everything was lost in a shuffle of decapitated cadences. This corresponded to the hipster's social behavior as jester, jongleur, or prestidigitator. But it was his own fate he had caused to disappear for the audience, and now the only trick he had left was the monotonous gag of pulling himself—by his own ears, grinning and gratuitous—up out of the hat.

The élan of jazz was weeding out of bebop because all enthusiasm was naive, nowhere, too simple. Bebop was the hipster's seven types of ambiguity, his Laocoön, illustrating his struggle with his own defensive deviousness. It was the disintegrated symbol, the shards, of his attitude toward himself and the world. It presented the hipster as performer, retreated to an abstract stage of *tea* and pretension, losing himself in the multiple mirrors of his fugitive chords. This conception was borne out by the surprising mediocrity of bebop orchestrations, which often had the perfunctory quality of vaudeville music, played only to announce the coming spectacle, the soloist, the great Houdini.

Bebop rarely used words, and, when it did, they were only nonsense syllables, significantly paralleling a contemporaneous loss of vitality in jive language itself. Blues and jazz were documentary in a social sense; bebop was the hipster's Emancipation Proclamation in double talk. It showed the hipster as the victim of his own system, volubly tongue-tied, spitting out his own teeth, running between the raindrops of his spattering chords, never getting wet, washed clean, baptized, or quenching his thirst. He no longer had anything relevant to himself to say—in both his musical and linguistic expression he had finally abstracted himself from his real position in society.

His next step was to abstract himself in action. *Tea* made this possible. Tea (marijuana) and other drugs supplied the hipster with an indispensable outlet. His situation was too extreme, too tense, to be satisfied with mere fantasy or animistic domination of the environment. Tea provided him with a free world to expatiate in. It had the same function as trance in Bali, where the unbearable flatness and de-emotionalization of "waking" life is compensated for by trance ecstasy. The hipster's life, like the Balinese's, became schizoid; whenever possible, he escaped into the richer world of tea, where, for the helpless and humiliating image of a beetle on its back, he could substitute one of himself floating or flying, "high" in spirits, dreamily dissociated, in contrast to the ceaseless pressure exerted on him in real life. Getting high was a form of artificially induced dream catharsis. It differed from *lush* (whisky) in that it didn't encourage aggression. It fostered, rather, the sentimental values so deeply lacking in the hipster's life. It became a *raison d'être,* a calling, an experience shared with fellow believers, a respite, a heaven or haven.

Under jive the external world was greatly simplified for the hipster, but his own role in it grew considerably more complicated. The function of his simplification had been to reduce the world to schematic proportions which could easily be manipulated in actual, symbolical, or ritual relationships; to provide him with a manageable mythology. Now, moving in this mythology, this tense fantasy of somewhereness, the hipster supported a completely solipsistic system. His every word and gesture now had a history and a burden of implication.

Sometimes he took his own solipsism too seriously and slipped into criminal assertions of his will. Unconsciously, he still wanted terribly to take part in the cause and effect that determined the real world. Because he had not been allowed to conceive of himself functionally or socially, he had conceived of himself *dramatically,* and, taken in by his own art, he often enacted it in actual defiance, self-assertion, impulse, or crime.

That he was a direct expression of his culture was immediately apparent in its reaction to him. The less sensitive elements dismissed him as they dismissed everything. The intellectuals *manqués,* however, the desperate barometers of society, took him into their bosom. Ransacking everything for meaning, admiring insurgence, they attributed every heroism to the hipster. He became their "there but for the grip of my superego go I." He was received in the Village as an oracle; his language was *the revolution of the word, the personal idiom.* He was the great instinctual man, an ambassador from the Id. He was asked to read things, look at things, feel things, taste things, and report. What was it? Was it *in there?* Was it *gone?* Was it *fine?* He was an interpreter for the blind, the deaf, the dumb, the insensible, the impotent.

With such an audience, nothing was too much. The hipster promptly became, in his own eyes, a poet, a seer, a hero. He laid claims to apocalyptic visions and heuristic discoveries when he *picked up;* he was Lazarus, come back from the dead, come back to tell them all, he would tell them all. He conspicuously consumed himself in a high flame. He cared nothing for catabolic consequences; he was so prodigal as to be invulnerable.

And here he was ruined. The frantic praise of the impotent meant recognition—*actual somewhereness*—to the hipster. He got what he wanted; he stopped protesting, reacting. He began to bureaucratize jive as a machinery for securing the actual—really the *false*—somewhereness. Jive, which had originally been a critical system, a kind of Surrealism, a personal revision of existing disparities, now grew moribundly self-conscious, smug, encapsulated, isolated from its source, from the sickness which spawned it. It grew more rigid than the institutions it had set out to defy. It became a boring routine. The hipster—once an unregenerate individualist, an underground poet, a guerrilla—had become a pretentious poet laureate. His old subversiveness, his ferocity, was now so manifestly rhetorical as to be obviously harmless. He was bought and placed in the zoo. He was *somewhere* at last—comfortably ensconced in the 52nd Street clip joints, in Carnegie Hall, and *Life*. He was *in-there* . . . he was back in the American womb. And it was just as unhygienic as ever.

# ROBERT BRUSTEIN

ROBERT BRUSTEIN had just completed his doctorate at Columbia University and was lecturing there in the School of Dramatic Arts when he attacked the Beat writers in "The Cult of Unthink" for *Horizon* magazine in September 1958. Brustein went on to publish *The Theatre of Revolt: Studies in Modern Drama* in 1964, among many other books. Currently he is Artistic Director of the American Repertory Theatre at Loeb Drama Center in Cambridge, Massachusetts.

## *The Cult of Unthink*

When a hitherto unknown actor named Marlon Brando eleven years ago assumed the role of Stanley Kowalski, the glowering, inarticulate

hero of Tennessee Williams' *A Streetcar Named Desire,* few people realized the symbolic importance of that creation. For Brando was to
personify an entire postwar generation of troubled spirits trying to find
an identity. Today we find his Kowalski wherever we look, whether in
our latest literature, our poetry, our painting, our movies, our popular
music, or on our city streets. In one guise or another he is the hero of
the Beat Generation.

This new ideal image, as Brando first gave it dramatic form and as
tribal followers from coast to coast have adopted it, is that of a man of
much muscle and little mind, often surly and discontented, prepared to
offer violence with little provocation. He peers out at the world from
under beetling eyebrows, his right hand rests casually on his right hip.
Walking with a slouching, shuffling gait, he scratches himself often and
almost never smiles. He is especially identified by the sounds that issue
from his mouth. He squeezes, he grunts, he passes his hand over his
eyes and forehead, he stares steadily, he turns away, he scratches, then
again faces his adversary, and finally speaks—or tries to.

The new hero has cut himself off from cultural and social life and
now seems close to abdicating even from himself. Whether he throws
words on a page, like the San Francisco novelist Jack Kerouac, or pig-
ment onto a canvas like the "action" painter Franz Kline, whether he
mumbles through a movie or shimmies in the frenetic gyrations of
rock-'n-roll, he is a man belligerently exalting his own inarticulateness.
He "howls" when he has the energy, and when he doesn't, sits around
"beat" and detached, in a funk. He is hostile to the mind, petulant toward tradition, and indifferent to order and coherence. He is concerned chiefly with indulging his own feelings, glorifying his own
impulses, securing his own "cool" kicks. His most characteristic sound
is a stammer or a saxophone wail: his most characteristic symbol, a
blotch and a glob of paint.

He exults in solitude and frequently speaks proudly of his "personal vision." Yet, while outwardly individualistic and antisocial, he is
inwardly conformist. He travels in packs, writes collective manifestoes, establishes group heroes like the late movie star James Dean,
and adheres to the ethics of the coterie. He is "existential" without
having developed any substantial existence. If he has a coherent philosophy, it is one of simple negation without any purposeful individual
rebellion to sustain it.

The novelists and poets now centering in San Francisco are the most striking examples of conformists masquerading as rebels. They travel together, drink together, "smoke pot" together, publish together, dedicate works to each other, share the same pony-tailed girls in faded blue jeans, wear a uniform costume, and take for their collective theme the trials and tribulations of their own troubled souls. "I saw the best minds of my generation destroyed by madness, starving hysterical naked," writes Allen Ginsberg, the most talented of the group, before launching into a description of the worst degradations to which the human animal can descend. The only horror not included in it is loneliness, for the Beat Generation suffers its degradations en masse.

Although they pretend to "disaffiliate" from the "Social Lie," Ginsberg, Kerouac, William Burroughs, Michael McClure, Michael Rumaker and other writers of the Generation are the Joiners of the new age, eschewing the Lions and the Shriners for a club whose rules, though more unusual, are no less strict. Their extremely limited language, derived from the "hip" talk of "cool" jazz musicians, is a coterie argot designed to exclude the common run of "squares" who don't "dig" their message. But the coterie's message has an automatism about it that exposes its communal roots. Only Ginsberg ever expresses anger, the emotion of rebellion. The rest are either "cool," detached, separated from the world and their own existences, or brimming full of an indiscriminate enthusiasm for everything.

Take Jack Kerouac. His novel *On the Road* (1957), is a picaresque work in which the author, under a pseudonym, speeds from place to place across the country, usually in a car at up to 110 miles per hour, embracing people, cities, plains, and mountains. The book has an unflagging Whitmanesque zing and demonstrates that Kerouac, like most Americans, worships pure physical energy:

> The only people for me are the mad ones, the ones who are mad to live, mad to talk, mad to be saved, desirous of everything at the same time, the ones who never yawn or say a commonplace thing, but burn, burn, burn like fabulous yellow roman candles exploding like spiders across the stars and in the middle you see the blue centerlight pop and everybody goes "Awww!"

Kerouac's most typical response is "Wow," but he makes sure to keep his feelings uncommitted and his energy undirected. In fact, he embraces everything on equal terms: "We love everything . . . we dig it all. We're in the vanguard of a new religion." And Kenneth Rexroth, a poet from another generation who is trying to give his own meaning to the movement, like an elder politician running on a young man's ticket, sees in this and other expressions like it a new affirmation of faith, reflecting a "reverence for life."

It is clear, however, that Kerouac's "reverence for life," like that of his friends, is actually a disguised disgust and boredom with life. For to be "desirous of everything at the same time" is really to be happy with nothing. It is no accident that Kerouac's characters are constantly seeking new kicks outside the pale of everyday experience: the experience of everyday life never touches them. In that speeding car, only the objects move (as if seen in a rearview projector giving the illusion of movement behind stationary actors) while the characters stand immobile. Never learning or growing or developing, they remain perpetually hungry until the inevitable disenchantment sets in:

> [I wished] I were a Negro, feeling that the best the white world offered was not enough ecstasy for me, not enough life, joy, kicks, darkness, music not enough night . . . I wished I were a Denver Mexican, or even a poor overworked Jap, anything but what I was so drearily, a "white man" disillusioned.

This attempt to identify one's self with dispossessed minorities is the hipster's effort to adopt a ready-made motivation for his rebellion. In its discontent with physical limitations, it also reflects an effort to escape from the self. This escape takes other forms in "dreams . . . drugs . . . waking nightmares, alcohol . . ." as poet Ginsberg, who celebrates the more sinister side of the movement, puts it. Under these influences, hallucinations are hailed as visions. Ginsberg's "angel-headed hipster" seeks "the ancient heavenly connection to the starry dynamo in the machinery of night," and if he can't find it with the aid of the various narcotics he mentions, he turns to "Plotinus Poe St. John of the Cross telepathy and bop kaballa," not to mention Zen Buddhism. For the hipster, these philosophies are designed to initiate him not into life but into nothingness. Thus:

> For just a moment I had reached the point of ecstasy that I had always wanted to reach, which was the complete step across chronological time into timeless shadows, and wonder-

ment at the bleakness of the mortal realm, and the sensation
of death kicking at my heels to move on . . .

Here Kerouac is explicitly celebrating the attractiveness of death, just
as Ginsberg frequently writes of his desire to curl up in the soft comfort of the womb. The other side of complete acceptance, then, is
complete rejection, withdrawal into the "cool" neutral realm of perfect
passivity. The opposite of "mad" is "beat"—and Kerouac defines "beat"
as "beatific." One might more accurately, in describing this movement,
talk of its reverence for death, since it leads its advocates into the bot-
tomless void.

Although it embodies a vague intellectuality, this literary movement is persistently anti-intellectual. "I DON'T KNOW I DON'T CARE AND
IT DOESN'T MAKE ANY DIFFERENCE," Kerouac affirms in his "philosophical final statement," and the stammering hero of his second book, *The
Subterraneans,* bears him out: "Details are the life of it," he shouts:
"say everything on your mind, don't hold it back, don't analyze or anything as you go along." Before this indiscriminate accumulation of details—the hallmark of the new writing—order, analysis, form, and
eventually coherence give way. The result is a style like automatic
writing or an Eisenhower press conference, stupefying in its unread-
ability. Most of the San Franciscans' works are like the modern "cool"
jazz that forms the background against which they are often read
aloud: the main theme founders and breaks down under a welter of
subjective variations. Kerouac, Ginsberg, McClure, and the others
fling words on a page not as an act of communication but as an act of
aggression; we are prepared for violence on every page.

Although the San Franciscans talk a great deal about "essences,"
the only feeling one gets from their work about the essence of life is
that it is upsettingly discontinuous and jerky and that it alternates between aggression and passivity. It is no accident that many of them are
followers of the late Wilhelm Reich, a maverick psychiatrist who
treated patients by placing them in the "orgone box" he had invented.
His box might well be the monument to their movement: for in it, cultural withdrawal is complete, will and intelligence are suspended, and
the emotions are at the mercy of mysterious "cosmic" stimuli.

The mixed aggression and passivity of the hipster literati are an index of the adolescent quality of their rebellion. So is their accent on

youth: about the only crime offensive to all of them is that of growing old. Juvenile delinquency, on the other hand, is often a subject for glorification, since it is an expression of spontaneous feelings. Dean Moriarty, one of the central characters of *On the Road* (and also the secret hero of Ginsberg's poem "Howl"), is too confused to speak clearly, but he expresses himself by stealing cars, taking drugs, and conning his friends. Moriarty's childish irresponsibility has in it something so poignant that Kerouac hails him as a "new kind of American saint." Other subjects for canonization by the San Franciscans are the motorcycle set—Ginsberg's "saintly motorcyclists" and Kerouac's "Texas poets of the night"—whose angelic deeds are daily immortalized in quite a different way on the country's police blotters. It is hardly a coincidence that the argot of teen-age gangs and of the hipster literati is almost identical. It is not so long a jump from the kick-seeking poet to the kick-seeking adolescent who, sinking his knife into the flesh of his victim, thanked him for the "experience."

It is significant that the heroes and saints of the Beat Generation are all death lovers and escapists. The junkies, the derelicts, the delinquents, the madmen, the criminals, and the Outsiders who people this literature have in common their paralysis in the face of all intelligible forms of behavior. In this they are counterparts of the personification created on the level of popular culture by Marlon Brando and aped by large numbers of Stanislavsky Method actors since. In *The Wild One,* for example, Brando played a "saintly motorcyclist," equipped with leather jacket, studded belt, and violent nature, of the type Ginsberg and Kerouac exalt in their writing. Brando, who has a strong social conscience, has expressed regret at his participation in this film and lately has even been attempting roles of a more articulate nature. But the success of his imitators—James Dean, Ralph Meeker, Ben Gazzara, Paul Newman, Rod Steiger, and countless others—testifies to the persistent popularity of a hero unlike any before seen in the movies.

Like the heroes of San Francisco literature, this hero is extremely withdrawn, but his subjectivity seems as much the result of the actor's technique as of the scenarist's concept. The famous Method of the Russian director Stanislavsky, as presently practiced in this country, exalts the actor's personality over the written word. That is, the actor imposes his experience on the part rather than—like, say, Sir Laurence Olivier—subordinates himself to it. The personality of many Method actors, however, rather than being an individual expression, is often a parody of Brando's playing of Stanley Kowalski. The result of this imitation is a culture hero with easily distinguishable traits. Important among them is that he is usually a delinquent of some kind and that—for all the dependence of his media on language—he cannot talk.

The hero's link with the Beat Generation is signified by the fact that he is invariably an outcast or a rebel who stands in a very uneasy relationship with society. His rebellion, like that of the San Francisco writers, is expressed as much through his costume (torn T shirt, leather jacket, blue jeans) as through his behavior, for in a world of suits and ties, a shabby, careless appearance is an open sign of alienation. Again as in the case of the San Franciscans, his rebellion seems to be unmotivated. It no longer has any political or social relevance, and it is obscured by his inability to describe it. Most often, he is a rebel without a cause, whose sense of grievance has turned inward on himself, making his grip on reality extremely uncertain. Although he often travels in groups, sometimes in juvenile gangs, he seems to be alienated even from his friends. He is a man whom nobody understands and who understands nobody. Toward the world of authority—his father, his teachers, and the police—he feels hostile and he seems to be submissive only with his girl friend. His confusion has isolated him within a self which he cannot comprehend and which, in consequence, causes him unspeakable pain.

In this character, the inarticulate hero appears in a number of movies that despite surface differences never seem to change in essential parts. More timorous than literature and subject to rigid production codes, these movies do not glorify the hero's delinquency (he is usually converted to righteousness before the end), but they do their best to exploit it. His violent nature, for example, is allowed expression but is channeled into the service of benevolence: it is directed always against the "bad guys" and helps the hero to move over to the right side.

In *On the Waterfront,* Marlon Brando is an ex-prizefighter who works on the docks. He is isolated even from his peers and can find consolation only in homing pigeons. When his brother is murdered, he decides, despite his hatred of the police, to inform on the labor racketeers who killed him and, at the end, engages in a bloody fist fight with the thugs. In *Rebel Without a Cause,* the young hero (James Dean) cannot come to terms with his family or gain acceptance by his adolescent contemporaries. To win the friendship of the latter, he agrees to play "chicken" with hot-rod cars, a game which results in the death of the gang's leader. Unable to tell the police or his father, he is attacked by the revenging gang. In *Edge of the City,* a friendless wanderer (John Cassavetes) on the run from the police, gets a job as a longshoreman and is shown the ropes by a fatherly Negro. When the Negro is slain in a brutal hook fight, he battles with the vicious foreman who killed his friend.

Despite the fact that it is invariably represented as a benevolent social gesture, the hero's violence, along with his inarticulateness, exposes his antisocial nature. He rejects communication with the outside world and yields to his basic impulses. Whatever intelligence he has is subordinated to his feelings. But even the emotions of this hero are blunted and brutalized. It is significant that he rarely exhibits anger, the civilized expression of the aggressiveness he feels, but only violence, its primitive expression. He remains "cool" until the moment comes to strike. Without a language, he cannot understand or express his feelings; he can only act them out. Like Melville's Billy Budd, who could express himself only with a blow because of his stuttering speech, the movie hero illustrates his feelings most characteristically with his fists.

Early this year, a rock-'n-roll jamboree at Boston led to riots, and it is clear that the Beat Generation hero, like certain rock-'n-roll singers, reflects anarchic impulses in the young. Rejection of coherent speech for mumbles, grunts, and physical gyrations is a symptom of this anarchy, for speech is an instrument of control. Rebelliousness has always been essential to any awakening of the young, for it leads them to question existing values, to pierce lifeless conventions, and to erect a moral or a social structure more true to life as they see it. But today's rebellion can define neither its own values nor those of the authority it rejects. Such juvenile rebellion, rather than being a true expression of individualism, stems from an impulse to belong and usually ends in some kind of conformity. The memorial cult that developed after the death of James Dean had no program except "togetherness." Similarly, the one reward to which the hero of these movies aspires is acceptance by the group. His conflict has been caused not by considered intellectual disagreement but by misunderstanding—that is, he is thought to be hostile because he cannot express his true feelings. But although most of these films end with the hero's acceptance by society or by the gang or by his father (as in the case of Dean's characters), nothing has truly been resolved. The inarticulate hero never makes the lonely step to maturity. When James Dean grows to middle age in *Giant*, his character doesn't change; he merely has some powder added to his hair.

The difference between the new rebellion and the earlier one of the 1930's in the theater can be seen in their contrasting types of expression. Although the new hero descends from the older "social-protest" drama (he wears the same shabby costume as the proletarian hero of those days), some highly significant changes have been made. The actors and writers of the old Group Theater were highly articulate people, rather than stammerers. John Garfield, Luther Adler, and Lee J. Cobb, the most representative actors in the group, were notable for their direct delivery, the intensity of their emotions, and their poetic intelligence; and Clifford Odets was one of America's most dynamic and eloquent playwrights. Furthermore, Odets' characters were fully engaged in the world and highly aware of the forces against which they were rebelling. One could disagree with the playwright's interpretation of social events, but only because one always knew precisely what his meaning was. The new acting and writing, on the other hand, is remarkable for its de-emphasis of language and its brutalization of character. The inarticulate hero portrays no feeling at all directly. He is persistently engaged in playing *against* his emotions.

A scene from *On the Waterfront* illustrates the two approaches. Brando, playing a dockworker, comes into conflict with the veteran Lee J. Cobb, playing a labor boss. The two actors confront each other across a table, both presumably fighting mad. Cobb communicates this directly, manipulating his bulk, slamming on the table, thrusting out his jaw, letting his power erupt across the room. Brando, on the other hand, suppresses his emotions, examining his fingers, shifting in his chair, surveying his antagonist with an intense but blank expression, stammering quietly, simmering rather than boiling. Both are using the subjective Stanislavsky Method, but the technique leads Cobb to reveal himself, Brando to hide. Cobb's anger is kinetic, explosive, articulate, while Brando's is repressed, internalized, and "cool." Brando is "beat"; he never raises his voice, but we know that the character he plays will momentarily spring into violence. Cobb has contact with things and people; Brando is alone in his own private world. . . .


Taken together in their inarticulateness, obscurity, and self-isolation, the assorted bearers of Beat Generation attitudes in the various arts in America show an increasing reluctance to come to grips with life. They seem to be engaged in a new kind of expatriation—this time more symbolic than geographic. Unlike the expatriates of the past, they are not moving toward what they see as culture and enlightenment, but away from it. Having abdicated the traditional responsibilities of the avant-garde—that of facing existing culture squarely and honestly if only to criticize, condemn, or demolish it—they seem determined to slough off all responsibility whatsoever. In this, the artists of the Beat Generation differ from Britain's Angry Young Men today, who not only have serious public and intellectual causes to fight for but are highly articulate about them. But we may take solace in the fact that America also has artists who are eloquent, individualistic, and above all sympathetic to the claims of the intelligence, and who no doubt will outlast the Kowalski cult of unthink.

# CHRISTOPHER BUCKLEY AND PAUL SLANSKY

CHRISTOPHER BUCKLEY joined with PAUL SLANSKY to pay the ultimate tribute to Beat poetry in the form of a "Howl" parody, "Yowl for Jay McInerney," the American novelist. It was published in *The New Republic* on December 8, 1986, to mark the thirtieth anniversary of "Howl for Carl Solomon." Buckley is the author of *The White House Mess* (1986) and *Wry Martinis* (1997). Slansky is a Los Angeles–based writer.

## Yowl
### For Jay McInerney

### I

I saw the best minds of my generation destroyed by stress
    frazzled overtired burnt-out,
jogging through suburban streets at dawn
    as suggested by the late James Fixx,
career-minded yupsters burning for an Amstel Light
    watching Stupid Pet Tricks,
who upwardly mobile and designer'd and bright-eyed and high sat up
    working in the track-lit glow of the Tribeca loft skimming
    through the Day Timer while padding the expense account,
who passed through universities and saved their asses hallucinating
                                        Grateful
    Dead posters and eating Sara Lee while watching the war on TV,
who were graduated and went on to law schools burning to save the
                                        world,
who brewed decaffeinated coffee doing their yoga in alligator shirts
    and listening to the latest Windham Hill Sampler,
who ate chocolate croissants in outdoor cafés and drank blush
    wine on Columbus Avenue washed down with a little Percodan
    with Dove bars with Diet Coke with Lean Cuisine,
stopping by on the way home for a pound of David's cookies
    telling each other of their fears of intimacy and their need
    for space and inability to commit—for now,
who watched Mary Tyler Moore reruns and wept for Rhoda and
                                        worried about
    acid rain and the mercury in the swordfish while strung out on
                                        cyclamates
    faces flushed with MSG even after specifically making a point of
    mentioning to the waiter not to put it in,
who prowled through uncertain money markets chewing Tums and
    doing lines with the Hispanics in the mail room
    sitting in the gents with baby-laxative runs while the boss buzzes
    and the secretary says you're on the phone to Bonn,

who stayed up too late working out their relationships 'n' things feeling
  the gnawing rat-fear that they hadn't been communicating lately
                                                            and
  the urgent pounding screaming need to think about their priorities,
yacketayakking analyzing thinking it through making constructive
  suggestions as the eastern sky flamed in raw Ralph Lauren pastels,
got to get away for a few days but the Hartmann luggage is being
  repaired oh,
who needs this wandering through Needless-Markup wailing (inside)
                                                            for
  the baby seals and the bunnies slaughtered for lipstick
  remembering all the unanswered anti-vivisection junk mail on the
  way to the appliances section to beg another blade for the Cuisinart,
who subscribed to *Gourmet* and the *American Lawyer* and after an
                                                       exhausting
  search found Jamaica time-shares in the classifieds for only
  $1200 a month coping as best they could with the Negro beach boys
  wanting to sell them ganja,
paying outrageous sums for bottled water and having to complain
  about the maid service and the warm orange juice knowing they
                                                       should
  have gone to Cape Cod instead where the Peugeot mopeds fart
                                                       carbon
  monoxide and the half-eaten lobster rolls rot in wax paper on the
  sidewalks and the Republican men in lime-green corduroys with
                                                       little
  orange elephants bray as their wives buy overpriced scrimshaw,
who nudged and nuzzled over margaritas and dreamed of endless
  throbbing hot sticky sex but Not tonite dear I have a yeast infection,
running on spongy Reeboks to sublimate their lust
  then plunging into *Bright Lights, Big City,*
who upped their nightly hits of Valium from two to five mgs and
  worried if they were going to be groggy in the morning,
who hollow-eyed and febrile read the theater reviews in unread
  issues of the *New Yorker* yes the *New Yorker,*
who watched re-reruns of Mary Tyler Moore and decided they hated
                                                       Rhoda,
who skimmed the Banana Republic catalog with brain-dead gaze
  wondering if they really needed Ethiopian saddlebags,

who padded back and forth to the john for endless glasses of water
                                                                    while
   worrying about refinancing at ten and an eighth and waited for the
   fiendish tweet of birds and the thud of the *Wall Street Journal*
   on the porch,
who took a little tootsky after their Yoplait just to get going
   and buzzzzzzzzzzzzzzzzzzzzzzzed along in the carpool
   yattering to the gray-flannelled bottisatvas in the backseat
   about rowing machines and Eddie Murphy's homo jokes,
ah Jay while you are not safe I am not safe and now *Ransom*
   is remaindered at Waldenbooks and you're really in a bind—
and who therefore drown in butter-flavored popcorn at the Cineplex
                                                                    as the
   answering machines cutely speak to strangers and Discover cards are
   mailed to the incorrect addresses while Mohawked clerks at Tower
   Records with little crucifixes in their ears play "Pillow Talk" and
   everything you want they only have in Beta.

## II

Yuck! Gross! Eeewww! Buying crack from the zombies in the
   park! Closing out the trust fund! Checking into the rehab!

## III

Jay McInerney! I'm with you at Area
   where the shark swims on the wall
I'm with you David Letterman on the tower
   where you drop watermelons and TVs and bowling balls
I'm with you Gary Hart in New Hampshire
   where you stammer and yammer about New Ideas
I'm with you Don Johnson in Miami
   where you don't wear socks
I'm with you Jerry Rubin on Wall Street
   where you only hear yippie when the Dow hits a high
I'm with you Donald Trump on Fifth Avenue
   where Steven Spielberg has an apartment in your building
I'm with you John McEnroe in England
   where you appear on world television treating people like scum

I'm with you Maria Shriver in Hyannisport
   where a wedding gift from Kurt Waldheim has arrived
I'm with you John Zaccaro at Middlebury
   where you pursue independent study projects
I'm with you Doctor Ruth on cable
   where you giggle with your guests about orgasm
I'm with you Ron Jr cavorting
   in your underwear on national television
I'm with you Mike Deaver in Bitburg
   where your mind was on buying a car
I'm with you Billy Crystal in too many places
   where your routines have not aged well
I'm with you Brooke Shields at Princeton
   where you—but who cares?
I'm with you on the Upper East Side
   pricing modems
I'm with you on the Upper East Side
   stopping into the Food Emporium for a quart of lo-fat milk
I'm with you on the Upper East Side
   eating sushi and Ecstacy
I'm with you on the Upper East Side
   looking for myself in *People* magazine

---

# WILLIAM S. BURROUGHS

WILLIAM S. BURROUGHS (1914–1997) enjoyed passing along
what he humorously called "my specialized bits of wisdom like
'always use poultry shears to cut off fingers' " and "Never participate in active or passive role in *any* shooting things off of, or
near one, or knife throwing or *anything similar,* and, if a by-
stander, always try to stop it" (letter to Allen Ginsberg, February 7, 1955). But unlike his friends Ginsberg and Kerouac,
Burroughs rarely gave his views on the phenomenon known as
the Beat Generation, with perhaps the notable exception of his
essay "Remembering Jack Kerouac." Burroughs wrote it for the
1982 conference sponsored by the Naropa Institute in Boulder,

Colorado, to commemorate the twenty-fifth anniversary of the publication of *On the Road*.

As the critic Vince Passaro observed, Burroughs lived long enough to have been "commercially morphed into the grand old man of American freakdom, the last living beatnik widow, a 'cool' face in a Nike ad, and a background vocalist on Tom Waits and Laurie Anderson records." But Passaro also understood that "in reality, however, Burroughs was a dangerous man, not only an actual killer but a theoretician of crime and resistance, someone who strove to forge the unspeakable into an art form. With his passing, the American literary world lost more than the thin, neatly dressed Beat icon that the mainstream obituaries described; it lost the last of its revolutionary modernists." "Remembering Jack Kerouac" was included in Burroughs's *The Adding Machine* (1985).

---

## Remembering Jack Kerouac

Jack Kerouac was a writer. That is, he wrote. Many people who call themselves writers and have their names on books are not writers and they can't write, like a bullfighter who makes passes with no bull there. The writer has been there or he can't write about it. And going there, he risks being gored. By that I mean what the Germans aptly call the Time Ghost. For example, such a fragile ghost world as Fitzgerald's Jazz Age—all the sad young men, firefly evenings, winter dreams, fragile, fragile like his picture taken in his twenty-third year— Fitzgerald, poet of the Jazz Age. He went there and wrote it and brought it back for a generation to read, but he never found his own way back. A whole migrant generation arose from Kerouac's *On the Road* to Mexico, Tangier, Afghanistan, India.

What are writers, and I will confine the use of this term to writers of novels, trying to do? They are trying to create a universe in which they have lived or where they would like to live. To write it, they must go there and submit to conditions that they may not have bargained for. Sometimes, as in the case of Fitzgerald and Kerouac, the effect produced by a writer is immediate, as if a generation were waiting to be written. In other cases, there may be a time lag. Science fiction, for example, has a way of coming true. In any case, by writing a universe, the writer makes such a universe possible.

To what extent writers can and do act out their writing in so-called real life, and how useful it is for their craft, are open questions. That is, are you making your universe more like the real universe, or are you pulling the real one into yours? Winner take nothing. For example, Hemingway's determination to act out the least interesting aspects of his own writing and to actually be his character, was, I feel, unfortunate for his writing. Quite simply, if a writer insists on being able to do and do well what his characters do, he limits the range of his characters.

However, writers profit from doing something even when done badly. I was, for one short week—brings on my ulcers to think about it—a very bad assistant pickpocket. I decided that a week was enough, and I didn't have the touch, really.

Walking around the wilderness of outer Brooklyn with the Sailor after a mooch (as he called a drunk) came up on us at the end of Flatbush: "The cops'll beat the shit out of us . . . you have to expect that." I shuddered and didn't want to expect that and decided right there that I was going to turn in my copy of the *Times,* the one I would use to cover him when he put the hand out. We always used the same copy—he said people would try to read it and get confused when it was a month old, and this would keep them from seeing us. He was quite a philosopher, the Sailor was . . . but a week was enough before I got what I "had to expect . . ."

"Here comes one . . . yellow lights, too." We huddle in a vacant lot. . . . Speaking for myself at least, who can always see what I look like from outside, I look like a frightened commuter clutching his briefcase as Hell's Angels roar past.

Now if this might seem a cowardly way, cowering in a vacant lot when I should have given myself the experience of getting worked over by the skinny short cop with the acne-scarred face who looks out of that prowl car, his eyes brown and burning in his head—well, the Sailor wouldn't have liked that, and neither would a White Hunter have liked a client there to get himself mauled by a lion.

Fitzgerald said once to Hemingway, "Rich people are different from you and me."

"Yes . . . they have more money." And writers are different from you and me. They write. You don't bring back a story if you get yourself killed. So a writer need not be ashamed to hide in a vacant lot or a corner of the room for a few minutes. He is there as a writer and not as a character. There is nothing more elusive than a writer's main character, the character that is assumed by the reader to be the writer himself, no less, actually doing the things he writes about. But this main character is simply a point of view interposed by the writer. The main character then becomes in fact another character in the book, but usually the most difficult to see, because he is mistaken for the writer himself. He is the writer's observer, often very uneasy in this role and at a loss to account for his presence. He is an object of suspicion to the world of nonwriters, unless he manages to write them into his road.

Kerouac says in *Vanity of Duluoz:* "I am not 'I am' but just a spy in someone's body pretending these sandlot games, kids in the cow field near St. Rota's Church. . . ." Jack Kerouac knew about writing when I first met him in 1944. He was twenty-one; already he had written a million words and was completely dedicated to his chosen trade. It was Kerouac who kept telling me I should write and call the book I wrote *Naked Lunch*. I had never written anything after high school and did not think of myself as a writer, and I told him so. "I got no talent for writing. . . ." I had tried a few times, a page maybe. Reading it over always gave me a feeling of fatigue and disgust, an aversion towards this form of activity, such as a laboratory rat must experience when he chooses the wrong path and gets a sharp reprimand from a needle in his displeasure centers. Jack insisted quietly that I did have talent for writing and that I would write a book called *Naked Lunch*. To which I replied, "I don't want to hear anything literary."

Trying to remember just where and when this was said is like trying to remember a jumble of old films. The 1940s seem centuries away. I see a bar on 116th Street here, and a scene five years later in another century: a sailor at the bar who reeled over on the cue of "Naked Lunch" and accused us—I think Allen Ginsberg was there, and John Kingsland—of making a sneering reference to the Swiss Navy. Kerouac was good in these situations, since he was basically unhostile. Or was it in New Orleans or Algiers, to be more precise, where I lived in a frame house by the river, or was it later in Mexico by the lake in Chapultepec Park . . . there's an island there where thousands of vultures roost apathetically. I was shocked at this sight, since I had always admired their aerial teamwork, some skimming a few feet off the ground, others wheeling way up, little black specks in the sky—and when they spot food they pour down in a black funnel . . .

We are sitting on the edge of the lake with tacos and bottles of beer. . . . "Naked Lunch is the only title," Jack said. I pointed to the vultures.

"They've given up, like old men in St. Petersburg, Florida. . . . Go out and hustle some carrion, you lazy buzzards!" Whipping out my pearlhandled .45, I killed six of them in showers of black feathers. The other vultures took to the sky. . . . I would act these out with Jack, and quite a few of the scenes that later appeared in *Naked Lunch* arose from these acts. When Jack came to Tangier in 1957, I had decided to use the title, and much of the book was already written.

In fact, during all those years I knew Kerouac, I can't remember ever seeing him really angry or hostile. It was the sort of smile he gave in reply to my demurrers, in a way you get from a priest who knows you will come to Jesus sooner or later—you can't walk out on the Shakespeare Squadron, Bill.

Now as a very young child I had wanted to be a writer. At the age of nine I wrote something called *Autobiography of a Wolf*. This early literary essay was influenced by—so strongly as to smell of plagiarism—a little book I had just read called *The Biography of a Grizzly Bear*. There were various vicissitudes, including the loss of his beloved mate . . . in the end this poor old bear slouches into a valley he knows is full of poison gases, about to die. . . . I can see the picture now, it's all in sepia, the valley full of nitrous yellow fumes and the bear walking in like a resigned criminal to the gas chamber. Now I had to give my wolf a different twist, so, saddened by the loss of his entire family, he encounters a grizzly bear who kills him and eats him. Later there was something called *Carl Cranbury in Egypt* that never got off the ground, really . . . a knife glinted in the dark valley. With lightning speed Carl V. Cranbury reached for the blue steel automatic . . .

These were written out painfully in longhand with great attention to the script. The actual process of writing became so painful that I couldn't do anything more for Carl Cranbury, as the Dark Ages descended—the years in which I wanted to be anything else but a writer. A private detective, a bartender, a criminal. . . . I failed miserably at all these callings, but a writer is not concerned with success or failure, but simply with observation and recall. At the time I was not gathering material for a book. I simply was not doing anything well enough to make a living at it. In this respect, Kerouac did better than I did. He didn't like it, but he did it—work on railroads and in factories. My record time on a factory job was four weeks. And I had the distinction to be actually fired from a defense plant during the War.

Perhaps Kerouac did better because he saw his work interludes simply as a means to buy time to write. Tell me how many books a writer has written . . . we can assume usually ten times that amount shelved or thrown away. And I will tell you how he spends his time: Any writer spends a good deal of his time alone, writing. And that is how I remember Kerouac—as a writer talking about writers or sitting in a quiet corner with a notebook, writing in longhand. He was also very fast on the typewriter. You feel that he was writing all the time; that writing was the only thing he thought about. He never wanted to do anything else.

If I seem to be talking more about myself than about Kerouac, it is because I am trying to say something about the particular role that Kerouac played in my life script. As a child, I had given up on writing, perhaps unable to face what every writer must: all the bad writing he will have to do before he does any good writing. An interesting exercise would be to collect all the worst writing of any writer—which simply shows the pressures that writers are under to write badly, that is, not write. This pressure is, in part, simply the writer's own conditioning from childhood to think (in my case) white Protestant American or (in Kerouac's case) to think French-Canadian Catholic.

Writers are, in a way, very powerful indeed. They write the script for the reality film. Kerouac opened a million coffee bars and sold a million pairs of Levi's to both sexes. Woodstock rises from his pages. Now if writers could get together into a real tight union, we'd have the world right by the words. We could write our own universes, and they would all be as real as a coffee bar or a pair of Levi's or a prom in the Jazz Age. Writers could take over the reality studio. So they must not be allowed to find out that they can make it happen. Kerouac understood this long before I did. "Life is a dream," he said.

My own birth records, my family's birth records and recorded origins, my athletic records in the newspaper clippings I have, my own notebooks and published books are not real at all; my own dreams are not dreams at all but products of my waking imagination. . . . "This, then, is the writer's world—the dream made for a moment actual on paper, you can almost touch it, like the endings of *The Great Gatsby* and *On the Road*. Both express a dream that was taken up by a generation."

Life is a dream in which the same person may appear at various times in different roles. Years before I met Kerouac, a friend from high school and college, Kells Elvins, told me repeatedly that I should write and that I was not suited to do anything else. When I was doing graduate work at Harvard in 1938, we wrote a story in collaboration, entitled "Twilight's Last Gleamings," which I used many years later almost verbatim in *Nova Express*. We acted out the parts, sitting on a side porch of the white frame house we rented together, and this was the birthplace of Doctor Benway.

" 'Are you all right?' he shouted, seating himself in the first lifeboat among the women. 'I'm the doctor!' "

Years later in Tangier, Kells told me the truth: "I know I am dead and you are too. . . ." Writers are all dead, and all writing is posthumous. We are really from beyond the tomb and no commissions. . . . (All this I am writing just as I think of it, according to Kerouac's own manner of writing. He says the first version is always the best.)

In 1945 or thereabouts, Kerouac and I collaborated on a novel that was never published. Some of the material covered in this lost opus was later used by Jack in *The Town and the City* and *Vanity of Duluoz*. At that time, the anonymous gray character of William Lee was taking shape: Lee, who is there just so long and long enough to see and hear what he needs to see and hear for some scene or character he will use twenty or thirty years later in his writing. No, he wasn't there as a private detective, a bartender, a cotton farmer, a pickpocket, an exterminator; he was there in his capacity as a writer. I did not know that until later. Kerouac, it seems, was born knowing. And he told me what I already knew, which is the only thing you can tell anybody.

I am speaking of the role Kerouac played in my script, and the role I played in his can be inferred from the enigmatically pompous Hubbard Bull Lee portrayals, which readily adapt themselves to the scenes between Carl and Doctor Benway in *Naked Lunch*. Kerouac may have felt that I did not include him in my cast of characters, but he is of course the anonymous William Lee as defined in our collaboration—a spy in someone else's body where nobody knows who is spying on whom. Sitting on a side porch, Lee was there in his capacity as a writer. So Doctor Benway told me what I knew already: "I'm the doctor . . ."

---

# CAROLYN CASSADY

CAROLYN CASSADY, a graduate of Bennington College (class of 1944) who went on to do graduate work in theater arts at the University of Denver, was another woman drawn into the Beat orbit with her marriage to Neal Cassady in 1948. Twenty years later, she began to write her reminiscences of her life with her husband, Neal, and his friend Jack Kerouac, which first appeared in the magazine *Rolling Stone*. Her book *Heart Beat: My Life with Jack & Neal* was published in 1976. She went on to write *Off the Road: My Years with Cassady, Kerouac, and Ginsberg* (1990), from which this excerpt is taken. There she described the continuation of her love affair with Kerouac when he came to visit her and Neal and their three children in 1952 after they left their small house in Russian Hill, near the North Beach district in San Francisco, and moved into their suburban home outside San Jose.

## From Off the Road

In August of 1952 I wistfully bid goodbye to the little house on Russian Hill where I had passed so many milestones and whose "possibilities" had gone unfulfilled.

I surveyed the new potential of the huge house we'd found in San Jose fifty miles to the south. We were on the edge of the city—then aptly nicknamed 'Nowheresville'—but the lovely valley surrounding it was too vast to explore from afar, so we'd settled on this lucky find until we could learn more about the area and Neal could see how the new location would affect his work.

The one-story house had been part of an old estate, and had eight rooms of various sizes in a puzzling arrangement and high ceilings but, oddly enough, no fireplace. It was surrounded with neglected flowerbeds and set back far enough from the street to allow for a large front yard dotted with fruit and nut trees. Behind was a paved courtyard separating our big house from a smaller, newer one. Our decision to rent it had been finalized when we had met the young couple, Dick and Marie Forest, who lived in the smaller house behind. They had a boy about Jami's age and a baby girl, and their eagerness to help us move and to adjust to a new town was a taste of neighborliness in the old tradition.

The Forests had no notion of the kind of life their new neighbors had been living, but I confidently expected we would become as organized, peaceful and conventional as they—except, perhaps, in one respect. Neal had talked away my fears and planted some marijuana seeds in the flowerbeds, tucked behind the shrubs under the front porch, and in the vacant lot next door, hoping to eliminate constant searching and high prices. However, it would be a long time before the harvest. He was pleased the Forests were so "square," figuring they wouldn't know what the plants were when they saw them.

Every room in our house was covered in layers of old wallpaper, and I tried to get Neal to release some pent-up energy by scraping it off the walls of our bedroom. It was a much bigger job than it looked, but he attacked it furiously, fighting every inch, and once started it had to be finished. When the job was completed at last, he was proud of the result and of himself. I painted the walls a deep royal blue, the ceiling above the molding white, made white tucked drapes out of old sheets and placed a white spread and yellow pillows on the bed. A red bulb in the overhead light turned the walls purple, the curtains, spread and ceiling pink, and the pillows orange. "Psychedelic" we would have said if the word had been invented then. Instead, we called it our "passion pit," each of us projecting our own aspirations.

The change in location looked most promising for all of us. Neal enjoyed playing chess with Dick, a droll storyteller and a delight to the children. Neal seemed more settled and was able to spend more time at home. The freight runs began and ended in San Jose, whereas formerly he had had to "deadhead" to and from San Francisco. I learned to forget how to read a timetable. Neal had gone to great lengths to teach me this complicated skill soon after he'd first been hired, but we had both come to regret it when I was able to figure out what time he *should* have come home.

Neal wanted to share this new house with Jack, plus which, Neal was out of tea [marijuana]. We had heard no more from Jack during our move, and assumed he'd gone off to his hut with the Indians. Neal decided to risk writing him at Bill's, fearing all along that Jack was angry with him for not being able to repay all of an old debt.

> Damn you for being in Mexico without me. Why in hell not give up the Indians to come back and tell me about them and to still earn about 2000 bucks on RR before the year's out? You can easily live in our big 9 room house here in sunny San Jose and ride about in my new station wagon.

He then apologized at length for not having any money (new station wagon to the contrary) saying, "Sept. 26 this the first paycheck I'll have enough clear to even buy the 3 dozen light bulbs this house needs." He understood that Jack was "surely mad as hell" at him:

> And rightly so, and I started letters and never sent them and I told Carolyn, who wants you back so desperately, to write you, and everything went to hell and I'm without even any help from Miss Green, and where the hell are you? I'll send you fare to get back here on, only hurry up or there won't be much RRing left . . . stay here until December then you'll have plenty to go east.

Before mailing the letter, we learned that Jack was in North Carolina with his mother, and I added a note saying I hoped he wasn't mad at us:

> Neal and I still not making it without you. He says to tell you he'll join you in December, and you'll both go booming on the Florida East Coast Line. I shouldn't doubt it, and I'll be saying just what Cathy did the other night, "Daddy and Jack both went off and left me."

Suddenly the Southern Pacific came up with a new ruling that no new men over 30 would be hired. Jack had just turned 30 in March, so

Neal rushed to write to him again and outlined in explicit detail not only how he could get around this ruling if he came immediately, but also how to travel on the trains at minimum expense—in such explicit detail, in fact, that Jack would have had to carry the letter in his hand all the way to be able to follow the complicated directions.

Jack agreed to come, but he left North Carolina before Neal's instructions arrived. The next word we received was a card from Denver. Neal went into a fit of expletives and dashed out to send Jack a telegram emphasizing the imminence of the hiring deadline. He even wired him $25.00 to prove the seriousness of the situation.

My spirits soared, my energy was electrified. Jack was coming back after only three months this time. Joyfully I hastened to make a room ready for him. We had brought the big plywood desktop from San Francisco, and it was reinstated in the bedroom next to ours. Although the room was nearer the rest of the household than had been his attic nook, it had French doors leading into a sunroom and thence to the front door.

Saturday afternoon Jack telephoned from San Francisco, and Neal told him to hop the "Zipper," the trainmen's nickname for the Zephyr, the fast through-freight to Los Angeles that stopped at San Jose. He said we'd meet him at the yard office. Neal had been called to work a freight to Watsonville, and I realized Jack and I would be alone this first night, and this thought, for the rest of the afternoon, caused a considerable lack of concentration on my household tasks.


I had to go along with Neal to meet the Zephyr, because Jack couldn't drive. The station wagon had broken down, but Neal now had a Model-A Ford to play with as well, and I enjoyed it too, once I got used to driving it in traffic. The night was inky black, and Neal parked near the far edge of the unpaved, weed-fringed parking lot next to the small wooden building that was the freight office. I stayed in the car while Neal went to check on his train. I could hear the Zephyr approaching. It screamed to a stop, clanging its bell and snorting steam that billowed orange and yellow in the lights from the office windows. Then, black-silhouetted against the engine's powerful shaft of white light, I saw two men coming toward me, Neal's lantern making crazy zig-zags as he pounded Jack on the back and punched him, boisterous and exuberant. Jack chuckled, trying to defend himself and looking shyly at the ground then sideways at Neal. When he saw me in the car he ran his fingers through his hair and shoved at his shirt-tail. I lit a cigarette to calm my nerves, trembling at the sight of the familiar hulk in the checkered shirt.

Jack climbed into the narrow back seat, dragging his sea bag with him, and Neal got into the driver's side. I was glad Neal had to wait awhile for his train and could carry the conversation. He asked Jack for details of his trip to California, lamenting the lost instructions, and then talked gaily about our house and how he anticipated showing Jack the sports they could see through the fence that divided our lot from the high school athletic field, "and all the pretty high school girls, and cheerleaderesses, and—oops, ma, sorry."

Jack giggled, and I smiled but said nothing, feeling Jack becoming increasingly attractive. Speech was even more difficult when our eyes met, and by the time Neal bounded off to catch his train the close air in the little car was dripping with desire. The darkness was warm and humid inside, and outside the fog wrapped a blanket around us.

"Let's don't go yet," Jack said softly. "Come back here."

As we embraced, all the memories welled up within me, resurrected by his sweet smells, strengthened by his absence. In my happiness I had to smile, and broke away from his kiss.

"Honestly, Jack, I feel like a high school girl myself—necking in the back seat of a car, yet."

Jack chuckled and groped for a poor-boy in his jacket pocket. After a few swallows apiece and distracted attempts at speech, he set the bottle on the shelf behind us and pulled me to him again. But when he attempted to change our positions his elbow struck the bottle, which flipped over and drenched us both. The spell broken, we laughingly tried to brush off the wine, but soon his ardor returned undampened, I was neither comfortable nor relaxed under these conditions, and when we were suddenly bathed in blinding light, we sprang apart, our breathing suspended. "Oh, sorry—I was looking for—" The voice and light faded away in the fog.

As I swung the car around the back of the house and parked, Dick was climbing his front steps, having just checked our children. I waved and called my thanks before leading Jack into the house. We had told the Forests of Jack's impending visit, that he was a published author who had come to continue his writing and to work on the railroad with Neal. We had shown them *The Town and the City,* and they had been properly impressed. Nothing was said, of course, of our shared affections, and I hoped we could manage not to shock them.

We made a brief tip-toe tour of the house, Jack pleased with its age and even its unique layout—he and I shared a mutual interest in old houses. He had a bath while I made him a snack and poured the wine. He ate with relish; we lingered over our wine until our shyness subsided, and then flowed together to the magnet of his bed. His tenderness and appreciation made it almost impossible for me to leave him and return to my own bed, but that was my absolute rule, since often one of the girls came to me during the night.

In the morning they were awake long before Jack and could hardly keep still in their impatience to see him. Even so, they were both stricken with an attack of shyness. But when Jack sat down for breakfast and talked to them, they jostled each other to climb on his lap. He asked them to show him around outside, and nothing could have pleased them more. A child hanging on each hand, they set out, both of the girls talking at once. The first place Jack wanted to see was the high school ballfield. They had to go through the Forests' yard, and little Chris rushed out to join in the tour. As I watched them through the pantry window I mused on how content Jack always appeared with children. He relaxed into a naturalness that contrasted with the frequent discomfort he displayed with adults, male or female. With children he had nothing to prove, nothing to be that was more than himself.

Neal arrived in time for a celebration dinner of Jack's favorite pizza, after which we had the Forests over to meet him, and the Hinkles were invited to join us. They had moved to San Jose too, and had bought a tract house on the outskirts of town. Everyone was gay and agreeable, Dick and Neal swapping Paul Bunyon yarns, the rest of us an appreciative audience to their antics, which Jack, too, appeared to enjoy despite his shyness. What relief I felt to see Neal happy again.

The next day the serious business of getting Jack hired on the railroad was begun. He was fearful and resistant, but Neal prodded and coached, and after a day or so Jack was accepted and began his two weeks of student training trips. Every evening on his return home we had to cheer and encourage him anew. When training was over

Jack signed on the extra-board, proud to be a "genu-wine" brakie and to sport the same paraphernalia as Neal. Another celebration was called for.

Jack soon found he much preferred stories about railroads to the work itself. His physique and kinetic responses were more suited to running and dodging on a football field than to the swift and agile moves necessary for freight-car switching. Although we kept reassuring him he'd improve in time, his clumsiness was agony to him. He loved the earthy railroad men as characters, but his sensitivity and paranoia caused him to resent their practice of identifying men through nicknames, his becoming "Keroway" which soon degenerated into "Caraway Seed." He was sure they all scorned and laughed at him. Neal, too, became more irritable, partially from sympathy for Jack, partially because he wanted to be proud of his friend, not listen to jokes at his expense, and partially (I suspected) because he didn't like Jack and me being alone together so much.

Once when Jack had a day off before he was called for a job, he asked me if the girls and I would like to go to San Francisco with him to visit our old haunts. The station wagon was running again, and we all set off in high spirits on an Indian summer day, the air heavy with the nostalgia inherent in autumn aromas. Our eager expectations were snuffed the minute we parked at Coit Tower. Cathy had to be taken to the emergency hospital and then straight home: she was diagnosed as having rheumatic fever, though it turned out to be osteomyelitis.

In spite of our abortive romantic excursion, Jack and I had lovely days at home, especially when Neal was off duty too. Our favorite pastimes enjoyed in San Francisco were revived. We read aloud, discussed books and authors, and usually recorded it all. (Having few tapes, which were expensive, we shortsightedly erased most of what we recorded.) The large, sparsely furnished dining room with the bay window had lots of space for the children to play while we three sat around the big round oak table. Neal juggled the fruit from the centerpiece, sending the girls scurrying under the table to retrieve those he'd drop. Sometimes Jack read to us from *Dr. Sax* in a great booming voice, spiced with W.C. Fields or Major Hoople imitations, while Neal, eyes sparkling above his grin, hissed "Yeah . . . yeah . . . yeaahh" after nearly every sentence, especially when Jack made reference to sex, which would make Jack break off his serious tones and giggle. In turn, Neal liked reading Proust aloud, saying "Listen to this, now. I want you to just listen to this—this is one paragraph, mind you just one paragraph . . ." and he'd read the intricate prose slowly and precisely, ignoring Jack's attempts to correct 'his French pronunciation. Other times we'd pass out our several copies of Shakespeare's plays, and each of us would take two or three parts, changing our voices to fit while Jack and Neal leaped about acting out their characters with exaggerated gestures.

And there were lovely evenings, too, when Jack and I were alone. We'd put the children to bed together, and he'd read them their stories, using all his range of voices. Jami was his special favorite still, and she'd fling her arms around his neck and give him big kisses on the cheeks, dissolving him into self-conscious mirth. Then we'd close their door and have our dinner in the big kitchen. Sometimes we were high and hilarious, other times sentimental and romantic.

One such night, when we had finished eating and I'd put our dishes in the sink, we sat dreamily sipping our wine in the flickering patterns of the candlelight, absorbing the music of blues and ballad, both of us silent and pensive. My mind was catching images drifting peacefully in the glowing atmosphere when Jack's voice broke the stillness like a great mellow gong, vibrating clear through me and reverberating in the air: "*God* . . . I love you."

I looked at him to be sure I'd heard right and met his blue eyes, so intense and piercing I had to look down again, and I couldn't even smile, my breath caught somewhere. All I could manage was a whisper I didn't think he heard: "I can't believe it."

But he said, slow and steady, "I could convince you."

I tried to gather up my scattered wits to say something, but my eyes wouldn't move from the ruby light in my glass, and I could feel his hadn't wavered. All I could do was slide my hand along the table to his, but I still couldn't look at him. I closed my eyes and breathed deeply.

"Let's dance," he said softly.

We floated close together, swaying, warm and blending—timeless. Soon I couldn't contain my joy in such a solemn mood. I broke away, filled our glasses and Jack loaded the phonograph with mambos. We danced and danced, abandoned to the music, sparks flying when we touched.

For years afterward, remembering this night, I'd think about Neal.

Why could he and I no longer have these romantic, emotional love scenes? No one had been more deeply romantic than Neal in the beginning. Did this always cease with the advent of marriage? Did we know each other too well? Nevertheless, I never forgot Jack's magic words; they have warmed me ever since.

Other memories of those golden months drift by in small but vivid snatches: my sitting on Jack's bed rocking Johnny if he'd wake up crying, Jack propped on one elbow, patting Johnny too, talking to me about his mother, planning where we would meet. He'd read me her letters, and I'd insert comments in his letters to her.

Then there were afternoons when Jack would sit for hours experimenting with the tape recorder, singing both lyrics and "scat," accompanying himself on a tiny pair of bongos I'd given him for a joke. These tapes I listen to now and recall the long fall afternoons, fragrant with the smell of burning leaves, which reminded both of us of our beloved New England, and I relive the quiet pleasure of our being together.

Almost daily he'd go on walks with the girls, listening to their prattle, teaching them to make poems—walks that left their cheeks ruddy, their little fists clenched around precious scraggly flowers he'd helped them pick.

All this pleasure and my partial descriptions of it to Neal pleased him less and less. Jack was now more interested in Neal's family than in Neal, whose lonely brooding on long runs stoked his jealousy and resentment. Where was his old partner in crime? Where his excuse and sidekick for his own private desires? Then the chill of winter arrived and with it, the cold rains and the colds in the noses. When the railroad work slowed, the men were home together more often, and the feeling of confinement increased the restlessness and irritation in them both as they waited and waited for the calls that never came. There was nothing interesting to do in San Jose, and San Francisco was too far to go without a good excuse. It was evident that wanderlust was tugging at Neal again and the Mexican sun at Jack, and in me the seed of dread began to sprout.

Neal found the necessary reasons to drive the new car to San Francisco more often as time went on, but he still couldn't persuade Jack to go with him or to cover up for him. For his part, Jack reverted to ranting and raving, growling and swearing at publishers, bitterly resenting his failure to be accepted and appreciated.

Nor was Jack blind to the cause of Neal's growing irascibility and resistance to his attempts to continue their former intellectual games. All Neal would talk to him about were his responsibilities and the expenses of the family. Jack got the message.

Telling me he thought maybe I should have one husband at a time, he insisted on moving to San Francisco and a skid-row hotel. Neal felt guilty but relieved and drove Jack to the city. Yet after less than a month, he persuaded Jack to return, establishing a better balance in all our affairs.

On April 5, 1958, seven months after the publication of Kerouac's *On the Road*, Neal Cassady was arrested by narcotics agents for possession of three marijuana cigarettes. In Carolyn Cassady's foreword to *Grace Beats Karma* (1993), the book of Neal's prison letters she edited, she gave the background of the setup that resulted in Cassady's incarceration in San Quentin until June 3, 1960.

## *Foreword to* Grace Beats Karma

This is how Neal described to me his crime and the incidents leading up to his arrest:

I was at a party at the Fergusons' apartment. When I said I had to go to work, a couple of guys offered to drive me to the depot. When we got there, I offered them a couple of joints in return and went to my locker to get them. I gave them three. Then, on my way home, it hit me; something told me they were narcs, and now I'm positive they were.

I think it's a trap. You see, a couple of months ago two other guys asked me to buy them some pot. They gave me forty dollars, and I said I'd try. I was sure they were agents, so I took the money to the racetrack. This, of course, told them I knew who they were. Somehow I think it's all connected.

Weeks went by and nothing happened, so we assumed Neal was safe. But on the morning of April 5 two agents came to the house, arrested him and took him to San Francisco. He was held for a week, but the Grand Jury threw out the case, and Neal returned to Los Gatos. He said that while held in the city jail, he learned that because he had recognized the two narcotics agents, he could "blow their cover," and they had ordered: "Get that kid off the streets." They beat him, he said, in the stomach, "where it wouldn't show," demanding he tell them who else was involved, something Neal would never do. They called him "uncooperative."

The next morning he was re-arrested. This time the District Attorney called a special meeting of the Grand Jury at midnight and changed the cast of collaborators, including the Public Defender Neal had been assigned the first time and who was sympathetic to Neal. A news item appeared in the papers declaring that according to the police Neal was the leader of a gang of marijuana smugglers and brought large quantities of marijuana from Mexico, transporting them on the Southern Pacific trains. The trains Neal worked went no farther south than Watsonville, nowhere near Los Angeles, let alone Mexico. This item, although later retracted, cost Neal his railroad job forever more. In the end, he was sentenced to two terms of five years to life for "selling" drugs.

He found time to write letters only after he was transferred to the county jail in San Bruno, a commute town south of San Francisco. At first Neal was allowed visits and correspondence only with women, with the exception of letters to his Godfather, Fr. Harley Schmitt, a Monsignor in Denver. His constant counsellor, Hugh Lynn Cayce, was excluded as were his "degenerate" male friends, Allen Ginsberg and Jack Kerouac. Ex-wives and lovers were welcomed as was Helen Hinkle and myself. Figure that.

The first time he was arrested and held for a week in San Francisco city jail his attitude had born the fruits of his metaphysical studies: he was calm, poised and assured, and he performed something of a miracle in spontaneously separating two battling thugs who shared his tiny cell, after which he nearly fainted thinking of the risk he'd taken. His release furnished further proof of the validity of the universal truths he had been learning and attempting to practice. Alas, when he was re-arrested and falsely accused, his faith deserted him to be replaced by anger and resentment, attitudes that had to be repressed. Unjustly condemned, his bitterness must have intensified, since he had sworn to me vehemently that he knew he would *never* go to jail again as long as he lived. Had he been allowed to remain at Vacaville, he might have been able to transcend them, and his prison experience could have been a blessing in disguise. Instead, his move to San Quentin plunged him further into fury, and old-fashioned willpower had to be employed.

Some compensation was afforded Neal in the person of an older wise counsellor, Gavin Arthur, who taught the Comparative Religion class at San Quentin and who considered Neal half Saint. Gavin could serve him also as a go-between to friends outside, and once he arranged for Ginsberg to address the class and thereby see Neal briefly. An attempt to unite Kerouac with Neal aborted due to Jack's indisposition and failure to appear.

These letters to me contain subject-matter Neal knew I would understand—even the Catholic theology neither of us approved. He later confirmed my assessment that the exercise of memorizing church dogma and repeating it by rote was a method he used to block thoughts of his unjust predicament and prevent the arousal of the fire-breathing dragon of rage coiled within, whose release would destroy him. I've often wondered whether his retreat to Catholicism was also an attempt to recapture some of the comfort afforded him in his early childhood by his contact with the only warmth, beauty and grace encountered in his otherwise harsh existence. The church must have been a magical and seductive fantasyland for such a sensitive boy.

In prison he had to engage his brilliant active mind in some uplifting occupation to counteract his dismal environment, so I heartily approved any method of controlling his thoughts and emotions. A further mental challenge lay in recording these thoughts in letters, stimulating creativity by playing with words, imitating Proustian non-stop sentences, devising games of alliteration and figuring out how to please or fool the censors. In addition, he could write down and perhaps clarify his efforts toward self-improvement and spiritual growth—a goal that had begun to obsess him from the time he was introduced to metaphysics in 1952. Learning the universal laws as exemplified by Jesus reunited him with the Christ he'd lost when Catholicism let him down, but in a vastly different context!

With this new vision he saw Jesus as the last in a long line of gu-
rus to enlighten the planet; a man who had, through many lifetimes,
perfected his natural attributes by freely willing to obey the universal
laws of nature and to use these powers to become again a co-creator
with the original Loving Intelligence or "God." His mission was now as
the "Way Shower," as He said, since we must all make the same journey. As Adam He had fallen—forgotten the Source of Life and used
his powers for selfish pleasures. By the time he was 30, Jesus had
learned to crucify the desires of his lower nature and to will to flow
with the constant stream of forces that move only toward good (God).
This good, as Jesus continually pointed out, is Spirit, the life-force of
everything and everyone, available to all. Cayce's informants likened
this force to electricity, that is, one that just *flows*; it cannot judge,
condemn, punish or play favorites. It just IS—all good—i.e., love.
Free will allows us to tune in and go along with it according to its laws,
or go our own way. Selfishness is the daddy of all "sin."

Everyone's purpose in life is the same. Each of us has unique
flaws to correct. On this planet of three-dimensional matter, and using
the five senses that go with it, we are provided with tailor-made opportunities (chosen by ourselves) to learn the particular individual
lessons that apply to our own past mistakes and to once again claim
and expand our innate powers by which we continue the creative evolution of our planet and ourselves. Either we go forward or backward;
we never stand still. "Each day there is put before you good and evil—
choose thou." Heaven and hell are within us and individually suited.
What we sow, we reap. No one and nothing outside ourselves can be
blamed as a cause; it is solely our own attitudes and responses to outside events that result in joy or pain.

I have merely skimmed the surface of some of the principle ideas
Neal had accepted and which informed his thoughts. Our introduction to these ideas was in a book by Gina Cerminara entitled *Many
Mansions*. There followed a frantic search for further verification, and
we found dozens of books, some of which had been in print for centuries, to augment and expand these theories, such as Madam
Blavatsky and the Theosophists (recommended by the Cayce informants), Max Heindel, Charles Fillmore, Teilhard de Chardin, Jakob
Boehm, Meister Eckhart and many many other Western and Eastern
thinkers. Along with the foundation texts of the Hindu, Buddhist,

Taoist and other world religions, the Christian Bible was illuminated and experienced in a more understandable and personal way.

The "miracles" therein could easily be explained by physics and have often been repeated, yet instead of diminishing the mystery, it is rendered all the more awesome. This view of the purpose of our being demands practical, provable action, and once one gets the hang of its application, even small daily occurrences take on the mantle of a miracle. The progress may be painfully slow, but the rewards are worth it. Neal and I learned that rather than "human nature never changes," everything depends on one's attitudes, and these can—indeed, *must*— change if growth is to go forward.

This, briefly, is how Neal saw things when these letters were written, addressed to another—his only—fellow-believer. What joy we had shared reading and discussing, delving, questioning, testing these brand-new ideas, especially after struggling so many years with philosophers and psychologists. They may have the questions and paint a picture of what appears, but here we thought we'd found the answers. In any case, we were delighted with the roadmap and the goal. I am aware that to many these tenets will sound shocking or absurd, and so they should if this is not their chosen path.

In spite of his constant efforts to become the man he longed to be, Neal's "miserable worm, worthless sinner" conditioning, compounded by his increased sense of guilt, remained triumphant to the end. Even after all the study and effort, he confessed to me that logically he could accept the truth that each of us has the mark of Cain, a divine spark, are "an idea in the mind of God," but he could never wholly believe—*know* it as true of himself. He remained "unworthy."

And, alas, in spite of all the personal love, the vows, the hopes he expresses in these letters, I was never to know the joy they promised. We did not rush into each other's arms when I collected him outside the prison gates. As in most of my visits to him, he could not conceal his resentment, and we drove away in nervous tongue-tied silence. With the children he was his warm best self—the man I'd married, but the affection and trust of our earlier years had been marred.

I had planned to travel to Scotland before his release because I was afraid of his resentment, so thinly veiled at our meetings. The trip was cancelled when I learned that unless a convict had a home to go to he would not be released. I certainly could not add that to my previous crime. Whether or not the family reunion in Michigan was a good idea, my intention was to give him some free time and space to think about his future. He offered me no new ideas; he wanted to stay and support his family. It wasn't many months, however, before the grueling work of tire-recapping and the boredom weakened his will and his self-discipline. He often left the county for San Francisco, and as the railroad continued to refuse him his beloved job, his resolve melted, his spiritual goals faded, and he sank further and further into a sadomasochistic mire. When I could no longer watch his physical flagellation, by work and drugs, I asked him for a divorce in order to free him from this burden of our support. He vigorously resisted until I conjured up another man he conceded would be a better influence on the children. Even then he took months to move out, and I saw him more frequently than before. The "other man" dematerialized.

Unknowingly at the time, I had removed the only remaining pillar that supported what little self-respect Neal had. The railroad job was one; his home and family the other. He had now learned that suicide was no longer an option, but after he left us he sought death in any other form.

He wanted his home, but I don't think he ever totally forgave me for not risking it to bail him out. That had been the most wrenching decision I've ever had to make. I longed to do anything to release him from that dehumanizing place and save us all from all it entailed, and although I felt that he'd be dumb not to run for the border, it wasn't so much a fear of that as of his sanity. Had he not gone on about that readily-available huge sum of money, I might have acted differently. It made no sense, and he would never explain it.

Away from us he didn't stop *talking* about his spiritual beliefs, and he earned the nickname the Preacher, but no one had "ears to hear," and his actions belied his words. Often, however, he allowed himself to commit minor misdemeanors, mostly traffic violations for which he was jailed for one or two weeks. I wondered if these were voluntary respites from the hedonistic life he was living. Whatever the reason, in five years from the end of his parole he was at last mercifully released from the prison of his own making. I have never stopped loving the man I knew he truly was, and in the end I learned to love him even as he appeared to be. Although I found life with him a long rough road, he had taught me the precious lesson of unconditional love. There is no greater gift.

These letters reveal a Neal few knew, not even his closest friends, and now I'll let him speak through them.

Since no letters of mine herein answered are available, should anyone be interested in the background, a general account is given in the book *Off the Road,* in which I describe my twenty years with Neal.

---

# NEAL CASSADY

NEAL CASSADY (1926–1968), the inspiration for Dean Moriarty, the central character in *On the Road,* met Kerouac in New York City in December 1946. A little more than two months later, only hours after getting on a Greyhound bus taking him back to Denver, Cassady began writing letters to Kerouac describing his road experience. Cassady's letters were a strong influence on Kerouac's literary style, freeing him from his obsession with the novels of Thomas Wolfe. Kerouac called Cassady's prose "kick-writing," as in Neal's letter to him in February 1951. This letter arrived a few months before Kerouac began the three-week burst of typing that resulted in *On the Road.*

---

### *Letter to Jack Kerouac,*
### *February 1951 (Excerpt)*

I enclose here a real quickie I whipped off in just a couple of hours. Actually I wrote this poor little start of a thing around the first of January before I came east for a visit. I don't feel badly as to its weak qualities because I just dashed it off without a pause.

My second trip from Denver to Los Angeles was not the starved struggle the first one had been. I established a pattern used in later years when hitchhiking south from my home town, that is, I always afterward left the city in the fashion I did this time. The policy was to be on Denver's southern outskirts at dawn and by not leaving the road for an instant, hope to gain Raton, New Mexico, by nightfall. I never failed to achieve this goal. It seems I possessed the inordinary luck to conquor this 250-odd mile distance by catching quick rides that often got me into New Mexico in the early PM. Conversely, once on Raton's highway junction—the right hand leg went to Texas and southeast, the left to the southwest and California—some blocks beyond the railroad underpass where the hotshot freights begin to pick up speed, I could never get a lift until I'd waited many hours. My first trip had switched its mode of travel at this point, when at midnight, after thumbing cars for eight full hours, I'd caught one of these hiball reefer trains and continued the balance of the journey by rail. A couple of years later I was to wait 2 days in this spot without being picked up by a friendly motorist. Now, however, I had the good fortune to make connections right away with one of the infrequently passing cars. He took me to Taos, and when I got out it was not yet dusk. I was cheered; this was making the fastest time ever and just escaping from the Raton Rut bouyed me no end. I was confident; I was happy.

I bounced along the narrow blacktop with eager strides, breathing deep of the clean mountain air, marveling at the luxuriant vermillion gold of the sunset. Adobe buildings lined the way; every tenth structure housed a bar. From out their open doors came loud Mexican music and the aroma of spiced food. Drunken Indians, their long black hair braided under strange hats, used the center of the hiway as a path upon which to stagger. Some were singsonging to themselves, none talked, and most passed me in dark silence with cold eyes. Ahead, half up a slight hill, I saw a white rancher leave one of these taverns and make for a pickup truck; he was finishing a bottle of beer as he slowly walked to the machine. I hurried to catch him and bum a ride. He sensed my intention before I had a chance to voice it, and looking me over for a second, he said, "Get in." He didn't take me far, but I soon caught another ride which took me into Santa Fe near middlenight.

I sauntered thru this city in a fine state of hunger—fine, I say, because I hadn't eaten since morning, and in my pockets was the money for a good feed. Knowing the unlikelihood of an auto stopping for me after nightfall, I anticipated taking in the sights I could of this State Capitol while hiking leisurely across it, then, settle in a cozy restaurant for a lengthy meal. I figured this program to get me "On the Road" and in position still in good time before dawn, so I followed it.

I recall as I passed the State Police barracks two stern troupers left its well-lit interior and crunched their swank boots on the gravel driveway for brief seconds before they piled into their radio-dispatched police car with automatic motions of tough efficiency. This flashing glimpse of their hard gestures and unslack jaws, clamped so tightly against the grim upper lip, and their faces immobile as steel emphasizing the sheen of their merciless eyes glittering with zeal to perform their duty made me shudder as I thought of the short shift they gave their prey. They spun the wheels and roared away while I was pitying any quarry they nabbed that night. Their ruthless tactics I well knew and couldn't escape a twinge of relief that I wasn't their intended victim. I went by crowded tourist cafes serving well-to-do travelers Mexican and American dishes, catering to their every wish, as their slick automobiles, parked in the rough street's high curb at an angle, patiently waited in quiet splendor to carry them away—escorted in magnificent style—when it was their whim to leave. The downtown area was packed with throngs of humanity, altho it was a late hour, and I don't think it was a Saturday night. The congested glob was heightened by the streets of alley width (20 ft. or so) along which cars crawled with exasperated honking. The sidewalks were over-flowing with people; men in cowboy apparel and otherwise, Indians, solemn and otherwise, Mexicans chattering and otherwise, whites drunk and otherwise, Indian girls encased in moccasins, Indian squaws encased in fat, Mexican chicks in tight skirts and provocative stride, old Mexican women in more fat and burdened with unwashed infants, white women of all kinds, waitresses, heiresses, etc., and kids, kids every place imaginable, leaping and yelling, lunging between cars in mid-block or quiet and morose, scuffling along with head down. Above all this mass of activity glared the lights. Edison's greatest invention hung over the gathered heads in astonishing profusion. There wonderous dissipators of darkness were in every color and all shapes. Countless thousands of lights squeezed into a square mile displayed a garish brilliancy that plunged the surrounding parts of town into seeming blackness. They blazed from every wall, shone down from every ceiling, illuminated every storefront from row upon row of arrayed bulbs. Gigantic markers jutted sharp fingers of flame beyond the rooftops. Enormous signs thrust out their bulk from the building face and drew the eye to multicolored letters proclaiming announcements with electric gleam. Long billboards in continuous circle covered the secondstorys with emblazoned script. Big single ones popped from the wall over every dazzled doorway. Smaller ones, controlled by hand chains, had been flicked on inside every building. The tiny ones were obliviated in this steady stream of lights aiding the streetlamps to rival the sun. Under a theater marquee engaged in combat with night by flashing bright blasts of garbled glare at regular intervals, I paused in midstep, struck with the size of this small city's electric bill. Most of their overhead must be electricity, paying sums I couldn't guess for the priviledge of this crazy glow. Were two thirds of the lights switched off, the remainder would still outshine Times Square with its artificial daylight. I envied the owners of the utilities company that supplied Sante Fe.

My supper was consumed in a gaudy restaurant decorated with a Mexican motif. I lingered over a second coffee until 3 AM, then, stepped to the hiway. Instant luck . . . amazing luck! A 1941 Packard cream convertable (this in 1942) screeched to a halt some hundred feet past me. I raced forward and got in beside a lone man. He was going (believe this) to Los Angeles!! What a trip! I've never had it so good. He raced at 80 per for several hundred miles, then, pulled over and slept for a few hours in the front seat; I had the back one. We stopped here and there as whim dictated: Grand Canyon, wayside pottery stands, etc. He bought all the meals. It was, all in all, a dream come true, save he didn't suggest I drive, and not to risk antagonizing him, I wouldn't ask.

We approached L.A. from the south, on hiway 101. Once in Venice, Calif. (actually a park of sprawling L.A.'s 444 sq. miles), I thanked him profusely and got out, within five blocks of the place I had traveled 1300 miles to reach. . . .

———

On October 16, 1958, Neal Cassady wrote his first letter to his wife, Carolyn, from his cell in San Quentin State Prison. Included in *Grace Beats Karma* (1993), it described his transport in leg irons from the California Medical Facility at Vacaville, where Cassady had been imprisoned since July 1958. At Vacaville, Neal told his wife that he had noticed the prison library's copy of *On the Road* was "always checked out."

## Letter to Carolyn Cassady

NAME *Neal Cassidy* [sic]
BOX NO. A-47667, SAN QUENTIN, CALIF.
DATE 10 P.M. 10/16, 1958

Dearest Dear Carolyn, wonder wife;
Even as they were striking my leg irons, that had, along with two sidearm carrying officers, locked door, barred windows & snow white pajamas worn—minus a half expected bright red or yellow bullseye on back—most adequately subdued any wild urge to disembark during the short bus ride from Vacaville, I began experiencing generation of a not inconsiderable self pity soon to become, while receiving procedure progressed, almost overpowering by virtue of those repeated shocks every new dismal view bordering sheer disbelief administered in seperate but accumulative blow to my so-sorry-for-myself sharpened conception as, now buffeted from both within & without into a bewildering numbness, I at last encountered, when first stumbling across the "Big Yard"—as the "cons" call it—in that characteristic state it seems to engender, a paradoxical one of hazelike concentration, the main source of what gloomy eminations my all too sympathetic mood had rendered it recipiant; that psychical wall each convict's dispair ridden tension made to exist inside the, high & wide tho they be, far weaker stone walls of this infamous old—1859 is chiseled atop the facade of one still used building—prison at which, accompanying 23 more, I finally arrived last week. After a troubled sleep, in sagging bunk beneath one of a thug who'd escaped 8 times, much disturbed by an anxiety dream concerning some just right blonde, fatty cheeked both above & below, presumably you since I personally know no other, & myself at a drive-in movie—remember that one in Kansas we attended so long ago?—the following day brought, undoubtedly with aid of a strong, yet abstractly felt of course, sorrow occasioned by news of the Holy Father's demise (predict canonization in half century; minimum time the church allows, incidently, today's Pontiff is John VIII, 872–882) reawakening to enough genuine inner cognition of my excep-

tional selfishness that a deeply shamed acknowledgement was forced from me of just how narrowly centered, esp. regarding my literary obligations toward you, I had become during this 6½-month immuration, or rather, bluntly put, I sensed in stark dismay how, despite all protestations, my previous ignoring of your very sensible wishes has now simply dwindled to a begrudged letter biquarterly. Along this line, the next day, another shared sadness, but in a far lighter vein of thought than the Pope's death, served for further perception into my always too weak realization of excessive self centeredness, i.e., the demise, real enuf, tho figuratively & collectively, of the Milwaukee Braves in the World Series. Much more, however, responsibility for lifting me from that blue funk of depression this place must naturally impress on "Fish"—new convicts—can be attributed to an increasing awareness over this last week of the balancing factor it equally imposes: compassion. Truly I've never seen, nor is there elsewhere in this noble country concentrated, surely not even in Sing Sing, such an assorted assemblege of absolutely pitiful misfits as are the 5,042 felons—latest count, which Radio KROW announced on 6 P.M. News as largest number here since 1942—in whose routine I am daily—& nightly, ugh—immured until at least Easter of 1960. Still, besides the main one of having those tough scabs encrusting my hardened heart ripped completely away, or anyway so loosen that eventual uprooting must come, thru its nigh-constant bleeding at the sight of these condemned misanthropics, the cloud this length of time constitutes has its lining, limited tho it be, in that I will be informed exactly one year from now—Oct.—when my release may come, thus avoiding nearly 100 days anxiety over this little item for, as you may recall, it previously was to be Jan. '60 before I'd be told the adult authority's—those who determine one's actual time inside—decision on how my 5 yrs. was to be split, now, thanks to being selected as an "inactive" member of a psychologically oriented experimentation instituted roughly 3 yrs. ago & called the "It" program—Intensive Treatment—I have, without further arbitration, fully met the requirements for this reward of finding my fate out some, to repeat, 3 months sooner. Another group, the "Active Its" therapeutically controlled in classes of 8 or 10 men meeting twice weekly for a year makes the whole endeavor ostensibly dedicated to our culturally warped scientific spirit in that, besides deciding who among us fortunate eligibles are to be in which group by drawing blindly from a hat, one group is matched individually with unknown partners to the other so that they can tell, long years hence, what percentage of these two groups returns—over 50% now do—the most often. Briefly as is possible for a redundant windbag I'll pause here to attempt explanation of why you've not heard from me ere now. My first letter, mailed a week ago and returned on Tue., was rejected for mailing account in elaborating via anti-Auguste Compte sired mathematical abstractions certain statements such as "Such sweeping plans as the 'It' program are, alas, as by its very nature all changes for the good of the majority based on charts, graphs, etc., determined solely by the placing of the final decimal point," violated rules of prison gossip & excessive writing; I plead guilt, to the latter esp. How are kiddies, Cayce, water pump & *most* important, you?

Love, Love, N.

# ANN CHARTERS

ANN CHARTERS wrote an essay describing her two days in August 1966 with Jack Kerouac at his home in Hyannis, Massachusetts, after he had invited her there to help her compile his bibliography. Eight months earlier, she had completed the requirements for her doctorate in American Literature at Columbia University, writing a dissertation on the effect of the landscape on a group of nineteenth-century authors in the Berkshires. Her admiration for Kerouac's books dated back to 1958, when she had responded to his description in *The Dharma Bums* of the bohemian scene around the Berkeley campus of the University of California where she had been an undergraduate.

## With Jack Kerouac in Hyannis

On a hot August morning I drove to Kerouac's house. He had mailed me directions to his home in Hyannis, Massachusetts, earlier in the month. Located close to the Joseph Kennedy Memorial Skating Rink, it was easy to find—a brown-shingled one-story house in a modest neighborhood of recently built Cape Cod and ranch houses separated by small lawns with no sidewalks. It was August 16, 1966.

Kerouac had written me, "This will be fascinating. I myself am beginning to need a bibliography. And I look forward to meeting a scholar and a gentlewoman." In his second letter, he penciled a postscript: "Throw these instructions away, rather, that is, bring 'em with you— 'Beatniks' look like Spooks in my mother's poor door at midnight—You understand."

After collecting Kerouac's books for years, I had agreed to compile his bibliography for a Contemporary Writers series published by the Phoenix Bookshop in New York. At that time Jack was receiving very little respect as a writer, but he was well known as an alcoholic recluse.

I arrived at Kerouac's front door at noon after a seven-hour drive from the East Village. When he opened the front door, I mistook him for his father. Dressed in a rumpled white V-neck T-shirt and baggy chinos, Kerouac looked much older and heavier than his photographs. The images of him on the covers of his books had made him look so wildly attractive that while I was coasting along the highways from New York City to Hyannis I had thought that I would be tempted to fall into bed with him. As I followed him into his house, I knew there was no danger of that happening.

Jack introduced me to his mother, Gabrielle, a stocky woman in a cotton housedress who came in from the kitchen wearing the kind of bib apron my mother used to wear. "Wait a minute, Charters is your married name. What is your real name?" Jack asked me. I told them "Danberg," and they had a quick exchange in Canadian French. I understood enough to say, "Yes, that's right. I'm Jewish." "Oh, you know what we're talking about. Then we'll talk in English," Jack said.

Kerouac walked me through the living room down the hall to his study, actually a sunny bedroom at the back of the house, filled with a twin bed, a desk, two chairs, a filing cabinet, a bureau, and several bookcases. His mother's bedroom was on one side of it, and his bedroom was further along the hall, separated from the study by a bathroom. We got right down to work—no small talk. I was impressed by the stacks of books and magazines Kerouac had piled up for me to look at. He told me to sit at his desk as we started to catalogue the "A" section of the American editions of his novels for his bibliography.

It was warm in the room. Jack sat behind me in a rocking chair beside an open window, directly in front of the whirring blade of a small electric fan. On top of the bookshelf near the fan, a can of malt beer was at the ready, with a juice glass of Johnny Walker Red beside that. The bottle of Scotch was kept in the kitchen. Throughout the afternoon he went there to refill his glass, always stopping first in the bathroom. Later at dinner he told me that he had finished one bottle and was halfway through the next.

While we worked, Kerouac took many trips down the short hallway. Once his mother bustled after him into the study, carrying a tray of baloney and egg salad sandwiches and pickles and potato chips and hot coffee. Jack didn't eat any sandwiches but he took a few potato chips and drank steadily. The alcohol didn't affect his concentration.

Jack kept passing me books so I could measure them and note their dimensions. After we'd been working for about three hours, he offered me half a benny. "I've taken one, it's keeping me going. I'll give you one too." I said no, I never used them. "Then okay, don't have any now." But I asked for some Scotch and he brought me a small shot in a juice glass, straight. Later when I asked for it, he brought me another.

All afternoon we heard the faint cries of children through the open windows of the house, filtered across Jack's narrow lawn with its half-dozen half-grown pine trees. Apparently we were in the flight path to the Hyannis airport. Once the noise of a jet filled the study and Jack said, "That's the *Caroline*. It's the only jet that comes here. It's Sargeant Shriver flying off to Washington. Fuck them."

Kerouac sat at the window that faced the house next door, one spindly tree between him and his neighbor. The other study window looked out on a backyard enclosed by a tall redwood fence where his mother was looking after my dog, an Irish setter I had brought along for company. Jack told me that he and Gabrielle had lived in the house only four months.

Before that, it had been a "bigger house" in St. Petersburg, Florida, filled I suppose with the same maple and chinz furniture, the mahogany spinet piano, the television set, and the same two framed pictures on the living room walls—a photograph of Jack as the handsome young author of *The Town and the City* over the sofa, and a large drawing by James Spanfeller of Kerouac's dead brother, Gerard, as a boy feeding the birds, one of the illustrations in *Visions of Gerard,* over his mother's favorite armchair.

Bookshelves lined three of the four walls of Jack's study. The upper shelves of the one near the desk contained paperbacks in French—Balzac, Celine, Flaubert, Hugo. Beside the desk, alongside the shortwave radio and Hermes portable typewriter, were more books: Shakespeare's tragedies, Emily Dickinson's poems, Balzac's *Quest of the Absolute,* Joyce's *Ulysses,* Boswell's *Life of Johnson,* Christopher Smart's *Poems,* and the *Complete Rabelais.*

Tacked to the walls over the desk and bookcases were large pages from an illustrated Japanese calendar. On one of them Jack had drawn a teacup and penned a haiku to spring. Over the light switch near the door were magazine cutouts of American Indians and four bird feathers arranged in a semicircle like a war bonnet. Jack had found the feathers on his lawn. He admired the Indians, he told me, because his mother's family was part Indian.

There were religious pictures cut out of magazines tacked above the bed and on the back of the door. Somebody had thumbtacked a small red felt pennant with "Hyannis" lettered on it to the wall above the desk. The new pennant and the magazine cutouts and the narrow maple bed made me feel like I was in a kid's room, but Jack's dedication to his writing was unmistakable.

Lined up neatly on the shelves were rows of foreign editions of Kerouac's novels, with well-thumbed copies of American editions alongside. His manuscripts and correspondence were organized just as carefully in manila folders in a tall green filing cabinet in one corner. Deep drawers in a built-in dresser contained little copy books and notebooks and carefully rolled teletype paper covered with typewriting—the raw material of Jack's books all grouped in separate bundles and tied with string and rubber bands.

Jack untied the string and showed me the first draft of *Doctor Sax* written in pencil on both sides of small, cheap notebook pages. Why, I asked, did he use such small notebooks? They were small enough to be slipped into his shirt or pants pockets, he told me. Then he could carry them and write anywhere. He flipped the pages carefully to show me that here and there in the *Sax* notebooks some lines were crossed out. "When I typed the book for the publishers, I wouldn't type what I crossed out. Now I don't cross anything out when I write."

I asked him why he used the rolls of white paper in his typewriter. "You know why you use a roll like that? So you don't have to change pages. The secret of narrative—Fielding, Richardson, Defoe, Dickens knew that—is that you get hot when you get disgusted. That's the time *not* to stop. Just roll along."

The tidy piles of books, magazines, and papers on the bed, the bookshelves, the radio, the bureau, and the portable TV were the result, Jack told me, of having "worked a week" to stack everything up neatly for his bibliography. He wanted it to be complete, "maybe a hundred pages," so that he could "be like that fellow in Cambridge, Edmund Wilson, always giving a little pamphlet away." He had kept copies of "99.5 percent" of his published work, and he had spent hours organizing "the neatest records you ever saw."

This surprised me, since I had gotten the impression he lived a chaotic life from his books, especially *Satori in Paris,* just published in *Evergreen Review.* But then at forty-four, Kerouac was still full of contradictions. A dozen years earlier, he was the lover who had come back to his mother's house in Queens for breakfast every morning during the passionate affair he had described in *The Subterraneans.*

Around seven-thirty that evening I took Kerouac back on the road. I told him that my dog needed a run on the beach before it got dark, and he said he would come along to pick up something at the liquor store. There was a whispered conference with his mother in the kitchen about cashing a check, but finally everything got straightened out. I greeted my dog in the backyard and crammed her into the back seat of my dusty orange Volkswagen Beetle.

Still talking to Gabrielle, Jack emerged from the house a few minutes later and got into the car. Right after he sat down he popped open another fresh can of malt beer. The metal flip-top was on the floorboards as a souvenir the next morning. I hadn't seen him palm it out of the refrigerator, but then fresh cans of beer kept appearing at his side all afternoon, like a W. C. Fields sleight-of-hand trick.

The beach was a few miles away through the center of Hyannis. Jack knew the stretch of road near his house, but closer to the ocean he became disoriented and asked me to put the headlights on to read the sign for beach parking. He had worn reading glasses in the study—"Never used to need 'em, but now I'm getting old"—but he'd left them at home.

I stopped the car in the middle of a deserted parking lot. We got out, the dog raced onto the sand toward the splashing waves, Jack stopped on his side of the car to take a leak, and I slipped off my sandals so I could walk more easily on the beach.

In the twilight the deserted beach reminded Kerouac of Tangier. That's where William Burroughs had told him that Whitman and Melville were both "homos" (Jack's term). He threw out his arms: "Here's how Burroughs did it." Jack pulled at the neck of his T-shirt, where the gold chain from his religious medal shone against his chest. His gray-blue eyes got very big and round.

"That's how Whitman came on with little boys. While Melville, he'd sidle up to them in a dark slouch hat." Jack hunched his shoulders up to meet his Indian black hair and narrowed his eyes. "He'd chuck them under the chin and whisper, 'How'd you like to come with me?'" I protested about Melville and Jack scowled. "Yes, he was a queer. Burroughs showed me a poem he'd written in Italy, a love poem to a boy."

We plodded through the soft sand to sit on some rocks and listen to the waves as the light disappeared. I asked him about the form of his novels. He answered impatiently. "I tell you, the novel is as dead as Queen Victoria coming down the street in Hyannis. I wrote only one novel, *The Town and the City.* That's according to what they taught me at Columbia. Fiction. Then I broke loose from all that and wrote picaresque narratives. That's what my books are. You know what that is? Picaresque narratives?"

Abruptly he stood up and shouted at me, "You know the difference between me and those boys Ginsberg, Burroughs, Snyder, Corso, Duncan? I'm the only one who laid down my life for my country. I'm still a Marine, you know, and that's why I don't mix with those beatniks. All those guys carrying signs for peace on their shoulders. Not me."

It was dark when I leashed my dog and we left the beach. "Just a minute, I'll meet you at the car. I want to take a leak." Jack walked away and stood on the hard sand near the water. Back in the car he seemed subdued, not saying much, and I wondered aloud about the chicken pie his mother was baking for dinner. "Naw, don't worry about her. Wait—we're passing the best bar in Hyannis. Stop the car, let's go in. I want to show it to you."

Suddenly he was in high humor. "You know, it's a funny thing about being famous. They don't believe you're you. You go into a bar and they say, 'Aw, go on, get out of here.'" The bartender was a blond young man in his early thirties whom Kerouac introduced as Al Hill. "So you're a writer, huh," Hill said to Kerouac. "Anything published?" Jack nodded, pouring Budweiser into his glass.

The bartender pushed a little. "How much do you make a year?" Kerouac screwed up his eyes and hesitated only a moment. "About as much as you do. Maybe $9,000." Hill replied with friendly scorn, "That's nothing. If you've published all them books you told me about, how come you don't make more?" He moved a little further down the bar to serve another customer.

Jack leaned over his beer, finished it quickly, left for the toilet, bought cigarettes, and reappeared. "Buy me another beer, please," he asked me. I did and he looked around the room. "This is the best bar in Hyannis. When I first came here to look for a house, I was so happy to be back in New England I got drunk and they arrested me twice. But the cops are good here. They didn't bring me in. Both times I only got a warning."

The bartender moved back. "Yes, you were so drunk the first night you came in here, I wouldn't serve you. You looked bad, too. You hadn't shaved." Kerouac raised his chin, granstanding: "I shaved today for this lady here." The bartender continued, "And you were wearing a funny hat." "Yes, my big straw hat. I found it in the swamps in Florida," Jack said. "What were you doing in the swamps?" asked Al. "I was taking a shortcut to the supermarket," Jack told him.

Somebody started to play a World War II song on the piano. Kerouac took my arm. "Come on, they have a piano bar." The pianist was a middle-aged blond woman who looked tired. Jack asked me, "Isn't she good?" I nodded. "What would you like her to play?" I said anything she wanted. Jack kept looking at me. "Wait a minute, you remind me a little of Joan Crawford. The movie star. I wrote a story about her once, 'Joan Rawshanks in the Fog.' You know it?"

Near Kerouac's house we made one more stop at the liquor store so he could pick up some champagne. ("My mother likes champagne. It's the only thing she can drink anymore.") Jack told me he wanted to celebrate the bibliography—he was having a good time. He made only one small pass during the two days we spent together, a shy kiss on my arm the next afternoon while I sat near him on the bed in his study looking at some book contracts.

The rest of the time he repeatedly asked the question, "You don't love your husband, do you?" I always answered, "Yes, I told you, I love him very much." At the end of the second afternoon, he said to shock me, "I don't need you anyway. I can do it to myself. Tell me, what does detumescence mean, my dear?" I replied, "To come down off of?" That was the only thing I said to Jack during our time together that he thought was funny.

---

# SAMUEL CHARTERS

SAMUEL CHARTERS first encountered the Beats in 1953, when he was a newly discharged Korean War veteran working in the San Francisco office of Dun & Bradstreet, a large commercial credit-rating agency. Neighbors across the street on Telegraph Hill were trying to start a paperback bookstore they wanted to call City Lights, but they were having problems with credit. Charters volunteered to prepare a credit report for them, wrote a highly favorable report on the potential for the paperback book in America, and gave them the highest possible credit rating. Two weeks later, when he stopped by the small space they had rented on Columbus Avenue, he found Peter Martin and Lawrence Ferlinghetti unpacking cartons of books. One of Charters's jazz essays was included in the New Orleans magazine *The Outsider,* which was also publishing Beat poetry, in the late 1950s. Charters wrote his essay on Lord Buckley for this anthology. For those of you who weren't there, the spinning wheel mentioned by Gandhi was an instrument against British mercantile interests. By manufacturing their own cloth, the Indians struck a blow for their own freedom.

## Hipsters, Flipsters, and Finger Poppin' Daddies

### A Note on His Lordship, Lord Buckley, the Hippest of the Hipsters

### 1. Like, Man, Groovy

In the beginning there were Hipsters—

> These two cats were walking across the Sahara desert, you dig, and one of the cats looks all around him and he says, "Man, I don't dig no water here."
> The other cat looks around and he says, "Yeah, man, but dig the crazy beach."

—And their view of life was not our own.

> This cat blew wild piano, you dig, and he got a gig with this other cat who blew bass, and the first night on the gig they're grooving and wailing and bopping and the cat who blew piano he wanted to dig a little of what was happening, so he got up and went to the other end of the room and it sounded so mellow he went back and got the cat who was wailing on the bass and he told him he should come and dig. So the cat who was grooving on the bass comes with him and the two of them are standing there and there's no sound, not one mellow tone. After a minute the cat who blew piano he gets real down and he says, "Man, wouldn't you know. Our first night on the gig and the sound system's blown."

If you have read "Howl" carefully, you remember, of course, that the greatest minds of Allen Ginsberg's generation were *hipsters*. As he wrote in line three, they were "Angel headed hipsters burning for the ancient heavenly connection to the starry dynamo in the machinery of night," which strains the point a little, but—it is hipsters that Ginsberg is describing. For Jack Kerouac, it is also the term *hipsters* that describes himself and his friends. He wrote in the opening sentence of his 1957 piece "About the Beat Generation," "The Beat Generation, that was a vision that we had, John Clellon Holmes and I, and Allen Ginsberg in an even wilder way, in the late Forties, of a generation of crazy, illuminated hipsters suddenly rising and roaming America, serious, curious, bumming and hitchhiking everywhere, ragged, beatific, beautiful in an ugly graceful new way. . . ." Out of the hipsters came the Beats, and for many of the Beats, like Kerouac, there was a continual disappointment that they weren't welcomed with the same kind of affection that was the general response to the hipster.

The hipster, however, was the day's wise fool, from whom little was expected except outrageous comments on the absurdity of what he saw around him. A definition of the term "hipster" in a 1959 newspaper column titled "Basic Beatnik" even used the word "courage." To be hip meant to be "equipped with enough wisdom, philosophy, and courage to be self-sufficient, independent of society, able to swing on any scene." Neal Cassady titled his description of his first meeting with William Burroughs "The History of the Hip Generation." None of the original group around Kerouac and Holmes was ever really comfortable calling themselves "Beat," but all of them would have insisted that they were "hip."

Words carry considerable weight, and like artifacts dredged up from the bottom of the sea, they come to us with so many scars and markings that they tell us much more than they intend, or than we intend when we use them. So a little rummaging in the genealogy of "hipster": The words "hipster" and "hip" are white variants of the African-American terms "hep" and "hep cat" and, as often happens, the terms made their way across the racial divide through music. The irrepressible vocalist, dancer, and slyly watchful showman Cab Calloway proclaimed that he was a hep cat. At the same time a popular Los Angeles white pianist and singer named Harry Gibson presented himself as Harry "the Hipster" Gibson. In its earliest 1930s connotations, a hipster was someone who was hung up on jazz. To be hip, in 1937, meant knowing a lot about jazz musicians.

"Hep" itself has its own past, and Partridge's *A Dictionary of Slang and Unconventional English* (Eighth Edition, 1984) suggests that the word is "Ultimately ex the ploughman's, or the driver's, 'Hep!' to his team of horses ('Get up!'); the horses 'get hep' or lively, alert." In country slang, the phrase "he's mighty hep" means "very shrewd." From the beginning the word has nothing but positive connotations, which contrasts it with all of the variant definitions of "beat" and "beatnik," which despite Kerouac's protests and his wistful attempt to use the word "beatitude" as a substitute, remained vaguely negative.

Norman Mailer's essay "The White Negro" (in *The Portable Beat Reader*) contains much that is indigestible today, but it does manage to describe what his generation thought about the hipster. Although the essay was written in 1957, before the word "beat" had become such a fixation with the media, Mailer carefully compares the two terms, and he is much more favorable to hip than to beat. In the same way that Ginsberg's "best minds" were hipsters, Mailer correctly found the locus of hip in the Negro, just as Kerouac did in his much reviled paragraph in *On the Road* when he rhapsodized about the pleasures of black life in the Denver ghetto. Mailer wrote,

> So no wonder that in certain cities of America, in New York, of course, and New Orleans, in Chicago and San Francisco and Los Angeles, in such American cities as Paris and Mexico, D.F., this particular part of a generation was attracted to what the Negro had to offer. In such places as Greenwich Village, a ménage à trois was completed—the bohemian and the juvenile delinquent came face-to-face with the Negro, and the hipster was a fact in American life. If marijuana was the wedding ring, the child was the language of Hip. And in this wedding of the white and the black it was the Negro who brought the cultural dowry.

Mailer was also conscious that this complicated relationship had evolved its own new language to suit the new situation:

> . . . the Negro, not being privileged to gratify his self-esteem with the heady satisfactions of universal condemnation, chose to move instead in that other direction where all situations are equally valid . . . and elaborated a morality of the bottom, an ethical differentiation between the good and the bad in every human activity from the go-getter pimp (as opposed to the lazy one) to the relatively dependable pusher or prostitute. Add to this, the cunning of their language, the abstract ambiguous alternatives in which from the danger of oppression they learned to speak ("Well, now, man, like I'm looking for a cat to turn me on. . . ."), add even more the profound sensitivity of the Negro jazzman who was the cultural mentor of a people, and it is not too difficult to believe that the language of Hip which evolved was an artful language, tested and shaped by an intense experience. . . .

In Kerouac's famous description at the beginning of *On the Road* of the kind of people who turn him on—the ones who burn and go off like rockets—he is describing Mailer's hipsters. Mailer, when he evokes the pain and the exhaustion of recording this experience, could have been describing Kerouac. It was at this point in his essay that Mailer contrasted hip with beat, and it is "beat" that comes off the loser.

> If, however, you agree with my hypothesis, if you as a cat are way out too, and we are in the same groove . . . why then you say simply "I dig," because neither knowledge nor imagination comes easily, it is buried in the pain of one's forgotten experience, and so one must occasionally exhaust oneself by digging into the self in order to perceive the outside. And indeed it is essential to dig the most, for if you do not dig you lose your superiority over the Square, and so you are less likely to be cool (to be in control of a situation because you have swung where the Square has not, or because you have allowed to consciousness a pain, a guilt, a shame or a desire which the other has not had the courage to face). To be cool is to be equipped, and if you are equipped it is more difficult for the next cat who comes along to put you down. And of course one can hardly afford to be put down too often, or one is beat, one has lost one's confidence, one has lost one's will, one is impotent in the world of action and so closer to the demeaning flip of becoming a queer, or indeed closer to dying, and therefore it is even more difficult to recover enough energy to try to make it again, because once a cat is beat he has nothing to give, and no one is interested any longer in making it with him. This is the terror of the hipster—to be beat. . . .

## 2. I Dig What the Man's Putting Down

In one of the hipster classics of the 1950s, the consciously satiric "interview" with the jazz musician "Shorty Peterstein," the interviewer asks him how he feels about the concept of Art. Peterstein thinks for a confused minute, then he says, "Art blows great, man. Art's the most."

My own personal definition of "beat" has always been elastic enough to include the hipster. How could you tell where one ended and the other began? Also, no matter how I arranged the figures of the

Beat pantheon, one hipster had to be included. What would the 1950s have been without Lord Buckley, the hippest of them all! Buckley's hipster monologues were part of our daily meditations. Without them, could there have been the 1950s? How will we know—since there he was.

I didn't know anything about him. Just his recordings. I don't think any of us knew much more. Buckley didn't make the jazz magazines, since what he was doing wasn't jazz, and his monologues were so far beyond the norms of popular television and radio that he didn't make the popular magazines either. A half century later, I found out that he was from Stockton, California. How could Lord Buckley be from Stockton, California? When he left there in the 1920s it must have had what—five thousand people? Ten thousand people? He was born part–Native American, and perhaps it's the Native American part that kept him from sinking into the dust and the drears of California's Central Valley. I still shake my head in disbelief at Stockton, but then I think of other unlikely places that saw the birth of the Beats. Kerouac from Lowell, Ginsberg from Paterson, McClure from Marysville, Kansas, Sanders from Kansas City, Ferlinghetti from Yonkers. I add Stockton to the list of home places.

Since in the 1950s I had already decided which side of the spiritual barricades I had dropped my backpack, I knew only the great, groovy, swinging monologues which Buckley recorded in Los Angeles in 1951. Those were the cool messages from his Lordship. Like just about everything else in the 1950s, a time when America was split into at least two worlds that hardly acknowledged each other, there was a different side to Buckley. I didn't know about it until a few months ago, when one of the Disciples of the Lord of Hip, which is what Buckley fans like to call themselves in weak moments, sent me a videocassette of Buckley's appearances on popular television programs in the 1950s, like Ed Sullivan's variety show. Since by that time I had already dropped out enough so that I didn't watch television, I didn't know that Buckley was also part of those patchy early days. I wouldn't have recognized him, except for his Salvador Dalí–ish waxed mustache and his general air of barely suppressed craziness.

Sullivan didn't seem to like him much, but it was hard to tell, on any of Sullivan's programs that I saw later, whether or not Sullivan liked anybody. He called him Dick Buckley, but usually added "His

Lordship." What Buckley did on Sullivan's network television show was a crazed, hipster version of an ancient skit that must go back to the Commedia del'arte. Buckley sat four people on a row of chairs, then crouched behind them, moving their heads and speaking all of their voices in a frantic dialogue that was on the level of the old "Who's on First?" routine of Abbott and Costello. Buckley's routine was popular enough that Sullivan brought him back several times to repeat it with different guests. On other shows Buckley had an even less sane sketch, if that's possible. He led a group of male studio audience volunteers into a routine that ended up with all of them with their shirts off and their trousers rolled up, doing wobbly gymnastic exercises on mats spread on the stage. These television appearances would never put him into anyone's list of early television greats, so it has to be the monologues that are Richard Buckley's—His Lordship's—ticket to the Hipster Valhalla.

Humor is infamous for not being humorous for long. Any decade's jokes become the tiresome drag of the next decade, but I still listen to the best of Buckley with pleasure. I don't know if he developed the hipster monologues in his long years as a nightclub comic, but the moment came, and some things that he had obviously been doing before melded with what he wanted to do now. Much of the impulse behind the monologues is a strain that winds its way through Western culture like rust in old pipes. We have always had two levels of culture, one that we could call the popular vernacular, and the other the historical intellectual. To soften the sense of exclusion, the popular vernacular culture continually appropriates and restates the iconic utterances of the historical intellectual. As a crude example, one of the staple jokes of the early minstrel shows in America was a version of the balcony scene from Shakespeare's *Romeo and Juliet* performed in blackface, with the dialogue rewritten in stage "Coon" dialect. If this kind of appropriation is not part of the cultural dialogue today, it is because American culture has become so diffuse and so hedged in with qualifications that no one can be certain of what is being included or excluded—or if there are even things that continue to be part of a common cultural language.

Buckley also turned to Shakespeare, and one of his most successful monologues was his hipster reworking of Marc Antony's speech from *Julius Caesar*. "Friends, Romans, Countrymen, lend me your ears" becomes "Hipsters, Flipsters, and Finger Poppin' Daddies, knock me your lobes." Now there is no way I can be certain of what anyone else hears in this monologue, since I am of the generation that was given Marc Antony's oration to memorize in high school. I hear it the same way that Buckley did. But it is his monologues that try for a broader sweep that give more of a glimpse of what Buckley meant to us half a century ago. For many, the mellowest was the most famous, "The Nazz."

When we see the word "Nazz" today, do we immediately think of Jesus Christ, the Nazarene? Probably many church-going people would know what the dialogue has as its subject, but I'm certain they wouldn't be the same people who listen to Buckley. There was still enough of a congruence in the 1950s that there were people who were offended by "The Nazz." No one should have been offended, though, since as Mailer said, hipsters were cool, and part of their cool was wonder. To Lord Buckley, Christ was one of the true hipster heroes.

> "He may not be no real preachin' cat to you, but I dig what the man's putting down."

Since there were limits to what Buckley could squeeze onto a long-playing vinyl record—and to what his nightclub audiences would sit still for—the Lord of Hip couldn't do all of the New Testament, but he managed to cover the miracle of the cripple restored to health, Jesus' walk on the water, and the miracle of the fishes and the loaves. This is the hipster's conception of the encounter between Jesus and the cripple:

> . . . the Nazz and his buddies was goofin' off down the boulevard one day and they run into a little cat with a bent frame, so the Nazz looks at this little cat with the bent frame, and he says,
>
> "What's the matter with you, Baby?"
>
> And the little cat with the bent frame, he say, "Well, my frame is bent, Nazz, it's been bent from the infirm."
>
> So the Nazz looked at this little cat with the bent frame and he put the golden arc of love on this here little kitty and looked right down into the windows of his soul and he said to the little cat, he said,
>
> "STRAIGHTEN!"

[Thunder sound effects and a roll on the studio Hammond organ]

The cat stood up straighter than an arrow and everybody jumpin' up and down sayin',

"Look what the Nazz put on that boy! You dug him before, dig him now!"

When the cripple is able to walk, there is considerable excitement. After that success the Nazz becomes so popular he doesn't have the time to meet with everyone who wants him. "They want him to gig here, they want him to do a gig there . . . but he can't make all that jazz." So the Nazz picks twelve cats to hang out and dig his lick. Buckley's coolest insight into the figure of Jesus comes as a quick sentence in the middle of a paragraph about something else: "He wants everybody to see through his eyes, so they can see how pretty it was."

Even more than the Beats, Buckley was the voice of wonder in the 1950s that changed into the self-conscious, self-proclaiming voice of the 1960s. Since we seem to have a need to establish connections that have a clear identity to satisfy our sense of history, followers of the True Hip know that Bill Cosby was performing some of Buckley's material in Greenwich Village clubs when Bob Dylan first came to New York. Dylan encountered Buckley through Cosby. For simpler devotees, it is enough to know that as an expression of Buckley's religious beliefs, His Hipness got around to establishing—very briefly—his own church. Charles Tacot, who contributed the notes to an Elektra LP reissue of the monologues based on his long, sorely tried friendship with Buckley, wrote that His Hipness "organized his own brand of religion (The Church of the Living Swing, America's first Jazz church), starring himself and a pair of belly-dancers, which had the distinction of being the only church performance ever raided by the vice squad."

Buckley's words on a page don't really convey the effect of his delivery. He shouts, whispers, pleads, wheedles, and insists—all with immeasurable joy. A Buckley monologue is a groove and a wail. It is also a conscious reworking of the language of the African-American church, and when Buckley has finished his story of the Nazz, he swings into a Louis Armstrong–influenced vocal on "When the Saints Go Marching In." For our generation, this kind of appropriation cuts uncomfortably closer and deeper than his description of Jesus as "groovy." Listeners coming upon Buckley for the first time will have to decide for them-

selves if they can get down with it, or if it wigs them out. My own take
on it is that if I can dig Bobby Short comping on Cole Porter, I can get
down with Buckley doing Reverend C. L. Franklin.

What I hold closest in my affection for Buckley's monologues are
the moments when he goes beyond appropriation and uses the new,
swinging language to make something different. It is his "The Hip
Gahn" that finally—for me—gives him his folding chair up there in
the pantheon. The monologue has no precedent, it was written with
love, and in the end it takes us places we never knew about but recognize as perfectly familiar once we look around and understand where
we have come. "The Hip Gahn" is Buckley's name for Mahatma
Gandhi, and the monologue is a take on Gandhi's role in modern India
that works with a deceptive layering of metaphor. Buckley begins the
story with Gandhi challenging a lion, the symbol of the colonial power,
the British lion.

> You see, India was bugged with the lion. Every time India
> get a little extra scarf in the cupboard, wham, here come the
> lion, chomp, brmmf, swoop up the scene, and there stands
> the poor Indian's scarf, and it bugged him to death. That was
> before the Hip Gahn blew in on the scene.

Gandhi backs up and takes off on a run, jumping on the lion's tail
so hard that the lion swoops the scene and that gasses India. As
thanks for what Gandhi has done, Mr. Rabidi, who is called something
like the Indian Parkiller, gathers musicians playing every kind of instrument in India and has them do a giant jam session for the Hip
Gahn. Mr. Rabidi tells them,

> "Boys, you know what to blow. 'When the *Saint* Goes
> Marching In.'"
> They say, "Groovy."
> Now here comes the Gahn with his twenty-six chicks, with
> the horn rim glasses, nineteen nanny goats, and two spinning
> wheels, and he looks so sharp and so fine and so groovy 'cause
> he got a nice clean white dow dow on and the love light
> is gleaming through his glasses and he's gassing the whole
> scene . . .
> The Indian Parkiller sits him down on some nice groovy
> sofa pillows, silken that is, and he cools the nanny goats and
> the chicks all cuddle and, cats and kitties, you never dug no
> session like those cats blew.

But it is the last twist of this tale that has forever endeared me to Buckley. Mr. Rabidi comes up to the Gahn when everybody has finished playing and asks,

"Did you dig the scene?
"Which one of the instruments did you dig the most?"

So the Hip Gahn looked at him and a love look come on his face and he say, "Well, baby," (low laugh), "the music of all India which I dig the most, the instrument—you ain't got here."

Mr. Rabidi, man, say, "What? What you sayin'?

I got the dong dong players
and the bang bang players
and the liberdee players
and the reed heads
and the lute heads
every head I could dig up to swing out of the jungle

and this cat tell me the one he digs the most, I ain't got here?"
"That's right."

So he said, "Well, sweet double hipness, great beloved non-stop beauty, straighten me, 'cause I'm ready."

And the Hip Gahn said, "That's right, that's right. Well, here's the lick."

He said, "Baby, the instrument of all India which I dig the music the most of, that swings my soul up in the great cathedral head of beauty, is the music of the

Hop a do do da diddle diddle de dat teh teh teh teh deda dit and da da dit pat pa pa."

He said, "The spinning wheel, baby.
De det det n dee dit n nallada de dat dat
Knock a little patch on the cat's pants,
Doot dootn doot do do dootn
Swing a coat on grandma.
De dat dat dat da da tauyu tauyu det det"
[All the riffs are approximate, of course. You can wig out on
your own groove.]

"Get a little juice on the table.
Da da da doo, doo, de dat, de dat
The spinning wheel, baby.

"I hope I didn't bring you down."

## 3. *The Sky Is High and So Am I*

"This lady is walking across Washington Square Park and it's late at night and she's worried about whether she's going to get home and she sees this hip cat sitting on a bench and she goes up to him and she says,

"Excuse me, do the crosstown buses run all night?"

And the cat looks at her and you can tell he's trying to get with what she has laid on him, and after a minute he gets this real cool smile and he says, "Doodah, doodah."

Now generally the hipster was just—well—different, and the serious baggage of drugs wasn't strung over his shoulders, but in this joke the hipster is obviously stoned. For those of you who didn't do all those American social studies in the early grades, the lady has laid on him something that the hipster almost gets. It's a complicated, subliminal allusion to Stephen Foster's song "Camptown Races," which opens with the line, "De Camptown ladies sing this song," and the refrain, of course, is "Doodah, doodah." The chorus of the song begins, "Gwine to run all night, gwine to run all day." Now people who thought the joke was funny—and that wasn't everybody—were digging all those things that this joke was saying: that hipsters get stoned, and when they're stoned, things get a little messed up. Drunk jokes have the same effect on audiences. Some people can't stop laughing, and other people just get very down and droopy. But the thing to notice here is how mellow the hipster is. It's late at night, and the lady isn't afraid to walk up to him in Washington Square Park and ask him a question, which he almost manages to understand. After dark, the real Washington Square Park in Greenwich Village was never so mellow, but the *perception* in the joke is that it is mellow, and perception is what we deal with in vernacular humor.

Language is a very useful indication of our popular perceptions. In the 1940s, when the hipster landed on the far shores of our consciousness, marijuana had been illegal for only a few years. The government's inquisition against herb and its users hadn't yet reached today's tidal wave proportions. What were the words hipsters used for it? "Mary Jane," "tea," "weed," "reefer." Very unworried. In *Junky,* Burroughs consistently uses the term "tea head" for marijuana users, instead of the much darker word "addict." The perception among people who knew what all the words meant was so calm and orderly that Cab Calloway had a hit song with the first line, "Talk about a reefer five feet long. . . ." The title of the song, "If You're a Viper," is a little less sanguine, but "viper"—for a tea head—was more of a joke than a worry. "The sky is high and so am I. . . ." ends the song.

Did a dark, cloudy drug nimbus hang over the hipsters and Buckley? The jazz musicians who were well known to the casual club audiences still mostly drank. Alcohol was the mainstream jazz musicians' drug of choice. If they also smoked, they kept it to themselves. Those in the know were aware that there was heavy drug use among the beboppers, but it was usually considered a bad problem, and not anything that anybody would want to imitate. There was no concern about hipsters being stoned, since nobody could be as manic as Buckley while stoned. Benzedrine was something else, but it was so casually available that you could buy it in every drug store in over-the-counter nasal inhalers. The United States government was just beginning to move with a campaign against the drugs they considered downers. There were still a few years to go before they added uppers to their continually growing list.

The hipster has gotten lost in the tumbleweeds of time, but as a journalist wrote, and Mailer quoted as an opening to "The White Negro," the hipster was "the only extreme nonconformist of his generation." Since he "does not try to enforce his will on others, Napoleon-fashion, but contents himself with a magical omnipotence never disproved but never tested . . . he exercises a powerful if underground appeal for conformists."

Before the Beats, there were the Hipsters. For many in that generation, that was as much as they wanted to test the new consciousness. With Lord Buckley, the new consciousness and the new language passed on a message of pleased—if slightly crazed—wonder, and wonder will always be in short supply in our tired and disillusioned world.

# GREGORY CORSO

GREGORY CORSO (1930–2001) was born in Greenwich Village, where he returned after beginning to write poetry in the state prison in Dannemora, New York. Befriended by Allen Ginsberg in 1950, Corso published his first book five years later, *The Vestal Lady on Brattle and Other Poems*, in Cambridge, Massachusetts. In 1960, New Directions published *The Happy Birthday of Death*, which included the surrealistic mock-battle wordplay of "Poets Hitchhiking on the Highway," first appearing in the little magazine *Coastlines* in the Summer 1957 issue. "Spontaneous Requiem for the American Indian," first included in *Yugen* 2 (1958), can also be found in Corso's *Elegaic Feelings American* (New York: New Directions, 1970) and *Mindfield* (New York: Thunder's Mouth, 1989). Corso has explained that in this poem, "Kiwago is the big bull buffalo. The white buffalo is Kiwago. Wakonda is the great sky god, but also earth god. Wakonda takes in the whole shot, whereas Talako is the sky god. Talako would be like Horus in Ancient Egypt, Hermes in Greece. Wakonda is more the great spirit."

## Poets Hitchhiking on the Highway

Of course I tried to tell him
but he cranked his head
        without an excuse.
I told him the sky chases
        the sun
And he smiled and said:
        "What's the use."
I was feeling like a demon
        again
So I said: "But the ocean chases
        the fish."
This time he laughed

and said: "Suppose the
   strawberry were
      pushed into a mountain."
After that I knew the
  war was on—
So we fought:
He said: "The apple-cart like a
      broomstick-angel
   snaps & splinters
      old Dutch shoes."
I said: "Lightning will strike the old oak
   and free the fumes!"
He said: "Mad street with no name."
I said: "Bald killer! Bald killer! Bald killer!"
He said, getting real mad,
    "Firestoves! Gas! Couch!"
I said, only smiling,
    "I know God would turn back his head
    if I sat quietly and thought."
We ended by melting away,
   hating the air!

## Spontaneous Requiem for the American Indian

Wakonda! Talako! deathonic turkey gobbling in the soft-
  footpatch night!
Blue-tipped yellow-tipped red-tipped feathers of whort dye
  fluffing in fire mad dance whaa whaa dead men red men
  feathers-in-their-head-men night!
Deerskin rage of flesh on the bone on the hot tobacco ground!
Muskhogean requiems america southeastern, O death of
  Creeks, Choctaws,
The youthful tearful Brave, in his dying hand trout, well-caught
  proud trout,
Softest of feet, fleet, o america dirge, o america norwegians
  swedes of quid and murder and boots and slaughter and
  God and rot-letters,

O pinto brays! O deatheme sled mourning the dying chief!
Berries, spruce, whortle, cranky corn, bitter wheat; o scarcity
of men!
High-throttled squawlark, sister warrior, teepee maid, scar
lover, crash down thy muskrat no longer thy flesh hand
and rage and writhe and pound thy Indianic earth with
last pang of love of love,
o america, o requiems—

Ghost-herds of uneaten left to rot animals thundering across
the plains
Chasing the ghost of England across the plains forever ever,
pompous Kiwago raging in the still Dakotas, o america—
America o mineral scant america o mineralize america o
conferva of that once
great lovely Muskhogean pool, o oil-suck america despite, oil
from forgetive days, hare to arrow, muskellunge to spear,
fleet-footed know ye speed-well the tribes thence outraced
the earth to eat to love to die,
o requiems, Hathor off-far bespeaks Wakonda,
heraldic henequen tubas whittled in coyote tune to mourn the
death of the going sun the going sled of each dying, sad
and dying, shake of man, the tremble of men, of each
dying chief slow and red and leather fur hot—
Shake slow the rattler, the hawk-teeth, the beetle-bells, shake
slow dirge, o dirge, shake slow the winds of winds, o
feathers withered and blown,
Dirge the final pinto-led sled, the confused hurt sad king of
Montanas,
Strike dumb the French fur trappers in their riverboat brool
mockery, no chant of death in such a wealth of muskrat
and beaver, shun them,
O slam squaw hysteria down on america, the covered wagon
america, the arrow flamed wagons of conquest, the death
stand of quakers and white-hooded hags and proud new
men, young and dead,
O Geronimo! hard nickel faced Washington Boliva of a dying
city that never was, that monster-died, that demons
gathered to steal and did,

O Sitting Bull pruneman Jefferson Lenin Lincoln reddeadman,
    force thy spirit to wings, cloud the earth to air, o the
    condor the vulture the hawk fat days are gone, and you
    are gone, o america, o requiems,
Dry valleys, deathhead stones, high Arizonas, red sun earth, the
    sled,
The weeping bray, the ponymarenight, the slow chief of death,
    wrinkled and sad and manless, vistaless, smokeless, proud
    sad dying—
Toward the coyote reach of peak and moon, howl of heyday,
    laugh proud of men and men, Blackfoot, Mohawk,
    Algonquin, Seneca, all men, o american, peaked there then
    bow
Thy white-haired straw head and, pinto imitated, die with the
    rising moon, hotnight, lost, empty, unseen, musicless,
    mindless; no wind—
In the grim dread light of the Happy Hunting Ground
A century of chiefs argue their many scalps, whacking the
    yellow strands of a child against the coaly misty harsh of
    tent;
It falls apart in a scatter of strewn, away, gone, no more, back
    free out of the quay, into the bladder seep of the bald dead
    seeking the hairless rawhead child of whiteman's grave;
O there is more an exact sorrow in this Indianical eternity,
Sure o america woof and haw and caw and wooooo whirl
    awhirl here o weep!
Indianhill woe! never was the scalp of men the prime knife in
    the heart of a savagengence era, Clevelandestroyer of
    manland, o requiems,
O thundercloud, thunderbird, rain-in-the-face, hark in the
    gloom, death,
And blankets and corn, and peaceful footings of man in quest
    of Kiwago, america, Kiwago, america, corn america,
    earthly song of a sad boy's redfleshed song in the night
    before the peered head intrusive head of laughing
    thunderbolt Zeus, o the prank, o the death, o the night,
Requiem, america, sing a dirge that might stalk the white wheat
    black in praise of Indianever again to be, gone, gone,
    desolate, and gone;

Hear the plains, the great divide, hear the wind of this night
    Oklahoma race to weep first in the dirge of mountains and
    streams and trees and birds and day and night and the
    bright yet lost apparitional sled,
The bowed head of an Indian is enough to bow the horse's
    head and both in unison die and die and die and never
    again die for once the night eats up the dying it eats up the
    pain and there is no Indian pain no pregnant squaw no
    wild-footed great-eyed boy no jolly stern fat white-furred
    chief of tobacco damp and sweet, o america america—
Each year Kiwago must watch its calves thin out; must watch
    with all its natural killers dead, the new marksmen of
    machines and bullets and trained studied eyes aim and fire
    and kill the oldest bull, the king, the Kiwago of the
    reminiscent plain—
Each year Wakonda must watch the motionless desert, the dry
    tearless childless desert, the smokeless desert, the
    Indianlessadly desert—
Each year Talako must watch the bird go arrowless in his peace
    of sky in his freedom of the mouth of old america, raw
    wild calm america,
O america, o requiem, o tumbleweed, o Western Sky, each year
    is another year the soft football doesn't fall, the thin strong
    arm of spear never raised, the wise council of gathered
    kings no longer warm with life and fur and damp and heat
    and hotcorn and dry jerky meat, each year no squaw titters
    her moony lover of hard love and necessary need of man
    and wife and child child, each year no child, no mien of
    life, good life, no, no, america, but the dead stones, the dry
    trees, the dusty going winded earth—requiem.
Pilgrim blunderbuss, buckles, high hat, Dutch, English, patent
leather shoes, Bible, pray, snow, careful, careful, o but feast,
turkey, corn, pumpkin, sweet confused happy hosty guests,
Iroquois, Mohawk, Oneida, Onondaga, Thanksgiving!
O joy! o angels! o peace! o land! land land land, o death,
O fire and arrow and buckshot and whisky and rum and death
    and land,
O witches and taverns and quakers and Salem and New
    Amsterdam and corn,

And night, softfeet, death, massacre, massacre, o america, o
    requiem—
Log-cabins, forts, outposts, trading-posts, in the distance,
    clouds,
Dust, hordes, tribes, death, death, blonde girls to die, gowns of
    ladies to burn, men of redcoats and bluecoats to die, boys
    to drum and fife and curse and cry and die, horses . . . to
    die, babies . . . to die;
Yeeeeeeeeeeeeeeeoooooooooooo!Harrrrrrrrrrrrrrraaaaaaaaa!
EEEEEEEeeeeeeeeEEEEEEaaaaaaaaaaaaaaah!
To die to die to die to die to die to die . . . america, requiem.
Corn, jerky, whortly, the Seneca in a deacon's suit, gawky,
    awkward, drunk,
Tired, slouched—the gowns and bright boots pass, the quick
take-your-partner-swing-to-the-left-swing-to-the-right hums
all is over, done, the Seneca sleeps, no sled, no pinto, no end,
but sleep, and a new era, a new day, a new light and the corn
grows plenty, and the night is forever, and the day;
The jetliner streams down upon Texas,
                    Requiem.


Motorcyclist Blackfoot his studded belt at night wilder than
bright hawk-eyes sits on his fat bike black smelly brusqued assy
about to goggleeye himself down golden ventures whizzing
faster than his ancestral steed past smokestacks bannershacks
O the timid shade of Kiwago now! the mad roar exhaustpipe
Indian like a fleeing oven clanking weeeeee weeeeeee no
feathers in his oily helmet O he's a fast engine of steam
zooming unlaurelled by but he's stupid he sits in Horn &
Hardart's his New York visit and he's happy with his short
girls with pink faces and bright hair talking about his big fat
bike and their big fat bike, O he's an angel there though sinister
sinister in shape of Steel Discipline smoking a cigarette in a
fishy corner in the night, waiting, america, waiting the end, the
last Indian, mad Indian of no fish or foot or proud forest haunt,
mad on his knees ponytailing & rabbitfooting his motorcycle,
his the final requiem the final america READY THE FUNERAL
STOMP goodluck charms on, tire aired, spikes greased, morose
goggles on, motor gas brakes checked! 1958 Indians, heaps of

leather—ZOOM down the wide amber speedway of Death,
Little Richard, tuba mirum, the vast black jacket brays in the
full forced fell.

---

# DIANE DI PRIMA

DIANE DI PRIMA, born in New York City the granddaughter of
Italian immigrants, lived in Greenwich Village with a group of
bohemian artists, writers, actors, and dancers after she dropped
out of Swarthmore College to become a writer. In *Memoirs of a
Beatnik* (1969), she gave a memorable description of how she
stopped cooking dinner for a dozen of her friends in a midtown
Manhattan tenement and walked over to a pier on the Hudson
River so she could be alone while she read Ginsberg's "Howl for
Carl Solomon" in the small black-and-white City Lights Pocket
Poets paperback edition in 1957. In di Prima's account, she elo-
quently expressed the excited "shock of recognition" of other
sympathetic readers encountering Beat poetry for the first time:

> I knew that this Allen Ginsberg, whoever he
> was, had broken ground for all of us—all few hun-
> dreds of us—simply by getting this published. I
> had no idea yet what this meant, how far it would
> take us. . . .
> For I sensed that Allen was only, could only be,
> the vanguard of a much larger thing. All the peo-
> ple who, like me, had hidden and skulked, writ-
> ing down what they knew for a small handful
> of friends—and even those friends claiming it
> "couldn't be published"—waiting with only a
> slight bitterness for the thing to end, for man's era
> to draw to a close in a blaze of radiation—all these
> would now step forward and say their piece. Not
> many would hear them, but they would, finally,
> hear each other. I was about to meet my brothers
> and sisters.

In 1961, a year after her first book of prose, *Dinners and Nightmares,* di Prima with her lover LeRoi Jones in her apartment on East Fourth Street began a little magazine that they titled *The Floating Bear, a newsletter.* Copies were mimeographed for free distribution. Surviving until 1969, despite insufficient funding, it published thirty-seven issues, making it one of the most successful Beat publications of all time (along with the thirteen issues of Ed Sanders's Lower East Side journal, *Fuck You: A Magazine of the Arts,* from 1962 to 1965). At the same time that di Prima and Jones were publishing their newsletter, they also founded New York Poets Theatre with Fred Herko, Alan Marlowe, and James Waring, which produced four seasons of one-act plays by poets. In 1973, di Prima was interviewed about her work with the magazine. Material from this interview became her introduction to a reprint edition of *The Floating Bear,* published by Laurence McGilvery in La Jolla, California. "Rant" is included in di Prima's collection *Pieces of a Song* (1990).

## The Floating Bear, a newsletter

Bear Number One, what I remember about it. We printed 250 copies. Our mailing list was just two pieces of paper with names scribbled on them, 117 names that we had gotten out of our address books. Painters, poets, dancers, those folks, and mostly from New York. It was in February 1961 and how it came about was that the year before A.B. Spellman and I had decided to do a magazine called *The Elephant at the Door.* One of the first manuscripts we got was from Russell Edson and he called it "The Horse at the Window." (There seem to have been a lot of animals around at the time.) Then, when it came to the point where A.B. had to reject his first manuscript, he decided that he didn't want to be an editor because he couldn't reject anybody. I just put all the manuscripts in a file drawer and forgot about it, and the next year LeRoi came up with the idea that we should do a newsletter that would go out free to writers. Then came the question of a name. Half kidding, I suggested calling it "The Floating Bear," which was a boat Winnie-the-Pooh made out of a honey pot. It had a

characteristic I was really fond of: "Sometimes it's a Boat, and sometimes it's more of an Accident." To my surprise, LeRoi liked it, and so
it became *The Floating Bear, a newsletter.*

Before that LeRoi had been doing some publishing for about two
and a half years. We were doing things together a lot, but not all the
time. It was very informal, he was kind of feeling the scene out. *Yugen*
ran for eight issues from 1958 to 1962. The early issues were very
rough, both in content and format: great things and real junk, side by
side. I used to go over to his house on 20th Street and paste them up
with his wife, Hettie. The later issues became more professional looking, and also the writing was more professional. It had become a regular little magazine instead of something done out of somebody's living
room.

LeRoi's early book publishing was behind him, too, at this point.
He had done the first Totem Press things himself, with the help of
Hettie and me, typing them up on an IBM typewriter and pasting
them up at home. Things like Charles Olson's *Projective Verse* (1959)
and Michael McClure's *For Artaud* (1959) were done with practically
no money at all. Later things, like *Second Avenue* (1960) by Frank
O'Hara and *Like I Say* (1960) by Philip Whalen were done in conjunc-
tion with Corinth Books, which was an offshoot of the Eighth Street
Bookshop. We still did the pasteup and all that, but more money was
available, the books began to look and feel a little more solid, and we
were a little more certain when they would come out.

A lot of what went into the early Bears was stuff that LeRoi got in
the mail through his having already published *Yugen*—people sending
him poems and things, and him slowly getting in touch with the main
body of writers who were working in that period. It wasn't simply one
clique of writers throughout the country. There were still a lot of people working quietly and separately in a lot of funny little places. Then,
too, we didn't know too much about the West Coast writers except for
a few well-publicized ones, like Ginsberg and Ferlinghetti. There were
a lot of people in the earlier issues whom I had not yet met or read, for
instance, I had never read Robin Blaser before I put him in the first issue of the Bear, but LeRoi had gotten his stuff in the mail.

Nearly everything that appeared in the Bear was published there
for the first time, except for obvious things like an excerpt from King
James VI or Ma Rainey, and then, in a much later issue, the long piece
by Grosseteste. In the later issues it would sometimes happen that

something would accidentally be a reprint, because we would hang onto material for a long time, and the writer would by then have sent it to another magazine which would print it first. But the intention was to publish only original material, and at first the intention was very much that it should be technically innovative material, or that it should introduce a new writer who hadn't been seen before. We often gave a whole issue, or a large part of an issue, to a new writer: Bill Berkson, A.B. Spellman, David Shapiro, George Stanley, etc.

We got hold of manuscripts all kinds of ways besides in the mail. For instance, I would go over to Frank O'Hara's house pretty often. He used to keep a typewriter on the table in the kitchen, and he would type away, make poems all the time, when company was there and when it wasn't, when he was eating, all kinds of times. There would be an unfinished poem in his typewriter and he would do a few lines on it now and again, and he kept losing all these poems. They would wind up all over the house. He was working full time at the Museum of Modern Art, and he never paid much attention to what was happening. The poems would get into everything and I would come over and go through, like, his dresser drawers. There would be poems in with the towels, and I'd say, "Oh, hey, I like this one," and he'd say, "OK, take it." Very often it would be the only copy. My guess is that huge collected Frank O'Hara has only about one-third of his actual work.

The John Wieners poems in Number 10 were from manuscripts that he had left around at different people's houses where he had stayed at one time or another. The really early stuff, from his Black Mountain days and right after, he had left at Frank O'Hara's house years and years ago. Frank just laid the manuscript on me. John also stayed at LeRoi's and left stuff there, and when I came out to the West Coast, I was given poems that he had left at Wallace Berman's pad when he'd been living with him on Scott Street in San Francisco (period of *The Hotel Wentley Poems*). There's a huge stack of unpublished John Wieners floating around somewhere.

John was better at hanging onto other people's work than to his own. Some of the work that he used when he edited Number 33 came from as far back as 1951. This issue was predominantly a street/junkie issue: beautiful, wasted chicks and hustlers that John had known in Boston, in San Francisco and New York. It's a very beautiful issue, I think.

The Kerouac things were really old, I mean the typescript looked old, so they were probably done around the mid-fifties. I don't know quite how we got them, probably from Allen Ginsberg. The Lamantia poems were old, too. They appear in various Bears, but they all come from one rather fat manuscript with a letter attached to it that LeRoi received from Phil when *Yugen* was going.

"Tear Gas" by Michael McClure in Number 37 came my way in a kind of interesting way. There was an issue of *The Realist,* Paul Krassner's magazine out of New York, that was devoted completely to the Diggers, and distributed free in San Francisco. And then there was a lot of leftover material that didn't get into it, most of it unsigned. This leftover stuff was sent to my house in San Francisco by Emmett Grogan, so that Ron Thelin could get hold of it. Ron was one of the editors of the *Oracle,* but the *Oracle* had folded by then, and Ron wasn't into doing anything with the manuscript, so he left it with me. I found the piece by Michael, and stuck it in the last Bear.

Apart from getting hold of out-of-the-way work and unpublished poets, our other major concern, at least for the first year or so, was speed: getting this new, exciting work into the hands of other writers as quickly as possible. I remember that the last time I saw Charles Olson in Gloucester, one of the things he talked about was how valuable the Bear had been to him in its early years because of the fact that he could get new work out that fast. He was very involved in speed, in communication. We got manuscripts from him pretty regularly in the early days of the Bear, and we'd usually get them into the very next issue. That meant that his work, his thoughts, would be in the hands of a few hundred writers within two or three weeks. It was like writing a letter to a bunch of friends.

There was a constant tug-of-war between LeRoi and myself about how much space we were going to give to what. LeRoi was much more into an analytic kind of thing. The letter in Number 5 is a pretty clear statement of what LeRoi's interest and concern with the Bear was at the beginning. That, and his statement on poetics in *New American Poetry* ("'HOW YOU SOUND?' is what we recent fellows are up to"), could be a map of where he was then. He was involved with our thought, our investigation into who we were and what our stance was in relation to our society and the world outside. He liked strong, politically aware poetry, and a lot of prose and criticism. I reacted more intuitively to what I read—didn't always intellectually "understand" the poems I was into. I had no articulate poetic theory at all, and I learned a lot from Roi. We didn't really agree about a lot of the poets, and this gave rise to a very healthy tension. We never argued about anything, but I'd say, OK, you can have three pages of Perkoff and I'll take three of O'Hara, whatever. I think it gave a fine editorial balance to the early Bears which was lacking when LeRoi left and I was editing later issues by myself.

What we did have in common was our consciousness that the techniques of poetry were changing very fast, and our sense of the urgency of getting the technological advances of, say, Olson, into the hands of, say, Creeley, within two weeks, back and forth, because the thing just kept growing at a mad rate out of that.

LeRoi could work at an incredible rate. He could read two manuscripts at a time, one with each eye. He would spread things out on the table while he was eating supper, and reject them all—listening to the news and a jazz record he was going to review, all at the same time. When LeRoi and I would get the manuscripts together for an issue they would be in all kinds of shape. I would type directly on the mimeograph stencils, and most editing decisions would happen while I was typing: lay out and edit and type all at one time. A prose piece would take, say, half a page more than we had expected, so we would decide to leave something else out. This didn't happen with the poetry because as much as possible I tried to keep the look of the page the same as the author's page. This was a big advantage of the Bear format. You didn't have to guess where to break the stanza if both you and the poet were using 8½ x 11 paper. Almost everybody writes on typewriters, and I felt that a lot of what they were doing had to do with the shape of their page.

For the first year or a little more we printed the Bear on a mimeograph machine at Larry Wallrich's Phoenix Bookshop and gave him fifty copies of each issue in exchange. Then Larry left for England and sold the shop to Bob Wilson, and about the same time we bought our own machine with money we had raised around New York. We still continued to take fifty copies of each issue to the Phoenix, only now we sold them to Bob Wilson. He often bought them in advance, to give us the money we needed for paper.

There wasn't much help around until Number 25, except for a few issues that came out early in 1962. It was mostly just LeRoi and me working. Of course, our friends were in and out all the time, and we did have some help with things like collating and addressing, because I would just lasso anyone who came in the door. Nobody could just come and visit me, ever, in any of my houses. I sort of resent it, even now. I like to hand them something, some cards or envelopes, and say, "While we're talking, would you mind putting those in alphabetical order?" or, "Would you mind writing addresses on these?" It's a very good way to keep extra people away, and it gets a lot done. Even so, there was an incredible amount of work involved, just answering letters, and reading all the manuscripts and rejecting them, and keeping that damn mailing list up. The people on the list were moving all the time. I bet they moved on the average at least once a year.

In the winter of 1961–1962 we held gatherings at my East 4th Street pad every other Sunday. There was a regular marathon ball thing going on there for a few issues. Whole bunches of people would come over to help: painters, musicians, a whole lot of outside help. The typing on those particular issues was done by James Waring who's a choreographer and painter. Cecil Taylor ran the mimeograph machine, and Fred Herko and I collated, and we all addressed envelopes. I would have the issues more or less edited ahead of time and the whole thing would be typed, run off, collated, and addressed in about a day and a half. Sometimes we would stay up together all Sunday night and have it in the mail by Monday morning. That petered out when it got to be spring and people had other things to do.

Anybody who asked for the Bear got put on the list. There was no charge until the last year or two, that is, the last four or five issues, when I started asking people for an initial contribution for postage. After the first couple of issues we always broke even. People would send us money, or stamps, or give us things. A lot of the money came from the New York painters, the abstract expressionists who were selling well at the time. At one time Al Leslie gave us 4000 copies of *The Hasty Papers* as a contribution. It's a very big—huge—magazine, or, as he called it, a "one-shot review," he had edited. He had printed 5000 of them and didn't know what to do with them; he was tired of paying the warehouse for storage. We didn't know what to do with them either, so we remaindered them to the Paperbook Gallery for ten cents each. That gave us $400—a fortune, because our expenses in those early days were very small. The first issue was four sheets, and we only needed a ream per two sheets because we did 250 copies, so we bought two reams of paper, maybe we bought three reams. And postage was much less, 3¢ or 4¢ a copy. We mailed to 117 people, so the cost of the whole issue was less than $25. By the end of the first year we were up to 500 copies, and by the time of the last few issues we were printing 1500 and mailing out 1250: about 250 abroad and 1000 all over the United States, and that's counting cutting back the mailing list all the time. We printed 2000 of Number 37, so that we would have 500 to give away around San Francisco to friends and other street people. Those late, thick issues cost two to three hundred dollars apiece to do. Postage is phenomenally high now, and especially postage to Europe.

Most of the extra copies were either given away to people who happened by, or to the writers who were in that particular issue. Later, when new people were added to the list, I would send them all the back issues that we still had around for a start. I tried not to keep any extras. I always considered the Bear a throwaway, and if we had an issue that wasn't going very well, we would bring a whole bunch of it someplace where they could be given away. I had two complete sets for a number of years, but I got rid of the last set, xeroxed it and sold the original, in June of 1968. Except for the copies that went to the Phoenix and the copies of the last issue, Number 37, that were given away in the Bay Area, the Bear was not distributed through bookstores.

There was a person on the *Floating Bear* mailing list, a black poet named Harold Carrington, who was in prison in New Jersey. The censor or somebody read all of his mail, of course, and however it happened issue Number Nine was reported for obscenity. I think the particular objection was to LeRoi's play *From the System of Dante's Hell,* and to William Burroughs' piece *Routine.* I guess they couldn't stand the idea of FDR and all those baboons. (Harold Carrington, by the way, got out of prison in 1965 at the age of 25, after having been there since he was 18. He went to Atlantic City, spent two weeks there, and O.D.'d. I had a lot of poems and letters from him and they were pretty far out. He'd write, "I've never seen a play. Is this what plays are like? I've just written one." Then he would send you a play he had written. It was very strange. Some of them have been printed in England.)

Anyway. We were arrested on October 18, 1961, and what went down was more or less like this. I heard a knock on my door early in the morning which I didn't answer because I never open my door early in the morning in New York City. In the morning in New York City is only trouble. It's landlords, it's Con Edison, it's the police, it's your neighbors wanting to know why you made so much noise last night, it's something awful, and before noon I never open my door. The people after being slightly persistent went away, and then I got a phone call which I did answer. It was Hettie, LeRoi's wife, informing me that if anybody came to the house I shouldn't let them in because it would be the postal authorities and the FBI looking to arrest me for *The Floating Bear* and that they had just taken LeRoi away. Hettie had opened the door, still sleepy, and they had marched right into the bedroom which was also the office and gotten LeRoi up. Then they searched it quite thoroughly, taking all kinds of little magazines and manuscripts and even a water pipe that LeRoi had made himself with a cork and some glass tubes. They were looking mainly for the Bear mailing list but I had it, so they took practically everything else in sight, including LeRoi, whom they arrested for sending obscenity through the mails. They asked him where I was, and he said immediately that I had left for California. Half asleep, this was his immediate reply: "Oh, her, she went away, she's not in New York City."

A little before noon they came back a second time and banged on the door again. I had an upstairs neighbor who was a very good friend, Freddie Herko, who had been very close to me for about ten years. We used to always communicate by the fire escape, not the doors that led to the hall. I called Freddie up and said, "Listen, the FBI's banging on the door. Why don't you come down the fire escape and talk to me." Freddie and his lover Alan Marlowe, who was later my husband, came down the fire escape to babysit my daughter Jeanne, who was four, and I showered and put on some very expensive clothes, which was how I figured I should go to court. Then I called up Roi's lawyer, Stanley Faulkner, and arranged to meet him at the courthouse to turn myself in so we could get LeRoi out. They wouldn't set bail on him until they had me too, so we went down to the courthouse and did this whole number. Stanley really pulls all kinds of 1930's, sentimental, C.P. tricks. And they work. I had told him we couldn't go to court in June because I was going to have LeRoi's baby then. This was only October, and I didn't even look pregnant yet, but Stanley went rushing around insisting that clerks move out of their offices so I could sit down and rest while the whole thing was going on. He had everybody so frightened that the guy who fingerprinted me kept saying "Excuse me" every time he took a different finger. He'd say "Excuse me" and then he would do the next finger, "Excuse me."

Meanwhile, LeRoi had been in a very small cell by himself all day and they hadn't allowed him any paper or books. I yelled and screamed and Stanley yelled and screamed, and we finally both got out with no bail. It was the first time for me and probably also for LeRoi of having that unpleasant experience of walking through a place like a courthouse while reporters flash lights at you. (A couple of papers ran stories on the arrest; the New York Post was one of them.)

The case never went to court. LeRoi requested a grand jury hearing on Stanley Faulkner's advice. Only one of us could testify and he did. He spent two days on the stand. The first day he was questioned by the D.A., and the second he brought in a ton of stuff that had one time or another been labeled "obscene": everything from Ulysses to Catullus. He read for hours to the grand jury, and they refused to return an indictment. Of course, we also had letters from people all over the world stating that the work of William Burroughs and LeRoi Jones was "literature" (whatever that is) and that we should be left alone.

1962 was a good time for people to be liberal that way with a very nice, literate, still polite, still cool LeRoi. Made them feel good. They had a chance to be really nice, and they haven't had many chances since, with any of us.

Even before the case was cleared, From the System of Dante's Hell was performed by the New York Poets Theatre. It was on the first program of the Theatre and was the first thing of LeRoi's ever staged. The other plays on the program were Michael McClure's Pillow and my Discontent of a Russian Prince, that I played in with Freddie Herko. LeRoi went to almost all of the rehearsals and I think that was when he really got the idea of working with the theater. He started to get the feeling of that sound and what you had to do to make it move, even though this one obviously hadn't been written to be performed. We expected all the time the plays were running that we were going to be busted again, but we weren't.

LeRoi resigned in 1963 after Number 25 came out, and after that the Bear got very long because it came out irregularly and we would have these backlogs of manuscripts we had accepted. Also, it made sense to do fewer, larger issues, because money was available in large lumps when it was available at all. I married Alan Marlowe in San Francisco in November of 1962, and sporadically he was very good at raising money and organizing things. In between, nothing happened. On and off he was a great theater producer, and we had the New York Poets Theatre. Officially it was the American Theatre for Poets, Inc., but it was always called the New York Poets Theatre. The whole scene got much bigger then in 1964 and 1965, kind of uncomfortably big for me in some ways.

When I left New York in September of 1962, I left the manuscript of Number 24 with a guy named Soren Agenoux, who was supposed to type it and mimeograph it and get it in the mail for me. I gave Soren enough bread to print a regular issue, but he spent part of it, naturally, so he ended up buying less paper and cheaper paper, and the copies didn't stand up very well. He printed about 500 copies instead of the 1000 we were doing by then, and he mailed out about 200 and put the rest in some cardboard boxes in the closet of a house in Brooklyn where he went to stay. The house belonged to Jerry Ayres who now lives in Hollywood and works for one of the film companies. Anyway, Jerry's wife decided one day that she wanted to clean her closet, and she threw out all the unmailed copies of Number 24, which is why it became the "scarce issue" that libraries and collectors keep looking for. Soren Agenoux isn't his real name, by the way, but he's used it so long I forget what his real name is. He was a great boon to me at that point. He not only lost issue 24, but he sublet my apartment and sold all my art books and distributed somehow to the community all my Art Nouveau French jewelry and my Egyptian scarab collection. Later he did an endless number of parodies of the Bear called *The Sinking Bear*. He mimeographed them at the Judson Church in New York. They were a kind of gay version of the Bear, cliquey and full of local speed-freak and theater news. I don't know how many *Sinking Bears* there were, but there were a lot, because Soren and his friends were very prolific, and the Judson Church bought the paper.

Number 25 I edited at Stinson Beach, California, and mailed from Topanga Canyon. It was printed at San Francisco State College. Someone knew some kids there who were able to use an office, and they mimeographed and collated it. We printed the usual number, but didn't mail to the whole list because we were very, very short of money. I mailed a few at a time, and went over the list and took the people I really cared about first.

After LeRoi left, the Bear was starting to get one-sided, so I asked various people to guest-edit some of the issues. Number 26 was guest-edited by Billy Linich. Billy was working for us for free, whenever he felt like it: helping with the mail and the Bear mailing list and all that, and I let him guest-edit an issue, which turned out to be very like *The Sinking Bear*. Lots of letters and puns and in-group jokes. Like, somebody would steal a painting off the walls of a theater, and seven other people would know about it, and there would be a lot of jokes about it, but only those seven people would know what was going on.

Billy also typed Numbers 27, 28 and 29, and did a lot of work for the New York Poets Theatre. In Number 29 there was a piece by John McDowell, and John had made just about every sentence into a separate paragraph, and Billy when he typed the issue made the whole thing into a lot fewer paragraphs, which made John not too happy. Billy by that time was also putting commas into people's poems, and things like that, but that particular piece made a controversy between Billy and me which made Billy go away. That was unfortunate, both because I liked Billy very much, and because it slowed us down even more than ever.

Then Billy moved in with Andy Warhol, and changed his name to Billy Name, and lined the walls of Andy's studio with tinfoil, which made Andy very famous. He worked for Andy for free for six or seven years. I saw him in San Francisco recently, and he was living on the street and had changed his name to Kingdom Unknown Name.

In March of 1965 I put together a print shop on the lower East Side to publish Poets Press books, and I typed and ran off the next few issues myself. Number 31 was edited by Alan Marlowe. Kirby Doyle did half of Number 32 before he left New York rather precipitously, and I finished editing the issue. Everything up to the Yvonne Rainer piece was chosen by Kirby, and the rest, which I put together, I just labeled Part II.

Number 33 was edited by John Wieners in the fall of 1966 while we were living at Timothy Leary's place in Millbrook, New York. We left to do a cross-country reading tour and the issue was typed and printed at the Detroit Artists Workshop. John Sinclair and friends had a whole commune there, and everybody who came in helped a little with it. Numbers 34 and 35 were done at the Hotel Albert in New York, and there was help there, too. John Braden, a young singer, and Lee Fitzgerald, who later became an actor, were living with us. John was 21, and Lee was in his late teens, and they did a lot of the work.

Then, when I moved back to the West Coast in 1968 to Oak Street in San Francisco, I had fourteen rooms and most of them were usually full. A kind of communal thing was going on: lots of people doing things, lots of people passing through. I can't even remember some of the kids. They stayed a few days in the basement on their way to somewhere and some of them ran the mimeograph machine. Michael Smith, the theater critic from the *Village Voice,* stayed with us on Oak Street, and he typed Bear 36. That issue was edited by Bill Berkson. I had a lot of trouble getting it out, because most of that East Coast poetry didn't seem very relevant out here. Numbers 36 and 37 were printed some months apart but they were mailed out simultaneously. I edited Number 37 in San Francisco and deliberately aimed for a West Coast feeling. A whole bunch of the last issue, Number 37, was stamped "free" and left at the Third Eye bookstore on Haight Street because I thought the people of the City of San Francisco should have it. I also left a handful at Cody's and Moe's in Berkeley. It was definitely a West Coast issue. The whole free city thing was going strong then, the Diggers and so on, and we wanted to have plenty of copies for everyone.

After Number 37 was mailed out, there was a period of about a year and a half when things were in a state of flux. But, by the spring of 1970 I knew for sure that the Bear was finished—I didn't want to do any more publishing for a long time. At that point, however, I still had stacks and stacks of accepted manuscripts.

I got in touch with Allen De Loach in Buffalo who does *Intrepid* magazine. I knew that *Intrepids* were usually covered by grants, either from the State University of New York at Buffalo or from the Coordinating Council of Little Magazines, so I asked Allen if I could guest-edit an issue using left-over Bear materials. He said yes. It took

a long time to edit the material—I guess I wound up using about half
of what I had—but I finally got it off to him. In the summer of 1971 he
put out a very thick issue which he called *The Intrepid-Bear Issue: Intrepid #20/Floating Bear #38*.

### Rant

You cannot write a single line w/out a cosmology
a cosmogony
laid out, before all eyes

there is no part of yourself you can separate out
saying, this is memory, this is sensation
this is the work I care about, this is how I
make a living

it is whole, it is a whole, it always was whole
you do not "make" it so
there is nothing to integrate, you are a presence
you are an appendage of the work, the work stems from
hangs from the heaven you create

every man / every woman carries a firmament inside
& the stars in it are not the stars in the sky

w/out imagination there is no memory
w/out imagination there is no sensation
w/out imagination there is no will, desire

history is a living weapon in yr hand
& you have imagined it, it is thus that you
"find out for yourself"
history is the dream of what can be, it is
the relation between things in a continuum

of imagination
what you find out for yourself is what you select
out of an infinite sea of possibility
no one can inhabit yr world

yet it is not lonely,
the ground of imagination is fearlessness
discourse is video tape of a movie of a shadow play
but the puppets are in yr hand
your counters in a multidimensional chess
which is divination
                & strategy


the war that matters is the war against the imagination
all other wars are subsumed in it.


the ultimate famine is the starvation
of the imagination


it is death to be sure, but the undead
seek to inhabit someone else's world


the ultimate claustrophobia is the syllogism
the ultimate claustrophobia is "it all adds up"
nothing adds up & nothing stands in for
anything else


THE ONLY WAR THAT MATTERS IS THE WAR AGAINST
                         THE IMAGINATION
THE ONLY WAR THAT MATTERS IS THE WAR AGAINST
                         THE IMAGINATION
THE ONLY WAR THAT MATTERS IS THE WAR AGAINST
                         THE IMAGINATION


ALL OTHER WARS ARE SUBSUMED IN IT


There is no way out of the spiritual battle
There is no way you can avoid taking sides
There is no way you can *not* have a poetics
no matter what you do: plumber, baker, teacher


you do it in the consciousness of making
or not making yr world
you have a poetics: you step into the world
like a suit of readymade clothes

or you etch in light
your firmament spills into the shape of your room
the shape of the poem, of yr body, of yr loves

A woman's life / a man's life is an allegory

Dig it

There is no way out of the spiritual battle
the war is the war against the imagination
you can't sign up as a conscientious objector

the war of the worlds hangs here, right now, in the balance
it is a war for this world, to keep it
a vale of soul-making

the taste in all our mouths is the taste of our power
and it is bitter as death

bring yr self home to yrself, enter the garden
the guy at the gate w/the flaming sword is yrself

the war is the war for the human imagination
and no one can fight it but you/& no one can fight it for you

The imagination is not only holy, it is precise
it is not only fierce, it is practical
men die everyday for the lack of it,
it is vast & elegant

*intellectus* means "light of the mind"
it is not discourse it is not even language
the inner sun

the *polis* is constellated around the sun
the fire is central

# ANN DOUGLAS

ANN DOUGLAS, a Distinguished Professor of American Literature at Columbia University, wrote the introduction to an anthology of almost fifty years of William S. Burroughs's work, *Word Virus: The William S. Burroughs Reader* (1998), edited by James Grauerholz and Ira Silverberg. Douglas is the author of *The Feminization of American Culture* (1977) and *Terrible Honesty: Mongrel Manhattan in the 1920s* (1995).

---

## "Punching a Hole in the Big Lie": The Achievement of William S. Burroughs

"When did I stop wanting to be President?" Burroughs once asked himself, and promptly answered, "At birth certainly, and perhaps before." A public position on the up-and-up, a career of shaking hands, making speeches, and taking the rap held no appeal for one who aspired to be a "sultan of sewers," an antihero eye-deep in corruption, drugs, and stoic insolence, watching "Old Glory float lazily in the tainted breeze."

Burroughs started out in the 1940s as a founding member of the "Beat Generation," the electric revolution in art and manners that kicked off the counterculture and introduced the hipster to mainstream America, a movement for which Jack Kerouac became the mythologizer, Allen Ginsberg the prophet, and Burroughs the theorist. Taken together, their best-known works—Ginsberg's exuberant take-the-doors-off-their-hinges jeremiad *Howl* (1956); Kerouac's sad, funny, and inexpressibly tender "true story" novel *On the Road* (1957); and Burroughs' avant-garde narrative *Naked Lunch* (1959), a Hellzapoppin saturnalia of greed and lust—managed to challenge every taboo that respectable America had to offer.

Over the course of his long career, Burroughs steadfastly refused to honor, much less court, the literary establishment. Invited in 1983 to join the august Academy and Institute of Arts and Letters, he remarked, "Twenty years ago they were saying I belonged in jail. Now they're saying I belong in their club. I didn't listen to them then, and I don't listen to them now." Adept in carny routines and vaudevillian sleights of hand, Burroughs was a stand-up comic, a deadpan ringmaster of Swiftian satire and macabre dystopias, who claimed an outsider role so extreme as to constitute extraterrestrial status. "I'm apparently some kind of agent from another planet," he told Kerouac, "but I haven't got my orders decoded yet."

Unlike Ginsberg and Kerouac, however, Burroughs, born in 1914 to a well-to-do Wasp family in St. Louis, was part of the American elite. Indeed, as he often noted, his personal history seemed inextricably intertwined with some of the most important and ominous events of the modern era. In the 1880s, his paternal grandfather had invented the adding machine, a harbinger of the alliance of technology and corporate wealth that made possible the monstrously beefed-up defense industry of the Cold War years. Burroughs' maternal uncle, Ivy Lee, a pioneer of public relations, had helped John D. Rockefeller Jr. improve his image after the Ludlow Massacre of 1914, in which Colorado state militia shot two women and eleven children in a dispute between miners and management. In the 1930s, Lee served as Hitler's admiring publicist in the United States, an achievement that Congressman Robert LaFollette branded "a monument of shame."

Thin, physically awkward, with a narrow, impassive, even hangdog face as an adolescent, Burroughs qualified easily as the most unpopular boy in town. One concerned parent compared him to "a walking corpse." (Burroughs agreed, only wondering whose corpse it was.) Already interested in drugs, homosexuality, and con artistry, devoid of team spirit and "incurably intelligent," he was at best a problematic student, a troubling presence at several select schools, among them the Los Alamos Ranch School in New Mexico, the site J. Robert Oppenheimer commandeered in 1943 for the scientists engaged in the Manhattan Project. Los Alamos birthed the bombs that destroyed Hiroshima and Nagasaki and brought into being what Burroughs sardonically referred to as "the sick soul, sick unto death, of the atomic age," the central theme of his work.

In 1936, Burroughs graduated from Harvard, a place whose pretensions he loathed; a blank space appeared in the yearbook where his photograph should have been. He then traveled to Vienna and saw for himself what the Nazi regime his uncle had promoted was up to. For Burroughs, as for Jean Genet, one of his literary heroes, Hitler became a seminal figure; he never forgot that everything Hitler had done was legal. During the 1940s, Burroughs worked as a drug pusher and a thief, but he was guilt-free; a life of petty crime was less "compromising" than the "constant state of pretense and dissimulation" required by any job that contributed to the status quo. When gangsters write the laws, as Burroughs was sure they did, not only in the Third Reich but in most of the post-WWII West, ethics become fugitives, sanity is branded madness, and the artist's only option is total resistance. "This planet is a penal colony and nobody is allowed to leave," Burroughs wrote in *The Place of Dead Roads* (1984). "Kill the guards and walk."

In September 1951, in a drunken attempt at William Tell–style marksmanship, Burroughs inadvertently shot and killed his wife, Joan, while the couple was living in Mexico with their four-year-old son, Billy. Burroughs never considered himself anything but homosexual. He saw his intermittent sexual relations with Joan as a stopgap measure when the "uncut boy stuff" he preferred was unavailable. Joan worshipped him, but he admitted to a friend that the marriage was in some sense "an impasse, not amenable to any solution." Regarding the feminine sex in general as a grotesque mistake of nature, a biological plot against male independence and self-expression, he never made a woman central to his fiction. Starring roles went instead to wickedly updated, flagrantly queer versions of the classic male hero, to tricksters, gunmen, pirates, and wild boys. Like Genet, Burroughs saw homosexuality (as opposed to effeminacy and faggotry, for which he had no tolerance) as inherently subversive of the status quo. Women were born apologists; (queer) men were rebels and outlaws. Nonetheless, Burroughs knew that rules are defined by their exceptions. He adored Joan's brilliantly unconventional mind and elusive delicacy. He never fully recovered from her death.

Cool, even icy in manner, acerbic in tone, Burroughs once remarked that all his intimate relationships had been failures—he had denied "affection . . . when needed or supplied [it] when unwanted." He had not responded to his father's sometimes abject pleas for love nor visited his mother in her last years in a nursing home. In 1981, after an impressive debut as a novelist, Billy Burroughs, who had been raised by his grandparents, died of cirrhosis, believing that his father had "signed my death warrant."

Although the cause of Joan's death was ruled "criminal imprudence" and Burroughs spent only thirteen days in jail, he held himself responsible. He had been "possessed," and, in the magical universe Burroughs believed we inhabit, to be the subject of a successful possession was the mark of carelessness, not victimhood. If you knew, as he did, that life is a contest between the invading virus of the "Ugly Spirit" and the vigilant, if existence is predicated on preternatural watchfulness, what excuse could there possibly be for falling asleep on the job? In a sea swarming with sharks, he remarked, it is strongly advisable not to look like a "disabled fish."

In the introduction to *Queer* (1985), he tells his readers that Joan's death "maneuvered me into a lifelong struggle in which I had no choice but to write my way out"; his art was grounded in his culpability. It mattered greatly to him that Calico, one of the beloved cats of his later years, who reminded him of Joan, had never been mistreated, had never required or suffered discipline at his hands. A matchless revisionist of received wisdom, Burroughs thought there was a very real point in closing the barn door after the horse had gone. Mistakes, he explained in *Exterminator!* (1973), are made to be corrected. Filled with the ironies of belatedness as it is, life is education to the last breath, and beyond.

In the same spirit, Burroughs rejected the notion that his familial and geographic proximity to the forces of darkness represented by corporate wealth, Hitler, and the Manhattan Project were "coincidence," a word he disdained. For his first novel, *Junky* (1953), he took his nom de plume, "William Lee," from his mother and his uncle; always uncannily alert to the subterranean implications of his friend's personae, Kerouac described *Junky* as the work of a "Goering-like sophisticate." Nor did Burroughs leave unexamined the class and race privileges to which he had been born. As a lifelong student of the ways in which power passes itself off as nature, he believed that nothing happens without our consent; we are always complicit in what we take to be our God-given circumstances. "To speak is to lie—to live is to collaborate."

"I don't mind people disliking me," Burroughs wrote in *Queer*. "The question is, what are they in a position to do about it?" In his case, the answer was "apparently nothing, at present," but he knew how and where his relative immunity was manufactured. He escaped the full rigor of the law not only in the case of Joan's death, but on various occasions when he was caught red-handed with illegal drugs, not because the wind is ever tempered to the shorn lamb, but because those who have usually get more. He always had some family funds at his disposal, and he was quite aware that he possessed, in Kerouac's word, "finish"—it was visible at all times that he did not belong to the "torturable classes."

Almost alone among the major white male writers of his generation, Burroughs viewed whiteness and wealth as in some sense criminal and certainly man-made, a con job passed off as a credential. Whites, he liked to complain, were the only ethnic group who marshaled an army before they had enemies. This hardly meant that Burroughs wanted, as both Genet and Kerouac on occasion said they did, to cease being white; he conducted no romance with negritude, an infatuation he took to be simply another form of the sentimentalism he disdained. He remained imperturbably himself in all climates, speaking no language but English despite the years he spent living in various parts of North Africa and Latin America. Strangers sometimes mistook him for a banking official, even a CIA or FBI agent, and he was never averse to trading on his patrician aura in a tight spot. "Keep your snout in the public trough" was a Burroughs maxim.

Burroughs remarked in *Junky* that one reason he drifted into a life of "solo adventure" and addiction was that a drug habit supplied the close-to-the-margin knowledge of emergency his comfortable background had forestalled. Yet, finally, his aim was not to undertake slumming expeditions among his social inferiors but to use his wit and his mind to write his way out of his condition. It was a task for which he was superbly equipped.

Among his contemporaries, only Thomas Pynchon and Kurt Vonnegut begin to match the wild brilliance of Burroughs' laconic extravaganzas of black humor. In one inspired moment in *The Place of Dead Roads* (1983), Burroughs' stand-in, William Hall, is driving on a dimly lit road at night, wondering if he'll be able to summon the "correct emotions" for the parents of the child he imagines himself running over. Suddenly a man swings into view, carrying a dead child under one arm; he slaps it down on a porch, and asks, "This yours, lady?"

None of Burroughs' peers were his equal in brainpower megawattage, in sheer, remorseless intelligence. In his own phrase, he was a "guardian of the knowledge," a Wittgenstein of the narrative form. A critique of the family is implicit in Burroughs' fantasy about the dead child; even the most hallucinatory inventions of his imagination are grounded in hard, clear, powerfully analytic and authoritative thought. Dickens and Tolstoy remind us that great authors need not be intellectual geniuses, but part of the special excitement and pleasure in reading Burroughs at his best lies in the shock of encountering someone so much smarter than oneself. Burroughs' work is an intellect booster, Miracle-Gro for the mind—the reader has been handed the strongest binoculars ever made and for the first time sees the far horizon click into focus.

Burroughs claimed that after one look at this planet, any visitor from outer space would say, "I WANT TO SEE THE MANAGER!" It's a Burroughs axiom that the manager is harder to locate than the Wizard of Oz, but Burroughs holds what clues there are to his whereabouts; his work draws the "Wanted, Dead or Alive" poster, and his delineations are executions, fearless and summary. "The history of the planet," he wrote, "is a history of idiocy highlighted by a few morons who stand out as comparative geniuses." In an essay titled "The Hundred-Year Plan," he compared Cold War politicians, bravely proffering patriotic stupidity, crass ignorance, and a gung-ho weapons program as qualifications for office, to prehistoric dinosaurs, whom he imagined gathering for a convention many millennia past. Faced with downscaling or extinction, a dinosaur leader announces, "Size is the answer . . . increased size. . . . It was good enough for me. . . . (Applause) . . . We will increase . . . and we will continue to dominate the planet as we have done for three hundred million years! . . . (Wild Applause)." In this arena, Burroughs believed his elite status worked for him. Revolutionaries are always disaffected members of the ruling class; only the enemy within can lay hands on top-secret information. The insider is the best spy.

Like Hemingway, like Ginsberg and Kerouac, Burroughs aspired to "write his own life and death," to leave something like a complete record of his experiment on the planet; by his own admission, there is finally only one character in his fiction—himself. In a guarded but uncannily astute review of *The Wild Boys* (1971), Alfred Kazin analyzed what he took to be the solipsism of Burroughs' narrative form; Burroughs wanted "to make the fullest possible inventory and rearrangement of all the stuff natural to him . . . to put his own mind on the internal screen that is his idea of a book." Yet Burroughs was not in any usual sense a confessional or autobiographical writer.

A leader of postmodern literary fashion in the 1960s, Burroughs early discarded the Western humanistic notions of the self traditionally associated with autobiography. In a 1950 letter, he commented severely on Ginsberg's recent discovery that he was "just a human like other humans." "Human, Allen, is an adjective, and its use as a noun is in itself regrettable." Burroughs took his starting point to be the place where "the human road ends." In his fiction, identity is an affair of ventriloquism and property rights—everything is potentially up for reassignment or sale. In a compulsive gambling session described in *Naked Lunch,* a young man loses his youth to an old one; lawyers sell not their skills, but their luck to the hapless clients they defend. Most things in Burroughsland function as addictive substances, and the "self" can be simply the last drug the person in question has ingested. Or it may be a random object, someone else's discard, an "article abandoned in a hotel drawer."

Yet if postmodernism is, as a number of its critics have said, a disavowal of responsibility, Burroughs was no postmodernist. In his view, the elite's last shot at virtue lay in taking responsibility for the consequences of its power, and Burroughs for one—and almost the only one in the ranks of recent, major, white male American authors—was willing not only to shoulder responsibility, but to extend it. In Burroughs' magical universe, if we are everywhere complicit, we are also everywhere active. "Your surroundings are *your* surroundings," he wrote in *The Soft Machine.* "Every object you touch is alive with your life and your will."

When Burroughs wrote, in a famous line from *Naked Lunch,* that he was merely a "recording instrument," he wasn't implying, as a number of his critics and fans have thought, that he made no choices, exerted no control over what he wrote, but rather that he wanted to learn how to register not the prepackaged information he was programmed by corporate interests or artistic canons to receive, but what was actually there. In a 1965 interview with *The Paris Review,* he explained that while the direction of Samuel Beckett, a novelist he admired greatly, was inward, he was intent on going "outward." For Burroughs, the "control machine" is almost synonymous with the Western psyche. The point, as he saw it, was to get outside it, to beat it at its own game by watching and decoding the extremely partial selections it makes from the outside world and then imposes on us as "reality."

Like Marshall McLuhan, himself a fan and brilliant expositor of Burroughs' work, Burroughs saw that Western man had "externalized himself in the form of gadgets." The media extend to fabulous lengths man's nervous system, his powers to record and receive, but without content themselves, cannibalizing the world they purportedly represent and ingesting those to whom they in theory report; like drugs inserted into a bodily system, they eventually replace the organism they feed—a hostile takeover in the style of *The Invasion of the Body Snatchers*. Instead of reality, we have the "reality studio"; instead of people, "person-impersonators" and image-junkies looking for a fix, with no aim save not to be shut out of the "reality film." But Burroughs believed that a counteroffensive might still be possible, that the enemy's tactics can be pried out of their corporate context and used against him by information bandits like himself. Computers might rule the world, but the brain is the first computer; all the information people have forgotten is stored there. The problem is one of access.

In the 1960s, as he developed the "cut-up" method of his first trilogy, *The Soft Machine* (1961), *The Ticket That Exploded* (1962), and *Nova Express* (1964), Burroughs became fascinated by tape recorders and cameras. A how-to writer for the space age for whom science fiction was a blueprint for action, dedicated to "wising up the marks," he instructed readers in the art of deprogramming. Walk down the street, any street, recording and photographing what you hear and see. Go home, write down your observations, feelings, associations, and thoughts, then check the results against the evidence supplied by your tapes and photos. You will discover that your mind has registered only a tiny fraction of your experience; what you left unnoticed may be what you most need to find. "Truth may appear only once," Burroughs wrote in his journal in 1997; "it may not be repeatable." To walk down the street as most people perform the act is to reject the only free handout life has to offer, to trample on the prince in a rush for the toad, storming the pawnshop to exchange gold for dross. What we call "reality," according to Burroughs, is just the result of a faulty scanning

pattern, a descrambling device run amok. We're all hard-wired for destruction, in desperate need of rerouting, even mutation.

How did this happen? How did Western civilization become a
conspiracy against its members? In his second trilogy, *Cities of the Red
Night* (1981), *The Place of Dead Roads* (1984), and *The Western Lands*
(1987), which taken as a whole forms his greatest work, Burroughs
fantasized the past which produced the present and excavated its
aborted alternatives, the last, lost sites of human possibility. The first
is the United States that disappeared in his boyhood, the pre- and just
post-WWI years when individual identity had not yet been fixed and
regulated by passports and income taxes; when there was no CIA or
FBI; before bureaucracies and bombs suffocated creative consciousness and superhighways crisscrossed and codified the American landscape—"sometimes paths last longer than roads," Burroughs wrote in
*Cities of the Red Night*. In the heyday of the gunman, of single combat, and of the fraternal alliances of frontier culture, the promises of
the American Revolution were not yet synonymous with exclusionary
elite self-interest. Now, however, Burroughs wrote, there are "so many
actors and so little action"; little room is left for the independent co-
operative social units he favored, for the dreams that he saw as the
magical source of renewal for whole peoples as well as individuals.

Globally, Burroughs located a brief utopian moment a century or
two earlier, a time when one's native "country" had not yet hardened
into the "nation-state" and the family did not police its members in the
interests of "national security"; before the discovery by Western buc-
caneers and entrepreneurs of what was later known as the Third
World had solidified into colonial and neocolonial empire, effecting a
permanent and inequitable redistribution of the world's wealth; before
the industrial revolution had produced an epidemic of overdevelop-
ment and overpopulation and capitalism had become an instrument of
global standardization.

Burroughs had no sympathy for the regimented, Marxist-based
Communist regimes of Eastern Europe. He saw the Cold War admin-
istrations of the U.S. and the U.S.S.R. not as enemies but as peers
and rivals vying to see who could reach the goal of total control first.
Yet both Burroughs and Karl Marx had an acute understanding of just
how revolutionary the impact of plain common sense could be in a
world contorted by crime and self-justification, and in a number of ar-

eas their interests ran along parallel lines. Unlike Ginsberg or Kerouac, Burroughs unfailingly provides an economic assessment of any
culture, real or imaginary, he describes; how people make a (legal or illegal) living is always of interest to him. Like Marx, he was certain that
"laissez-faire capitalism" could not be reformed from within: "A problem cannot be solved in terms of itself." He, too, saw the colonizing
impulse that rewrote the world map between the sixteenth and nineteenth centuries as a tactic to "keep the underdog under," an indispensable part of capitalism's quest for new markets and fresh supplies
of labor.

Burroughs never accepted the geopolitics that divided the American continent into separate southern and northern entities. Both were
part of the same feeding system, though the South was the trough, the
North the hog. Traveling in Colombia in search of the drug *yagé* in
April 1953, Burroughs reported to Ginsberg that he was mistaken for a
representative of the Texaco Oil Company and given free lodging and
transportation everywhere he went. In fact, as Burroughs knew, Texaco had surveyed the area, discovered no oil, and pulled out several
years before. The Colombian rubber and cocoa industries, totally dependent on American investment, were drying up as well. Colom-
bians, however, refused to believe it; they were still expecting the
infrastructure of roads, railroads, and airports that U.S. industry could
be counted on to build to expedite the development, and removal, of a
Third World country's material wealth. Burroughs had no more sympathy for the losers in the neocolonial con game than he did for any
other "mark." "Like I should think some day soon boys will start climbing in through the transom and tunneling under the door" was his derisive comment on Colombian delusions about U.S. investment.

The literary critic Tobin Siebers, writing about post-WWII literary
culture, has speculated that the postmodern disavowal of agency, almost entirely the work of First World, white, male writers and theo-
rists, is both an expression and an evasion of racial and economic
guilt. Looking at the defining phenomena of the twentieth century, its
holocausts, genocides, gulags, and unimaginably lethal weapons of destruction, who would want to advertise himself as part of the group
that engineered and invented them? Postmodernism allows whites to
answer the question "Who's responsible?" by saying, "It looks like me,
but actually there is no real 'me'"—no one, in postmodernspeak, has a

firmly defined or authentic self. In the universe of total, irreversible complicity postmodernism posits, the cause-and-effect sequence of individual action and consequence, motive and deed, is severed. Where Burroughs breaks with the postmodern position is that in his fiction, though everyone is complicit, everyone is also responsible, for everyone is capable of resistance. There are no victims, just accomplices; the mark collaborates with his exploiter in his own demise.

"We make truth," Burroughs wrote in his journal shortly before his death on August 2, 1997. "Nobody else makes it. There is no truth we don't make." What governments and corporations assert as truth is nothing but "lies"; such bodies are inevitably "self-righteous. They have to be because in human terms they are wrong." For Burroughs as for the postmodernists, identity was artifice, but for him it was made that way, betrayed that way, and can be remade differently. To deny the latter possibility is the last and worst collusion because it's the only one that can be avoided. Burroughs' final trilogy is a complex, funny, impassioned attempt, with one always aware of the death sentence under which it apparently operates, to "punch a hole in the big lie," to parachute his characters behind the time lines of the enemy and make a different truth.

As he explained it in *Cities of the Red Night*, what Burroughs had in mind was a globalization of the Third World guerrilla tactics that defeated the U.S. in Vietnam. He prefaces the novel with an account of an actual historical personage, Captain Mission, a seventeenth-century pirate who founded an all-male, homosexual community on Madagascar, a libertarian society that outlawed slavery, the death penalty, and any interference in the beliefs and practices of its members. Although Captain Mission's relatively unarmed settlement didn't survive, Burroughs elaborates what its "New Freedoms" could have meant if it had: fortified positions throughout the Third World to mobilize resistance to "slavery and oppression" everywhere.

Despite his scorn for those lining up to welcome their destroyers, Burroughs did not traffic with the racialized thinking that—in historical fact—buttressed and excused the empire-building process, the definition of Third World people of color as inherently lazy, dishonest, incorrigibly irrational, and unable to look after their own welfare. The Western virtues of rationality and instrumentalism were largely suspect to Burroughs in any case; he shared the so-called primitive belief in an animistic universe which the skeptical West categorically rejected. In *Cities of the Red Night,* Burroughs is explicit that whites would be welcome in his utopia only as "workers, settlers, teachers, and technicians"—no more "white-man boss, no Pukka Sahib, no Patróns, no colonists." As he recounts the history of seven imaginary cities in the Gobi desert thousands of years ago, Burroughs explains that before the destruction of the cities by a meteor (itself a forerunner of late-twentieth-century nuclear weaponry), an explosion which produced the "Red Night" of the title, all the people of the world were black. White and even brown and red-skinned people are "mutations" caused by the meteor, as was the albino woman-warrior whose all-female army conquered one of the original cities, reducing its male inhabitants to "slaves, consorts, and courtiers."

Burroughs' cosmological myth resembles the Black Muslim fable, embraced notably by Elijah Muhammad and Malcolm X, about the creation of a white race of "devils" by an evil black scientist named Yacub intent on destroying the all-black world that has rejected him. Yet Burroughs never signed up for the fan clubs of the Third World revolutionaries so compelling to young, left-wing Americans in the 1960s; to his mind, heroes like Che Guevara were simply devices for those running the "reality film," a gambit designed to leave the "shines cooled back . . . in a nineteenth century set." Burroughs claimed to belong to only one group, the "Shakespeare squadron"; in the historical impasse in which he lived, language was his only weapon.

Language as he found it, however, was rigged to serve the enemy, an ambush disguised as an oasis—in the West, language had become the "word virus," the dead heart of the control machine. Burroughs' avant-garde experiments in montage, the cut-up, and disjunctive narrative were attempts to liberate Western consciousness from its own form of self-expression, from the language that we think we use but which, in truth, uses us. "Writers are very powerful," Burroughs tells us; they can write, and "unwrite," the script for the reality film.

Defending *Naked Lunch* during the obscenity trial of 1966 as an example of automatic writing, Norman Mailer noted that "one's best writing seems to bear no relation to what one is thinking about." Many post-WWII writers showed a quickened interest in the random thought that reroutes or classifies the plan of a novel or essay, but Burroughs came closest to reversing the traditional roles of design and chance. For him, conscious intent was a form of prediction, and prediction is only possible when the status quo has reason to assume it will meet no significant opposition. In his fiction, the continuity girl, the person who keeps the details of one sequence of film consistent with the next, has gone AWOL; there are no shock absorbers. Jump cuts replace narrative transitions; straight chronological, quasi-documentary sequences are spliced with out-of-time-and-space scenes of doom-struck sodomy and drug overdoses. Lush symbolist imagery and hard-boiled, tough-guy slang, the lyric and the obscene, collide and interbreed. Burroughs' early style was founded on drug lingo and jive talk; he was fascinated by their mutability, their fugitive quality, the result of the pressure their speakers were under to dodge authority and leave no records behind. His later work elaborates and complicates this principle. No one form of language can hold center stage for long. Fast-change artistry is all; sustained domination is impossible.

The novelist Paul Bowles, a friend of Burroughs', thought the cut-up method reflected an "unsatisfied desire on the part of the mind to be anonymous," but it also came out of Burroughs' need to work undercover, at the intersections where identities and meanings multiply faster than language can calculate or record. The cut-up method was not a refusal of authorship. The writer still selects the passages, whether from his own work, a newspaper, a novel by someone else, or a sign glimpsed out a train window, which he then cuts up and juxtaposes. You always know what you're doing, according to Burroughs. Everyone sees in the dark; the trick is to maneuver yourself into the position where you can recognize what you see.

The first step is to realize that the language, even the voice that you use, are not your own, but alien implants, the result of the most effective kind of colonization, the kind that turns external design into what passes for internal motivation and makes what you are allowed to get feel like what you want. In *The Ticket That Exploded*, Burroughs challenged his readers to try and halt their "subvocal speech," that committee meeting inside the head that seldom makes sense and never shuts up, the static of the self, the lowest idle of the meaning-fabricating machine. Who are you talking to? Burroughs wants to know. Is it really yourself? Why has Western man "lost the option of silence"? The nonstop monologue running in our heads is proof of

ANN DOUGLAS / 145

possession, and the only way to end it is to cut the association lines by which it lives, the logic by which we believe that "b" follows "a" not because it in fact does, but because we have been aggressively, invasively conditioned to think so. Like the Jehovah who is its front man, Western language has become prerecorded sequence, admitting of no alternatives.

"In the beginning was the word," the Bible says, but the only beginning the line really refers to, Burroughs reminds us, is the beginning of the word itself, the recorded word, literacy as the West understands it, a period that makes up only a tiny fraction of human history. Burroughs suggests that people try communicating by pictures, as the Chinese and Mayans did, even by colors and smells; words are "an around-the-world oxcart way of doing things." English as spoken shuts out the infinite variations in which meaning presents itself; the body thinks too, though the Western mind can only imperfectly translate its language. Burroughs wanted to abolish "either/or" dichotomies from our speech, change every "the" to an "a," and root out the verb "to be," which is not, as it claims, a description of existence, but a "categorical imperative of permanent condition," a way of programming people to disavow change, no matter how imperative.

Burroughs' ambitions amounted to nothing less than an attempt to uproot and transform Western concepts of personhood and language, if not personhood and language themselves, to produce a new emancipation proclamation for the twenty-first century. Inevitably, in his last novel, *The Western Lands,* he judged his attempt a failure, but he also noted that even to imagine success on so radical a scale was victory. By the time of his death, Burroughs was recognized as one of the major American writers of the postwar era and he had become a formative influence, even a cult figure, for several generations of the young, leaving his mark on punk rock, performance art, and independent film.

When Norman Mailer shared a podium with Burroughs at the Jack Kerouac School of Disembodied Poetics of the Naropa Institute in Boulder in 1984, he found him an impossible act to follow. The kids loved him, Mailer noted with some envy; they laughed uproariously at his every line. They knew he was "authentic." The critic Lionel Abel thought that Burroughs and his Beat colleagues had established the "metaphysical prestige" of the drug addict and the criminal; though modern skepticism destroyed the belief in transcendence, the human "need for utterness," not to be denied, had found its satisfaction in "trans-descendence." In a cameo role in Gus Van Sant's *Drugstore Cowboy* (1989), a movie about young addicts in Seattle, with his dead-white poker face, dark, quasi-clinical garb, and low-pitched, deliberate, nasal intonation, Burroughs is clearly an iconic apparition from the underground, the hipster as Tiresias, the master of "the crime," as he described it in *Naked Lunch*, "of separate action."

Burroughs was never comfortable with the "Beat" label. In a 1969 interview with Daniel Odier, while acknowledging his close personal friendships with several of the Beat writers, he remarked that he shared neither their outlook nor their methods. Kerouac believed that the first draft was always the best one and emphasized spontaneity above all else; Burroughs counted on revision. He used the word "beat" sparingly and literally, to mean "no fire, no intensity, no life," while Kerouac and Ginsberg said it meant "high, ecstatic, saved." Unlike Ginsberg, Kerouac, or Gregory Corso, whose entire careers can be seen as part of the Beat movement, Burroughs belongs to another literary tradition as well, that of the avant-garde novelists headed by Vladimir Nabokov, Thomas Pynchon, John Hawkes, William Gaddis, John Barth, and Don DeLillo. His affinities with their direct forebears, T. S. Eliot and Ernest Hemingway in particular, are defining ones; for all his innovations, he is visibly carrying on the work of high modernist irony, as Kerouac and Ginsberg most decidedly are not, and this fact may account for the willingness of the American critical establishment to grant Burroughs a more respectful hearing than it has yet accorded his Beat peers.

Nonetheless, the affinities between Burroughs and the Beats are stronger than those he had with any other group. When he first met the much younger Ginsberg and Kerouac in 1944, he instantly took on a mentor role, handing Kerouac a copy of Oswald Spengler's *Decline of the West*, with an instruction to "EEE di fy your mind, my boy, with the grand actuality of fact." Ginsberg said that while Columbia University (where both Ginsberg and Kerouac had been students) taught them about "the American empire," Burroughs instructed them about the "end of empire." As John Tytell has pointed out, their pathway to "beatitude" sprang directly out of his "nightmare of devastation." In Tangiers in 1955, as Burroughs began the work that would become

*Naked Lunch*—a book that Kerouac named and that he and Ginsberg helped to type and revise—he wrote Kerouac that he was trying to do something similar to Kerouac's "spontaneous prose" project, whose guidelines Kerouac had written out in 1953 at Ginsberg's and Burroughs' request; Burroughs was writing "what I see and feel right now to arrive at some absolute, direct transmission of fact on all levels."

Kerouac's extended, astute, funny, and loving portraits of Burroughs as "Will Dennison" in *The Town and the Country* (1950) and "Old Will Lee" in *On the Road* not only served as advance publicity for *Naked Lunch,* but by Burroughs' own admission helped to elaborate the persona he adopted. In his essay "Remembering Kerouac," Burroughs said that Kerouac had known Burroughs was a writer long before he himself did. Over the course of his long life, Burroughs had other seminal, creative friendships and partnerships, most notably with the avant-garde artist Brion Gysin. Yet in some not altogether fanciful sense, Burroughs became what Kerouac and Ginsberg had first imagined and recognized him to be.

The novelist Joyce Johnson, a friend of Kerouac's, claims that the Beat Generation "has refused to die." Unlike the "Lost Generation" of the 1920s headed by F. Scott Fitzgerald and Hemingway which, within a decade, as the "Jazz Age" gave way to the Depression, was decisively repudiated by its own members, the Beat movement continues even today, a half century after its inception, sustaining its veterans and attracting new members—those for whom the respectable is synonymous with boredom and terror, if not crime, who regard the ongoing social order as suffocating, unjust, and unreal, who believe that honesty can still be reinvented in a world of lies and that the answers, if there are any, lie not in the political realm but in the quest for new forms of self-expression and creative collaboration across all traditional class, race, and ethnic boundaries, in fresh recuperative imaginings of ourselves and our country, in physical, spiritual, and metaphysical explorations of roads still left to try. "What's in store for me in the direction I don't take?" Kerouac asked.

Burroughs deconstructed the word, but he never abandoned it; it was, after all, his "fragile lifeboat," the "mainsail to reach the Western lands." Though he turned to painting as his main artistic outlet and published no novels after 1987, he continued to write, as Kerouac and Ginsberg had, up to the very day he died. If he had never been known as a Beat writer, if there had been no Beat movement, his avant-garde experiments in form, his wit, his mastery of language would ensure his inclusion in college courses on the post-WWII narrative. But it is his talismanic power to beckon and admonish his readers, to reroute their thoughts and dreams, that has made him widely read outside the academy as well as within it, and this is what he shares with his Beat companions and no one else, certainly not with the reclusive Thomas Pynchon or the at times grotesquely overexposed Norman Mailer. Like Ginsberg and Kerouac, Burroughs is there yet elsewhere. He, too, practiced literature as magic.

The uncannily perceptive Herbert Huncke, a hustler, homosexual, addict, and writer, was the fourth seminal figure of the first Beat circle. Initially, he had been troubled by Burroughs' coldness. On one occasion, however, when Burroughs passed out drunk in his apartment, Huncke saw a different man. Awake, Burroughs was "the complete master of himself," Huncke wrote in *The Evening Sun Turns Crimson* (1980), but asleep, he seemed a "strange, otherworld" creature, "relaxed and graceful," touched with a mysterious beauty, "defenseless and vulnerable . . . lonely and as bewildered as anyone else." At that instant, Huncke said, "a certain feeling of love I bear for him to this day sprang into being." At moments, Kerouac glimpsed in Burroughs "that soft and tender curiosity, verging on maternal care, about what others think and say" that Kerouac believed indispensable to great writing. Burroughs was a Beat writer because he, too, wanted to decipher what he called the "hieroglyphic of love and suffering," and he learned about it largely from his relations with other men.

In the age that coined the word "togetherness" as a synonym for family values, the Beats, each in his own style, mounted the first open, sustained assault in American history on the masculine role as heterosexual spouse, father, and grown-up provider. In the midst of the Cold War crusade against all deviations from the masculine norm, in the era that could almost be said to have invented the idea of classified information, they openly addressed homosexuality, bisexuality, and masturbation in their work, declassifying the secrets of the male body, making sexuality as complex as individual identity, and pushing their chosen forms to new limits in the process.

Though Kerouac did not consider himself homosexual, he had intermittent sex with Ginsberg throughout the 1940s and early 1950s.

Ginsberg and Burroughs had also been lovers, and their deep and steady friendship outlasted their physical affair. Shortly before his death from cancer on April 5, 1997, Ginsberg telephoned Burroughs to tell him that he knew he was dying. "I thought I would be terrified," Allen said, "but I am exhilarated!" These were his "last words to me," Burroughs noted in his journal; it was an invitation a "cosmonaut of inner space," in his favored phrase of self-description, could not fail to accept. He died four months later.

Some of Burroughs' last journal entries were about Allen and "the courage of his total sincerity." Though Kerouac's self-evasions had strained Burroughs' patience long before Kerouac's death in 1969, he always loved the passage in *On the Road* in which Kerouac spoke of feeling like "somebody else, some stranger . . . my whole life was a haunted life, the life of a ghost." Burroughs, too, knew what it was to be "a spy in somebody else's body where nobody knows who is spying on whom." In *The Western Lands,* Burroughs imagined a new kind of currency, underwritten not by gold or silver but by moral virtues and psychological achievements. Rarest of all are the "Coin of Last Resort," awarded those who have come back from certain defeat, and the "Contact Coin," which "attests that the bearer has contacted other beings." Finally, love between men was simply love, and love, Burroughs wrote in his journal the day before he died, is "What there is. Love."

## Selected Bibliography

Abel, Lionel. "Beyond the Fringe." *Partisan Review.* 30 (1963): 109–112.

Burroughs, William S. "Final Words." *The New Yorker.* (August 18, 1997): 36–37.

Fiedler, Leslie A. "The New Mutants." *Partisan Review.* 32 (1965): 505–525.

Huncke, Herbert *The Herbert Huncke Reader.* Ed. Benjamin G. Schafer. New York: William and Morrow Company, 1997.

Johnson, Joyce. "Reality Sandwiches." *American Book Review.* 18 August–September (1997): 13.

Kazin, Alfred. "He's Just Wild about Writing." *The New York Times Book Review.* (December 12, 1971): 4, 22.

Kerouac, Jack. *Vanity of Duluoz: An Adventurous Education, 1935–1946.* 1968; rpt., New York: Penguin Books, 1994.

Knickerbocker, Conrad. "William Burroughs: An Interview." *The Paris Review*. 35 (1965): 13–49.

McCarthy, Mary. "Burroughs' *Naked Lunch*." *William S. Burroughs at the Front: Critical Reception, 1959–1989*. Ed. Jennie Skerl and Robin Lydenberg. Carbondale: Southern Illinois University Press, 1991: 33–39.

McLuhan, Marshall. "Notes on Burroughs." *The Nation* (December 28, 1964): 517–519.

Morgan, Ted. *Literary Outlaw: The Life and Times of William S. Burroughs*. 1988; rpt., New York: Avon Books, 1990.

Siebers, Tobin. *Cold War Criticism and the Politics of Skepticism*. New York: Oxford, 1993.

Tanner, Tony. *City of Words: American Fiction 1950–1970*. London: Jonathan Cape, 1971.

Tytell, John. *Naked Angels: Kerouac, Ginsberg, Burroughs*. New York: Grove Weidenfeld, 1976.

Watson, Steven. *The Birth of the Beat Generation: Visionaries, Rebels, and Hipsters, 1944–1960*. New York: Pantheon, 1995.

# WILLIAM EVERSON

WILLIAM EVERSON (1912–1995), a major figure of the San Francisco Poetry Renaissance, published his first of many volumes of poems, *These Are the Ravens*, in 1935. From 1951 to 1969 he was in the Dominican Order as Brother Antoninus; he left the order to marry in 1969. Two years later Everson became poet-in-residence at the University of California at Santa Cruz, where he was also a master printer at the campus's Lime Kiln Press. In addition to creating his books of poetry and criticism, he edited and printed superb hand-press editions of the works of the poet Robinson Jeffers.

Everson wrote his essay "Dionysus and the Beat Generation" in 1959, after the success of Ginsberg's and Kerouac's books brought a great deal of mostly hostile critical attention to the Beat writers. The essay was published in *Fresco*, Summer 1959, and included in *Earth Poetry* (1980), edited by Lee Bartlett.

## Dionysus and the Beat Generation

### The Reemergence of the Dionysian Spirit in Contemporary Life

The Beat Generation is perhaps the most significant American example of a universal trend: the reemergence in the twentieth century of the Dionysian spirit. Its mood of positive repudiation, as summed up in the phrase "I don't know; I don't care; and it doesn't make any difference," is counter-balanced by an opposite mood of negative affirmation: "Beat means beatitude." Before Dionysus was depotentiated in Greek culture to the status of a cheerful wine-god, his was a primordial orgiastic mystery-cult infiltrating from Thrace, disputing the worship of various local deities, and cursing with orgiastic madness those who refused him propitiation.

The art form principally associated with Dionysus was dithyrambic verse (a wild poetry of spontaneous enthusiasm). Thus the insistence of the Beat Generation to combine jazz and poetry is quite symptomatic of the Dionysian tendency. Even the Beat novel is an open effort to sustain lyric intensity over the whole course of the work. Kerouac's essay "The Essentials of Spontaneous Prose" in the *avant garde* quarterly *The Evergreen Review,* which was, characteristically, held up for ridicule by *Time,* is a transparent technique for achieving the true dithyrambic deeps: "If possible," he says, "write 'without consciousness' in semi-trance . . . allowing subconscious to admit in own uninhibited interesting necessary and so 'modern' language what conscious art would censor, and write excitedly, swiftly, with writing-or-typing-cramps, in accordance (as from center to periphery) with laws of orgasm." Nothing could be more explicit.

The end of the Dionysian movement is always ecstasy, a going out of oneself, the loss of Ego to forces greater than it. Dionysus in his own realm of field and forest is nothing dangerous; he represents simply the flow of unconscious life in the whole psyche. But over against him stands Apollo, god of light and consciousness, the guardian of civilization and culture, education, commerce and civic virtue. To the civilizing Apollonian attitude, with its premium on rational conscious-ness and ego-integrity, nothing is more abhorrent, and hence more dangerously seductive, than the dark irrational urge. Ego fears to lose everything before the ecstatic force, and it organizes all its powers of persuasion and coercion to check the spontaneous effect.

Refusing any concession it seeks first to persuade, to admonish and convert, but it rarely knows how. Trying to be rational it simply rational-izes. The god of light does not understand the darkness, and, finding persuasions ineffectual, only repressive action remains. Dionysus is locked up. But locking him up, repressing the irrational unconscious, is not the end of the matter, only its postponement. Man is a rational ani-mal, but an animal for all that, and Dionysus is unkillable. Unless his voice be heard, unless the irrational be given its healthful place in the whole psyche, sooner or later the god will break out. And the humiliated outrage with which he makes his emergence bodes ill for consciousness and Apollo when darkness drops over the earth. The terrible and mag-nificent might of Apollonian Rome fell once, and it fell forever.

If rational persuasion, or enforced repression, is so often ineffec-tual in dealing with the feared influx, it is because the latter is usually a sign, in advanced cultures, of some deficiency in the Apollonian atti-tude itself, some awful skeleton in its own closet. The annihilation of the American Indian, the enslavement of the African Negro, the hys-terical atom-bombing of the Orientals, persist as a terrible fear and a compulsive guilt in the American unconscious. The solution, after a thorough examination of conscience, true contrition followed by a heart-felt confession, would call for the incorporation of genuine ec-static and mystical needs in the interplay of the collective psyche. The Apollonian, however, in his civilized fear, calls ecstasy Satanic, and stands ready to strike again.

Now it is a theological truism that Satanic influence over the mind of man is maintained principally by virtue of human blindness, human ignorance; and though Dionysus is indeed blind, he is never ig-norant: he knows himself thoroughly. It is the Apollonian refusal to recognize its own variety of blindness—hubris, pride—that enables the Satanic spirit to exploit any ecstatic impulse against it. This is the real sin of the civilized. It was not Dionysus, remember, who crucified the Christ, but a rational Apollonian Roman governor and his religious counterpart the high priest. Perhaps depth psychology's greatest contribution is to have discovered that the desperate failure of Apollonian culture to effect any genuine synthesis with the unconscious is bringing its own doom down on its head.

But apparently this is something neither Pilate nor Caiaphas is ever prepared to concede: it is safer to crucify. In the upshot Dionysus and Agape, the Good Thief and the Christ, share the cross together, and Barabbas goes free. For though it is the purpose of this paper to distinguish between Dionysus and Christ rather than identify them, one fact they do share in common. In some places the cult of Dionysus took the form of Zagreus, meaning "torn-to-pieces," the god whose dismembered body rose each spring to redeem the people from the ravages of winter. "Beat means beatitude" indeed—but in a sense which perhaps neither City Hall nor the Beats have sufficiently grasped.

Genuine religious cultures, cultures not utterly dominated by the Apollonian attitude, are not so vulnerable to the inroads of the ecstatic, for their authentic mystical character militates against the sharp crystallization of the ego-centric attitude, and permits a more balanced interplay between the instinctual, rational and intuitional elements of the psyche. Nazism, the major revival of the Dionysian spirit in our time, is indicative of the fate awaiting a highly developed technology when its atheistic humanism denies the validity of any ecstatic outgoing—especially the subsuming mysticism of religious aspiration in which the twin forces of the Apollonian and the Dionysian attitudes are most properly harmonized and annealed. The twentieth century is Apollonian to a painful excess, and the war between the two forces is everywhere discernible. It is a commonplace that the repressive action of Prohibition led straight to an orgy of alcoholism. And though this Protestant example comes conveniently to mind, secular Catholicism is not without instances of its own Apollonian blindness. Such an episode as the protestation against the naming of Walt Whitman Bridge is only the most trifling, if indeed the most embarrassing, of an all too frequent trend. It is their utter lack of perspective which makes these episodes such dangerous symptoms.

The problem is complete because of the double character of the "unconscious" forces paired below and above the Ego. There is a God far greater than Apollo, that master of the finite world of humanized effects. Transcendently greater is *Yahweh,* He Who Is, incomprehensible in His infinity and incommunicable in His otherness. Ego stands against the uprush of Dionysus from below and the downrush of the Spirit from above—both ecstatic factors, and both feared by it. For Ego is actually a kind of conscious differential, militating between the instincts and the intellective intuition, subject to tremendous invasions from either quarter. On Pentecost the populace took the disciples to be drunk. It was an easy mistake to make—to Apollo both Eros and Agape are fools. King Pentheus, taken for a beast and killed by his own mother at the Dionysian revels, and St. Paul, struck from his horse and rendered impotent on the road to Damascus, are both types that Ego dreads to contemplate. Confronted with these fearful alternatives it compulsively freezes, rigidifies around such static civilized norms as it has acquired, and depends upon common sense and coercion to carry it through, projecting with anxious hostility against the reveler and the prophet wherever it finds them. But in the end it will give in or go down. Proud King Pentheus and the Pharisee Saul each in his own way witnesses to the fate of the Apollonian attitude.

In fallen man the problem is endemic and has but one solution: voluntary expiation of the Ego. On the Cross we see the true Person, symbol of the perfect synthesis between body and soul, instinct and intelligence, Eros and Agape, crucified between the demonic mob and the pharisaical Ego. The role of the Christian in any age is precisely this, which is nothing less than the functionalism of the Cross, taking into himself in an act of ego-annulment the brutalities of each. If it is not accepted willingly, then it follows as a matter of course, consequent upon a kind of divine archetypal necessity. There will always be a victim. Was it not the inability of the Jews to grasp this functionalism which led to their repudiation of Golgotha, and which accounts for their subsequent tragic history? But for the Christian martyr it is not much different—the same law is at work. St. Bernadette of Lourdes underwent a "trial" before incredulous Apollonian judges and "crucifixion" by a contemptuous Apollonian superior in order to conform to that Christ-archetype and expiate the materialistic sins of her century. And we breath a sigh of relief that our egoistic culture was saved, and hope for another saint to stand up and save it again—any one but ourselves.

These are terrible fates to the Ego, the willing and the unwilling alike. But what will become of that true Apollonian, the solid citizen, that "square" of the Beats, be he statesman or churchman, who complacently overlooks the conventional sins of his time: racial injustice, institutionalized graft, legalized pornography, administrative corruption, convenient prostitution, yet contemptuously rejects any genuine manifestation of the spirit, whether it be Dionysian or of the Holy Ghost, lest it upset the customary equanimity of his life? Christ forgave both the hot and the cold but for the lukewarm he poured out the apotheosis of his scorn.

So once again we see, along with the revival of the religious spirit, the rise of the repressed Dionysian. It is the endeavor of the Beat Generation to fuse Eros and Agape in a profane synthesis, but by settling for ecstasy at any price, it roves restlessly from the delirium of sensational licentiousness to compulsive flights at the infinite through drugs or dithyrambic aestheticism. It has in its favor the repudiation of all philistine values, a salutary contempt for the attitudes of "this world" to a degree that puts many a Christian to shame, and an earnest quest for actual existential engagement. But because in its protest against stodginess it repudiates true order, not simply the Apollonian order of contingent effects, but the veritable order of interior synthesis, it oscillates between an orgiastic sexuality and an incoherent elation. The way of perfection is hard, rigorous, and disenchanting, as the great religions have ever taught.

All efforts to find a means to circumvent the desperate straits of Ego in some experimental transcendent participation must fail. Were such gnostic endeavors truly efficacious, God would never have instituted the sacrifice of Golgotha. It is not possible in fallen man for the Dionysian and Apollonian attitudes to make a natural resolving synthesis—even a tragic one, as Nietzsche thought he saw in the birth of tragedy. Aesthetic resolution to tragic drama, the Greek catharsis, is indeed a genuine climactic, but it is obvious from the course of history that it could not effect the deliverance of man from the opposed tensions within him. Only in the Tragedy of Calvary was the final catharsis achieved, assumed by the divine promethean, the God-Man of universal expiation. And if Christian history seems as sorry to the skeptic as any other, it is the individual Christian's failure to accommodate himself to the truth in which his faith is hearted that must be blamed. For it is only in the efficacy of that total Archetype that each man can approach, through his own interior abnegation, the expiatory act that achieves his beatitude. Only when through contemplation he understands and realizes and *knows* that each day that Sacrifice must be relived within himself—only then can he accommodate his actions to the divine reality at work within his soul, truly participate in his own perfection.

Yet the fact that the Beat Generation, in spite of its dangerous recklessness, has produced valid art testifies at least to its essential seriousness, its preoccupation with the real, rather than the pseudo. For by the very fact of delivering itself over in a kind of trust, to the deepest forces of the psyche, it has, in some instances, succeeded in liberating art from the preoccupation with surfaces which has dominated it since the Renaissance. In so doing it has, be it ever so blindly, exposed the essential seriousness of the disordered human soul. Those who are saddened rather than ostracized to see young men and women damage themselves in an effort to achieve authenticity must understand the need of youth for self-immolation will manifest itself, if not in good ways then in bad ones; that the world of "civilization-as-usual" (offered as the chief preoccupation of reasonable men) is no longer capable of stemming the uprush of ecstatic forces from the repressed instinctual and spiritual life of man. In the end, both the Apollonian and the Dionysian must learn that only a supernatural culture, the culture of basic Christian mystical life, hearted in the sacraments, subsumed in collective ritual, the Liturgy, and cruxed on the profound knowledge of expiatory self-sacrifice in the Christ-immolation, is capable of healing the disordered human psyche, torn since Adam between the counter-claiming forces of Instinct, Ego and Intuition. If the twentieth century is breaking up, it is because nowhere on earth has it been able to effect any such synthesis.

———

In 1975, Everson exchanged a series of letters with his editor Lee Bartlett, discussing in greater depth what Everson envisioned as "the re-emergence of the Dionysian attitude in American poetry" heralded by the Beats. The letters were printed in *Sparrow 63*, issued by the Black Sparrow Press in December 1977.

## Four Letters on the Archetype

### Note by Lee Bartlett

In late July, 1975, William Everson and I spent an evening together in Davis going over a manuscript I was editing, *Earth Poetry: Selected Essays & Interviews of William Everson* (Oyez, Berkeley). During the course of our discussion, we talked at length about a critical study I was starting—a Jungian analysis of the Dionysian archetype in 19th and 20th century American poetry—which was to take as its starting point Everson's essay "Dionysus and the Beat Generation" (*Fresco,* Summer 1959). His basic contention in that essay, and in our discussion, was that the frontal attack of the Beats on Modernist poets and New Critics was a re-enactment of the archetypal conflict between the Dionysian impulse toward the primitive, the ecstatic, and the unconscious, and the Apollonian tendency toward culture, education, and the ego. In poems like "Howl," Everson saw the re-emergence of the Dionysian attitude in American poetry. A few days after our talk, I received the following note.

Aug. 2, 1975

Dear Lee:

The cruciality of the shift from Newtonian to Einsteinian physics for contemporary art came to me on reading "Frost as Modern Poet" in *The Pastoral Art of Robert Frost* by John L. Lynen, Yale, 1960.

Of course the assertion that these facts cut the whole ground out from under Modernism is an extension of my own.

Bill

The shift validated the subjectivization of value over against Newtonian objectivization—hence the validation of the Dionysian vs Apollonian psychological perspectives. Right? But of course the American *experience* was prior to the proof.

Then, between August 2 and August 8, came the following four letters rapid-fire.

I

August 2, 75
Swanton

Dear Lee:

In my card (just posted) I pointed to Lynen on "Frost as Modern Poet" as giving a provisional sketch of the situation in science which produced Modernism. The quote is from Whitehead:

> There persists . . . throughout the whole period [from Copernicus to Einstein] the fixed scientific cosmology which presupposes the ultimate fact of an irreducible brute matter, or material, spread throughout space in a flux of configurations. In itself such a material is senseless, valueless, purposeless. It just does what it does do, following a fixed routine imposed by external relationships which do not spring from the nature of its being.

He notes that Frost accepts this view and meets it through stoicism. So did Williams. Both rejected Symbolist solutions. What Williams did was to adopt grass-roots American positivism and regionalism as the positivistic basis of culture, no more. I spoke of him as a key figure due to his approximate relationship to the Beats, which is deceptive, and has made the scene so hard to get straight. He was a formative influence on Ginsberg, Snyder, and Whalen, yet he was not a dionysian. Nor was he a precisionist in the refined aesthetic sense of Zukofsky. But much more a precisionist than symbolist, which is what I take to be the two sides of Modernism (imagism & symbolism) both exploiting high-consciousness, Apollonian clarity.

(I'm beginning to believe it must have been Einstein who opened up the cosmos for Jeffers, enabling his Emersonian transcendentalism to find an objective scientific basis. For pantheism enabled him to accept the scientific world view and at the same time retain the dionysian perspective. But it's something I'll have to develop elsewhere.)

I became a dionysian through Jeffers, but it was Lawrence who enabled me to make it whole within myself—subjectivize the Jeffersian cosmos as the pattern of my soul. In your study your problem will be to get from the Modernists to the Beats. I think the line is through Lawrence via Rexroth. "The line" in the sense of a short-circuit. The *real* line, decreed by the archetype but missed because of the cultural warpage, was Emerson—Whitman—Jeffers—Everson. When I discovered Lawrence I had yet to hear of Rexroth, but it was Lawrence who brought us together. It was as Lawrentians we faced the world of the formalists. Rexroth, like Williams, was an "experimentalist," if objectivist, etc., first, then discovered the dionysian when he came West—avowedly through Lawrence but actually through Jeffers. When I spoke of Williams as a key figure I meant one to be wary of. Rexroth is to the Beat Generation what Williams is thought to be: the real link to the authentic dionysian root in Lawrence. (But it was the impact of Whitmanian America that shaped and liberated that dionysian strain in Lawrence. Today it is hard to credit the passion with which Lawrence took on the whole continental precisionist Establishment, and did it in terms which the American counter-culture today validates.)

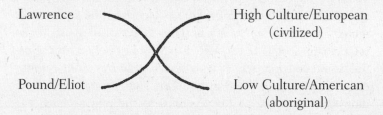

Lawrence — High Culture/European (civilized)

Pound/Eliot — Low Culture/American (aboriginal)

To get back to Rexroth. The split in him between objectivist precisionism and dionysian orgiastic-celebration is awesome. This is why he was able to weld together the precisionist-derived Pound-Williams-Olson side of the attack on the formalists (the attack on stasis), and the Whitmanesque-

Lawrentian-Reichian side of the same confrontation. But after the emergence he was unable to hold it together—the precisionist side triumphed because it was the only side high-conscious enough for the academic poets, poets jarred loose and shaken off by the Beat triumph, to relate to. If you are an iron-filing and some lightning bolt sparks at your magnet, the only other magnet you can gravitate to can be some other corresponding iron-filing precisionist, with Father Pound pumping away at the generator. That's why the dionysian-apollonian equation is so basic—it separates the sheep from the goats.

Yrs,
Bill

**2**

August 7, 1975
Swanton

Dear Lee:

If we think of the pre-Einsteinian scientific situation as imposing an increasing pressure of objectivization in consciousness, then the response of Modernism was to refine the image in direct conformation (brilliance, crystalization, sharpness, precision, definition, etc.) and the objectivization of the symbol in indirect conformation. The objectivized symbol was used to telescope the time-span to present science with a verifiable art-function which its (science's) norms could authenticate. Thus the symbol was not used properly, as in dionysian art, as the aperture to the energies of the unconscious, but objectively and controlled to afford measure to the mind, to make decisive judgments on history and time, to achieve a stasis that could be verified judgmentally.

I never read *Time & Western Man*—just picked up the quote I mentioned somewhere. Will have to check this out.

Actually, the two Englishmen who brought the dionysian back into American awareness in the pre-Beat era were Lawrence and Dylan Thomas. When Rexroth blurbed *The Residual Years* in 1948, he used Lawrence as the opening wedge. When Leslie Fiedler rose to the bait in August 1949 *Partisan Review,* he mostly attacked the blurb; it is significant that he coupled me with Dylan Thomas as my fellow "traveler in emotional excess." The sensational life and death were directly responsible for a shift in perspective, and helped pave the way for the Beats. It is significant that Bob Dylan took his name.

Thomas had been published here before the war but his impact had not been all that great. It was his platform appearances that did it. He had a Shakespearean manner which gave him immense authority and enabled the dionysian aspect to ride in behind its prestige. His first American tour was immensely successful (1950?). Then his legend began to grow and he emerged as a true dionysian, so that by the time of his death it had become his image. The *impact* of Lawrence actually came later with legalization of *Lady Chatterley's Lover.* As a poet he never has had in the States the renown that Thomas has. Nevertheless, he is a more root figure. He developed his dionysian platform in the pre-Einsteinian era and came by it through painful thought and conflict. Thomas you might say was one of the first fruits of the Einstein revolution. He quickened in its soil. Lawrence's *concepts* are more enduring, thus he is the more important long-range influence.

Yrs,
Bill

3

August 8, 1975
Swanton

Dear Lee:

In my sketch yesterday I should have mentioned Rexroth's issuance of Lawrence's *Selected Poems* in 1946 or '47. It was Rexroth's opening Salvo—his Introduction, I mean—and it took them by surprise. "Intellectual truancy!" I remember one reviewer squeaked. Rexroth had been quietly perfecting his polemical skills in the small anarchist publications, but this one was his opening blast, and it's still around today. This issuance has to qualify what I said about Lawrence's impact on the counter-culture coming with *Lady Chatterley* a decade later.

This was followed rapidly by *Paterson*—or maybe the two hit together, I don't remember the dates. Anyway, these two events were the prime dionysian strikes during the late forties. Then Dylan coming to sustain it across the New Critical triumph of the fifties until the arrival of the Beats.

Going back to the twenties—or, say, to the teens. It was Lawrence in England and Sandburg in America who carried what I call "the uses of imprecision" along with the precisionist breakthrough in the Revolution of the Word—both wings striking at the dead past—Victorian formalism. In the twenties on the international scene, precisionism triumphed with *The Waste Land, Ulysses,* etc. Williams' *Autobiography* chronicles this period well, and his dilemma as an American author.

Actually, the precisionists didn't triumph all that much in America. I think of the power displayed by Sandburg, O'Neill, Jeffers, Millay, Thomas Wolfe, and others across the twenties—all dionysians. In *Exiles Return* Malcolm Cowley has written eloquently of the difficulties encountered by the expatriates (precisionist) in this period.

The Depression put a stop, or at least a severe check,

to this upwelling tension of the twenties. Economic issues swept all fields of expression, but the dionysians kept their hand in through the populist roots from the teens that Sandburg had drawn on. Steinbeck emerged as Jeffers began to fall in the background under the charge of fascism. Steinbeck and Saroyan—powerful dionysian voices in the later thirties. At this time Rexroth changed from an objectivist-precisionist to a Lawrentian dionysian, and when the war came became a pacifist. Lawrence dies, but Henry Miller emerges in Paris . . . one expatriate who is pure anti-precisionist/dionysian.

During the war Rexroth brooded deeply, wrote his best poetry, and began to put it all together. Looking back on it, it seems to me the only mistake he made was his rejection of Jeffers. Other than that, he saw the gleam of the future in the combination of Lawrentian passionate eroticism, populist-anarchist-pacifist collective surge and American precisionist adhesion through Bill Williams. I was to be his Lincolnesque populist pacifist—the "pome-splitter," Duncan a celebrative dionysian aesthete with formalist adhesions to the precisionists, Lamantia a dionysian surrealist. It would have worked if we could have held together but the personality problems blew it up. Thus San Francisco.

In the early fifties, the scene shifts to Black Mountain. Olson, Creeley, et al. Precisionism refinding itself against the stuffy New Critical academic triumph. Pound, the master. Duncan admires and falls under Olson's spell.

Late fifties. The scene shifts back to San Fran. Snyder, Whalen, & Welch arrive from Reed, Williams their mentor. Ginsberg and Kerouac arrive from New York. Duncan returns. Lamantia has converted back to Catholicism. I am in the Dominicans. Rexroth pulls it together, provides just the right touch to make it coalesce. The feuds of the forties are forgotten. The S. F. Renascence and on its heels the Beat Generation.

The problem is compounded by the universal and ever-present problem of formalism. Formalism might be defined as the codification of the precisionism of the past. When this happens, both the neo-precisionist avant-garde and the dionysian ecstatics combine to overthrow it. Thus Pound and Lawrence both assailed post-Victorianism, exhausted formalism. Thus too Olson, Creeley, et al., neo-precisionists, combined with Ginsberg, Corso, Kerouac, et al., imprecisionists with gusto, to overthrow New Critical formalism.

> Post-Victorianism was a formalism of *practice*.
> New Criticism was a formalism of *method*—its best achievement in practice was the early Lowell.

> I remember when I first met Olson in 1947 he had just come from Pound at St. Elizabeth's. He was calling for a new approach to Pound even then, saying that New Critics like Tate had nothing more to say, whereas he and Kenner offered a fresh approach.

But once the revolution is won, the movement tends to fragment, and the neo-precisionists usually capture the control because their methods can be codified, whereas the dionysians depend on subjective spontaneity. The triumph of projective verse broke down the New Critical progeny and compelled them to adopt its methods in order to advance. The Beats fell away, only Ginsberg by sheer personal charisma and platform skill maintained his place. But Bukowski following close in the dionysian strain, versifying Henry Miller's crude sexuality.

Something tells me I've covered all this in earlier letters.

Yrs,
Bill

P.S. I'm thinking now about my place in this development. As a dionysian, I moved in with the Beat sweep, and especially on platform and in sensational publicity ran with the pack. I espoused "erotic mysticism," and did it right up to my leaving the Order. That all fits together. But my deeper roots are in Jeffers, another problem. If Rexroth had welded Jeffers into the movement it would have gained power and substance. As it was, his offering had to go forward through me. Since leaving the Order my own place is compromised. I haven't found a new strain. My peers are more comfortable with me, but hardly know how to fit me in. Except in the group readings, where I'm a natural. But my resistance to projectivism bewilders them. Actually, I'm still ingesting the past, getting it together for a new emergence. But I don't think it will be a *group* emergence for some time. The new formalism is not yet jelled enough to produce a revolt. Actually the women poets are carrying the new creative tension right now, but how permanent it is is hard to say.

The place of Jeffers in the dionysian movement is to bring a strain of negativity over-against the populist utterance. If we think of Emerson as the fountainhead, and Whitman and Thoreau as the twin strains of positive and negative, then Jeffers follows Thoreau. It downgrades humanity in order to upgrade Nature and God.

**4**

August 8, 1975
Swanton

Dear Lee,

In this morning's letter, already sealed, I drew up two lists under the dionysian setting: positive & negative. These two lists tend to themselves divide, the negative side between the skeptical and religious, the positive side between the passionate and critical.

DIONYSIAN

Other Worldly    ⋀    This Wordly

| Religious | (−) | Skeptical | Hot/Passionate | (+) | Cool/Critical |
|---|---|---|---|---|---|
| Melville | | Thoreau | Whitman | | Williams |
| Jeffers | | Frost | Lawrence | | Olson |
| early Everson | | Robinson | Ferlinghetti | | Snyder |
| | | | Wolfe | | Creeley |
| | | | Thomas | | Duncan |
| | | | Sandberg | | Levertov |
| | | | Corso | | Whalen |
| | | | Ginsberg | | |
| | | | Rexroth | | |
| | | | Miller | | |
| | | | O'Neill | | |
| | | | Cummings | | |
| | | | Patchen | | |
| | | | Bukowski | | |
| | | | Steinbeck | | |
| | | | late Everson | | |
| | | | Lew Welch | | |
| | | | Kerouac | | |
| | | | Kesey | | |
| | | | McClure | | |

This side takes a pessimistic          This side takes an affirmative &
view of human life.                    optimistic view of human life.

To get some background on this way of looking at things, see the diagram of the Archetypal Feminine in Erick Neuman's *The Great Mother*. See also his *Origins and History of Consciousness*.

Yrs,

Bill

Sept. 21, 1977
Swanton

Dear Lee:

I have yours of the 19th suggesting publication of my 1975 letters to you on the tension between apollonian and dionysian tendencies in recent American poetry. I do not know how persuasive these letters will be since I did not document my contention that modernism is the product of nineteenth century scientism and was rendered obsolete by the Einsteinian revolution in physics.

Modernism dies hard. Only recently Denis Donoghue in *The New York Review of Books* attacked Yeats for his departure from modernist tenets—his interest in the occult, his emphasis on lifestyle as opposed to aesthetic detachment, his dependence on regionalist incentives, his imprecisionist technique—all factors validated by Einsteinian perspectives. It's as if Shakespeare, seventy-five years after Copernicus, were being assailed because his practice did not accord with the Music of the Spheres!

Publication would also seem imprudent for other reasons. For one thing I brag on myself, making myself the issue of a new American mainstream: Emerson-Whitman-Jeffers-Everson! For another, I play fast and loose with categories, arbitrarily assigning people in ways they might resent. This seems to be part of the teaching process—all right in the classroom, but best not publish! Still, perhaps these letters will stand as sketches merely, loose formulations intended to be suggestive rather than final. So let it roll!

Yrs,
Bill

# LAWRENCE FERLINGHETTI

LAWRENCE FERLINGHETTI, co-founder of the City Lights Book Store and publisher of City Lights Books in San Francisco, is the author of more than a dozen books of poetry, two volumes of plays, and two novels. He wrote his "Note on Poetry in San Francisco" for the Spring 1958 issue of the *Chicago Review.*

In his "Note on Poetry in San Francisco," Ferlinghetti's description of his walk "thru Chinatown . . . with a famous academic poet" might have been a reference to Robert Lowell, a traditional East Coast poet two years older than Ferlinghetti, who was impressed by the poetry readings he attended when he visited the city in March 1957. There, in what Lowell later called "the era and setting of Allen Ginsberg," he found that "all about very modest poets were waking up prophets." Lowell wrote in *The Contemporary Poet as Artist and Critic* (1964, edited by Anthony Ostroff) that the street poetry he heard in San Francisco made him dissatisfied with his writing as an academic poet. Rereading his own work after listening to Beat poetry, Lowell felt that the style of his poems "seemed distant, symbol-ridden and willfully difficult. I began to paraphrase my Latin quotations, and to add extra syllables to a line to make it clearer and more colloquial." At the same time, Lowell had his reservations. He admitted that he was "no convert to the 'beats.' I know well too that the best poems are not necessarily poems that read aloud. Many of the greatest poems can only be read to one's self, for inspiration is no substitute for humor, shock, narrative, and a hypnotic voice, the four musts for oral performance. Still, my own poems seemed like prehistoric monsters dragged down into the bog and death by their ponderous armor."

In recent years Ferlinghetti has continued to describe the achievement of what he calls the "rebel band" of Beat Generation poets, as in section 12 of his "Work-in-Progress," an ongoing long poem excerpted in his New Directions volume *A Far Rockaway of the Heart* (1997). "A Buddha in the Woodpile" was included in *These Are My Rivers* (1993).

## *Note on Poetry in San Francisco*

There are all kinds of poets here, writing very dissimilar types of poetry.
. . . But I should say that the kind of poetry which has been making the
most noise here is quite different from the "poetry about poetry," the
poetry of technique, the poetry for poets and professors which has
dominated the quarterlies and anthologies in this country for some
time and which of course is also written in San Francisco. The poetry
which has been making itself heard here of late is what should be
called street poetry. For it amounts to getting the poet out of the inner
esthetic sanctum where he has too long been contemplating his complicated navel. It amounts to getting poetry back into the street where
it once was, out of the classroom, out of the speech department, and—
in fact—off the printed page. The printed word has made poetry so
silent. But the poetry I am talking about here is spoken poetry, poetry
conceived as oral messages. It "makes it" aloud. Some of it has been
read with jazz, much of it has not. A new "ashcan" school? Rock and
roll? Who cares what names it's called. What is important is that this
poetry is using its eyes and ears as they have not been used for a number of years. "Poetry about poetry," like much non-objective painting,
has caused an atrophy of the artist's senses. He has literally forgotten
(taken leave of) his senses. (I walked thru Chinatown recently with a
famous academic poet, and he never saw the whole schools of fish
gasping on counters, nor heard what they breathed.)

And finally, in some larger sense, it all adds up to the beginning of
a very inevitable thing—the *resocialization* of poetry. But not like the
Thirties.

## From *Work-in-Progress*

And Pablo Neruda
      that Chilean omnivore of poetry
         who wanted to
            put everything in

and take nothing out
(of his *Canto General*)
said to me in Cuba Libre Hilton 1959
"I love your wide open poetry"
by which he meant a certain kind of
*poesia norteamericana*
and its rebel band who
rose over the rooftops of
tenement boneyards
intent on making out
And made out of madness
a hundred years of beatitude

"So boring I'm snoring"
cried Joe Public
before *they* came along
and busted out the sides
of Poetry Chicago
and various New Yorkerish
poetasters
out of their Westchester cradles
endlessly rocking
on the Times Square Shuttle
between the Times Book Review
and the Algonquin
while lady critics and professors
moaned about poetic pederasts
at Columbia
They cruised Times Square and America
and cruised into history
"waving genitals and manuscripts"
And tuned their holy unholy voices
to a wide open society
that didn't yet exist
And so jump-started
the stalled merrygoround
of American ecstasy
left along East River's
echoing shores

after Old Walt stepped off
Brooklyn Ferry
into the heart of America

## A Buddha in the Woodpile

If there had been only
one Buddhist in the woodpile
In Waco Texas
to teach us how to sit still
one saffron Buddhist in the back rooms
just one Tibetan lama
just one Taoist
just one Zen
just one Thomas Merton Trappist
just one saint in the wilderness
of Waco USA
If there had been only one
calm little Gandhi
in a white sheet or suit
one not-so-silent partner
who at the last moment shouted *Wait*
If there had been just one
majority of one
in the lotus position
in the inner sanctum
who bowed his shaved head to the
Chief of All Police
and raised his hands in a mudra
and chanted the Great Paramita Sutra
the Diamond Sutra
the Lotus Sutra
If there had somehow been
just one Gandhian spinner
with Brian Wilson at the gates of the White House
at the Gates of Eden
then it wouldn't have been
Vietnam once again

and its "One two three four
What're we waitin' for?"
If one single ray of the light
of the Dalai Lama
when he visited this land
had penetrated somehow
the Land of the Brave
where the lion never
lies down with the lamb—
But not a glimmer got through
The Security screened it out
screened out the Buddha
and his not-so-crazy wisdom
If only in the land of Sam Houston
if only in the land of the Alamo
if only in Wacoland USA
if only in Reno
if only on CNN CBS NBC
one had comprehended
one single syllable
of the Gautama Buddha
of the young Siddhartha
one single whisper of
Gandhi's spinning wheel
one lost syllable
of Martin Luther King
or of the Early Christians
or of Mother Teresa
or Thoreau or Whitman or Allen Ginsberg
or of the millions in America tuned to them
If the inner ears of the inner sanctums
had only been half open
to any vibrations except
those of the national security state
and had only been attuned
to the sound of one hand clapping
and not one hand punching
Then that sick cult and its children
might still be breathing

the free American air
of the First Amendment

---

# HENRY LOUIS GATES, JR.

HENRY LOUIS GATES, JR., distinguished educator and prolific writer on black culture, was fascinated by the double life of the writer Anatole Broyard, whose essay "A Portrait of the Hipster" (*Partisan Review*, 1948) was the first to discuss the emergence of the hipster in the United States. Broyard was born into an African-American family, but he "passed" as a white man when he began his career as a writer in New York City. Gates described Broyard's complicated life in a *New Yorker* profile on June 17, 1996. W. E. B. Du Bois Professor of Humanities at Harvard University, Gates is also director of the Institute for Afro-American Research there.

## *White Like Me: Anatole Broyard*

In 1982, an investment banker named Richard Grand-Jean took a summer's lease on an eighteenth-century farmhouse in Fairfield, Connecticut; its owner, Anatole Broyard, spent his summers in Martha's Vineyard. The house was handsomely furnished with period antiques, and the surrounding acreage included a swimming pool and a pond. But the property had another attraction, too. Grand-Jean, a managing director of Salomon Brothers, was an avid reader, and he took satisfaction in renting from so illustrious a figure. Anatole Broyard had by then been a daily book reviewer for the *Times* for more than a decade, and that meant that he was one of literary America's foremost gatekeepers. Grand-Jean might turn to the business pages of the *Times* first, out of professional obligation, but he turned to the book page next, out of a sense of self. In his Walter Mittyish moments, he sometimes imagined what it might be like to be someone who read and wrote about books for a living—someone to whom millions of readers looked for guidance.

Broyard's columns were suffused with both worldliness and high culture. Wry, mandarin, even self-amused at times, he wrote like a man about town, but one who just happened to have all of Western literature at his fingertips. Always, he radiated an air of soigné self-confidence: he could be amiable in his opinions or waspish, but he never betrayed a flicker of doubt about what he thought. This was a man who knew that his judgment would never falter and his sentences never fail him.

Grand-Jean knew little about Broyard's earlier career, but as he rummaged through Broyard's bookshelves he came across old copies of intellectual journals like *Partisan Review* and *Commentary,* to which Broyard had contributed a few pieces in the late forties and early fifties. One day, Grand-Jean found himself leafing through a magazine that contained an early article by Broyard. What caught his eye, though, was the contributor's note for the article—or, rather, its absence. It had been neatly cut out, as if with a razor.

A few years later, Grand-Jean happened on another copy of that magazine, and decided to look up the Broyard article again. This time, the note on the contributor was intact. It offered a few humdrum details—that Broyard was born in New Orleans, attended Brooklyn College and the New School for Social Research, and taught at New York University's Division of General Education. It also offered a less humdrum one: the situation of the American Negro, the note asserted, was a subject that the author "knows at first hand." It was an elliptical formulation, to be sure, but for Anatole Broyard it may not have been elliptical enough.

Broyard was born black and became white, and his story is compounded of equal parts pragmatism and principle. He knew that the world was filled with such snippets and scraps of paper, all conspiring to reduce him to an identity that other people had invented and he had no say in. Broyard responded with X-Acto knives and evasions, with distance and denials and half denials and cunning half-truths. Over the years, he became a virtuoso of ambiguity and equivocation. Some of his acquaintances knew the truth; many more had heard rumors about "distant" black ancestry (wasn't there a grandfather who was black? a great-grandfather?). But most were entirely unaware, and that was as he preferred it. He kept the truth even from his own children. Society had decreed race to be a matter of natural law, but he wanted race to be an elective affinity, and it was never going to be a fair fight. A penalty was exacted. He shed a past and an identity to become a writer—a writer who wrote endlessly about the act of shedding a past and an identity.

Anatole Paul Broyard was born on July 16, 1920, in New Orleans to Paul Broyard and Edna Miller. His father was a carpenter and worked as a builder, along with his brothers; neither parent had graduated from elementary school. Anatole spent his early years in a modest house on St. Ann Street, in a colored neighborhood in the French Quarter. Documents in the Louisiana state archives show all Anatole's ancestors, on both sides, to have been Negroes, at least since the late eighteenth century. The rumor about a distant black ancestor was, in a sense, the reverse of the truth: he may have had one distant white ancestor. Of course, the conventions of color stratification within black America—nowhere more pronounced than in New Orleans—meant that light-skinned blacks often intermarried with other light-skinned blacks, and this was the case with Paul and his "high yellow" wife, Edna. Anatole was the second of three children; he and his sister Lorraine, two years older, were light-skinned, while Shirley, two years younger, was not so light-skinned. (The inheritance of melanin is an uneven business.) In any event, the family was identified as Negro, and identified itself as Negro. It was not the most interesting thing about them. But in America it was not a negligible social fact. The year before Anatole's birth, for example, close to a hundred blacks were lynched in the South and anti-black race riots claimed the lives of hundreds more.

While Anatole was still a child, the family moved to the Bedford-Stuyvesant area of Brooklyn, thus joining the great migration that took hundreds of thousands of Southern blacks to Northern cities during the twenties. In the French Quarter, Paul Broyard had been a legendary dancer, beau, and *galant;* in the French Quarter, the Broyards—Paul was one of ten siblings—were known for their craftsmanship. Brooklyn was a less welcoming environment. "He should never have left New Orleans, but my mother nagged him into it,"

Broyard recalled years later. Though Paul Broyard arrived there a master carpenter, he soon discovered that the carpenters' union was not favorably inclined toward colored applicants. A stranger in a strange city, Paul decided to pass as white in order to join the union and get work. It was strictly a professional decision, which affected his work and nothing else.

For Paul, being colored was a banal fact of life, which might be disguised when convenient; it was not a creed or something to take pride in. Paul did take pride in his craft, and he liked to boast of rescuing projects from know-nothing architects. He filled his home with furniture he had made himself—flawlessly professional, if a little too sturdily built to be stylish. He also took pride in his long legs and his dance-hall agility (an agility Anatole would share). It was a challenge to be a Brooklyn *galant,* but he did his best.

"Family life was very congenial, it was nice and warm and cozy, but we just didn't have any sort of cultural or intellectual nourishment at home," Shirley, who was the only member of the family to graduate from college, recalls. "My parents had no idea even what the New York *Times* was, let alone being able to imagine that Anatole might write for it." She says, "Anatole was different from the beginning." There was a sense, early on, that Anatole Broyard—or Buddy, as he was called then—was not entirely comfortable being a Broyard.

Shirley has a photograph, taken when Anatole was around four or five, of a family visit back to New Orleans. In it you can see Edna and her two daughters, and you can make out Anatole, down the street, facing in the opposite direction. The configuration was, Shirley says, pretty representative.

After graduating from Boys High School, in the late thirties, he enrolled in Brooklyn College. Already, he had a passion for modern culture—for European cinema and European literature. The idea that meaning could operate on several levels seemed to appeal to him. Shirley recalls exasperating conversations along those lines: "He'd ask me about a Kafka story I'd read or a French film I'd seen and say, 'Well, you see that on more than one level, don't you?' I felt like saying 'Oh, get off it.' Brothers don't say that to their sisters."

Just after the war began, he got married, to a black Puerto Rican woman, Aida, and they soon had a daughter. (He named her Gala, after Salvador Dali's wife.) Shirley recalls, "He got married and had a child on purpose—the purpose being to stay out of the Army. Then Anatole goes in the Army anyway, in spite of this child." And his wife and child moved in with the Broyard family.

Though his military records were apparently destroyed in a fire, some people who knew him at this time say that he entered the segregated Army as a white man. If so, he must have relished the irony that after attending officers' training school he was made the captain of an all-black stevedore battalion. Even then, his thoughts were not far from the new life he envisioned for himself. He said that he joined the Army with a copy of Wallace Stevens in his back pocket; now he was sending money home to his wife and asking her to save it so that he could open a bookstore in the Village when he got back. "She had other ideas," Shirley notes. "She wanted him to get a nice job, nine to five."

Between Aida and the allure of a literary life there was not much competition. Soon after his discharge from the Army, at war's end, he found an apartment in the Village, and he took advantage of the G.I. Bill to attend evening classes at the New School for Social Research, on Twelfth Street. His new life had no room for Aida and Gala. (Aida, with the child, later moved to California and remarried.) He left other things behind, too. The black scholar and dramatist W. F. Lucas, who knew Buddy Broyard from Bed-Stuy, says, "He was black when he got into the subway in Brooklyn, but as soon as he got out at West Fourth Street he became white."

He told his sister Lorraine that he had resolved to pass so that he could be a writer, rather than a Negro writer. His darker-skinned younger sister, Shirley, represented a possible snag, of course, but then he and Shirley had never been particularly close, and anyway she was busy with her own life and her own friends. (Shirley graduated Phi Beta Kappa from Hunter College, and went on to marry Franklin Williams, who helped organize the Peace Corps and served as Ambassador to Ghana.) They had drifted apart: it was just a matter of drifting farther apart. Besides, wasn't that why everybody came to New York—to run away from the confines of family, from places where people thought they knew who and what you were? Whose family *wasn't* in some way unsuitable? In a *Times* column in 1979 Broyard wrote, "My mother and father were too folksy for me, too colorful. . . . Eventually, I ran away to Greenwich Village, where no one had been born of a mother and father, where the people I met had sprung from their own brows, or from the pages of a bad novel. . . . Orphans of the avant-garde, we out-distanced our history and our humanity." Like so much of what he wrote in this vein, it meant more than it said; like the modernist culture he loved, it had levels.

In the Village, where Broyard started a bookstore on Cornelia Street, the salient thing about him wasn't that he was black but that he was beautiful, charming, and erudite. In those days, the Village was crowded with ambitious and talented young writers and artists, and Broyard—known for calling men "Sport" and girls "Slim"—was never more at home. He could hang out at the San Remo bar with Dwight Macdonald and Delmore Schwartz, and with a younger set who yearned to be the next Macdonalds and the next Schwartzes. Vincent Livelli, a friend of Broyard's since Brooklyn College days, recalls, "Everybody was so brilliant around us—we kept duelling with each other. But he was the guy that set the pace in the Village." His conversation sparkled—everybody said so. The sentences came out perfectly formed, festooned with the most apposite literary allusions. His high-beam charm could inspire worship but also resentment. Livelli says, "Anatole had a sort of dancing attitude toward life—he'd dance away from you. He had people understand that he was brilliant and therefore you couldn't hold him if you weren't worthy of his attention."

The novelist and editor Gordon Lish says, "Photographs don't suggest in any wise the enormous power he had in person. No part of him was ever for a moment at rest." He adds, "I adored him as a man. I mean, he was really in a league with Neal Cassady as a kind of presence." But there was, he says, a fundamental difference between Broyard and Kerouac's inspiration and muse: "Unlike Cassady, who was out of control, Anatole was *exorbitantly* in control. He was fastidious about managing things."

Except, perhaps, the sorts of things you're supposed to manage. His bookstore provided him with entrée to Village intellectuals—and them with entrée to Anatole—yet it was not run as a business, exactly. Its offerings were few but choice: Céline, Kafka, other hard-to-find translations. The critic Richard Gilman, who was one of its patrons, recalls that Broyard had a hard time parting with the inventory: "He had these books on the shelf, and someone would want to buy one, and he would snatch it back."

Around 1948, Broyard started to attract notice not merely for his charm, his looks, and his conversation but for his published writings. The early pieces, as often as not, were about a subject to which he had privileged access: blacks and black culture. *Commentary*, in his third appearance in its pages, dubbed him an "anatomist of the Negro personality in a white world." But was he merely an anthropologist or was he a native informant? It wasn't an ambiguity that he was in any hurry to resolve. Still, if all criticism is a form of autobiography (as Oscar Wilde would have it), one might look to these pieces for clues to his preoccupations at the time. In a 1950 *Commentary* article entitled "Portrait of the Inauthentic Negro," he wrote that the Negro's embarrassment over blackness should be banished by the realization that "thousands of Negroes with 'typical' features are accepted as whites merely because of light complexion." He continued:

> The inauthentic Negro is not only estranged from whites— he is also estranged from his own group and from himself. Since his companions are a mirror in which he sees himself as ugly, he must reject them; and since his own self is mainly a tension between an accusation and a denial, he can hardly find it, much less live in it. . . . He is adrift without a role in a world predicated on roles.

A year later, in "Keep Cool, Man: The Negro Rejection of Jazz," he wrote, just as despairingly, that the Negro's

> contact with white society has opened new vistas, new ideals in his imagination, and these he defends by repression, freezing up against the desire to be white, to have normal social intercourse with whites, to behave like them. . . . But in coolness he evades the issue . . . he becomes a pacifist in the struggle between social groups—not a conscientious objector, but a draft-dodger.

These are words that could be read as self-indictment, if anybody chose to do so. Certainly they reveal a ticklish sense of the perplexities he found himself in, and a degree of self-interrogation (as opposed to self-examination) he seldom displayed again.

In 1950, in a bar near Sheridan Square, Broyard met Anne

Bernays, a Barnard junior and the daughter of Edward L. Bernays, who is considered the father of public relations. "There was this guy who was the handsomest man I have ever seen in my life, and I fell madly in love with him," Bernays, who is best known for such novels as "Growing Up Rich" and "Professor Romeo," recalls. "He was physically irresistible, and he had this dominating personality, and I guess I needed to be dominated. His hair was so short that you couldn't tell whether it was curly or straight. He had high cheekbones and very smooth skin." She knew that he was black, through a mutual friend, the poet and Blake scholar Milton Klonsky. (Years later, in a sort of epiphany, she recognized Anatole's loping walk as an African-American cultural style: "It was almost as if this were inside him dying to get out and express itself, but he felt he couldn't do it.")

After graduation, she got a job as an editor at the literary semi-annual *Discovery*. She persuaded Broyard to submit his work, and in 1954 the magazine ran a short story entitled "What the Cystoscope Said"—an extraordinary account of his father's terminal illness:

> I didn't recognize him at first, he was so bad. His mouth was open and his breathing was hungry. They had removed his false teeth, and his cheeks were so thin that his mouth looked like a keyhole. I leaned over his bed and brought my face before his eyes. "Hello, darlin'," he whispered, and he smiled. His voice, faint as it was, was full of love, and it bristled the hairs on the nape of my neck and raised goose flesh on my forearms. I couldn't speak, so I kissed him. His cheek smelled like wax.

Overnight, Broyard's renown was raised to a higher level. "Broyard knocked people flat with 'What the Cystoscope Said,'" Lish recalls. One of those people was Burt Britton, a bookseller who later co-founded Books & Co. In the fifties, he says, he read the works of young American writers religiously: "Now, if writing were a horse race, which God knows it's not, I would have gone out and put my two bucks down on Broyard." In "Advertisements for Myself," Norman Mailer wrote that he'd buy a novel by Broyard the day it appeared. Indeed, Bernays recalls, on the basis of that story the Atlantic Monthly Press offered Broyard a twenty-thousand-dollar advance—then a staggeringly large sum for a literary work by an unknown—for a novel of which "Cystoscope" would be a chapter. "The whole literary world was waiting with bated breath for this great novelist who was about to arrive," Michael Vincent Miller, a friend of Broyard's since the late fifties, recalls. "Some feelings of expectation lasted for years."

Rumor surrounded Broyard like a gentle murmur, and sometimes it became a din. Being an orphan of the avant-garde was hard work. Among the black literati, certainly, his ancestry was a topic of speculation, and when a picture of Broyard accompanied a 1958 *Time* review of a Beat anthology it was closely scrutinized. Arna Bontemps wrote to Langston Hughes, "His picture . . . makes him look Negroid. If so, he is the only spade among the Beat Generation." Charlie Parker spied Broyard in Washington Square Park one day and told a companion, "He's one of us, but he doesn't want to admit he's one of us." Richard Gilman recalls an awkwardness that ensued when he stumbled across Anatole with his dark-skinned wife and child: "I just happened to come upon them in a restaurant that was not near our usual stomping grounds. He introduced me, and it was fine, but my sense was that he would rather not have had anyone he knew meet them." He adds, "I remember thinking at the time that he had the look of an octoroon or a quadroon, one of those—which he strenuously denied. He got into very great disputes with people."

One of those disputes was with Chandler Brossard, who had been a close friend: Broyard was the best man at Brossard's wedding. There was a falling out, and Brossard produced an unflattering portrait of Broyard as the hustler and opportunist Henry Porter in his 1952 novel, "Who Walk in Darkness." Brossard knew just where Broyard was most vulnerable, and he pushed hard. His novel originally began, "People said Henry Porter was a Negro," and the version published in France still does. Apparently fearing legal action, however, Brossard's American publisher, New Directions, sent it to Broyard in galley form before it was published.

Anne Bernays was with Broyard when the galleys arrived. Broyard explained to her, "They asked me to read it because they are afraid I am going to sue." But why would he sue, she wanted to know. "Because it says I'm a Negro," he replied grimly. "Then," Bernays recalls, "I said, 'What are you going to do?' He said, 'I am going to make them change it.' And he did."

The novel went on to be celebrated as a groundbreaking chronicle of Village hipsters; it also—as a result of the legal redactions—reads rather oddly in places. Henry Porter, the Broyard character, is rumored to be not a Negro but merely "an illegitimate":

> I suspect [the rumor] was supposed to explain the differ-
> ence between the way he behaved and the way the rest of us
> behaved. Porter did not show that he knew people were talk-
> ing about him this way. I must give him credit for maintaining
> a front of indifference that was really remarkable.
>
> Someone both Porter and I knew quite well once told me
> the next time he saw Porter he was going to ask him if he was
> or was not an illegitimate. He said it was the only way to clear
> the air. Maybe so. But I said I would not think of doing it. . . .
> I felt that if Porter ever wanted the stories about himself
> cleared up, publicly, he would one day do so. I was willing to
> wait.

And that, after all, is the nature of such secrets: they are not what cannot be known but what cannot be acknowledged.

Another trip wire seems to have landed Broyard in one of the masterpieces of twentieth-century American fiction, William Gaddis's
"The Recognitions." Livelli explains, "Now, around 1947 or '48,
William Gaddis and Anatole were in love with the same gal, Sheri
Martinelli. They were rivals, almost at each other's throats. And Willie
was such a sweetheart that he had a mild approach to everything, and
Anatole was sort of a stabber: he injected words like poison into conversations." When "The Recognitions" came out, in 1955, "Anatole
caught on to it right away, and he was kind of angry over it." The
Broyard character is named Max, and Gaddis wrote that he "always
looked the same, always the same age, his hair always the same short
length," seemingly "a parody on the moment, as his clothes carica-
tured a past at eastern colleges where he had never been." Worse is his
"unconscionable smile," which intimates "that the wearer knew all of
the dismal secrets of some evil jungle whence he had just come."

Broyard's own account of these years—published in 1993 as
"Kafka Was the Rage"—is fuelled by the intertwined themes of writing
and women. Gaddis says, "His eyes were these great pools—soft, gentle pools. It was girls, girls, girls: a kind of intoxication of its own. I always thought, frankly, that that's where his career went, his creative
energies."

Anne Bernays maintains, "If you leave the sex part out, you're only telling half the story. With women, he was just like an alcoholic with booze." She stopped seeing him in 1952, at her therapist's urging. "It was like going cold turkey off a drug," she says, remembering how crushing the experience was, and she adds, "I think most women have an Anatole in their lives."

Indeed, not a few of them had Anatole. "He was a pussy gangster, really," Lucas, a former professor of comparative literature, says with Bed-Stuy bluntness. Gilman recalls being in Bergdorf Goodman and coming across Broyard putting the moves on a salesgirl. "I hid behind a pillar—otherwise he'd know that I'd seen him—and watched him go through every stage of seduction: 'What do you think? Can I put this against you? Oh, it looks great against your skin. You have the most wonderful skin.' And then he quoted Baudelaire."

Quoting Baudelaire turns out to be key. Broyard's great friend Ernest van den Haag recalls trolling the Village with Broyard in those days: "We obviously quite often compared our modus operandi, and what I observed about Anatole is that when he liked a girl he could speak to her brilliantly about all kinds of things which the girl didn't in the least understand, because Anatole was really vastly erudite. The girl had no idea what he was talking about, but she loved it, because she was under the impression, rightly so, that she was listening to something very interesting and important. His was a solipsistic discourse, in some ways." Indeed, the narrator of "What the Cystoscope Said" tells of seducing his ailing father's young and ingenuous nurse in a similar manner:

> "Listen," I said, borrowing a tone of urgency from another source, "I want to give you a book. A book that was written for you, a book that belongs to you as much as your diary, that's dedicated to you like your nurse's certificate." . . . My apartment was four blocks away, so I bridged the distance with talk, raving about *Journey to the End of the Night,* the book she needed like she needed a hole in her head.

Broyard recognized that seduction was a matter not only of talking but of listening, too, and he knew how to pay attention with an engulfing level of concentration. The writer Ellen Schwamm, who met Broyard in the late fifties, says, "You show me a man who talks, and I'll show you a thousand women who hurl themselves at his feet. I don't mean just talk, I mean dialogues. He *listened*, and he was willing to speak of things that most men are not interested in: literature and its effect on life." But she also saw another side to Broyard's relentless need to seduce. She invokes a formulation made by her husband, the late Harold Brodkey: "Harold used to say that a lot of men steal from women. They steal bits of their souls, bits of their personalities, to construct an emotional life, which many men don't have. And I think that Anatole needed something of that sort."

It's an image of self-assemblage which is very much in keeping with Broyard's own accounts of himself. Starting in 1946, and continuing at intervals for the rest of his life, he underwent analysis. Yet the word "analysis" is misleading: what he wanted was to be refashioned— or, as he told his first analyst, to be *transfigured*. "When I came out with the word, I was like someone who sneezes into a handkerchief and finds it full of blood," he wrote in the 1993 memoir. "I wanted to discuss my life with him not as a patient talking to an analyst but as if we were two literary critics discussing a novel. . . . I had a literature rather than a personality, a set of fictions about myself." He lived a lie because he didn't want to live a larger lie: and Anatole Broyard, Negro writer, was that larger lie.


Alexandra Nelson, known as Sandy, met Broyard in January of 1961. Broyard was forty, teaching the odd course at the New School and supporting himself by freelancing: promotional copy for publishers, liner notes for Columbia jazz records, blurbs for the Book-of-the-Month Club. Sandy was twenty-three and a dancer, and Broyard had always loved dancers. Of Norwegian descent, she was strikingly beautiful, and strikingly intelligent. Michael Miller recalls, "She represented a certain kind of blonde, a certain kind of sophisticated carriage and a way of moving through the world with a sense of the good things. They both had marvellous taste."

It was as if a sorcerer had made a list of everything Broyard loved and had given it life. At long last, the conqueror was conquered: in less than a year, Broyard and Sandy were married. Sandy remembers his aura in those days: "Anatole was very hip. It wasn't a pose—it was in his sinew, in his bones. And, when he was talking to you, you just felt that you were receiving all this radiance from him." (Van den Haag says, "I do think it's not without significance that Anatole married a blonde, and about as white as you can get. He may have feared a little bit that the children might turn out black. He must have been pleased that they didn't.")

While they were still dating, two of Broyard's friends told Sandy that he was black, in what seemed to be a clumsy attempt to scare her off. "I think they really weren't happy to lose him, to see him get into a serious relationship," she says. "They were losing a playmate, in a way." Whatever the cultural sanctions, she was unfazed. But she says that when she asked Broyard about it he proved evasive: "He claimed that he wasn't black, but he talked about 'island influences,' or said that he had a grandmother who used to live in a tree on some island in the Caribbean. Anatole was like that—he was very slippery." Sandy didn't force the issue, and the succeeding years only fortified his sense of reserve. "Anatole was very strong," she says. "And he said about certain things, 'Just keep out. This is the deal if you get mixed up with me.'" The life that Broyard chose to live meant that the children did not meet their Aunt Shirley until after his death—nor, except for a couple of brief visits in the sixties, was there any contact even with Broyard's light-skinned mother and older sister. It was a matter of respecting the ground rules. "I would try to poke in those areas, but the message was very direct and strong," Sandy explains. "Oh, when I got angry at him, you know, one always pushes the tender points. But over time you grow up about these things and realize you do what you can do and there are certain things you can't."

In 1963, just before their first child, Todd, was born, Anatole shocked his friends by another big move—to Connecticut. Not only was he moving to Connecticut but he was going to be commuting to work: for the first time in his life, he would be a company man. "I think one of his claims to fame was that he hadn't had an office job—somehow, he'd escaped that," Sandy says. "There had been no real need for him to grow up." But after Todd was born—a daughter, Bliss, followed in 1966—Anatole spent seven years working full-time as a copywriter at the Manhattan advertising agency Wunderman Ricotta & Kline.

Over the next quarter century, the family lived in a series of eighteenth-century houses, sometimes bought on impulse, in places like Fairfield, Redding, Greens Farms, and Southport. Here, in a land of leaf-blowers and lawnmowers, Bed-Stuy must have seemed almost comically remote. Many of Broyard's intimates from the late forties knew about his family; the intimates he acquired in the sixties did not, or else had heard only rumors. Each year, the number of people who knew Buddy from Bed-Stuy dwindled; each year, the rumors grew more nebulous; each year, he left his past further behind. Miller says, "Anatole was a master at what Erving Goffman calls 'impression management.'" The writer Evelyn Toynton says, "I remember once going to a party with Sandy and him in Connecticut. There were these rather dull people there, stockbrokers and the usual sorts of people, and Anatole just knocked himself out to charm every single person in the room. I said to him, 'Anatole, can't you ever *not* be charming?'" Miller observes, "He was a wonderful host. He could take people from different walks of life—the president of Stanley Tools or a vice-president of Merrill Lynch, say, and some bohemian type from the Village—and keep the whole scene flowing beautifully. He had perfect pitch for the social encounter, like Jay Gatsby."

It was as if, wedded to an ideal of American self-fashioning, he sought to put himself to the ultimate test. It was one thing to be accepted in the Village, amid the Beats and hipsters and émigrés, but to gain acceptance in Cheever territory was an achievement of a higher order. "Anatole, when he left the Village and went to Connecticut, was able not only to pass but even to be a kind of influential presence in that world of rich white Wasps," Miller says. "Maybe that was a shallower part of the passing—to be accepted by Connecticut gentry."

Broyard's feat raised eyebrows among some of his literary admirers: something borrowed, something new. Daphne Merkin, another longtime friend, detected "a 'country-squire' tendency—a complicated tendency to want to establish a sort of safety through bourgeoisness. It was like a Galsworthy quality."

Even in Arcadia, however, there could be no relaxation of vigilance: in his most intimate relationships, there were guardrails. Broyard once wrote that Michael Miller was one of the people he liked best in the world, and Miller is candid about Broyard's profound influence on him. Today, Miller is a psychotherapist, based in Cambridge, and the author, most recently, of "Intimate Terrorism." From the time they met until his death, Broyard read to him the first draft of almost every piece he wrote. Yet a thirty-year friendship of unusual intimacy was circumscribed by a subject that they never discussed. "First of all, I didn't *know*," Miller says. "I just had intuitions and had heard intimations. It was some years before I'd even put together some intuition and little rumblings—nothing ever emerged clearly. There was a certain tacit understanding between us to accept certain pathways as our best selves, and not challenge that too much." It was perhaps, he says a little sadly, a limitation on the relationship.

In the late sixties, Broyard wrote several front-page reviews for the *Times Book Review.* "They were brilliant, absolutely sensational," the novelist Charles Simmons, who was then an assistant editor there, says. In 1971, the *Times* was casting about for a new daily reviewer, and Simmons was among those who suggested Anatole Broyard. It wasn't a tough sell. Arthur Gelb, at the time the paper's cultural editor, recalls, "Anatole was among the first critics I brought to the paper. He was very funny, and he also had that special knack for penetrating hypocrisy. I don't think he was capable of uttering a boring sentence."

You could say that his arrival was a sign of the times. Imagine: Anatole Broyard, downtown flaneur and apostle of sex and high modernism, ensconced in what was, literarily speaking, the ultimate establishment perch. "There had been an awful lot of very tame, very conventional people at the *Times,* and Broyard came in as a sort of ambassador from the Village and Village sophistication," Alfred Kazin recalls. Broyard had a highly developed appreciation of the paper's institutional power, and he even managed to use it to avenge wrongs done him in his Village days. Just before he started his job at the daily, he published a review in the *Times Book Review* of a new novel by one Chandler Brossard. The review began, "Here's a book so transcendently bad it makes us fear not only for the condition of the novel in this country, but for the country itself."

Broyard's reviews were published in alternation with those of Christopher Lehmann-Haupt, who has now been a daily reviewer at the *Times* for more than a quarter century, and who readily admits that Broyard's appointment did not gladden his heart. They hadn't got along particularly well when Lehmann-Haupt was an editor at the *Times Book Review,* nor did Lehmann-Haupt entirely approve of Broyard's status as a fabled libertine. So when A. M. Rosenthal, the paper's managing editor, was considering hiring him, Lehmann-Haupt expressed reservations. He recalls, "Rosenthal was saying, 'Give me five reasons why not.' And I thoughtlessly blurted out, 'Well, first of all, he is the biggest ass man in town.' And Rosenthal rose up from his desk and said, 'If that were a disqualification for working for the New York *Times*'—and he waved—'this place would be empty!' "

Broyard got off to an impressive start. Lehmann-Haupt says, "He had a wonderful way of setting a tone, and a wonderful way of talking himself through a review. He had good, tough instincts when it came to fiction. He had taste." And the jovial Herbert Mitgang, who served a stint as a daily reviewer himself, says, "I always thought he was the most literary of the reviewers. There would be something like a little essay in his daily reviews."

Occasionally, his acerbic opinions got him in trouble. There was, for example, the storm that attended an uncharitable review of a novel by Christy Brown, an Irish writer who was born with severe cerebral palsy. The review concluded:

> It is unfortunate that the author of "A Shadow on Summer" is an almost total spastic—he is said to have typed his highly regarded first novel, "Down All the Days," with his left foot— but I don't see how the badness of his second novel can be blamed on that. Any man who can learn to type with his left foot can learn to write better than he has here.

Then, there was the controversial review of James Baldwin's piously sentimental novel of black suffering, "If Beale Street Could Talk." Broyard wrote:

> If I have to read one more description of the garbage piled up in the streets of Harlem, I may just throw protocol to the winds and ask whose garbage is it? I would like to remind Mr. Baldwin that the City Health Code stipulates that garbage must be put out in proper containers, not indiscriminately "piled."

No one could accuse Broyard of proselytizing for progressive causes. Jason Epstein, for one, was quick to detect a neoconservative air in his reviews, and Broyard's old friend Ernest van den Haag, a longtime contributing editor at *National Review*, volunteers that he was available to set Broyard straight on the issues when the need arose. Broyard could be mischievous, and he could be tendentious. It did not escape notice that he was consistently hostile to feminist writers. "Perhaps it's naïve of me to expect people to write reasonable books about emotionally charged subjects," one such review began, irritably. "But when you have to read and review two or three books each week, you do get tired of 'understanding' so much personal bias. You reach a point where it no longer matters that the author's mistakes are well meant. You don't care that he or she is on the side of the angels: you just want them to tell the truth."

Nor did relations between the two daily reviewers ever become altogether cordial. Lehmann-Haupt tells of a time in 1974 when Broyard said that he was sick and couldn't deliver a review. Lehmann-Haupt had to write an extra review in less than a day, so that he could get to the Ali-Frazier fight the next night, where he had ringside seats. Later, when they discussed the match, Broyard seemed suspiciously knowledgeable about its particulars; he claimed that a friend of his had been invited by a television executive to watch it on closed-circuit TV. "I waited about six months, because one of the charming things about Anatole was that he never remembered his lies," Lehmann-Haupt says, laughing. "And I said, 'Did you see that fight?' And he said, 'Oh, yeah—I was there as a guest of this television executive.' That's why he couldn't write the review!"


Broyard had been teaching off and on at the New School since the late fifties, and now his reputation as a writing teacher began to soar. Certainly his fluent prose style, with its combination of grace and clarity, was a considerable recommendation. He was charismatic and magisterial, and, because he was sometimes brutal about students' work, they found it all the more gratifying when he was complimentary. Among his students were Paul Breslow, Robert Olen Butler, Daphne Merkin, and Hilma Wolitzer. Ellen Schwamm, who took a workshop with him in the early seventies, says, "He had a gourmet's taste for literature and for language, and he was really able to convey that: it was a very sensual experience."

These were years of heady success and, at the same time, of a rising sense of failure. An arbiter of American writing, Broyard was racked by his inability to write his own magnum opus. In the fifties, the Atlantic Monthly Press had contracted for an autobiographical novel—the novel that was supposed to secure Broyard's fame, his place in contemporary literature—but, all these years later, he had made no progress. It wasn't for lack of trying. Lehmann-Haupt recalls his taking a lengthy vacation in order to get the book written. "I remember talking to him—he was up in Vermont, where somebody had lent him a house—and he was in agony. He banished himself from the Vineyard, was clearly suffering, and he just couldn't do it." John Updike, who knew Broyard slightly from the Vineyard, was reminded of the anticipation surrounding Ellison's second novel: "The most famous non-book around was the one that Broyard was not writing." (The two non-book writers were in fact quite friendly: Broyard admired Ellison not only as a writer but as a dancer—a high tribute from such an adept as Broyard.)

Surrounded by analysts and psychotherapists—Sandy Broyard had become a therapist herself by this time—Broyard had no shortage of explanations for his inability to write his book. "He did have a total writer's block," van den Haag says, "and he was analyzed by various persons, but it didn't fully overcome the writer's block. I couldn't prevent him from going back to 'The Cystoscope' and trying to improve it. He made it, of course, not better but worse." Broyard's fluency as an essayist and a reviewer wasn't quite compensation. Charles Simmons says, "He had produced all this charming criticism, but the one thing that mattered to him was the one thing he hadn't managed to do."

As the seventies wore on, Miller discussed the matter of blockage with his best friend in relatively abstract terms: he suggested that there might be something in Broyard's relationship to his family background that was holding him back. In the eighties, he referred Broyard to his own chief mentor in gestalt therapy, Isador From, and From became perhaps Broyard's most important therapist in his later years. "In gestalt therapy, we talk a lot about 'unfinished business': anything that's incomplete, unfinished, haunts the whole personality and tends, at some level, to create inhibition or blockage," Miller says. "You're stuck there at a certain point. It's like living with a partly full bladder all your life."

Some people speculated that the reason Broyard couldn't write his novel was that he was living it—that race loomed larger in his life because it was unacknowledged, that he couldn't put it behind him because he had put it beneath him. If he had been a different sort of writer, it might not have mattered so much. But Merkin points out, "Anatole's subject, even in fiction, was essentially himself. I think that ultimately he would have had to deal with more than he wanted to deal with."

Broyard may have been the picture of serene self-mastery, but there was one subject that could reliably fluster him. Gordon Lish recalls an occasion in the mid-seventies when Burt Britton (who was married to a black woman) alluded to Anatole's racial ancestry. Lish says, "Anatole became inflamed, and he left the room. He snapped, like a dog snapping—he *barked* at Britton. It was an ugly moment." To people who knew nothing about the matter, Broyard's sensitivities were at times simply perplexing. The critic Judith Dunford used to go to lunch with Broyard in the eighties. One day, Broyard mentioned his sister Shirley, and Dunford, idly making conversation, asked him what she looked like. Suddenly, she saw an extremely worried expression on his face. Very carefully, he replied, "Darker than me."

There was, finally, no sanctuary. "When the children were older, I began, every eighteen months or so, to bring up the issue of how they needed to know at some point," Sandy Broyard says. "And then he would totally shut down and go into a rage. He'd say that at some point he would tell them, but he would not tell them now." He was the Scheherazade of racial imposture, seeking and securing one deferral after another. It must have made things not easier but harder. In the modern era, children are supposed to come out to their parents: it works better that way around. For children, we know, can judge their parents harshly—above all, for what they understand as failures of candor. His children would see the world in terms of authenticity; he saw the world in terms of self-creation. Would they think that he had made a Faustian bargain? Would they speculate about what else he had not told them—about the limits of self-invention? Broyard's resistance is not hard to fathom. He must have wondered when the past would learn its place, and stay past.

Anatole Broyard had confessed enough in his time to know that confession did nothing for the soul. He preferred to communicate his truths on higher frequencies. As if in exorcism, Broyard's personal essays deal regularly with the necessary, guilt-ridden endeavor of escap-

ing family history: and yet the feelings involved are well-nigh universal. The thematic elements of passing—fragmentation, alienation, lim-
inality, self-fashioning—echo the great themes of modernism. As a
result, he could prepare the way for exposure without ever risking it.
Miller observes, "If you look at the writing closely enough, and listen
to the intonations, there's something there that is like no writer from
the completely white world. Freud talked about the repetition compulsion. With Anatole, it's interesting that he was constantly hiding it
and in some ways constantly revealing it."

Sandy speaks of these matters in calmly analytic tones; perhaps
because she is a therapist, her love is tempered by an almost professional dispassion. She says, "I think his own personal history continued to be painful to him," and she adds, "In passing, you cause your
family great anguish, but I also think, conversely, do we look at the anguish it causes the person who is passing? Or the anguish that it was
born out of?"

It may be tempting to describe Broyard's self-positioning as arising
from a tortured allegiance to some liberal-humanist creed. In fact, the
liberal pieties of the day were not much to his taste. "It wasn't about
an ideal of racelessness but something much more complex and interesting," Miller says. "He was actually quite anti-black," Evelyn Toynton says. She tells of a time when she was walking with him on a
street in New York and a drunken black man came up to him and
asked for a dollar. Broyard seethed. Afterward, he remarked to her, "I
look around New York, and I think to myself, If there were no blacks
in New York, would it really be any loss?"

No doubt this is a calculation that whites, even white liberals,
sometimes find themselves idly working out: How many black mug-
gers is one Thelonious Monk worth? How many Willie Hortons does
Gwendolyn Brooks redeem? In 1970, Ellison published his classic essay "What America Would Be Like Without Blacks," in *Time*; and one
reason it is a classic essay is that it addresses a question that lingers in
the American political unconscious. Commanding as Ellison's arguments are, there remains a whit of defensiveness in the very exercise.
It's a burdensome thing to refute a fantasy.

And a burdensome thing to be privy to it. Ellen Schwamm recalls that one of the houses Broyard had in Connecticut had a black jockey on the lawn, and that "he used to tell me that Jimmy Baldwin had said to him, 'I can't come and see you with this crap on your lawn.' " (Sandy remembers the lawn jockey—an antique—as having come with the house; she also recalls that it was stolen one day.) Charles Simmons says that the writer Herbert Gold, before introducing him to Broyard, warned him that Broyard was prone to make comments about "spades," and Broyard did make a few such comments. "He personally, on a deeper level, was not enamored of blacks," van den Haag says. "He avoided blacks. There is no question he did." Sandy is gingerly in alluding to this subject. "He was very short-tempered with the behavior of black people, the sort of behavior that was shown in the news. He had paid the price to be at liberty to say things that, if you didn't know he was black, you would misunderstand. I think it made him ironical."

Every once in a while, however, Broyard's irony would slacken, and he would speak of the thing with an unaccustomed and halting forthrightness. Toynton says that after they'd known each other for several years he told her there was a "C" (actually, "col," for "colored") on his birth certificate. "And then another time he told me that his sister was black and that she was married to a black man." The circumlocutions are striking: not that *he* was black but that his birth certificate was; not that *he* was black but that his family was. Perhaps this was a matter less of evasiveness than of precision.

"Some shrink had said to him that the reason he didn't like brown-haired women or dark women was that he was afraid of his own shit," Toynton continues. "And I said, 'Anatole, it's as plain as plain can be that it has to do with being black.' And he just stopped and said, 'You don't know what it was like. It was horrible.' He told me once that he didn't like to see his sisters, because they reminded him of his unhappy childhood." (Shirley's account suggests that this unhappy childhood may have had more to do with the child than with the hood.)

Ellen Schwamm remembers one occasion when Broyard visited her and Harold Brodkey at their apartment, and read them part of the memoir he was working on. She says that the passages seemed stilted and distant, and that Brodkey said to him, "You're not telling the truth, and if you try to write lies or evade the truth this is what you get. What's the real story?" She says, "Anatole took a deep breath and said, 'The real story is that I'm not who I seem. I'm a black.' I said, 'Well, Anatole, it's no great shock, because this rumor has been around for years and years and years, and everyone assumes there's a small percentage of you that's black, if that's what you're trying to say.' And he said, 'No, that's not what I'm trying to say. My father could pass, but in fact my mother's black, too. We're black as far back as I know.' We never said a word of it to anybody, because he asked us not to.'"

Schwamm also says that she begged him to write about his history: it seemed to her excellent material for a book. But he explained that he didn't want notoriety based on his race—on his revealing himself to be black—rather than on his talent. As Toynton puts it, Broyard felt that he had to make a choice between being an aesthete and being a Negro. "He felt that once he said, 'I'm a Negro writer,' he would have to write about black issues, and Anatole was such an aesthete."

All the same, Schwamm was impressed by a paradox: the man wanted to be appreciated not for being black but for being a writer, even though his pretending not to be black was stopping him from writing. It was one of the very few ironies that Broyard, the master ironist, was ill equipped to appreciate.


Besides, there was always his day job to attend to. Broyard might suffer through a midnight of the soul in Vermont; but he was also a working journalist, and when it came to filing his copy he nearly always met his deadlines. In the late seventies, he also began publishing brief personal essays in the *Times*. They are among the finest work he did—easeful, witty, perfectly poised between surface and depth. In them he perfected the feat of being self-revelatory without revealing anything. He wrote about his current life, in Connecticut: "People in New York City have psychotherapists, and people in the suburbs have handymen. While anxiety in the city is existential, in the country it is structural." And he wrote about his earlier life, in the city: "There was a kind of jazz in my father's movements, a rhythm compounded of economy and flourishes, functional and decorative. He had a blues song in his blood, a wistful jauntiness he brought with him from New Orleans." (Wistful, and even worrisome: "I half-expected him to break into the Camel Walk, the Shimmy Shewobble, the Black Bottom or the Mess Around.") In a 1979 essay he wrote about how much he dreaded family excursions:

> To me, they were like a suicide pact. Didn't my parents know that the world was just waiting for a chance to come between us?
> Inside, we were a family, but outside we were immigrants, bizarre in our differences. I thought that people stared at us, and my face grew hot. At any moment, I expected my father and mother to expose their tribal rites, their eccentric anthropology, to the gape of strangers.
> Anyone who saw me with my family knew too much about me.

These were the themes he returned to in many of his personal essays, seemingly marking out the threshold he would not cross. And if some of his colleagues at the *Times* knew too much about him, or had heard the rumors, they wouldn't have dreamed of saying anything. Abe Rosenthal (who did know about him) says that the subject never arose. "What was there to talk about? I didn't really consider it my business. I didn't think it was proper or polite, nor did I want him to think I was prejudiced, or anything."

But most people knew nothing about it. C. Gerald Fraser, a reporter and an editor at the *Times* from 1967 until 1991, was friendly with Broyard's brother-in-law Ambassador Franklin Williams. Fraser, who is black, recalls that one day Williams asked him how many black journalists there were at the *Times*. "I listed them," he says, "and he said, 'You forgot one.' I went over the list again, and I said, 'What do you mean?' He said, 'Shirley's brother, Anatole Broyard.' I was dumbstruck, because I'd never heard it mentioned at the *Times* that he was black, or that the paper had a black critic."

In any event, Broyard's colleagues did not have to know what he was to have reservations about *who* he was. He cultivated his image as a trickster—someone who would bend the rules, finesse the system—and that image only intensified his detractors' ire. "A good book review is an act of seduction, and when he did it there was nobody better," John Leonard says, but he feels that Broyard's best was not always offered. "I considered him to be one of the laziest book reviewers to come down the pike." Soon a running joke was that Broyard would review only novels shorter than two hundred pages. In the introduction to "Aroused by Books," a collection of the reviews he published in the early seventies, Broyard wrote that he tried to choose books for review that were "closest to [his] feelings." Lehmann-Haupt says dryly, "We began to suspect that he often picked the books according to the attractiveness of the young female novelists who had written them." Rosenthal had shamed him for voicing his disquiet about Broyard's reputation as a Don Juan, but before long Rosenthal himself changed his tune. "Maybe five or six years later," Lehmann-Haupt recalls, "Rosenthal comes up to me, jabbing me in the chest with a stiffened index finger and saying, 'The trouble with Broyard is that he writes with his cock!' I bit my tongue."

Gradually, a measure of discontent with Broyard's reviews began to make itself felt among the paper's cultural commissars. Harvey Shapiro, the editor of the *Book Review* from 1975 to 1983, recalls conversations with Rosenthal in which "he would tell me that all his friends hated Anatole's essays, and I would tell him that all my friends loved Anatole's essays, and that would be the end of the conversation." In 1984, Broyard was removed from the daily *Times* and given a column in the *Book Review*.

Mitchel Levitas, the editor of the *Book Review* from 1983 to 1989, edited Broyard's column himself. He says, "It was a tough time for him, you see, because he had come off the daily book review, where he was out there in the public eye twice a week. That was a major change in his public role." In addition to writing his column, he was put to work as an editor at the *Book Review*. The office environment was perhaps not altogether congenial to a man of his temperament. Kazin recalls, "He complained to me constantly about being on the *Book Review*, because he had to check people's quotations and such. I think he thought that he was superior to the job."

Then, too, it was an era in which the very notion of passing was beginning to seem less plangent than preposterous. Certainly Broyard's skittishness around the subject wasn't to everyone's liking. Brent Staples, who is black, was an editor at the *Book Review* at the time Broyard was there. "Anatole had it both ways," Staples says. "He would give you a kind of burlesque wink that seemed to indicate he was ready to accept the fact of your knowing that he was a black person. It was a real ambiguity, tacit and sort of recessed. He jived around and played with it a lot, but never made it express the fact that he was black." It was a game that tried Staples' patience. "When Anatole came anywhere near me, for example, his whole style, demeanor, and tone would change," he recalls. "I took that as him conveying to me, 'Yes, I am like you. But I'm relating this to you on a kind of recondite channel.' Over all, it made me angry. Here was a guy who was, for a long period of time, probably one of the two or three most important critical voices on literature in the United States. How could you, actively or passively, have this fact hidden?"

Staples pauses, then says, "You know, he turned it into a joke. And when you change something basic about yourself into a joke, it spreads, it metastasizes, and so his whole presentation of self became completely ironic. *Everything* about him was ironic."

There were some people who came to have a professional interest in achieving a measure of clarity on the topic. Not long before Broyard retired from the *Times,* in 1989, Daphne Merkin, as an editor at Harcourt Brace Jovanovich, gave him an advance of a hundred thousand dollars for his memoirs. (The completed portion was ultimately published, as "Kafka Was the Rage," by Crown.) Merkin learned that "he was, in some ways, opaque to himself," and her disquiet grew when the early chapters arrived. "I said, 'Anatole, there's something odd here. Within the memoir, you have your family moving to a black neighborhood in Brooklyn. I find that strange—unless they're black.' I said, 'You can do many things if you're writing a memoir. But if you squelch stuff that seems to be crucial about you, and pretend it doesn't exist . . .'" She observes that he was much attached to aspects of his childhood, but "in a clouded way."

When Broyard retired from the *Times,* he was nearly sixty-nine. To Sandy, it was a source of some anguish that their children still did not know the truth about him. Yet what was that truth? Broyard was a critic—a critic who specialized in European and American fiction. And what was race but a European and American fiction? If he was passing for white, perhaps he understood that the alternative was passing for black. "But if some people are light enough to live like white, mother, why should there be such a fuss?" a girl asks her mother in "Near-White," a 1931 story by the Harlem Renaissance author Claude McKay. "Why should they live colored when they could be happier living white?" Why, indeed? One could concede that the passing of Anatole Broyard involved dishonesty; but is it so very clear that the dishonesty was mostly Broyard's?

To pass is to sin against authenticity, and "authenticity" is among the founding lies of the modern age. The philosopher Charles Taylor summarizes its ideology thus: "There is a certain way of being human that is *my* way. I am called upon to live my life in this way, and not in imitation of anyone else's life. But this notion gives a new importance to being true to myself. If I am not, I miss the point of my life; I miss what being human is for *me*." And the Romantic fallacy of authenticity is only compounded when it is collectivized: when the putative real me gives way to the real us. You can say that Anatole Broyard was (by any juridical reckoning) "really" a Negro, without conceding that a Negro is a thing you can really be. The vagaries of racial identity were increased by what anthropologists call the rule of "hypodescent"—the one-drop rule. When those of mixed ancestry—and the majority of blacks are of mixed ancestry—disappear into the white majority, they are traditionally accused of running from their "blackness." Yet why isn't the alternative a matter of running from their "whiteness"? To emphasize these perversities, however, is a distraction from a larger perversity. You can't get race "right" by refining the boundary conditions.

The act of razoring out your contributor's note may be quixotic, but it is not mad. The mistake is to assume that birth certificates and biographical sketches and all the other documents generated by the modern bureaucratic state reveal an anterior truth—that they are merely signs of an independently existing identity. But in fact they constitute it. The social meaning of race is established by these identity papers—by tracts and treatises and certificates and pamphlets and all the other verbal artifacts that proclaim race to be real and, by that proclamation, make it so.

So here is a man who passed for white because he wanted to be a writer, and he did not want to be a Negro writer. It is a crass disjunction, but it is not his crassness or his disjunction. His perception was perfectly correct. He *would* have had to be a Negro writer, which was something he did not want to be. In his terms, he did not want to write about black love, black passion, black suffering, black joy; he wanted to write about love and passion and suffering and joy. We give lip service to the idea of the writer who happens to be black, but had anyone, in the postwar era, ever seen such a thing?

Broyard's friend Richard A. Shweder, an anthropologist and a theorist of culture, says, "I think he believed that reality is constituted by style," and ascribes to Broyard a "deeply romantic view of the intimate connection between style and reality." Broyard passed not because he thought that race wasn't important but because he knew that it was. The durable social facts of race were beyond reason, and, like Paul Broyard's furniture, their strength came at the expense of style. Anatole Broyard lived in a world where race had, indeed, become a trope for indelibility, for permanence. "All I *have* to do," a black folk saying has it, "is stay black and die."

Broyard was a connoisseur of the liminal—of crossing over and, in the familiar phrase, getting over. But the ideologies of modernity have a kicker, which is that they permit no exit. Racial refusal is a forlorn hope. In a system where whiteness is the default, racelessness is never a possibility. You cannot opt out; you can only opt in. In a scathing review of a now forgotten black author, Broyard announced that it was time to reconsider the assumption of many black writers that " 'whitey' will never let you forget you're black." For his part, he wasn't taking any chances. At a certain point, he seems to have decided that all he had to do was stay white and die.

In 1989, Broyard resolved that he and his wife would change their life once more. With both their children grown, they could do what they pleased. And what they pleased—what he pleased, anyway—was to move to Cambridge, Massachusetts. They would be near Harvard, and so part of an intellectual community. He had a vision of walking through Harvard Square, bumping into people like the sociologist Daniel Bell, and having conversations about ideas in the street. Besides, his close friend Michael Miller was living in the area. Anne Bernays, also a Cambridge resident, says, "I remember his calling several times and asking me about neighborhoods. It was important for him to get that right. I think he was a little disappointed when he moved that it wasn't to a fancy neighborhood like Brattle or Channing Street. He was on Wendell Street, where there's a tennis court across the street and an apartment building and the houses are fairly close to-gether." It wasn't a matter of passing so much as of positioning.

Sandy says that they had another the-children-must-be-told con-versation shortly before the move. "We were driving to Michael's fiftieth-birthday party—I used to plan to bring up the subject in a place where he couldn't walk out. I brought it up then because at that point our son was out of college and our daughter had just graduated, and my feeling was that they just absolutely needed to know, as adults." She pauses. "And we had words. He would just bring down this gate." Sandy surmises, again, that he may have wanted to protect them from what he had experienced as a child. "Also," she says, "I think he needed still to protect himself." The day after they moved into their house on Wendell Street, Broyard learned that he had prostate cancer, and that it was inoperable.


Broyard spent much of the time before his death, fourteen months later, making a study of the literature of illness and death, and pub-lishing a number of essays on the subject. Despite the occasion, they were imbued with an almost dandyish, even jokey sense of incon-gruity: "My urologist, who is quite famous, wanted to cut off my testi-cles. . . . Speaking as a surgeon, he said that it was the surest, quickest, neatest solution. Too neat, I said, picturing myself with no balls. I knew that such a solution would depress me, and I was sure that depression is bad medicine." He had attracted notice in 1954 with the account of his father's death from a similar cancer; now he recharged his writing career as a chronicler of his own progress toward death. He thought about calling his collection of writings on the sub-ject "Critically Ill." It was a pun he delighted in.

Soon after the diagnosis was made, he was told that he might have "in the neighborhood of years." Eight months later, it became clear that this prognosis was too optimistic. Richard Shweder, the anthro-pologist, talks about a trip to France that he and his wife made with Anatole and Sandy not long before Anatole's death. One day, the two men were left alone. Shweder says, "And what did he want to do? He wanted to throw a ball. The two of us just played catch, back and forth." The moment, he believes, captures Broyard's athleticism, his love of physical grace.

Broyard spent the last five weeks of his life at the Dana Farber Cancer Institute, in Boston. In therapy sessions, the need to set things straight before the end had come up again—the need to deal with unfinished business and, most of all, with his secret. He appeared willing, if reluctant, to do so. But by now he was in almost constant pain, and the two children lived in different places, so the opportunities to have the discussion as a family were limited. "Anatole was in such physical pain that I don't think he had the wherewithal," Sandy says. "So he missed the opportunity to tell the children himself." She speaks of the expense of spirit, of psychic energy, that would have been required. The challenge would have been to explain why it had remained a secret. And no doubt the old anxieties were not easily dispelled: would it have been condemned as a Faustian bargain or understood as a case of personality overspilling, or rebelling against, the reign of category?

It pains Sandy even now that the children never had the chance to have an open discussion with their father. In the event, she felt that they needed to know before he died, and, for the first time, she took it upon herself to declare what her husband could not. It was an early afternoon, ten days before his death, when she sat down with her two children on a patch of grass across the street from the institute. "They knew there was a family secret, and they wanted to know what their father had to tell them. And I told them."

The stillness of the afternoon was undisturbed. She says carefully, "Their first reaction was relief that it was only this, and not an event or circumstance of larger proportions. Only following their father's death did they begin to feel the loss of not having known. And of having to reformulate who it was that they understood their father—and themselves—to be."

At this stage of his illness, Anatole was moving in and out of lucidity, but in his room Sandy and the children talked with humor and irony about secrets and about this particular secret. Even if Anatole could not participate in the conversation, he could at least listen to it. "The nurses said that hearing was the last sense to go," Sandy says.

It was not as she would have planned it. She says, gently, "Anatole always found his own way through things."

The writer Leslie Garis, a friend of the Broyards' from Connecticut, was in Broyard's room during the last weekend of September,

1990, and recorded much of what he said on his last day of something like sentience. He weighed perhaps seventy pounds, she guessed, and she describes his jaundice-clouded eyes as having the permanently startled look born of emaciation. He was partly lucid, mostly not. There are glimpses of his usual wit, but in a mode more aleatoric than logical. He spoke of Robert Graves, of Sheri Martinelli, of John Hawkes interpreting Miles Davis. He told Sandy that he needed to find a place to go where he could "protect his irony." As if, having been protected by irony throughout his life, it was now time to return the favor.

"I think friends are coming, so I think we ought to order some food," he announced hours before he lapsed into his final coma. "We'll want cheese and crackers, and Faust."

"Faust?" Sandy asked.

Anatole explained, "He's the kind of guy who makes the Faustian bargain, and who can be happy only when the thing is revealed."


A memorial service, held at a Congregationalist church in Connecticut, featured august figures from literary New York, colleagues from the *Times*, and neighbors and friends from the Village and the Vineyard. Charles Simmons told me that he was surprised at how hard he took Broyard's death. "You felt that you were going to have him forever, the way you feel about your own child," he said. "There was something wrong about his dying, and that was the reason." Speaking of the memorial service, he says, marvelling, "You think that you're the close friend, you know? And then I realized that there were twenty people ahead of me. And that his genius was for close friends."

Indeed, six years after Broyard's death many of his friends seem to be still mourning his loss. For them he was plainly a vital principle, a dancer and romancer, a seducer of men and women. (He considered seduction, he wrote, "the most heartfelt literature of the self.") Sandy tells me, simply, "You felt more alive in his presence," and I've heard almost precisely the same words from a great many others. They felt that he lived more intensely than other men. They loved him—perhaps his male friends especially, or, anyway, more volubly—and they admired him. They speak of a limber beauty, of agelessness, of a radiance. They also speak of his excesses and his penchant for poses. Perhaps, as the bard has it, Broyard was "much more the better for being a little bad."

And if his presence in American fiction was pretty much limited to other people's novels, that is no small tribute to his personal vibrancy. You find him reflected and refracted in the books of his peers, like Anne Bernays (she says there is a Broyard character in every novel she's written) and Brossard and Gaddis, of course, but also in those of his students. His own great gift was as a feuilletonist. The personal essays collected in "Men, Women and Other Anticlimaxes" can put you in mind of "The Autocrat of the Breakfast-Table," by Oliver Wendell Holmes, Sr. They are brief impromptus, tonally flawless. To read them is to feel that you are in the company of someone who is thinking things through. The essays are often urbane and sophisticated, but not unbearably so, and they can be unexpectedly moving. Literary culture still fetishizes the novel, and there he was perhaps out of step with his times. Sandy says, "In the seventies and eighties, the trend, in literature and film, was to get sparer, and the flourish of Anatole's voice was dependent on the luxuriance of his language." Richard Shweder says, "It does seem that Anatole's strength was the brief, witty remark. It was aphoristic. It was the critical review. He was brilliant in a thousand or two thousand words." Perhaps he wasn't destined to be a novelist, but what of it? Broyard was a Negro who wanted to be something other than a Negro, a critic who wanted to be something other than a critic. Broyard, you might say, wanted to be something other than Broyard. He very nearly succeeded.

Shirley Broyard Williams came to his memorial service, and many of his friends—including Alfred Kazin, who delivered one of the eulogies—remember being puzzled and then astonished as they realized that Anatole Broyard was black. For Todd and Bliss, however, meeting Aunt Shirley was, at last, a flesh-and-blood confirmation of what they had been told. Shirley is sorry that they didn't meet sooner, and she remains baffled about her brother's decision. But she isn't bitter about it; her attitude is that she has had a full and eventful life of her own—husband, kids, friends—and that if her brother wanted to keep himself aloof she respected his decision. She describes the conversations they had when they did speak: "They always had to be focussed on

something, like a movie, because you couldn't afford to be very intimate. There had to be something that would get in the way of the intimacy." And when she phoned him during his illness it was the same
way. "He never gave that up," she says, sounding more wistful than re-
proachful. "He never learned how to be comfortable with me." So it
has been a trying set of circumstances all around. "The hypocrisy that
surrounds this issue is so thick you could chew it," Shirley says
wearily.

Shirley's husband died several months before Anatole, and I think
she must have found it cheering to be able to meet family members
who had been sequestered from her. She says that she wants to get to
know her nephew and her niece—that there's a lot of time to make
up. "I've been encouraging Bliss to come and talk, and we had lunch,
and she calls me on the phone. She's really responded very well. Considering that it's sort of last-minute."

Years earlier, in an essay entitled "Growing Up Irrational," Anatole
Broyard wrote, "I *descended* from my mother and father. I was *extracted*
from them." His parents were "a conspiracy, a plot against society," as
he saw it, but also a source of profound embarrassment. "Like every
great tradition, my family had to die before I could understand how
much I missed them and what they meant to me. When they went into
the flames at the crematorium, all my letters of introduction went with
them." Now that he had a wife and family of his own, he had started to
worry about whether his children's feelings about him would reprise his
feelings about his parents: "Am I an embarrassment to them, or an accepted part of the human comedy? Have they joined my conspiracy, or
are they just pretending? Do they understand that, after all those years
of running away from home, I am still trying to get back?"

# ALLEN GINSBERG

ALLEN GINSBERG (1926–1997) found his calling as a poet
after he moved to San Francisco from New York City in 1954
and created "Howl for Carl Solomon" the following year. In

Ginsberg's letter to his California friend John Allen Ryan on September 9, 1955, written shortly after Ginsberg had moved to a cottage at 1624 Milvia Street in Berkeley, he described his plans for a poetry reading at the 6 Gallery. Before Ryan left for Mexico, he had been active in the art world of San Francisco, forming the Progressive Art Workers group with the artists Wally Hedrick, David Simpson, Hayward King, Deborah Remington, and Paula Webb, who all, according to Rebecca Solnit in *Secret Exhibition: Six California Artists of the Cold War Era* (1990), had "leftist leanings and avant-garde aspirations." Ryan had also been one of the six artists and poets—with Jack Spicer, Hedrick, Simpson, King, and Remington—who founded the 6 Gallery in San Francisco, which opened in September 1954.

Shortly after the repeat performance of the "6 Poets at 6 Gallery" reading in Berkeley, while at his job loading baggage onto Greyhound buses in Oakland on May 18, 1956, Ginsberg wrote a letter to the poet Richard Eberhart, whom he had met at the Berkeley reading. Eberhart, a fifty-one-year-old traditional writer, had been commissioned by *The New York Times* for an article about the San Francisco poetry scene, which appeared in September 1956. In his article Eberhart began by stating that "the West Coast is the liveliest spot in the country in poetry today. It is only here that there is a radical group movement of young poets." Acknowledging that "poetry here has become a tangible social force, moving and unifying its auditors, releasing the energies of the audience through spoken, even shouted verse, in a way at present unique to this region," Eberhart offered guarded praise for Ginsberg's "Howl for Carl Solomon" as "the most remarkable poem of the young group."

> My first reaction was that it is based on destructive violence. It is profoundly Jewish in temper. It is Biblical in its repetitive grammatical build-up. It is a howl against everything in our mechanistic civilization which kills the spirit, assuming that the louder you shout the more likely you are to be heard. Its positive force and energy come from a redemptive quality of love, although it destructively catalogues evils of our time from physical deprivation to madness.

In 1975 Eberhart recalled that he had been delighted to get Ginsberg's long letter twenty years before, impressed "at his meticulous approach to his work." In Eberhart's career as an instructor of poetry, he would "every now and then" read Ginsberg's letter to his classes: "It always stimulated students, made them think, opened their minds to heady discussions." In 1975, when Ginsberg wrote an explanation of his letter, he added that "what I didn't say to Eberhart" was that " 'Howl' is really about my mother, in her last year at Pilgrim State Hospital—acceptance of her, later described in 'Kaddish' detail." And that most readers of "Howl" (including Eberhart) missed "the element of parody and humor in characterization of certain nutty cases alluded to" in the first part of the poem. With hindsight Ginsberg also explained that he had an ulterior motive in writing his letter to Eberhart: "The campaign of vilification and denigration that the first 'Beat' texts met—interpreted from *Partisan Review* thru *Time* and even in FBI files as incomprehensible anti-social wild-eyed hate-filled irrational rebellious protest—was what I was foreseeing and trying to avoid as politely and straightforwardly as possible."

Ginsberg's essay "Poetry, Violence, and the Trembling Lambs" first appeared in the *San Francisco Chronicle*, "This World" section, on July 26, 1959.

## Letter to John Allen Ryan

Sept 9 [1955] Berkeley

Dear Johnny:

Your letter September Something received, and also your previous one, and the poems, and I think one of mine crossed in the mails; and I also wrote Univac (no relation to Kerouac) (latter a Breton name) you would be in D.F. [Mexico City]; I hope you did meet; and that you were not too much of a cool Zen & that he was not too much of a mahayana sourpuss; and that Garver put you on one way or another.

I got the mss. back thanks. And one day I ran into McClure too—his address is 3077 Sacramento Street SF Cal and his phone No. if you feel like phoning him is Walnut 1-8064.

[Wally] Hendrix asked me if I wanted to organize a poetry reading at the Six, and I didnt several months ago, not knowing of any poetry around worth hearing, but changed my fucking mind, & so you will be glad to know the tradition continues with a Gala evening sometime in a month or so or shorter, the program being Rexroth as introducer, McClure reading new poems (he thinks, it's partly true, he's found his own natural voice—it sounds a little tightassed to me, but he is writing well and that's maybe the way god built him), Lamantia putting in an appearance to read John Hoffman's work (which I havent really seen for years, if it isn't poetry it'll be a great social occasion), myself to read a long poem the first scrap of which I sent to Kerouac, you might look at it if you see him again I dont have a copy or I'd send you a piece (it's more or less up the alley of your SF recollections in tranquillity [sic]), and a bearded interesting Berkeley cat name of Snyder, I met him yesterday (via Rexroth suggestion) who is studying oriental and leaving in a few months on some privately put up funds to go be a Zen monk (a real one). He's a head, peyotlist, laconist, but warmhearted, nice looking with a little beard, thin, blond, rides a bicycle [sic] in berkeley in red corderoy & levis & hungup on indians (ex anthropology student from some indian hometown) and writes well, his sideline besides zen which is apparently calm scholarly & serious with him. Interesting person. If anybody else turns up along the way to read we may add somebody else. When Kerouac gets to SF probably I'll try set up another program, Myself, Jack & Neal Cassady (whom you didnt know in SF?). You might send this bit of 6 gossip to [Jack] Spicer, he'll probably be pleased that something is being done to continue there. And you might send me any advice on organizing these readings that you can remember from previous experience.

Yes I'm studying literature at Berkeley, I may be able to make a selfsupporting proposition via some kind of sinacure [sic] in 6 months, according to what vague promises I've wheedled out of [Josephine] Miles, [Mark] Shorer & a nice one named [Thomas] Parkinson, ex SF Anarchist now Eng. Prof. here. I'll be working scholarly like on prosody problems.

I have a house here for 35 a month, backyard cottage & private backyard, quite big, filled with vegetables & flowers, ideal Camden Whitman cottage, I write a lot, depression, solitude, last night a rare half hour of a kind of animistic ecstasy & weeping in garden, the vines with leaves turned top up in the night as they were left during the hours of day when the gracious sun rayed on them, the father is merciful; I had a vision of that as I havent had in maybe 7 years; a relief, a drop of sweetness. I did some writing & it looks like Chrs. Smart. Tell Jack if you see him; but well I'll write.

I dont know what Woods will do, havent seen him, will find out & inform you. I still have wooden Joe's music. Peter still looking around in SF, for a place.

Love, as ever
Allen

## A *Letter to Eberhart*

[May 18, 1956]
Berkeley

Dear Mr Eberhart:

Kenneth Rexroth tells me you are writing an article on S.F. poetry and asked for a copy of my MSS. I'll send it.

It occurred to me with alarm how really horrible generalizations might be if they are off-the-point as in newspapers.

I sat listening sans objection in the car while you told me what you'd said in Berkeley. I was flattered and egotistically hypnotized by the idea of recognition but really didn't agree with your evaluation of my own poetry. Before you say anything in the *Times* let me have my say.

1) The general "problem" is positive and negative "values." "You don't tell me how to live," "you deal with the negative or horrible well but have no positive program" etc.

This is as absurd as it sounds.

It would be impossible to write a powerful emotional poem

without a firm grasp on "value" not as an intellectual ideal but as an emotional reality.

You heard or saw *Howl* as a negative howl of protest.

The title notwithstanding, the poem itself is an act of sympathy, not rejection. In it I am leaping *out* of a preconceived notion of social "values," following my own heart's instincts—*allowing* myself to follow my own heart's instincts, overturning any notion of propriety, moral "value," superficial "maturity," Trilling-esque sense of "civilization"; and exposing my true feelings—of sympathy and indentification with the rejected, mystical, individual even "mad."

I am saying that what seems "mad" in America is our expression of natural ecstasy (as in Crane, Whitman) which suppressed, finds no social form organization background frame of reference or rapport or validation from the outside and so the "patient" gets confused thinks he is mad and really goes off rocker. I am paying homage to mystical mysteries in the forms in which they actually occur here in the U.S. in our environment.

I have taken a leap of detachment from the Artificial preoccupations and preconceptions of what is acceptable and normal and given my yea to the specific type of madness listed in the Who section.

The leap in the imagination—it is safe to do in a poem.

A leap to actual living sanctity is not impossible, but requires more time for me.

I used to think I was mad to want to be a saint, but now what have I got to fear? People's opinions? Loss of a teaching job? I am living outside this context. I make my own sanctity. How else? Suffering and humility are forced on my otherwise wild ego by lugging baggage in Greyhound.

I started as a fair-haired boy in academic Columbia.

I have discovered a great deal of my own true nature and that individuality which is a value, the only social value that there can be in the Blake-worlds. I see it as a "social value."

I have told you how to live if I have wakened any emotion of compassion and realization of the beauty of souls in America, thru the poem.

What other value could a poem have—now, historically maybe?

I have released and confessed and communicated clearly my true feelings tho it might involve at first a painful leap of exhibition and fear that I would be rejected.

This is a value, an actual fact, not a mental formulation of some second-rate sociological-moral ideal which is meaningless and academic in the poetry of H——, etc.

*Howl* is the first discovery as far as *communication* of feeling and truth, that I made. It begins with a catalogue sympathetically and *humanely* describing excesses of feeling and idealization.

Moloch is the vision of the mechanical feelingless inhuman world we live in and accept—and the key line finally is "Moloch whom I abandon."

It ends with a litany of active acceptance of the suffering of soul of C. Solomon, saying in effect I am *still* your amigo tho you are in trouble and think yourself in a void, and the final strophe states the terms of the communication

"oh starry spangled shock of MERCY"

and mercy is a real thing and if that is not a value I don't know what is.

How mercy gets to exist where it comes from perhaps can be seen from the inner evidence and images of the poem—an act of self-realization, self-acceptance and the consequent and inevitable relaxation of protective anxiety and selfhood and the ability to see and love others in themselves as angels without stupid mental self deceiving moral categories selecting *who* it is safe to sympathize with and who is not safe.

See Dostoyevsky and Whitman.

This process is carried to a crystal form in the *Sunflower Sutra* which is a "dramatic" context for these thoughts.

"Unholy battered old thing O sunflower O my soul
I LOVED you then."

The effect is to release self and audience from a false and self-denying self-deprecating image of ourselves which makes us feel like smelly shits and not the angels which we most deeply are.

The vision we have of people and things outside us is obviously (see Freud) a reflection of our relation to our self.

It is perhaps possible to forgive another and love another only after you forgive and love yourself.

This is why Whitman is crucial in development of American psyche. He accepted himself and from that flowed acceptance of all things.

The *Sunflower Sutra* is an emotional release and exposition of this process.

Thus I fail to see why you characterize my work as destructive or negative. Only if you are thinking an out-moded dualistic puritanical academic theory ridden world of values can you fail to see I am talking about *realization* of love. LOVE.

The poems are religious and I meant them to be and the effect on audience is (surprising to me at first) a validation of this. It is like "I give the primeval sign" of Acceptance, as in Whitman.

The second point is technical. This point would be called in question only if you have not Faith. I mean it is beside the true point and irrelevant because the communication, the *sign* of communication if successfully made should begin and end by achieving the perfection of a mystical experience which you know all about.

I am also saying have faith that I am finally referring to the Real Thing and that I am trying to communicate it.

Why must you deny your senses?

But as to technique—[Ruth] Witt-Diamant said you were surprised I exhibited any interest in the "Line" etc.

What seems formless tho effective is really effective thru discovery or realization of rules and meanings of forms and experiments in them.

The "form" of the poem is an experiment. Experiment with uses of the catalogue, the ellipse, the long line, the litany, repetition, etc.

The latter parts of the first section set forth a "formal" esthetic derived in part incidentally from my master who is Cezanne.

The poem is really built like a brick shithouse.

This is the general ground plan—all an accident, organic, but quite symmetrical surprisingly. It grew (part III) out of a desire to build up rhythm using a fixed base to respond to and elongating the response still however containing it within the elastic of one breath or one big streak of thought.

As in all things a reliance on nature and spontaneity (as well as much experience writing and practicing to arrive at spontaneity which IS A CRAFT not a jerk-off mode, a craft in which near-perfection is basic too) has produced organic proportion in this case somewhat symmetrical (i.e. rationally apprehensible) proportion.

This is, however, vague generalization.

The Long Line I use came after 7 yrs. work with fixed iambic rhyme, and 4 yrs. work with Williams' short line free form—which as you must know has its own mad rules—indefinable tho they be at present—

The long line, the prose poem, the spontaneous sketch are XX century French forms which Academic versifiers despite their continental interests (in XIX century French "formal" forms, Baudelaire) have completely ignored. Why?

This form of writing is very popular in S.A. and is after all the most interesting thing happening in France.

Whitman
Apollinaire
Lorca

Are these people credited with no technical sense by fools who by repeating the iambic mouthings of their betters or the quasi-iambic of Eliot or the completely irrational (tho beautiful) myth of "clear lucid form" in Pound—who works basically by ear anyway and there isn't any clear mentally formulizable form in him anyway, no regular countable measure*—I'm

*An error here, as Pound attempted to approximate classical quantitative measure. (Allen Ginsberg, 1975)

straying—people who by repeating etc., are exhibiting no technical sensitivity at all but merely adeptness at using already formulated ideas—and *this* is historically no time for that—or even if it were who cares, I don't. I am interested in discovering what I do *not* know, in myself and in the ways of writing—an old point.

The long line—you need a good ear and an emotional ground-swell and technical and syntactical ease facility and a freedom "esprit" to deal with it and make of it anything significant. And you need something to say, i.e. clear realized feelings. Same as any free verse.

The lines are the result of long thought and experiment as to what unit constitutes *one speech-breath-thought*.

I have observed my mind
   "     "        "        "  speech

       1.) Drunk
       2.) Drugged
       3.) Sober
       4.) Sexy etc.

And have exercised it so I can speak *freely,* i.e. without self-conscious inhibited stoppings and censorships which latter factors are what destroy speech and thought rhythm.

We think and speak rhythmically all the time, each phrasing, piece of speech, metrically equivalent to what we have to say emotionally.

Given a mental release which is not mentally blocked, the breath of verbal intercourse will come with excellent rhythm, a rhythm which is perhaps unimprovable.

[Unimprovable as experiment in any case.

Each poem is an experiment

Revised as little as possible.

So (experiments) are many modern canvasses as you know. The sketch is a fine "Form."]

W.C. Williams has been observing speech rhythms for years trying to find a regular "measure"—

he's mistaken I think.

There is no measure which will make one speech the exact length of another, one line the exact length of another.

He has therefore seized on the phrase "relative measure" in his old age.

He is right but has not realized the implications of this in the long line.

Since each wave of speech-thought needs to be measured (we speak and perhaps think in waves)—or what I speak and think I have at any rate in *Howl* reduced to waves of relatively equally heavy weight—and set next to one another they are in a balance O.K.

The technique of writing both prose and poetry, the technical problem of the present day, is the problem of Transcription of the natural flow of the mind, the transcription of the melody of actual thought or speech.

I have leaned more toward capturing the inside-mind-thought rather than the verbalized speech. This distinction I make because most poets see the problem via Wordsworth as getting nearer to actual *speech*, verbal speech.

I have noticed that the unspoken visual-verbal flow inside the mind has great rhythm and have approached the problem of Strophe, Line and stanza and measure by listening and transcribing (to a great extent) the coherent mental flow. Taking *that* for the model for Form as Cezanne took Nature.

This is not surrealism—they made up an artificial literary imitation.

I transcribe from my ordinary thoughts—waiting for extra exciting or mystical moments or near mystical moments to transcribe.

This brings up problems of image, and transcription of mental flow gives helpful knowledge because we think in sort of surrealist (juxtaposed images) or haiku-like form.

A haiku as the 1910–20's imagists did *not* know, consists of 2 visual (or otherwise) images stripped down and juxtaposed—the charge of electricity created by these 2 poles being greater when there is a greater distance between them—as in Yeats' phrase "murderous innocence of the sea"—2 opposite poles reconciled in a flash of recognition.

The mind in its flow creates such fantastic ellipses thus the key phrase of method in *Howl* is "Hydrogen Jukebox" which tho quite senseless makes in context clear sense.

Throughout the poem you will see traces of transcription, at its best see the last line of *Sunflower Sutra,* "mad locomotive riverbank sunset frisco hilly tincan evening sitdown vision."

This is a curious but really quite logical development of Pound–Fenelossa–Chinese Written Character–imagist W.C. Williams' practice.

I don't see the metrics or metaphors as revolution, rather as logical development, given my own interests, experiences, etc. and time.

This (explanation) is all too literary as essentially my purpose has been to say what I actually feel (not what I want to feel or think I should feel or fit my feelings into a fake "Tradition" which is a *process* really not a fixed set of values and practices anyway—so anybody who wants to hang on to traditional metrics and values will wind up stultified and self-deceived anyway despite all the sincerity in the world). Everybody thinks they should learn academically from "experience" and have their souls put down and destroyed and this has been raised to the status of "value" but to me it seems just the usual old fake death, caused by fear and lack of real experience. I suffered too much under Professor T——, whom I love, but who is a poor mental fanatic after all and not a free soul— I'm straying.

2) *The poetry situation in S.F.*

The last wave was led by Robert Duncan, highly over-literary but basic recognition of the spontaneous free-form experiment. He left for Mallorca and contacted Robert Creeley, editor of *Black Mountain Review,* they came friends and Duncan who dug Williams, Stein, etc. especially the Black Mountain influence of Charles Olson who is the head peer of the East Coast bohemian hipster-authors post Pound. Olson's *Death of Europe* in *Origin* last year (about a suicide German boy)—"oh that the Earth/had to be given/to you/this way" is the first of his poems I've been able to read but it is a great breakthrough of feeling and a great modern poem I think.

Creeley his boy came here [San Francisco] last month and made contact with us—and next issue of *Black Mountain Review* will carry me, Whalen and:

1) William S. Burroughs, a novelist friend of mine in Tangier. Great Man.

2) Gary Snyder, a Zen Buddhist poet and Chinese Scholar 25 years old who leaves next week for further poetry study in a Zen monastery in Kyoto.

3) Jack Kerouac, who is out here and is the Colossus unknown of U.S. Prose who taught me to write and has written more and better than anybody of my generation that I've ever heard of. Kerouac you may have heard of but any review of the situation here would be ultimately historically meaningless without him since he is *the* unmistakable fertile prolific Shakespearean *genius*—lives in a shack in Mill Valley with Gary Snyder. Cowley (Malcolm) is trying to peddle him in N.Y.C. now* and can give you info. Kerouac invented and initiated my practice of speech-flow prosody.

I recount the above since anything you write will be irrelevant if you don't dig especially Kerouac—no shit, get info from Kenneth [Rexroth] or Louise Bogan who met him if you don't take my word.

The W.S. Burroughs above mentioned was Kerouac's and my mentor 1943–1950.

I have written this in the Greyhound between loading busses and will send it on uncensored.

I've said nothing about the extraordinary influence of Bop music on rhythm and drugs on the observation of rhythm and mental processes—not enough time and out of paper.

*Yours Allen Ginsberg*

---

* Cowley as editor at Viking was having difficulty persuading the management to publish *On the Road*. (Allen Ginsberg, 1975)

May 18 [1956]
I am off to the Arctic part of Alaska on a USMSTS resupply
ship for the DEW line radar installation. Mail for me will be
forwarded—A. Ginsberg c/o Phil Whalen, 1624 Milvia Street,
Berkeley, Cal. See you next Xmas.

*Allen*

*(The following pages were appended to Ginsberg's letter.)*

## Summary

### *I. Values*

1) *Howl* is an "affirmation" of individual experience of God, sex, drugs,
absurdity etc. Part I deals sympathetically with individual cases.
Part II describes and rejects the Moloch of society which con-
founds and suppresses individual experience and forces the individual to consider himself mad if he does not reject his own
deepest senses. Part III is an expression of sympathy and identification with C.S. [Carl Solomon] who is in the madhouse—saying
that his madness basically is rebellion against Moloch and I am
with him, and extending my hand in union. This is an affirmative
act of mercy and compassion, which are the basic emotions of the
poem. The criticism of society is that "Society" is merciless. The alternative is private, individual acts of mercy. The poem is one such.
It is therefore clearly and consciously built on a *liberation* of basic
human virtues.

To call it work of nihilistic rebellion would be to mistake it completely. Its force comes from positive "religious" belief and experience. It offers no "constructive" program in sociological terms—no
poem could. It does offer a constructive human value—basically
the *experience*—of the enlightment of mystical experience—without which no society can long exist.

2) *Supermarket in California* deals with Walt Whitman. Why?

He was the first great American poet to take action in recognizing his individuality, forgiving and accepting *Him Self,* and automatically extending that recognition and acceptance to all—and
defining his Democracy as that. He was unique and lonely in his
glory—the truth of his feelings—without which no society can long

exist. Without this truth there is only the impersonal Moloch and self-hatred of others.

Without self-acceptance there can be no acceptance of other souls.

3) *Sunflower Sutra* is crystallized "dramatic" moment of self-acceptance in modern terms.

"Unholy battered old thing, O sunflower O my soul, I *loved* you then!"

The realization of holy self-love is a rare "affirmative" value and cannot fail to have constructive influence in "Telling *you* (R.E.) [Richard Eberhart] how to live."

4) *America* is an unsystematic and rather gay exposition of my own private feelings contrary to the official dogmas, but really rather universal as far as private opinions about what I mention. It says—"I am thus and so I have a right to do so, and I'm saying it out loud for all to hear."

## II. Technique

A. These long lines or Strophes as I call them came spontaneously as a result of the kind of feelings I was trying to put down, and came as a surprise solution to a metrical problem that preoccupied me for a decade.

I have considerable experience writing both rhymed iambics and short line post-W.C.W. [William Carlos Williams] free verse.

*Howl*'s 3 parts consist of 3 different approaches to the use of the long line (longer than Whitman's, more French).

1. Repetition of the fixed base "Who" for a catalogue.
    A. building up consecutive rhythm from strophe to strophe.
    B. abandoning of fixed base "who" in certain lines but carrying weight and rhythm of strophic form continuously forward.
2. Break up of strophe into pieces within the strophe, thus having the strophe become a new usable form of stanza—Repetition of fixed base "Moloch" to provide cement for continuity. *Supermarket* uses strophe stanza and abandons need for fixed base. I was experimenting with the form.
3. Use of a fixed base, "I'm with you in Rockland," with a reply in which the strophe becomes a longer and longer streak of speech, in

order to build up a *relatively* equal nonetheless free and variable structure. Each reply strophe is longer than the previous. I have measured by ear and speech-breath, there being no other measure for such a thing. Each strophe consists of a set of phrases that can be spoken in one breath and each carries relatively equal rhetorical weight. Penultimate strophe is an exception and was meant to be—a series of cries—"O skinny legions run outside O starry spangled shock of mercy O victory etc." You will not fail to observe that the cries are all in definite rhythm.

The technical problem raised and partially solved is the breakthrough begun by Whitman but never carried forward, from both iambic stultification and literary automatism, and unrhythmical shortline verse, which does not yet offer any kind of *base* cyclical flow for the build up of a powerful rhythm. The long line seems for the moment to free speech for emotional expression and give it a measure to work with. I hope to experiment with short-line free verse with what I have learned from exercise in long.

B. Imagery—is a result of the *kind* of line and the kind of emotions and the kind of speech-and-interior flow-of-the-mind transcription I am doing—the imagery often consists of 1920's W.C.W. [Williams] imagistically observed detail collapsed together by interior associative logic—i.e., "hydrogen jukebox," Apollinaire, Whitman, Lorca. But *not* automatic surrealism. Knowledge of Haiku and ellipse is crucial.

## Poetry, Violence, and the Trembling Lambs

Recent history is the record of a vast conspiracy to impose one level of mechanical consciousness on mankind and exterminate all manifestations of that unique part of human sentience, identical in all men, which the individual shares with his Creator. The suppression of contemplative individuality is nearly complete.

The only immediate historical data that we can know and act on are those fed to our senses through systems of mass communication.

These media are exactly the places where the deepest and most personal sensitivities and confessions of reality are most prohibited, mocked, suppressed.

## National Subconscious

At the same time there is a crack in the mass consciousness of America—sudden emergence of insight into a vast national subconscious netherworld filled with nerve gases, universal death bombs, malevolent bureaucracies, secret police systems, drugs that open the door to God, ships leaving Earth, unknown chemical terrors, evil dreams at hand.

Because systems of mass communication can communicate only officially acceptable levels of reality, no one can know the extent of the secret unconscious life. No one in America can know what stereotypes of mass communication disapprove and deny the insight. The police and newspapers have moved in, mad movie manufacturers from Hollywood are at this moment preparing bestial stereotypes of the scene.

The poets and those who share their activities, or exhibit some sign of dress, hair, or demeanor of understanding, or hipness, are ridiculed. Those of us who have used certain benevolent drugs (marijuana) to alter our consciousness in order to gain insight are hunted down in the street by police. Peyote, an historic vision-producing agent, is prohibited on pain of arrest. Those who have used opiates and junk are threatened with permanent jail and death. To be a junky in America is like having been a Jew in Nazi Germany.

A huge sadistic police bureaucracy has risen in every state, encouraged by the central government, to persecute the illuminati, to brainwash the public with official lies about the drugs, and to terrify and destroy those addicts whose spiritual search has made them sick.

Deviants from the mass sexual stereotype, quietists, those who will not work for money, or fib and make arms for hire, or join armies in murder and threat, those who wish to loaf, think, rest in visions, act beautifully on their own, speak truthfully in public, inspired by Democracy—what is their psychic fate now in America? An America, the greater portion of whose economy is yoked to mental and mechanical preparations for war?

Literature expressing these insights has been mocked, misinterpreted, and suppressed by a horde of middlemen whose fearful allegiance to the organization of mass stereotype communication prevents them from sympathy (not only with their own inner nature but) with any manifestation of unconditioned individuality. I mean journalists, commercial publishers, book-review fellows, multitudes of professors of literature, etc., etc. Poetry is hated. Whole schools of academic criticism have risen to prove that human consciousness of unconditioned Spirit is a myth. A poetic renaissance glimpsed in San Francisco has been responded to with ugliness, anger, jealousy, vitriol, sullen protestations of superiority.

And violence. By police, by customs officials, post-office employees, by trustees of great universities. By anyone whose love of Power has led him to a position where he can push other people around over a difference of opinion—or Vision.

## Great Stakes

The stakes are too great—an America gone mad with materialism, a police-state America, a sexless and soulless America prepared to battle the world in defense of a false image of its Authority. Not the wild and beautiful America of the comrades of Whitman, not the historic America of Blake and Thoreau where the spiritual independence of each individual was an America, a universe, more huge and awesome than all the abstract bureaucracies and Authoritative Officialdoms of the World combined.

Only those who have entered the world of Spirit know what a vast laugh there is in the illusory appearance of worldly authority. And all men at one time or other enter that Spirit, whether in life or death.

## Trembling Lambs

How many hypocrites are there in America? How many trembling lambs, fearful of discovery? What Authority have we set up over ourselves, that we are not as we Are? Who shall prohibit an art from being published to the world? What conspirators have power to determine our mode of consciousness, our sexual enjoyments, our different labors and our loves? What fiends determine our wars?

When will we discover an America that will not deny its own God? Who takes up arms, money, police, and a million hands to murder the consciousness of God? Who spits in the beautiful face of Poetry which sings of the Glory of God and weeps in the dust of the world?

# JOHN CLELLON HOLMES

JOHN CLELLON HOLMES (1926–1988) wrote the first article on the Beat Generation, "This is the Beat Generation," for *The New York Times* in 1952, shortly after the publication of his first novel, *Go*, an autobiographical fiction dramatizing the chaotic lives of his friends Allen Ginsberg, Jack Kerouac, Neal Cassady, and others in their group. Holmes went on to publish two more novels and several essay collections, including *Gone in October: Last Reflections on Jack Kerouac* (1985).

"This is the Beat Generation" and "The Philosophy of the Beat Generation" (1958) were included in *Nothing More to Declare* (1967). Later Holmes grouped them as "cultural essays" in *Passionate Opinions* (1988), one of three books of essays published by the University of Arkansas, where he taught creative writing. (The two others were the collection of travel essays *Displaced Person* [1987] and the biographical essays titled *Representative Men* [1988].) Shortly before Holmes's death from cancer, he wrote in his *Maine Daybook*:

> I am calm at last.

> Multitudes of natural life
> busy all around me
> assure me like a good memory
> of time's benevolence.

## This is the Beat Generation

Several months ago, a national magazine ran a story under the heading "Youth" and the subhead "Mother Is Bugged At Me." It concerned an eighteen-year-old California girl who had been picked up for smoking marijuana and wanted to talk about it. While a reporter took down her ideas in the uptempo language of "tea," someone snapped a picture. In view of her contention that she was part of a whole new culture where one out of every five people you meet is a user, it was an arresting photograph. In the pale, attentive face, with its soft eyes and intelligent mouth, there was no hint of corruption. It was a face which could only be deemed criminal through an enormous effort of righteousness. Its only complaint seemed to be: "Why don't people leave us alone?" It was the face of a beat generation.

That clean young face has been making the newspapers steadily since the war. Standing before a judge in a Bronx courthouse, being arraigned for stealing a car, it looked up into the camera with curious laughter and no guilt. The same face, with a more serious bent, stared from the pages of *Life* magazine, representing a graduating class of ex-GIs, and said that as it believed small business to be dead, it intended to become a comfortable cog in the largest corporation it could find. A little younger, a little more bewildered, it was this same face that the photographers caught in Illinois when the first non-virgin club was uncovered. The young copywriter, leaning down the bar on Third Avenue, quietly drinking himself into relaxation, and the energetic hotrod driver of Los Angeles, who plays Russian roulette with a jalopy, are separated only by a continent and a few years. They are the extremes. In between them fall the secretaries wondering whether to sleep with their boyfriends now or wait; the mechanic beering up with the guys and driving off to Detroit on a whim; the models studiously name-dropping at a cocktail party. But the face is the same. Bright, level, realistic, challenging.

Any attempt to label an entire generation is unrewarding, and yet the generation which went through the last war, or at least could get a drink easily once it was over, seems to possess a uniform, general quality which demands an adjective . . . The origins of the word "beat" are obscure, but the meaning is only too clear to most Americans. More than mere weariness, it implies the feeling of having been used, of being raw. It involves a sort of nakedness of mind, and, ultimately, of soul; a feeling of being reduced to the bedrock of consciousness. In short, it means being undramatically pushed up against the wall of oneself. A man is beat whenever he goes for broke and wagers the sum of his resources on a single number; and the young generation has done that continually from early youth.

Its members have an instinctive individuality, needing no bohemianism or imposed eccentricity to express it. Brought up during the collective bad circumstances of a dreary depression, weaned during the collective uprooting of a global war, they distrust collectivity. But they have never been able to keep the world out of their dreams. The fancies of their childhood inhabited the half-light of Munich, the Nazi-Soviet pact, and the eventual blackout. Their adolescence was spent in a topsy-turvy world of war bonds, swing shifts, and troop movements. They grew to independent mind on beachheads, in gin mills and USOs, in past-midnight arrivals and pre-dawn departures. Their brothers, husbands, fathers, or boy friends turned up dead one day at the other end of a telegram. At the four trembling corners of the world, or in the home town invaded by factories or lonely servicemen, they had intimate experience with the nadir and the zenith of human conduct, and little time for much that came between. The peace they inherited was only as secure as the next headline. It was a cold peace. Their own lust for freedom, and the ability to live at a pace that kills (to which the war had adjusted them), led to black markets, bebop, narcotics, sexual promiscuity, hucksterism, and Jean-Paul Sartre. The beatness set in later.

It is a postwar generation, and, in a world which seems to mark its cycles by its wars, it is already being compared to that other postwar generation, which dubbed itself "lost." The Roaring Twenties, and the generation that made them roar, are going through a sentimental revival, and the comparison is valuable. The Lost Generation was discovered in a roadster, laughing hysterically because nothing meant anything anymore. It migrated to Europe, unsure whether it was looking for the "orgiastic future" or escaping from the "puritanical past." Its symbols were the flapper, the flask of bootleg whiskey, and an attitude of desperate frivolity best expressed by the line: "Tennis, anyone?" It was caught up in the romance of disillusionment, until even that became an illusion. Every act in its drama of lostness was a tragic or ironic third act, and T. S. Eliot's *The Waste Land* was more than the dead-end statement of a perceptive poet. The pervading atmosphere of that poem was an almost objectless sense of loss, through which the reader felt immediately that the cohesion of things had disappeared. It was, for an entire generation, an image which expressed, with dreadful accuracy, its own spiritual condition.

But the wild boys of today are not lost. Their flushed, often scoffing, always intent faces elude the word, and it would sound phony to them. For this generation conspicuously lacks that eloquent air of bereavement which made so many of the exploits of the Lost Generation symbolic actions. Furthermore, the repeated inventory of shattered ideals, and the laments about the mud in moral currents, which so obsessed the Lost Generation, do not concern young people today. They take these things frighteningly for granted. They were brought up in these ruins and no longer notice them. They drink to "come down" or to "get high," not to illustrate anything. Their excursions into drugs or promiscuity come out of curiosity, not disillusionment.

Only the most bitter among them would call their reality a nightmare and protest that they have indeed lost something, the future. For ever since they were old enough to imagine one, that has been in jeopardy anyway. The absence of personal and social values is to them, not a revelation shaking the ground beneath them, but a problem demanding a day-to-day solution. *How* to live seems to them much more crucial than *why*. And it is precisely at this point that the copywriter and the hotrod driver meet and their identical beatness becomes significant, for, unlike the Lost Generation, which was occupied with the loss of faith, the Beat Generation is becoming more and more occupied with the need for it. As such, it is a disturbing illustration of Voltaire's reliable old joke: "If there were no God, it would be necessary to invent him." Not content to bemoan His absence, they are busily and haphazardly inventing totems for Him on all sides.

For the giggling nihilist, eating up the highway at ninety miles an hour and steering with his feet, is no Harry Crosby, the poet of the Lost Generation who planned to fly his plane into the sun one day because he could no longer accept the modern world. On the contrary, the hotrod driver invites death only to outwit it. He is affirming the life within him in the only way he knows how, at the extreme. The eager-faced girl, picked up on a dope charge, is not one of those "women and girls carried screaming with drink or drugs from public places," of whom Fitzgerald wrote. Instead, with persuasive seriousness, she describes the sense of community she has found in marijuana, which society never gave her. The copywriter, just as drunk by midnight as his Lost Generation counterpart, probably reads *God and Man at Yale* during his Sunday afternoon hangover. The difference is this almost exaggerated will to believe in something, if only in themselves. It is a *will* to believe, even in the face of an inability to do so in conventional terms. And that is bound to lead to excesses in one direction or another.

The shock that older people feel at the sight of this Beat Generation is, at its deepest level, not so much repugnance at the facts, as it is distress at the attitudes which move it. Though worried by this distress, they most often argue or legislate in terms of the facts rather than the attitudes. The newspaper reader, studying the eyes of young dope addicts, can only find an outlet for his horror and bewilderment in demands that passers be given the electric chair. Sociologists, with a more academic concern, are just as troubled by the legions of young men whose topmost ambition seems to be to find a secure berth in a monolithic corporation. Contemporary historians express mild surprise at the lack of organized movements, political, religious, or otherwise, among the young. The articles they write remind us that being one's own boss and being a natural joiner are two of our most cherished national traits. Everywhere people with tidy moralities shake their heads and wonder what is happening to the younger generation.

Perhaps they have not noticed that, behind the excess on the one hand, and the conformity on the other, lies that wait-and-see detachment that results from having to fall back for support more on one's capacity for human endurance than on one's philosophy of life. Not that the Beat Generation is immune to ideas; they fascinate it. Its wars, both past and future, were and will be wars of ideas. It knows, however, that in the final, private moment of conflict a man is really fighting another man, and not an idea. And that the same goes for love. So it is a generation with a greater facility for entertaining ideas than for believing in them. But it is also the first generation in several centuries for which the act of faith has been an obsessive problem, quite aside from the reasons for having a particular faith or not having it. It exhibits on every side, and in a bewildering number of facets, a perfect craving to believe.

Though it is certainly a generation of extremes, including both the hipster and the radical young Republican in its ranks, it renders unto Caesar (i.e., society) what is Caesar's, and unto God what is God's. For the wildest hipster, making a mystique of bop, drugs, and the night life, there is no desire to shatter the "square" society in which he lives, only to elude it. To get on a soapbox or write a manifesto would seem to him absurd. Looking at the normal world, where most everything is a "drag" for him, he nevertheless says: "Well, that's the Forest of Arden after all. And even *it* jumps if you look at it right." Equally, the young Republican, though often seeming to hold up Babbitt as his culture hero, is neither vulgar nor materialistic, as Babbitt was. He conforms because he believes it is socially practical, not necessarily virtuous. Both positions, however, are the result of more or less the same conviction—namely that the valueless abyss of modern life is unbearable.

For beneath the excess and the conformity, there is something other than detachment. There are the stirrings of a quest. What the hipster is looking for in his "coolness" (withdrawal) or "flipness" (ecstasy) is, after all, a feeling of somewhereness, not just another diversion. The young Republican feels that there is a point beyond which change becomes chaos, and what he wants is not simply privilege or wealth, but a stable position from which to operate. Both have had enough of homelessness, valuelessness, faithlessness.

The variety and the extremity of their solutions are only a final indication that for today's young people there is not as yet a single external pivot around which they can, as a generation, group their observations and their aspirations. There is no single philosophy, no single party, no single attitude. The failure of most orthodox moral and social concepts to reflect fully the life they have known is probably the reason for this, but because of it each person becomes a walking, self-contained unit, compelled to meet, or at least endure, the problem of being young in a seemingly helpless world in his own way.

More than anything else, this is what is responsible for this generation's reluctance to name itself, its reluctance to discuss itself as a group, sometimes its reluctance to be itself. For invented gods invariably disappoint those who worship them. Only the need for them goes on, and it is this need, exhausting one object after another, which projects the Beat Generation forward into the future and will one day deprive it of its beatness.

Dostoyevski wrote in the early 1880s that "Young Russia is talking of nothing but the eternal questions now." With appropriate changes, something very like this is beginning to happen in America, in an American way; a re-evaluation of which the exploits and attitudes of this generation are only symptoms. No single comparison of one generation against another can accurately measure effects, but it seems obvious that a lost generation, occupied with disillusionment and trying to keep busy among the broken stones, is poetically moving, but not very dangerous. But a beat generation, driven by a desperate craving for belief and as yet unable to accept the moderations which are offered it, is quite another matter. Thirty years later, after all, the generation of which Dostoyevski wrote was meeting in cellars and making bombs.

This generation may make no bombs; it will probably be asked to drop some, and have some dropped on it, however, and this fact is never far from its mind. It is one of the pressures which created it and will play a large part in what will happen to it. There are those who believe that in generations such as this there is always the constant possibility of a great new moral idea, conceived in desperation, coming to life. Others note the self-indulgence, the waste, the apparent social irresponsibility, and disagree.

But its ability to keep its eyes open, and yet avoid cynicism; its ever-increasing conviction that the problem of modern life is essentially a spiritual problem; and that capacity for sudden wisdom which people who live hard and go far, possess, are assets and bear watching. And, anyway, the clear, challenging faces are worth it.

## The Philosophy of the Beat Generation

Last September a novel was published which *The New York Times* called "the most beautifully executed, the clearest and most important utterance" yet made by a young writer; a book likely to represent the present generation, it said, as *The Sun Also Rises* represents the twenties. It was called *On the Road,* by Jack Kerouac, and it described the experiences and attitudes of a restless group of young Americans, "mad to live, mad to talk, mad to be saved," whose primary interests seemed to be fast cars, wild parties, modern jazz, sex, marijuana, and other miscellaneous "kicks." Kerouac said they were members of a Beat Generation.

No one seemed to know exactly what Kerouac meant, and, indeed, some critics insisted that these wild young hedonists were not really representative of anything, but were only "freaks," "mental and moral imbeciles," "bourgeois rebels." Nevertheless, something about the book, and something about the term, would not be so easily dismissed. The book became the object of heated discussion, selling well as a consequence; and the term stuck—at least in the craw of those who denied there was any such thing.

Providing a word that crystallizes the characteristics of an entire generation has always been a thankless task. . . . But to find a word that will describe the group that is now roughly between the ages of eighteen and twenty-eight (give or take a year in either direction) is even more difficult, because this group includes veterans of three distinct kinds of modern war: a hot war, a cold war, and a war that was stubbornly not called a war at all, but a police action.

Everyone who has lived through a war, any sort of war, knows that beat means not so much weariness, as rawness of the nerves; not so much being "filled up to *here*," as being emptied out. It describes a state of mind from which all unessentials have been stripped, leaving it receptive to everything around it, but impatient with trivial obstructions. To be beat is to be at the bottom of your personality, looking up; to be existential in the Kierkegaard, rather than the Jean-Paul Sartre, sense.

What differentiated the characters in *On the Road* from the slumbred petty criminals and icon-smashing Bohemians which have been something of a staple in much modern American fiction—what made them *beat*—was something which seemed to irritate critics most of all. It was Kerouac's insistence that actually they were on a quest, and that the specific object of their quest was spiritual. Though they rushed back and forth across the country on the slightest pretext, gathering kicks along the way, their real journey was inward; and if they seemed to trespass most boundaries, legal and moral, it was only in the hope of finding a belief on the other side. "The Beat Generation," he said, "is basically a religious generation."

On the face of it, this may seem absurd when you consider that parents, civic leaders, law-enforcement officers and even literary critics most often have been amused, irritated or downright shocked by the behavior of this generation. They have noted more delinquency, more excess, more social irresponsibility in it than in any generation in recent years, and they have seen less interest in politics, community activity, and the orthodox religious creeds. They have been outraged by the adulation of the late James Dean, seeing in it signs of a dangerous morbidity, and they have been equally outraged by the adulation of Elvis Presley, seeing in it signs of a dangerous sensuality. They have read statistics on narcotics addiction, sexual promiscuity and the consumption of alcohol among the young—and blanched. They have lamented the fact that "the most original [literary] work being done in this country has come to depend on the bizarre and the offbeat for its creative stimulus"; and they have expressed horror at the disquieting kind of juvenile crime—violent and without an object—which has erupted in most large cities.

They see no signs of a search for spiritual values in a generation whose diverse tragic heroes have included jazzman Charlie Parker, actor Dean and poet Dylan Thomas; and whose interests have ranged all the way from bebop to rock and roll; from hipsterism to Zen Buddhism; from vision-inducing drugs to Method Acting. To be told that this is a generation whose almost exclusive concern is the discovery of something in which to believe seems to them to fly directly in the face of all the evidence.

Perhaps all generations feel that they have inherited "the worst of all possible worlds," but the Beat Generation probably has more claim to the feeling than any that have come before it. The historical climate which formed its attitudes was violent, and it did as much violence to ideas as it did to the men who believed in them. One does not have to be consciously aware of such destruction to feel it. Conventional notions of private and public morality have been steadily atrophied in the last ten or fifteen years by the exposure of treason in government, corruption in labor and business, and scandal among the mighty of Broadway and Hollywood. The political faiths which sometimes seem to justify slaughter have become steadily less appealing as slaughter has reached proportions that stagger even the mathematical mind. Orthodox religious conceptions of good and evil seem increasingly inadequate to explain a world of science-fiction turned fact, past enemies turned bosom friends, and honorable diplomacy turned brink-of-war. Older generations may be distressed or cynical or apathetic about this world, or they may have somehow adjusted their conceptions to it. But the Beat Generation is specifically the *product* of this world, and it is the only world its members have ever known.

It is the first generation in American history that has grown up with peacetime military training as a fully accepted fact of life. It is the first generation for whom the catch phrases of psychiatry have become such intellectual pablum that it can dare to think they may not be the final yardstick of the human soul. It is the first generation for whom genocide, brainwashing, cybernetics, motivational research—and the resultant limitation of the concept of human volition which is inherent in them—have been as familiar as its own face. It is also the first generation that has grown up since the possibility of the nuclear destruction of the world has become the final answer to all questions.

But instead of the cynicism and apathy which accompanies the end of ideals, and which gave the Lost Generation a certain poetic, autumnal quality, the Beat Generation is altogether too vigorous, too intent, too indefatigable, too curious to suit its elders. Nothing seems to satisfy or interest it but extremes, which, if they have included the criminality of narcotics, have also included the sanctity of monasteries. Everywhere the Beat Generation seems occupied with the feverish production of answers—some of them frightening, some of them foolish—to a single question: how are we to live? And if this is not immediately recognizable in leather-jacketed motorcyclists and hipsters "digging the street," it is because we assume that only answers which recognize man as a collective animal have any validity; and do not realize that this generation cannot conceive of the question in any but personal terms, and knows that the only answer it can accept will come out of the dark night of the individual soul.

Before looking at some of those answers, it would be well to remember what Norman Mailer, in a recent article on the hipster, said about the hip language: "What makes [it] a special language is that it cannot really be taught—if one shares none of the experiences of elation and exhaustion which it is equipped to describe, then it seems merely arch or vulgar or irritating." This is also true to a large extent of the whole reality in which the members of the Beat Generation have grown. If you can't see it the way they do, you can't understand the way they act. One way to see it, perhaps the easiest, is to investigate the image they have of themselves.

A large proportion of this generation lived vicariously in the short, tumultuous career of actor James Dean. He was their idol in much the same way that Valentino was the screen idol of the twenties and Clark Gable was the screen idol of the thirties. But there was a difference, and it was *all* the difference. In Dean, they saw not a daydream Lothario who was more attractive, mysterious and wealthy than they were, or a virile man of action with whom they could fancifully identify to make up for their own feelings of powerlessness, but a wistful, reticent youth, looking over the abyss separating him from older people with a level, saddened eye; living intensely in alternate explosions of tenderness and violence; eager for love and a sense of purpose, but able to accept them only on terms which acknowledged the facts of life as he knew them: in short, themselves.

To many people, Dean's mumbling speech, attenuated silences, and rash gestures seemed the ultimate in empty mannerisms, but the young generation knew that it was not so much that he was inarticulate or affected as it was that he was unable to believe in some of the things his scripts required him to say. He spoke to them right through all the expensive make-believe of million-dollar productions, saying with his sighs, and the prolonged shifting of his weight from foot to foot: "Well, I suppose there's no way out of this, but we know how it *really* is. . . ." They knew he was lonely, they knew he was flawed, they knew he was confused. But they also knew that he "dug," and so they delighted in his sloppy clothes and untrimmed hair and indifference to the proprieties of fame. He was not what they wanted to be; he was what they *were*. He lived hard and without complaint; and he died as he lived, going fast. Or as Kerouac's characters express it:

"We gotta go and never stop going till we get there.

"Where we going, man?

"I don't know, but we gotta go."

Only the most myopic, it seems to me, can view this need for mobility (and it is one of the distinguishing characteristics of the Beat Generation) as a flight rather than a search.

Dean was the product of an acting discipline known as The

Method (taught at New York's Actors Studio), which has proved irresistibly attractive to young actors and has filled the screens and stages of America in recent years with laconic, slouching youths, who suddenly erupt with such startling jets of emotional power that the audience is left as shaken and moved as if it had overheard a confession. The primary concern of The Method is to find the essence of a character, his soul, and the actor is encouraged to do this by utilizing emotions in his own experience that correspond to those in the script. Non-Method actors sometimes complain that disciples of The Method coast along during the greater part of a role, hoarding their emotional resources for the climactic scenes. To which Method actors might reply that only the climactic scenes in most plays and movies have any deep human truth to them, and that the rest is only empty dialogue building toward the moment when the character reveals himself.

An example of this might well be the movie *On the Waterfront*, conceived by its writer, Budd Schulberg, and its director, Elia Kazan, as a social exposé of conditions among longshoremen, centralized in the figure of a young ex-boxer mixed up in a corrupt union. Marlon Brando's electrifying performance of this role, however, so interiorized the character that the social overtones seemed insignificant beside the glimpse of a single human soul caught in the contradictions and absurdity of modern life. It was exactly as if Brando were saying in scene after scene: "Man is not merely a social animal, a victim, a product. At the bottom, man is a spirit." As a theory of acting keyed to this proposition, The Method is preeminently the acting style of the Beat Generation.

Critics constantly express amazement at the willingness, even the delight, with which this generation accepts what are (to the critics) basically unflattering images of itself. It was noticed, for instance, that the most vociferous champions of the film, *The Wild Ones* (which gave a brutal, unsympathetic account of the wanton pillage of a California town by a band of motorcyclists), were the motorcyclists themselves. Equally, most juvenile delinquents probably saw, and approved of, the portrait of themselves offered in *Rebel Without a Cause*, even though they laughed at the social-worker motivations for their conduct that filled the script. One can only conclude that what they see and what adults see are two different things. The standards by which adults judge the behavior portrayed have scant reality to them, for these standards are based on social and moral values that do not take into consideration their dilemma, which might be described as the will to believe even in the face of the inability to do so in conventional terms.

All too often older people make the mistake of concluding that what lies beneath this is an indifference to values of any kind, whereas almost the reverse is true. Even the crudest and most nihilistic member of the Beat Generation, the young slum hoodlum, is almost exclusively concerned with the problem of belief, albeit unconsciously. It seems incredible that no one has realized that the only way to make the shocking juvenile murders coherent at all is to understand that they are specifically moral crimes. The youth, who last summer stabbed another youth and was reported to have said to his victim, "Thanks a lot, I just wanted to know what it felt like," was neither insane nor perverted. There was no justification for his crime, either in the hope of gain or in the temporary hysteria of hate, or even in the egotism of a Loeb and Leopold, who killed only to prove they could get away with it. His was the sort of crime envisaged by the Marquis de Sade a hundred and fifty years ago—a crime which the cruel absence of God made obligatory if a man were to prove that he was a man and not a mere blot of matter. Such crimes, which are no longer rarities and which are all committed by people under twenty-five, cannot be understood if we go on mouthing the same old panaceas about broken homes and slum environments and bad company, for they are spiritual crimes, crimes against the identity of another human being, crimes which reveal with stark and terrifying clarity the lengths to which a desperate need for values can drive the young. For in actuality it is the *longing* for values which is expressed in such a crime, and not the hatred of them. It is the longing to do or feel something meaningful, and it provides a sobering glimpse of how completely the cataclysms of this century have obliterated the rational, humanistic view of Man on which modern society has been erected.

The reaction to this on the part of young people, even those in a teen-age gang, is not a calculated immorality, however, but a return to an older, more personal, but no less rigorous code of ethics, which includes the inviolability of comradeship, the respect for confidences, and an almost mystical regard for courage—all of which are the ethics of the tribe, rather than the community; the code of a small compact group living in an indifferent or a hostile environment, which it seeks not to conquer or change, but only to elude.

On a slightly older level, this almost primitive will to survive gives rise to the hipster, who moves through our cities like a member of some mysterious, nonviolent Underground, not plotting anything, but merely keeping alive an unpopular philosophy, much like the Christian of the first century. He finds in bop, the milder narcotics, his secretive language and the night itself, affirmation of an individuality (more and more besieged by the conformity of our national life), which can sometimes only be expressed by outright eccentricity. But his aim is to be asocial, not antisocial; his trancelike "digging" of jazz or sex or marijuana is an effort to free *himself*, not exert power over others. In his most enlightened state, the hipster feels that argument, violence and concern for attachments are ultimately Square, and he says, "Yes, man, yes!" to the Buddhist principle that most human miseries arise from these emotions. I once heard a young hipster exclaim wearily to the antagonist in a barroom brawl: "Oh, man, you don't want to interfere with him, with his kick. I mean, man, what a *drag!*"

On this level, the hipster practices a kind of passive resistance to the Square society in which he lives, and the most he would ever propose as a program would be the removal of every social and intellectual restraint to the expression and enjoyment of his unique individuality, and the "kicks" of "digging" life through it. And, as Norman Mailer said in the afore-quoted article, "The affirmation implicit in [this] proposal is that man would then prove to be more creative than murderous, and so would not destroy himself." Which is, after all, a far more spiritual, or even religious, view of human nature than that held by many of those who look at this Beat Generation and see only its excesses.

This conviction of the creative power of the unfettered individual soul stands behind everything in which the members of this generation interest themselves. If they are curious about drugs, for instance, their initial reason is as much the desire to tap the unknown world inside themselves as to escape from the unbearable world outside. "But, man, last night," they will say, "I got so high I knew *everything*. I mean, I knew *why*."

In the arts, modern jazz is almost exclusively the music of the Beat Generation, as poetry (at least until Kerouac's novel) is its literature. If the members of this generation attend to a wailing sax in much the same way as men once used to attend the words and gestures of sages, it is because jazz is primarily the music of inner freedom, of improvisation, of the creative individual rather than the interpretive group. It is the music of a submerged people, who *feel* free, and this is precisely how young people feel today. For this reason, the short, violent life of alto-saxist Charlie Parker (together with those of Dean and Dylan Thomas) exerts a strong attraction on this generation, because all three went their own uncompromising way, listening to their inner voices, celebrating whatever they could find to celebrate, and then willingly paying the cost in self-destruction. But if young people idolize them, they have no illusions about them as martyrs, for they know (and almost stoically accept) that one of the risks of going so fast, and so far, is death.

But it is perhaps in poetry where the attitude of the Beat Generation, and its exaggerated will to find beliefs at any cost, is most clearly articulated. In San Francisco, a whole school of young poets has made a complete break with their elegant, university-imprisoned forebears. Some of them subscribe to Zen Buddhism, which is a highly sophisticated, nonrational psychology of revelation, and wait for satori (wisdom, understanding, reconciliation). Some are Catholic laymen, or even monks, and pray for the redemption of the world. Many of them resemble mendicant friars, or the Goliard balladeers of the Middle Ages, carrying everything they own on their backs, including typewritten copies of their poems to be left, as one of them put it, in art galleries, latrines, "and other places where poets gather." All of them believe that only that which cries to be said, no matter how "unpoetic" it may seem; only that which is unalterably true to the sayer, and bursts out of him in a flood, finding its own form as it comes, is worth the saying in the first place. Literary attitudes, concern about meter or grammar, everything self-conscious and artificial that separates literature from life (they say) has got to go. . . . One of them, Allen Ginsberg, whom *Life* Magazine has called the most exciting young poet in America, has written a long, brilliant and disordered poem called "Howl." It contains a good many expressions and experiences that have never been in a poem before; nevertheless, its aim is so clearly a defense of the human spirit in the face of a civilization intent on destroying it, that the effect is purifying. " 'Howl' is an 'Affirmation' by individual experience of God, sex, drugs, absurdity," Ginsberg says.

The same might be said of *On the Road*. Most critics spent so much time expressing their polite distaste for the sordidness of some of the material that they completely failed to mention that in this world, the world of the Beat Generation, Kerouac unfailingly found tenderness, humility, joy, and even reverence; and, though living in what many critics considered a nightmare jungle of empty sensation, his characters nevertheless could say over and over:

"No one can tell us that there is no God. We've passed through all forms . . . Everything is fine, God exists, we know time . . . Furthermore we know America, we're at home . . . We give and take and go in the incredibly complicated sweetness . . ."

Whatever else they may be, these are not the words of a generation consumed by self-pity over the loss of their illusions; nor are they the words of a generation consumed by hatred for a world they never made. They seem rather to be the words of a generation groping toward faith out of an intellectual despair and moral chaos in which they refuse to lose themselves. They will strike many people as strange words, coming as they do from the lips of a young man behind the wheel of a fast car, racing through the American night, much as Kerouac's reply to *Nightbeat*'s John Wingate seemed strange, when he was asked to whom he prayed. "I pray to my little brother, who died, and to my father, and to Buddha, and to Jesus Christ, and to the Virgin Mary," he said, and then added: "I pray to those five *people*. . . ."

But if this grouping of a saint, a sage and a savior with two twentieth-century Americans seems strange, it is only because many of us have forgotten (or have never known) how real the spiritual experience can be when all other experiences have failed to satisfy one's hunger. The suggestion, at least in Kerouac's book, is that beyond the violence, the drugs, the jazz, and all the other "kicks" in which it frantically seeks its identity, this generation will find a faith and become consciously—he believes that it is unconsciously already—a religious generation.

Be that as it may, there are indications that the Beat Generation is not just an American phenomenon. England has its Teddy Boys, Japan its Sun Tribers, and even in Russia there are hipsters of a sort. Everywhere young people are reacting to the growing collectivity of modern life, and the constant threat of collective death, with the same disturbing extremity of individualism. Everywhere they seem to be saying to their elders: "We are different from you, and we can't believe in the things you believe in—if only because *this* is the world you have wrought." Everywhere, they are searching for their own answers.

For many of them, the answer may well be jail or madness or death. They may never find the faith that Kerouac believes is at the end of their road. But on one thing they would all agree: the valueless abyss of modern life is unbearable. And if other generations have lamented the fact that theirs was "the worst of all possible worlds," young people today seem to know that it is the only one that they will ever have, and that it is *how* a man lives, not why, that makes all the difference. Their assumption—that the foundation of all systems, moral or social, is the indestructible unit of the single individual—may be nothing but a rebellion against a century in which this idea has fallen into disrepute. But their recognition that what sustains the individual is belief—and their growing conviction that only spiritual beliefs have any lasting validity in a world such as ours—should put their often frenzied behavior in a new light, and will certainly figure large in whatever future they may have.

---

# HERBERT HUNCKE

HERBERT HUNCKE (1915–1996), born into an unhappy middle-class family in Chicago, was the original hipster who served as the prototype for Jack Kerouac's invention of the Beat Generation. A high school dropout in his teens, a heroin addict in his twenties, Huncke drifted to New York City in the mid-1940s, where he met Burroughs, Ginsberg, and Kerouac. He had started writing short sketches and poetry before he became their friend, believing in the simple aesthetic "Say whatever comes into your mind." As Ann Douglas understood, "For Kerouac and Ginsberg, 'beat,' a bit of drug-world slang they picked up from Huncke, came to mean being high, ecstatic, saved, lying in the gutter in order at last to see the stars, but Huncke always used 'beat' in its root sense, to signify the defeated, those not open to the insult of rehabilitation, those unable or unwilling to 'make it.'"

Near the end of his life, Huncke's prose poem "The Nee-dle" was one of his favorite selections when he read aloud to his friends. It was published posthumously in *The Herbert Huncke Reader* (1997), edited by Benjamin G. Schafer. In the earlier narrative from *Guilty of Everything,* published by Paragon House in 1990, Huncke described the Lower East Side scene in the spring of 1961, shortly after Allen Ginsberg and Peter Orlovsky had left New York City for a two-year trip around the world. At this time Huncke was living with a loose group of friends, including Bill Heine, Alexander Trocchi (the Scottish author of the Beat novel *Cain's Book,* published by Grove Press in 1960), Ginsberg's friend Elise Cowen, and the young poet Ja-nine Pommy Vega. The section concludes with Huncke's ac-count of a party in New York City for William Burroughs in 1964 or 1965 after the American publication of *Naked Lunch.*

---

## The Needle

There are innumerable ways of wooing. On one's knees while gazing fondly into the eyes of the one being wooed, and then words—so I am told—are effective. Not to mention the ever handy kiss, or stroking, touching tenderly, and, of course, inspired endearments; but nothing surpasses the wicked needle. How titillating that first tiny prick. Both slightly painful, although not quite, as the eye watches and then quickly looks away, only to once again become aware of the tiny point pressed against the outer casing of the waiting vein, one instant in re-jecting and then hopefully anticipating the moment of penetration and recognizing the sensation felt as that little point has entered the flow-ing blood already seen through the glass of the first syringe, beginning a pressured course sending it back to rejoin the original stream diluted with a wondrous new sensation—once known, never forgotten. Con-tinue then this strange communication. I've known the needle well and wondered at the occasional gentle touch—both shy and deter-mined—once or twice cruelly—yet always inwardly charming. Strange still at this late period, knowing the arrival of the death entity. The end already started. Reaching neither timidly nor eagerly. Offering the last of rapid heartbeat. In fullness, never suspected as part of the finishing experience, nor imagine contemplation as possible. Wishing deeply it be known and accepted. Thusly the perfect bringing together of our involving magnetism, richly charred with the old and the new.

## *From* Guilty of Everything

Now that Allen [Ginsberg] and Peter [Orlovsky] were gone they weren't the focal point any longer. When they left for India there were still three weeks left on their rent, so I moved into their place for the three weeks. Naturally, the first thing Bill [Heine] did was bring over several of his friends and take the place over.

When Bill first hit New York he was an innocent little drummer boy—but a good good one. How he originally got involved in the Village scene I don't know. All of a sudden, it seemed, he blossomed into a leader. He had been very close to Trocchi, and when Trocchi left, Bill took his place. Trocchi had to leave because his place was raided one night by the cops and because of various legal problems; he decided the best thing to do for the time being was to split the scene rather than come to the attention of the cops.

Bill came with several strange and powerful personalities in tow. I say powerful because they emanated a certain amount of energy that you could almost feel when in their presence. Very dynamic people.

Bill, incidentally, was one of the most creative persons I've ever known. He could take a white sheet, fold it in such a way that it was the size and shape of a skull, wrap yards of silk thread around it to keep it together, and then inject it with a huge hypodermic needle filled with paint. He would draw various colors up into the needle and jab it into the sheet again and again. He'd work on it for about an hour and then snip the threads and open up the sheet until it fell apart like a chrysalis with the most exquisite colorings you've ever seen. He made the most beautiful hangings, and every time he left a pad invariably there'd be one of these hangings left on the wall of the place. It was all so fantastic, actually, what with all the ritual that went into it.

When Bill unloaded his shoulder bag he'd pull out more from his store of tricks. He had a brass Buddha, all kinds of precious and semi-

precious stones—amethyst, topaz, carnelian—and he'd fashion an altar for himself. It got to be a nightly ritual with him. In fact, it got so
he didn't even take it down after he settled in.

At one point I tried to get him to show his work in a gallery, but
the gallery people weren't willing to take the risk, saying that the only
way the hangings could be appreciated properly would be to have
them stretched and exhibited in such a way that light would be able to
shine through them. They did not have the facilities to accommodate
him. He did have beautiful stuff, no question about that. In fact, he
was probably the first to invent tie-dye. When I first met him, no one
had ever heard of tie-dye. It's amazing how popular it's become since
then.

Bill had something about him too that attracted a certain type of
person to him. For example, there was this young chick named Rita
who happened on the scene for a short time. She'd wear long black
dresses and black boots. She knew a great deal about stones and
wood, things that I'm sure she must have studied at one time. She also
wrote some very good poetry. And there were times, as well, when
she'd become completely inarticulate. You know, I don't know what finally became of her. She may be dead, although I ran into someone
not too long ago that told me she'd been in the hospital. I'd rather that
she be dead, I think, than end in a hospital, because she was such a
free individual. She loved her freedom. She was the kind of person
that would run down the street and laugh simply because she was running, or who would put on a dance performance on a corner for the joy
of it.

There were many others in Bill's orbit, some that I did not cotton
to. I found a few just a little too treacherous for me. When we left
Allen's, and had sort of wrecked the place, Bill, Janine, and myself
moved in with Elise once more. Eventually, we found a place of our
own on East Sixth Street.

It was a fine layout. We had the floor clear through. It had apparently been a warehouse at one time, and the people that owned the
building had converted the first-floor section into a storage place, with
an office in front, and rented out the other two floors. The place was
protected by the police, oddly enough. It was funny because, God
knows, some of the scenes that went down there—if the police had
had any inkling of what was going on, we'd have all ended up doing

some kind of time. But we were never bothered, not once in the whole time we were there.

We decorated the place with hangings and paintings, and it got so that we were having amphetamine jam sessions up there at all hours of the night. I soon discovered that the father of the family that rented the floor above ours had been sentenced to a five-year bit and they were perfectly satisfied in their quiet. I don't believe it would've mattered to them if we'd torn the place down. We had things pretty much our own way there, and it turned out to be a fantastic spot.

Allen had left a few pieces of furniture behind, so we moved them over to this new place. It was in the apartment that Janine and Bill began the intensity of their relationship. It began to function in a way that everyone who came into our place was aware of the tension that was being built up. I tried to stick around because I was worried about Janine. I could not figure Bill out, to be honest, and I did not know what he had in mind. After all, Janine was something of a child.

One night she came to me crying, saying, "I don't want to be Bill's old lady." She was furious with the idea that Bill had been referring to her as his old lady. And there were other scenes like when Bill would come running out of his room cursing and damning everything, with a hypodermic needle pointed at his eye. I don't know what it had been about, but Janine was weeping and hysterical, and Bill was shouting, "What do you want me to do? Put my eye out with this thing?" The whole dramatic bit. I'd have to sit back and watch this and hope like hell nothing serious would come of it.


From that point on, our scene became even more outrageous. There'd usually be ten or twelve people in the place at a time and the record player would be going full blast with Charlie Parker, of course, or with some incredibly fine Afghanistan teahouse records. Also, a friend of Allen's had made some beautiful recordings of the kef festivals in Morocco where everyone pitches in and sings, beats on drums, blows whistles. Ravi Shankar was becoming popular about then in America, and we had too some fantastic Indian records. So there was music going day and night, and a continual stream of people. Some were painting, some were building things or making things—just a lot of action and movement.

Alex Trocchi moved into the apartment. At that time there was still a case pending against him which would finally force him into sneaking out of the city again, across the Canadian border, and eventually into leaving for England from Canada. When he was living with us, though, he and Bill would do some remarkable things together with wood and knives. I can remember Trocchi with this knife that must have been a regulation hunter's knife. He had acquired at least two- or three-inch-long tracks on his arms as an addict, and he'd allow them to scab over. He had a habit of standing with one of these knives underneath a bright lightbulb, picking the scabs off with the point of the knife.

The scene continued on all that summer and into fall, and then it went kaput. Too many notorious people came into the place. There were scenes, there were fights, there were people running out into the streets. Then it got so bad that some got to burning each other. A guy would come up with thirty or forty dollars to cop an ounce of A with and someone else would go south with it. Also, too many junkies came into the scene.

So things fell apart and it was partially due to Janine too. I finally convinced her that she had better get out of there. I didn't want to see her doing a lot of the things that I knew would occur if she'd kept on. I didn't want to see her on the streets hustling.

Bill had set guard over her for so long that it was nearly impossible to get to her. I couldn't even talk with her without seeming to interfere. One night I waited until Bill was asleep and I got hold of Janine and said to her, "Look, you've got to get out of here."

"I just can't walk out without telling him," she said.

"That's the only way you're going to get out," I said. "You've had your share of grief. Now you've got to split. I want you to get out of here, go home for a little while, think things over, and, if you want to come back, why all right, come on back. But meanwhile you've got to split now." After arguing with her and being afraid Bill was going to wake any minute and find me, I got her outside and said, "Now, I'm going to get you on the bus for Jersey to see your people."

Bill went absolutely insane, threatening to kill people. He tore up and down the streets looking for her. It was unbelievable the way he ran through the stairways of old tenement buildings in the neighborhood, hoping to somehow locate her.

*[After the loss of the Sixth Street apartment, Huncke moved to Avenue C with the poet John Wieners.]*

I was flat broke again. I hadn't been able to score anything, and was sick besides. I had given up as far as stealing was concerned, given up breaking into cars. As a matter of fact, I wasn't doing much of anything that was illegal, other than use drugs—just petty stuff, like clipping somebody for a ten-dollar bill or giving someone a tale of woe. Yet I have to admit I *was* up against it.

I was staying with poet John Wieners on Avenue C, and one night we were both so sick I decided that someone had to go out and get something. So I started out cruising the streets, one after another. I'd made it all the way to Fifty-ninth Street on foot and hadn't found a thing. The streets were bare. In disgust I started back down Fifth Avenue. I didn't have carfare home. I got to Twenty-eighth Street, and between Fifth and Madison there are two or three nice hotels, second-rate commercial affairs. I had on several occasions prior to then cracked a couple of cars on this street, and they'd been successful enterprises. I'd always kept this area sort of in reserve when I'd felt desperate.

I cut down this street. I was cold, tired, disgusted. There was a station wagon pulled up near the entrance to one of the hotels. As I passed it I glanced in and sitting on the front seat were two moneybags. I said to myself, My God, what is this? I checked around, stopping in my tracks. I went back, gave the door a little twist, and pulled it open. I reached in and snatched one of those bags, got it open a bit, glancing around all the while. I couldn't believe anyone could be so stupid. This thing was packed with money, and I didn't know what I should do.

What I ended up doing was grabbing hold of that bag and hauling ass down the street. There was a boardwalk around this new office building going up at Madison and Twenty-eighth, so I walked over there and stepped inside. I set the moneybag down and thought, Well, what the hell, I might as well go back and get the other bag.

When I returned to the car, I decided at first to let it stay because it was just too heavy for me. I thought, God, walking down the street with two moneybags will be more than anyone can handle. If they stop me, I'm really stuck. But then I saw an attaché case and grabbed that, dumping the money in it. There were a couple of bottles of whiskey inside, too.

My conclusion about the circumstances was that these people were with a whiskey company and they had run some sort of contest or something. They were from Canada because the money was in Canadian currency. What were they doing in New York? I'd seen two or three of those cardboard advertising cutouts so I guessed they were in town for some sort of special occasion. I was so skeptical of it all, though, that I wasn't even sure it was the real thing. How could it be? Nevertheless, I took it.

The following morning I went to a bank with a couple of the bills and told them I'd like to exchange them. They gave me ninety-two cents on the dollar. Fantastic. But I didn't know exactly how I should exchange all of the money because I figured the theft would be in the papers. I looked for some mention of it that day but there was none. What I did was take about two hundred dollars' worth of bills in at a time, and I hit several different places where they changed money.

Then I moved into a hotel on Washington Square and stayed there for quite a while. It was an odd period of time for me. Janine was in a bad way and I was worried about her. I had sort of rescued her and I brought her up to the room. She just laid up for two or three days until she began to feel better. I got some food and fruit into her because she was terribly run down, both mentally and physically.

There was also a fellow at the time who'd sort of attached himself to me because I had given him a little money and straightened him out. His name was Joel and he was very gay and very strange. He looked something like Harpo Marx with his big bushy hair, large nose, and strange features.

I said, "Joel, why don't the three of us—you, me, and Janine—go up to Canada? We'll take this money with us and spend it, and no-body's going to be the wiser." And that's what we did. We cashed in enough to get bus tickets.

I wanted to be as inconspicuous as possible, though of course I could've chosen better traveling companions. Joel, who had an incredible sense of humor, had brought along a large suitcase into which he had packed *Naked Lunch,* and many other avant-garde books and underground publications—the type that had already created a little disturbance here and there.

Well, they refused us entry into the country. Janine looked to them like an underage girl. They wanted to know exactly who we were and what we intended to do in Canada. I suppose we were three wild-looking people. And we hadn't thought to provide ourselves with some money to cover traveling expenses.

"How long are you going to be in Canada?"

"I don't know, several weeks," I replied.

"And what are you going to do for money?" I couldn't very well tell them I was sitting on an attaché case filled with a couple thousand dollars.

Finally they said, "We're very sorry. We can't let you all in." I said that I would stand good for the other two, but then they saw all these weird books in Joel's bag. They found *Naked Lunch* and had a fit. He told them that he was here to spread the good word. So that was the end of that.

I didn't want to go right back to New York, so I said, "Look, we'll try to find someplace to stay." We ended up in a small town dead on the border of the States and Canada, a beautiful place called Elizabethville. I spoke to a taxi driver and he took us to an inn. It was a nice place, a house that had been built, according to the proprietor, sometime shortly after Washington had traveled through these parts. The inn had been handed down through the family since then. I guess they catered mostly to hunting parties and people of that sort.

I put Janine in a room by herself, and she slept for two days. She had been on amphetamine and was by this time exhausted. Joel and I were using, and I had brought plenty of stuff with me. If they'd searched me, we'd have been in trouble for sure.

We laid up in the inn for about five days. They didn't know where we'd come from, and we were very quiet about it. We took long walks, and prowled about the countryside admiring the big pine trees and fields and the whole bit. In three or four days Janine had the color back in her cheeks, and she looked just beautiful. We got to eating, and the lady of the house could cook. Oh God—big thick steaks, baked potatoes, homemade apple pies. It turned out very well.

But now I wanted to get back to the city. I got on a train just as the customs agents were getting off. They'd ridden down from Montreal, getting off at Elizabethville, and I simply caught the train there and came back into New York. I had some money left and I checked into a hotel myself, and got a room for Joel and Janine so they would have a place when they returned. I called them long distance and told them everything was fine, come on back. When they did, things went along fairly smoothly for a while until the money was gone.

That money did not last very long, though—about a month is all. I'd given about two or three hundred dollars to John Wieners, and I don't know how much I spent on the three of us. What I wanted to do, incidentally, was to go to Spain, but the Iberian lines were so expensive that I thought, Well, shit, it'll cost me a thousand dollars before I'm through buying a ticket.

One morning I woke up and found that Joel had helped himself to a good part of the cash and had taken it on the lam. He left me a note: "Really, you have enough." He was so shy about apologizing for it when I ran into him again.

During this time it was suddenly announced that the great Mr. William Burroughs was back in town. This is late '64–'65. *Naked Lunch* had finally been published in the States and it created an unbelievable stir. People would run up to Allen on the street and talk to him about Burroughs and his book. There was a whole cult established before Burroughs even put his nose into the scene. Many people did not know that he'd written a book before called *Junky*. But even so, it was a generally accepted fact that Burroughs was the outstanding writer of his time, and when word got out that he was back in the city everybody was anxious to meet him. I was sort of anxious to see Bill myself. Allen would tell me, "Well, I heard from Bill and such-and-such is happening."

Of course I'd read *Naked Lunch* immediately. I enjoyed the book and even peeked into it later from time to time, but I found his satire a little too biting, a little too cold. I think he has an incredible style—there's no getting around that. As a writer he is a master, and he had certainly ripped the covers off present social standards. But there is that coldness—he's forgotten the human element somehow, it seems to me.

Anyway, all the young writers and artists were waiting to see him.

It was finally arranged for him to come to this place where everyone was reading, and when the night rolled around the place was jammed. People were lined up out on the street. Of course, he took his sweet time about getting there. There was a loudspeaker so they could announce him, and he arrived in his dignified, reserved way. Everyone was gaping. It was all quite amusing.

Not long afterward, a woman named Panna Grady decided to give a party for him. Allen and Peter had met Panna in San Francisco not long before. She was a Hungarian countess and, in fact, one of the most gracious women I have ever met in my life. There was no affectation—just naturally genteel. She was a real lady in the truest sense of the word. She'd made a terrific impression upon me and I didn't realize until later on that she had a title. Of course, there were many comments to the effect that a woman that had been raised with her advantages would naturally have charm and grace. It was partially due to that, but there was an inner quality to her I truly believe was part of her, regardless.

Later she told me how she had met Allen and Peter. She had given a party and the two poets were invited. She'd stepped out into her garden during the evening and there were Allen and Peter, stark naked, dancing in the moonlight. She said it gave her such a thrill and that it was something she'd never forgotten. On the strength of that she immediately developed an interest in both of them, though in Ginsberg she recognized his potential as a major poet. She became a patron of literature, and of the arts in general.

Panna, I believe, has had experiences of all kinds. She's had lesbian lovers and men lovers, but her weakness was Irish poets. Her ex-husband is an Irish poet, a man by the name of Grady. As I understand it, without knowing all the details, after they married he became even more of a heavy drinker. He finally became so unbearable that she had to divorce him. They'd had a child, Ella, and she too was beautiful. She was being raised with all the advantages, spoke several languages, just like her mother.

As it turned out, Panna had a crush on Burroughs. She told Allen that she would give a party to welcome him back to New York after being abroad for so long. She believed she could handle a hundred guests and asked Allen to select some of Burroughs's closer friends. Allen passed the invitation along to me, telling me she was a friend of Bill's and that she was very wealthy. She had an apartment in the

Dakota building, up on Seventy-second Street, an absolutely incredible place. It was furnished very simply in antiques. When someone scratched a dining table that dated back several hundred years, I commented saying, "Oh, that's a shame." She replied, "Oh no, Herbert. You see these marks? That happened probably a hundred years ago. And these? Fifty years ago. This just happened now." I thought that was such a beautiful way of accepting it instead of fussing about it.

She had a bar with two bartenders serving drinks as rapidly as they could. There were two gigantic rooms that overlooked Central Park, and in one she'd set up the bar and the other was her music room. She'd moved all the furniture out of it and had this incredible hi-fi system going, blasting all the best music. Folks were really letting their hair down. The dining room table was piled with baked hams, bowls of fruit, everything you could imagine.

Cabs were pulling up as though it was a nightclub. I never saw anything like it. As one group of people left, another mob would arrive. She hadn't expected anything like that. I was amazed at her ability to stand at the door and, with all the charm and grace of a hostess, greet the people whom you'd think twice about before speaking to on the street. The only thing that she stipulated was that there be no press people. *Life* magazine tried to do a spread on it, but she wouldn't allow it. She wanted no notoriety, but, by God, word of mouth was enough for it to get around.

It happened that at least four hundred people came to the party, and finally Panna had to call down to the desk and tell them to turn people away.

Of course they stripped the place down. I don't know whether she lost personal things or not. Some of the women's bags were rifled, but other than that there was no stealing. LeRoi Jones arrived with several of his friends, and when he couldn't get in, he got in a very heated argument with the doorman. They ended up in a fight and he broke the man's arm. Of course, Panna handled all the expenses for that, but it was too bad because it spoiled an otherwise exciting evening.

Burroughs and I had a chance to speak briefly at the party. I said to him, "Well, Bill, you're looking well."

"I feel well," he said. "I've decided there'll be no more drugs in my life. Anybody that uses drugs is a damn fool. I won't have any more to do with narcotics."

"Your first love has always been alcohol anyway," I replied.

"I guess it has." Then he confided, "This affair is for me but I don't like this kind of thing. As soon as I possibly can, I'm gong to leave."

"You must admit, it's quite a turnout," I told him.

Panna, though, hardly got a chance to speak with Bill, as he was one of the first to leave. He'd put in his appearance; but I guess they arranged to meet for lunch or something before he left. When I got ready to leave, she stopped me and said, "I hear you're a good friend of Bill's."

"I'm not really a close friend," I told her, "though I have been associated with him on and off for some time."

Then she said, "Well, feel free to give me a call," and she gave me her phone number.

When I left, I decided that I *would* get in touch with her. I must admit that it occurred to me that she might be able to help me financially. It was so obvious that she had money and, in fact, Allen had said to me, "Herbie, perhaps Panna can be of some assistance to you." At the time I was barely existing. I'd lost my place on Attorney Street and was living with Bryden on Eleventh Street. But I wanted to get out of there and get a place of my own. It occurred to me that if I could get hold of a couple hundred dollars, I could pay the rent on an apartment and have a little something left to operate on as well. This was the plan anyway. I make plans. I get just so far and then things get all screwed up, always, but my intentions are good. At least most of the time they've been good.

I finally called and she said, "Oh yes, I'm seeing Robin this afternoon, but why don't you come on up?" Robin was an artist friend of Burroughs's who'd done several covers for his books. Most of his stuff was abstract, and a lot of it looked like Oriental calligraphy. He was very British. I'd met him for the first time at Panna's party—she'd made a point of introducing him to me—and he said, "Oh, I've heard a great deal about you, Huncke. It's a pleasure to meet you." He'd been draped in sartorial splendor, a white suit and the whole bit: a typical Englishman in many ways but something of a soldier of fortune, who had become close friends with Burroughs while he was in Tangier. They would travel back and forth from London to Tangier, and I guess Robin had come through with Bill when he returned to New York.

When I arrived at Panna's, Robin was there showing her some of his pictures. She wrote out a check to him for four hundred dollars for four of them. I said very little. At last she turned to me: "Now, what can I do for you?"

"I'm in a bad situation financially," I said, "and it occurred to me that possibly you'd be willing to help me."

"Well, what can you tell me about Bill? Maybe if you can tell me something nice about Bill, I can be of some assistance to you. What sort of man is he? I hear that you lived with him in Texas with his wife, Joan."

"Yes, I did." And I told her a little bit about Texas and about our relationship there. And I said something to the effect that I'd stopped and spoken with him the night of the party, and that he didn't like big crowds of people but that he did say he thought she was a very charming lady.

"Oh," she said, "that's worth a hundred dollars," and she sat down and wrote me a hundred-dollar check just like that. "Keep in touch," she told me, and I said, "Oh, I will, of course, and thank you very much."

---

# JOYCE JOHNSON

JOYCE JOHNSON, author of three novels, documented her unrequited love affair with Jack Kerouac more than a quarter-century ago in her prize-winning memoir *Minor Characters* (1984). She continued to explore this major event in her life in her book *Door Wide Open* (2000), presenting her correspondence with Kerouac along with her commentary on their relationship. She was aware, as she said, that although Kerouac did not return her feelings, she "became intent on saving him through showing him that he was loved."

## *From* Minor Characters

It's an evening the previous May, 1956. A small makeshift theater in Berkeley. An audience gathered in response to a post-card invitation.

Young people, mostly—poets and students, wives and girlfriends of same. The theater is dark, but there are line drawings tacked on the walls. If you walk up to them and look closely, you will see that they are drawings of two naked men, Allen Ginsberg and Peter Orlovsky, in acts of love.

The audience is unshockable, at one with the thin, intense young man in black raveled sweater who gets up on the tiny stage to read from his as yet unpublished manuscript. "I saw the best minds of my generation destroyed by madness . . ." Or if there is shock, it's the shock of recognition popping off in a series of electrical synapses. ". . . starving hysterical naked / dragging themselves through the negro streets at dawn looking for an angry fix, / angelheaded hipsters . . ."

The poet reads in that low, oddly compelling voice he had even when he was seventeen and first met Jack Kerouac on the Columbia campus—that almost diffident voice with the power hidden in it. "Moloch!" he shouts, the power rising to the surface. "Moloch whose love is endless oil and stone! Moloch whose soul is electricity and banks! Moloch whose poverty is the specter of genius!"

Each indictment of Moloch sets off boos and hisses. Like a prophet of a coming revolution, Allen captures the crowd, finishing in a rainbow razzmadazzle of all the colored stage lights on the board and the forward rush of fellow poets to grip his hands, and the embrace of Kerouac.

Jack, who has given Allen's poem its title, is drunk again, as he was the first time Allen ever read *Howl* publicly—the October night at the Six Gallery when the San Francisco Renaissance was actually born. There, too, Jack had played the buffoon, uproariously good-natured on the sidelines, plying the audience with jugs of wine. Since 1951, he has written eleven books himself. Faithfully, Allen plans to list them in the dedication to the upcoming City Lights edition of *Howl*, with the ironic notation "All these books will be published in heaven."

One curious thing is that despite appearances this reading in May is not a starting point but a reenactment. The same poets, the audience arriving knowing what to expect, and thus part of the performance themselves. The ritual of a movement that's less than a year old but maturing quickly.

Cautiously turned on by what he sees, a visiting poet from the East, Richard Eberhart, writes an article for the *New York Times Book*

*Review.* Something new is stirring in San Francisco, a revolution in consciousness. Neglecting indigenous West Coast poets like Kenneth Rexroth, Robert Duncan, and Michael McClure—and sowing the seeds of rivalry—he devotes most of the article, which will be published early the following September, to Allen Ginsberg.

By the time Jack Kerouac came down from his mountain, a photographer from *Mademoiselle* had flown in and was trying to line up the San Francisco Renaissance poets for a group portrait. Not wishing to be photographed with Allen Ginsberg and his circle, Michael McClure and Kenneth Rexroth made appointments for separate sessions. "Hand in hand, it's got to be," Allen insisted. He was torn between disappearing and moving the revolution elsewhere.


In the fall of '56, having narrowly survived my twentieth year, I was just turning twenty-one. My crash course in the depths of human experience sometimes made me feel extremely old. This was not entirely an unpleasant feeling but new and strange, like walking around in an exotic garment that suddenly made you impervious to everything but didn't connect you to most of the people you knew in your everyday life. Once you'd touched bottom, what was there to be afraid of anymore? I was continually lonely, but very fearless. Life seemed grey but not impossible.

I found a new job at another literary agency and got a little more money. I moved into a new apartment of my own that happened to be around the corner from Alex's. I worked on the novel about Barnard I'd begun in Hiram Haydn's workshop. Elise and Alex were characters in it. By making Alex into a character, I took away his power to hurt me. Just like me, my heroine would have an affair with the Alex character and end up alone. But in my fictional rearrangement of life, it was she who was going to leave him after their one and only night together. I rewarded her with a trip to Paris. I typed forty letters a day and dreamed of taking off myself.

There was a restlessness in everyone I knew. Journeys seemed imminent. Elise and Sheila actually went to Rockefeller Center one day on their lunch hours and applied for passports, had their pictures taken and everything, even though neither of them had a dime.

The Sunday the article on Allen appeared, Elise called and read it to me over the phone, her voice taut with excitement. With that, our collective travel fantasies switched over to San Francisco, city of poets and accessible by Greyhound bus, whose hilly streets in our imaginations took on a perpetual golden haze. I thought about San Francisco the way I'd thought about the Village when I was thirteen, before I ever went there. Could it possibly be what it was said to be? A vision of community into which I would somehow fit. I didn't seem to fit into the rest of America, although I did it better than Elise. It took great effort and vigilance to report to my job on Madison Avenue, my hair wound into a chignon around a horrible doughnut-shaped thing called a rat. My office identity seemed as precarious as my hair style. Someday they would find me out. I had broken the law, I had slept with men, I had contempt for the books the MCA Literary Agency was attempting to sell to publishers. The lives of my superiors seemed desiccated rather than enviable. Only the publication of my novel would transform my existence into what I wanted it to be.

Elise, although she wouldn't come out and say it, wanted to go to San Francisco for purposes of love. This worried me. What if Allen Ginsberg wouldn't be so glad to see her? It had been three years since that night on East Seventh Street that she still talked about. I myself had come to place value on forgetting as a way of getting through life. Lovers you couldn't forget were dangerous. Allen Ginsberg had somehow always been legendary, even before he became famous in the *New York Times*.

A Barnard friend of mine worked for *Mademoiselle*. I visited her there one day and she showed me proofs of the article they were going to run on the San Francisco Renaissance. There was a photo of Allen with three other men, a cherubic hoodlum named Gregory Corso, a scholarly Philip Whalen, and a writer who had a crucifix around his neck and tangled black hair plastered against his forehead as if he'd just walked out of the rain. He looked wild and sad in a way that didn't seem appropriate to the occasion. This was Jack Kerouac, whose reputation was underground. Like the others, he was said to frequent North Beach, a run-down area where there were suddenly a lot of new coffee shops, jazz joints, and bars, as well as an excellent bookstore called City Lights that was the center of activity for the poets. Thus several thousand young women between fourteen and twenty-five were given a map to a revolution. *Mademoiselle* made it its business to keep up with things.

I remembered the man with the dark, anguished face and the name that was unlike anyone else's, the harsh music of its three syllables. Soon afterward I found it on a book at the office. A battered copy of *The Town and the City* was on a shelf where they put things that weren't active any more. I asked what it was doing at MCA, and was told it was the work of a talented but very terrible person who had briefly been handled by the agency. He had grown more and more enraged and unreasonable as his various novels proved impossible to place. Sometimes he seemed under the influence of alcohol—or worse, probably. Then one day an equally crazy Mr. Ginsberg had turned up without an appointment, demanding the return of the three manuscripts and announcing that *he* was Jack Kerouac's agent. Good riddance!

I asked if I could borrow Kerouac's book. I took it home and never brought it back.

---

# HETTIE JONES

HETTIE JONES, poet, children's book author, and memoirist, dedicated her book *How I Became Hettie Jones* (1990) to her two daughters, Kellie and Lisa (their father was the writer and activist LeRoi Jones), adding the poem

> *pat my bro*
> *pat my sister*
> *see we tender*
> *women*
> *live*
> *on.*

Before the opening chapter of her book, Hettie quoted a line from a novel that she had admired in the 1950s, *Two Serious Ladies* (1943), written by Jane Bowles, one of her favorite authors, who was also the wife of a strong personality: "The idea

... is to change first of our own volition and according to our own inner promptings before they impose completely arbitrary changes on us." This excerpt from *How I Became Hettie Jones* describes how the impecunious fledging co-publisher of *Yugen* magazine got her job as subscription manager and copy editor at the *Partisan Review*.

---

## *From* How I Became Hettie Jones

It's a sunny late September morning on Morton Street. We're hanging around, reading the paper. Roi's in a chair, one of the two the landlord said I might keep, and which, were we your typical fifties couple, we would now think of as "our furniture." Except we never think about furniture. Like money, it's simply what you come across. Luckily, we don't think much about food either—except the dollar salad at Café San Remo, split between the two of us, with lots of free bread and butter. (I haven't learned to cook.)

But we're living on love, of course. Last night we went to an Ionesco play, *The Bald Soprano,* and laughed louder than anyone else in the audience. That's another thing I like about us—we make noise. We play. He jumps over fire hydrants and tries to vault parking meters, eek. I whistle in the street, and tell him how my mother used to tell me to stop that. And when I am my usual antic self, the look of pleasure on him is like grace. With no effort, or adjustment, I can't imagine life without him.

And there's a way we approach the fact of our being together that has none of the high seriousness the world seems to wish on it. Little Rock, Arkansas, has just refused to integrate its schools. Federal troops were called. But nothing touches *us;* people stop and stare and we sail on—what else should we do, fall on our knees and ask their permission? Sometimes I still want to toss my head or stick out my tongue or shriek *We are not illegal* but I have learned, and I am learning every day.

Today I'm sprawled on the bed, thinking about what to do next. I've just finished reading the new, hot book *On the Road.* I love Jack Kerouac's footloose heroes, who've upset complacent America simply by driving through it! I don't know whether Roi and I are among "the mad ones, the ones who are mad to live, mad to talk, mad to be saved," but I know I don't want to go on the road right now, not while New York is the best place in the world. Nothing could tempt me away.

Though nagging my peace is the fact that Dick's dollar an hour is not enough anymore. Besides, he's running out of money himself and is thinking of closing the *Changer* and moving to California. I heave an elaborate sigh, a shoo-in for attention.

"What's the matter?" Roi comes up out of the *Book Review*.

"Hand me the want ads," I say gloomily.

He smiles at my terrible expression, but he'll be out of work soon too. "I'll read them," he offers.

I smile at him. How generous. But I don't hold much hope. I'll never find a job that's anything like the one at the *Record Changer*. It's probably back to the straight world for me. But where? What? And I don't *want* to. "Lots of luck," I say to Roi, and bury my face in the magazine.

Then in a few minutes he says, "Hey, look at this," and I hear disbelief. "Look at this," he says again. "*Partisan Review* wants a subscription manager."

"*Partisan Review!*" I jump off the bed. "Stop teasing me," I mutter, and crash down beside him, poking pages out of the way. "Let me see."

And, indeed, there it is. "Well, *I'm* a subscription manager," I say, incredulous. And then we're all over each other, laughing. But we remember to save the ad and the phone number.


The next day William Phillips, one of the editors, had nearly the same reaction. "You're really a subscription manager?" he asked. It must have seemed unlikely, not the kind of specialization expected from a drama major. But he was impressed by the fact that I'd done film research for Eric Barnaow at Columbia. (I didn't tell him I'd done that *once*.)

"And you *know* the magazine," he said doubtfully.

"Know *Partisan*? Why, of course," I said. "A friend of mine was discharged from the Air Force for reading it!"

This seemed to reassure William Phillips, who hired me on the spot. I left in a hazy euphoria. Eighty dollars a week and all those words! I couldn't imagine anything better, anything more thrilling—and the two, cluttered, scruffy rooms on Union Square confirmed all my rebellious suspicions. Here was real upward mobility—plus I got my job through *The New York Times*! What a joke!

Running downtown to spread the news, I caught my wide grin in Fifth Avenue's windows, above that same brown dress I'd worn home from Newport. And I'd been hired in my old clothes! Was it my direct eye, my innocent confidence? I'm curious now, I never thought of *why* then. The world was my oyster, that's all. And the pearls! . . .


Those two rooms were soon what the ads called a "one-girl office," since added to subscriptions were also "all phases magazine management." With literary quarterlies, international journals, *Dissent, Midstream, Hudson, Poetry, Kenyon, Encounter,* the London *Times*—and books, books! An ocean of words and opinion surrounded me like the Jiffy bag fuzz I'd scatter each morning in my rush to open the mail.

And as Union Square was familiar, I preferred to hole up, noon hours, in the grimy-windowed *Partisan* office, with a peanut butter and jelly sandwich and whatever I happened to be reading.

In a very short time I discovered myself barely educated, with great intellectual gaps where everyone else had stored movements and cultures. What had I learned at Mary Washington—Roi called it my "teacup college"—except an illusion of independence from the men who called the shots? "That's the trouble with you young people today, no sense of history!" William would yell cheerfully, shaking his finger at me. Yet he was always kindly instructive, and I liked watching him edit, the care for the precise word, the very generosity of honing another person's argument. When I began to take charge of business with the printer, and there were times when a line here or there had to be saved, we would spread out the proofs and go over them. The content dissolved in the pleasure of sweet manipulation.

Still my mind balked at the academic focus on criticism, the same texts run over and over like obligatory laps. I imagined the nine letters of N.e.w. C.r.i.t.i.c. as the nine Supreme Court justices, presiding over all that was robed and respectable. And Moby-Dick, solid and impenetrable, with all these critics sliding down his sides. I knew William was right but sometimes I felt defensive, as if it were only *his* history he thought I should know. Where was the guide to my situation, cultural or political—where was my life in all these pages? I felt, as always, that I had no precedent. Except—to give credit where it's certainly due—the time William said to me, with a terrible look of astonishment: "What! You've never read Tillie Olsen!"

Fortunately, neither an acceptable Moby-Dick analysis, nor an enlightened Lenin approach, is much to the point in running a magazine, even a literary one, and with a sly acuity of eye and ear I could fudge it. The past regretted, I had no complaints about my present education. William's co-editor, the critic Philip Rahv, also seemed to trust me and like William was willing to teach.

"Copyedit this," he said to me one day, putting a manuscript into my hand.

"But I've never . . . How do you do it?" I said.

He hesitated, frowning, then patted my shoulder. "Just make it right," he said reassuringly. "And change it from English to American."

That I felt I could do. By luck I had grammar by ear, and knowing American was high on my list. What I didn't tell Philip, or William—not just yet—was that I thought we were defining American now, we of the "misalliance," we of the new world, the one that hadn't yet livened their pages.


One windy late fall Friday just after we moved to Chelsea, Roi and I went out to hear Jack Kerouac read his poetry. Jack's life had so far led from working-class Lowell, Massachusetts, where he'd been a football star, past Columbia University, the Merchant Marine, Mexico, both coasts, two marriages, many liaisons, and a child he wouldn't acknowledge. In the year since *On the Road* he'd been celebritized, endlessly criticized, pressed for definitions of Beat. The attention hadn't helped. I didn't know him, and after our one brief meeting at Jazz on the Wagon I'd only caught glimpses of him haggard, drunk, and surrounded.

The reading was at a newly opened, out-of-the-way place, the Seven Arts Coffee Gallery, a second-floor storefront on Ninth Avenue in the forties, the transient neighborhood near the bus terminal. The audience, mostly friends, numbered only about thirty. Unexpectedly Jack was sober, all slicked down and lumberjacked up, an engineer scrubbed clean for the evening (on the West Coast he'd worked as a trainman). I decided I liked this good-looking, friendly man whom everyone loved and admired, and I certainly admired his work, so when the reading began I sat alone at a table up front to pay attention. He noticed. He kept catching my eye and reading to me, and he was marvelous: relaxed, confident, full of humor and passion—and he wanted the meaning *clear*. At the end we all stomped and whistled and clapped and cheered.

A crowd of thirty, thus inspired, needs a big enough place to party. Our new house was a straight mile downtown, just off Ninth Avenue, and we had nothing but party space to offer, so after the reading we just brought the audience home, to 402 West Twentieth Street, a once elegant six-room parlor facing the weatherbeaten brick of the Episcopal Seminary.

In the arrival melee of coats and drinks and glasses and ash trays, I caught some puzzled glances from Jack, who looked as if he couldn't place me, as if he'd read to me as an interested stranger, and only now had noticed the burgeoning rest of me. To whom was this pregnant woman attached? I saw him whisper the question to Allen, who pointed to Roi.

The connection seemed to please Jack enormously—his face lit in the strangest, gleaming little grin. The music was on and a few people were already dancing. Suddenly he ducked and wove his way through them—fast, as if in a scrimmage—to Roi, who was at the other end of the two adjoining front rooms. Then dragging bewildered Roi by the hand he maneuvered back to me and grabbed me too, and then, with amazing strength, he picked us both up at once—all 235 pounds of us, one in each arm like two embarrassed children—and held us there with an iron grip and wouldn't let go!

What a pleasure to meet this funny, visionary Jack, who appeared to have such sympathy in him, a sweetness similar to Roi's that I found attractive. Word got out and soon the party of thirty grew to fifty, and all night Jack kept running to me with different people: "I didn't remember who she was," he kept saying, "but she was listening so hard at the reading, she was really listening to me—she *understood* what I said!"

That Friday night party never ended. Soon we had a studio couch and a folding cot, one or two weekly boarders, twenty or more weekend regulars, occasional bashes for hundreds. Under these circumstances, being the one who understands can get you a rep for sufferance. The writer Hubert (Cubby) Selby, Jr., once said, to my surprise, "I always meant to apologize for those years we crashed all over you." But never having to manage alone made all the difference to me, as never having to go home alone—or always having a home to go to—made all the difference to them. Twentieth Street was a young time, a wild, wide-open, hot time, full of love and rage and heart and soul and jism. Like everyone else, I tried to get my share.

Billie Holiday had been at Jack's reading, or at least she was outside the Seven Arts in a car. It was the poet Joel Oppenheimer, bearded and bespectacled and wild-eyed as a young Trotsky, who approached her while the rest of us kept a respectful distance. In the darkness the turned-up collar of his black overcoat seemed all of a piece with his hair and beard, and he must have been a sight to Billie, whose mouth opened slightly in surprise when, leaning into the open window of the car, he said, with all his avant-garde elliptic-profundo: "Thanks, Lady. Just . . . thanks."

"Thanks?" Billie said. "For what?"

# BOB KAUFMAN

BOB KAUFMAN (1925–1986), who moved to San Francisco after serving for twenty years in the U.S. Merchant Marine, was active in the East Bay "poetry renaissance" in the 1950s and early 1960s. As the poet Anne Waldman recognized, Kaufman was "the quintessential urban Beat poet." He organized poetry readings at the Co-Existence Bagel Shop and other cafés in North Beach, close to the City Lights Bookshop, and often ran afoul of the San Francisco police for his insistence on free speech. His wife, Eileen Kaufman, was with him in November 1963 when he became so distraught at the news of John F. Kennedy's assassination that he took a vow of silence that lasted a decade. During that time, in 1967, City Lights published a book of Kaufman's poetry, *Golden Sardine*, as volume twenty-one in its Pocket Poets series.

"Abomunist Manifesto," one of Kaufman's most imaginative exercises, using jazz rhythms and street speech, was first published as a broadside by City Lights in 1958; it was included in Kaufman's first poetry collection, *Solitudes Crowded with Loneliness,* issued by New Directions in 1959. Kaufman produced his "Abomunist Manifesto" as a parody of the Communist Manifesto, written (as the critic Jack Foley recognized) "not by Marx or Engels but by 'Bomkauf,'" a reference to the threat of the superbomb brandished by both the United States and the Soviet Union during the Cold War.

---

## *Abomunist Manifesto*

ABOMUNISTS JOIN NOTHING BUT THEIR HANDS OR LEGS,
    OR OTHER SAME.

ABOMUNISTS SPIT ANTI-POETRY FOR POETIC REASONS
    AND FRINK.

ABOMUNISTS DO NOT LOOK AT PICTURES PAINTED
    BY PRESIDENTS AND UNEMPLOYED PRIME MINISTERS.

IN TIMES OF NATIONAL PERIL, ABOMUNISTS, AS REALITY
    AMERICANS, STAND READY TO DRINK THEMSELVES
    TO DEATH FOR THEIR COUNTRY.

ABOMUNISTS DO NOT FEEL PAIN, NO MATTER HOW MUCH
    IT HURTS.

ABOMUNISTS DO NOT USE THE WORD SQUARE EXCEPT WHEN
    TALKING TO SQUARES.

ABOMUNISTS READ NEWSPAPERS ONLY TO ASCERTAIN THEIR
    ABOMINUBILITY.

ABOMUNISTS NEVER CARRY MORE THAN FIFTY DOLLARS
    IN DEBTS ON THEM.

ABOMUNISTS BELIEVE THAT THE SOLUTION OF PROBLEMS
    OF RELIGIOUS BIGOTRY IS, TO HAVE A CATHOLIC
    CANDIDATE FOR PRESIDENT AND A PROTESTANT
    CANDIDATE FOR POPE.

ABOMUNISTS DO NOT WRITE FOR MONEY; THEY WRITE
    THE MONEY ITSELF.

ABOMUNISTS BELIEVE ONLY WHAT THEY DREAM ONLY
    AFTER IT COMES TRUE.

ABOMUNIST CHILDREN MUST BE REARED ABOMUNIBLY.

ABOMUNIST POETS, CONFIDENT THAT THE NEW LITERARY
    FORM "FOOT-PRINTISM" HAS FREED THE ARTIST
    OF OUTMODED RESTRICTIONS, SUCH AS: THE ABILITY TO
    READ AND WRITE, OR THE DESIRE TO COMMUNICATE,
    MUST BE PREPARED TO READ THEIR WORK AT DENTAL
    COLLEGES, EMBALMING SCHOOLS, HOMES FOR UNWED
    MOTHERS, HOMES FOR WED MOTHERS, INSANE ASYLUMS,
    USO CANTEENS, KINDERGARTENS, AND COUNTY JAILS.
    ABOMUNISTS NEVER COMPROMISE THEIR REJECTIONARY
    PHILOSOPHY.

ABOMUNISTS REJECT EVERYTHING EXCEPT SNOWMEN.

## Notes Dis- and Re- Garding Abomunism

Abomunism was founded by Barabbas, inspired by his dying
    words: "I wanted to be in the middle, but I went too
    far out."
Abomunism's main function is to unite the soul with oatmeal
    cookies.
Abomunists love love, hate hate, drink drinks, smoke smokes,
    live lives, die deaths.
Abomunist writers write writing, or nothing at all.
Abomunist poetry, in order to be compleatly (Eng. sp.)
    understood, should be eaten . . . except on fast days,
    slow days, and mornings of executions.

Abomunists, could they be a color, would be green,
    and tell everyone to go.
Uncrazy Abomunists crazy unAbomunists by proxy kicky
    tricks, as follows:
  By telling psychometric poets two heads are better
    than none.
  By selling middle names to impotent personnel managers.
  By giving children brightly wrapped candy fathers.
  By biting their own hands after feeding themselves.
  By calling taxis dirty names, while ordering fifths
    of milk.
  By walking across hills, ignoring up and down.
  By giving telescopes to peeping Toms.
  By using real names at false hotels.
Abomunists who feel their faith weakening will have to
    spend two weeks in Los Angeles.
When attacked, Abomunists think positive, repeating over
    and under: "If I were a crime, I'd want to be
    committed . . .
        No! . . . Wait!"


### Further Notes

*(taken from "Abomunismus und Religion" by Tom Man)*

Krishnamurti can relax the muscles of your soul,
Free your aching jawbone from the chewinggum habit.
Ouspensky can churn your illusions into butter and
Give you circles to carry them in, around your head.
Subud can lock you in strange rooms with vocal balms
And make your ignorant clothing understand you.
Zen can cause changes in the texture of your hair,
Removing you from the clutches of sexy barbers.
Edgar Cayce can locate your gallstones, other organs,
On the anarchistic rockpiles of Sacramento.
Voodoo Marie can give you Loas, abstract horses,
Snorting guides to tar-baby black masses.
Billy can plug you into the Christ machine. Mail in your
Mind today. Hurry, bargain God week, lasts one week only.

## $$ Abomunus Craxioms $$

Egyptian mummies are lousy dancers.
    Alcoholics cannot make it on root beer.
Jazz never made it back down the river.
    Licking postage stamps depletes the body fluids.
Fat automobiles laugh more than others, and frink.
    Men who die in wars become seagulls and fly.
Roaches have a rough time of it from birth.
    People who read are not happy.
People who do not read are not happy.
    People are not very happy.
These days people get sicker quicker.
    The sky is less crowded in the West.
Psychiatrists pretend not to know everything.
    Way out people know the way out.
Laughter sounds orange at night, because
    reality is unrealizable while it exists.
Abomunists knew it all along,
    but couldn't get the butterscotch down.

## Excerpts from the Lexicon Abomunon

*At election time, Abomunists frink more, and naturally, as hard-core Abo's, we feel the need to express ourselves somewhat more abomunably than others. We do this simply by not expressing ourselves (abomunization). We do not express ourselves in the following terms:*

*Abommunity:* n. Grant Avenue & other frinky places.
*Abomunarcosis:* n. Addiction to oatmeal cookies & liverwurst.
*Abomunasium:* n. Place in which abomunastics occur, such
    as bars, coffee shops, USO's, juvenile homes, pads, etc.
*Abomunastics:* n. Physical Abomunism.
*Abomunate, The:* n. The apolitical CORPUS ABOMUNISMUS.
*Abomunette:* n. Female type Abomunist (rare).
*Abomunibble:* v. 1. To bite a daisy. 2. How poets eat.
*Abomunicate.* v. To dig. (Slang: to frink.)
*Abomunics:* n. Abomunistic techniques.

*Abomunificance:* n. The façade behind the reality of double-talking billboards.

*Abomunify:* v. To (censored) with an Abomunette, or vice versa.

*Abomunik:* n. Square abomuflack.

*Abomunism:* n. Footprintism. A rejectory philosophy founded by Barabbas and dedicated to the proposition that the essence of existence is reality essential and neither four-sided nor frinky, but not non-frinky either.

*Abomunist:* n. One who avows Abomunism, disavowing almost everything else, especially butterscotch.

*Abomunitions:* n. Love, commonly found in the plural state, very.

*Abomunity:* n. A by-product of abomunarcosis, also obtained by frinking. (Thus: Frinkism.)

*Abomunize:* v. To carefully disorganize—usually associated with frinking.

*Abomunoid:* adj. Having some Abomunistic qualities such as tragictories, pail faces, or night vision.

*Abomunology:* n. The systematic study of Abomunism; classes every other Frinksday, 2 a.m.

*Abomunosis:* n. Sweet breath.

*Abomunosophy:* n. Theoretical Abomunism.

*Abomunull:* n. 1. They. 2. One who is not quite *here.*

*Abomusical:* adj. Diggable sounds.

*Abomutiny:* n. Regimentation. v. To impose organization from without, i.e., without oatmeal cookies.

*Frink:* v. To (censored). n. (censored) and (censored).

*Frinkism:* n. A sub-cult of Abomunism, not authorized nor given abomunitude by Bomkauf.

*Frinky:* adj. Like (censored).

—*Compiled by* BIMGO

## Abomunist Election Manifesto

1. Abomunists vote against everyone by not voting for anyone.
2. The only proposition Abomunists support are those made to members of the opposite sex.
3. Abomunists demand the abolition of Oakland.

4. Abomunists demand low-cost housing for homosexuals.
5. Abomunists demand suppression of illegal milk traffic.
6. Abomunists demand statehood for North Beach.
7. The only office Abomunists run for is the unemployment office.
8. Abomunists support universal frinkage.
9. Abomunists demand split-level ranch-type phonebooths.
10. Abomunists demand the reestablishment of the government in its rightful home at ?

## Still Further Notes Dis- & Re- Garding Abomunism

*The following translation is the first publication of the Live Sea Scrolls, found by an old Arab oilwell driller. He first saw them on the dead beds of the live sea. Thinking they were ancient bubblegum wrappers he took them to town to trade in for hashish coupons. As chance would have it, the hashish pipes were in the hands of a visiting American relief official, who reluctantly surrendered them in return for two villages and a canal. We developed the cunic script by smearing it with tanfastic sun lotion, after which we took it down to the laundromat and placed it in the dryer for two hours ($1.20). We then ate four pounds of garlic bread & frinked; then we translated this diary. We feel this is one of the oldest Abomunist documents yet discovered.*

MONDAY—B.C.—minus 4—10 o'sun, a.m.

Nazareth getting too hot, fuzz broke up two of my poetry readings last night. Beat vagrancy charge by carrying my toolbox to court—carpenters O.K. Splitting to Jeru. as soon as I get wheels.

TUESDAY—B.C.—minus 3—8 o'sun, p.m.

Jeru. cool, Roman fuzz busy having a ball, never bother you unless someone complains. Had a ball this morning, eighty-sixed some square bankers from the Temple, read long poem on revolt. Noticed cats taking notes, maybe they are publisher's agents, hope so, it would be crazy to publish with one of those big Roman firms.

WEDNESDAY—B.C.—minus 2—11 o'sun, a.m.

Local poets and literary people throwing a big dinner for me tonight, which should be a gas. Most of the cats here real cool, writing real far out—only cat bugs me is this Judas, got shook up when I refused to loan him thirty pieces of silver, he seems to be hung on loot, must be a lush.

THURSDAY—B.C.—minus 1—10 o'sun, p.m.

I am writing this in my cell. I was framed. How can they give the death sentence on charges of disorderly conduct and having public readings without a permit? It's beyond me. Oh well, there's always hope. Maybe that lawyer Judas is getting me can swing it. If he can't, God help me.

FRIDAY—Neutral—5 o'sun, a.m.

Roman turnkey was around passing out crosses. The two thieves have good connections so they got first crack at them—I got stuck with the biggest one. One of the guards doesn't dig my beard and sandals—taunted me all night. I'm going to be cool now, but tomorrow I'll tell him to go to hell, and what's so groovy is: he will. . . . somebody coming. I feel sort of abomunable. Barabbas gets a suspended sentence and I make the hill. What a drag. Well, that's poetry, and I've got to split now.

**Boms**

1. Stashed in his minaret, towering
   Over the hashish wells, Caliph
   Ralph inventoried his popcorn hoard
   While nutty eunuchs conced his concubines.

2. Movies about inventors' lives and glass-encased
       historical documents do not move me as much as
       drinking or hiccupping in the bathtub.

3. Filled with green courage we sneezed political,
   Coughing our dirty fingernails for President.

4. Ageless brilliant colored spiders webbing eternally,
   Instead of taking showers under the fire hydrants
       in summer.

5. Unruly hairs in the noses of statues in public gardens
   Were placed there by God in a fit of insane jealousy.

6. Single-breasted suits, dancing in the air,
   Turned up their cuffs at double-breasted suits
   Plodding down the street.

7. Greedy burglars stole my mother and father,
   And gave me a free pass to the circus and I like stripes.

8. Misty-eyed, knee-quaking me, gazing on the family
        Home,
   Realizing that I was about to burn it down.

9. Waterspouts, concealed in pig knuckle barrels, rumbled,
   As tired storms whispered encouragement.

10. Angry motives scrambled for seating space,
    Shaking their fist at the moon.

11. Liver salesmen door to doored back pats,
    Disturbing chimneysweeps sleeping on roofs.

12. Daily papers suicided from tree tops,
    Purpling the lawn with blueprints.

13. Caribou pranced in suburban carports,
    Hoofmarking the auto-suggestions.

14. Pentagonal merit badges flowed
    Gracefully over the male nurses' heads.

15. Disordered aquariums, dressed in shredded wheat,
    Delivered bibles to pickles crying in confessionals.

## Abomunist Rational Anthem

*(to be sung before and after frinking)*

Derrat slegelations, flo goof babereo
Sorash sho dubies, wago, wailo, wailo.

Geed bop nava glid, nava glied, nava
Speerieder, huyedist, hedacaz, ax, O, O.

Deeredition, Boomedition, squom, squom, squom,
Dee beetstrawist, wapago, wapago, loco,
        locoro, locoest
Voometeyereepetiop, bob, bop, bop, whipop.

Dearat, shloho, kurritip, plog, mangi, squom pot,
Clopo jago, bree, bree, asloopered, akingo labiop,
Engpop, engpop, boint plolo, plolo, bop bop.

*(Music composed by Schroeder.)*

## Abomunist Documents

*(discovered during ceremonies at the Tomb
of the Unknown Draftdodger)*

Boston, December 1773

Dear Adams:

I am down to my last can of tea, and cannot afford to score for
more as the British Pushers have stamped a new tax on the
Stuff, I know that many Colony Cats are as hung as I am, so
why don't we get together on the Night of the Sixteenth and
Go down to the Wharf and swing with a few Pounds. I think
it will be cooler if we make the Scene dressed as Indians, the
British Fuzz will not know who the Tea-Heads are, it will be
very dark so we will have to carry torches, tell the Cats not to

goof with the torches and start a Fire, that would ruin the whole Scene.

Later,<br>HANCOCK

West Point, December 1778

Dear Wife:

I am trying my best to raise the Money for the Rent, but the Army has no funds for Personal Hardships. I sounded George about Promotion, but the Virginia Crowd seems to be in Control so even my hero status can't be any good. Met a very nice English Cat named André, and he has offered to see if he can swing a Loan for me. I don't know where he can get so much money, but since he has been so nice, it would be traitorous to ask.

P.S. He was telling me how much cheaper it is to live in England. Maybe when this is over we can settle there. I have been doing a lot of drawing in my spare time, and tonight I promised to show André some of my sketches, if I can find them, they are all mixed up with my defense plans and I've broken my glasses. Have to close now. I can hear André sneaking in, the chances he takes. He really loves Art.

Yours, faithfully,<br>BENEDICT

**Abomnewscast . . . on the Hour . . .**

America collides with iceberg piloted by Lindbergh baby. . . . Aimee Semple Macpherson, former dictator of California, discovered in voodoo nunnery disguised as Moby Dick. . . . New hit song sweeping the country, the Leopold & Loeb Cha-cha-cha. . . . Pontius Pilate loses no-hitter on an error, league split over scorer's decision, Hebrew fireballer out for season with injured hands. . . . Civilian Defense Headquarters unveils new bomb shelter with two-car garage, complete with indoor patio and barbecue unit that operates on radioactivity, comes in decorator colors, no down payment for vets, to be sold only to those willing to sign loyalty oath. . . . Forest Lawn Cemetery opens new subdivision of split-level tombs for middle-income group. . . . President inaugurates new policy of aggressive leadership, declares December 25th Christmas Day. . . . Pope may allow priests to marry, said to be aiming at one big holy family. . . . Norman Rockwell cover, "The Lynching Bee" from "Post" Americana series, wins D.A.R. Americanism award. . . . Russians said to be copying TV format with frontier epic filmed in Berlin, nuclear Wagon Train features Moiseyev Dancers. . . . Red China cuts birthrate drastically, blessed events plummet to two hundred million a year. . . . Cubans seize Cuba, outraged U.S. acts quickly, cuts off tourist quota, administration introduces measure to confine all rhumba bands to detention camps during emergency. . . . Both sides in Cold War stockpiling atomic missiles to preserve peace, end of mankind seen if peace is declared, UN sees encouraging sign in small war policy, works quietly for wider participation among backward nations. . . . End of news. . . . Remember your national emergency signal, when you see one small mushroom cloud and three large ones, it is not a drill, turn the TV off and get under it. . . . Foregoing sponsored by your friendly neighborhood Abomunist. . . . Tune in next world. . . .

---

# EILEEN KAUFMAN

EILEEN KAUFMAN was a journalist in San Francisco before her marriage to Bob Kaufman in 1958. Together with Allen Ginsberg, they founded the magazine *Beatitude* the following spring, which lasted a year. Eileen Kaufman transcribed her husband's oral poetry, edited his first poetry collection for New Directions, and supported him and their son by writing articles and reviews of musical events for the *Los Angeles Free Press*, *Billboard* magazine, and *Music World Countdown*. In 1973 she began her memoir, *Who Wouldn't Walk with Tigers?* After Kaufman's death in 1986, she presented her transcriptions of his poetry after 1980 to the Mugar Museum and Library of the

Letters section of Boston University. Since many readers in France regarded Bob Kaufman as "the black Rimbaud," Eileen Kaufman arranged to deposit the manuscripts of his poetry before 1980 in the Bibliothèque Archives at the Sorbonne in Paris.

---

## *From* Who Wouldn't Walk with Tigers?

Mark Green had been clueing me that there was really nothing going on in North Beach at the moment, but when Jack Kerouac, Allen Ginsberg, Bob Kaufman, and Neal Cassady came back, there really would be something happening.

The third week in May, Mark seemed unduly excited. He whispered to me, "That one there—in the red beret—that's Bob Kaufman."

I looked over. I saw a small, lithe brown man/boy in sandals . . . wearing a red corduroy jacket, some nondescript pants and striped t-shirt. A wine-colored beret was cocked at a precarious angle on a mop of black curly hair . . . and he was spouting poetry. A policeman came in and told Bob to cool it. He stopped—only until the cop left. Then once more, he began. This time, he jumped up on the nearest table in the Bagel Shop. "Hipsters, Flipsters and Finger-poppin' daddies, knock me your lobes." He was quoting one of his idols, Lord Buckley.

Next, he began to shout some of his own poetry. Everyone was laughing, listening to this poet. When he left the Bagel Shop, everyone within hearing seemed to leave with him. We all wandered over across the street to what was then Miss Smith's Tea Room. And Bob proceeded to hold court at a large round table like a latter-day François Villon.

Flashing black eyes dancing as he spoke, gesticulating as a European does. I couldn't believe this. It all seemed to me like a scene from one of my favorite operas that I had sung the year before.

Rodolfo from "La Bohème" must have appeared like this bard . . . even down to the black goatee. And watching Bob hold court in the Tea Room at the huge table filled with artist friends and admirers, generally leaving the bill for the enthralled tourist . . . it seemed very much that scene from Bohème wherein Musetra joins Marcello,

Mimi, Rodolfo, and their artist friends, leaving her wealthy escort to pay their outrageous bill.

I think I began to play Mimi subconsciously—in the hope that this dynamic Rodolfo would notice me. No luck that evening, but a few nights later, still recuperating from my first head spinning peyote trip, instead of going off to Sacramento to write copy—I remained in the pad which my friend with the MGA and I maintained for weekends. We sublet it to Joe Overstreet, a painter, during the week.

There were four rooms with a long hall connecting them. One in back—a storeroom—a small kitchen, a bathroom, a tiny living room, and the bedroom which Joe used.

Lucky for me that I kept the apartment and used it. For it was on this night that Skippy, Bob Kaufman's old lady, chanced to throw him out.

I was still asleep beside Mark Green when I heard the voice I recognized from the Bagel Shop.

"Let me in. I need a cuppa' coffee . . . you know?"

That voice was hoarse and low. If you ever heard it, you could never mistake it for another. After ten minutes of Bob's pleading, Joe Overstreet came in and said, "For God's sake, somebody, get Bob Kaufman a cup of coffee so we can all get some sleep."

I got up, curious to see the small brown bard again. I went to the window. Mark was visibly annoyed. I padded over and opened the door. "Just a minute, o.k.?"

Suddenly I was looking into the deepest brown eyes I have ever seen—a well I was to explore for many years. I asked him in. Bob never stopped his monologue.

"Hey, man . . . my old lady, she threw me out . . . and I need a cuppa' coffee . . . Can you give me a cup, huh? I don't even have a dime . . ." and on . . . and on, while I slipped on my poncho over black leotards and t-shirt.

We walked down Kearny, crossing Broadway, over to the original old Hot Dog Palace on Columbus, where El Cid now sprawls on the triangle. Bob sat on a stool near the door. It was such a tiny place that anywhere you sat, it was near the door.

I paid for three cups of coffee for Bob while I drank hot chocolate. All the time we were there, he was charming everyone within earshot with his poetry, his quotations of great poetry of the ages, and his extraordinary insights. I was so completely overwhelmed by this young poet that I lost all sense of time, forgot my surroundings . . . everything banal.

Bob was teaching. Money was not important . . . a fact that I was fast coming to believe . . . Living was. Awareness is all. High on Life.

Time drifted by in the Hot Dog Palace. Bob was rapping on every subject known to Man . . . giving us all a show . . . expounding on history, literature, politics, painting, music . . . He kept repeating after every heavy subject that his old lady had thrown him out . . . truly confused that such a thing could be.

We finally left the stand. We walked in the damp San Francisco fog up the Kearny Steps. It might have been the Steppes of Central Asia. It might have been Hawaii. I was neither hot nor cold. I could only hear that hoarse, low voice.

When we got to the flat, I asked Mark for the key to his apartment on Telegraph Hill. I didn't want to disturb Joe further. We three walked to Mark's pad below Coit Tower.

Bob kept up a running conversation, and Mark went to the kitchen to look for food and tea. We just couldn't talk to each other enough. There were so many things we had to find out about each other all at once. Bob had seen a poem of mine which Mark had pinned on the Bagel Shop wall, without my knowledge.

Then Bob quoted one of his own poems to me. "An African Dream."

In black core of Night, it explodes
Silvery thunder, rolling back my brain,
Bursting copper screens, memory worlds
Deep in star-fed beds of time,
Seducing my soul to diamond fires of night.
Faint outline, a ship—momentary fright,
Lifted on waves of color,
Sunk in pits of light,
Drummed back through time,
Hummed back though mind,
Drumming, cracking the night,
Strange forest songs, skin sounds
Crashing through—no longer strange,

Incestuous yellow flowers tearing
Magic from the earth,
Moon-dipped rituals, led
By a scarlet god.
Caressed by ebony maidens
With daylight eyes,
Purple garments,
Noses that twitch,
Singing young girl songs
Of an ancient love
In dark, sunless places
Where memories are sealed,
Burned in eyes of tigers.
Suddenly wise, I fight the dream.
Green screams enfold my night.

I was overwhelmed. Here was a real poet. He reminded me of Coleridge, my childhood favorite. Bob was not one of those schlock artists who write just to be doing something. This man was real, a genuine poet with that calling.

I thrilled every time I looked into his dark, serious eyes. It wasn't hypnotism, because I was fully conscious. But the dynamic glance and depth of this poet's eyes was too much to bear for seven hours. This is how long we talked. We had to get through to each other immediately. I knew that I had suddenly fallen in love with a poet. I had been entranced—from the moment Bob began to talk . . . running down the hill, hand in hand, to the Hot Dog Palace.

We left Mark at his pad (I can't really say that I considered his feelings. I was too mad about Bob Kaufman). My Rodolfo and I wandered back to my flat hand in hand. Joe slept on—unaware of the changes I was experiencing. We sat down on a mattress in the back room and talked softly.

"You are my woman, you know," said Bob. I just gazed at him with newly opened eyes, now wide in disbelief.

He whispered, "You don't believe me now . . . but you'll see."

His arm was around my shoulders. I was standing next to him. I swayed a little then, and he caught me in his arms, broke my balance, and together—we fell laughing onto the bare mattress. He was laughing at me, and I was laughing because, well, I was a little scared and kind of high from our meeting and subsequent conversation.

Suddenly, I sat up straight and leaned over Bob, letting my hair fall into his face. He took hold of my long, loose hair with one hand and pulled me down to him. Then he kissed me. Except for holding hands or casually putting his arm about my shoulders, that was the first actual physical contact with him.

I shivered, and he pulled my hair a little harder, and consequently me closer. How did I feel? Like sunsets and dawns and balmy midnights and ocean voyages. My pulse was dancing a wild Gypsy rhythm, and I felt alive! We searched each other's mouths for a time. Then, as if we had found an answer there . . . without a word, we broke apart . . . and each began to undress the other.

It was a simple task for me, because Bob wore only trousers, t-shirt and sandals. I was eager to feel his strong brown body. It seemed a long time until I was in his arms and stroking that sensual body. This man—with the body of Michelangelo's David—wanted me—and yes, oh yes, I certainly wanted him—for as long as he would have me.

When you find your soul mate, there can be no question, no hesitation, no games. You have been lovers before in many other lives, so you are attuned to each other immediately.

Why else is there love at first sight? Hollywood is often chided for its use of music coming out of nowhere in a big love scene. Believe me, there is music then—music from the spheres.

Without the slightest formal introduction on my part to Eastern eroticism, Bob and I became Tantric lovers spontaneously that morning. That was my second psychedelic trip in two weeks in North Beach.

It is true that your soul leaves your body during a very passionate love embrace. It happened to me just that way. And I suspect that Bob experienced a bit of magic too . . . as he held me throughout the entire tidal wave.

When I caught my breath, I looked at him and smiled. I noticed that he was lying beside me drenched and spent. He said it again. "You see? You are my woman. You have absolutely no choice in the matter."

For the first time, I began to think. How can you ponder what is happening in a vortex . . . at the eye of the hurricane . . . in a whirlpool? You can only swing with it and hope you don't go under permanently. Was I going under? Up to this point, I hadn't even cared.

But now, I leaned on one elbow and looked down into Bob's smiling eyes. I said it as well as I could. "It's just all too overwhelming for me, Bob Kaufman. Go away please and leave me for a few hours . . . till maybe 6 tonight, o.k.? I really have to think about everything that's happened last night and this morning."

Bob's smile faded.

"But hold me now. We can talk later," I added.

He brightened and seemed to understand. He turned on his side, folded me back into his arms, and went to sleep. I may have slept, but I heard him when he got up to dress. I opened my eyes and said sleepily . . . "See you around 6 tonight . . . on Grant."

Bob said, "Then you'll be my old lady. You have no . . ."

I put my fingers over his mouth lightly. "Tell you then. I really have to be alone all day to think it out. Bye."

Bob kissed me lightly on the mouth and vanished. He was gone as suddenly as he had arrived.

I danced the rest of the day through in a hazy kind of mist. I wasn't high on peyote any longer. I was high on Bob Kaufman. Maybe contact high—maybe more, since he had all kinds of dope available to him . . . and he has never been known to turn down any of it!

I dressed slowly, brushing my hair overtime, taking a little more care with the black eyeliner . . . too excited to eat anything, I threw on my poncho and ran out the front door. We didn't have a clock in the pad, and I wasn't going to be late for this important decision.

I ran down Green Street, turned the corner at Grant. Walking down past the Bagel Shop, I saw Bob on the opposite side of the street. He stared at me intently and clenched his teeth, as he has a way of doing when asking a silent question. I just nodded. He came bounding across the street. I said, "You're right. *I'm your woman.*" And he hugged me tightly in answer.

We started to the Bagel Shop. Bob read a few victory poems there, drank a few beers and laughed a lot. He told everyone, "Meet Eileen, my old lady."

That very night, I got my first taste of life with a poet. And that taste has since stayed in my mouth. I could never love a lesser man than an artist.

Bob began to hold court in the Coffee Gallery about 7:30 in the evenings, and for several hours while the locals and the tourists brought him beer, wine, champagne—anything, he, in turn, would speak spontaneously on any subject, quote great poetry by Lorca, T. S. Eliot, e e cummings, or himself. I would just sit adoringly at his side.

I wish that I had been able to tape every conversation, every fragment, because each time Bob speaks it is a gem in a crown of oratory. His wit . . . Cities should be built on one side of the Street . . . His one-liners . . . Laughter sounds orange at Night . . . and his prophecies—all are astounding. Bob's entire monologue is like a long vine of poetry which continually erupts into flowers.

In the late '50s the Coffee Gallery was arranged differently. After the management took over from Miss Smith, the Gallery became the "other" place in the 1300 block on Grant.

There was no partition for the entertainment section, and jazz was played throughout the place any time the musicians fell by. Spontaneity was the key word in our life style in North Beach. This is what made it "the scene," for one never knew in advance just who might show to read a poem, dance, play some jazz, or put on a complete play.

The tourists were delighted to buy a pitcher of beer, bottle of champagne, or anything we wanted—just to be a part of the life emanating from our table. The Life was, for the most part, Bob, and his hilarious monologues, sparkling wit and funky comments. Even the "Mr. Jones" who didn't know what was happening in the late '50s knew that *something* groovy was going on, and he would *buy* his way into it, by God, if he couldn't get in any other way! That's where we accumulated our camp followers, hangers-on and groupies.

Some nights Bob would really get it on. In the early evening he would be writing on note paper, napkins, finally toilet paper, just to get his speeding thoughts down. I began to keep these valuable fragments for him so that he could finish the poems when he got home.

In the early morning, Bob would wander out and take one of his dawn-morning walks—harking back to walks with his great-grand-mother. Sometimes I would go with him. Other days I would sleep in. Bob and I would begin our Grant Avenue odyssey around three or four each afternoon. And whatever happened would happen. We would run down the hill, laughing, and brighten the lives of tourists, adding to the disorder of the day. We proceeded to urge on any musical activity in Washington Square. (New Yorkers, please note: We have our own in North Beach.) Bob might recite a poem or write a new one in the Bagel Shop . . . or we might drink wine or smoke grass at someone's subterranean pad. We spent a lot of time on the rooftops smoking hash.

When I met Bob Kaufman, King of North Beach, my values changed overnight. I had been a greedy, mercenary career girl whose only object was to get it while you can. But the very night I met Bob, I could see these values totally changing. When Bob read "African Dream" to me, I knew I had met a genius.

And so I knew at once what my life would be: Tempestuous, Adventurous, Passionate, but always new experiences. I reached out for Bob Kaufman, the man and his poetry. And he made my life a shambles. It was not as though I didn't ask for it. I knew at a glance and after one night that this man could create my life or destroy it. The life I had known was in ashes, and like the Phoenix, my new life had begun. It was to be everything I had seen in the flash of an African Dream . . . and more. Suddenly wise, I did not fight the Dream.

---

# ALFRED KAZIN

ALFRED KAZIN (1915–1997) wrote a perceptive review of Burroughs's novel *The Wild Boys* for *The New York Times Book Review* on December 12, 1971. A leading American literary critic and reviewer, Kazin began his long career with *On Native Grounds: An Interpretation of Modern American Prose Literature* (1942, 1956) and continued with his widely read *A Walker in the City* (1951), *Contemporaries* (1962), and *Bright Book of Life: American Novelists and Storytellers from Hemingway to Mailer* (1973), among many other titles.

## He's Just Wild About Writing

William S. Burroughs is a great autoeroticist—of writing, not sex. He gets astral kicks by composing in blocks, scenes, repetitive and identical memories galvanizing themselves into violent fantasies, the wild mixing of pictures, words, the echoes of popular speech. It is impossible to suspect him of any base erotic motives in his innumerable scenes of one adolescent boy servicing another like a piece of plumbing; nor should one expect a book from him different from his others. Burroughs is the purest writer in Barney Rosset's grove, and not just because in this book he more than ever turns his obsession with cold, callous homosexual coupling into a piece of American science fiction.

The fact is, he is mad about anything that he can get down on paper. He loves, literally, being engaged in the act of writing, filling up paper from the scene immediately present to him. Composition by field, as the Black Mountain poets used to say; plus composition by frenzy and delight, and in any direction. Words, horrid isolate words, those symbols of our enslavement, are replaced by the a-b-c of man's perception of simultaneous factors—the ability to drink up the "scanning pattern." Get it down when it is still hot, vibrant, and wild to your consciousness! The literary impulse is more demonic to Burroughs than sex was to Sade, but can be just as nonconductive to onlookers.

*The Wild Boys* is Burroughs' fifth or sixth or seventh book. The gang of totally sadistic homosexual young Snopeses who come into the book in the last third are not important except as a culmination of the continual fantasy of boys in rainbow-colored jockstraps coldly doffing them; nor are they important to the book. Nothing here is any more important than anything else, except possibly Burroughs' unusually tender memories of adolescent sex around the golf course and locker rooms in his native St. Louis in the 1920s. But the wild boys are apaches of freedom, and so are different from the "thought-control mob," the narcotics cops, and the despots of the communications monopolies who are the villains of Burroughs' other books—especially *Nova Express*. The wild boys in this book are a positive force for freedom: i.e., they have such an aversion to women (to Burroughs, women are the thought-control mob in infancy) that the boys continue the race by artificial insemination and thus, *Gott zu dank,* a "whole generation arose that had never seen a woman's face nor heard a woman's voice."

This book in texture is like Burroughs' other books—*Naked Lunch, The Soft Machine, Nova Express, The Ticket That Exploded,* and for all I know, *Skirts* and *Who Pushed Paula,* published under a pseudonym and which I have never seen. The book is essentially a reverie in which different items suddenly get animated with a mar-velously unexpected profusion and disorder. Anything can get into it, lead its own life for a while, get swooshed around with everything else. Reading it does communicate Burroughs' excitement in composition and in the arbitrarily zany rearrangements that he calls "cut-ups." Ac-tually, he is a cutup who writes in action-prose, kaleidoscopic shifts, spurts, eruptions, and hellzapoppins. But with all the simultaneous and cleverly farcical reversals, noises, revolver shots, sadomasochistic scenes on and off the high wire, the book is inescapably a reverie, the private Burroughs dream state. Whole scenes collide and steal up on each other and break away as if they were stars violently oscillating and exploding in the telescopic eyepiece of an astronomer who just happens to be gloriously soused.

Burroughs became an imaginative force in our self-indulgent liter-ature of disaster with *Naked Lunch*. He was able to turn his addiction to morphine, to "junk," into a really amazing ability to scrutinize the contents of his restlessly bold, marvelously episodic imagination. His aversion to the hallucinogens (LSD and the like) is significant. He did not want to have *his* mind changed—Burroughs does not need inspi-ration! He wanted, in the tradition which is really his own, for he tran-scribes sexual fantasy into *literary* energy, to make the fullest possible inventory and rearrangement of all the stuff natural to him. He wanted to put his own mind on the internal screen that is his idea of a book.

More than anyone else I can think of in contemporary "fiction," he showed himself absolutely reckless in writing for his own satisfaction only. And yet he was so inventive, brilliant, funny in his many wild im-provisations (he writes scenes as other people write adjectives, so that he is always inserting one scene into another, *turning* one scene into another), that one recognized a writer interested in nothing but his own mind. He was more crazily "dirty" than anyone else (ah, those hanged men having their last involuntary sex thrill) yet one could not put him down as another tiresome Sixth Avenue sex store between covers.

Burroughs from *Naked Lunch* on showed himself a man who had gone very far in his own life and had put just about everything into his system—to please his imagination. He was an addict from 30 to 45. He had an insatiable sort of mind; he was well educated, had a taste for slumming, yet had some marked resemblances to his brilliant grandfather Burroughs, who did not invent the adding machine but thought up the little gadget that kept it steady, and to his uncle Ivy Lee, the public-relations man for old John D. Rockefeller who helped to sweeten that fetid reputation.

Burroughs worked in advertising and, typically, as an exterminator. His travels in Latin America and North Africa show an unmistakably upper-class American taste for practicing discomfort (rather like Theodore Roosevelt proving that he was not a weakling). He has for all his flights into the ether a penetrating common sense about American racketeering, political despotism, police agencies, plus a real insight into how machines work and how the innumerable objects, stimuli, and drugs in contemporary life affect the organism. He has put himself to some ruthless tests, for he has the natural curiosity of a scientist, a fondness for setting up ordeals, and above all an inborn gift for subjecting himself to anything as an experiment. "Experiment" is indeed the great thing in and behind all his work. He is the subject; he is the performing surgeon; he is the paper on which the different stages of the operation are described; he is the result.

Burroughs is indeed a serious man and a considerable writer. But his books are not really books, they are compositions that astonish, then pall. They are subjective experiences brought into the world for the hell of it and by the excitement of whatever happens to be present to Burroughs' consciousness when he writes. There is an infatuation with the storeroom of his own mind that represents a strange lapse somewhere, for Burroughs is smart, perky, courageous, but seems inextricably wired into his adolescence. He believes so screamingly in freedom for himself that one hesitates to admit how boring the wholly personal can be. The self, taken as nothing but itself, its memories, fantasies, random cruelties, is a depressive.

All stream of consciousness writing, in order to rise above the terrible fascination with itself, has to find something other than itself to love. Burroughs is mired in the excitement of writing. A book is something he doesn't really care about. He has invented an instant conduit from his mind to a TV screen before which he sits in perfect self-love. There is no end in sight; hair will grow even in the grave. But what Burroughs has never realized is that a mind fascinated by itself alone is unconsciously lonely, therefore pessimistic.

Burroughs' whole aesthetic and his suspicion of every political idea are the same: let me alone! Even his endlessly fascinated, obsessive recall of homosexual intercourse says—let me alone! There is no love making, no interest in love, not even much interest in the sensation of orgasm. The emphasis is on emission as the end product. The idea is to show in how many different scenes and with how many coldly selected partners one can do it. But repetition, that fatally boring element in Burroughs' "cut-ups," turns the coupling into an obsessive primal scene that never varies in its details. The technical arrangements never vary, but they are described with such unwearied relish that the "wild boys" and their sadistic knives, scissors, gougers, castrators, etc., etc., seem like the embroidery of a cruel dream, not wickedness.

Jean Genet is a hero to Burroughs, but Genet's masturbatory fantasies were undergone in prison, and were in the service of love. Genet is indeed an addict of love, which is why his novels and plays are crowded with people. Burroughs seems to me the victim of solitude. He expresses it in the coldness with which partners are dismissed: "The boy shoved the Dib's body away as if he were taking off a garment." The comic moments in *The Wild Boys* are not situations but jokes: "Bearded Yippies rush down a street with hammers breaking every window on both sides leave a wake of screaming burglar alarms strip off the beards, reverse collars and they are fifty clean priests throwing petrol bombs under every car WHOOSH a block goes up behind them."

No situation, no line, no joke, lasts very long with Burroughs. He once noted that morphine "produces a rush of pictures in the brain as if seen from a speeding train. The pictures are dim, jerky, grainy, like old film." And Burroughs does give the impression of reliving some private scene. Everything turns in on itself. Outside, the planets and constellations reel to prove that life has no meaning, that there is not and cannot be anything else but our own sacred consciousness. Everything outside is *hell*. But as if to prove that life in the United States does imitate art, I open up the *Sunday Times* at random and find an advertisement for the *Capitalist Reporter* that cries out: "Money! Opportunity Is All Around You! . . . American treasures are all around you—attic, church bazaar, house-wrecking yards, thrift shops, etc. Old bottles, obsolete fishing lures, prewar comics. . . . names and addresses of people who buy *everything,* from old mousetraps to dirigibles to *used electric chairs* [author's italics]."

---

# JOAN HAVERTY KEROUAC

JOAN HAVERTY KEROUAC (1930–1990) became Jack Kerouac's second wife in a short ceremony before a Manhattan judge on November 17, 1950, after having known Jack for only a few weeks. Four days after his marriage, in a letter to Neal Cassady, Kerouac described her as a "dressmaker, designer, model," although when he met his future wife she was working as a seamstress. Joan had come to New York City from her home in Albany, New York, as the result of a friendship she had made with Bill Cannastra, one of Kerouac's homosexual friends, who later accidentally committed suicide by putting his head out of the window of a moving subway car. The day after Kerouac's wedding, Ginsberg wrote Cassady that Joan struck him as " 'sensitive' and troubled (trying to be on own from family in the big city at age 20) . . . full of a kind of self-effacing naivete." Seven months later, after Jack had written the book that would be published as *On the Road* while Joan supported him with her earnings as a waitress at the Brass Rail restaurant, she learned that she was pregnant. Kerouac accused her of committing adultery with a Puerto Rican busboy who worked at the restaurant and said that he was unwilling to become the father of her child. Joan returned to her family in Albany, where her daughter Janet was born February 16, 1952.

During the last decade of her life, before she died of breast cancer, Joan worked on a memoir. Edited by John Bowers, it was published in 2000 by Creative Arts Book Company in Berkeley, California, as *Nobody's Wife.* In this chapter from the memoir, Joan describes her first meeting with Neal Cassady in February 1951, while she and Jack were still sharing his mother Gabrielle's apartment in Richmond Hill, New York. Soon afterward, Joan took the waitressing job at the Brass Rail and found an apartment in Manhattan at 454 West Twentieth Street. Jack joined her there, moved in the large wooden desk that his mother had kept for him in her cramped apartment, and taped together a long roll of paper. Encouraged by Joan's questions about his travels with Cassady, Jack started a speed-typing marathon fueled with black coffee and Benzedrine that resulted three weeks later in the so-called "teletype" manuscript of *On the Road*.

---

## Meeting Neal Cassady

I heard footsteps on the stairs and got up, planning to take my coffee to the sewing room so I wouldn't have to talk to Jack. But instead, there was a knock on the door. I opened it warily.

There, hopping from one foot to the other, beaming his delight at having reached his destination at last, stood Neal Cassady. I recognized him instantly from the descriptions Jack had written of him.

"Neal! Come in!" I said.

"Ah, me, ah, me! So this is the little wife!" He came inside, dropped his gear and rubbed his gloveless hands in abandoned glee. "And where is *he*? The now honorable married man?"

I started to tell him Jack was out, but he said "No, don't wake him, little darling. Just show me where he is and I'll sit on his bed till he wakes. I've got nothing else to do now that I'm here. Oh, my feet! So sore!"

"He's not here, Neal. Come sit down. I just got home myself so I don't know where he is."

"Well, well! Not *here* you say. We'll just have to sit down then. That is definitely the first order of business. To sit down and take off the shoes. Oh, my poor poor feet."

"Here, Neal. Let me take your coat. I'll hang it in the hall closet. And you could probably use something to eat."

"No, no." He handed me his coat. "When your good husband gets home will be soon enough."

"Some coffee? It's hot."

"Would there be, perchance, a cold beer? And as I was saying about my poor feet, what I could really use and would fully appreciate, my sweet darling, is a pair of your husband's clean socks, washed by your own lovely, slim young hands, no doubt. And because I couldn't put such precious socks on these dirty, sweaty, travel-sore feet, might I have a pan of warm water, some soap and a towel? The order of the aforementioned items doesn't matter, except for the beer. Let's start with that, shall we?"

It was impossible not to smile, to delight in the way Neal spoke. He might have sounded pompous, with his archaic expressions and run-on phrasing, but it all seemed so obviously tongue-in-cheek. He exaggerated a set of giddy mannerisms to an unforgettable extreme. I brought the requested articles and sat in fascinated silence as he immersed his feet and gulped his beer in rapturous comfort.

"Ah, ah. So good! How very warm this soak is. And how very good it is to be here. Let me tell you, my dear, this last little bit of the trip just about finished me. Only thing that kept me going was my desire, my intense desire to see dear Jack and his sweet wife. And now here you are and here we are and you must, you absolutely must tell me all about your sweet young girlhood and how you came to love this great man who is now your husband."

I blinked. As he talked, the sound of Jack's proposal to me echoed in my memory. I had been unable until now to reconcile the audacity and presumptuousness he'd shown that night with the timid, suspicious personality I had now come to know so well. Now I saw that, in order to get the job done, and reinforced by the smoking of a lot of grass, Jack had become the embodiment of Neal. He had done it in the same way he automatically became W. C. Fields when he drank. The garb or disguise of one hero or another allayed his fears and suspicions and enabled him to surge forth and meet the challenge, whatever it was.

"Ah, it's so warm in here, and so cold, so damnably cold outside in this town. But never mind! We'll all soon be in San Francisco together. You, Carolyn, old Jack and me. What times we'll have!"

He talked nonstop and there was so much energy about him he seemed to be jumping out of his skin.

"So you came to this big, confused city and found the man of your dreams. From some clean wind-swept state? Ah, yes. Oh, yes. I see it in your eyes, eyes that have looked at far horizons. Was it perchance Minnesota, land of sky blue waters, land of milk and honey?"

There was no need to answer him. He answered all his own questions with bigger-than-life, better-than-life answers. Now he drew his feet out of the water, and wrapped them in the towel, telling me of Texas, and how the nights felt and the stars looked and the air smelled. He was revving himself up in anticipation of Jack's arrival, talking of cars and escapades, jail memories and women and nights and blues.

And I wanted him to write it all down, or better yet record it. No matter how faithful the reproduction, I was sure text could never capture the vitality and intensity of the voice I now heard, describing everything in such a way that I lived it just by listening. He had the quality of a jazz musician inspiring the audience to answer with "yeah!" or to shout "go!" That quality in Neal's monologue was as elusive to the printed page as James Moody's horn. Sounds, sights and personalities came to life as he talked, assuming monumental proportions. Listening, I became aware of his phenomenal ability to perceive an event on several different levels and in terms of several disciplines at once, without losing the thread of one while he picked up another. To listen was to hear social commentary, poetry, philosophy, geography and natural history.

We exchanged childhood stories. Watching him talk and expound and move, I remembered a sociology student I'd known, who had told me officiously that all who resist the socialization process will wind up either in prison or in a mental institution. He believed that no individual was capable of forming a behavior code or a value system without society's dictum. His arrogant pronouncement had infuriated me, yet I realized how close I had come to mental illness in creating the superficial character I inhabited, trying to escape detection as a social anarchist.

And here was Neal, raw and alive. Not the well-mannered, numbed excuse for a living being that I was. Had he experienced ostracism and revised his outward behavior? I doubted it, but then he'd spent time in jail.

"Did you find it hard to resist the mold?" I asked him.

"I'm sure it was harder for you, my dear," he said. "I had nothing to resist. No mold was presented to me until it was too late. The die was cast."

"I'm glad," I said. "And I'm glad Jack has a friend like you. But if the world were inhabited by people like you and me, there'd be no or-der at all. Do you ever think about that?"

"Ah, but it isn't, you see." He laughed. "And this is by a divine de-sign. We have our place."

"I haven't found mine."

"Well, neither have I. But it doesn't matter. The place is there whether we recognize it or not."

I smiled. "But don't you think we might be more useful if we rec-ognized it?"

"Ah, now there's the question. There's the question. You and Car-olyn would find a lot to talk about. You have the same philosophic bent. To me it doesn't matter. I just do it."

At the sound of footsteps on the stairs I took away the pan, towel and soap. "I'll put your socks in with Jack's laundry," I told Neal.

He put his finger to his lips and took his shoes to the bedroom.

I opened the door as Jack arrived. Peering at my face, he asked "What are you looking so mysterious about?"

I didn't answer but stepped back to let him in, wanting to see his face when he saw Neal. He put out his hand to touch a familiar ob-ject, a book of Neal's left on the desk. His eyes widened as Neal came padding out of the bedroom in sock feet. The complete abandon with which Jack dropped the things he had been carrying, and his shouted "*Nee* hul" with a catch in the throat like a sob, told me that *this,* if any-one, was the being Jack loved more than himself.

They whacked each other on the back and laughed and shouted till they almost cried. "You old devil!" "You bastard, you!" "Son of a gun!"

I went to the kitchen to start dinner, leaving them in a confusion of punches and hugs like two puppies on the couch.

"How about some beer in here!" Jack called, and it was delivered.

"How long can you stay, Neal?" he asked.

"I planned on a week."

"All right! I am entirely at your disposal, except for one night when we're going to the Duke Ellington concert with Henri Cru. Remember the crazy Marseillaise I told you about?"

"Well, ahem. Yes, of course, but I want to spend some time with Allen too. You understand that, dear Jack. Tonight though, *tonight!* I just want to dig you and your wife in your marriage situation and we'll get our plans together for your trip, because I will hear no excuses. You'll have to live not just near us but absolutely next door, or failing that, in the same house. So happy for you, man! And she's thin! Remember what I told you about skinny girls? They're the best! And wasn't it a delight to get to know her body? All of it, starting from the toes, I mean. Do you see what I meant now? There's nothing like knowing, I mean really *knowing* a woman."

"Yeah, yeah," Jack said uncertainly. "Hey man, don't you want to go into town tonight? Look up some people, find some girls? After dinner, of course."

It would have been impossible not to hear the conversation. I came to the doorway to get Jack's attention.

"Your mother's late. I wonder what's keeping her."

"Union meeting again. There's trouble at the factory."

"Isn't that luck?" Neal asked me. "Gabe thinks I'm leading her only son astray. And she's right, of course. Quite right. Quite right. Ahem! If she were here she'd hasten my departure, wouldn't she, Jack?"

I assumed there would be three for dinner and got back to the stove. Their conversation continued in hushed tones until they came to stand in the doorway, Neal a little behind Jack, nudging him, whispering "Go on!" and pushing him toward me in the manner of one little boy urging another to ask his mom if they can have some cookies.

"Neal, you're staying for dinner, aren't you?" I asked.

"Oh, yes! Dinner!" he said, pushing Jack a little farther.

Jack finally came up to me and said, "Ah . . . I want to talk to you. Come into the bedroom for a minute." I checked the stove to be sure I wouldn't burn anything, and followed him into the bedroom, passing Neal, who rocked on his heels, beaming at our departure.

Jack sat on the edge of the bed and motioned to me to sit beside him.

"Now, darling," he began. I immediately gave him a highly suspicious look, because he had never called me that before.

"What I want to ask is this. You find Neal attractive, don't you?"

"He's very unusual and interesting. I enjoy listening to him."

"Never mind that!" he said. "He's physically attractive to you, isn't he?"

"Not particularly."

"Ah, g'wan. He is too. Anyway, he finds *you* very attractive."

"I'm flattered." I was beginning to get the picture. "Let's go have dinner." I stood up to go.

"Now wait a minute. Listen, please. Neal's like a brother to me. We've always shared everything and . . . , well, I want you to know that if you and Neal . . . , well, you'd have my permission. That is, it wouldn't bother me a bit if . . . , well, I'd be proud." He lost confidence and stammered at the rage he saw growing in me.

"*You're* giving *me* permission to sleep with Neal?"

"Shh!"

"I don't need your permission. It isn't yours to give. If I wanted someone else I'd just leave you. It would be that simple."

"Now wait. I don't mean it like that. I'd be with you, of course. The three of us together. Please. He wants to and we've done this before. It's nothing new for Neal and me. You see, there's no jealousy between us. You have to understand what a great buddy, what a great brother he is to me. Be reasonable. Don't insult him, please."

I tried to soften a bit. I could see what he was going through. He was under the strongest kind of peer pressure. He had followed Neal in every scheme, every prank, every wild drive and chase after women, and he was afraid he'd be diminished in Neal's eyes if he stopped here. Neal's curiosity about his friend's wife was understandable. Probably more men experienced that curiosity than ever voiced it or satisfied it. But it was not my problem. I certainly didn't feel the kind of slavish loyalty to Jack that might have made a *menage à trois* possible, though Jack would have loved to be able to say, "Look. My woman will do anything I want her to."

"I understand, Jack, and I won't feel any jealousy if you and Neal take a subway into town and find a girl you can share. You're free." And I couldn't help adding a little nastily, "I give you my permission."

"But it wouldn't be the same. It's because you're my wife that he wants you."

"I understand that too. But Jack, last November when you realized that I was the 'Cathy' Bill had been talking about, you must have known that nothing like what you have in mind could ever take place."

"I would have thought that a girl like Bill described would have been amenable to her husband's wishes by now! Listen, Neal is a great lover. Women just fall in love with him after one night. He could show you what it's all about . . . probably show me what I'm doing wrong. Just be agreeable. Everything will be much better for us as a result. You'll see. It'll be all right."

"Jack, the last thing I want is to know what it's all about."

"Oh, why do you have to be such a goddamned prude!"

"Because not all A are B," I said coldly. "Shall we have dinner? You can show your friend what a great domestic your wife is, and he'll never have to know she's a lousy lay."

"To hell with dinner!" he said, going back to the living room and slamming the door. "Damned haughty broad!" he shouted to Neal. "If I were any kind of a man I'd beat her."

"Now, now. That's no way to talk," Neal reasoned with Jack. "Why, you should be proud that she's so loyal. I'm disappointed, of course. Would have liked to know the delights you find in such a sweet girl. But I'm so happy for you, dear Jack. No matter! We'll go to the big city and we'll have a ball. But why forsake dinner? Make up to her, old man, and tell her you love her. You'll have to do it sooner or later."

I decided to make an appearance rather than sulk. Jack was sulky enough for both of us, and Neal was being the man of the two.

"No offense intended, Neal," I said. "Let's not let the food get cold."

"I don't hold it against you in the least, my girl. Ahem, no pun intended. Your prerogative I'm sure, and my loss, though I have been told by certain ladies that, ah, well, it was worth the trip. Your devotion to your husband is completely understood. Yes! Even admired, I might say. Now Jack, let's enjoy this lovely meal your wife has prepared."

Jack was sullen through dinner, not looking at me, as Neal told endless stories of his travels and played his flute. I was more relaxed than I had been in a long, long time. If Jack could give me permission to sleep with Neal, he could hardly object if I made my liking for him obvious by speaking to him and laughing at him. And could Neal misinterpret my animation? Now that we knew where we stood, communication was direct and comfortable.

Neal was working on the Southern Pacific Railroad and had come all the way across the country on his pass, a change from hopping freights and hitching rides. There was no doubt in my mind that the man was brilliant, with no use for a formal education. He was all the more alive and raw for not having had a benefit like that. By avoiding education, Neal Cassady had managed to retain that inborn knowledge of how to survive and love every minute of it.

We sat after dinner and lingered over coffee for hours, and Jack eventually lost his dark mood as the life at the table won out. As soon as he began to participate, I sat back and watched. He had become more interesting to me since Neal's arrival. I was witnessing the difference between *The Town and the City* and *On the Road,* the difference between the brooding Ti-Jean and the laughing, charming Jack I had seen at Lucien's party, the difference between the shy man who wanted an unworldly wife and the adventurous man who wanted a sexually liberated party girl.

I wondered about the forces that had brought these two together, and about the exchanges between them. An obvious product of their meeting was Jack's book in progress. But what effect had Jack had upon Neal? There was no way for me to know, since my knowledge of him was after the fact.

I wondered what kind of a writer Jack would have become had he not met Neal. I had seen some of Neal's letters to Jack—no, Jack had read portions of them to me. I knew that pieces of those letters had to remain private. I secretly believed that only Neal could write like Neal. But would he? Would his writings portray his essential quality, or did Jack find it necessary to immortalize him?

They were talking now about boxcars they had known and shared. And Neal spoke of boxcars he had shared with his father and other hoboes long before that. As I listened I could hear the train whistle and the sound of the cars coupling in the yard, and I could smell the cars, see the wheat fields in the dawn and dew passing by, just as though I were watching from the open door of a boxcar. I could see Omaha, and hear the conductor in the passenger cars calling it out as a stop, "*Oh* maha. Oma hah? Ohhh ma ha."

And not for the first time, I regretted not having been born a male. This was the closest I could come to it, sitting in the company of males, with a relationship (or lack of one) established, so there was no need or place for the usual male-female games. Just real talk about real things and real experiences.

Soon, though, they tired of talk, remembering that other need that must be satisfied, the one I would have no part in, because I couldn't be a companion. Only a tool.

Jack and I waited at Henri Cru's apartment for the limousine which
would take us to the Duke Ellington concert at Carnegie Hall. I had
thought the limousine was being rented in the nature of a joke, and I
had hoped that Henri's tie, hand-painted with replicas of our tickets,
was a joke, too. But here was Henri, wearing the tie in front of his mirror, rolling the edge of his pink shirt collar between his fingers to get it
to lie just right, just exquisitely. And neither Jack nor Henri saw that it
was obscene.

"Don't you see this as an insult to the Duke?" I asked Jack.

"Look. Dig Henri," he said, smiling at the reflection, not even
hearing me. "See how he has to get that collar to roll just right? Nothing haphazard for old Henri! He's a perfectionist."

"Some day the importance of little details will be meaningful to
you, Jack, dear boy," Henri said. "You'll put your dreadful plaid shirts
aside in favor of silk ones."

"But I'm not wearing a plaid shirt tonight, Henri. Don't you think
this is appropriate?" He pulled at the front of his white dress shirt.

"It's acceptable, but not unique. One day the ordinary will not be
good enough for you."

"You sound like my wife, for crying out loud," Jack said.

"I resent that," I objected. "There's a difference between distinction and vulgarity." Henri looked at me suspiciously in the mirror, and
Jack wanted it spelled out.

"You're distinctive and he's vulgar?"

"Let's just say that Henri aspires to the subtle insult." I was relieved when Henri smiled in agreement. "Not that he succeeds," I
added.

His date sat on the edge of her chair, uncomfortably stuffed into
something grotesquely fashionable. Even if it had been tastefully
done, what was to be gained by this superficial display? How far could
a phony image go in terms of self-respect?

Three short rings told Henri the limousine was ready, and we
went downstairs to be helped into it by the chauffeur. As we pulled
away from the curb, Neal came running across the street to hang on
Jack's door. The chauffeur had to stop to avoid dragging him into traffic, though the look on his face said he would have liked to do just

that. Jack opened the window and hastily introduced Neal to Henri, who pointedly ignored him.

"Hey, Jack! Can't you give me a lift to Forty-second Street?" Neal rubbed his hands together, his breath visible in the frosty night. "I'm about to freeze my balls in this durned cold." Jack looked at Henri for an answer, but all he got was a negative shake of the head and a look of displeasure.

"No, man. I'm sorry. Can't do it," Jack said, and Neal turned without a word and ran up the street in the direction we were heading, his thin coat flapping behind him in the wind.

"That's a lousy way to say goodbye to a friend," I said.

"But it's not *time* for saying goodbye to Neal, don't you see?" Jack answered impatiently. "I've already done that. It's time for the concert now. And there's no way to put the two things together."

I had a fleeting vision of the four of us in our absurd finery, bearing Neal into Carnegie Hall on our shoulders, like a hero in rags. That was the only way I could see all this pomp serving any purpose.

"Couldn't Neal come to the concert with us?" I asked Henri.

"No, no!" he said emphatically. "Absolutely out of the question."

How sad, how unspeakably sad that anyone should need these props to enjoy a night of good music. Neal would have enjoyed it in his ragged old coat, and I was sure that if the Duke had compared Neal's appreciation with Henri's, he would have chosen the wild man in rags. Too much of life was like this, expensive wrappings attempting to compensate for the poverty of contents.

Too bad, Neal, old buddy. It's not time for someone real like you. You'd spoil our make-believe, reminding us that we're all cold, much of the time, in a thin coat on a winter street.

# KEN KESEY

KEN KESEY, author of *One Flew Over the Cuckoo's Nest* (1962), cast an I Ching prophecy (the Book of Changes, an ancient Chinese divination text) on December 28, 1984, for Ann Charters, who had traveled to his Oregon farm to photograph him and his "Further" schoolbus, parked inside a barn not far from his house. This had been the vehicle driven by Neal Cassady during the Merry Pranksters' trip across the United States in 1964. Now the bus resides permanently in the Smithsonian Institution in Washington, D.C., a part of American cultural history.

*For Ann:*

Up in the sunny rainy room doing a dual ching:

8--7--9--9--7--8

PREPONDERANCE OF THE GREAT

The superior man is unconcerned and unduanted.

Nine in third:
The ridgepole sags to the breaking point. Misfortune.

Nine fourth:
The ridgepole is braced. Good fortune.
If there are ulterior motives, it is humiliating.

THE ABYSMAL
(WATER)

If you are sincere, you have success in your heart, and whatever you do succeeds.

The superior man walks in lasting virtue and carries on the business of teaching.

*Respectfully,*

*Ken Kesey*

*12/28/84*

# JOANNE KYGER

JOANNE KYGER was part of the group of young writers studying with the San Francisco poets Robert Duncan and Jack Spicer when she met Gary Snyder in 1958. She remembered that "Gary came to our Sunday poetry group and read from *Myths and Texts* sitting cross-legged on a table with Jack Spicer sitting cross-legged under the table." Spicer asked her, "Do you like this Boy Scout poetry?" and she answered that she "did indeed, very much." Two years later Kyger left San Francisco to join Snyder in Japan, where they were married and traveled together for four years. There she kept the diary later published as *Japan and India Journals: 1960–1964.* On returning to San Francisco, Kyger divorced Snyder and published the first of her many books of poetry, *The Tapestry and the Web,* in 1965. "Tapestry" was first published in Jack Spicer's magazine *J* (1958) in San Francisco. The other two poems were written in Japan.

————

## Tapestry

              the eye
           is drawn
        to the Bold
   DESIGN ——— the
           .Border.
      .California flowers.
   nothing promised that   isn't shown.


         Implements:


           shell
           stone


   .Peacock.

## It Is Lonely

It is lonely
I must draw water from the well 75 buckets for the bath
I mix a drink—gin, fizz water, lemon juice, a spoonful
                              of strawberry jam
And place it in a champagne glass—it is hard work
        to make the bath
And my winter clothes are dusty and should be put away
In storage. Have I lost all values I wonder
        the world is slippery to hold on to
When you begin to deny it.
Outside outside are the crickets and frogs in the rice fields
Large black butterflies like birds.


## My Father Died This Spring

My father died this spring
                Well, I had meant to write more often
To a kind of hell it must be, with all unresolved difficulties.
        I had greens with vinegar last night—that's something
    in common
                And I would have told him that—adding it
        to a list of possible conversations
With the pictures on his dressing table
        of all his daughters
but he wasn't flinging out his arms to keep a soul there.
                You can't say he wasn't strange
        and difficult.
                How far does one go
    to help a parent like a child—when he waits
        at the employees entrance in old clothes
                and I don't want him.
                                Well he'll be there waiting
    for me. Demands just, wanted, or not
        are to be met.
And let me see, yes the demon large
        impossible and yields without vanishing

no power, no satisfaction
　　　sitting on the back porch drinking beer
　　following me to the sick squirrels in the cellar.
And the material things, calling cards
　　　engraved watches, trunks that married life brings
　　　　full of stuff
he left behind 10 years ago. The golf clubs. The fact is
　　　there was a man, a married man,
　　and an old man. It's impossible to know,
　　　　but blood does bring curiosity.

*9.15.63*

---

# WAYNE LAWSON

WAYNE LAWSON published his article "The Beats" in the *Encyclopedia Americana* 1958 Annual.

---

## *The Beats*

In the last ten years, a group of shabby young individuals who like to be known as the Beats have attracted considerable attention to themselves in the United States. Like the American Communists of the 1930's, the Paris existentialists of the 1940's and England's Angry Young Men of recent years, the Beats are conspicuous because they deliberately break every rule and ridicule every aspiration of the normal "good" citizen of their society.

It is easy to recognize the Beat. He has developed a fairly standard uniform, a pretty rigid set of tastes and a small, strict vocabulary which serves him in describing anything and everything. He is likely to wear dungarees, sandals and a black turtle-neck sweater. He was formerly given to beards, but recently beat imitators have started wearing beards and so the true Beat has shaved his off.

The Beat prefers to live in beat communities. Such communities are usually in the free-and-easy, Bohemian sections of large cities. Favorite locations are the North Beach area of San Francisco. Venice West in Los Angeles and Greenwich Village in New York. The furnishings of the Beat's "pad" are standard: a bare mattress, crates that serve as tables and bookcases, a hot plate and a few pans, a phonograph and loud-speaker and a typewriter. Lighting is provided by bare bulbs, or candles stuck in wine bottles.

Actually, the costume and habitat of the Beats are very little different from those of that eternal cliché, the Bohemian artist. It is in his tastes and ideas that the Beat is, to a degree at least, original. The Beat is in revolt against society. He wants to be an outsider. More properly phrased, he wants to free himself and "bug the Squares." This is a packed sentence and certainly wants clarification, for it is at the very heart of beat thinking.

We—you and I—are the Squares. A person is square if he hopes to advance in a career, marry and settle down in a comfortable home. A person is square if he openly expresses love of family, country and church, or if he approves of television or almost any other creation of modern scientific technology. In short the honest, average man is square; and he is square because he goes along with his age, because he is conscientious about his politics as well as his personal ethics, because he feels that he can improve himself along conventional lines, but mainly because he is not "hip," or beat.

It is from being square in any way that the Beat, or Hipster, wants to free himself. It is from the present-day world, which he thinks is futile and doomed and meaningless, that the Beat sets out to escape.

These definitions are admittedly simple. But their implications are clear. If the Beats have found a foolproof salvation, then there is the remote possibility that our society is in danger of being outmoded and overturned by them. If not, then they are merely a small group of malcontents and their movement in time will peter out as so many like it have done in times past.

In order to decide which of these alternatives is likely to come to pass, it is worth investigating the beliefs and mores of the Beats. It is already apparent that the Beats feel that our society is dull, empty and dying if not dead. They feel, as a result, that any escape from that society is good.

Their heroes are the bums, "winos," "junkies" (drug addicts) and jazz musicians. Beats admire the Negro because he is discriminated against and because he has made the glorious contribution of a floating, forlorn, hypnotic form of jazz which they consider the art counterpart of being "gone," or "high," on wine, marijuana or whatever.

The words "gone," "high" and "swinging" are frequent in beat lingo. They denote a state of complete detachment, of perfect release, from the square world. The Beats liken this state to that reached by those whom they call the Zen "lunatics" in the Japanese religion of Zen Buddhism. Zen itself is actually a religion based on strict discipline, a striving after perfect holiness and an intuitive insight into truth and the ultimate nature of things. The word "Zen" means "meditation" and the Zen Buddhists believe that they can escape from the crassness of the material world through meditation on and identification with the eternal reality. The Beats are hardly willing to undergo the rigors of Zen or any other religion. They really only substitute a drugged state for one of religious mysticism. The best that can be said is that they "dig" Zen—that is, they appreciate it. They don't find Zen square.

Such are the things that take up the Beat's time and occupy his mind. Since he abhors anything as conventional as a job, he has plenty of free time. He may spend it talking in espresso coffee houses, listening to jazz records or hitchhiking around the country. What is certain is that the Beat's life—however uncomfortable or lacking in nutrition it may be—is very far from exhausting or even productive. That is why the Beats are no danger to normal society. Their revolt is too negative. They have nothing very alluring with which to replace the society they condemn.

To say that the Beats are unproductive is in a sense misleading. The small nucleus of beat writers who are responsible for the whole craze have produced a fairly sizable literature and have made a very handsome income from it. Their names are known to the most ardent Squares and their methods of artistic creation are well worth discussing. Most serious writers in America consider the literary Beats to be young men who have lost their erasers. On a TV panel discussion, Truman Capote described them as "typists, not writers!" But to the average Beat their work is gospel.

At the top of the heap is novelist and short-story writer Jack Kerouac. Onetime football player for Columbia University, later filling-station attendant, sports writer and railroad brakeman, Kerouac settled down in San Francisco in 1949 and began writing his novels of disillusionment and frustration. It was Kerouac who coined the phrase "the Beat Generation" for the young men in the land who felt "done in" by a smug, arid society. His best-known novels are *On the Road* and *The Dharma Bums*. He says that he never rewrites a word. He just sticks a roll of paper in the typewriter and bangs out eight or ten feet of words a day. His style amounts to a relaxed narration in "hip" language of his personal experiences.

In 1953 a group of Kerouac's friends joined him in San Francisco. Public awareness of beatdom dates from that year. In this group was Allen Ginsberg, the poet, who is probably the most talented of the Beats. His little book *Howl and Other Poems* has sold over 33,000 copies. "Howl" is a nightmarish catalogue of the horrors of the modern world and a frank catalogue of the Beats' attempts to escape this modern inferno. It is not a pretty poem by any means. And yet it is perhaps the best Beat work to date by literary standards.

Ginsberg and other Beat poets began the craze for public readings of their works. The readings began in coffee houses and jazz places on the West coast. According to report, they are often feverish affairs. At the height of one of them, Ginsberg undressed completely to demonstrate Nakedness.

Other Beat writers include Gregory Corso, Philip Lamantia, Mike McClure, John Clellon Holmes, Lawrence Ferlinghetti, William S. Burroughs and many others. Several anthologies of their stories, poems and essays are available. One is called *The Beat Generation and the Angry Young Men,* edited by Gene Feldman and Max Gartenberg. More recent is *The Beats,* edited by Seymour Krim.

In addition to published works and public recitations, the Beats have also made a movie. It is called *Pull My Daisy,* is narrated by Jack Kerouac and stars, among others, Allen Ginsberg and Gregory Corso. It is something of a joke—loose, formless, perhaps half serious. It has the same careless, silly and sardonic touch that characterizes the Beats' printed matter.

And there is not much more to say about the Beats. They are in revolt against the Squares. Meanwhile the Squares think little or nothing of the Beats. They give them the foolish, derisive name of Beatniks. Many people feel that the beat craze is almost finished. Many

Beats feel it has scarcely begun. However, whether the Beats are approaching the heights or whether they are on their last legs, their influence and their art do not amount to much. Whether they were angry at America, Americans, the world or themselves when they began the whole new Bohemianism, we may never know. Unless they produce something more universal than they have so far, no one will care.

# A. ROBERT LEE

A. ROBERT LEE, an English professor of literature now teaching in Japan, wrote about the "Black Beats" in a collection of essays on *The Beat Generation Writers,* which he edited, published by Pluto Press in London in 1996. Two years later he revised his article in his book *Designs of Blackness: Mappings in the Literature and Culture of Afro-America.* The later version of the essay is included here.

## Black Beats: The Signifying Poetry of LeRoi Jones/Imamu Amiri Baraka, Ted Joans, and Bob Kaufman

Already well known and virtually revered in ultrahip literary circles, Roi had become by then a Greenwich Village luminary. Along with New York's Ted Joans and San Francisco's Bob Kaufman, he was among a handful of mid-century African American poets whose early reputations are identified with the Beat Generation. We're talking here of course about a literary movement shaped, loosely speaking, by Whitmanesque confessionalism, the modernist iconoclasm of Ezra Pound, T.S. Eliot and William Carlos Williams, as well as by ab-

stract expressionist painting, Eastern mysticism, drug
culture, and jazz.

Al Young, "Amiri Baraka (LeRoi Jones)," in J.J. Phillips,
Ishmael Reed, Gundars Strads and Shawn Wong (eds.),
*The Before Columbus Foundation Poetry Anthology* (1992)[1]

Williams was a common denominator because he
wanted American Speech, a mixed foot, a variable measure. He knew American life had out-distanced the
English rhythms and their formal meters. The language
of this multi-national land, of mixed ancestry, where
war dances and salsa combine with Country and Western, all framed by African rhythm-and-blues confessional.

*The Autobiography of LeRoi Jones/Amiri Baraka* (1984)[2]

I cannot deny that I am Ted Joans Afro American negro
colored spade spook mau mau soul-brother coon jig
darkie, etc.

Ted Joans, *Tape Recording at the Five Spot* (1960)[3]

Let us blow African Jazz in Alabama jungles and wail
savage lovesongs of unchained fire.

Bob Kaufman, "Jazz *Te Deum* for
Inhaling at Mexican Bonfires,"
*Solitudes Crowded with Loneliness* (1965)[4]

Allen Ginsberg's "Howl" (1956), the Grand Anthem of Beat poetry, has
"the best minds of my generation . . . dragging themselves through the
negro streets at dawn." In *On the Road* (1957) Jack Kerouac invokes
Harlem as quintessential "Jazz America" while his narrator in *The Subterraneans* (1958) recalls "wishing I were a Negro" when in Denver's
"colored section." In "The Philosophy of the Beat Generation," a key
manifesto first published in *Esquire* in 1958, John Clellon Holmes eu-
logizes Charlie Parker, Bird, as black godfather to the movement.
Gregory Corso, for his part, puts him alongside Miles Davis in "For
Miles" (*Gasoline,* 1958), recalling a set

when you & bird
wailed five in the morning some wondrous
yet unimaginable score.

Norman Mailer, whose "The White Negro" (1957) served as apologia for Beat and hipster alike, found himself arguing that "the Negro's equality would tear a profound shift into the psychology, the sexuality, and the moral imagination of every White alive." Could it ever be doubted that in virtually all white-written Beat poetry and fiction, or associated manifestos, Afro-America supplied a touchstone, a necessary black vein of reference and inspiration?[5]

Yet black Beat writers themselves might well be thought to have gone missing in action. Only LeRoi Jones, still to metamorphose into Imamu Amiri Baraka, was reported in dispatches. That, however, had as much to do with his Greenwich Village sojourn—and to an extent the small magazine publication of his Projective early verse—as with any fuller recognition of the life begun in Newark, New Jersey, continued in the Air Force as gunner and weatherman, and given an ambiguous education in the ways of the black middle class at Howard University. Rather, he seemed a literary one-off caught in the shadow of an already senior Beat pantheon of Kerouac, Ginsberg, Burroughs, Corso, Ferlinghetti, Clellon Holmes, di Prima and the rest.

But Jones/Baraka, in fact, did have company: Ted Joans, self-styled surrealist troubadour; Bob Kaufman, "Abomunist," born into a large New Orleans black Jewish family (a lineage acknowledged in his "Bagel Shop Jazz"), seaman, Zen practitioner yet San Francisco rowdie, and above all jazz and performance poet; A.B. Spellman, the poet of *The Beautiful Days* (1965) and the jazz historian of *Four Lives in the Bebop Business* (1966); and Archie Shepp, verse-writing jazzman.[6] Yet despite all of these, and whatever its varied borrowings from black culture, the Beat phenomenon rarely seemed to speak other than from, or to, white America.

Jones hardly failed to acknowledge, at the time or later, this oversight towards his black fellow-writers. Thinking back on his founder and co-editor role in the journals *Yugen* (1958–62) and *The Floating Bear* (1961–63), which published not only Beats but Black Mountaineers like Charles Olson and Robert Creeley, and New York School virtuosi like Frank O'Hara and Kenneth Koch, he recalled in his *Autobiography*:

I was "open" to all schools within the circle of white poets of all faiths and flags. But what had happened to the blacks? What had happened to me? How is it that only the one colored guy?[7]

The same held not only for *Yugen* but for the host of other magazines which printed his early work, whether *Kulchur, Penny Poems, Locus-Solus, Nomad/New York, Fuck You: A Magazine of the Arts, Naked Ear, Quicksilver, Combustion* or *Red Clay Reader.*[8] It was no doubt further symptomatic, or at least some continuance of the assumed *status quo,* that he made himself the only black contributor to his own anthology of "popular modernism," *The Moderns* (1963).[9]

This "white social focus," as he came to term it—which also included his marriage in 1958 to Hettie Cohen, white, Jewish, his editorial collaborator on *Yugen,* and recently the affecting, unrecriminatory memoirist of *How I Became Hettie Jones* (1990)—would bring on a major turnabout in both his life and art.[10] The process notably gained impetus from his transforming visit to Cuba out of which, and against America's usual Cold War stance, he found himself inveighing in "Cuba Libre": "the Cubans, and the other *new* peoples (in Asia, Africa, South America) don't need us, and we had better stay out of their way."[11] Then, as Watts exploded in 1962, Harlem, Chicago and Bedford-Stuyvesant in 1964 (and all the cities in their wake), and as Dixie racism led to the Birmingham school-bombing in 1963 and newly emboldened Klan and White Citizens Councils activity (the latter first begun in Mississippi in 1954), so Jones/Baraka himself increasingly took to black nationalism.

His poem "BLACK DADA NIHILISMUS" bore the mark of this new Africanism, a millennial black resolve and threat:

> may a lost god damballah, rest or save us
> against the murders we intend
> against his lost white children
> black dada nihilismus.[12]

*Dutchman* (1964), his celebrated one act play, would further explore the myth of white and black America locked in unending subterranean contest.[13] This transformation had been much foreshadowed in his voluminous essay work, whether *Blues People: Negro Music in White*

*America* (1963) and *Black Music* (1967), which paid homage to Afro-America's unique jazz and blues, or *Home: Social Essays,* his wide-ranging, activist expressions of social and ideological critique.[14]

His personal life took its own symbolic turn when he moved from Greenwich Village to Harlem, breaking not only with white bohemia but with Hettie Jones (née Cohen) and their daughters. Suddenly he became a black figure of controversy. The media typecast him as a voice of black terrorism, race hatred, the politics of accusation and hate. By 1965 the proof seemed conclusive: the FBI were called in to investigate his Harlem theater work and its funding through the HARYOU-ACT (Harlem Youth Act), arrested him and, among other things, accused him of building a gun arsenal. The Black Arts Movement was deemed to be cause for alarm, his own leadership a danger.

Ginsberg, Kerouac and their fellow Beats may well have aroused shock by their language, their sexual and other mores, for a Middle America which twice had voted Eisenhower into office (in 1952 and 1956) and had become gridlocked in consumerism and Cold War ideology. But even they did not anticipate the sheer headiness and impact of Black Power. Not without cause, Robert Lowell, in his WASP confessional poem, "Memories of West Street Lepke," called the 1950s "tranquillized,"[15] and J. D. Salinger, in *The Catcher in the Rye* (1951), supplied Holden Caulfield's "phony" as the *mot clef* for generational ennui.[16]

Afro-America had not lacked markers: Baldwin, Ellison, Brooks, Hayden, Hansberry and a young LeRoi Jones himself all counted. But the kind of politics and affiliation which caused Jones to Africanize (and Islamize) his name to Baraka, become a founder of the Black Arts Movement, take up the cause of Black Power first through community activism (initially in Harlem, then Newark) and, from 1974 onwards, through Third World Marxism, had yet to be fully embarked upon. Black, at this stage, conveyed more a style of consciousness, a source of being cool. There was a while to go before a piece like Ted Joans's "TWO POEMS" could assume widespread assent when it spoke of:

> those TWO
> beautiful words BLACKPOWER.

All three poets, rather, typically took up the Beat interest in Zen and Eastern transcendental spirituality—though linking it to blues and to Africa as a prime source of reference. Similarly, if their poetry could be sexually celebratory and playful, in the style of Ginsberg, it could also broach the racial taboos of sex, a Beat articulation (long continued in Joans and Kaufman) of the purported black senses. Given a heritage derived from slavery and formed as much by jazz, spirituals and rap as by Blake, Whitman, Williams and Pound, who was culturally better placed to have adapted Beat to a black dispensation, or in that honored African American usage, to have made it signify?[17]

A number of linked references back help situate Baraka as Beat poet. First, in the *LeRoi Jones/Amiri Baraka Reader* (1991), he himself (or his editor William J. Harris) supplies precise dates for his Beat phase, namely 1957–62.[18] These, in his *Reader's* words constituted "bohemian" years before "ethnic consciousness" gave way to "political consciousness." The *Autobiography*, however, gives the circumstances and flavor of his relationship to the movement:

> I'd come into the Village *looking*, trying to "check," being open to all flags. Allen Ginsberg's *Howl* was the first thing to open my nose, as opposed to, say, instructions I was given, directions, guidance. I dug *Howl* myself, in fact many of the people I'd known at the time warned me off it and thought the whole Beat phenomenon a passing fad of little relevance. I'd investigated further because I was looking for something. I was precisely open to its force as the statement of a new generation. As a line of demarcation from "the silent generation" and the man with the . . . gray flannel skin, half brother to the one with the gray flannel suit. I took up with the Beats because that's what I saw taking off and flying somewhere resembling myself. The open and implied rebellion—of form and content. Aesthetic as well as social and political. But I saw most of it as Art, and the social statement as merely our lives as dropouts from the mainstream. I could see the young white boys and girls in their pronouncements of disillusion with and "removal" from society as related to the black experience. That made us colleagues of the spirit.[19]

A 1980s interview sets these remembrances within a wider historical perspective:

> Beat came out of the whole dead Eisenhower period, the whole of the McCarthy Era, the Eisenhower blandness, the whole reactionary period of the 50s. The Beat Generation was a distinct reaction to that, a reaction not only to reactionary politics, reactionary life style of American ruling class and sections of the middle class, reaction to conservatism and McCarthyism of that period. Also reaction to the kind of academic poetry and academic literature that was being pushed as great works by the American establishment. So it was a complete reaction: socially, politically, and of course artistically to what the 50s represented. That whole opening and transformation of course had its fullest kind of expression in the 60s in the Black Liberation Movement.[20]

There also remains the Beat aesthetic as Baraka fashioned it in the late 1950s, published under the rubric "How Do You Sound?" in "The Statements on Poetics" section of Donald Allen's *The New American Poetry* (1960).[21] Revealingly, Black Power, black cultural nationalism at least, nowhere features in an explicit way. Rather, Baraka takes aim at New Critical academicism, with its emphasis on formal prerequisites and design, advocating open forms and fields of expression. The formulation, right down to the abbreviations and punctuation, shows the residual mark of Charles Olson, together with a Ginsbergian, and behind that a Whitmanesque, will to inclusiveness:

> "HOW DO YOU SOUND??" is what we recent fellows are up to. How *we* sound; our peculiar grasp on, say: a. Melican speech, b. Poetries of the world, c. Our selves (which is attitudes, logics, theories, jumbles of our lives, & all that), d. And the final . . . The Totality of Mind: Spiritual . . . God?? (or you name it): Social (zeitgeist): or Heideggerian *umwelt*.
> MY POETRY is anything I think I am. (Can I be light & weightless as a sail?? Heavy & clunking like 8 black boots.) I CAN BE ANYTHING I CAN. I make a poetry with what I feel is useful & can be saved out of all the garbage of our lives. What I see, am touched by (CAN HEAR) . . . wives, gardens, jobs, cement yards where cats pee, all my interminable artifacts . . . ALL are a poetry, & nothing moves (with

any grace) pried apart from all these things. There cannot be closet poetry. Unless the closet be wide as God's eye.

And all that means that I *must* be completely free to do just what I want, in the poem.[22]

Given the self-liberative urgings, the affirmations and the learning lightly worn (or, as it were, spoken), this might be thought virtually a Beat poem in its own imaginative right, or at least a prose equivalent. Certainly it links directly to the poems which make up his *Preface to a Twenty Volume Suicide Note* (1961), the volume which taken in retrospect has most become associated with his part in the Beat movement.[23]

> You are as any other sad man here
> american

Jones has his speaker confide in "Notes for a Speech," the collection's closing poem which ruefully, ironically, echoes Countee Cullen's 1920s-written "Heritage":

> What is Africa to me: . . .
> *One three centuries removed*
> *From the scenes his fathers loved,*
> *Spicy grove, cinnamon tree.*
> *What is Africa to me?*

Jones's black bohemian would seem to have lost touch not only with Africa but with African American life and origins. Yet even as he considers this double deracination, the measure of his lament sounds blues-like and drawn from the most intimate repertoire of his own blackness. This also applies in "Preface to a Twenty Volume Suicide Note" as title poem, which opens proceedings on a note of generalized alienation ("Nobody sings anymore") only to have that same alienation challenged by the sight of his young, cross-racial daughter, Kellie Jones, at prayer.[24]

Other poems in *Preface* do a similar about-turn. In "For Hettie," his affectionate, roistering mock complaint at his pregnant wife's "left-handedness" obliquely suggests the different pushes and pulls of his love for her. In "For Hettie in Her Fifth Month" he attempts, with a hint of William Carlos Williams's "The Red Wheel Barrow," to catch both the otherness of pregnancy itself and of the unborn child—the latter as

> one of Kafka's hipsters,
> parked there
> with a wheelbarrow.

A related kind of otherness, that of inter-racial sexual life with all its supposed mystique and taboos, shows through in blues vignettes like "Symphony Sid" ("A man, a woman shaking the night apart") or "Theory of Art" ("blackness, strange, mocked").

At a different level are the poems dedicated to his co-Beats. "One Night Stand," for Ginsberg, teases the triumphalist fervor of the New Bohemia ("We entered the city at noon! The radio on . . ."), a funny-wry vision of Beat's legions dressed in motley fashion and full of pose:

> We *are* foreign seeming persons. Hats flopped so the sun
> can't scald our beards; odd shoes, bags of books & chicken.
> We have come a long way, & are uncertain which of the masks
> is cool.

"Way Out West," for Gary Snyder, explores perceptual process from:

> As simple an act
> as opening the eyes

to:

> Closing the eyes. As
> simple an act. You float . . .

Whether an America of Sheridan Square or a Greece of Tiresias, in the poem's span of reference, the poet's vision doubles as always mutualizingly outer and inward. Snyder's Zen affinities undoubtedly had aroused an answering note in Jones.

The most Beat cum "projective verse" composition in *Preface,* however, is to be found in "Look for You Yesterday, Here You Come Today," its title taken from an old blues, as if to give added emphasis to the memories of an American childhood fast giving way to a meaner, tougher adult human order. The note is nostalgic yet a nostalgia itself chastised and mocked. The speaker, duly bearded, literary, confides:

> I have to trim my beard in solitude.
> I try to hum lines from "The Poet In New York"

Similarly, he acknowledges that his own pose can hardly keep up with an undermining diversity of experience:

> It's so diffuse
> being alive.

"Terrible poems come in the mail." A dark Strindbergian feeling comes over him at his wife's pregnancy. Frank O'Hara, the poem reports, prefers the importance of his own silence to "Jack's incessant yatter." The poet's own thoughts, in a Baudelairean put-down of self-consciousness, in turn become:

> Flowers of Evil
> cold & lifeless
> as subway rails.

Only "dopey mythic worlds hold," a childhood pop culture arcade which includes Tom Mix

> dead in a Boston Nightclub
> before I realized what happened

and other heroes from Dickie Dare to Captain Midnight, Superman to the Lone Ranger ("THERE *MUST* BE A LONE RANGER!!!" runs his insistence). These stalwarts (they have company in the title-figure reference to a Dashiell Hammett hero in "The Death of Nick Charles" and to Lamont Cranston as The Shadow in "In Memory of Radio") lag behind in time and place, tokens of a lost, simpler, altogether more secure childhood order. The nostalgia is palpable:

> My silver bullets all gone
> My black mask trampled in the dust
>
> & Tonto way off in the hills
> moaning like Bessie Smith.

One just about hears a Jones ready to move on from Beat self-absorption into politicization, with Bessie Smith, blues, *black* popular heritage as a route towards more committed ends and purposes.

In this respect few poems in *Preface to a Twenty Volume Suicide Note* assume a blacker animus than "Hymn for Lanie Poo" (the nickname for his sister, Sandra Elaine). Freely associative in range, it develops a montage of skillfully parodic, if at times rueful, slaps at white social norms and their emulation by America's black middle class. Rimbaud's *Vous êtes de faux Nègres* offers the point of departure, with sequences to follow guying, in turn, white America's taste for primitivizing superstitions about sunburnt black skin, Lanie's Gatsbyesque

> coming-out party
> with 3000 guests
> from all parts of the country

and the typical superficiality of most culture talk about race. Jones's ending takes especial aim at black bourgeois assimilationism and, as he sees it, the inevitable outcome of so obviously wrong a cultural turning:

> Smiling & glad/in
> the huge & loveless
> white-anglo sun/of
> benevolent step
> mother America.

If the form (and tone) can be said to be Beat, it rests in the poem's spontaneous voices and transitions. Certainly the playful iconoclasm can scarcely be missed in

> The god I pray to
> got black boobies
> got steatopygia . . .

Similarly the poem's "I" vaunts a touch of self-irony in

> it's impossible
> to be an artist and bread
> winner at the same time.

With a perhaps irreverent eye, or ear, to Ginsberg and Snyder, there is also a show of mock oceanic feeling:

> Each morning
> I go down
> to Gansevoort St.
> and stand on the docks.
> I stare out
> at the horizon
> until it gets up
> and comes to embrace
> me. I make believe
> it is my father.
> This is known
> as genealogy.

"Hymn for Lanie Poo" yields a kind of flyting, at once regretful and angrily comic, at how black America has begun to buy into and imitate white middle-class American life. The phantasmagoria is not only plentiful but apt:

> A white hunter, very unkempt,
> with long hair,
> whizzed in on the end of a vine.
> (spoke perfect english too.)

From the start, and some time ahead of his Black Nationalist and Marxist phases, Jones's poetry clearly involved a subtle overlap of both personal and a more inclusive racial feeling. As brief an affiliation as it may have been for the then LeRoi Jones, Beat—Beat poetry—had assumed its own mediating black textures.

Black Beat writing yields no more companionable a presence than Ted Joans. "Afro-surrealist," jazz adept, trumpeter, painter by early training, and lifelong performance poet, even into his sixties he continues to maintain the role of international stroller player with alternating bases in Manhattan, Paris and Mali. His insistence has always been upon an oral poetry, a talking blues or jazz, by his own count one of "funk" and "afrodisia."

The connection to the Beat Movement began with his arrival in New York City in 1951, from Indiana, and an early link-up with Jack Kerouac. Their friendship, evidently full of warmth and unhampered by racial lines, Joans recalls in "The Wild Spirit of Kicks," written to commemorate Kerouac's death in October 1969, and marked out by allusions to blues and jazz (including Kerouac's own "Mexico City Blues") and to the Beat icon of "the road":

JACK IN RED AND BLACK MAC
RUSHING THROUGH DERELICT STREWN
    STREETS OF NORTH AMERICA
JACK IN WELLWORN BLUE JEANS AND
    DROOPYSWEATER OF SMILES
RUNNING ACROSS THE COUNTRY LIKE A
    RAZOR BLADE GONE MAD
JACK IN FLOPPY SHIRT AND JACKET
    LOADED WITH JOKES
OLE ANGEL MIDNIGHT SINGING MEXICO
    CITY BLUES
IN THE MIDST OF BLACK HIPSTERS AND
    MUSICIANS
FOLLOWED BY A WHITE LEGION OF COOL
    KICK SEEKERS
POETRY LIVERS AND POEM GIVERS
PALE FACED CHIEFTAIN TEARING PAST

THE FUEL OF A GENERATION
AT REST     AT LAST

JK SAYS HELLO TO JC
JOHN COLTRANE, THAT IS[25]

Joans's prolific output, almost thirty titles in all beginning from *Jazz Poems* (1959) and *All of Ted Joans and No More* (1961) and running through to *Wow: Selected Poems of Ted Joans* (1991), has perhaps met its best success in two late-1960s (and still available) collections, *Black Pow-Wow: Jazz Poems* (1969) and *Afrodisia* (1970).[26] Both exhibit Joans's quickfire wit and wordplay, a largely free-form poetry in which blues, jazz, sex, Black Power. Africa and surrealist motif (his debt to André Breton is acknowledged in "Nadja Rendezvous") plait one into another.[27]

His own working credo especially shows through in "Passed on Blues: Homage to a Poet," a celebration of Langston Hughes, which opens on the following mellow note:

> the sound of black music
> the sad soft low moan of jazz ROUND ABOUT MIDNIGHT
> the glad heavy fat screaming song of happy blues
> That was the world of Langston Hughes.

The poem works its way through a montage of references to Harlem nights, Jesse Simple bars, downhome food (whether "pinto beans," "hamhocks in the dark," "grits" or "spareribs"), "the A-Train," "the dozens," "the rumping blues," "migrated Dixieland," "the jitterbug," "rent parties," Fats Waller's "Ain't Misbehavin' " and "sweaty, hard-working muscle." These, as he says, constitute:

> THE WORLD OF THE POET LANGSTON HUGHES
> BLACK DUES!
> BLACK NEWS!

This is both a homage to Hughes's lyric genius and to Afro-America's first city, a "sonata of Harlem." It also bespeaks Joans's own considerable inventive talent, his ventriloquist fusion of Beat and jazz.

This fusion extends throughout most of *Black Pow-Wow* and *Afrodisia*. In the former, in "O Great Black Masque," for instance, he invokes a negritude embracing Bouaké and Alabama, Mali and Manhattan, which suggests the cadences of the black spiritual and of Whitman. In "For the Viet Congo," an indictment of black Third World exploitation set out in capitalized typescript, he simulates what might be a newspaper "Report from the Front" made over into verse form. The comic, teasing side to Joans comes through in his "No Mo' Kneegrow," written while flying over Dixie ("I'M FLYING OVER AL-ABAMA . . . WITH BLACK POWER IN MY LAP") and which, according to his own gloss, "can be sung to the tune of 'Oh! Susannah,' a short but apposite piece of satiric wordplay on the price of racial deference; or in "Uh Huh," a line-up of seemingly muttered banalities which take aim at "THE COLORED WAITING ROOM"; or in "Santa Claws" which opens with "IF THAT WHITE MOTHER HUB-BARD COMES DOWN MY BLACK CHIMNEY . . ." and goes on to lampoon Santa as some white patriarchal "CON MAN."

Nor can there be any mistaking the angrier Joans in his well-known "The Nice Colored Man," which offers a column of therapeutic, detoxifying variations on the word "nigger," beginning from "Nice Nigger Educated Nigger Never Nigger Southern Nigger" and working through to:

> Eeny Meeny Minee Mo
> Catch Whitey by His Throat
> If He Says—Nigger CUT IT!

This gathers yet greater force from the fact that Joans's own father was killed by whites in a 1943 Detroit race riot; the schoolyard race ditty is sardonically turned about face, inside out.

The poems which invoke jazz likewise become the thing they memorialize, though benignly and out of deepest need and affection, as in "They Forget Too Fast," written in memory of Charlie Parker, "Jazz Is My Religion" ("it alone do I dig"), or "Jazz Must Be a Woman," a sound poem made up of the accumulating and run-on names of jazz's greats. One hears a near perfect blues sense of pitch in the carefully interspaced "True Blues for Dues Payer," Joans's elegy to Malcolm X written in North Africa:

> As I blew   the second chorus   of Old Man River
> (on an old gold trumpet loaded with blackass jazz)
> a shy   world traveling   white Englishman pushed a French-
> Moroccan
> newspaper   under my Afroamerican eyes
> there it said   that you were dead   killed by a group
> of black assassins   in black Harlem in the black of night

As I read    the second page    of bluesgiving news
(with wet eyes and trembling cold hands)
I stood    facing east    under quiet & bright African sky
I didn't cry    but inside    said goodbye to you whom I confess
I loved    Malcolm X

*Afrodisia* reflects more of Joans's African sojourns and his resolve
to link Afro-America back to the mother continent. The opening
poem, "Africa," so envisions Africa as

Land of my mothers, where a black god made me.
My Africa, your Africa, a free continent to be.

"Afrique Accidentale," another Hughes-like montage which parallels
the Mississippi with the Niger, Greenwich Village with the Sudan, re-
enacts his own African *Wanderjahr,* that of a "jiving AfroAmerican" in
search of the half-mythic and cleverly multispelled Timbuctoo.

I have traveled a long way on the Beat bread I made
now I'm deep in the heart of Africa,
the only Afroamerican spade

he says teasingly, yet pointedly, of his own true black homecoming.
The concluding lines make the point even more emphatic:

so now lay me down to sleep
to count black rhinos, not white sheep
Timbukto, Timbucktoo, Thymbaktou!
I do dig you!
Timbuctu, Timbouctou
I finally made you
Timbuctoo
Yeah!!

Throughout, Joans's surrealism shows its paces. In "No Mo Space
for Toms" he takes an absurdist tilt at colonialism; in "The Night of
the Shark," he concocts a priapic mock creation parable; and in
"Harlem to Picasso" he lowers a satiric eye on Euro-American artistic
borrowings from Africa with all the accompanying talk of primitivism:

Hey PICASSO why'd you drop Greco-Roman &
other academic slop then picked up on my
black ancestors sculptural bebop?

In "Jazz Anatomy," the poem itself becomes surreal while invoking
surrealism in painting and music. The body, Magritte-like, turns into a
combo, a line-up:

> my head is a trumpet
> my heart is a drum
> both arms are pianos
> both legs are bass viols
> my stomach the trombone
> my nose the saxaphone
> both lungs are flutes
> both ears are clarinets
> my penis is a violin
> my chest is a guitar
> vibes are my ribs
> my mouth is the score
> and my soul is where the music lies

Taken with the plentiful erotica, at its best in poems like "I Am
the Lover" and "Sweet Potato Pie" (and at its quasi-sexist, dated worst
in a poem like "Cuntinent"), Joans has long earned his reputation.
"Whenever I read a poem of my own creation," he has written, "I intentionally lift it off the page and 'blow it' just as I would when I was a
jazz trumpeter." Veteran of both Beat and blues, friend to Kerouac and
Ginsberg as to "Bird," "Dizzy" and "Monk," black surrealist and long-
time European and Africa sojourner, his continues to be a truly ongoing and live performance.

---

Though born in New Orleans of a Catholic black mother and Jewish
white father, raised in the Lower East Side (whose human variety he
warms to while condemning the squalor and poverty in pieces like
"East Fifth St. (N.Y.)" and "TeeVeePeople"), and with 20 years in the
Merchant Marine, Bob Kaufman has long been best known as a drugs

and poetry doyen of San Francisco. Despite several jail terms, or the self-denying and Buddhist 10 year vow of silence from 1963 to 1973 taken to memorialize John Kennedy's assassination, his adopted city, on his death in January 1986, appointed April 18 "Bob Kaufman Day" as well as naming a street after him. It was also Kaufman who helped coin the term Beat when editing the magazine *Beatitude* (the journalist Herb Caen claims Beatnik), no doubt appropriately so for the voice which once told America in "Benediction":

> Everyday your people get more and more
> Cars, television, sickness death dreams.
> You must have been great
> alive.

A degree of fame came in the 1950s and early West Coast 1960s with his work on *Beatitude,* and then Lawrence Ferlinghetti's City Lights Books published his Abomunist poems and broadsides. More, however, resulted from his jazz accompanied and Dadaist poetry readings, not to mention the legendary street and bar "happenings." At his death he was usually to be thought of as San Francisco's own one-off bohemian, a Beat irregular.

His different Abomunist papers (*Abomunist Manifesto* [1959], *Second April* [1959] and *Does the Secret Mind Whisper?* [1960]),[28] each an anarcho-surreal parody of all "isms" and issued under the name Bomkauf, argued for a Beat-derived "rejectionary philosophy." A synthesis of terms like bomb, anarchist, communist, Bob, make up the term "abomunism." In *Abomunist Manifesto,* telegram style, he lays out its implications as follows:

ABOMUNIST POETS CONFIDENT THAT THE NEW LITERARY FORM "FOOTPRINTISM" HAS FREED THE ARTIST OF OUTMODED RESTRICTIONS, SUCH AS: THE ABILITY TO READ AND WRITE, OR THE DESIRE TO COMMUNICATE, MUST BE PREPARED TO READ THEIR WORK AT DENTAL COLLEGES, EMBALMING SCHOOLS, HOMES FOR UNWED MOTHERS, HOMES FOR WED MOTHERS, INSANE ASYLUMS, USO CATEENS, KINDERGARTENS, AND COUNTY JAILS. ABOMUNISTS NEVER COMPROMISE THEIR REJECTIONARY PHILOSOPHY.

Whatever the noise, the heat, the often dire turns in his life, which went with "abomunism," Kaufman managed poetry of genuine distinction as borne out in his three principal collections, *Solitudes Crowded with Loneliness, Golden Sardine* (1967) and *The Ancient Rain: Poems 1956–1978* (1981).[29]

In *Solitudes* Kaufman strikes his own Beat affinity in "Afterwards, They Shall Dance," a poem in which he claims lineage with Dylan Thomas ("Wales-bird"), Billie Holiday ("lost on the subway and stayed there . . . forever"), Poe ("died translated, in unpressed pants"), and the *symboliste* master, Baudelaire. Only a dues-paying *black* Beat, however, would end in terms which resemble both Ginsberg's "Sunflower Sutra" and a dreamy, flighted blues:

> Whether I am a poet or not, I use fifty dollars's worth
> of air every day, cool.
> In order to exist I hide behind stacks of red and blue poems
> And open little sensuous parasols, singing the nail-in-
> the-foot-song, drinking cool beatitudes.

Nor can the Beat connection be missed in "West Coast Sounds—1956," one of his best-known San Francisco compositions, in which he identifies Ginsberg. Corso, Rexroth, Ferlinghetti, Kerouac, Cassady and himself as co-spirits for a changed America, even to the point of crowding the West Coast. The insider Beat reference, playful throughout, is unmistakable, whether to hipsters or squares, jazz or being high:

> San Fran, hipster land,
> Jazz sounds, wig sounds,
> Earthquake sounds; others,
> Allen on Chesnutt Street,
> Giving poetry to squares
> Corso on knees, pleading,
> God eyes.
> Rexroth, Ferlinghetti,
> Swinging, in cellars,
> Kerouac at Locke's,
> Writing Neal
> On high typewriter,

Neal, booting a choo-choo,
On zigzag tracks.
Now, many cats
Falling in,
New York cats,
Too many cats,
Monterey scene cooler,
San Franers, falling down.
Canneries closing.
Sardines splitting,
For Mexico.
Me too.

This has to be put alongside poems like "Ginsberg (for Allen)," his surreal, larky homage to the author of "Howl" ("I have proof that he was Gertrude Stein's medicine chest," "I love him because his eyes leak"); or "Jazz *Te Deum* for Inhaling at Mexican Bonfires," a hymn to the human need for exuberance ("Let us walk naked in radiant glacial rains and cool morphic thunderstorms"); or "A Remembered Beat," with its play of opposites, to the one side Charlie Parker as "a poet in jazz," Mexico and the "hidden Pacific," and to the other, coercive "organization men" and "television love"; or "War Memoir," his contemplative, Hiroshima haunted lament at nuclear folly; or "Jail Poems," his 34 part, movingly self-inquisitorial, sequence:

I sit here writing, not daring to stop,
For fear of seeing what's outside my head.

*Solitudes Crowded with Loneliness* made for an auspicious debut.

Though far less even (a suspicion arises that some of the poems were unfinished), *Golden Sardine* has its own triumphs. The untitled opening poem, a sequence of "reels" as Kaufman calls them, portrays Caryl Chessman on death row awaiting the electric chair. Norman Mailer's telling of the execution of Gary Gilmore in *The Executioner's Song* (1979) might well have been anticipated.

Kaufman opens his poem in images which deliberately jar, as though writing a kind of deliberately fractured and discontinuous death chant:

This is a poem about a nobody.
Charlie Chaplin & Sitting Bull walk hand in hand through
the World Series.
The scene opens with Dim Pictures of Animal Sadness, the
Deathbed of the last Buffalo in Nebraska . . . CARYL
CHESSMAN WAS AN AMERICAN BUFFALO.

Chessman's own voice weaves into the voices about him, a killer but
also a sacrificial killing. A mix of verse and prose, its typeface variously
in italics or capitalized, the whole exudes a fierce compassion, a
gallery of witness and indictment.

Poems like "Round About Midnight," "Tequila Jazz," "His Horn,"
or "Blue O'Clock," give testimony to Kaufman's belief in jazz as a healing intimacy, its power to subdue chaos. His poem "On," a sequence
of one line imagist scenes, envisages an America of further disjunc-
ture, beginning "On yardbird corners of embryonic hopes, drowned
in a heroin tear" and moving through to "On lonely poet corners of
low lying leaves & moist prophet eyes." The view is one from the
Beat or hipster margins, appalled at American conformity, "comicbook seduction" and the "motion picture corners of lassie & other
symbols."

Kaufman as Beat, however, is perhaps most to be heard in "Night
Sung Sailor's Prayer" in which America's "born losers, decaying in sorry
jails" become some of humanity's holiest (as they do in Ginsberg's
"Footnote to Howl"). The note is indeed beatific, Kaufman as poet of
spirit over materiality:

Sing love and life and life and love
All that lives is Holy.
The unholiest, most holy of all.

In his Introduction to *The Ancient Rains: Poems 1956–1978*, Kaufman's editor, Raymond Foye, rightly characterizes the later work as
"some of the finest . . . of his career—simple, lofty, resplendent." Two
poems especially do service. In "War Memoir: Jazz, Don't Listen to at
Your Own Risk," he makes jazz a counterweight, a moral balance, to
war and rapacity:

While Jazz blew in the night
Suddenly we were too busy to hear a sound.

He again focuses on the memory of Hiroshima and Nagasaki:

busy humans were
Busy burning Japanese in atomicolorcinescope
With stereophonic screams,
What one-hundred-percent red-blooded savage would waste precious
                                                              time
Listening to Jazz, with so many important things going on.

For Kaufman, jazz, "living sound," restores and harmonizes, an act of
life over death. Or as he himself puts it:

Jazz, scratching, digging, bluing, swinging jazz,
And we listen
And we feel
And live.

In "Like Father, Like Sun," with Lorca as tutelary spirit, he in-
vokes the engendering hope of the Mississippi and the "Apache,
Kiowa, and Sioux ranges" as against a "rainless," "fungus" America.
The ending looks to a pluralized, uncoercive, universal nation, to
America as "poem" or "ample geography" as might have been derived
from Emerson's visionary essay "The Poet":[30]

The poem comes
Across centuries of holy lies, and weeping heaven's eyes,
Africa's black handkerchief, washed clean by her children's honor,
As cruelly designed anniversaries spin in my mind.
Airy voice of all those fires of love I burn in memory of.
America is a promised land, a garden torn from naked stone.
A place where the losers in earth's conflicts can enjoy their triumph.
All losers, brown, red, black, and white; the colors from the Master
                                                              Palette.

Kaufman's "Like Father, Like Sun" no doubt bespeaks his own
pains, his own losses and, throughout, his own will to redemption. But

it also brings to bear a quite specific cultural credential: "Africa's black handkerchief" as progenitor and cornerstone. In shared spirit with Jones/Baraka and Joans, this would signify America made subject to a black beatitude and so reminded of its own best promise as the multi-cultural apotheosis of all "colors."

## Notes

1. J.J. Phillips, Ishmael Reed, Gundars Strads and Shawn Wong (eds), *The Before Columbus Foundation Poetry* (New York: W.W. Norton, 1992).
2. Imamu Amiri Baraka, *The Autobiography of LeRoi Jones/Amiri Baraka* (New York: Freundlich Books, 1984), p. 159.
3. Ted Joans, *Tape Recording at the Five Spot,* reprinted in Seymour Krim (ed.), *The Beats* (Greenwich, Connecticut: Fawcett World Library, 1960), pp. 211–13.
4. Bob Kaufman, *Solitudes Crowded with Loneliness* (New York: New Directions, 1965).
5. Allen Ginsberg, *Howl and Other Poems* (San Francisco: City Lights Books, 1956); Jack Kerouac, *On the Road* (New York: Viking, 1957) and *The Subterraneans* (New York: Grove, 1958); John Clellon Holmes, "The Philosophy of the Beat Generation," reprinted together with his two other Beat essays, "This is the Beat Generation" and "The Game of the Name" in *Nothing More to Declare* (New York: Dutton, 1967); Gregory Corso, *Gasoline* (San Francisco: City Lights Books, 1958); and Norman Mailer, *The White Negro* (San Francisco: City Lights Books. 1957).
6. Bob Kaufman, "Bagel Shop Jazz," reprinted in *Solitudes Crowded with Loneliness,* pp. 77–86; A.B. Spellman, *The Beautiful Days* (New York: Poets Press, 1965) and *Four Lives in the Bebop Business* (New York: Schocken, 1966), later retitled *Black Music: Four Lives* (New York: Schocken, 1970).
7. *The Autobiography of LeRoi Jones/Amiri Baraka,* p. 157.
8. A full list of these early magazine publications is to be found in Werner Sollors, *Amiri Baraka/LeRoi Jones: The Quest for a "Populist Modernism"* (New York: Columbia University Press, 1978), pp. 301–28.
9. LeRoi Jones (ed.), *The Moderns: An Anthology of New Writing in America* (New York: Corinth Books, 1963).
10. *How I Became Hettie Jones* (New York: E.P. Dutton, 1990). The first two chapters, especially, touch on these early years.

11. "Cuba Libre" first appeared in *Evergreen Review* and was republished in *Home: Social Essays* (New York: William Morrow & Co., 1966).

12. "BLACK DADA NIHILISMUS," in *The Dead Lecturer* (New York: Grove Press, 1964).

13. *Dutchman* was published in *Dutchman* and *The Slave* (New York: William Morrow & Co., 1964).

14. *Blues People: Negro Music in White America* (New York: William Morrow & Co., 1963); *Black Music* (New York: William Morrow & Co., 1967).

15. Robert Lowell, "Memories of West Street and Lepke," in *Life Studies* (New York: Farrar, Straus & Cudahy, 1959).

16. J.D. Salinger, *The Catcher in the Rye* (Boston: Little, Brown, 1951).

17. Full-length contextual anthologies, studies and memoirs include Gene Feldman and Max Gartenberg (eds.), *The Beat Generation and the Angry Young Men* (New York: Citadel, 1958); Lawrence Lipton, *The Holy Barbarians* (New York: Julian Messner, 1959); Krim (ed.), *The Beats*; Donald M. Allen (ed.); *The New American Poetry: 1945–60* (New York: Grove Press, 1960); Elias Wilentz (ed.), *The Beat Scene* (New York: Corinth, 1961); Thomas A. Parkinson (ed.), *A Casebook on the Beat* (New York: Crowell, 1961); LeRoi Jones (ed.), *The Moderns*; Richard Weaver, Terry Southern and Alexander Trocchi (eds.), *Writers in Revolt* (New York: Frederick Fells, 1963); *Wholly Communion* (London: Lorrimer Films, 1965); *Astronauts of Inner Space: An International Anthology of Avant-Garde Activity* (San Francisco: Stolen Paper Review, 1966); Leslie Garrett, *The Beats* (New York: Scribner's, 1966); Clellon Holmes, *Nothing More to Declare*; Tina Morris and Dave Cunliffe (eds.), *Thunderbolts of Peace and; Liberation* (Blackburn, England: BB Books, 1967); M.L. Rosenthal, *The New Modern Poetry* (New York: Macmillan, 1967); David Kherdian, *Six Poets of the San Francisco Renaissance* (Fresno, California: Giligia Press, 1967); Diane di Prima, *Memoirs of a Beatnik* (New York: Olympia Press, 1969); David Metzer (ed.), *The San Francisco Poets* (New York: Ballantine, 1971); Nick Harvey (ed.), *Mark in Time: Portraits & Poetry/San Francisco* (San Francisco: Glide, 1971); Bruce Cook, *The Beat Generation* (New York: Scribner's, 1971); Laurence James (ed.), *Electric Underground: A City Lights Reader* (London: New English Library, 1973); Yves Le Pellec (ed.), *Beat Generation* (New York: McGraw Hill, 1976); Ed Sanders, *Tales of Beatnik Glory* (New York: Stonehill, 1975); David S. Wirshup (ed.), *The Beat Generation & Other Avant-Garde Writers* (Santa Barbara, California: Anacapa Books, 1977); Lee Bartlett (ed.), *The Beats: Essays in Criticism* (Jefferson,

North Carolina: McFarland, 1981); Arthur and Kit Knight (eds.), *The Beat Vision: A Primary Sourcebook* (New York: Paragon House Publishers, 1987).

18. Amiri Baraka, *The LeRoi Jones/Amiri Baraka Reader,* edited by William J. Harris (New York: Thunder's Mouth Press, 1991).

19. *The Autobiography of LeRoi Jones/Amiri Baraka,* p. 156.

20. Arthur and Kit Knight (eds.), *The Beat Vision: A Primary Sourcebook,* p. 131.

21. Allen (ed.), *The New American Poetry.*

22. Allen (ed.), *The New American Poetry,* p. 424.

23. LeRoi Jones, *Preface to a Twenty Volume Suicide Note* (New York: Totem Press/Corinth, 1961).

24. A considerable critical bibliography has now built up around Jones/Baraka. See Donald B. Gibson (ed.), *Five Black Writers* (New York: New York University Press, 1970); Letitia Dace, *LeRoi Jones: A Checklist of Works By and About Him* (London: Nether Press, 1971); Theodore Hudson, *From LeRoi Jones to Amiri Baraka: The Literary Works* (Durham, North Carolina: Duke University Press, 1973); Stephen Henderson, *Understanding the New Black Poetry: Black Speech and Black Music as Poetic References* (New York: Morrow, 1973); Donald B. Gibson (ed.), *Modern Black Poets: A Collection of Critical Essays* (Englewood Cliffs, New Jersey: Prentice Hall, 1973); Esther M. Jackson, "LeRoi Jones (Imamu Amiri Baraka): Form and Progression of Consciousness," *College Language Association Journal,* Vol. 17, No. 1 (September 1973); Kimberley Benston, *Baraka: The Renegade and the Mask* (New Haven, Connecticut: Yale University Press, 1976); Kimberley Benston (ed.), *Imamu Amiri Baraka (LeRoi Jones): A Collection of Essays* (Englewood Cliffs, New Jersey: Prentice Hall, 1978); Thomas M. Inge *et al.* (eds.), *Black American Writers: Bibliographical Essays, Volume 2: Richard Wright, Ralph Ellison, James Baldwin, and Amiri Baraka* (New York: St. Martin's Press, 1978); Henry C. Lacey, *To Raise, Destroy, and Create: The Poetry, Drama and Fiction of Imamu Amiri Baraka (LeRoi Jones)* (Troy, New York: The Whitson Publishing Company, 1981); William J. Harris, *The Poetry and Poetics of Amiri Baraka: The Jazz Aesthetic* (Columbia, Missouri: University of Missouri Press, 1985).

25. Reprinted in Arthur and Kit Knight (eds.), *The Beat Vision,* p. 289. His connection with Kerouac and other Beats is chronicled in the interview which follows with Gerald Nicosia, pp. 270–83.

26. Ted Joans, *Jazz Poems* (New York: Rhino Review, 1959), *All of Ted Joans and No More: Poems and Collages* (New York: Excelsior Press, 1961), *Wow:*

*Selected Poems of Ted Joans* (1991), *Black Pow-Wow: Jazz Poems* (New York: Hill and Wang, 1969) and *Afrodisia* (New York: Hill and Wang, 1970).

27. Ted Joans, "The Beat Generation and Afro-American Culture," *Beat Scene Magazine*, No. 13 (December 1991), pp. 22–23. The same issue contains a brief profile, "Ted Joans in Paris," by Jim Burns, p. 13.

28. All three of these manifestos, the originals now collector's items, are republished in Kaufman, *Solitudes Crowded with Loneliness*.

29. *Golden Sardine* (San Francisco: City Lights Books, 1967) and *The Ancient Rain: Poems 1956–1978* (New York: New Directions, 1981). For bearings on Kaufman, see Barbara Christian, "Whatever Happened to Bob Kaufman?," in Bartlett (ed.), *The Beats*, pp. 107–14; Arthur and Kit Knight (eds.), *The Beat Vision*, and Joans, "The Beat Generation and Afro-American Culture," pp. 22–23.

30. As given in Emerson's "The Poet," in *Essays: Second Series* (1844): "America is a poem in our eye; its ample geography dazzles the imagination."

---

# NORMAN MAILER

NORMAN MAILER, co-founder of *The Village Voice* in 1955, published *The White Negro: Superficial Reflections on the Hipster* as a City Lights pamphlet in 1957. His essay began "Probably we will never be able to determine the psychic havoc of the concentration camps and the atom bomb upon the unconscious mind of almost everyone alive in these years." Mailer took the hipster as a heroic figure "whose values and lifestyle" might inspire emulation. The hipster knew that

> if the fate of twentieth century man is to live with death from adolescence to premature senescence, why then the only life-giving answer is to accept the terms of death, to live with death as immediate danger, to divorce oneself from society, to exist without roots, to set out on that uncharted journey into the rebellious imperatives of the self.

In 1959 Mailer included "The White Negro" in *Advertisements for Myself,* along with a footnote to the essay titled "Hipster and Beatnik," which had originally appeared in *The Village Voice.* For the next few years Mailer continued to write about "The Hip and the Square" in *The Village Voice,* defining "hip" as "an exploration into the nature of man, and its emphasis is on the Self rather than Society. . . . Hip is an American existentialism, profoundly different from French existentialism because Hip is based on a mysticism of the flesh, and its origins can be traced back into all the undercurrents and underworlds of American life. . . ." In the 1960s Mailer was the recipient of the National Book Award for *Miami and the Siege of Chicago* (1968) and the Pulitzer Prize for *The Armies of the Night* (1969).

---

## Hipster and Beatnik

### A Footnote to
### "The White Negro"

Hipster came first as a word—it was used at least as long ago as 1951 or 1952, and was mentioned in the New Directions blurb on Chandler Brossard's *Who Walk in Darkness.* It came up again from time to time, notably in Ginsberg's *Howl* ("Angel-headed hipsters"), and was given its attention in *The White Negro.* Then came *On the Road,* and with Kerouac's success, the Beat Generation (a phrase first used by him many years ago, and mentioned several times in articles by John Clellon Holmes) was adopted by the mass-media. Beatnik came into existence a year later, in the summer or fall of 1958, the word coined by a San Francisco columnist, Herb Caen. The addition of "nik" however—"nik" being a pejorative diminutive in Yiddish—gave a quality of condescension to the word which proved agreeable to the newspaper mentality. "Beatnik" caught on. But one no longer knew whether the Beat Generation referred to hipsters or beatniks or included both, and some people to avoid the label of beatnik began to call themselves Beats.

Since there is no authority to order this nomenclature, it is anyone's right to set up his surveyor's marks as he chooses, and I will make the attempt here, for I think there are differences, and they should be noted.

The Beat Generation is probably best used to include hipsters and beatniks. Not too many seem to use the word Beats; it is uncomfortable on the tongue; those who refuse to let it die seem to use it as an omnibus for hipsters and beatniks, a shorthand for saying the Beat Generation. This last term is itself an unhappy one, but since it has entered the language, one may as well live with it. Still, it must be said that the differences between hipsters and beatniks may be more important than their similarities, even if they share the following general characteristics: marijuana, jazz, not much money, and a community of feeling that society is the prison of the nervous system. The sense of place is acute—few care to stay away for long from the Village, Paris, North Beach, Mexico, New Orleans, Chicago and some other special cities. Hipster and Beatnik both talk Hip, but not in the same way— the beatnik uses the vocabulary; the hipster has that muted animal voice which shivered the national attention when first used by Marlon Brando.

Now the differences begin. The hipster comes out of a muted rebellion of the proletariat, he is, so to say, the lazy proletariat, the spiv; nothing given to manual labor unless he has no choice. The beatnik— often Jewish—comes from the middle class, and twenty-five years ago would have joined the YCL. Today, he chooses not to work as a sentence against the conformity of his parents. Therefore he can feel moral value in his goodbye to society. The hipster is more easygoing about the drag and value of a moneyless life of leisure.

Their bodies are not the same. A hipster moves like a cat, slow walk, quick reflexes; he dresses with a flick of chic; if his dungarees are old, he turns the cuffs at a good angle. The beatnik is slovenly—to strike a pose against the middle-class you must roil their compulsion to be neat. Besides—the beatnik is more likely to have a good mind than a good body. While he comes along with most hipsters on the first tenet of the faith: that one's orgasm is the clue to how well one is living—he has had less body to work with in the first place, and so his chances for lifting himself by his sexual bootstraps are commonly nil, especially since each medieval guild in the Beat Generation has invariably formed itself on a more or less common sexual vitality or lack of it. The boys and girls available to the average beatnik are as drained as himself. Natural that the sex of the beatnik circles in, and mysticism becomes the Grail—he ends by using his drug to lash his mind into a higher contemplation of the universe and its secrets, a passive act, onanistic; the trance is coveted more than any desire to trap it later in work or art. The beatnik moves therefore onto Zen, the search for a lady ends as a search for *satori*—that using a drug goes against the discipline of Zen is something he will face later.

The hipster has a passing respect for Zen, he doesn't deny the experience of the mystic, he has known it himself, but his preference is to get the experience in the body of a woman. Drugs are a gamble for him, he gambles that the sensitivity of his libido on marijuana will help him to unlock the reflexes of his orgasm. If marijuana and the act take more out of him than he gets back, he is not likely to consider himself in good shape. Whereas a beatnik might. Who cares about impotence if one finds within it the breath of a vision? The beatnik, then, is obviously more sentimental—he needs a God who will understand all and forgive all. The hard knowledge of the hipster that you pay for what you get is usually too bitter for the beatnik. But then, the hipster is still in life; strong on his will, he takes on the dissipation of the drugs in order to dig more life for himself, he is wrestling with the destiny of his nervous system, he is Faustian. The beatnik contemplates eternity, finds it beautiful, likes to believe it is waiting to receive him. He wants to get out of reality more than he wants to change it, and at the end of the alley is a mental hospital.

If a hipster has a fall, it is to death or jail. Psychosis is not for him. Like a psychopath, he is juggling the perils of getting your kicks in this world, against the hell (or prison) of paying for them in the next. The hipster looks for action, and a bar with charge is where he goes when marijuana has turned him on—the beatnik, more at home with talk, can be found in the coffeehouse. The poet is his natural consort, his intellectual whip, even as the criminal, the hip hoodlum, and the boxer are the heart of knowledge for the hipster who ducks the psychotic relations between beatniks as too depressing, a hang-up, they go nowhere which can nourish him. The beatnik is in the line of continuation from the old bohemian, and nowhere near in his tradition to the hipster whose psychic style derives from the best Negroes to come up from the bottom. Yet the beatnik is to the Left of the other, for the hipster is interested in exploring the close call of the Self, and so has to collaborate more with the rhythms and tastes of the society he quit. It is not that the hipster is reactionary, it is rather that in a time of crisis, he would look for power, and in the absence of a radical spirit in the American air, the choices of power which will present themselves are more likely to come from the Right than the moribund liberalities of the Left. The beatnik, gentle, disembodied from the race, is often a radical pacifist, he has sworn the vow of no violence—in fact, his violence is sealed within, and he has no way of using it. His act of violence is to suicide even as the hipster's is toward murder, but in his mind-lost way, the beatnik is the torch-bearer of those all-but-lost values of freedom, self-expression, and equality which first turned him against the hypocrisies and barren cultureless flats of the middle-class.

For years now, they have lived side by side, hipster and beatnik, white Negro and crippled saint, their numbers increasing every month as the new ones come to town. They can be found wherever one knows to look, in all their permutations and combinations, in what is finally their unclassifiable and separate persons. I have exaggerated some tendencies, and made some divisions, but I have also blurred the spectrum of individuality by creating two types who never exist so simply in the real life of any Village ferment. If there are hipsters and beatniks, there are also hipniks and beatsters like Ginsberg and Kerouac, and across the spectrum like a tide of defeat—rebellion takes its price in a dead year and a deadened land—there are the worn-out beats of all too many hipsters who made their move, lost, and so have ended as beatniks with burned-out brains, listening sullenly to the quick montage of words in younger beatniks hot with the rebellion of having quit family, school, and flag, and on fire with the private ambition to be charged one day so high as to be a hipster oneself.

---

# EDWARD MARSHALL

EDWARD MARSHALL wrote his poem "Leave the Word Alone" in 1955 and published it two years later in *Black Mountain Review* Number 7. Allen Ginsberg remembered that he saw the poem in manuscript in San Francisco in 1956, when Robert Creeley showed it to him. In 1979 Marshall's poem was published as a small pamphlet by the Pequod Press in New York City, a limited edition handset by R'lene Dahlberg. In an introduction to the pamphlet, Ginsberg disclosed the effect of "Leave the Word Alone" on him. Apparently Marshall's poem led to the composition of "Kaddish" much as Kenneth Rexroth's poem "Thou Shalt Not Kill" (1953–54), another long poem Ginsberg had seen in manuscript in San Francisco, had impressed him earlier and unconsciously helped to shape the theme and imagery of "Howl for Carl Solomon."

Here telling about his mother, as I told of mine in *Kaddish* [1958–59]—so here's Marshall's original Confession, that inspired my own; I copied his freedom of form, and wildness of line, and homeliness of personal reference. . . .

I remember kneeling before Marshall over a decade ago 8th Avenue 28th Street N Y thanking him for displaying a model memorial family poem, model of what's now tritely called "confessional" poem as if confession to Lord or Priest were socially appropriate but confession of consciousness to fellow humans to break the human ice (as G. Corso named a mood) were somehow emotionally degraded. . . .

Re-reading the text I'm amazed that in this time the poem and poet haven't become classic, known to all youths in Nixon years of impersonal secret thought with hidden feeling and uptightness dominating Nation from White House down to street robber—everybody in America a thief living off thievery from man or nature, thus secretive & shamed of inner thought—So that this poem, and the type of poem that rises from it, emotional medicine to the Nation. . . .

I know it's strange to praise another Poet's work for influencing your own, but I have fame and name and shame of money where Marshall has none, yet much of my reputation rests on an original breath of inspiration that came from Edward

Marshall's own body's lone unlaureled Prana intelligence, lung.

Marshall explains his breaththrough, in an extra fragment of *The Word*: "for it was the Holy
Spirit / that made me jump out of my seat—"

---

### Leave the Word Alone

*I.*

Leave the word alone it is dangerous.
Leave the Bible alone it is dangerous.
Leave all barbed wires alone they are
dangerous.

When you go to the country *au campagne* watch for
the cows . . . beware of moo-her
moo-her—moo-her.

There aren't too many bulls, but there are harsh
fathers who still insist on impregnation
at 35 while he is 41.

That was twenty three years ago and now she is in
an insane asylum because she
wanted to read the Bible and
her health book.

She reads nothing now for she is catatonic, dementia-
praecox among the wolverine
gang of girls who
couldn't get what they
wanted in the '29 crash.

Lena went to the asylum at the age of 35 having just
had a child and when that baby came to
visit her she said pretty baby,

you have a very beautiful
    baby and that baby is
        now I.

II.

If I can finish this poem without cracking up and becoming
  victorious, onslaught resurrection.
    It was the first of August that she couldn't
      take it any longer—pressure
      and she ran away.
The neighbors came and Papa Harry as I called him later
  invited all the neighbors to take part in
   a hunting search—ordered a lot
    of bread and made sandwiches.
On the farm Harry got fat and no longer was called Edward.
  I am Edward Junior and always knew of my own father
    as Papa Harry and it was not healthy
      either for I did not know that
        he was the stocky guy that
          gave the sperm to my mother,
            still in the asylum.
Yes, she is still in the asylum not too far from my Concord
  N. H. residence—and I stayed in the
    same asylum nineteen years after
      she was admitted and I was
      there for 5 months.
Harry—He almost had her there after my second sister
  was born, but Lena did not go to the hospital.
    When I was six the boy out back said my mother was crazy
    and I thought he didn't like my mother
      (present) who is my
      aunt by marriage.
Vernon—he heard loose talk from his mother
  but I always thought Vernon's mother odd and
    his sister Irene liked to play
      around with me before I
      understood sex and
Vernon used to get pleasure sticking paper up

my rectum and he was
   Greek-American. Father
      worked at St. Clair's ice-cream shop.


Later Vernon got a puppy from the same farm where I
   was born and then I got a puppy but
      it died of rotten pears in the backyard.
David, my cousin, asked when I was going back to live
   with my mother and father (I thought I
      was living with them) (they were my
         aunt and uncle).
You naughty boy, if you don't watch out I shall send you
   back to the farm with Papa Harry—
      You must appreciate what I do and I was confused
         for I didn't know I came from a fertile
            process and I didn't understand
               how babies came until I was 12—
                  Honte!   Honte!   Shame!
I didn't understand how I was born until a smart Greek boy
   a few blocks over got to talking about it one night
      when we were sleeping in a pup tent.
         You are dumb!
It wasn't long before I knew more about the subject than he did
   and he was dumb about Greek love
      but when I didn't know about babies
         he said his younger sister did.
Never shall that be anymore. And that
   same year I was adopted.
My father let my aunt-by-marriage adopt me—
   he was broke, it was World War 2
      and he wasn't living on the farm.
I was adopted then he got involved with some women.
   And when one woman found he didn't
      have any money she withdrew the
         alienation of affection suit against him.
And Harry visited the hospital to see my
   mother—faint recognition.
      She was gone—not gone, asleep—no more
      Bible.

Lena was once a school teacher after she graduated
　　from Normal School.
　　　　Then she was a teacher down in the Hollow
　　　　　　when she met Harry thru robust Eva who
　　　　　　　　afterwards kept house for sister Lena.


With a little honey-moon at Rye Beach they came to
　　the farm in Chichester where
　　　　she slaved til 35.
"Get those potatoes ready for the working-men" but
　　she kept reading the Bible and
　　　　Harry wasn't good in taking
　　　　　　her to Church Sunday
　　　　　　　　and she enjoyed church so.
The religion was in the dining room where all the
　　tramps would come in and sit and
　　　　when she felt injured there was
　　　　　　the health book nearby
　　　　　　　　and no relatives from up-country understood.
And the sister in Boston was getting
　　ready for the mental hospital.
She (Olive) died three or four years ago of tuberculosis,
　　and while I was a patient at NHSH
　　　　I met Dr. Quimby from Sandwich who tended
　　　　　　my grandmother or Lena and Olive's mother.
Dr. Quimby was manic depressive and yet
　　he always went back up-country to practice.
In his last years Papa Harry went with Bertha who
　　my adopted mother couldn't stomach.
　　　　Immoral—living together!
　　　　Immoral!
But the kind relatives would answer—but a man
　　is entitled to a house-keeper who housekeeps
　　　　for him. It is the property she
　　　　　　wants. So it was.
But Bertha never got the property—not one cent when
　　Harry died ("passed on" to Christian-Science-Bertha).
Sister Marguerite had the chance to buy some of the estate
　　woodlot to help pay off the

funeral bill to that funeral
    parlor in Gloucester where they
        tried to make my father alive after he
            died! Blasphemy!
And he died a year before my grandmother died.
    And when my grandmother died she got the
        same treatment—to make her alive.
My grandmother was a Saint and she would have been horrified
    to have them make her alive when she is alive
        in some of our memories. Blasphemy!
            Burn down that funeral home
                and to the pyre, to the pyre!
                    And the funeral home still sends bills,
                        and not because of fire.
They send bills because they said they did a lot to make
    both of them alive and my uncle (by marriage)
        from New Jersey and a Presbyterian—when he
            went by the bier he kissed her and I thought
                it disgusting but he never sent
                    anything for her bill.
W. C. Williams as the Irish would say—I dig you—
    Come and show us how to perform a funeral.
        And show us Congregationalists the way.
In the house in West Gloucester I used to love to go up
    the back way steps and smell the home-made soap
        and working men's bread but that dynasty
            is gone—it went after my
                grandfather died.
Gloucester and Chichester—two kingdoms gone!
    One by the ocean—Pigeon's Cove
        near large estates not occupied.
            Chichester where even Harry Kelley has given up.
Chichester—an inland cranberry marsh and
    swamp and sweet-smelling hay
        brings back Antipas, George and Moses Marshall.
            And they were truly Georgian, indeed!
And if I wish to use sweet-smelling hay—that is all
    right! sweet peas are a fact in
        Chichester and Gloucester.
Are you to take anything from man's collected

experience? If you do—you are a traducer and I shall
    stamp on you. And what business
        did you have giving me a Rorschach?
Me? Child destined to take a Rorschach, no, damn it!
    No, Professor Fowler! you gave me a Rorschach and
        yet a year later I saw you with a cute number with
        shorts on Main St., Concord.

Children destined to take a Rorschach get back to your
    parents—never leave them—know
        their sex organs, if possible.
Children to take a Rorschach get back to your parents—
    Antipas, Moses, George, what do you think
        an insult to thee who gave
        us and you were healthy too.
Lena, child, grand-child of Rhoda Straw that one
    Indian—whatever happened to you?
        Did the grand-son of Antipas expect too much of you?
The Marshalls and Watsons and Harrises are the healthy
    types but there is a bad clot—Indian half-breeds.
        Who will ever know?
When I asked my other great-aunt to list all
    the insane relatives, there are two,
        your mother and her sister,
        but I know that there were more.
And at the death of my great-aunt I met my great Uncle
    John and he was in an asylum for a while
        and great Uncle Sam who wanted to be a minister
        got struck in the head by a base-ball bat,
        and that affected his mentality
        so he had a chicken-farm.
Great Uncle Sam is supposed to have had
    a couple of nice looking children.
        The Pitmans from the Straws, no doubt
        the cause of that insanity when Rhoda
        waked at morn on the lake
        and saw the black cloud over head.
And she cursed the lake as Kierkegaard's father
    cursed on a hill in Denmark.
Rhoda you have a long line of descendants—too much
    to carry, indeed too much?

I don't believe my own mother ever thought of Rhoda
  but Rhoda is a fact because I traced her back
    in the genealogy book and save for
      a couple of clergy with M.A. degrees
        the tree looked rather bad on the whole.
I have that Nova Scotian blue-blood and that is why
  I am able to survive—under Steve and
    the cock-roach society. (Steve not to be
      confused with the cock-roach society).
No guilt by association I cry and I suppose
  that was my father's argument about Bertha
    but he was limited in the provoked image.
Rhoda Straw was never limited in images they were too heavy
  and the dust was under her feet and between her toes
    and the milkweed in her hair
      but that is the story of one girl.
And is she thankful for someone of hers to bang on the
  typewriter as my mother banged on
    the asylum wall until catatonia won out?
I am rigid and will often curl up on my bed and if my
  back bone was ever snapped then I would
    go like Lena and hang from the nails
      and hang by my bones.
My sister did visit her and she said
  it was a pitiful sight and not to be seen again.
    I never did see her although
      I slept a few yards away
        but that was in an admissions building.
Well I am here writing on blue paper and I must watch myself
  for I hear a spoken word telling me to do many things—
    to read this and that:
You must read Williams, Olson, and that D. H. Lawrence—
  I suppose I must—that is the punishment of all
    who have stepped over the crescent
      and stepped on the hot of the grit.
There was no fireplace where I was born and that was because
  the house I was born in was a put-up job
    originally to house summer boarders for the
      well-to-do Shaws next door.
Wood stoves, yes—And when I was born was in June

and when winter came I was not on the farm
  but I was living with my aunt and uncle
    in the Congregationalist town of Pittsfield.
I never stayed over on the farm in winter until
  I was in my teens and then I spent my time
    looking over the parsing books and McGuffy readers
     of my mother and I found out
      that she was a member of a German club
      and could speak a little.
That was when girls were allowed at New Hampton
  but after World War I boys got more sexy
    after hearing rumors about France
    and the expatriates.
A tract for the age was coming (End of an Age)
  W. R. Inge.
I don't know whether my mother read Eliot or Joyce
  but I found Longfellow
    and a rather nice copy at that.
O, I found her wedding dress and it tore easily
  and the brides-maid clothes were there—what Olive wore
    and Eva played an old-fashioned harp.
When I was in high school I was talking to a neighbor
  down the farm road. And my daughter went
    with your uncle when he was in high school
    and you look just like him.
I couldn't say for I had never seen Uncle Arthur.
  He was my mother's little brother—very tall
    athletic looking and he was an expert carpenter.
When I go to that town—Chichester
  I find out about myself and when I hear
    the moo-her I shiver and I say
     is it my mother?
And when I dream, I dream of riding on a bicycle
  from Concord to Durham where I went to college
    for a year.
And when I get half way—Chichester—a valve leaks
  in my tube and it is just to annoy me.
Chichester will not let me alone
  and I haven't let it alone.
Sometimes I hear cries and cries when I go through

Center Road to the farm where the blueberry bushes
    are high and in the upper pasture and fields
        the sheep-nose apples wither and the pears rot—
           the ice-house is turned about and no barn
              where the cupola looked everywhere.
The barn burned down to get fire insurance—
    a motive brought out—never proven.
And there was an attempt to get a veteran who was to
    get farm machinery from the government to cultivate the land
        but it never worked.
My soul is Chichester and my origin is a womb
    whether one likes it or not.
And the womb is Lena's who read the Bible and health book
    and she couldn't get to church and no one cared
        and she ran down the Center Road
           where one thought that she was going
              to run to the quicksand—suicide?
She read the Bible and she did go out and work in the garden
    but the daughters weren't scrubbed
        and all was scurvy.
She was fed well in the asylum
    and the strength of nervous energy was manifested:
        a heavy table tossed up and turned over.
And don't think this mere journalism for when the
    child was brought she said: "You have a beautiful child."


And this is the most painful process that I have had
    to go through for a long while
        and I am a Christian because I know how deep
           and sore is the womb from which I came;
And I know that the wages of sin is death and that the
    sins of the fathers are visited upon the children;
And I know that the gift of God is eternal life for the
    one who could go through the trauma
        and write of it. And it is not
           my fingers that write this.
It is Lena; it is Rhoda Straw—
    it is the sore womb and that is fertility.
It is a painful process but it is a process I must go through
    to stay out of the asylum—

perhaps that bear cave by Newfound Lake
   where animals—bears, lynx—have made their
      imprint on Rhoda's paths.

*Boston, October, 1955*

---

# IAN MARSHALL

IAN MARSHALL included his personal account of finding the
spirit of "Howl for Carl Solomon" while on a long hiking trip at
Bear Mountain, New Jersey, in his book *Story Line: Exploring
the Literature of the Appalachian Trail* (1998). Marshall had begun his walk on Springer Mountain in Georgia; he concluded it
on the summit of Mount Katahdin in Maine. A professor of
English at Pennsylvania State University–Altoona, he has hiked
all but a couple of hundred miles of the 2,150-mile-long Appalachian Trail.

## Where the Open Road Meets Howl

The coyote paces along a wall of his chain-link cage, his toenails clicking on concrete. He stops at the corner of the cage, his ears tilt forward, his silvery eyes find mine. Then his brows drop and he turns
away, toenails clicking, moving back and forth along that one wall,
pausing each time to stare at me.

---

Even before I got to the coyote cage, I thought that Bear Mountain,
part of the Palisades Interstate Park Commission in New York, was a
zoo, in the same way that people call Yankee Stadium the "Bronx Zoo."
It's a hectic, crowded place, maybe two hundred people on the summit by midday on a bright Sunday in May. There's an observation
tower on top, with panoramic views. A road winds its way up here, and

looking to the west, out to New Jersey, I hear behind me some motor-cycles grring, a helicopter in front of me whirring. To the south-southwest, about forty miles away, lies New York City. Even on a clear day, the view is hazy. The city looks like some barely discernible range in the distance, an outcropping of cliffs. Only when I look steadily for more than a few seconds do I see that the shapes are too evenly rec-tangular to be natural.

Heading down the mountain, toward Bear Mountain Inn, I see a man, woman, and child hiking up. The little boy is engrossed by some-thing he sees in a stream; the man looks away from me as I approach. His T-shirt, emblazoned with the name of a motor oil, bulges at the belly. The woman is wearing cut-off jeans and lacy leotards. When I say Hi, accustomed as I am to the camaraderie of the trail, she looks at me suspiciously, as if she thinks I've mistaken her for someone I know.

Around Hessian Lake at the bottom of the mountain, thousands of people are picnicking. There's some sort of dog competition under-way, and dogs of all sorts are wandering around, leashed, many with bandanas around their necks. (I've got one there, too, kept handy to mop up sweat rolling into my eyes on uphill climbs, or to be doused in streams so I can carry their coolness with me. Apparently, I'm au courant in dog fashion.) Radios are playing salsa, lighter fluid and charcoal briquettes scent the air, I hear people speaking Spanish and Chinese. New York City has come to the woods.

The trail follows an asphalt walkway through the park, leading past a statue of Walt Whitman, with an excerpt from "Song of the Open Road" engraved on a rock next to the statue. The lines give a good indi-cation of what all these people, including me, are looking for here:

> Afoot and light-hearted I take to the open road
> Healthy, free, the world before me,
> The long brown path before me leading wherever I choose.
>
> . . . . .
>
> Henceforth I ask not good fortune, I myself am good fortune.
> Henceforth I whimper no more, postpone no more, need
> nothing,
> Done with indoor complaints, libraries, querulous criticisms,
> Strong and content I travel the open road.
>
> . . . . .

Camerado, I give you my hand!
I give you my love more precious than money,
I give you myself before preaching or law;
Will you give me yourself? Will you come travel with me?
Shall we stick by each other as long as we live?

More than anything I've ever read, these lines capture, I think, the essence of what the trail has to teach, the sense that the world lies before us, leading us wherever we choose, nothing to fear. While a long hike can be psychically as well as physically demanding, once they adjust to life on the trail many thru-hikers discover that the hike is a joywalk. In part that may be because they are in such good physical shape that they're on an endorphin high. In part it's because they are living a simple life that consists of hiking from point A to point B, with nothing more stressful weighing them down than deciding where to plot tomorrow's point B. But somehow the effects last a lifetime. Whatever lies ahead in life, thru-hikers move on confident that they can get there. And if worse comes to worst, well, you can always go hiking. The trail teaches us to see life as an open road and to hike it "strong and content," to appreciate each step along the way and to anticipate without trepidation the next step, the next turn in the trail.

That's the sort of lighthearted assurance conveyed by Whitman's poem. And Whitman's long, irregular lines, breaking out of the confining boundaries of traditional meters, sprawling across the page, enact the themes of the poem, each line finding its own end point, determining its own rhythm, flaunting its liberation from constraint and conformity, boldly moving into the open spaces beyond the usual margins. Elsewhere in "Song of the Open Road" Whitman proclaims, "I think heroic deeds were all conceiv'd in the open air, and all free poems also. . . . From this hour I ordain myself loos'd of limits and imaginary lines." The shifting meters of Whitman's poetry are akin to the rhythms of hiking, which is itself songlike, joyfully melodic, kept to the beat of footstep and pulse, at times allegro, at times adagio, making your heart beat hard and fast on an uphill climb, or, on the flat stretches, encouraging the streamlike meanderings of barely conscious meditation, with the luff of boots on earth repeating the mantra. Terra profundo.

Maybe New Yorkers find the open road on the Thruway heading north to Bear Mountain. But I'm not so sure. Even if a highway is part of the open road, we can't see it or feel it because we're going too fast, or because the impetus that projects our senses onto the world is something other than our own bodies. Maybe Bear Mountain is just one of many places where highways intersect the open road. You can see it from there, but all you can do by car is cross it.

The part of "Song of the Open Road" that's not contained on the plaque by the monument specifies that the open road leads through, or is one with, the natural world:

Now I see the secret of the making of the best persons,
It is to grow in the open air and to eat and sleep with the earth.
. . . . .
The efflux of the soul is happiness, here is happiness,
I think it pervades the open air, waiting at all times.
. . . . .
The earth is rude, silent, incomprehensible at first, Nature is rude and
    incomprehensible at first,
Be not discouraged, keep on, there are divine things well
    envelop'd. (110–11)

Recalling the pantheism of the transcendentalists, Whitman contends that the "divine things" of nature exist behind their surfaces, in spiritual meaning that is represented by the physical world, in an existence in the transcendental realm that can be better apprehended through intuition than intellect: "Paths worn in the irregular hollows by the roadsides . . . are latent with unseen existences," he writes; "Objects" in nature "call from diffusion my meanings and give them shape"— they are symbols that clarify meaning by representing moral and spiritual values in physical terms (108).

Among the moral values of nature celebrated by Whitman is democracy. The road to the natural world is open and equally available to all:

Here the profound lesson of reception, not preference nor denial,
The black with his woolly head, the felon, the diseas'd, the illiterate
    person, are not denied;
The birth, the hasting after the physician, the beggar's tramp, the
    drunkard's stagger, the laughing party of mechanics,

The escaped youth, the rich person's carriage, the fop, the eloping
    couple,
The early market-man, the hearse, the moving of furniture into the
    town, the return back from the town,
They pass, I also pass, any thing passes, none can be interdicted,
None but are accepted, none but shall be dear to me. (108)

By the end of that stanza Whitman is not just celebrating the open
road but seeming to speak for it. His poem has become the open road,
welcoming all, invigorating all with a taste of the freedom of the open
road, imparting its spirit, singing this song on the page.

    Whitman's invitation to all his readers to join him on the open
road leads to the poem's conclusion, the other stanza preserved on the
plaque, in those lines addressed to a "Camerado." The spirit of com-
panionship and community that those lines evoke are evident whenever hikers meet or walk together on the trail. But they are what
seemed sorely lacking amid the crowds atop Bear Mountain or around
Hessian Lake or in my encounter with the family on my way down the
mountain. Whitman warns in the poem that "He traveling with me
needs the best blood, thews, endurance" and "courage and health."
Then he adds a warning note: "Come not here if you have already
spent the best of yourself."

    It seems that the crowds around Hessian Lake brought something
less than the best of themselves on their search for the open road.
They are oblivious to the hand that Whitman offers, unwilling even to
make eye contact with a stranger. They have brought their fear and
isolation with them on their journey, and so, for all the miles of pavement under their wheels, they have yet to take their first step on the
open road.

---

Below the engraved lines on the rock, Whitman's name is inscribed,
the "Walt" half-covered by earth. Every autumn, I surmise, leaves pile
up in the crevice where the rock meets the ground, and every winter
the leaves decompose, building soil. With a twig I scrape away at the
dirt, several decades' worth, enough to make the whole name visible.
Behind me, Walt watches.

The statue of Whitman stands about eight feet high, atop a boulder that big all around. Walt holds his hat in his right hand, is just setting his weight onto his right foot, his left hand forward as he strides. His beard is full and flowing to the right, his eyes level, looking slightly left, over the head of an admirer of the statue. The tarnished bronze of the statue is green and black, Walt's forehead and left sleeve especially green. The statue was presented to the Park Commission in 1940 by William Averell Harriman as a memorial to his mother, Mary Williamson Harriman, on the thirtieth anniversary of her gift of ten thousand acres of land and one million dollars to establish the Bear Mountain and Harriman State Park sections of Palisades Park. That land contains the first stretch of trail designated as part of the A.T. In the hour that I spend at the statue, taking notes, nobody stops to look—not at the statue, at least.

The poet Louis Simpson must have sat about where I am. In a 1960 poem entitled "Walt Whitman at Bear Mountain," and addressed to Walt, Simpson writes: "As for the people—see how they neglect you! / Only a poet pauses to read the inscription." Even in 1960 Simpson saw here the sort of tawdry suburbanization that troubles me. "The Open Road goes to the used-car lot," he complains to Walt. "Where is the nation you promised?" Among the signs of our decay, writes Simpson, are "the realtors, / Pickpockets, salesmen, and the actors performing / Official scenarios" who have "contracted / American dreams"—in the process either ignoring or co-opting Whitman's visions of what America ought to be, and could be. Simpson ends the poem with a note of hope, though—an optimistic vision of "The clouds . . . lifting from the high Sierras, / The Bay mists clearing." I move on past the statue, still following the white paint blazes marking the Appalachian Trail, into the zoo.

---

In separate cages, in various stages of boredom are a bobcat, a red fox, three black bears, an osprey, several red-tailed hawks, a bald eagle, a turkey buzzard, some owls, and a deer. But what catches my attention most is the eastern coyote, *canis latrans*. He's big—not fox-sized, as I'd always imagined, but about the size of a mature German shepherd. A sign on the cage says that eastern coyotes are larger than western ones. They may have returned east from the west to thrive on lush eastern vegetation, or they may be natives that dwindled when forests of the eastern United States were cleared for farm and pasture land in the nineteenth century, but have flourished anew as the woods have returned. This one's fur is a mixture of gray and white and tawny, with some thin patches. Except for his regular pauses to stare back at me, he paces incessantly. And fast. He manages to sustain a quick trot even within the twenty-foot-square confines of his cage.

I can see more diverse wildlife here in the Bear Mountain Zoo than I'd see in several weeks of hiking in the woods. And I must admit that I'm fascinated. But it's a guilty pleasure I feel. A zoo is worse than a prison—it's like a concentration camp, for the inmates have committed no crime. They are incarcerated for being different, for being something other than *homo sapiens*. But still I'm curious, and I look. And the coyote paces.

The paved path leads out of the zoo, past the reptile house and a historical museum and onto the Bear Mountain Bridge. Used to be that hikers had to pay a ten-cent toll, but now the trail enters the bridge just past the toll booth. Walking across, heading east, you can see pleasure boats and commercial liners. Downstream is Manhattan, upstream is West Point.

On my first hike on this portion of the trail, when I was with three friends, we'd heard that hikers could stay for the night at Graymoor Monastery, about five miles or so up the trail. Mark and I were moving fast, well ahead of Bob and Joe Dunes, and we got to the monastery around dinnertime. We knocked at a building on the monastery grounds, asked if this was the place where hikers could sleep, and a guy wearing jeans and a plaid shirt—very unmonklike attire, we thought—said, "Sure, I suppose so, come on in." Turns out that we were in a drying-out place for homeless people from New York City. The monks drove into the city in a van, offered meals and a bed to the homeless, and brought them back to the monastery. The man in charge said we should lock up our packs in a closet. We were assigned bunks but slept little, kept awake by the groans and shouts of men suffering from delirium tremens. Bob and Joe never showed up.

The sound of piped-in electronic church bells woke us in the early morning. Mark and I were led into a cafeteria, seated at a long table, and served a breakfast of pancakes, corn flakes, and coffee. The homeless men were somber, but sobered-up and kind. All of them seemed to know about us and added to our allotted portions of breakfast. After breakfast Mark and I got our packs and hit the trail early, still wondering what had happened to Bob and Joe. We left a note tacked to a tree, telling them where we were headed for that night, figuring they'd catch up to us. The trail that day followed lots of dirt roads. The only people we met were a couple of middle-aged women out for the day bird-watching. We helped them pinpoint their position on their county map. They were amused by Mark's T-shirt—"cunning linguist," it read, though he was no language specialist. Later we ran into some threatening domestic dogs that we fended off with our hiking sticks. That night we slept under the clouds (Joe had the tent in his pack) on a grassy spot by Canopus Lake and woke up to a drizzle, then walked eight miles, getting soaked more by the wet brush than by the rain itself, to a lean-to with a galvanized tin roof. We got there by midday. Then the storm hit in earnest. A few hours later Bob and Joe arrived, happy and wet. They had stopped at a different building at the monastery and had been welcomed into the monks' residence, pampered with a private room with a shower, a hot dinner of thick stew, and a bacon-and-egg breakfast. They were having such a good time scrubbing at weeks-old sweat and grime in the showers and talking with the monks—who looked *very* monklike dressed in dark robes— that they didn't set out on the trail until the afternoon. One of the monks they talked with kept feeding them chocolate chip cookies, which he stored in the cowl behind his head.

We shared stories of our stay in the monastery, then settled down in the lean-to to wait out the storm, the tapping of rain on tin drifting in and out of our consciousness. Sometime in the dwindling light of late afternoon, Joe took from his pack a slim volume of poetry, a City Lights "Pocket Poets" edition of Allen Ginsberg's Beat Generation classic, *Howl and Other Poems*. We took turns reading, Joe, Mark, and I reading the three parts of the title poem. First the "who" part, a catalog of the calamitous sorrows of America's disaffected seekers—"who vanished into nowhere Zen New Jersey leaving a trail of ambiguous picture postcards of Atlantic City Hall." Then the "Moloch" part, a catalog of the materialist forces of modern society which, like the angry Old Testament god, demand human sacrifice—"Moloch whose mind is pure machinery! Moloch whose blood is running money! Moloch whose fingers are ten armies! Moloch whose breast is a cannibal dynamo! Moloch whose ear is a smoking tomb!" Then the address to Carl Solomon, a catalog of empathic woe for Ginsberg's friend confined to a mental institution—"I'm with you in Rockland / where we hug and kiss the United States under our bedsheets the United States that coughs all night and won't let us sleep." Finally, Bob read the "Footnote to Howl," the "everything is holy" part, a catalog of beatific, democratic inclusion—"Holy the solitudes of skyscrapers and pavements!" Ginsberg's poem is the howl of someone or something wounded deep in the soul, of something trapped. Its setting—and target—is urban America. But somehow on that wet day, the reading fit our mood, even as we believed ourselves to be afoot and lighthearted and free-spirited out on the open road of the Appalachian Trail.

Perhaps it was the accompanying percussion of the rain on the roof, perhaps it was the company, perhaps it was the events of the past two days, perhaps it was relief at seeing my friends were okay—whatever it was, that reading of *Howl* was the most moving encounter with a literary work that I've ever had. Moreso even than when I heard Ginsberg himself read the poem several years later to a packed ballroom of scholars at the Modern Language Association's annual conference in New York City. There in the dripping lean-to, I was awash with sadness for the institutionalized—Ginsberg's friend Carl Solomon locked up in an insane asylum, the homeless men shrieking and crying out their alcoholic woes in the monastery, even the city dwellers rushing from their desperate work all week to their desperate picnics at Bear Mountain on the weekend and then back to the city. Perhaps my pity was patronizing and misplaced. After all, Ginsberg asserts in the "Footnote" that "The bum's as holy as the seraphim! the madman is holy as you my soul are holy!" (134) But my sympathy grew out of some sense of connection. I wanted all the mad, the desperate, the unhappy to fit with us under the pinging, leaking roof of that lean-to, and I wanted them to walk a mile or two with us on vibram souls down a gloriously muddy trail.

I wanted to share the open road. I wanted them to look up and realize that they were standing right on it and all they needed to do was start walking. But maybe I was wrong. Surrounded by walls of steel and glass and concrete, forced there by necessity, by responsibilities, by circumstances, by all that they'd never seen or even read about of the world around them—perhaps they were as securely caged as the coyote behind chain-link in the Bear Mountain Zoo.

Using the same long line as Whitman, Ginsberg makes that line not so much a means of conveying expansiveness and freedom as it is a vessel for pouring out vast internal anguish. In *Howl* he defines his poetics as the attempt "to recreate the syntax and measure of poor human prose and stand before you speechless and intelligent and shaking with shame, rejected yet confessing out the soul to conform to the rhythm of thought in his naked and endless head" (130–31). Any expansiveness, it seems, is contained by the skull. Ginsberg took his epigraph for *Howl* from Whitman's *Song of Myself*: "Unscrew the locks from the doors! / Unscrew the doors themselves from their jambs!" But in Ginsberg's poem those lines seem more like a plea than a fait accompli. Throughout, images of containment predominate. Seedy apartments and dingy hotel rooms, alleyways, railroad yards, bathhouse partitions, cardboard boxes that serve as shelter under dark bridges—that is the claustrophobic geography of *Howl*. Ginsberg speaks of the disaffected of his generation "who chained themselves to subways for the endless ride from Battery to holy Bronx on benzedrine until the noise of wheels and children brought them down shuddering mouth-wracked and battered bleak of brain all drained of brilliance in the drear light of Zoo" (126). Not only is their mad rush for experience conducted while bound by constraint, it ends in containment. In the second part of *Howl* Ginsberg calls the monster-god of modern America "Moloch the incomprehensible prison! Moloch the crossbone soulless jailhouse and Congress of Sorrows!" (131). In the final section the images of confinement are most explicit, as Ginsberg expresses his empathy with Carl Solomon, locked up in an insane asylum, screaming in a straitjacket. As wide-ranging as the poem is, depicting scenes from across America, again and again the horrors of contemporary American society are presented in images of containment. The most geographically expansive line, where the montage moves beyond the borders of the United States, ends in the ultimate state of confinement, the coffin: Ginsberg writes of his friends "who retired to Mexico to cultivate a habit, or Rocky Mount to tender Buddha or Tangiers to boys or Southern Pacific to the black locomotive or Harvard to Narcissus to Woodlawn to the daisychain or grave" (130).

On the rare occasions when *Howl* moves to the great outdoors, the images of openness are either unappealing or equally terrifying. He speaks for those "who lit cigarettes in boxcars boxcars boxcars racketing through snow toward lonesome farms in grandfather night" (127). The moon casts a "wartime blue floodlight," the sky is "tubercular" (128–29). In his madness Carl Solomon's soul has gone adrift someplace outside himself: "I'm with you in Rockland / where fifty more shocks will never return your soul to its body again from its pilgrimage to a cross in the void" (133). Loneliness, violence, sickness, emptiness—that's how *Howl* describes open space. It's no wonder that the poem ends with an image of retreat to cozy containment: the poet says to his friend, "in my dreams you walk dripping from a sea-journey on the highway across America in tears to the door of my cottage in the Western night" (133). Despite the anxieties about imprisonment that the poem has expressed, ultimately confinement offers refuge from the terror, the exposure, of openness.

---

The road from Whitman to Ginsberg had led us from Bear Mountain to Graymoor Monastery to the comforting confinement of tin-roofed Farmer's Mills Shelter. But it hadn't been just the journey of a couple of days. In a sense we'd traveled the path of American culture over the space and time of a century. Whitman and Ginsberg are kindred spirits—they even look alike, with long flowing beards, and both give open expression to their homosexuality in their poems, and both rely on long, rhythmic lines structured around the anaphoric catalog. Those long lines are declarations of freedom, from both poetic tradition and social constraint. But the emphasis must have been different for the two poets. Whitman could still feel himself part of the mainstream of American society, celebrating its virtues and its progress, no matter how revolutionary his poetic line. Ginsberg, on the other hand, no matter how out of step with American society he and his fellow Beats may have felt, could still feel himself part of a poetic tradition. His long poetic line owed something to jazz rhythms, and something to Hebrew prayer, and to William Blake, and mad Christopher Smart, and most of all to Whitman, an influence Ginsberg acknowledges in "A Supermarket in California," addressed to Whitman. There Ginsberg calls Whitman "dear father, graybeard, lonely old courage teacher."

But if "A Supermarket in California" pays poetic tribute to Whitman, in its perspective on American society it measures Ginsberg's distance from Whitman every bit as much as *Howl* does when compared to "Song of the Open Road." It's the distance of a century—with Civil War and the "triumph" of the Industrial Revolution and Darwinism and Freud and two world wars, mustard gas and the hydrogen bomb, the advent of the technological era, Vietnam, and IBM, and "plasticwasp9to5america" all marked on the measuring stick. It's the distance from nineteenth-century American optimism to twentieth-century ennui. In "A Supermarket in California," Whitman is pictured not as some heroic poetic pathfinder but as a "childless, lonely old grubber, poking among the meats in the refrigerator and eyeing the grocery boys." He seems a pathetic figure, a decline stemming more from the change in the American setting than in the poet or the man. Ginsberg is accompanied in his imagination by his friend and mentor, and the two poets "stroll dreaming of the lost America of love past blue automobiles in driveways, home to our silent cottage"—the shelter of containment, akin to the cottage refuge he dreams of offering Carl Solomon at the end of *Howl*. On the way there, Ginsberg and Whitman travel a road that has been paved over, the pedestrian making way for the Buick and the Chevy. Tellingly, the cars they see remain parked in driveways in front of the indistinguishable houses of suburbia. Ginsberg's friends among the Beats at least pulled out of the driveway and took to the highway, looking to get *somewhere,* they knew not where. But Jack Kerouac's version of *On the Road* is a far and frenzied, desperate cry from Whitman's contented vision of the open road.

What I found at Bear Mountain, from the motorcyclers whining their way to the summit to get a glimpse of the city they'd come from and would return to, to the crowds dousing themselves in the incense of charcoal briquettes and sealing themselves off from their neighbors with the sound-boundaries emitting from their radios, to the lonely statue of Walt Whitman to the cages of the zoo—that was the spirit of *Howl*. But amid the howls of the homeless being squeezed and shaken by the d.t.'s, and amid the clink of spoons on plain porcelain bowls of corn flakes within the walls of Graymoor Monastery, and under the storm-drummed tin roof of Farmer's Mills Shelter where four friends read aloud to one another and maybe to a couple hundred million or so people well out of earshot—there I felt the spirit of the open road.

The storm let up in the morning, though we were splattered with intermittent rain most of the day. The trail, heading northeast toward Connecticut, wound through some nice open meadows and tall hemlock woods with bracken and Christmas ferns lining the path of mossy ground—"as soft as you could want to walk on," said Bob. The next night we stayed in another leaking lean-to. Falling asleep, I thought of the coyote, of his silent pacing, and of the city, too.

---

# MARY MCCARTHY

MARY MCCARTHY (1912–1989), a prominent novelist, memoirist, and critic, wrote her review of Burroughs's *Naked Lunch* for the first issue of *New York Review of Books* in 1963. Later the same year she published *The Group,* a best-selling realistic novel that followed the lives of eight Vassar graduates in the 1930s. While in the process of finishing *The Group,* in August 1962 McCarthy attended a five-day writers' conference in Edinburgh on the future of the novel, where in a panel on the first day she introduced William Burroughs and explained that, along with the novels of Vladimir Nabokov, she thought that Burroughs's *Naked Lunch* represented the best of contemporary fiction. Although her own fiction was nothing like Burroughs's writing, she noted with approval that his novel *Naked Lunch* "is laid everywhere and is sort of speeded up like jet travel and it has that somewhat supersonic quality. It also has some of the qualities of Action Painting." Later in the conference Burroughs was so lucid and impressive in his explanation of what he was doing in his work that he became an instant celebrity, championed by both McCarthy and Norman Mailer. At this time *Naked Lunch* had only been published abroad by the Olympia Press. After the Edinburgh writers' conference, Barney Rosset of Grove Press began to ship his edition of Burroughs's novel to bookstores in the United States. In January 1963, the owner of a Boston bookstore was arrested for selling it. More than three years later, on July 7, 1966, along with *The Memoirs of Fanny Hill, Naked Lunch* was ruled not obscene in a landmark decision by the Massachusetts Supreme Court.

## *Burroughs'* Naked Lunch

Last summer at the International Writers' Conference in Edinburgh, I said I thought the national novel, like the nation-state, was dying and that a new kind of novel, based on statelessness, was beginning to be written. This novel had a high, aerial point of view and a plot of perpetual motion. Two experiences, that of exile and that of jet-propelled mass tourism, provided the subject matter for a new kind of story. There is no novel, yet, that I know of, about mass tourism, but somebody will certainly write it. Of the novel based on statelessness, I gave as examples William Burroughs' *The Naked Lunch,* Vladimir Nabokov's *Pale Fire* and *Lolita.* Burroughs, I explained, is not literally a political exile, but the drug addicts he describes are continually on the move, and life in the United States, with its present narcotics laws, is untenable for the addict if he does not want to spend it in jail (in the same way, the confirmed homosexual is a chronic refugee, ordered to move on by the Venetian police, the Capri police, the mayor of Provincetown, the mayor of Nantucket). Had I read it at the time, I might have added Günter Grass' *The Tin Drum* to the list: here the point of view, instead of being high, is very low—that of a dwarf; the hero and narrator is a displaced person, born in the Free City of Danzig, of a Polish mother (who is not really a Pole but a member of a minority within Poland) and an uncertain father, who may be a German grocer or a Polish postal employee. In any case, I said that in thinking over the novels of the last few years, I was struck by the fact that the only ones that had not simply given me pleasure but interested me had been those of Burroughs and Nabokov. The others, even when well done (Compton-Burnett), seemed almost regional.

This statement, to judge by the British press, was a shot heard round the world. I still pick up its reverberations in Paris and read about them in the American press. I am quoted as saying that *The Naked Lunch* is the most important novel of the age, of the epoch, of the century. The only truthful report of what I said about Burroughs was given by Stephen Spender in *Encounter,* October 1962. But nobody seems to have paid attention to Spender any more than anyone paid attention to what I said on the spot. When I chided Malcolm Muggeridge in person with having terribly misquoted me in the *New Statesman,* he appeared to think that there was not much difference between saying that a book was one of two or three that had interested you in the last few years and saying that it was one of the "outstanding novels of the age." According to me, the age is still Proust, Joyce, Kafka, Lawrence, Faulkner, to mention only the "big names," but to others evidently the age is shrinking to the length of a publishing season, just as a literary speaker is turned into a publisher's tout. The result, of course, is a disparagement of Burroughs, because if *The Naked Lunch* is proclaimed as the masterpiece of the century, then it is easily found wanting. Indeed, I wonder whether the inflation of my remarks was not at bottom malicious; it is not usually those who admire Burroughs who come up to me at parties to announce: "I *read* what you said at Edinburgh." This is true, I think, of all such publicity; it is malicious in effect whatever the intention and permits the reader to dismiss works of art and public figures as "not what they are cracked up to be." A similiar thing happened with *Dr. Zhivago,* a wonderful book, which attracted much hatred and venom because it was not Tolstoy. Very few critics said it was Tolstoyan, but the impression got around that they had. Actually, as I recall, the critics who mentioned Tolstoy in connection with Pasternak were those bent on destroying Pasternak's book.

As for me, I was left in an uncomfortable situation. I did not want to write to the editors of British newspapers and magazines, denying that I had said whatever incontinent thing they had quoted me as saying. This would have been ungracious to Burroughs, who was the innocent party in the affair and who must have felt more and more like the groom in a shotgun literary wedding, seeing my name yoked with his as it were indissolubly. And the monstrousness of the union, doubtless, was what kept the story hot. In the end, it became clear to me that the only way I could put an end to this embarrassment was by writing at length what I thought about *The Naked Lunch*—something I was reluctant to do because I was busy finishing a book of my own and reluctant, also, because the whole thing had assumed the proportions of a *cause célèbre* and I felt like a witness called to the stand and obliged to tell the truth and nothing but the truth under oath. This is not a normal critical position. Of course the critic normally tries to be truthful, but he does not feel that his review is some sort of pay-off or eternal reckoning, that the eye of God or the world press is staring into his heart as he writes. Now that I have written the present review, I am glad, as always happens, to have made a clean breast of it. This is what I think about Burroughs.

"You can cut into *The Naked Lunch* at any intersection point," says Burroughs, suiting the action to the word, in "an atrophied preface" he appends as a tailpiece. His book, he means, is like a neighborhood movie with continuous showings that you can drop into whenever you please—you don't have to wait for the beginning of the feature picture. Or like a worm that you can chop up into sections each of which wriggles off as an independent worm. Or a nine-lived cat. Or a cancer. He is fond of the word "mosaic," especially in its scientific sense of a plant-mottling caused by a virus, and his Muse (see etymology of "mosaic") is interested in organic processes of multiplication and duplication. The literary notion of time as simultaneous, a montage, is not original with Burroughs; what is original is the scientific bent he gives it and a view of the world that combines biochemistry, anthropology, and politics. It is as though *Finnegans Wake* were cut loose from history and adapted for a Cinerama circus titled "One World." *The Naked Lunch* has no use for history, which is all "ancient history"—sloughed-off skin; from its planetary perspective, there are only geography and customs. Seen in terms of space, history shrivels into a mere wrinkling or furrowing of the surface as in an aerial relief-map or one of those pieced-together aerial photographs known in the trade as (again) mosaics. The oldest memory in *The Naked Lunch* is of jacking-off in boyhood latrines, a memory recaptured through pederasty. This must be the first space novel, the first serious piece of science fiction—the others are entertainment.

The action of *The Naked Lunch* takes place in the consciousness of One Man, William Lee, who is taking a drug cure. The principal characters, besides Lee, are his friend, Bill Gains (who seems momentarily to turn into a woman called Jane); various members of the Narcotic Squad, especially one Bradley the Buyer; Dr. Benway, a charlatan medico who is treating Lee; two vaudevillians, Clem and Jody; A.J., a carnival con man, the last of the Big Spenders; a sailor; an Arab called Ahmed; an archetypal Southern druggist, Doc Parker ("a man don't have no secrets from God and his druggist"); and various boys with whining voices. Among the minor characters are a number of automobiles, each with its specific complaint, like the oil-burning Ford V–8; a film executive; the Party Leader; the Vigilante; John and Mary, the sex acrobats; and a puzzled American housewife who is heard complaining because the Mixmaster keeps trying to climb up under her dress. The scene shifts about, from New York to Chicago to St. Louis to New Orleans to Mexico to Malmö, Tangier, Venice, and the human identities shift about too, for all these modern places and modern individuals (if that is the right word) have interchangeable parts. Burroughs is fond too of the word "ectoplasm," and the beings that surround Lee, particularly the inimical ones, seem ectoplasmic phantoms projected on the wide screen of his consciousness from a mass séance. But the haunting is less visual than auditory. These "characters," in the colloquial sense, are ventriloquial voices produced, as it were, against the will of the ventriloquist, who has become their dummy. Passages of dialogue and description keep recurring in different contexts with slight variations, as though they possessed ubiquity.

The best comparison for the book, with its aerial sex acts performed on a high trapeze, its con men and barkers, its arenalike form, is in fact with a circus. A circus travels but it is always the same, and this is Burroughs' sardonic image of modern life. The Barnum of the show is the mass-manipulator, who appears in a series of disguises. *Control,* as Burroughs says, underlining it, *can never be a means to anything but more control—like drugs,* and the vicious circle of addiction is reenacted, worldwide, with sideshows in the political and "social" sphere—the "social" here has vanished, except in quotation marks, like the historical, for everything has become automatized. Everyone is an addict of one kind or another, as people indeed are wont to say of themselves, complacently: "I'm a crossword puzzle addict, a hi-fi addict," etc. The South is addicted to lynching and nigger-hating, and the Southern folk-custom of burning a Negro recurs throughout the book as a sort of Fourth-of-July carnival with fireworks. Circuses, with their cages of wild animals, are also dangerous, like Burroughs' human circus; an accident may occur, as when the electronic brain in Dr. Benway's laboratory goes on the rampage, and the freaks escape to mingle with the controlled citizens of Freeland in a general riot, or in the scene where the hogs are let loose in the gourmet restaurant.

On a level usually thought to be "harmless," addiction to platitudes and commonplaces is global. To Burroughs' ear, the Bore, lurking in the hotel lobby, is literally deadly (" 'You look to me like a man of intelligence.' Always ominous opening words, my boy!"). The same for Doc Parker with his captive customer in the back room of his pharmacy (". . . so long as you got a legitimate condition and an RX from a certified bona feedy M.D., I'm honored to serve you"), the professor in the classroom ("Hehe hehe he"), the attorney in court ("Hehe hehe he," likewise). The complacent sound of snickering laughter is an alarm signal, like the suave bell-tones of the psychiatrist and the emphatic drone of the Party Leader ("You see men and women. *Ordinary* men and women going about their ordinary everyday tasks. Leading their ordinary lives. That's what we need. . . .").

Cut to ordinary men and women, going about their ordinary everyday tasks. The whine of the put-upon boy hustler: "All kinda awful sex acts." "Why cancha just get physical like a human?" "So I guess he come to some kinda awful climax." "You think I am innarested to hear about your horrible old condition? I am not innarested at all." "But he comes to a climax and turns into some kinda awful crab." This aggrieved tone merges with the malingering sighs of the American housewife, opening a box of Lux: "I got the most awful cold, and my intestines is all constipated." And the clarion of the Salesman: "When the Priority numbers are called up yonder I'll be there." These average folks are addicts of the science page of the Sunday supplements; they like to talk about their diseases and about vile practices that paralyze the practitioner from the waist down or about a worm that gets into your kidney and grows to enormous size or about the "horrible" result of marijuana addiction—it makes you turn black and your legs drop off. The superstitious scientific vocabulary is diffused from the laboratory and the mental hospital into the general population. Overheard at a lynching: "Don't crowd too close, boys. His intestines is subject to explode in the fire." The same diffusion of culture takes place with modern physics. A lieutenant to his general: "But chief, can't we get them started and they imitate each other like a chained reaction?"

The phenomenon of repetition, of course, gives rise to boredom; many readers complain that they cannot get through *The Naked Lunch*. And/or that they find it disgusting. It *is* disgusting and sometimes tiresome, often in the same places. The prominence of the anus, of feces, and of all sorts of "horrible" discharges, as the characters would say, from the body's orifices, becomes too much of a bad thing, like the sado-masochistic sex performances—the auto-ejaculation of a hanged man is not everybody's cantharides. A reader whose erogenous zones are more temperate than the author's begins to feel either that he is a square (a guilty sentiment he should not yield to) or that he is the captive of a joyless addict.

In defense, Swift could be cited, and indeed between Burroughs and Swift there are many points of comparison; not only the obsession with excrement and the horror of female genitalia but a disgust with politics and the whole body politic. Like Swift, Burroughs has irritable nerves and something of the crafty temperament of the inventor. There is a great deal of Laputa in the countries Burroughs calls Interzone and Freeland, and Swift's solution for the Irish problem would appeal to the American's dry logic. As Gulliver, Swift posed as an anthropologist (though the study was not known by that name then) among savage people; Burroughs parodies the anthropologist in his descriptions of the American heartland: "the Interior: a vast subdivision, antennae of television to the meaningless sky. [. . .] Illinois and Missouri, miasma of mound-building peoples, groveling worship of the Food Source, cruel and ugly festivals." The style here is more emotive than Swift's, but in his deadpan explanatory notes ("This is a rural English custom designed to eliminate aged and bedfast dependents"), there is a Swiftian laconic factuality. The "factual" appearance of the whole narrative, with its battery of notes and citations, some straight, some loaded, its extracts from a diary, like a ship's log, its pharmacopoeia, has the flavor of eighteenth-century satire. He calls himself a "Factualist" and belongs, all alone, to an Age of Reason, which he locates in the future. In him, as in Swift, there is a kind of soured utopianism.

Yet what saves *The Naked Lunch* is not a literary ancestor but humor. Burroughs' humor is peculiarly American, at once broad and sly. It is the humor of a comedian, a vaudeville performer playing in "One," in front of the asbestos curtain of some Keith Circuit or Pantages house long since converted to movies. The same jokes reappear, slightly refurbished, to suit the circumstances, the way a vaudeville artist used to change Yonkers to Renton when he was playing Seattle. For example, the Saniflush joke, which is always good for a laugh: somebody is cutting the cocaine/the morphine/the penicillin with Saniflush. Some of the jokes are verbal ("Stop me if you've heard this atomic secret" or Dr. Benway's "A simopath [. . .] is a citizen convinced he is an ape or other simian. It is a disorder peculiar to the army and discharge cures it"). Some are "black" parody (Dr. Benway, in his last appearance, dreamily, his voice fading out: "Cancer, my first love"). Some are whole vaudeville "numbers," as when the hoofers, Clem and Jody, are hired by the Russians to give Americans a bad name abroad: they appear in Liberia wearing black Stetsons and red galluses and talking loudly about burning niggers back home. A skit like this may rise to a frenzy, as if in a Marx Brothers or a Clayton, Jackson, and Durante act, when all the actors pitch in. *E.g.*, the very funny scene in Chez Robert, "where a huge icy gourmet broods over the greatest cuisine in the world": A.J. appears, the last of the Big Spenders, and orders a bottle of ketchup; immediate pandemonium; A.J. gives his hog-call, and the shocked gourmet diners are all devoured by famished hogs. The effect of pandemonium, all hell breaking loose, is one of Burroughs' favorites and an equivalent of the old vaudeville finale, with the acrobats, the jugglers, the magician, the hoofers, the lady-who-was-sawed-in-two, the piano-player, the comedians, all pushing into the act.

Another favorite effect, with Burroughs, is the metamorphosis. A citizen is turned into animal form, a crab or a huge centipede, or into some unspeakable monstrosity, like Bradley the Narcotics Agent who turns into an unidentifiable carnivore. These metamorphoses, of course, are punishments. The Hellzapoppin effect of orgies and riots and the metamorphosis effect, rapid or creeping, are really cancerous onslaughts—matter on the rampage multiplying itself and "building" as a revue scene "builds" to a climax. Growth and deterioration are the same thing: a human being "deteriorates" or grows into a one-man jungle. What you think of it depends on your point of view; from the junky's angle, Bradley is better as a carnivore eating the Narcotics Commissioner than he was as "fuzz"—junky slang for the police.

*The Naked Lunch* contains messages that unluckily for the ordinary reader are somewhat arcane. Despite his irony, Burroughs is a prescriptive writer. He means what he says to be taken and used literally, like an Rx prescription. Unsentimental and factual, he writes as though his thoughts had the quality of self-evidence. In a special sense, *The Naked Lunch* is coterie literature. It was not intended, surely, for the general public, but for addicts and former addicts, with the object of imparting information. Like a classical satirist, Burroughs is dead serious—a reformer. Yet, as often happened with the classical satirists, a wild hilarity and savage pessimism carry him beyond his therapeutic purpose and defeat it. The book is alive, like a basketful of crabs, and common sense cannot get hold of it to extract a moral.

On the one hand, control is evil; on the other, escape from control is mass slaughter or reduction to a state of proliferating cellular matter. The police are the enemy, but as Burroughs shrewdly observes in one passage: "A *functioning* police state needs no police." The policeman is internalized in the robotized citizen. From a libertarian point of view, nothing could be worse. This would seem to be Burroughs' position, but it is not consistent with his picture of sex. To be a libertarian in politics implies a faith in Nature and the natural, that is, in the life-principle itself, commonly identified with sex. But there is little affection for the life-principle in *The Naked Lunch,* and sex, while magnified—a common trait of homosexual literature—is a kind of mechanical man-trap baited with fresh meat. The sexual climax, the jet of sperm, accompanied by a whistling scream, is often a death spasm, and the "perfect" orgasm would seem to be the posthumous orgasm of the hanged man, shooting his jism into pure space.

It is true that Nature and sex are two-faced, and that growth is death-oriented. But if Nature is not seen as far more good than evil, then a need for control is posited. And, strangely, this seems to be Burroughs' position too. *The human virus can now be treated,* he says with emphasis, meaning the species itself. By scientific methods, he implies. Yet the laboratory of *The Naked Lunch* is a musical-comedy inferno, and Dr. Benway's assistant is a female chimpanzee. As Burroughs knows, the Men in White, when not simple con men, are the fuzz in another uniform.

*The Naked Lunch,* Burroughs says, is "a blueprint, a How-To Book. [. . .] How-To extend levels of experience by opening the door at the end of a long hall." Thus the act of writing resembles and substitutes for drug-taking, which in Burroughs' case must have begun as an experiment in the extension of consciousness. It does not sound as if pleasure had ever been his motive. He was testing the controls of his own mechanism to adjust the feed-in of data, noting with care the effects obtained from heroin, morphine, opium, Demerol, Yage, cannabis, and so on. These experiments, aiming at freedom, "opening a door," resulted in addiction. He kicked the imprisoning habit by what used to be known as will power, supplemented by a non-addictive drug, apomorphine, to whose efficacy he now writes testimonials. It seems clear that what was involved and continues to be involved for Burroughs is a Faustian compact: knowledge-as-power, total control of the self, which is experienced as sovereign in respect to the immediate environment and neutral in respect to others.

At present he is interested in scientology, which offers its initiates the promise of becoming "clears"—free from all hang-ups. For the novel he has invented his cut-out and fold-in techniques, which he is convinced can rationalize the manufacture of fictions by applying modern factory methods to the old "writer's craft." A text may be put together by two or three interested and moderately skilled persons equipped with scissors and the raw material of a typescript. Independence from the vile body and its "algebra of need," freedom of movement across national and psychic frontiers, efficiency of work and production, by means of short cuts, suppression of connectives, and other labor-saving devices, would be Uncle Bill Burroughs' patent for successful living. But if such a universal passkey can really be devised, what is its purpose? It cannot be enjoyment of the world, for this would only begin the addictive process all over again by creating dependency. Action, the reverse of enjoyment, has no appeal either for the author of *The Naked Lunch*. What Burroughs wants is out, which explains the dry, crankish amusement given him by space, interplanetary distances, where, however, he finds the old mob still at work. In fact, his reasoning, like the form of his novel, is circular. Liberation leads to new forms of subjugation. If the human virus can be treated, this can only be under conditions of asepsis: the Nova police. Yet Burroughs is unwilling, politically, to play the dread game of eugenics or euthenics, outside his private fantasy, which, since his intelligence is aware of the circularity of its utopian reasoning, invariably turns sardonic. *Quis custodet custodes ipsos?*

*March, 1963*

# Joanna McClure

Joanna McClure lived in San Francisco as the wife of the poet Michael McClure and taught in a nursery school as a specialist in early childhood development and parent education for many years. In 1957, two years after the birth of their daughter, Jane, Joanna McClure began writing poetry that she showed to others. Michael remembered that "through all those years from the mid-1950s to the publication of her first book, *Wolf Eyes,* in 1974, [Joanna] McClure wrote quietly, unheralded, and often in the middle of the night in ecstasy, or pain, or drunkenness, or a state of joy. There is probably no more honest, intense, or personal portrait of a period than is made through her poetry—for she is a very sensuous and sensual as well as musical poet." The four poems included here are from the period 1957 through 1963.

### 1957

Dear Lover,

Here on the eve of everything and humility,
The new shoes—the new tooth—
Can't quite fill the gap left
By Khrushchev, the rally, the gas chamber,
The satellite beaming down from the moon.

Your nerves ajar,
Mine apart.
Ghostliness, the promise of a
Dark change, hovers
Without motion
Between us—

Blocking the beautiful love felt two nights ago
And renewed by this pressure—

The pleasure of its discovery still fresh
Again last night.

Where are we?
Why the pain—so sane
And yet without purpose,
    our plight.

You say you are an American—of the continent—
But it doesn't help your twitching nerves
Or the discouragement of being here, now, at this time
Sat upon by the pressure of these lunatic affronts.

I come from dusty desert mountains
Where people only killed other people, bad people,
And rattlesnakes and deer to eat
And valued their horse and families.

I have only lately learned to wear pointed shoes
                        with delicate straps
And realize the value of a pearl choker with
High delicate necklines and short black gloves
Topped by wild cropped blond hair.
And I am glad & would wear them through a war
If I had to.

But these are not the battles I choose
These are only discoveries, like last night's love,
Which I want to fill a lifetime with
In order to stand a symbol of the things I still
                        believe in . . .
Desires for freedom, bodily beauty, tenderness,
        & your love & your Desire for change &
                Truth.
There isn't anyone on our side, just here
        where we stand.

And it's been too long
To make it all all right again.

I can't defend them anymore
Or, more painful, can not disengage
    from this time or place and have no
                      desire
For any other time or place but my own.
A stubborn Determination born somewhere
                          in the struggle.

I've turned down too many Gods to
Start inventing my own now
Or believe in yours either.

I only sit & wait & care for you
And worry—for I wanted to spend my life
Fighting with you . . . but
I wonder—what happens to us
When everything breaks apart.

My femininity is not willing to carry
    me along through sudden change.
I wanted to die slowly of old age.
The sliced lily plant, still green, hurts me.
I have no heart for wars I can't fight
Or bombs that destroy.

## A Letter to My Daughter
## Who Will Be Four Years Old

Dear Jane (Katie)—

I like you in all your guises,
                disguises
And costumes. I love you
              wailing
   sitting, flailing, teasing.
I love your round tow head
  and your round toes.
I love your round cheeks and

your round nose and your
    shiny eyes—red like a cat's,
Or round and big with the threat
    "if you don't, I'll cry."
I like your teasing and playing,
    chuckling with unrestrained glee
    at your newest trick.
I love you busy and excited, on the street,
    creating your own world,
    using ours—"Hi, Hi—(a nice man)"
    and off again.
Every day like a kaleidoscope,
    turning it this way and that,
    rearranging, delighted, or
    MAD—IT WON'T WORK—FIX IT.
Dancing—arched, self consciously beautiful
                    movements—
So vitally aware of each gesture,
Standing also, stopped, directly aware
    of the applause, stopped for one
    moment in the pleasure of an
    audience—surveying it—your domain
    and on
To the next step, the next game, the
Next room, the next boredom which
    creates the cry, the demand:
        "I never have *anyone* to play with.
        *Who's* going to play with me?
        You *told* me we would . . ."


And so pushing, manipulating, charming,
    pouting or—
    "I'll tell my grandmother if you don't!"
    eyes opened wide with simulated rage—
    testing.


And how am I to ever write a poem
    about you?
For there's no end to you

And I have forgotten the beginning
Which lay in a deep desire I felt
    for your father who was going away for
    a few days
And really had nothing to do with you.
    Except maybe that
The desire was strong enough to set in
Motion a little girl who will never stop
    growing, becoming a living love.
    A living tribute to love, an offering to the world & to love!

*(1959)*

## The Hunt

*lines from Michael*

"The hunt matters.
Run—the legs are meant for running"

I sing it to myself
Leaping up Cole Street
Around and up Ashbury

Remembering the contrast
Of putting heel to cement—
Planting myself up hill.

*(1963)*

## Piece

Fur purse
You are not mine
    though I made you.

Mad husband
I coveted
    your insanity

    *(1963)*

---

# MICHAEL McCLURE

MICHAEL McCLURE met his future first wife, Joanna, at the University of Arizona, introduced her to the works of Béla Bartók, James Stephens, William Butler Yeats, and Ezra Pound, and followed her to San Francisco in 1954, hoping to study painting with Mark Rothko and Clyfford Still. In the fall of 1955 McClure met Allen Ginsberg at a W. H. Auden reading at the San Francisco Poetry Center. McClure had been attending Robert Duncan's poetry workshops and Kenneth Rexroth's literary soirees, and as McClure tells the story, he mentioned to Ginsberg that he had been invited by the artist Wally Hedrick to put together a poetry reading at the 6 Gallery. Ginsberg volunteered to do it, with the understanding that McClure would be on the program, along with McClure's friend Philip Lamantia, a surrealist poet. Rexroth agreed to be the master of ceremonies and gave Ginsberg the address of Gary Snyder, who was studying Asian languages and philosophy at UC Berkeley. Snyder brought along his friend from Reed College, the poet Philip Whalen. A prolific author of many books of poems, essays, and plays, McClure has described the "6 Poets at 6 Gallery" event in *Scratching the Beat Surface* (1982), as well as in an essay for *The Beat Generation Galleries and Beyond* (1996), from which this account is taken. To announce the reading on October 7, 1955, Ginsberg bought a stack of two-penny postcards and sent them to people on the mailing list of the San Francisco Poetry Center. On the reverse side of the postcard, Ginsberg mimeographed the following message:

## 6 POETS at 6 GALLERY

Philip Lamantia reading mss. of late John Hoffman—Mike McClure, Allen Ginsberg, Gary Snyder & Phil Whalen—all sharp new straightforward writing—remarkable collection of angels on one stage reading their poetry. No charge, small collection for wine and postcards. Charming event.

Kenneth Rexroth, M.C.
8 PM Friday Night October 7, 1955
6 Gallery 3119 Fillmore St.
San Fran

## *Poetry of the 6*

The first beautiful show of San Francisco art that I saw was in the North Beach bar—The Place. I was sitting at a little square-topped table in the smoky and crowded neighborhood artists' bar and looked up and saw a group of small unframed gouaches. Each one was a daub or smear of black or red, or mixed black and red, on weathered posterboard with maybe an occasional drip or splash of blue and purple. There was an alchemical and visionary intensity to these almost shabby and entirely elegant works by Jay DeFeo. I had the sense at that moment that I was in the right place at the right time. It was 1954 and I knew for sure that I wanted to be in cowtown Frisco smelling the dark, salt smell of the Pacific and hearing the Chinese and Italian voices on the streets and not in Paris drinking in the last drops of Existentialism.

I had arrived in San Francisco hoping to study with Clyfford Still to add the experience of gestural expressionism and "spiritual autobiography" to the poetics I was beginning to formulate. On arriving, I found that Clyfford Still had already departed for parts unknown to me. Shortly after seeing the DeFeo work, I began to fall into a poetry scene so rich that I was engaged and dazzled by it—studying poetry with Robert Duncan and attending Kenneth Rexroth's literary evenings. Early in 1955 I was an actor in a staged reading of Robert

Duncan's madcap and mind-spinning musical play *Faust Foutu,* or "Faust Fucked." The play was presented at the Six Gallery which looked like it had once been an automobile repair shop before being converted into a rambling gallery space. Duncan had been, with painter Jess, a founder of the recently closed Ubu Gallery and had already given recitals of his poetry at the new Six Gallery. It was the natural place for his "outsider" and entirely outspoken play to take place.

Before this event, Duncan had always given solo reading-performances of the play, which was something like a rollicking amalgam of Goethe's *Faust,* Brecht, and a masque by Ben Jonson if Johnson had been a French surrealist. We were all game for the event though none of us were actors or singers. In the opening scenes of the play *The Master of Ceremonies* was painter Fred Snowden, *The Poet* was Robert Duncan, *The Muse* was North Beach poet Jack Spicer, *Faust* was experimental film-maker Larry Jordan, *Margueritte* was spoken by Duncan's friend Ida Hodes, the Scottish poet and balladeer Helen Adam took two roles—*The Nurse* and *Greta Garbo*—Jess played *Faust's Mother* and I spoke the lines for *A Boy.* Later in the performance painter Harry Jacobus and poet and song-writer James Keilty took roles.

We all sat at a long table on a little dais in the large room. Self-consciously, and as forwardly as we could, we belted out and mumbled and sang the play. Poet Spicer leaned towards the audience with his harsh voice and boyishly innocent but leering expression. Jess spoke his lines with the immense clarity and irony that we see in his collages. Faust chanted out his songs with loud, untrained voice. The whole event was held together with the thread of Duncan's presence. We did not act out the play with body gestures, the performance was a test of the play for its success on the ear: for its sound and its songs and its meaning. When it ended, Duncan, trembling and cock-eyed with pleasure stood up, took off his pants and showed the nakedness of the poet. All of us knew we'd done something outrageous, something that took a little courage in the silent, cold gray, cold war, chill fifties of suburban tract homes, crew cuts, war machines, and censorship.

Some months later in 1955, Wally Hedrick asked me if I would put together a poetry reading for the Six Gallery and I agreed. Not long before this meeting with Hedrick I'd met a poet from New York at a local party honoring W. H. Auden. Allen Ginsberg and I were sympatico about many things in the art of poetry. We'd gotten together and Ginsberg had shown me letters and poems from a young unknown genius named Jack Kerouac. During one session I told Allen about the Six Gallery reading and due to my lack of time Allen volunteered to shoulder the arrangements for the event.

On October 7th, 1955, five young poets and poet-philosopher Kenneth Rexroth, who was to M.C. the event, showed up at the Six Gallery. Ginsberg had met two new poet friends, Philip Whalen and Gary Snyder, and invited them to be in the reading. Besides Rexroth and Allen, I already knew the other reader, the American surrealist poet Philip Lamantia.

The October show at the Six Gallery was "Crate Sculpture" by Fred Martin. The pieces looked as if Martin had taken wooden fruit crates, broken them, and swathed them in muslin or some other light cloth then dipped them in plaster. I recall enjoying the sculptures which were part of the early days of the assemblage movement—I saw the pieces of Martin's in relationship to both Manuel Neri's work and Bruce Connor's mysterious collages of wallboard and window frames and found materials. In Rexroth's guffawing and generous introduction, championing the five totally unknown poets, he referred jovially to the Crate Sculptures as something that looked like "furniture for Japanese dwarfs." That gives an oddly appropriate description of the scale and furniturelike effect of the pieces, but I remember thinking, at that moment, that the sculptures gave me some of the mystical feeling of Morris Graves' Buddhist-centered works. There was a flagrant airiness as well as a plaster heaviness about the pieces: flamboyant, careless, monumental and mystical all at once. The sculptures probably were exactly right and appropriate to be the setting for the six of us at the Six Gallery.

Even in those days the young Philip Whalen was a good-sized man. Standing there on the low wooden dais with his stomach forward and a slight arch to his back, he held his pages up to his eyes as he read. Whalen showed such an insouciance and near-pedagogical indifference to the genius of his own deep scholarship that the poems seemed to break off in the air in hunks as they were spoken and hang there like visionary American cartoons. These poems he was reading, and that I was hearing for the first time, seemed to owe as much to

Krazy Kat and Smokey Stover as they did to the Patriarchs of Zen and William Carlos Williams.

(If the six of us presenting our art that night had to agree on one artist hero that we held in common, the first draw would have given us William Carlos Williams.) Williams was calling for the use of what he saw as the American language—our own natural everyday speech—as the language of verse. Here was Whalen who had apparently, out of nowhere, managed to master American language in his poetry and then, not stopping there, had harnessed it to his interest in metamorphosis, and his almost pragmatic religious and scientific understanding of the physical and historical universes—real and unreal. One poem—a kind of play in which Whalen comically and crankily read both voices—was about a bourgeois married couple turning into giant parakeets. Other poems were explorations of wild nature and the nature of Buddhism. Sometimes the little audience, 150 or so, would suck in their breath with delight and sometimes laugh out loud with surprised pleasure.

Gary Snyder, slender and coyote-eyed, dressed in old levi jeans like Whalen and Ginsberg, read the first poems that I'd heard that presented Nature in a way that was wholly devoid of urban man and without a trace of the sentiment that until that time accompanied nearly all poems of nature. It was Deep Nature that Snyder was calling up and showing us in his "Berry Feast" poem.

Man and woman were not absent in these poems but it was non-Western man and womankind that peopled the poems, and in the poems they were given the exact same respect, reverence and irreverence that was given to bears and to deer and to jays. The poems Gary read were as flinty as the edges of an old trail and as new as the flecks of foam on a rock at the edge of Puget Sound. Almost shocking in the midst of the forming and reforming perceptions of nature and non-Western man was Snyder's good humor. There was no pouty literariness in either Snyder or Whalen or in their poetry. Snyder was as much a scholar-poet as any of the finest in the English tradition. In fact, it was already clear that we were not only hipster-outsiders and literary outlaws and anarchists and surrealists and Buddhists, we were all also scholars of nature and our own art of poetry. Snyder's presence on stage and his words had the effect of catalyzing some of those who heard into a more definite orientation towards wild nature, and it caused some there to make immediate re-evaluations of their nature experiences. Snyder's erect, comfortable, equipoised presence on stage had a lot to say to the audience about the value of poetry—his words were as revolutionary as any heard since then.

Philip Lamantia had much grace in his physical presence and appearance and voice. He had decided to read, posthumously, the prose poems of his heroin-addicted friend John Hoffman. When he read these works they seemed to make themselves present in the air in orange stripes and trails of luminous colors.

I was twenty-three years old and the youngest to read; it was the first time I had read my poetry to an audience. Listening to a surviving audiotape of the event I was surprised by my sureness and my presence. I read a poem for the deaths of one hundred killer whales who had been machine-gunned from boats by NATO service men, near the coast of Iceland. It was a poem of outrage and anguish that called upon Goya to be the tutelary witness of this mass murder, and that closed with a call to D. H. Lawrence to witness the mindless assassination of these great erotic beings whom he had addressed in his poem "Whales Weep Not." I read another poem which was simultaneously an experiment with negative and positive space and the poem's physicality as an object of consciousness. The poem linked together Buddha's Fire Sermon and my perceptions of physical anthropology. I was looking, as we all were, for a poetics that would go beyond the unloved art of poetry which was at that moment the bastard stepchild of twittery academics. Some of my poems were about beauty as I then understood it—and the body as I understood it. The poetry was then, as it is now, irretrievably and subjectively searching for liberation, for nature, for physicality and for what I call soul-making. I had fallen into the rich art and nature of Northern California and was blossoming with poems that did, after all, begin to contain what I'd hoped to get from Clyfford Still. I was taking my first steps in projective verse and voice, and petals were trembling around my head.

Sometime this night during the first public reading of Ginsberg's "Howl," Jack Kerouac who was there and drunk and sometimes rolling over the floor among the audience seated on the concrete floor, began shouting, "Go . . . Go . . ." in time with Ginsberg's voice.

Bespectacled, vulnerable and almost willowy in stature, Allen began his poem in a clear, precise and measured voice, "I saw the best minds of my generation destroyed by madness . . ." And as he entered the sweep of his new master work he moved into the realm of the bardic. But more than anything else, in my memory is the growing awareness, of first one person and then another that a challenge was being thrown out to the grim, fearful and war-obsessed fifties. The ominous and overwhelming powers of censorship—both those powers of the brutal government and the self-censoring processes of the individual in propagandized society—had been challenged. But there was something more, in this act of nerve and bravery there was a generosity. This poem was not only a condemnation of society in a prophetic mode; it also kindly offered a helping hand. If this young and vulnerable man could speak out so clearly, broaching one unmentionable subject after another, why could not anyone do the same? Further, if it was possible to speak so, then why could one not go a step further and act?

The reading of "Howl" was like a series of awakening shocks—each one a bit harsh in its sudden newness but also exhilarating in the unveiling of the unspoken—or the secretly spoken—obvious. The homosexual, the pothead, the artist, the gagged professor, the downtrodden aging failure, the aspiring bright spirit, the soul in growth in the automobile graveyard, the victimized boy and girl, the politically suspect, the fearful idealist, the budding voice of revolt against brutal mechanized greed, the crazed neurotic caught in the pinchers of mindless social conformity, the older woman with secret dreams of freedom, the conscientious objector, the dejected parents wondering about the future of their child, and those who were defying (or almost ready to defy) racism and the creators of nuclear armaments for the final war, *everyone,* heard a humane voice that was greeting them with a new sounding *hello.* At the end of the reading the audience was on their feet with the realization that a new limit of individual expression had been reached. Almost everyone there, from anarchist carpenter to society lady, was willing to put their toe on that new line and to refuse to be made to step back without a struggle.

The Six Gallery on October 7th, 1955, was the venue of the first group reading of what has come to be known as the Beat Generation. The Beat Generation has proved, over the decades, to be the first literary wing of a worldwide environmental movement that was barely conceived of at that time. Allen Ginsberg's field has become the politics of the change of individual consciousness. Gary Snyder is a Pulitzer

Prize–winning explorer of deep ecology. Philip Whalen has received dharma transmission and is a practicing *sensei* and priest. As ever, I am a mammal patriot pursuing biology and the understanding of spirit.

---

# FRED W. MCDARRAH

FRED W. MCDARRAH, consulting picture editor and photographer at *The Village Voice* since 1959, started his "Rent-A-Beatnik" service that year through tongue-in-cheek ads in the *Voice,* offering to furnish "Beatniks" for New York parties. McDarrah recalled that his classified ad read, "ADD ZEST TO YOUR TUXEDO PARK PARTY . . . RENT A BEATNIK. Completely equipped: Beard, eye shades, old Army jacket, Levi's, frayed shirts, sneakers or sandles [*sic*] optional. Deductions allowed for no beard, baths, shoes, or haircuts. Lady Beatniks also available, usual garb: all black (Chaperone required)." Beatniks rented for forty dollars a night, a sum that McDarrah split evenly with what he called "the talent." "Props like bongo drums, guitars, or candle-topped Chianti bottles cost extra. . . . At these parties, guests sometimes outdid the Beatniks with fake beards, dark glasses, and outlandish attire." McDarrah's party service was so successful that *Mad* magazine followed suit with a (mock) "Rent-A-Square" advertisement.

In August 1960 McDarrah published an essay titled "Anatomy of a Beatnik" in the little magazine *Saga* as a response to Paul O'Neil's "The Only Rebellion Around," an attack on the Beats in *Life* magazine. McDarrah knew the models who had posed for the two-page photograph accompanying the *Life* article that illustrated "The Well-Equipped Pad." In a list under the photograph, *Life* catalogued what it called "all the essentials of uncomfortable living." The list consisted of the following items, a handy guide for potential Beatniks everywhere:

1. Beat chick dressed in black
2. Coal stove for heating baby's milk, drying chick's leotards and displaying crucifix-shaped Mexican cow bells

3. Naked light bulb
4. Hot plate for warming espresso coffee pot and bean cans
5. Marijuana for smoking
6. Posters from old poetry readings and jazz concerts
7. Paperback library of Beat classics
8. Crates which serve as tables and closets
9. Hi-fi loudspeaker
10. Typewriter with half-finished poem
11. Bearded Beat wearing sandals, chinos, and turtle-necked sweater, studying a record by the late saxophonist Charlie Parker
12. Italian wine bottle
13. Empty beer cans
14. Ill-tended plant
15. Current jazz favorite of Beats, Miles Davis's *Kind of Blue*
16. Guitar
17. Record player
18. Beat poetry leaflet (Kaufman's *Abomunist Manifesto*)
19. Bare mattress
20. Bongo drums for accompanying poetry reading (guitar is also used)
21. Cat
22. Beat baby, who has gone to sleep on floor after playing with beer cans

More recently, McDarrah and his wife, Gloria, collaborated on the book *Beat Generation: Glory Days in Greenwich Village* (1996).

━━━━━━

## Anatomy of a Beatnik

Scratch a beard . . . find a Beatnik. It doesn't even make any difference whether you're actually a rabbi, a university professor, a concert musician, a real, live honest to goodness poet, a grocery clerk, or a bus driver. The beard symbol has become so strong that it doesn't matter what or who you are. If you've got a beard, you're a Beatnik.

This symbol system has become such a "thing" in this country that nobody knows what to believe anymore, perhaps because nobody cares; everybody wants the fake, the phony, the spurious anyway. Here's a classic description of America's Beatnik taken from a major Negro magazine: ". . . Unwashed, bearded, free-loving, pseudo-intellectual, reefer-smoking, nonworking, self-styled artists or writers living in protest of something or other."

*Time* magazine says Beatniks are "a pack of oddballs who celebrate booze, dope, sex and despair." The same magazine calls Allen Ginsberg "the discount-house Whitman of the Beat Generation." They also call Jack Kerouac the "latrine laureate of Hobohemia."

*Time*'s poison pen sister, another four-letter-word magazine, was perhaps more successful in twisting the pliable minds of Americans. Last fall it published an incendiary piece called "The Only Rebellion Around." It was written by staff writer Paul O'Neil, who is apparently mixed up with fruit flies since he used the expression five times in one paragraph.

Carried away by College Composition I and II, O'Neil opened his remarkably twisted tale by saying: "If the United States today is really the biggest, sweetest and most succulent casaba ever produced by the melon patch of civilization, it would seem only reasonable to find its surface profaned—as indeed it is—by a few fruit flies. But reason would also anticipate contented fruit flies, blissful fruit flies, fruit flies raised by happy environment to the highest stages of fruit fly development. Such is not the case. The grandest casaba of all, in disconcerting fact, has incubated some of the hairiest, scrawniest and most discontented specimens of all time: The improbable rebels of the Beat Generation, who not only refuse to sample the seeping juices of American plenty and American social advances but scrape their feelers in discordant scorn of any and all who do."

The illustration of the "well-equipped pad," which accompanied the *Life* feature by O'Neil was so funny it was offensive. I happen to know the girl who posed for the photograph. I'm sure she needed the model fee. She is married to a struggling painter. Both are good people who mind their own business. Their two children are just about the most attractive kids anyone could imagine. Nevertheless, in the illustration she is pegged as "the beat chick dressed in black" surrounded by "a naked light bulb, a hot plate for warming espresso coffee pot and bean cans, a coal stove for heating baby's milk, drying chick's leotards and displaying crucifix-shaped Mexican cow bells." The real killer remark was a "beat baby, who has gone to sleep on the floor after playing with beer cans." You can imagine how that went over in Dubuque.

Gilbert Millstein of the *New York Times* told me, "We're the innocents." And I guess he's right. How incredibly innocent we must be to be not only fooled but also taken. O'Neil's *Life* article went on and on with cheap drivel, lies, phony stories, misquotes, slander and slaughter of some of my best friends. An apology for a malicious misquote between Allen Ginsberg and Dame Edith Sitwell did not appear in the magazine's Letters column until seven weeks after the original article was published.

Let me use just one more example of how this erroneous impression of the Beat Generation is perpetuated. Last winter the poetry editor of the *Saturday Review,* John Ciardi, wrote about the Beat Generation as "not only juvenile but certainly related to juvenile delinquency through a common ancestor whose best name is Disgust. The street gang rebellion has gone for blood and violence. The Beats have found their kicks in an intellectual pose, in drugs (primarily marijuana but also Benzedrine, mescaline, peyote, assorted goofballs, and occasionally heroin) and in wine, Zen, jazz, sex, and carefully mannered jargon. . . .

"The Beats wear identical uniforms. They raise nearly identical beards. . . . They practice an identical aversion to soap and water. They live in the same dingy alleys. They sit around in the same drab dives listening to the same blaring jazz with identical blanked-out expressions on their identical faces. And any one of them would sooner cut his throat than be caught doing anything 'square. . . . ' "

It seems clear that the mighty U.S. press has caught on its journalistic meat hook a new scapegoat, a whipping boy, a real live sucker, the so-called Beatnik. It doesn't matter if the facts are straight; after all, we need a little entertainment anyway. The hell with the Truth and down with the Facts. It's better to lay it on the Beatniks than to reflect too seriously on the headlines in the morning paper:

Whites Buy Out Gun Shop As Race Rift Widens in Africa . . . City to Intensify Battle on Crime . . . House Expands Inquiry into Federal Power Commission and Gas Industry . . . Child Kidnapped, Abductors Ask $100,000 . . . Militia Aids Castro in Hunt for Rebels. . . . New Haven Asks Another Fare Increase . . . Mistress Stabs Wealthy Sales Executive. . . .

I could go on and on. Allen Ginsberg puts it much better than I can. "Life is a nightmare for most people, who want something else. . . . People want a lesser fake of Beauty. . . . We've seen Beauty face to face, one time or another and said, 'Oh my God, of course, so that's what it's all about, no wonder I was born and had all those secret weird feelings!' Maybe it was a moment of instantaneous perfect stillness in some cow patch in the Catskills when the trees suddenly came alive like a Van Gogh painting or a Wordsworth poem. Or a minute listening to, say, Wagner on the phonograph when the music sounded as if it was getting nightmarishly sexy and alive, awful, like an elephant calling far away in the moonlight."

What Allen describes here are a few basic necessities of life, the things that make us what we are, Truth, Love and Beauty. As I see it there is very little else in the world that means anything. And this is what the real meaning of the Beat Generation is. This is what the so-called Beatnik wants. The Beat wants his life to mean something to himself. He is looking for an Order. Whether he finds it in poetry, painting, music, plumbing, carpentry, weight-lifting, selling shoes, or no matter what, he must find meaning for his life.

He wants a hero he can genuinely believe in, not like the figure all too frequently presented today, a hero in the form of a professional soldier who won the Bronze Star and half a dozen battle stars, a soldier who carries in his wallet a souvenir photograph of a Red Chinese soldier he bayoneted.

Essentially, it's a matter of living, of awareness, of sensitivity to nature . . . that single miracle ingredient of life that is present when you stand on top of a hill and face the sunny sky and want to scream at the top of your lungs how wonderful it is to be alive.

The trouble is, most people don't have time for such luxuries of the spirit. They're too mixed up, as Jack Kerouac says, in "hustling forever for a buck among themselves . . . grabbing, taking, giving, sighing, dying, just so they could be buried in those awful cemetery cities beyond Long Island City."

In deciding what he is pursuing, Jack writes, in his fine book, *On the Road*, ". . . they danced down the streets like dingledodies, and I shambled after as I've been doing all my life after people who interest me because the only people for me are the mad ones, the ones who are mad to live, mad to talk, mad to be saved, desirous of everything at the same time, the ones who never yawn or say a commonplace thing, but burn, burn, burn like fabulous Roman candles exploding like spiders across the stars. . . ."

I talked to my friend Edwin Fancher about Beatniks and the Beat Generation as we were driving out to Brooklyn to a Methodist church where they were holding a Convocation of Youth. The theme was Man's Strength, Man's Distress. The program consisted of the Beat film *Pull My Daisy,* a lecture on "What Is the Beat Generation?" and a poetry reading by LeRoi Jones, the editor of *Yugen,* which is a pocket-sized literary magazine publishing many Beat writers. The lecture was to be given by Ed.

I first met Ed Fancher at a party nearly a dozen years ago on a snowy New Year's Eve. He was living in the Village and going to the New School for Social Research. He is about 36, a veteran of the war in Europe, has always worn a beard and is a practicing psychologist. Five years ago he started a weekly newspaper in Greenwich Village, *The Village Voice.*

Fancher says that "it is a movement of protest. The Beat looks at the world we live in, everything that is part of our way of life, including finding out what is holy. . . . They live in a world gone mad and no one cares but them. Not only is the Beat Generation interested in intellectual work, they themselves are very social people. It's an attempt to cry out that what we need is a sense of society. If it's necessary to be part of a crazy, offbeat group, all right, that's better than being detached.

"I think the Beats have achieved popularity in America because they correspond to a very deep sense of unrest in America. Americans don't want to think about the real issues of concern; they want to stick their heads in the sand and avoid anything important. They forget that the Beat Generation does feel it's better to have vitality than to be dead at the core like the rest of America. Many Americans are dead at the core and don't know it. The Beats are interested in religion because they live in a society where no one is interested in it. They live in a hostile society and they are struggling to find the meaning of life outside of that dead society."

The religious theme that Ed Fancher talks about was brought up again by Howard Hart. I don't think it makes much difference that he's a Catholic. I've known Howard for about ten years, from the days when the up-and-coming literary set and the *Catholic Worker* crowd used to hang out in the White Horse Tavern and swill down steins of half 'n' half. Howard has been a drummer and has been writing poetry for a great many years. He's the same age as I and is represented in my picture book *The Beat Scene*. Howard says this about the Beat Generation:

"It's an obvious manifestation of the fact that the whole structure of American life is phony. The clothes and the manner immediately call attention to them [the Beats] because they are declaring something which is really a fact and they want to proclaim it. More than protest, there is an affirmative thing there . . . they are really looking for God . . . and after all, God is love. If they didn't have so much of a longing for God in their hearts they wouldn't come on so strong. It's a real search that gives them a kind of right to flaunt themselves even when they haven't got the talent or anything. . . ."

Bernard Scott is another who has some interesting comments to offer. Bud is 31 and is the associate minister of Judson Memorial Church in the heart of Greenwich Village. The church has an adjoining art gallery and sponsors a literary magazine called *Exodus*, which Bud edits. He says, "I always use the term Beatnik to designate a kind of part-time, imitation Bohemianism that was brought up to date with the Beat Generation. The definition of Beatniks rose out of the Beat Generation. It's really nothing more than a couple of dozen writers who helped to define what was happening to people consciously. In fact I remember when I was going to school right after the second war, I was hitchhiking across the country and doing all kinds of weird things. And when the Beat writers came on the scene, I found they were defining me and talking about the things I knew for the first time. They were the articulate spokesmen. I don't associate myself with the Beat Generation in an orthodox, stylistic sense any more, but I welcomed what I saw. They described experiences I knew and they were the first writers to do it.

"When you meet a Beat at a Village party he never asks you what you do because he's not interested in your economic definition. But what you do is one of the first questions you are asked on the outside. Our culture defines people in terms of their utility. The Beat wants to know what you are thinking, what's licking inside of you, how real you are in your heart, what you've got to say, can you help me see anything, can you turn me on . . . ?"

Somewhat apart from the Beats are the Hipsters, devotees of a philosophy best expressed by Norman Mailer, the author of *The Naked and the Dead*.

I see Norman around the *Village Voice* newspaper office quite a bit since he was one of the paper's founders, and I frequently run into him at parties. At one party I heard him being interviewed for a Monitor radio broadcast so his comments on Hip were abbreviated:

"I would say that Beat is more idyllic than Hip; it assumes that finally all you have to do is relax and find yourself and you'll find peace and honesty with it. Hip assumes that the danger of the modern world is that whenever anyone relaxes that is precisely the moment when he is ambushed. So, Hip is more than a philosophy of ambition, less destructive of convention than Beat. There is more respect for the accretion of human values. As an example, manners are important in Hip; the Beats say all manners are square. . . . The Beat writers seem to be getting better, more exciting. It may become a very powerful force in our literature. I think the Beat has opened the way to more excitement in our lives. . . ."

Another statement of the Hipster philosophy comes from Ted Joans, the 31-year-old poet and one of the more interesting characters living in Greenwich Village. He says, "I'm a hipster. I'm concerned with the moral revolution in America; revolution through peace and love; we're the richest people in the world and yet we don't have truth and love. It's not what's up front that counts, it's what's in your heart and brain. There is nothing wrong with material possessions. But you should use them and not let them use you. I think everybody wants to conform, but the future of the world lies in the hands of the nonconformists. . . ."

It's difficult for me to remember when I first ran into Mimi Margeaux. Maybe it was at a party, perhaps in a coffee shop. I might have even been formally introduced to her, as unlikely as it sounds. Mimi is 25. She is a beautiful girl, with thousands of friends, has traveled on the road frequently between her home in Chicago and San Francisco, New York, Mexico City, a thousand places. Mimi has been associated with the Beat movement for a long time. She knows all the poets, the painters and all the rest. I was walking down MacDougal Street one day when I met her and asked if she would join me in a beer at the Kettle of Fish, one of the Village's staple Beat haunts. Her conversation was characteristically candid: "There really are two kinds of Beats, people like [Kenneth] Patchen, the jazz musicians, [Norman] Mailer, Jack [Kerouac], Allen [Ginsberg], they're really Hipsters. The Beatniks are younger kids who are taking advantage of the trend. They don't know what they're rebelling against. They just can't get along with their parents so they run away from home.

"I would say I'm a Hipster, but people think I'm a Beatnik."

"The longest I've held a job is about six months. In fact my whole working career is only about a year. Most of the time I've lived from saved money, unemployment, living at home, living with friends, and I was married. . . . I get along."

Then there's John Mitchell, who has a coffee shop called the Gaslight, right next door to the Kettle. For a couple of years the Gaslight has been sponsoring Beat poets reading from their work. Just about every poet in New York has read there at one time or another, and the shop has gained a national reputation. Recently Mitchell published an anthology of poetry called *The Gaslight Review,* which included the work of most of the poets who have read there. John is in his early thirties and is very well informed about the Beat Generation since he has lived in the Village for years and is right in the center of all the activity.

"I've been accused of being a Beatnik," he says. "Maybe it's the way I dress. Maybe I act peculiar and people become hysterical and anything that looks different to them is a Beatnik. Being Beat is really an attitude. I sympathize with these young people. I was raised during the Depression and I can have more fun with five cents than these kids can have with fifty dollars.

"With the Bomb and all, I don't blame these kids for flipping. They're rejecting the incredible mess that the adults have created in the world. Every time you pick up a newspaper you find another corrupt government official exposed. To quote Frank Lloyd Wright, this country went from barbarism to decadence without a period of culture in between. I think the Beat protest is a healthy thing.

"There is a difference between the Bohemians of twelve years ago and the Beats. Five years ago people who came here were rejecting society but they weren't raising hell; they were dejected and defeated. The old-time Bohemians were really beaten down by society. These kids haven't given up. It's a much healthier movement. The Beats aren't a formal movement, but they know what they don't want. They don't want cold wars, hot wars, military service, all the rest. One of the things they reject is a political party in a group. Some good will come from all this. It's a healthy thing and a lot of people are involved. The American people put them down because they're afraid that they don't want change and these [Beats] might change their ways. The last big thing in this country like the Beat Movement was the marches on Washington during the Depression. This movement will be stronger."

I also talked to Jack Micheline, a poet who is associated with the Beat movement. Jack is in his early thirties and has put in his time on the road, so to speak. I'd call Jack a loner. He has a lot of friends, but he pretty much sticks to himself and his writing, which is a spontaneous, brick-and-mortar, concrete big-city type of writing.

"I want to get away from politics," Jack said. "I might have been politically active but it's all corrupt. I want to see better things happen that would help this country. I think the Beat is growing in all the arts. I've been told that the vitality of my work is identified with the Beat Generation. I'm anti-materialistic, the way I live, the way I feel, the way I think. I have no interest in becoming a millionaire. I'm interested in growing as a writer. Aside from my work I'm interested in girls.

"The Beat Generation is a way of life. All my life I've been rebelling against something or other. The reason for my rebellion is that I want to be able to be what I want, do what I want, without being restricted. I fight to remain myself. If my life means anything to me it has nothing to do with Beatniks. I've met a lot of people who weren't Beat who taught me a lot, who showed me things. A Beatnik is somebody running away from himself. Today they dress up in old clothes and hang around coffee houses. In the 1930s they joined the Communist Party. A Beatnik is the first stage of rebellion against society. Perhaps there will be an overthrow of the old order and not everything will be keyed to the machine age. You might say this is a rebellion against escalators."

The Beat Generation was practically founded in the East Harlem apartment of Mary Nichols, a 33-year-old mother of three children. Mary now lives in the Village and is a newspaper reporter and very active in politics. "I was a little girl out of Swarthmore College in those days," she says, "and I was terrified by that *Go* bunch, Clellon Holmes, Louis Simpson, Allen Ginsberg, all the rest. I moved to the

Village to get away from all those Bohemians. Of course, they didn't have a name then. Everybody smoking pot, inviting me to wild parties, and I thought, my goodness, they are an amoral group.

"I'm not a Beatnik but I think I understand some of them. I'm really quite bourgeois myself. But if someone accused me of being bourgeois, I might say I was Beat. I don't care for labels. I suppose the way I'm living is Beat, but I'm not satisfied with it. In my wildest dreams I want to die in the St. Regis Hotel.

"It's a question of anxiety, I think, that produces the Beat Generation. It may be an anxiety for order and security, which is a funny thing to say about them, but they want a security that's more cosmic than what the average square wants. . . . Beatniks are really very political in a strange way. I think there is a relation between their rejection of politics and their concern over the H-Bomb. You can't reject something unless you're involved in it.

"I think the security the Beat person wants is knowing that he's not going to be annihilated in the next ten years. When I really think about it, I think it's possible that the human race will be destroyed in my lifetime. Perhaps that's why I always look so happy. There may be so little time, it doesn't seem worth being any other way."

---

# DAVID MELTZER

DAVID MELTZER has resisted putting a label on his work as a poet. In *The Outlaw Bible of American Poetry,* he wrote that "I've been tagged by the Beat team, the SF Renaissance brokers, as well as the Psychedelic '60s mythographers." Raised in Los Angeles, he "fell into the postwar artist scene, primarily under the mentorship of Wallace Berman & Bob Alexander . . . & felt comfortable in the hipster urban marginal counterculture which had some of its roots in the earlier left Popular Front arts movements of the late '30s & war years." Feeling that Ginsberg and Kerouac were "elders, not my peers," Meltzer worked compatibly alongside Rexroth and Ferlinghetti reading poetry to jazz after he moved to the East Bay. To earn a living for his family, he helped start San Francisco's New College and developed courses in poetics and philosophy with Diane di Prima and other writers. A gifted musician as well as the author of many books, including *The San Francisco Poets* (1971) and *Reading Jazz* (1993), Meltzer says that most of his poetry celebrates "domestic life & kabbalah. But I was always clear that the mystery is ordinary & that the ordinary is the mystery." In recent years, his long poem *Beat Thing* has been an ongoing project.

### *From* Beat Thing

It was the Bomb
*Shoah*
*Khurbn*
it was Void
spirit    cry
crisis disconnect
no subject but blank
unrelenting busted time
no future
suburb expands into past
present nuclear (get it) family
'droids Pavlov minutiae
it was Jews w/ blues
reds nulled & jolted
Ethel & Julius brain smoke
pyres of shoes & eyeglasses
weeping black G.I.s
open Belsen gates
things are going to look different when
you get outside
understand that beforehand
this book doesn't kid you
& don't forget the third effect
radioactivity the power to
shoot off invisible atomic rays

even if the all clear's sounded
don't rush to leave the safe place
Geiger counts light leaks from
ash hand reaches up for your eyes
yes
the atomic bomb is a terrible weapon
BUT
not as terrible as most of us believe

Tillich tells us "it's the destiny of historical
man to be annihilated not by a cosmic event but
by the tensions in his own being & history"[1]

EIGHT SIMPLE AIR RAID RULES:

ALWAYS shut the windows and doors.
ALWAYS seek shelter.
ALWAYS drop flat on your stomach.
ALWAYS follow instructions.
NEVER look up.
NEVER rush outside after a bombing.
NEVER take chances with food or water.
NEVER start rumors.[2]

Furthermore, acquaintance with addicts proves
that "hypes" like being "hypes." They enjoy
being a "hype" as a hypochondriac enjoys being
a hypochondriac. They will argue that liquor
affects people worse than heroin, that drunks
are often noisy and argumentative, while all a
"hype" wants is to be left alone. They dislike
the social scorn, the inconvenience of having to
hide their addiction, but they enjoy the effect of
the drug which keeps them from facing reality.
    The juice of the poppy wrecks the body and

1. "The Power of Self Destruction," by Paul Tillich in *God and the H-Bomb,* edited
by Donald Keys. New York: Bernard Geiss Associates, 1961. Page 24.
    2. *How to Survive an Atomic Bomb,* by Richard Gerstell. New York: Bantam Books,
1950. Pages 138–139.

warps the spirit. The life of the addict is a
living death.[3]

. . . . . . . . . .

Okay, what drugs did Beat Things do
unstoppable Golems clunk up Frisco hills &
crash through glass Nob Hill doors hit waxed tile floors
bugged or goofy prophets hex profit outreach
for more upward agility let me list the ways
wisdom sways through barroom doors
hardline juicers boozers lushes dipsos
unpeel *Gemeinschaft* onion loops to steal
wise guy shifts in benny flipbook blur or
muggles giggles & pelvis wiggles sizzle
electric rootsystems light up epidermal cowl
dong bulb wired into cervical ark clutch
do redbirds sleepers newtime absinthe cafe blur
glazed out head down in a pool of dream drool
or nosedive into ether rag to regain the sky
flow through doors opening quicker than tics
or laser toke of opium tar brocades cocoon
or blade coke lines moon zoom cold precise
crater edges overburdened white light
into everything into everything else
or enbalm w/ smack your skin bongo
drum taut in feeze dry heat hit rush
wipe away clouds too loud your eyes
walled w/ shades fall in lay back land in Nod
or buttons boiled in aluminum pot on hotplate
eat every thorn drink up the soup & loop out
fight payphone octopus wires
get Bellevue to strap me down
or potcake chomped at Coffee Gallery
weary of Tina's definitive Jalapa trip blitz
which rewrote her itinerary or ripped on Hollywood
Boulevard bus en route to Silverlake everybody knows I'm

3. *The Inside Story of Narcotics*, by Jim Vaus. Grand Rapids: Zondervan Publications, 1953. Page 39.

out of it & they're all stark narcs behind shades I can't see
through or spiked punch electric surge flash flush
infusion of never-ending nerve-end or am
T's scribe for canned Squibb prophecies
whose raw socket volcano rockets wisdom
uncoiled levels connect reassemble
scribble down what can't make sense in the morning
or first meth death Maclaine the poet piper kino eye
head spent flying hours scavenging brass doorknobs from
Western Addition demolition or Valo
inhalers boing microsecond infinite or paregoric
or bowel block Cheracol coughsyrup or
lung sandblast hashpipe hit & run into Sierra
Sound w/ Clark, J.P., Denny, & David to lay
heavy tracks through endless tunnel or wormless
tequila w/ Stephanie atop stacked highs
in redwood canyon ready to descend & start again
or painting Cameron's Scott Street flat w/ Army surplus
ether-based khaki paint rocket beyond Coleridge
to meet in tantric blur or popping buttons w/ Dean
in his hungry Porsche grumbling to Idell's idyll
through California hills to Riverside or in Jack
the Baptist's VW van to Isla Vista drinking
beer toking weed or 60's New Year's Eve
Nancy in aluminum foil dress smoke up
scale grass in Roscoe bathroom & downstairs
dance random hippie sway or all day
all night dexy writing monkey gibber
gargantuan nothing splatter of commas
& semicolons or tons of nutmeg cons grind
into gel caps for joint jump or knot guts
'shrooms twist through slime showrooms
shiny bloody brain furls slopped into chrome
trays or Hedricks' home brew knocked flat back
on bathroom tilefloor fixed on ceiling mazda or
hurl in trunk of farewell party or Dino spike
smoke funnel kiss lung puncture blast off or
buzzed Crosby on Van Damme topdeck sings
Beatles to David & Tina below or achingly

clear blow-torqued bluegrass livingroom session w/ Greg
or Mount Rushmore heads in Romero's Portrero
pad & Angel LP Yehudi explains ragas Ravi
Shankar unravels our spines or February birthday
for Artie WB & me ozoned on floor watch
*Magnificent Ambersons* Larry Jordan projects onto
fold-out screen or Jim Hall/Red Mitchell at Keystone
while I nod out between bars Chris is alert or
drive a car one eye open & another eye shut or
dive w/ snorkel into cocaine Himalayas or do
Ali Baba hookah bubble pipe on foam-filled pillow
or day/night speed through the Apple's allures to home
& feel warm sleep cement inch up from toes fill rills &
ruts of busy buzzy brain brings erase & jazz on the radio
or Larkin Street deep flu fever a flask of cognac lacquers
or Sturdy tripping at Coffee & Confusion gets our music
really gets into it or T & me reenter & roulette restless
LPs on the phono & wind up weeping to worn 10" Pete
Seeger LP driven by unstandard time heart waver voice or
at Black Hawk with the Halseys waiting for Monk's set
or it could go on w/ Fentanyl patches IV insert new drip
protein into catheter click whir plugged-in pump or
short-circuit Ativan planchettes your ballpoint message
dream knot maze tangled baby scrawl or more liquid
morphine sucked out of clear plastic dose-measured tube
& sleep                          . . . . . . . . . . . .

ka-chung

Beat ephemera fills up shoeboxes mice nest in

Beat lounge acts at Ramada Inn bars near airports

Beat cruise mingle w/ Beat survivors sit at Captain's table w/ poete du
jour & dance to elderly bebop band at night win costume-contest feed
    sharks
masterpieces harpoon beached wails have a bunch of books signed by
    blind
bard riffing disenchanties adored singing up from the waxed floor his
    high
led to

Beat correspondence school ads on TV John Saxon reads off the course
offerings

Beat fairs rent space w/ tables of books, berets, records, leotards,
videocassettes, CDs, posters, 8 x 10 glossies, period antiquities in
bakelite, chrome, tigerskin pincushion vinyl, pushbutton cherry gizmos,
classic Tupperware in stacks (it's really the looks not the books)

Beat things shrink inside outsize sweaters wedge into room corners
   away
from lone candle jammed in wax caked wine bottle; Beat gamins & Jack
   Spratt
artistes shade-goggled eyes above black turtleneck rims
Beat wax museums in Fisherman's Wharf downtown Lowell McDougal
   Street &
Beat Thing Hall of Fame wing of Planet Hollywood on Sunset Boulevard

Beat leftovers second-stringers impersonators at Beat fests & contests
for the best Kerouac & Burroughs while in another hotel Elvises spangle
   glitter
lip curl compete for credibility

Beat karaoke franchises

Beat Generation (the musical) touring show at burb malls & civic
   centers;
Beat 900 numbers for phone bop prosody or Mamie Van Doren clone
   phone sex
bongo

Beat flesh pixeled jigsaw bricolage CD Roms; Beat DNA flash-frozen
   sperm &
eggs at Better Baby Boutiques new stock added weekly as oldtimers
   give it
up before drying up

Beat bulk lurch to lunch through plateglass posh chez cafe doors pour
   blood
over crisp white linen tablecloths fans magic act away for wall hangings

Beat thing headbutts into corporate conference room where suits hold out
pens for him to marathon grab as he signs contract after contract stacks up
a big deal

the agent Charlie McCarthy's a propped up Beat body against press conference wall

Beat superstar on MTV fastcut scratch 50's newsreel footage intercut w/
sitcom knows best voices over Kurt Loder asks Burroughs about killing his
wife

Beat CEO of media congealment spars w/ Bill Gates in razor-sharp khakis &
Italian soft leather loafers for global ownership of poetry on Charlie Rose

Beat creature from black lagoon dips spoon into tub of Ben & Jerry Kerouac
Carmel Walnut Chunk Satori

Beat nix sticks pen into toxic state of inc (orporation) to finish epic PR
for Disney Beatsville urban mall themepark

Beat infomercial Anne Waldman hosting looks cool in new do & black silk
sheath & stockings insouciant red beret w/ Beat bodyguards Ginsberg
Burroughs on each side of the overlit divan
Beat website with pot leaf wreathed logo of Ginsberg Kerouac Burroughs mother son holyghost
Beat tour jackets T-shirts numbered prints of Beat photos by Redl Stoll
McDarrah framed offered round the clock on Beat shopping channel

Beat Gap line of chinos lumberjack flannel shirts Dr. Dean beat shades Joe

Camel unfiltered beat smokes Armani blue black basement zoots to suit
   up in
& walk down to theme bar restaurant Coolsville chain owned by three
publishers owned by a transglobal media conglomerate owned by a
   network of
oil companies owned by a consortium of arms dealers owned by a clot
   of drug
producers owned by a massive webwork of Swiss bankers & German
   brokers in
silent partnership with Japanese alchemists in collusion with Chinese
gerontologists as proxies for Reverend Moon


Beat mercenary high steppers bottom feeders set up emporia marts in
   college
towns & fast food dance halls troughs underwrit by Dr Pepper's new
   beat
cola & McDonald's beat meat subs espresso shakes Bongo Burgers
   Cool Slaw


Beat cross country tours in refurbished Chevys & fintailed Caddies
   driven
by fast-talking clean-cut Neal-like tour guides who park at neo-beat
   motels
stapled along 66 w/ bar jukeboxes stocked w/ hop rhythm 'n' blues &
   haiku
cocktail napkins


Beat Blockbuster shelves filled w/ old & new A & B Hollywood beat
   flicks
plus full stock of alternative beat video readings performances of survivor
beats sub-beats micro-beats in Xerox wrapper hand-lettered plastic cases
along w/ second & third generation beat-identified groups performers &
momentarily cool souls


Beat motif lap dancers beret-ribbed rubbers XXX loops gay road
   buddies XXX
dildoes rebel leather flight jackets slave jeans w/ snap open back flap for
bongo beat fisting

Beat outfits w/ gold leaf Burroughs signature on barrel, HH
  monogrammed
smack baggies, Gallo special edition Thunderbird label reproduces page
  from
*On the Road* scroll comes in cases of 24 poorboy screwtop bottles only
  &
isn't sold downtown, Cassady nickel & dime bags w/ mini silkscreen
  · photo of
Neal in white T-shirt & deluxe kilo limited silkscreened last photo of
  Neal
on tightrope walking railroad tracks somewhere in Mexico numbered &
  signed
by Kesey, bonus presentation set of gold bullets in brass plaque plush
lined case w/ certificate of authenticity numbered & signed by William
  Lee . . .

David Meltzer wrote in *Reading Jazz* that "when I think of the
'spirit' of jazz I mean improvisation and the willingness to improvise. In and out of control at once, a conduit of/for invention. Present tense. Awake and alert to the cues and clues the
music allows. Receiving and transmitting. At once." He thought
Kerouac was the most successful of the Beat poets who
recorded their reading of poetry to jazz. When Kerouac performed, he understood that jazz was more than the background
to his poems; instead, he made the "spirit" of the music inter-
active with the poetry. Meltzer observed that Kerouac's

> sessions of haiku call-and-response with tenor
> saxophonists Al Cohn and Zoot Sims are wonder-
> ful examples of dialogues absent in the other
> records. (Even backed up by Steve Allen's pedes-
> trian cocktail jazz piano, Kerouac overcame the
> music's distracting lacklusterness with an elan in-
> trinsic both to his performance style and relation-
> ship with language and jazz sensibility.)

## Poetry & Jazz

## Text

I.

Okay what was poetry & jazz all about? how was it done? who did it? did it really make it? Nobody knows its origins while many claim to be its progenitor: Rexroth says he did it in Chicago with Jelly Roll Morton in the late 20s early 30s; ruth weiss claims to have started it all in 1946 in New Orleans; Vachel Lindsay in the 20s with his "fat black bucks . . . . boomalay boomalay" and "Daniel Jazz" (with marginalia cueing the jazz band); Langston Hughes did it in Harlem during the 20s Renaissance. Maybe it's all moot or, as they used to say in the 50s, "a matter of semantics." Poets have been singing their stuff probably starting in the caves moving into Babylonia Mesopotamia *shir hasharim* Bible plains chanting Kali and Kwan-Yin mantrum and plectrum Sapphic lyre into qawalli singing Sufis rapidfire fanning gutstrings duende cante troubadour courts of tzaddikim ecstatic upholding the universe *nigunim* into Brit balladeers across winter drifts to Schoenberg's *sprechstimme* and Louis Armstrong's amnesia inspired *Heebie Jeebies* 1926 glossolalia; Edith Sitwell ratatatat to *Facade* Walton's teadance jazz band hotcha; the Weimar cabaret and pop operas like Ernst Krenek's *Jonny spielt auf* in 1926, Kurt Weill and Bert Brecht's 1928 *Die Dreigroschenoper,* it's rumored Jean Cocteau played a mean drum kit in Paris Jazz Age joints. How about Gilbert & Sullivan, especially the "patter songs"? The Zurich Dada art demolition derby Cabaret Voltaire cats like Tzara? The "talking blues" form made popular in the Popular Front days of the 40s by Woody Guthrie? From Africa West to Delta South to Kansas City to Broadway, through blues griots, post-pogrom Jews Hart, Gershwin, Berlin, Dorothy Fields, Harburg, African-American poet James Weldon Johnson, Andy Razaf; Duke's recitatives; swing shift into bop mad mouths: Babs Gonsalves Leo Watson Slim Gaillard "putty putty"; acoustic blues poets like Robert Johnson, Blind Willie McTell; urban electric bluesmen like Little Walter, Howling Wolf; the constant stream of rural poetry from poet-singers called hillbilly, cowboy, country—like Jimmie Rodgers and Hank Williams; you get the drift? Post WW2 glossolaliacal Letterists led by Isidore Isou (which rooted into the late 60's Situationist International)? Any way you look at it (or hear it), we're dealing with kinds of song and we all know poetry started as song before being silenced, stamped into paper into a shut book, and another long history of enchantment, *encantare*. So, again, what is this thing called poetry and jazz? "What is this thing called love?"

## 2.

Okay, what was poetry and jazz in the halcyon daze of the Beat 50s in 'Frisco? Essentially it was poets holding onto the paper of their poems as cripts and cribs to recite to the accompaniment of a small jazz group. Flip the coin and clear the table. It's confession time. In the late 50s, as a lad, I too read my poems to jazz at The Jazz Cellar in North Beach; the same place Ferlinghetti and Rexroth strutted their stuff at. (Also Rod McKuen. He'd sometime do Sunday afternoon performances which I regret I never attended.) I was a kid, a bebop true believer barely drinking age, while the poets on stage were, jeez, fuckin' middleaged. The Beats were over-the-hill guys; they didn't, like, swing. Rexroth, Ferlinghetti, and Kenneth Patchen read alerting and often alarming words while the musicians played in the background. Listen to the "live" Fantasy recordings of Rexroth and Ferlinghetti. Both are formidable poets, public charmers and disarmers, but neither seemed connected to the jazz comped behind their words. The words came first, music second. As a greenhorn poet, my jazz poets were singers. Whatever poetry was it wasn't jazz. Jazz was dialogic not logocentric.

The impact of jazz and jazz culture on European and American poets, writers, artists, musicians, was permanently profound; the idiom signified new freedoms and permission to pilfer and transform, create and recreate a fantasy of slavery redeemed by white folk into masks of modernism. The new gets old as soon as it's announced as the new. Haute yearns to get down as long as they can take a cab back home. Both blacks and whites in the States took jazz and blues as an outcast (and cast away) art more profound than the uptown thunder of concert halls.

Barry Wallenstein writes, "The performance of jazz is not unlike

the performing language of poetry, one could note how improvised solos break away from the original harmonic and melodic structure. Similarly, in much of modern poetry, especially free verse, the range of
improvisatory gesture is immense."[1] The writing process is solitary
confinement, silent, on the page, the inward jumps and skips serve the
page. When the poet performs words on the page it's like a musician
reading sheet music. But it's not the same; it's a different creative act.
Poet and musician are interpreting marks on paper, but they're not
improvising, i.e., inventing on the spot alternate ways of expressing
words and music, creating new moments in time that are ineffable
and beyond captivity.

## Back to North Beach

During the quick burnout of the Beat moment in the late 50s, green-
backs galore were made off a dissident anti-materialist movement, just
as now nouveaux techno riche resell the Beat thing. Then entre-
prenurial zeal flourished in hit-&-run boutiques, galleries, cafes,
opened up and down Grant Avenue (like today's Valencia Street yuppie glut of high-end 50s redux shoppes, pubic goatees, exotic dogs,
multicultural themepark eateries, shades, capris, beanbag chairs, &c.,
all further oversold by umbilical computer throb lines). Daily Gray
Line Bus tours to North "Beat" Beach, and on weekends, suburban
beatnik wannabes donned black tights, berets, shades, goatees, bongos, and in nervous fibrillating groups ventured into the go-man-go
vortex, often predated on by hipster slicksters and tricksters. Hey,
baby, it's the looks (style, surface), not the books.

By the way, nostalgia.com tripsters, the 50s expressed and repressed the death of Western Civ revealed in Hiroshima, Nagasaki,
and the Holocaust. Business was good; a startlingly abundant postwar
economy after the Great Depression and its antidote World War 2. Affordable incredible stuff shaped out of new cheap malleable materials;
insaturation of a creditcard economy, a buy-now-pay-later trance trig-
gered by motivationally researched ads (concocted by Leftist Euro-

1. "Poetry and Jazz: A Twentieth Century Wedding," by Barry Wallenstein in *Black
American Literature Forum*. Volume 25, Number 3, 1991; p. 595. One of the more astute
takes on the genre.

pean exiles from Fascism), the rise of advertising as a major cultural power. And, uh, the fabulous Cold War, the Military Industrial Complex, Reds versus Feds, decades of top-down crunching of any or all dissent. Ah, the "cool" Fifties.

3.

In the late 50s Jonathan Williams, publisher of trailblazing Jargon Press (early publishers of Olson's *Maximus,* Creeley, Mina Loy, Lorine Neidecker, Stuart Z. Perkoff, &c.), drove a van through the States peddling his books to likely bookstores, art galleries, eccentrics, and rank strangers. He parked his van on La Cienega before the Ferus Gallery where Ed Keinholz, Bob Alexander and Walter Hopps struggled to curate the premiere avant-garde gallery in Los Angeles, site of Andy Warhol's first West Coast show and Wallace Berman's first public one-man show. I used to hang out there, a scussy 19-year-old poet from Brooklyn in exile. Went with Jonathan and a crew of others on a field trip to Venice, California to visit Lawrence Lipton, P. T. Barnum of the "Venice West" sideshow. Lipton, from Lodsz, had been a newspaperman with a street-smart desire for the uptown heights of Literature. Cigar clenched between choppers, Lipton proclaimed the coming revolution of the word, a world of voice spooled out of reel-to-reel tapes and the relatively recent LP. His book of toney *National Enquirer* wireservice Walter Winchell dit dit dot dot on the Venice enterprise, *The Holy Barbarians,* celebrated dissident stirrings with a rapt prose adhering to Euro-Romantic fixation with the heroic Self. The proviso was that he, Maestro Lipton, was the Toscanini or DeMille of the project. All would ultimately follow his lead as capo of the spoken word, jazz & poetry crusade. Man, books were dead, obsolete; the poet had better get with it and jam the jive and riff the raff. He proceded to perform his poetry which was, alas, cornball. The *poete maudit* hipster subcult of Venice was more realized by Stuart Z. Perkoff and his posse of Frank Rios and Tony Scibella. But these, again, were younger guys, hipsters, and deep into the subculture which, in those days, meant drugs as much as jazz as much as art. The profound and influential artist of that time and geography was Wallace Berman whose mantra was, loud and proud, "Art Is Love Is God." As I recall, the Southland was a great place for image; movie folks and artists did well. Not young bebop baptized poets.

4.

Exiled from Brooklyn to L.A. in '54, left for S.F. in '57. With a crew of hungry poets and artists, we spent all night hanging the annual art show at L.A.'s Barnsdell Park, were paid cash under the table and fed breakfast at the house of some hip Board member, and cut loose. Berman and I were driven to Burbank Airport to hop a cheapo Pacific Air flight to 'Frisco. He was going for a long weekend, I was going to stay. Had a job waiting at Paper Editions as a warehouse worker through Norman Rose, managing the operation, whose "pad" he graciously let me stay in. (It was a former radio repair shop on Larkin Street near California. I slept in the window counter, the window covered with ricepaper slapped into place with a mixture of Wilhold and water. We had a toilet and a sink and $25 monthly rent. Not much else.) In those days you could go to the plane toilet and turn on and zone out gazing through a round glass porthole. (People smoked cigarettes everywhere. It was the rule of cool and the law of the land. There was even a cigarette called "Kools.") A full moon night. When herb's bell rang, Luna was cushioned by dark cloudbanks lacked with radiant edges, shining like a radium watchface.

5.

The Jazz Cellar was a basement club on Green Street off Grant Avenue. The long staircase leading down to it took up more space than the club itself which was a narrow room with a bar on one side, a row of tables and chairs on the other side, and a small stage where the band played. When I started there on an off-night in 1958, the house band consisted of Bill Weisjahn, piano, Max Hartstein, drums, and club-owner Sonny Wayne, drums, with regular appearances by valve trombonist Frank Phipps and multi-reed player Leo Wright.

What happened when it happened? I'd make a "head arrangement" of my poems, i.e., a spine of elements, incomplete clues and prompts (like filecards or a fakebook) in order to improvise beyond the finished entity set deep on the page. (If poetry is the page, ideally poetry and jazz should be beyond the page. A potential form, open ended, dependent on the interactions of musical elements in musician and poet. We'll get back to that.)

I'd indicate the tempo and general ozone of sound like blues, samba, or generic bebop ballad, and tell the bass to walk the first chorus, followed by the drum in dialogue with the bass, then the piano's chorus in a trio format before jumping in for my chorus. We'd improvise, stretching out choruses until each of us said our say and could bring the work to a close. Sometimes it would be voice and drum or bass and voice, pushing each other into deeper dialogue. That was always the key to the process. Whatever would happen was unknown yet entered into with faith to knowing. Irregardless. No different than any kind of ordinary profound. Equilibirum, the dream. Receiving and transmitting all at once; shaping and being shaped.

Ah the good old bad old days. Maybe I got $20 a night at The Cellar, a once a week gig, which went for the usual fuel: cigarettes, rent, biscotti, Chinatown feasts on the cheap (another story). As a poet in those days I was too young to know much except the pulse of music and the often inscrutable paradox of words on paper and their shape-shifting flux of meaning. My workingclass immigrant Brooklyn popularfront coming of age propelled both by Old World and New World energies: *shtetl* orthodox Judaism and CP/USA storefront; Euro classical music and High Culture backup systems back to back (or toe to toe) with Boogie Woogie, Duke Ellington, Bebop, hipster culture, comicbooks, radio, movies, and sanctuary in Public Libraries, pushed me out into a new world that ultimately couldn't renew itself, fixed as it was in irreconcilable oppositions made more acute in 1945 in the faces of the Holocaust, Hiroshima and Nagasaki.

6.

As the beboppers turned pop music and blues inside-out to create an avant-garde, the "Beats" turned the Euro-American modernist avant-garde into a populist movement. One of the Beats' more radical gestures was returning poetry to people, not academicians and New Critic Calvinists. The beboppers, in turn, took jazz away from the body, the dance floor, into the mind of a seated person in a club digging the music as if in Carnegie Hall deep into a Bartók string quartet. The very body and spontaneity white Beat poets celebrated and fetishized in African-American expressivity, black Bebop innovators were relocating into a new formalism. The Beats claimed both a disaf-

filiated and populist stance even though most of the movement's assigned progenitors were as traditionally literary as the Enemy, as well
as privileged. The difference was seeking acceptance by rejecting the
accepted. A familiar strategy. Yesterday's anti-boogy warriors become
today's high culture heroes for the class they violated and desecrated.
Masochism, schism, or flux? Bebop led the way to Free Jazz and the
Black Arts movements which was a slave rebellion in the '60s out of
the familiar unresolved politics of race and art. From these movements emerged a new jazz and poetry more connected to a renewed
populist energy multicultural gumbo of inner-city creativity and defiance which turned on and nourished not only mall malaise but
became a global phenomena thanks to increasingly affordable tech-
nologies. Like Reggae, hip-hop is insurgent pleasure; agit-prop where
the rapper, the MC, the word wizard, holds forth against the beats and
mixes of the DJ. It's what jazz and poetry fussed with and pretended
but never owned. Baraka, Jayne Cortez, Gil Scott-Heron, The Last Poets, KRS-1, NWA, Michael Frante, Sistah Souljah, are just some of
the different generations of performers, stylists doing it. Much of the
groundwork for hip-hop was mulched by The Black Arts movement in
the 60s, one that also worked to unite factions and redefine cultural
perimeters in the same way the Beat moment worked. But the Black
Arts movement was never accorded the ever increasing cultural value
that the Beats have accumulated.

7.

Am flown down to Hollywood by Jim Dickson, owner and producer of
Vaya Records, Lord Buckley's first label. I'm 22 and it's 1959. Miles
Davis and Coltrane are on Columbia. Bird's been dead four years. My
first book of poetry has been printed (a two-fer shared with Donald
Schenker's first book), hand-set by Don and Alice Schenker on the
late Weldon Kees's press in a Potrero Hill basement. I knew Jim in
L.A. earlier when he was married to the actress Diane Varsi, who I
knew through Dean Stockwell. I remember Dean, Diane and yours
truly going to a Hollywood Boulevard movie house to see a restored
print of Citizen Kane, the same theater I earlier saw the first run of
Salt of the Earth before it was sucked into McCarthy era anticommu-
nist limbo.

Jim had caught me at The Cellar and set me up to perform a one-nighter at the Club Renaissance on Sunset Boulevard and do an after-hours recording session. Flew down with a handful of books to sell in the club's store and did a two-set gig.

You've got to visualize the Renaissance. It was sunk beneath the lip of a hill on Sunset and its rear was a glass Cinemascope panorama scoping out nighttime L.A. From The Cellar to the Renaissance. Top of the world, ma.

In the band was Allan Eager, a tenor sax hero of mine, and Bob Dorough was the pianist, but I draw a blank on the bass player and drummer. To be trading fours with these guys was astounding. Lots of glitter in the house. Show biz hipsters, actors, artists; it was (ugh) an "in" place. This was the moment of James Dean and Brando where the "movie star" was now an Artist, no longer a plank of glitter meat for an eroding Studio system evaporating into TV's reign of error.

An opulently huge space, lit seductively to create intimacy in between sets. A massive bar and barfood I couldn't imagine. (Earlier, when I lived in L.A. I'd go with other scroungy writer types to Rand's Round Up, "All You Can Eat" for something like $1.98, for our daily meal. We worked out a wolfish strategy: go for the high protein meats, fowl and fish, and hedge on easy landfill of potato salad, macaroni, rolls, fries, onion rings, &c. We figured the meat cost more than the rest of it and in our own way we were beating the system and denting the profit of Rand's Round Up.)

Each set was an awakening; we'd assign each poem to blues and standards whose changes had gotten innate for me, or freeform. Count tempo down and, bam! move into it. Permutations of vocal and instrumental solos, duos, ensemble riffing. When the club closed we recorded a group of poems for an LP to be issued by Vaya Records.

In dawn's early blight Jim and I went to his place to drink and smoke weed. He was a WW2 vet who came back to a United States that was sleepwalking into an immensely reductive paradigm shift of stupefying abundance and regulation. Even rebellion became market managed. He was a founding member of the Hell's Angels, composed mostly of vets who had nothing left to gain, deracinated by the moral contradictions of War and amped up in the face of a sleepy postwar world and its fatuous denial of complicity in the collapse of Western Civ.

Little sleep that night and then off to Burbank to catch my PSA flight back to the Bay Area.

Net result: a few books sold at the club and a toecurling acetate sent to us weeks later. It wasn't the music or spirit of the voice but my dorky poetry.

8.

What came first: the beatnik or the image of the beatnik? Not a trick question. The word was coined, as our forebears remind us, by S.F. *Chronicle* columnist Herb Caen c. 1958, whose daily local chitchat column was the Bay Area version of Walter Winchell's Manhattan daily must-read. The moniker was a play on coldwar panic around the arms and space race, directly referring to the Soviet Union's 1957 satellite "sputnik" which means "fellow traveler of Earth." It was a panic play on rebellion and nonconformity, diminishment via mockery, like "yuppie." It also intended to dis suburban effluvia seeking kicks in North Beach, i.e., "slumming." Paradoxically, it minted a new identity one could grow into and out of at a moment's notice. A new and renewable archetype, a mask, a comicbook safe house called "beatnik."

9.

In media's magic-act of erasing difficulty, the beatnik became a hipster Mickey Mouse whose four white minstrel gloved fingers on each hand emanated immense cuddly safety, not danger. Maynard G. Krebs, highschool beatnik jazzhead whose mantra yelp "Work?" made clear his shiftlessness and de facto that of the beatnik or artist. Then the generic anonymous jazz-poet dressed in black turtleneck, beret, shades, pants, riffing to a beat bongo player's laidback paradiddles at Mother's waterfront dive in *Peter Gunn* or in *Mad Comics* or *The New Yorker*. The instantly camp flicks: as a young hipster & disdainful beatnik, movies like *The Man with the Golden Arm* and *The Subterraneans* were sublimely unauthentic, especially the M.G.M.ing of Kerouac's novella which premiered in San Francisco. Local poets, artists, beatniks, & other marginals & harmless colorful folk were given free passes to attend the opening. We sauntered into the red plush carpet of the Warfield Theater & laughed ourselves to near puke at the idiocy on the screen: a bent remix of Judy Garland/Mickey Rooney movies with Leslie Caron as Judy, Mickey played by George Peppard wearing the same dazed preppy Wildroot glaze as in *Breakfast at Tiffany's* (another fiction deprogrammed by Metro) pretending to be Jack Kerouac. The City Lights Bookstore set came off the same backlot street Gene Kelly danced & sang in the rain upon. Literal bends set in when Gerry Mulligan pretended to be a paper doll pastiche of Pierre Delattre, Grant Avenue's Bread & Wine Mission minister. The obligatory jazz club scene in mandatory smoke smogged haze as beat poet Roddy McDowall, a giggly graft of Corso and Ginsberg, incants irate yet inexplicable Them/Us (Squares v. Hip) verse. Everpresent cool dude bangs bacchantic on a pair o' bongos; another remote cat bends over his tenor sax, another burrows into the piano, forehead almost touching the keyboard. The poet and jazz trope also trooped into comicbooks, pop music, op-ed cartoons, in the same way hip-hop does today. But what was it and—was it? It was, it wasn't, just like the "Beat Generation" was and wasn't. As always the past is more "now" than it was then. . . .

On the other hand, poetry & jazz (whatever it is) hasn't gone away and is always more or less than it's imagined to be. If the 50s poets were vanguardists, all that's followed in its wake is worthy of regard: freeform radio, adverts, hip hop, spoken word, the mainstreaming of cowboy poetry, poetry slams, presidential townhall debates, wherever words with insinuating beats and musical MSG are agents of seduction and transformation. The edge of the word, its utopic anger and optimism, coexists with its evil twin in a cacophony of power and powerlessness, smeared and glossed by a massive unmeaning making industry; where the word wounded, it is now affirms, reassures; where history had the potential for insight it now is cataracted by hindsight and certainty. When it gets down to essentials, whatever was Beat—the gesture of reading poetry to jazz as an act of inconclusive solidarity—resonates in different currents and will continue to mutate despite the fact that nobody was or will be sure about what it was when it was and what it is when it is and what is left. . . .

# HENRY MILLER

HENRY MILLER (1891–1980), author of the autobiographical novels *Tropic of Cancer* (1934) and *Tropic of Capricorn* (1938), so sexually explicit that they weren't published in America until Grove Press brought them out in the early 1960s, felt a kinship with Jack Kerouac, whom Miller understood also empathized with social outcasts. In 1957 Miller's sketch "Big Sur and the Good Life" was published in "The San Francisco Scene" issue of *Evergreen Review,* along with Ginsberg's "Howl," Kerouac's "October in the Railroad Earth," Rexroth's "San Francisco Letter," and poems by Ferlinghetti, McClure, Snyder, Whalen, and others. The following year, Miller sent a letter to Pat Covici, senior editor at Viking, expressing his enthusiasm for Kerouac's *The Dharma Bums:*

> From the moment I began reading the book I was intoxicated. . . . No man can write with that delicious freedom and abandonment who has not practiced severe discipline. . . . Kerouac could and probably will exert tremendous influence upon our contemporary writers young and old. . . . We've had all kinds of bums heretofore but never a Dharma bum, like this Kerouac.

In 1959, from his home in Big Sur, California, Miller contributed a generous preface to Kerouac's next novel, *The Subterraneans.*

------

## *Preface to* The Subterraneans

Jack Kerouac has done something to our immaculate prose from which it may never recover. A passionate lover of language, he knows how to use it. Born virtuoso that he is, he takes pleasure in defying the laws and conventions of literary expression which cripple genuine, untrammeled communication between reader and writer. As he has so well said in "The Essentials of Spontaneous Prose"—"Satisfy yourself first, then reader cannot fail to receive telepathic shock and meaning-excitement by same laws operating in his own human mind." His integrity is such that he can give the semblance, at times, of running counter to his own principles. (*Cancer! Schmanser!* What's the difference, so long as you're healthy!) His learning, by no means superficial, he can bandy about as something of no consequence. Does it matter? Nothing matters. Everything is of equal importance or non-importance, from a truly creative standpoint.

Yet you can't say he's cool. He's hot, red hot. And if he's far out, he's also near and dear, a blood brother, an alter ego. He's there, everywhere, in the guise of Everyman. The observer and the observed. "A gentle, intelligent, suffering prose saint," Allen Ginsberg says of him.

We say that the poet, or genius, is always ahead of his time. True, but only because he's so thoroughly *of* his time. "Keep moving!" he urges. "We've had all this a thousand million times before." ("Advance always!" said Rimbaud.) But the stick-in-the-muds don't follow this kind of talk. (They haven't even caught up with Isidore Ducasse.) So what do they do? They pull him down off his perch, they starve him, they kick his teeth down his throat. Sometimes they are less merciful—they pretend he doesn't exist.

Everything Kerouac writes about—those weird, hauntingly ubiquitous characters whose names may be read backwards or upside down, those lovely, nostalgic, intimate-grandiose stereopticon views of America, those nightmarish, ventilated joy-rides in gondolas and hot rods—plus the language he uses (à la Gautier in reverse) to describe his "earthly-heavenly visions," surely even the readers of *Time* and *Life,* of the Digests and the Comics, cannot fail to discern the rapport between these hypergolic extravaganzas and such perennial blooms as the *Golden Ass,* the *Satyricon,* and *Pantagruel.*

The good poet, or in this case the "spontaneous Bop prosodist," is always alive to the idiomatic lingo of his time—the swing, the beat, the disjunctive metaphoric rhythm which comes so fast, so wild, so scrimmaged, so unbelievably albeit delectably mad, that when transmitted to paper no one recognizes it. None but the poets, that is. He "invented it," people will say. Insinuating that it was souped up. What they should say is: "He *got* it." He got it, he dug it, he put it down. ("You pick it up, Nazz!")

When someone asks, "Where does he get that stuff?" say: "From you!" Man, he lay awake all night listening with eyes and ears. A night of a thousand years. Heard it in the womb, heard it in the cradle, heard it in school, heard it on the floor of life's stock exchange where dreams are traded for gold. And *man*, he's sick of hearing it. He wants to move on. He wants to *blow*. But will you let him?

This is the age of miracles. The day of the killer-diller is over; the sex maniacs are out on a limb; the daring trapeze artists have broken their necks. Day of wonders, when our men of science, aided and abetted by the high priests of the Pentagon, give free instruction in the technique of mutual, but total, destruction. Progress, what! Make it into a readable novel, if you can. But don't beef about life-and-letters if you're a death-eater. Don't tell us about good "clean"—no fallouts!—literature. Let the poets speak. They may be "beat," but they're not riding the atom-powered Juggernaut. Believe me, there's nothing clean, nothing healthy, nothing promising about this age of wonders—except the telling. And the Kerouacs will probably have the last word.

---

# GILBERT MILLSTEIN

GILBERT MILLSTEIN published his review of Kerouac's *On the Road* in *The New York Times* on September 5, 1957. Joyce Johnson bought an early edition of the paper, which she and Kerouac read together under a streetlamp on upper Broadway. Johnson remembered that she "felt dizzy reading Millstein's first paragraph—like going up on a Ferris wheel too quickly and dangling out over space, laughing and gasping at the same time." She also recalled that after they returned to her apartment to go back to sleep, "Jack lay down obscure for the last time in his life. The ringing phone woke him the next morning and he was famous."

## *Review of* On the Road

"On the Road" is the second novel by Jack Kerouac, and its publication is a historic occasion in so far as the exposure of an authentic work of art is at any great moment in an age in which the attention is fragmented and the sensibilities are blunted by the superlatives of fashion (multiplied a millionfold by the speed and pound of communications).

This book requires exegesis and a detailing of background. It is possible that it will be condescended to by, or make uneasy, the neo-academicians and the "official" avant-garde critics, and that it will be dealt with superficially elsewhere as merely "absorbing" or "intriguing" or "picaresque" or any of a dozen convenient banalities, not excluding "off-beat." But the fact is that "On the Road" is the most beautifully executed, the clearest and the most important utterance yet made by the generation Kerouac himself named years ago as "beat," and whose principal avatar he is.

Just as, more than any other novel of the Twenties, "The Sun Also Rises" came to be regarded as the testament of the "Lost Generation," so it seems certain that "On the Road" will come to be known as that of the "Beat Generation." There is, otherwise, no similarity between the two; technically and philosophically, Hemingway and Kerouac are, at the very least, a depression and a world war apart.

### The "Beat" Bear Stigmata

Much has been made of the phenomenon that a good deal of the writing, the poetry and the painting of this generation (to say nothing of its deep interest in modern jazz) has emerged in the so-called "San Francisco Renaissance," which, while true, is irrelevant. It cannot be localized. (Many of the San Francisco group, a highly mobile lot in any case, are no longer resident in that benign city, or only intermittently.) The "Beat Generation" and its artists display readily recognizable stigmata.

Outwardly, these may be summed up as the frenzied pursuit of every possible sensory impression, an extreme exacerbation of the nerves, a constant outraging of the body. (One gets "kicks"; one "digs" everything, whether it be drink, drugs, sexual promiscuity, driving at high speeds or absorbing Zen Buddhism.)

Inwardly, these excesses are made to serve a spiritual purpose, the purpose of an affirmation still unfocused, still to be defined, unsystematic. It is markedly distinct from the protest of the "Lost Generation" or the political protest of the "Depression Generation."

The "Beat Generation" was born disillusioned; it takes for granted the imminence of war, the barrenness of politics and the hostility of the rest of society. It is not even impressed by (although it never pretends to scorn) material well-being (as distinguished from materialism). It does not know what refuge it is seeking, but it is seeking.

As John Aldridge has put it in his critical work, "After the Lost Generation," there were four choices open to the post-war writer: novelistic journalism or journalistic novel-writing, what little subject-matter that had not been fully exploited already (homosexuality, racial conflict), pure technique (for lack of something to say), or the course I feel Kerouac has taken—assertion "of the need for belief even though it is upon a background in which belief is impossible and in which the symbols are lacking for a genuine affirmation in genuine terms."

Five years ago, in the Sunday magazine of this newspaper, a young novelist, Clellon Holmes, the author of a book called "Go," and a friend of Kerouac's, attempted to define the generation Kerouac had labeled. In doing so, he carried Aldridge's premise further. He said, among many other pertinent things, that to his kind "the absence of personal and social values . . . is not a revelation shaking the ground beneath them, but a problem demanding a day-to-day solution. *How* to live seems to them much more crucial than *why*." He added that the difference between the "Lost" and the "Beat" may lie in the latter's "will to believe even in the face of an inability to do so in conventional terms": that they exhibited "on every side and in a bewildering number of facets a perfect craving to believe."

## Those Who Burn, Burn, Burn

That is the meaning of "On the Road." What does its narrator, Sal Paradise, say? " . . . The only people for me are the mad ones, the ones who are mad to live, mad to talk, mad to be saved, desirous of everything at the same time, the ones who never yawn or say a commonplace thing, but burn, burn, burn like fabulous yellow roman candles. . . ."

And what does Dean Moriarty, Sal's American hero-saint say? "And of course no one can tell us that there is no God. We've passed through all forms. . . . Everything is fine, God exists, we know time. . . . God exists without qualms. As we roll along this way I am positive beyond doubt that everything will be taken care of for us—that even you, as you drive, fearful of the wheel . . . the thing will go along of itself and you won't go off the road and I can sleep."

This search for affirmation takes Sal on the road to Denver and San Francisco, Los Angeles and Texas and Mexico; sometimes with Dean, sometimes without; sometimes in the company of other beat individuals whose tics vary, but whose search is very much the same (not infrequently ending in death or derangement: the search for belief is very likely the most violent known to man).

There are sections of "On the Road" in which the writing is of a beauty almost breathtaking. There is a description of a cross-country automobile ride fully the equal, for example, of the train ride told by Thomas Wolfe in "Of Time and the River." There are the details of a trip to Mexico (and an interlude in a Mexican bordello) that are, by turns, awesome, tender and funny. And, finally, there is some writing on jazz that has never been equaled in American fiction, either for insight, style or technical virtuosity. "On the Road" is a major novel.

# CZESLAW MILOSZ

CZESLAW MILOSZ, Polish poet, novelist, and essayist who has spent his life in exile since 1939, now lives in California. In 1936, his second book of poems established his reputation; in 1980, he won the Nobel Prize for literature. "To Allen Ginsberg" is from Milosz's twenty-third book published in English, *Facing the River* (1995), translated by the author and Robert Haas.

---

## *To Allen Ginsberg*

Allen, you good man, great poet of the murderous century, who persisting in folly attained wisdom.

I confess to you, my life was not as I would have liked it to be.

And now, when it has passed, is lying like a discarded tire by the road.

It was no different from the life of millions against which you rebelled in the name of poetry and of an omnipresent God.

It was submitted to customs in full awareness that they are absurd, to the necessity of getting up in the morning and going to work.

With unfulfilled desires, even with the unfulfilled desire to scream and beat one's head against the wall, repeating to myself the command "It is forbidden."

It is forbidden to indulge yourself, to allow yourself idleness, it is forbidden to think of your past, to look for the help of a psychiatrist or a clinic.

Forbidden from a sense of duty but also because of the fear of unleashing forces that would reveal one to be a clown.

And I lived in the America of Moloch, short-haired, clean-shaven, tying neckties and drinking bourbon before the TV set every evening.

Diabolic dwarfs of temptations somersaulted in me, I was aware of their presence and I shrugged: It will pass together with life.

Dread was lurking close, I had to pretend it was never there and that I was united with others in a blessed normalcy.

Such schooling in vision is also, after all, possible, without drugs, without the cut-off ear of Van Gogh, without the brotherhood of the best minds behind the bars of psychiatric wards.

I was an instrument, I listened, snatching voices out of a babbling chorus, translating them into sentences with commas and periods.

As if the poverty of my fate were necessary so that the flora of my memory could luxuriate, a home for the breath and for the presence of bygone people.

I envy your courage of absolute defiance, words inflamed, the fierce maledictions of a prophet.

The demure smiles of ironists are preserved in the museums, not as everlasting art, just as a memento of unbelief.

While your blasphemous howl still resounds in a neon desert where the human tribe wanders, sentenced to unreality.

Walt Whitman listens and says, "Yes, that's the way to talk, in order to conduct men and women to where everything is fulfillment. Where they would live in a transubstantiated moment."

And your journalistic clichés, your beard and beads and your dress of a rebel of another epoch are forgiven.

As we do not look for what is perfect, we look for what remains of incessant striving.

# JOYCE CAROL OATES

JOYCE CAROL OATES, prolific storyteller and essayist, reviewed *The Selected Letters of Jack Kerouac 1940–1956* and *The Kerouac Reader* for *The New Yorker* on March 27, 1995, two weeks after Kerouac's (posthumous) seventy-third birthday. Briefly feeling him a kindred spirit in this review, Oates marveled at the thought of the books that Kerouac, a speed typist, might have written if, like her, he had lived long enough to have access to a word processor.

---

## *Down the Road*

Those whom the gods wish to destroy, they first make famous. Much as the young, brash, prodigiously gifted George Gordon, Lord Byron, woke one morning in London, in March, 1812, to find himself famous and the trajectory of his brilliant and fated life set before him, so, too, did the brash, prodigiously gifted, not so young (thirty-five-year-old) Jack Kerouac wake one morning in New York, in September, 1957, to find himself a literary celebrity and the course of his less brilliant but equally fated life set before him. From such rocket launchings there can be no return to safe obscurity.

The occasion of Byron's meteoric ascent was the publication of "Childe Harold's Pilgrimage," Cantos I and II; the occasion of Kerouac's was the publication of his second novel, "On the Road," which was blessed with the unlikely imprimatur of the *Times* in the kind of fluke review that can determine not just an artist's career but his or her subsequent life. Dismissed by other reviewers as subliterary trash, "On the Road" was declared by the *Times'* reviewer not just "an authentic work of art" but "a historic occasion" and yet more: "The most beautifully executed, the clearest and the most important utterance yet made by the generation Kerouac himself named years ago as 'beat.'" Wild! Zen lunacy! Few except literary insiders could appreciate the delicious irony of this review, itself something of a historic occasion: it was written by a young man named Gilbert Millstein, who was filling in for a vacationing Orville Prescott, the famously conservative regular reviewer who would surely have loathed "On the Road" if he'd condescended to read it at all.

Both "Childe Harold" and "On the Road" are, of course, pilgrimages: the former an account, in Spenserian stanzas, of a highly self-absorbed and romantic-minded young man's travels in such exotic places as Portugal, Spain, Albania, and Asia Minor; the latter an account, in rhapsodic, head-on, first-person prose, of a young man's travels across the United States hitchhiking and in the manic company of the charismatic Dean Moriarty (in life, the infamous Neal Cassady). Byron's Childe Harold is a transparency through which the twenty-four-year-old poet speaks his mind and his heart with self-dramatizing bravura; Kerouac's Sal Paradise is a twenty-five-year-old aspiring writer identical in most respects to Kerouac—word-obsessed, yearning, and wild to perform "our one and noble function of the time, move." Both pilgrims are force fields of romance and youthful ardor, emblematic of their very different, yet kindred, eras; Kerouac's Sal Paradise is the more rawly adolescent, if not juvenile, yet is possessed of an irresistible, undauntable, Whitmanesque enthusiasm, which fairly leaps off the page:

> What is that feeling when you're driving away from people and they recede on the plain till you see their specks dispersing?—it's the too-huge world vaulting us, and it's good-by. But we lean forward to the next crazy venture beneath the skies.

Jack Kerouac, self-designated "madman bum and angel," resembles Byron's friend and fellow-wanderer Percy Shelley as much as he does Byron, in the way he combines narcissism and idealism, passionately fuelled by religious-mystical yearning: not the sublime Neoplatonism of the young expatriated English Romantic but the American-style, San Francisco–based Buddhism of the fifties and sixties—although Kerouac, a lapsed Roman Catholic of French-Canadian background, would retain theistic-Christian imagery throughout his life. In an alcoholic stupor recorded in his 1962 novel "Big Sur," his alter ego Jack Duluoz hallucinates a cross.

Of course, there are differences between Byron and the merely Byronic novelist. Byron, like Shelley, would develop brilliantly as a poet, following his precocious debut; Kerouac's prose seems to have scarcely developed at all. The peak of lyricism he reached in "On the Road" would be regained only sporadically throughout the rest of his career. But all of them shared a Rimbaudian belief in deranging their senses in the service of their art. Byron and Shelley were geniuses of the English language, but hardly geniuses of living. Byron died, utterly worn out, at thirty-six; Shelley, in a sailing accident so reckless as to seem near-suicidal, at twenty-nine. Jack Kerouac, if no genius, was one of those prodigies (not unlike Jack London) whose talents come to seem very much a matter of imaginative vigor, physical recklessness, the energies of youth, and adolescent disdain for self-censure and the wise, boring constraints of their elders. (Such iconic masculine figures exert an irresistible appeal. As the flamboyant filmmaker Ken Russell took on, with controversial results, Byron and Shelley, so now Francis Ford Coppola will take on Kerouac and Cassady in a film version of "On the Road." When Coppola recently called an open audition in New York, more than three thousand hopefuls turned up.)

In a flood of prose—millions of hyperthermic words!—Kerouac would squander his writerly gifts as he would, in sexual liaisons as fleeting as those of fruit flies, squander his seed. He believed in neither revision nor remorse. From the evidence of his "true-life novels" and his letters, it seems that Kerouac could not have written with such a zestful lack of inhibition if not for regular jolts of alcohol and drugs. In the 1968 novel "Vanity of Duluoz" the narrator speaks ruefully of "the drugs, the morphine, the marijuana, the horrible Benzedrine we used to take . . . by breaking open Benzedrine inhalers and removing the soaked paper and rolling it into poisonous little balls that made you sweat and suffer. . . . My hair had begun to recede from the sides. I wandered in Benzedrine depression hallucinations." As early as the mid-nineteen-forties, Kerouac was hospitalized for thrombophlebitis from Benzedrine abuse.

Whatever the costs of its composition, "On the Road" came to be enshrined in Beat legend as an ecstatic experience, the first triumph of what Kerouac called "spontaneous prose," the "new literature" that would render all old literature obsolete. Written on one continuous paragraph on a hundred-and fifty-foot roll of teletype paper [sic] that ran through Kerouac's typewriter, it was completed in a manic energy surge of twenty days. This famous bout of composition was quickly

bested by the dervish-author, who went on to write "The Subterraneans" in three uninterrupted days, and the stage adaptation of "On
the Road" in a single night. (Just think if Kerouac had had a word
processor.) Kerouac's football-player stamina—he attended Columbia
on a sports scholarship—kept him going, but in later years he would
lose as many as ten pounds in a single writing session and emerge de-
pleted, depressed, even suicidal. Violent mood swings increasingly
characterized his life and his art as he grew, rapidly, older.

Two valuable new collections, "The Portable Jack Kerouac" (Viking;
$27.95) and "Jack Kerouac: Selected Letters 1940–1956" (Viking;
$29.95), both edited by Ann Charters, suggest that our response to
Kerouac's writing is largely our response to Kerouac's emotions—and
to the characters, the "dharma bums" and others, who aroused his
emotions to fever pitch. The great (although, it appears, sexually un-
consummated) love of Kerouac's life was the handsome son of a
Denver skid-row derelict, Neal Cassady. By the time Cassady was
twenty-one, according to Dennis McNally's 1979 biography of Kerouac, "Desolate Angel," he had stolen five hundred cars and spent fifteen months in jail. He was an aspiring writer, like Kerouac, yet was
even more expansive in his grandiloquence. He was a manic woman-
izer, a tireless carouser. And what physical prowess! He could run a
hundred yards in less than ten seconds and masturbate five or six
times a day, every day. Cassady met Kerouac in 1947 and took him on
the road in 1949, in a brand-new Hudson, driving from New York City
to New Orleans and from there to San Francisco. His fictional alter
ego, Dean Moriarty, is a wild man you would not wish to encounter
rushing toward you on a two-lane country highway. Sometimes Moriarty drives naked, insisting that his passengers disrobe, too. He seems
always to be drunk or stoned, or both; isn't above casual theft (from
poor folk); and is given to yelling, "Oh man, what kicks!" As Sal Paradise explains it:

> They danced down the streets like dingle-dodies, and I
> shambled after as I've been doing all my life after people who
> interest me, because the only people for me are the mad ones,
> the ones who are mad to live . . . the ones who never yawn or
> say a commonplace thing, but burn, burn, burn like fabulous
> yellow roman candles exploding like spiders across the stars

and in the middle you see the blue centerlight pop and everybody goes "Awww!"

Virtually all of Kerouac's novels after "On the Road," notably "The
Subterraneans" (1958), "The Dharma Burns" (1958), "Visions of Cody"
(1959), "Doctor Sax" (1959), "Big Sur" (1962), "Desolation Angels"
(1965), and "Vanity of Duluoz" (1968), are, like the metafictional experiments of the sixties and seventies, as much about the process of creation as about their ostensible subjects. In each novel, a Kerouac alter
ego travels with delirious Beat friends and gorgeous women through a
vertiginous rush of vivid settings, from Seattle to Tangier, recalling
events in the "sheer joy of confession," as Kerouac named it in his essay "The Origins of Joy in Poetry."

Most of the excerpts from novels and prose pieces in "The
Portable Jack Kerouac" contain inspired passages—lyric language em-
ulating jazz riffs—set beside passages that are not so inspired. Kerouac
is capable of scintillating speech and also of speech as undifferentiated as the sound of a gravel truck unloading. This is the inevitable
result of the author's "kind of new-old Zen Lunacy poetry, writing
whatever comes into your head as it comes." (The story "Good
Blonde," originally published in *Playboy*, and the essay "On the Road
to Florida," about a trip taken in the company of his photographer-
friend Robert Frank, are exceptions to Kerouac's usual unstoppered
flow, being conventionally structured, and they are, in fact, extremely
readable.) But to say that Kerouac's work is uneven is simply to say
that it is Kerouac's work.

In "The Dharma Bums," there is a wonderfully narrated mountain-
climbing episode with the California poet Japhy Ryder (a.k.a. Gary
Snyder), and a funny pricking of Beat-Buddhist pretensions:

> I went over to an old cook [in San Francisco's Chinatown]
> and asked him, "Why did Bodhidharma come from the West?"
> . . . "I don't care," said the old cook, with lidded eyes, and I
> told Japhy and he said, "Perfect answer, absolutely perfect.
> Now you know what I mean by Zen."

Kerouac is capable of humor both lunatic and ironic, "goofy" (a favorite Beat word) and chilling. In his story "The Mexican Girl" his boy
romantic's eye is as shrewed as Nathanael West's:

Sunset and Vine!—what a corner! Now there's a corner! Great families off jalopies from the hinterlands stood around the sidewalk gaping for sight of some movie star and the movie star never showed up. When a limousine passed they rushed eagerly to the curb and ducked to look: some character in dark glasses sat inside with a bejeweled blond. "Don Ameche! Don Ameche!" "No George Murphy! George Murphy!" They milled around looking at one another. Luscious little girls by the thousands rushed around with drive-in trays; they'd come to Hollywood to be movie stars and instead got all involved in everybody's garbage. . . . Handsome queer boys who had come to Hollywood to be cowboys walked around wetting their eyebrows with hincty fingertip. Those beautiful little gone girls cut by in slacks in a continuous unbelievable stream; you thought you were in heaven but it was only Purgatory and everybody was about to be pardoned, paroled, powdered and put down; the girls came to be starlets; they up-ended in drive-ins with pouts and goosepimples on their bare legs. . . . Hollywood Boulevard was a great screaming frenzy of cars; there were minor accidents at least once a minute; everybody was rushing off toward the farthest palm . . . and beyond that was desert and nothingness.

Set pieces of sustained drama include sharply recalled episodes of boyhood angst in the "gloomy bookmovie" of "Doctor Sax," and of an opium overdose—in the company of the brilliantly sinister junkie Bull Hubbard (a.k.a. William Burroughs)—in "Desolation Angels." In "Big Sur" there is a blackly comic nightmare interlude with a distraught woman named Billie who threatens to kill herself and her young son if the alcohol-dazed Jack Duluoz refuses to love her, and the terrifying lucidity of a true Zen epiphany in a retreat in Raton Canyon, as Duluoz tries to meditate, to regain some measure of his lost, pre-"King of the Beatniks" innocence:

I remember seeing a mess of leaves suddenly go skittering in the wind and into the creek, then floating rapidly down the creek towards the sea, making me feel a nameless horror even then of "Oh my God, we're all being swept away to sea no matter what we know or say or do"—And a bird who was on a crooked branch is suddenly gone without my even hearing him.

"Big Sur" even features a prescient evocation of an aging literary hero:

> "No!" I almost yell, "I mean I'm so exhausted I don't wanta
> do anything or see anybody"—(already feeling awful guilt
> about Henry Miller anyway, we've made an appointment with
> him about a week ago and instead of showing up . . . at seven
> we're all drunk at ten calling long distance and poor Henry
> just said "Well I'm sorry I don't get to meet you Jack but I'm
> an old man and at ten o'clock it's time for me to go to bed.")

Ann Charters has assembled a highly readable "Portable Jack Kerouac" and an intermittently engaging "Selected Letters." The anthology would have been stronger if she had included the whole of "On
the Road" and omitted Kerouac's poems—his "pomes," as he often referred to them. As it is, some of "On the Road"'s strongest passages,
among them the wry, memorable ending, are missing. Still, it is an attractive gathering. Charters, who has written a biography of Kerouac,
is too loyal to him, or too diplomatic, to acknowledge the obvious: that
such a volume allows for judicious editing of the kind that, in life, Kerouac so disdained.

Unfortunately, the "Selected Letters" ends in 1956, shortly before
the publication of "On the Road," and if it is of lesser interest this is
primarily because Kerouac's life so intimately fed his fiction that to
have read the fiction is to already know the life in a more urgent, dis-
tilled form. Also, the letters—for all their rhapsodizing on life, writing,
and Buddhism—do not demonstrate a striking intelligence, still less a
particularly original imagination. Yet they do throw off sparks of raw,
coruscating emotion. There are letters to family members, to his first
wife, Edith Parker, and to editors and literary acquaintances (among
them Alfred Kazin, whom Kerouac seems to have besieged with manuscripts and requests) as well as to the real-life models of his fictional
characters. Most of the letters, though, are to that same small gathering of people upon whom Kerouac was emotionally fixed.

The most warmly effusive (and longest) letters are, of course, to
Neal Cassady, to whom Kerouac poured out his heart as if writing to a
mirror self, rehearsing the nostalgic novels "Doctor Sax," "Visions of
Gerard," "Maggie Cassidy." Kerouac even volunteered to type Cassady's voluminous "scrawls," out of a passion for pure writing: "It's the
work itself I want, want to see the ordered sentences typed up neat on

perfect pages under a soft lamp, wild prose describing the world as it raced through my brain and cock once."

The most interesting letters are those to Allen Ginsberg, whom Kerouac admired as a poet and an intellectual yet could not resist chiding. He could swerve, in the course of a seemingly amicable note, into sudden hostility:

> September 6, 1945
>
> The quality of my friendship for you is far purer than yours could ever be for me. . . . There's nothing that I hate more than the condescension you begin to show whenever I allow my affectionate instincts full play with regard to you; that's why I always react angrily against you. It gives me the feeling that I'm wasting a perfectly good store of friendship on a little self-aggrandizing weasel.

Or into inept superiority:

> July 14, 1955
>
> Don't study Greek and Prosody at Berkeley get away from this Pound kick. Pound is an Ignorant Poet—how many times do I have to tell you that it's a Buddhist, AN EASTERN FUTURE ahead—Greeks and Poem styles are child's play. . . . The Greeks are a bunch of Ignorant Cocksuckers as any fool can plainly see. . . . I like Dickinson and Blake. . . . But even they are Ignorant because they simply don't know that everything is empty IN AND OUT IN TEN THOUSAND INFINITE DIRECTIONS OF THE UNDISTURRED LIGHT . . . please, Allen, wake up . . .
>
> All's I need is a drink. . . . I drink eternally. Drink always and ye shall never die. Keep running after a dog, and he will never bite you; drink always before the thirst, and it will never come upon you.

For an artist whose work is gaining strength and inward authority, failure can be nurturing; success, particularly premature success, can be devastating. Kerouac, long accustomed to the vicissitudes and camaraderie of a marginal literary existence, began to crack up almost immediately after the publication of "On the Road." His canonization as spokesman for a new Beat Generation assured him an ineradicable identity, which would follow him to the grave, and beyond. His drinking escalated. His friendships foundered. His affairs became ever more desperate and short-lived. (Impotence, a result of chronic alcoholism, did not help.) His relationships with editors, always uneasy, seem to have worsened under the strain of his egomania, for of what service was even a brilliant editor like Malcolm Cowley to a compulsive writer who believed that "as it comes, so it flows, and that's literature at its purest"? Celebrated by the media in one season, Kerouac was virulently, viciously, jeeringly, and indefatigably assailed by it in seasons to follow. Yet he had his fans—stoned acolytes of "On the Road"—who followed him everywhere they could, and whom he feared and despised. Our vision of Kerouac, provided by the author himself, is of a man aging before our eyes, as in a horror film. By the time of his notorious *Paris Review* interview, in 1967, an embittered and incoherent Kerouac had revised (that is, repudiated) his personal emotional history:

> Oh the beat generation was just a phrase I used in the 1951 written manuscript of *On the Road* to describe guys like Moriarty who run around the country in cars looking for odd jobs, girlfriends, kicks. It was thereafter picked up by West Coast leftist groups and turned into a meaning like "beat mutiny" and "beat insurrection" and all that nonsense; they just wanted some youth movement to grab onto for their own political and social purposes. I had nothing to do with any of that. I was a football player, a scholarship college student, a merchant seaman.

Politically reactionary, anti-intellectual, distrustful of a new "Pepsi generation of twisting illiterates," and even of anti–Vietnam War agitation, Kerouac retreated to cramped quarters in St. Petersburg, Florida, with his mother and his third wife, Stella. His life was a succession of late-night drunken telephone calls, days of television, fits of working on a manuscript tentatively titled "The Beat Spotlight." In February, 1968, he learned that Neal Cassady was dead, at forty-one, of a lethal combination of tequila and Seconal. Kerouac survived him only briefly, dying in October, 1969, at forty-seven. He was drinking, writing in his notebook, eating from a can of tuna fish, and watching "The Galloping Gourmet" when he was stricken.

The evidence of Jack Kerouac's œuvre is that, for all its flaws, it, and he, deserved to be treated better by the censorious "literary" critics of his time. Kerouac was dismissed as a "beatnik" by many commentators who had not troubled to read his work, still less to read it with sympathy. "The Portable Jack Kerouac" may well be seminal in a re-evaluation of Kerouac's position in the literature of mid-twentieth-century America—a richly varied affluence of "high" and "low" art that permanently changed the course of our fiction. The era is distinguished by tales of mordant flight from domesticity, bounded by Paul Bowles' cult novel "The Sheltering Sky" (1949) and John Updike's "Rabbit, Run" (1960). Between them stand such disparate works as J. D. Salinger's "The Catcher in the Rye," Vladimir Nabokov's "Lolita," Allen Ginsberg's "Howl," Norman Mailer's "The White Negro," and William S. Burroughs' "Naked Lunch." "On the Road" is a classic of the era to set beside these.

---

# PAUL O'NEIL

PAUL O'NEIL was a staff writer for *Life* magazine when he wrote his article on the Beats, "The Only Rebellion Around." It appeared in the issue of November 30, 1959, introduced by the caption "The Beats mount the only rebellion around—but they shabbily bungle the job in arguing, sulking, and bad poetry." O'Neil's article shared the spotlight with a movie review of *On the Beach*—"Dire drama on the death of the world: *On the Beach* imagines man's last hours before atomic extinction"—and a picture story on "Dress-up time: rich gowns at luxurious parties bring in more-elegant-than-ever U.S. social season—in color."

## *The Only Rebellion Around*

If the U.S. today is really the biggest, sweetest and most succulent casaba ever produced by the melon patch of civilization, it would seem only reasonable to find its surface profaned—as indeed it is—by a few fruit flies. But reason would also anticipate contented fruit flies, blissful fruit flies—fruit flies raised by happy environment to the highest stages of fruit fly development. Such is not the case. The grandest casaba of all, in disconcerting fact, has incubated some of the hairiest, scrawniest and most discontented specimens of all time: the improbable rebels of the Beat Generation, who not only refuse to sample the seeping juices of American plenty and American social advance but scrape their feelers in discordant scorn of any and all who do.

This penetrating threnody has been going on ever since the Korean War, but it is astonishing how seldom the noise has been understood. The wide public belief that the Beats are simply dirty people in sandals is only a small if repellent part of the truth. Any attempt to list the collective attitudes of Beatdom, it must be admitted, would be foolhardy in the extreme. Most of its members are against collectiveness of any description, a great many of them even refuse to admit there is any such thing as a Beat Generation, and most of them spend hours differing vehemently with their own kind. Individual Beats, however, in the course of what might be described as the Six Year War Against the Squares, have raised their voices against virtually every aspect of current American society: Mom, Dad, Politics, Marriage, the Savings Bank, Organized Religion, Literary Elegance, Law, the Ivy League Suit and Higher Education, to say nothing of the Automatic Dishwasher, the Cellophane-wrapped Soda Cracker, the Split-Level House and the clean, or peace-provoking, H-bomb.

Beat philosophy seems calculated to offend the whole population, civil, military and ecclesiastic—particularly and ironically those radicals of only yesterday who demanded a better world for the ill-fed, ill-clothed and ill-housed of the Great Depression and who still breathe heavily from proclaiming man's right to work and organize. Hard-core Beats want freedom to disorganize and thus to ensure full flowering of their remarkable individualities. They are against work and they are often ill-fed, ill-clothed and ill-housed by preference. The Negro, it is true, is a hero to the Beat (as are the junkie and the jazz musician), and he is embraced with a fervor which San Francisco's anarchist poet Kenneth Rexroth sardonically defines as "crow-jimism." But it seems doubtful that antisegregationists or many Negroes could take comfort in this fact. The things the Beat treasures and envies in the Negro are the irresponsibility, cheerful promiscuity and subterranean defiance which were once enforced in him during his years of bondage. A middle-class Negro would be hopelessly square. Novelist Norman Mailer, a devoted follower of hipsterism, calls the Beat movement the cult of the White Negro and glibly suggests that its members seek the "constant humility" of Negro life in order to emulate its "primitive . . . joy, lust, and languor. . . ." But the Beat Generation can be much more accurately described as a cult of the Pariah. It yearns for the roach-guarded mores of the skid road, the flophouse, the hobo jungle and the slum, primarily to escape regimentation. It shares these with Negroes, when it does, only by coincidence.

## Squares Are Tragic Saps

Unlike England's Angry Young Men who know what they want of society and bay for it with vehemence, the Beat finds society too hideous to contemplate and so withdraws from it. He does not go quietly, however, nor so far that his voice is inaudible, and his route of retreat is littered with old beer cans and marijuana butts. The industrious square, he cries, is a tragic sap who spends all the juices and energies of life in stultifying submission to the "rat race" and does so, furthermore, with no more reward than sexual enslavement by a matriarchy of stern and grasping wives and the certainty of atomic death for his children. Thus, say the Beats, the only way man can call his soul his own is by becoming an outcast.

Little of this is as remarkable as the Beats like to think. Bohemianism is not new to big American cities, and the whiskery bum was a familiar U.S. figure long before the advent of the western railroad. The recluse and the neurotic artist are as old as time, and most of the Beats' more outrageous attitudes were trumpeted long ago by nihilists, Dadaists and a thousand and one convocations of those crackpots and screwballs who have bloomed so luxuriantly down through the American years. There is, however, one enormous difference. While most of the forerunners of Beatdom were ignored by the general populace, the Beat Generation itself has attracted wide public attention and is exerting astonishing influence.

It is seldom out of the news for long, and there are few Americans today to whom the word Beat or the derisive term, Beatnik, does not conjure up some sort of image—usually a hot-eyed fellow in beard and sandals, or a "chick" with scraggly hair, long black stockings, heavy eye make-up and an expression which could indicate either hauteur or uneasy digestion. "Beat talk," a narrow and repetitive argot mostly stolen from jazz musicians, narcotic addicts and prostitutes, is rapidly becoming a part of American idiom. It relies heavily on such words as "cat," "dig," "bug" and "cool," substitutes "Spade" for Negro, "head" for narcotic user, and utilizes the word "like" as a means of beginning almost any sentence.

A Beat-inspired fad for public recitation of verse has not only caught on in big cities and college towns but has given the very word poetry a new and abrasive connotation. A calculated vulgarity is part of the Beat act, and a good many of these performances are conducted in an atmosphere not unlike that which attended the bare-knuckle prize-fights of the last century. Awareness of the Beat message is almost a social necessity today, and the name-dropper who cannot mention Beat Novelist Jack Kerouac (*On the Road, The Dharma Bums*), Allen Ginsberg (the Shelley of the Beat poets whose *Howl and Other Poems* has sold 33,000 copies) or Lawrence Lipton (author of last summer's best-seller *The Holy Barbarians*) is no name-dropper at all.

Armies of Americans experience a sense of tongue-clucking outrage at the antics of Beatdom's more strident practitioners, but most of them also experience a morbid curiosity about them. All sorts of entrepreneurs have rushed in to capitalize on this fact. The cellar night-clubs, espresso shops and coffeehouses which have lately sprung up are a direct result of public interest in the Beat Generation. Although they are patronized mostly by young hounds of the Volkswagen and Tweeter-Woofer cliques, they are popularly believed to be the sort of dens in which Beatniks hang out. In some cases their proprietors keep a tame or house Beat on the premises to shout crude verse at the customers. A radio soap opera, *Helen Trent,* now includes a Beat character, and a Beatnik has been drawn into the comic strip *Popeye.* M-G-M's motion picture *The Beat Generation* is dedicated to the proposition that Beats are terrible fellows with women, and the cover blurb of the paperback *Beatnik Party* states invitingly that they are "crazed with strange desires" and victims of "sinful passions."

The pervasive rag, tag, and bobtail of humanity which has set off all this uproar is a confusingly diffuse phenomenon, but it can be roughly divided into three main groups. The bulk of it is comprised of those mobs of "sick little bums" who emerge in any generation—the shabby and bearded men, the occasional pallid and sullen girls—who startle the tourists in San Francisco's North Beach section, inhabit the dreary "pads" of Venice West in Log Angeles, and lounge in the doorways and cheap cafeterias of New York's Greenwich Village. People very like them distributed pamphlets for the Communists in the 1930s, or muttered of anarchism and cadged drinks in the speakeasies of the 1920s, and then as now thirsted cunningly for the off-beat cause which could provide them with some sense of martyrdom and superiority. They are talkers, loafers, passive little con men, lonely eccentrics, mom-haters, cop-haters, exhibitionists with abused smiles and second mortgages on a bongo drum—writers who cannot write, painters who cannot paint, dancers with unfortunate malfunction of the fetlocks. Around this bohemian cadre wanders a second group—an increasing corps of amateur or weekend Beats who have jobs and live the comfortable square life but who seek the "cool" state of mind, spread the Beat message and costume themselves in old clothes to ape the genuinely unwashed on Saturday nights.

Both these groups, however, are only reflections of the most curious men of influence the 20th Century has yet produced: the Beat poets. The poets, almost to a man, are individualistic and antisocial to the point of neuroticism. They are dissidents so enthralled with their own egos and so intent on bitter personal complaint that they would be incapable of organizing juvenile delinquents in a reform school. But the Beat Generation is their baby for all that, and the country's current Beat-consciousness is their doing. This is not to say that the bums, hostile little females and part-time bohemians of the Beat Generation would not have been bums, hostile little females and part-time bohemians anyhow. But without the slightest missionary intent the poets have provided them with a name, the fuel of self-justification and attitudes guaranteed to "bug the squares."

The chief architects of the Beat Generation are Poet-Novelist Jack Kerouac and Poet Allen Ginsberg, the only valid guide-posts to be used in determining just when it all began. In a large sense Beatdom is a product of postwar disillusionment and restlessness. One Beat poet maintains that the real beginnings occurred as early as 1949 when a good many of today's Beat activators and heroes were living in gritty desolation on the fringes of Greenwich Village and sneering at New

York's leftover bohemianism. But since this poet is a narcotic addict who also recalls with vast nostalgia that 1949 was a year when the price of heroin fell from $10 to 30¢ a capsule in New York "and like you could buy it at the corner grocery store," this view must be discounted as sentimentality. Beatdom's year of emergence must be set at 1953. This was the twelvemonth when Ginsberg and a good many other bohemians followed Kerouac (who had begun his western visitations in 1949) to San Francisco, decided this was the place, and began scratching away at works which set much of the tone of the Beat world and steered American bohemianism toward the West.

Kerouac is a husky, dark-haired fellow of French-Canadian ancestry who might be described as the only *avant-garde* writer ever hatched by the athletic department at Columbia University. Impressed by his prowess as a high school star in Lowell, Mass., Columbia football scouts brought him to New York to play at Baker Field—but also brought him within range of big-city bohemianism. Kerouac began reading Thomas Wolfe, grew "black, broody and poetic," tired of his labors as a subsidized halfback and in 1941, his sophomore year, abruptly walked out on the team and higher education. In the years afterward he worked variously as a sportswriter, a gas station attendant, a merchant mariner and a railroad brakeman and bummed around the country with other garrulous wanderers. One of these companions, Neal Cassady, became Dean Moriarty, the hero of Kerouac's second published work, *On the Road,* and is consequently regarded as a Beat saint. (Cassady, known to his more jocular intimates as the "Johnny Appleseed of the Marijuana Racket," is currently doing five years in San Quentin for selling same.)

Kerouac's contributions to Beatdom are priceless. In *On the Road* he celebrated the Beat tradition of bumming across the country and the delights of drinking with cheap Mexican tarts, and he is widely heralded for coining the phrase "the Beat Generation." He denies publicly that he has ever rewritten a line (anyone who has sampled the goulash-like texture of his prose would be inclined to believe him implicitly) and has thus contributed heavily to one of the Beat Generation's guiding misapprehensions: that anything which pops into the Beat mind is worth putting down on paper. Kerouac has also been a leader in the use of uninhibited or "natural" public behavior. One of his finest hours occurred one night last fall when he took part, with other Beat poets, in a "reading" at Manhattan's Hunter College. The audience, bored and restive after a half hour of Kerouac reciting Kerouac, called on him to spare them further suffering, and he gave vent to his feelings by lurching noisily back and forth across the stage during the rest of the program, at one point trying on another speaker's hat and later attempting to wrest back the microphone.

Although Allen Ginsberg has been less publicized, his contributions to Beatdom are probably more important than Kerouac's. Ginsberg, a slight, dark, bespectacled and harmless-looking fellow of 33, grew up in Paterson, N.J. Ginsberg's mother was sent to a public insane asylum when he was very young and spent her declining years there (Ginsberg himself spent eight months in a mental hospital in 1949), and this experience seems to have induced in him a wildly articulate and unreasoning sense of terror and protest, which, combined with a shameless exhibitionism, has dominated his life. Ginsberg, like Kerouac, attended Columbia University. He was suspended for writing an obscene and derogatory three-word phrase about Jews on a clouded classroom window with his forefinger. This act confounded as well as mortified university officials ("But he's a Jew himself!" cried one professor) and has caused thousands of man hours of excited Beat conversation ever since.

No Beat work has so startled the public or so influenced the Beat mind as Ginsberg's long poem, "Howl," an expression of wild personal dissatisfaction with the world which was written in 1955 while he was encamped in a furnished room in San Francisco. "Howl" begins:

"I saw the best minds of my generation destroyed by madness, starving hysterical naked,/dragging themselves through the negro streets at dawn looking for an angry fix . . ." and goes on to discuss "angelheaded hipsters . . . who were expelled from the academies for crazy & publishing obscene odes on the windows of the skull. . . ." "Howl," as it gathers steam and momentum, reflects Ginsberg's public and repeated boasts that he is a homosexual, and his habit of implying that he is a heroin addict (he is not). It also makes free with perverse allusion in a fashion calculated to make the squares run for the cops. Both its literary style and the fact that it was pronounced fit for human consumption in 1957 after an obscenity trial in San Francisco seem to have made a profound impression on lesser Beats.

Ginsberg's influence, however, extends beyond poetry. He has been one of the first to insist that the Beat Generation is a religious phenomenon and that Beat (i.e., resigned, abject, pooped, put-upon,

disgusted) really stands for Beatitude. "I have seen God," says Ginsberg. "I saw him in a room in Harlem." Ginsberg is also among the
most vehement of the Beats who insist that U.S. citizens have a constitutional right to all the narcotics they want, a right that is being
abridged by the government in Washington. Like most Beats he is
a marijuana smoker and is particularly enraged because this weed
"which is better for you than whisky" is illegal. He also cries that
there is a plot between the Mafia and the Administration to keep
up the price of heroin, morphine and cocaine. Listening to him deliver his opinions on this subject is an experience very much like
sharing a room with a wind machine. Only political venality, he implies, prevents legalized addiction and cheap narcotics for American
addicts. "We're treating junkies," he says, "like the Nazis treated the
Jews."

Ginsberg has a built-in sense of the theatrical and can out-
embarrass most humans—although he met his match in an odd interview with Britain's equally theatrical Dame Edith Sitwell last year.
"My, you *do* smell bad, don't you," said Dame Edith on being introduced. "What was your name again? Are you one of the action poets?"
Ginsberg, genuinely taken aback at this beastliness from one he had
fondly conceived to be a fellow genius, reached nervously for a cigarette. "Is that a narcotic one?" cried his inquisitor. "Does it contain
heroin?" "No," said Ginsberg, struggling like a western badman trying
to get a six-gun out of his bedroll, "but I've got some here. Do you
want a shot?" "Oh, dear no," said Dame Edith. "Dope makes me come
out all over spots." This, however, was only a minor setback.*

---

*[Dame Sitwell's rejoinder, which follows, appeared in *Life*, February 8, 1960: "Sirs:
My attention has been called to a most disgusting report in your paper—one mass of
lies from beginning to end—which pretends to describe my meeting with Mr. Allen
Ginsberg. . . . There is not one word of truth in a single sentence of it.

Mr. Ginsberg *never* offered me heroin, and as I have never, in my life, taken
heroin, it can scarcely 'bring me out in spots' (an affliction from which, incidentally, I
do not suffer).

The English upper classes do not use the expression 'My!' (we leave that to persons of your correspondent's breeding). Nor do we tell people who are introduced to us
that they 'smell bad.'

This is the most vulgar attack, actuated evidently by an almost insane malice,
probably by some person whom I have refused to receive socially, that I have ever seen.

You had better apologise, publically, both to Mr. Ginsberg and me immediately."
*Life* replied, "The anecdote . . . had been widely circulated at Oxford. Mr. Ginsberg joins Dame Edith in denying it and *Life* apologizes to both.]

Ginsberg is the lion of the poetry-reading circuit. He declaims his own startling verse with wild fervor, and hecklers attack him at their peril. At a recitation in Los Angeles last year a man stood up and demanded to know what Ginsberg was "trying to prove." "Nakedness," said Ginsberg. "What d'ya mean, nakedness?" bawled the unwary customer. Ginsberg gracefully took off all his clothes.

Although hundreds of Beats write poetry, or say they do, only about a dozen are of any note. Ginsberg's leading disciple is Gregory Corso, who shares a dingy slum apartment off Manhattan's Bowery with him and a tousled, sheeplike young man named Peter Orlovsky. (Orlovsky, who occasionally writes a poem of his own, is noted mostly for being Ginsberg's constant companion.) Corso, who served a stretch in Dannemora before producing such poems as *Don't Shoot the Warthog* and *Bomb,* is described by admirers as a "charming child of the streets." He boasts that he has never combed his hair "although I guess I'd get the bugs out of it if I did."

### A Fix at the Altar

Philip Lamantia and Mike McClure of San Francisco are leading exponents of a Beat cult which believes true poetic effects are best achieved through an "ecstatic illumination" induced by what Lamantia calls "the heroic medicines": heroin, opium, mescaline, marijuana, peyote. Lamantia is a tiny, erratic and gentle being with dark hair cropped short along his forehead and a pale, delicate, saintlike face. He has been a heroin addict, although he professes to have kicked the habit by smoking opium for nine months. He is a Catholic and an impassioned student of theology who has convinced himself that the use of drugs to obtain visions does not conflict with the canons of the Church ("Philip," say his raffish friends, "is trying to get a fix at the altar"). Lamantia was a contributor to the surrealist magazine, *View,* at 15 and was much praised by its readers. Now 31 and convinced that life has been "a ball," he lives in fleabag hotels on money doled out by his widowed mother. Unlike many of his colleagues, he can be a delightful conversationalist, but his poetry is often close to gibberish. "Christ," which leads off a volume of his verse entitled *Ekstasis,* begins thus:

Death,          sunrises
Beatific  the  winter's
rise.   Blanch   light
on rivers seen unseen
Born CRYSTAL FLESH
FISH  IN  A  CLOUD
LIGHT          LIFE

McClure, another small, handsome man, is married (to a working schoolteacher) and has a baby daughter. He was employed until recently as an attendant and towel dispenser at Riley's gym, a San Francisco muscle-building emporium, but has abandoned gainful toil and hopes he has "quit working forever." McClure has achieved hallucination by eating peyote buds, but he gave up the practice last autumn on the theory that his new visionary look at the world would last his lifetime without further medication. He has since endured an emotional letdown he calls "my nine-month dark night of the soul." He is convinced, however, that scientists are preparing to alter the chemical make-up of the human race so that everyone will eventually be born with the privilege of "peyote vision." After that? "All will be chaos, carnage and beauty."

For sheer horror no member of the Beat Generation has achieved effects to compare with William S. Burroughs, who is regarded by many seekers after coolness as the "greatest writer in the world." A Harvard man and an offshoot of the wealthy St. Louis family, Burroughs is now 45, a pale, cadaverous and bespectacled being who has devoted most of his adult life to a lonely pursuit of drugs and debauchery. He has, first in Mexico and then in Tangier, dosed himself with alcohol, heroin, marijuana, kif, majoun and a hashish candy—a regimen he once punctuated with a trip to South America to sample a native drug called yage. Between agonizing periods of ineffectual withdrawal he has rubbed shoulders with the dregs of a half dozen races. His works are three, *Junkie, Queer* and a last masterpiece, *The Naked Lunch,* recently published in Paris.

*The Naked Lunch* could be described as an effort to communicate the degradations of addiction in epic tones: ". . . you pinch up some leg flesh and make a quick stab hole with a pin. Then fit the dropper *over not in* the hole and feed the solution slow and careful. . . ." Interspersed are hallucinatory scenes indicative of the "peeled nerves of junk sickness. . . ." "Did any of you ever see Dr. Tetrazzini perform? I say 'perform' advisedly because his operations were performances. He would start by throwing a scalpel across the room into the patient and then make his entrance like a ballet dancer. . . ."

To this list of major Beat poets one peripheral figure, Lawrence Ferlinghetti, must be added. Ferlinghetti, a wartime naval lieutenant commander who studied in Paris under the G.I. bill, is the founder of San Francisco's City Lights Pocket Bookshop, which has become headquarters for Beatdom. A tall, quiet, pleasant man, Ferlinghetti encourages, publishes and defends Beat writers—and, ironically enough, writes better Beat poetry than most of them. Dozens of Beats have lately dashed off poems about the Crucifixion, but none of them has produced anything so startling as one of Ferlinghetti's efforts which was delivered before San Francisco television cameras with a dance interpretation by a girl named Avril Weber:

He was a kind of carpenter
　from a square type place like Galilee
Who said the cat who really laid it on us all was his Dad
They stretch him on this tree to cool. . . .
He just hang there in his tree, looking real petered out and real cool. . . .
And real dead. . . .

The bulk of Beat writers are undisciplined and slovenly amateurs who have deluded themselves into believing their lugubrious absurdities are art simply because they have rejected the form, style and attitudes of previous generations and have seized upon obscenity as an expression of "total personality." They insist that poetry, until they leapt upon the scene, was written simply for other poets "and not for the people," but most of them not only write for but about each other and regard the "people" as residents of Squaresville. While bawling of individuality, scores of them mimic each other as solemnly as pre-school tots in play period.

If the general level of Beat writing is appalling, however, it is impossible to honestly discount all Beat literature. The astonishing views, self-defeating abhorrence of form, and pitiful personal lives of its authors have led a great many critics to do so, but it is too easy to forget that Poe was a drunk, Coleridge an opium eater and Vincent van Gogh a madman, and that a great deal of the world's art has a disconcerting way of getting produced by very odd types. A few Beat writers demonstrate that gift of phrase and those flashes of insight which bespeak genuine talent.

Allen Ginsberg, even at his most unreasonable, communicates excitement like a voice yelling from inside a police car. A young Negro, Robert Kaufman, who has produced a long, jumbled poem entitled *Abomunist Manifesto,* is capable of humor. "Abomunists," he announces, "never carry more than fifty dollars in debts on them," and he adds gravely that "licking postage stamps depletes the body fluids." Jack Kerouac has been unable (although he comes close) to disguise a real feeling for life as it is lived along the truck roads and tenderloins of America. For all his hideous preoccupation with man's lowest appetites, William Burroughs has a terrible and sardonic eye and a vengeful sense of drama, both made more startling by the fact that he has found the will to write at all. The Beat movement embraces undiscovered talent too: the young, troubled and dedicated artist often feels, today, that it is the only haven to which he can turn in his search for encouragement and understanding.

The Beat Generation, however, is primarily important in the U.S. as the voice of nonconformity, the fount of what might be described as a sort of nonpolitical radicalism. The Ginsbergs, Kerouacs and Corsos, like the dissidents who emulate them, are social rebels first and poets only second. Even as writers they seem more intent on revenging themselves on the squares and yowling at the world than on triumphs of literary composition. A great deal of their verse is written to be read aloud before audiences, and the most noted of them are performers, even demagogues, whose big moments have been public exhibitions of personal as well as literary eccentricity. If the poets did nothing but influence other lesser Beats, moreover, they would have to be considered the leaders of a social rebellion. It is a curious rebellion—unplanned, unorganized and based on a thousand personal neuroses and a thousand conflicting egos, but it is oddly effective withall. No matter what else it may be, it is not boring, and in the U.S. of the 1950s it is the only rebellion in town.

The Beat message is being spoken in innumerable unlikely places. Knots of self-professed Beats have come to the surface in Paris,

Athens, Manchester and Prague—although the members of these overseas lodges, like Belgian baseball players, seem a little unsure of just what is expected of them and are doubtless unlikely to make the double play. In the U.S. there are few colleges without a cell of bearded Beatniks and fewer yet where some overtones of Beat philosophy have not crept into the minds of students in general.

Hairy evangelists of Beatdom have even collected troupes of semi or weekend Beats in the Midwest and South. In Cleveland an ex-sailor, ex-cook, ex-taxi driver named Wil Martin has become the flag-bearer by being "against creeping meatballism and voidism." Texas Beats are mostly types which California Beats scorn as "tourists," but their espresso shops have been burgeoning like locoweed in Houston, Dallas, Lubbock and Amarillo. Atlanta's Beats are considered by experts to be "not complete in their thinking," but still they work hard at noncornponity after business hours.

Bongo drums are beaten at Atlanta's all-night Beat parties, marijuana cigarettes ("left-wing Luckies" in the South) are sometimes smoked and, more daring yet, carefully selected Negroes are invited to rub shoulders with the jean-clad white folks. The Beats mix socially with Negroes in Washington, D.C., too, and as a result embryo nonconformists in both cities sometimes decide they have hopped the wrong rattler. "I was never so completely outraged as at the first Beat party I went to," says one indignant Atlanta belle who had planned to become a Scarlett O'Hara of the local weirdos. "We climbed a lot of rickety stairs, dodging the rats. The first thing I saw was a big smile with about 68 white teeth in a big black face. I was completely bug-eyed. But not the others. They were too far out. They just sat around looking foggy."

Secondary Beatsmanship is practiced, with local variations and an increasing snobbishness, in a good many other U.S. cities. But the true, hard-core Beats (who "put down" part-time Beats—occasionally—by taking one look and slowly shaping the word "wow" with the lips) hive almost exclusively in New York and on the West Coast, specifically in Los Angeles and San Francisco.

There are no fewer than 2,000 Beats in Los Angeles, mostly in the crumbling suburb of Venice West. They live with such basic furnishings as a mattress, a few cans of tinned food and a record player, recorder or set of bongo drums in abandoned stores or cheap rooms near the hot dog stands which mark the Pacific shore. San Francisco's North Beach section, because of its long tradition of bohemianism and because of its memories of early Beats, must still be considered the capital of Beatdom. Grant Street is its main drag, and two dingy, placard-plastered hangouts, The Co-existence Bagel Shop and The Place, are its Stork Club and "21." There are probably less than a thousand Beats in San Francisco now, some living in industrial districts and some camped in barren rooms over the spaghetti factories and Chinese sweatshops at the foot of Telegraph Hill, but they exhibit that air of uniqueness to be found in inhabitants of any temple. Beat existence and Beat attitudes are roughly similar, however, in both western gathering grounds.

Beat life is not nearly so enlivened by debauchery as the poets might suggest, the public might suspect or the Beats themselves might hope. True Beats seldom have much more money than is necessary for bare existence. Some get allowances from presumably sorrowing parents. Some work from time to time, usually at menial or unskilled tasks, but almost invariably they quit as soon as the rent money is put by or a foundation for unemployment checks adequately laid. Few indulge in heroin or even whiskey, if only because they can seldom afford either. By and large they smoke marijuana when they can get it (Chicago "pot" is prized, New York marijuana considered inferior stuff) and drink cheap wine or beer. A bottle of wine or a few cans of beer, in fact, is adequate excuse for a Beat party, which consists, in many cases, simply of sitting on somebody's floor and listening silently to phonograph records.

### The Rare Pad-sharing Chick

Beatdom is largely a male society, perhaps 10% of which is Negro. Few Beats are homosexual, although they tend to regard homosexuality with vast forbearance, and for all their wild talk about sex, the Beat orgy is largely a figment of their imagination. There are relatively few female Beats, and—girls being the practical creatures they are—the "pad-sharing chicks" about whom Beats talk so fondly and with such vehemence are few and far between. Even then they are usually so dominated by their own jangling complaints that romance seldom blooms for long. The boon Beats really seem to want from femininity, furthermore, is financial support, and the "chicks" who are willing to support a whiskery male are often middle-aged and fat. "The mature bohemian," according to North Beach maxim, "is one whose woman works *full* time."

By their very nature and appearance, Beats make cops nervous and property owners indignant, and no small part of Beat existence is spent in hopeless though wildly vocal scuffling with authority. The Los Angeles police, perhaps out of ennui produced by long acquaintance-ship with other curious cults, seem to suffer the Beats with philosoph-ical calm, although Venice homeowners have lately banded together to protest their existence, decry their propensity for making night hideous, and to moan about property values.

San Francisco's police have gone out of their way to give Beats a bad time. At one point they parked prowl cars or paddy wagons in front of the Bagel Shop and The Place for hours on end and pointedly questioned everyone who went in or out. "But," explains Police Cap-tain Charles Borland, "we do that with *any* problem bar." Still, it can-not be denied that cops have problems too. "First the Beatniks came to North Beach," says Captain Borland. "Then the tourists came to stare at them. Then the paddy hustlers and boosters came to work on the tourists. When I was a lieutenant I spent years south of Market [San Francisco's tenderloin]. I wish I could go back to those Third Street bums. On Third Street they get back in the doorways when they see the wagon coming. But these North Beach bums! These Beatniks! They want to argue with the officer. They stand around drinking and throwing bottles on the pavement, and they sit on the curbs—dirty, unsightly and using bad language. How about a woman coming down the sidewalk with a baby carriage? We get complaints. And these Beatniks argue with the officer. They're always arguing with the officer."

Talk—endless talk—forms the warp and woof of Beat existence. Talk and the kind of exhibitionism that almost always moves the aver-age man to uncertainty and embarrassment are the Beat's weapons against the world. Mostly he is incapable of anything else. Beats are seldom ignoramuses—wild or not, theirs is a world of ideas and a sur-prising number of them have at least some college education. But Dr. Francis J. Rigney, a young San Francisco psychiatrist who has recently completed a massive study of the Beat Generation based on members of the North Beach community, feels that at least 60% of the Beats with whom he communicated were so psychotic or so crippled by tensions, anxieties and neuroses as to be incapable of making their way in the ordinary competitive world of men, and that another 20% were hovering just within the boundaries of emotional stability.

What sort of heirs are these to the long and stirring history of unpopular dissent in America? The 1950s, granted, have not been years calculated to produce a Thomas Paine or to inspire a crusade for the rights of the working man. The Beat Generation has achieved its effects in part by default and in part as a result of the very prosperity it rejects. But, default or no, who ever heard of rebels so pitiful, so passive, so full of childish rages and nasty, masochistic cries? What would an old-time Wobbly have thought if he had encountered one on his way out of town after burning a bunkhouse or dynamiting a tipple? What would Thomas Jefferson, that advocate of the cleansing qualities of revolution, have been moved to say if he had known rebelliousness in America would come to this?

The Beat Generation is not alone in the U.S. in questioning the values of contemporary society, in feeling spiritually stifled by present-day materialism, and in growing restive at the conformity which seems to be the price of security. But only the Beats have actually been moved to reject contemporary society in voicing their quarrel with those values. There they are—crouching at the roadside in rags like those rascally Holy Men of the Orient who may slit purses but nevertheless remind the fat and prosperous that the way to salvation may yet be hard and bitter. There they prance and gesture, living in poverty (in the Age of Supermarkets), rejecting the goodies of the suburbs (in the Age of Togetherness), babbling of marijuana and mescaline (in the Age of Vic Tanny) and howling about their souls, misshapen as their souls may appear to be.

A hundred million squares must ask themselves: "What have we done to deserve this?"

# PETER ORLOVSKY

PETER ORLOVSKY was traveling and living in India with Allen
Ginsberg in 1962 when they collaborated on "Letter to Charlie
Chaplin." Orlovsky wrote the letter while staying with Gins-
berg, Gary Snyder, and Joanne Kyger as the guest of Radhika
Jayakar, a wealthy translator whom Ginsberg had met in New
York City. Jayakar's home in Bombay was very luxurious after
the nearly two months that the poets had spent traveling on
third-class trains and sleeping on the floors of ashrams in
Almora, the Punjab, Pathankot, Jaipur, and Ellora. The poets
enjoyed their stay in Bombay so much that on May 11, 1962,
Ginsberg urged Kerouac to leave his home in Orlando, Florida,
and join them: "Even the journalists are gentle and would accept you as a saint-saddhu, not a mean beatnik—you'll see how
much gentleness you're missing in Machineryland."

---

## Collaboration: Letter to Charlie Chaplin

Our Dear Friend Charles:

Love letter for you. We are one happy poet & one unhappy
poet in India which makes 2 poets. We would like come visit
you when we get thru India to tickle yr feet. Further more
King in New York is great picture,—I figure it will take about
10 yrs before it looks funny in perspective. Every few years we
dream in our sleep we meat you.
Why dont you go ahead & make another picture & fuck everybody. If you do could we be Extras. We be yr Brownies free of
charge.
Let us tell you about Ganesha. He is elephant-faced god with
funney fat belley human body. Everyone in India has picture
of him in their house. To think of him brings happy wisdom
success that he gives after he eats his sweet candey. He neither exists nor does not exist. Because of that he can conquer

aney demon. He rides around on a mouse & has 4 hands. We salute yr comedy in his name.

Do you realize how maney times we have seen yr pictures in Newark & cried in the dark at the roses. Do you realize how maney summers in Coney Island we sat in open air theatre & watched you disguised as a lamp-shade in scratchey down stairs eternity. You even made our dead mothers laugh. So, remember everything is alright. We await your next move & the world still depends on yr *next move*.

What else shall we say to you before we all die? If everything we feel could be said it would be very beautiful. Why didn't we ever do this before? I guess the world seems so vast, its hard to find the right moment to forget all about his shit & wave hello from the other side of the earth. But there is certainly millions & millions of people waveing hello to you silently all over the windows, streets & movies. Its only life waveing to its self.

Tell Michael to read our poems too if you ever get them. Again we say you got that personal tickle-tuch we like-love.

Shall we let it go at that? NO, we still got lots more room on the page—we still to emptey our hearts. Have you read Louis Ferdinand Celine?— hes translated into english from French—Celine vomits Rasberries. He wrote the most Chaplin-esque prose in Europe & he has a bitter mean sad uggly eternal comical soul enough to make you cry.

You could make a great picture about the Atom Bomb!

Synops:

> a grubby old janitor with white hair who cant get the air-raid drill instructions right & goes about his own lost business in the basement in the midst of great international air-raid emergencies, sirens, kremlin riots, flying rockets, radios screaming, destruction of the earth. He comes out the next day, he cralls out of the pile of human empire state building bodies, & the rest of the picture, a hole hour the janitor on the screen alone makeing believe he is being sociable with no-

body there, haveing a beer at the bar with invisible boys, reading last years newspapers, & ending looking blankly into the camera with the eternal aged Chaplin-face looking blankly, raptly into the eyes of the God of Solitude.

> There is yr fitting final statement Sir Chaplin,
> you will save the world if ya make it—but yr fi-
> nal look must be so beautiful that it doesn't
> matter if the world is saved or not.

Okay I guess we can end it now. Forgive us if you knew it all before. Okay

Love & Flowers
Peter Orlovsky, Allen Ginsberg

*1962 Bombay*

---

# GRACE PALEY

GRACE PALEY, born in New York City as the daughter of a Jewish doctor who had emigrated to the United States from Czarist Russia, is the author of three widely praised volumes of short stories: *The Little Disturbances of Man* (1959), *Enormous Changes at the Last Minute* (1974), and *Later the Same Day* (1985). "A Conversation with My Father" is from the second collection, originally published in 1971 in *New American Review.*

Paley has said that this autobiographical story is essentially "about generational differences, about different ways of looking at life." She understood that

> What my father thought could be done in the world
> was due to his own history. What I thought could be
> done in the world was different, not because I was a
> more open person, because he was also a very open
> person, but because I lived in a particularly open

time, the late 1960s. The story I wrote for him was
about all these druggies. It was made up, but it was
certainly true. I could point out people on my block
[Paley lives in Greenwich Village] whose kids became junkies. Many of them have recovered from
being junkies and are in good shape now.

## A Conversation with My Father

My father is eighty-six years old and in bed. His heart, that bloody motor, is equally old and will not do certain jobs any more. It still floods
his head with brainy light. But it won't let his legs carry the weight of
his body around the house. Despite my metaphors, this muscle failure is not due to his old heart, he says, but to a potassium shortage.
Sitting on one pillow, leaning on three, he offers last-minute advice
and makes a request.

"I would like you to write a simple story just once more," he says,
"the kind de Maupassant wrote, or Chekhov, the kind you used to
write. Just recognizable people and then write down what happened to
them next."

I say, "Yes, why not? That's possible." I want to please him, though
I don't remember writing that way. I *would* like to try to tell such a
story, if he means the kind that begins: "There was a woman . . ." followed by plot, the absolute line between two points which I've always
despised. Not for literary reasons, but because it takes all hope away.
Everyone, real or invented, deserves the open destiny of life.

Finally I thought of a story that had been happening for a couple
of years right across the street. I wrote it down, then read it aloud.
"Pa," I said, "how about this? Do you mean something like this?"

Once in my time there was a woman and she had a son. They
lived nicely, in a small apartment in Manhattan. This boy at
about fifteen became a junkie, which is not unusual in our
neighborhood. In order to maintain her close friendship with
him, she became a junkie too. She said it was part of the
youth culture, with which she felt very much at home. After a
while, for a number of reasons, the boy gave it all up and left

the city and his mother in disgust. Hopeless and alone, she grieved. We all visit her.

"O.K., Pa, that's it," I said, "an unadorned and miserable tale."

"But that's not what I mean," my father said. "You misunderstood me on purpose. You know there's a lot more to it. You know that. You left everything out. Turgenev wouldn't do that. Chekhov wouldn't do that. There are in fact Russian writers you never heard of, you don't have an inkling of, as good as anyone, who can write a plain ordinary story, who would not leave out what you have left out. I object not to facts but to people sitting in trees talking senselessly, voices from who knows where. . . ."

"Forget that one, Pa, what have I left out now? In this one?"

"Her looks, for instance."

"Oh. Quite handsome, I think. Yes."

"Her hair?"

"Dark, with heavy braids, as though she were a girl or a foreigner."

"What were her parents like, her stock? That she became such a person. It's interesting, you know."

"From out of town. Professional people. The first to be divorced in their county. How's that? Enough?" I asked.

"With you, it's all a joke," he said. "What about the boy's father? Why didn't you mention him? Who was he? Or was the boy born out of wedlock?"

"Yes," I said. "He was born out of wedlock."

"For Godsakes, doesn't anyone in your stories get married? Doesn't anyone have the time to run down to City Hall before they jump into bed?"

"No," I said. "In real life, yes. But in my stories, no."

"Why do you answer me like that?"

"Oh, Pa, this is a simple story about a smart woman who came to N.Y.C. full of interest love trust excitement very up to date, and about her son, what a hard time she had in this world. Married or not, it's of small consequence."

"It is of great consequence," he said.

"O.K.," I said.

"O.K. O.K. yourself," he said, "but listen. I believe you that she's good-looking, but I don't think she was so smart."

"That's true," I said. "Actually that's the trouble with stories. People start out fantastic. You think they're extraordinary, but it turns out as the work goes along, they're just average with a good education. Sometimes the other way around, the person's a kind of dumb innocent, but he outwits you and you can't even think of an ending good enough."

"What do you do then?" he asked. He had been a doctor for a couple of decades and then an artist for a couple of decades and he's still interested in details, craft, technique.

"Well, you just have to let the story lie around till some agreement can be reached between you and the stubborn hero."

"Aren't you talking silly now?" he asked. "Start again," he said. "It so happens I'm not going out this evening. Tell the story again. See what you can do this time."

"O.K.," I said. "But it's not a five-minute job." Second attempt:

Once, across the street from us, there was a fine handsome woman, our neighbor. She had a son whom she loved because she'd known him since birth (in helpless chubby infancy, and in the wrestling, hugging ages, seven to ten, as well as earlier and later). This boy, when he fell into the fist of adolescence, became a junkie. He was not a hopeless one. He was in fact hopeful, an ideologue and successful converter. With his busy brilliance, he wrote persuasive articles for his high-school newspaper. Seeking a wider audience, using important connections, he drummed into Lower Manhattan newsstand distribution a periodical called *Oh! Golden Horse!*

In order to keep him from feeling guilty (because guilt is the stony heart of nine tenths of all clinically diagnosed cancers in America today, she said), and because she had always believed in giving bad habits room at home where one could keep an eye on them, she too became a junkie. Her kitchen was famous for a while—a center for intellectual addicts who knew what they were doing. A few felt artistic like Coleridge and others were scientific and revolutionary like Leary. Although she was often high herself, certain good mothering reflexes remained, and she saw to it that there was lots of orange juice around and honey and milk and vitamin pills. However, she never cooked anything but chili, and that no more than once a week. She explained, when we talked to her, seriously, with neighborly concern, that it was her part in the youth culture and she would rather be with the young, it was an honor, than with her own generation.

One week, while nodding through an Antonioni film, this boy was severely jabbed by the elbow of a stern and prosely-tizing girl, sitting beside him. She offered immediate apricots and nuts for his sugar level, spoke to him sharply, and took him home.

She had heard of him and his work and she herself pub-lished, edited, and wrote a competitive journal called *Man Does Live by Bread Alone*. In the organic heat of her continu-ous presence he could not help but become interested once more in his muscles, his arteries, and nerve connections. In fact he began to love them, treasure them, praise them with funny little songs in *Man Does Live*. . . .

> the fingers of my flesh transcend
> my transcendental soul
> the tightness in my shoulders end
> my teeth have made me whole

To the mouth of his head (that glory of will and determina-tion) he brought hard apples, nuts, wheat germ, and soybean oil. He said to his old friends, From now on, I guess I'll keep my wits about me. I'm going on the natch. He said he was about to begin a spiritual deep-breathing journey. How about you too, Mom? he asked kindly.

His conversion was so radiant, splendid, that neighborhood kids his age began to say that he had never been a real addict at all, only a journalist along for the smell of the story. The mother tried several times to give up what had become with-out her son and his friends a lonely habit. This effort only brought it to supportable levels. The boy and his girl took their electronic mimeograph and moved to the bushy edge of another borough. They were very strict. They said they would not see her again until she had been off drugs for sixty days.

At home alone in the evening, weeping, the mother read and reread the seven issues of *Oh! Golden Horse!* They seemed to her as truthful as ever. We often crossed the street to visit and console. But if we mentioned any of our children who were at college or in the hospital or dropouts at home, she would cry out, My baby! My baby! and burst into terrible, face-scarring, time-consuming tears. The End.

First my father was silent, then he said, "Number One: You have a nice sense of humor. Number Two: I see you can't tell a plain story. So don't waste time." Then he said sadly, "Number Three: I suppose that means she was alone, she was left like that, his mother. Alone. Probably sick?"

I said, "Yes."

"Poor woman. Poor girl, to be born in a time of fools, to live among fools. The end. The end. You were right to put that down. The end."

I didn't want to argue, but I had to say, "Well, it is not necessarily the end, Pa."

"Yes," he said, "what a tragedy. The end of a person."

"No, Pa," I begged him. "It doesn't have to be. She's only about forty. She could be a hundred different things in this world as time goes on. A teacher or a social worker. An ex-junkie! Sometimes it's better than having a master's in education."

"Jokes," he said. "As a writer that's your main trouble. You don't want to recognize it. Tragedy! Plain tragedy! Historical tragedy! No hope. The end."

"Oh, Pa," I said. "She could change."

"In your own life, too, you have to look it in the face." He took a couple of nitroglycerin. "Turn to five," he said, pointing to the dial on the oxygen tank. He inserted the tubes into his nostrils and breathed deep. He closed his eyes and said, "No."

I had promised the family to always let him have the last word when arguing, but in this case I had a different responsibility. That woman lives across the street. She's my knowledge and my invention. I'm sorry for her. I'm not going to leave her there in that house crying. (Actually neither would Life, which unlike me has no pity.)

Therefore: She did change. Of course her son never came home again. But right now, she's the receptionist in a storefront community clinic in the East Village. Most of the customers are young people, some old friends. The head doctor has said to her, "If we only had three people in this clinic with your experiences. . . ."

"The doctor said that?" My father took the oxygen tubes out of his nostrils and said, "Jokes. Jokes again."

"No, Pa, it could really happen that way, it's a funny world now-adays."

"No," he said. "Truth first. She will slide back. A person must have character. She does not."

"No, Pa," I said. "That's it. She's got a job. Forget it. She's in that storefront working."

"How long will it be?" he asked. "Tragedy! You too. When will you look it in the face?"

# THOMAS PARKINSON

THOMAS PARKINSON (1920–1997) was one of the professors in the English Department at the University of California at Berkeley—along with biographer Mark Schorer and poet Josephine Miles—who encouraged Ginsberg to think of enrolling as a graduate student there in the fall of 1955. Six years later, Parkinson acknowledged the help of both Ginsberg and Lawrence Ferlinghetti in compiling *A Casebook on the Beat* (1961), a pioneering academic anthology of Beat writing and criticism for the Thomas Y. Crowell Company as part of their series of "Literary Casebooks." Previous anthologies had included *A Casebook on Ezra Pound* and *A Casebook on Dylan Thomas*. In his preface to what he called "The pros and cons of the beat movement—with 39 pieces of beat writing—Kerouac, Ginsberg, and others," Parkinson explained that "since the editor has been rather deeply involved in the literature here treated, he has felt it necessary to present his own views, not as editorial views but as one of several comments." Instead of presenting his essay "Phenomenon or Generation" as an introduction to the anthology, Parkinson included it as a commentary in the last section of the book.

## The Beat Writers: Phenomenon or Generation

When the beat writers emerged in 1956 they struck so responsive a chord that they became the most widely discussed phenomenon of the late 1950s. If they represented a "generation," they replaced a remarkably short-lived and little-lamented "silent generation" which had dominated the first five years of the 1950s. Even in the accelerated pace of twentieth-century living, two generations per decade rather crowds things. Whether they represented an entire generation or a spasm of revulsion, the beat writers attained symbolic status, as did the until-then little-remarked Bohemian communities of New York's Greenwich Village and San Francisco's North Beach. When the San Francisco columnist Herb Caen dubbed the members of current Bohemia "beatniks," the derisive appellation stuck. Beatnik life became a subject of general interest, and that special nexus of jazz, Buddhism, homosexuality, drugs, and squalor was graphed and discussed in a wide range of media that reached a large audience.

It was easy to deride the nonconformist existentialist costumes, the sheer unpleasantness of texture in the dreary fakeries of beatnik art, and no one could defend the aimless self-destructiveness and occasional pointless criminality of conduct. But two basic problems were not so easily dismissed. The first was the genuine vigor and force of Allen Ginsberg and Jack Kerouac, the extraordinary wit and hilarity of Lawrence Ferlinghetti and Gregory Corso, the obvious intelligence, learning, and decency of Gary Snyder and Philip Whalen, the hard integrity of Michael McClure—in short, the simple literary expertise of several gifted writers who participated in many of the excitements and obsessions of current Bohemia. The second problem, essentially social, was how to estimate the importance of this extra-official mode of life. Was it spindrift or the point of an iceberg, this sudden revelation of resentment and bad feeling? Was it American Bohemia newly garbed, new beatnik being old bum writ bold? One commentator closed his very unfriendly article with somber tone: "A hundred million squares must ask themselves: 'What have we done to deserve this?'" A hundred million seems a modest estimate, but whatever the census, the refrain of puzzled commentators was a steady and repeated "What's wrong?" To many people the chief force of the beat movement was the suggestion that all was not well with our unrivaled happiness.

If not puzzled, commentators were pleased to see that the tradition of revolt was not dead, and many a patronizing phrase approved of youth having its fling. A surprising number of people seemed to assume that rebellion per se, whatever its means or ultimate goal, is a good thing. After ten years of literary dandies carefully machining their Fulbright poems in a social atmosphere of cold war and general stuffiness, the beats were welcomed. What troubled the most tolerantly disposed critics, however, was the refusal of beat and beatnik to play their proper social role. Their elders had a hazy rosy memory of their own daring youth in which they had been true radicals, that is, left New Dealers relatively active in political affairs. To their sense of things, the true rebel might take his origins in blank resentment of the world, but he went on to formulate his motives in terms of some ideal mode of social organization. But the beat movement simply denied the role of social critic and took an indifferent and passive posture before the problems of the world. Fallout, population, medical care, legal justice, civil rights—the beats were concerned actively with these problems when they impinged on the printing of books with certain taboo words, or on the problems of dope addicts cut off from their source of supply, or on the rights of poets to say slanderous things about policemen. Otherwise their approach was sardonic, apocalyptic, or impudent.

With very few exceptions, the beat and beatnik compose a social refusal rather than a revolt: as Allen Ginsberg announced to his audience in Chile, he is a rebel, not a revolutionist. They take no particular pleasure in tearing down a social fabric that they see as already ruined, and their attitude toward society is suspicious and evasive rather than destructive. When their attitude becomes destructive, the result is pointless antisocial acts; they then cease to be beat and become unemployed delinquents. Many beatniks are college students who, after two or more years of college, are not certain that they intend to go on into the business and professional worlds that swallow up the graduates of American colleges and universities. So they take a year off and loaf and invite their souls on Grant Avenue or Bleecker Street or the Left Bank. Some find the atmosphere so congenial that they linger through several years, and a few of them become permanent Bohemians. In such an atmosphere the tone is naturally anti-academic and antiofficial.

In this sense the beatnik world is a continuation of the Bohemian world already familiar to observers of American life. The beats are differentiated from past Bohemians by their religiosity (Zen Buddhism, Christ-as-beatnik with sandals and beard), experimental interest in hallucinogenic drugs and occasional dabbling in addictive drugs, proximity to criminality (largely through association with drugs), and fascination with moral depravity for its own sake. The traditional antidomesticity of the Bohemian world is still prevalent, as well as the concomitant relaxation of sexual mores in this predominantly male society.

The differences between the intellectual and religious concerns of current Bohemia and those of the 1920s or 1930s are modes of differentiating the attitudes of those eras from our own. It seems to me fairly plain that American Bohemia in reacting against suburbia tends to produce a reverse image of the society that makes the hydrogen bomb, throws its money around an idiot frenzy, and refuses to vote for school bonds; the same moral flaccidity, the same social irresponsibility, the same intellectual fraudulence operate throughout the two worlds that are, finally, not opposed. Freud in the 1920s meant sexual liberation, whereas psychoanalysis in Bohemia and suburbia in the 1950s was primarily a mode of keeping going. The borderline between beatnik and psychiatric patient shifts constantly, claiming one and releasing another, and a surprising number of people in current Bohemia are under psychiatric care. This in turn reflects the rising commitment rate of American mental hospitals and the steady increase in the numbers of people seeking psychiatric aid so that they can continue their business and professional life. The indifference toward politics exhibited by Bohemia is matched by the neglect and cynicism of suburbia. The beatnik contempt for simple comfort and cleanliness is the counterpart of mindless possessiveness, status-seeking, and other elaborate forms of greed.

It would be easy to multiply points of comparison: the gray flannel suit and the existentialist costume, the smiling religious purveyor of togetherness and the egotism of Christ-as-beatnik, ranch house and pad, cocktails and marijuana. But it was not merely the direct parody that attracted so much attention; rather, the illusion of community promoted by the hip jargon, the agreed values, the common rites, and relaxed tone—this was the chief source of attraction and interest. What was sought by commentator and reader alike was a way of life that would answer their feeling of pointlessness and guilt in looking at their own unrewarding accumulation of commodities. The beatniks not only evaded a society that, even its friendliest critics are quick to admit, has lost all community of motive; they went further and created an impenetrable community that turned the well-adjusted member of suburbia into a frustrated outsider. They shaped a way of life at once public and arcane. No wonder that the spectacle of Grant Avenue has produced so many dances of uncomprehending rage.

And yet is it not pathetic that the alternatives of American society should be posed in terms of Beatville and Squareville? If the beat and beatnik are the only answer to the wasteful cupidity of suburbia, then the country is in a very nasty spot. In truth, there is a vast fund of good sense and social responsibility in this country, and the only problem is to allow its voice to be heard more clearly and loudly. And if a rebellion is necessary, it will be fostered by people who have a sense of commitment to the insulted and injured of the world, who feel and act on an ideal of human conduct that sponsors change in individual experience, and who do not waste their substance on pointless conformity and aimless complaint. Some of those people live in suburbia, some in Bohemia, and many of them just anywhere; they respond to and shape their environment, and from such responsible shaping come the seeds of community and, finally, civilization.

In talking about the social phenomenon of the beat and beatnik, I deliberately distinguished between the two terms. The term "beat" I take to be descriptive, and its primary reference is to a group of writers, especially, who participate in certain common attitudes and pursue common literary aims. They may use the beatnik milieu as their subject and their ideas and attitudes may be widely shared by current Bohemia. The beatnik, on the other hand, is either not an artist or an incompetent and nonproductive one. The beatnik provides the atmosphere and audience of Grant Avenue and analogous areas, and he is frequently an engaging person. He may write an occasional "poem," but he has no literary ambitions.

The beat writer, on the other hand, is serious and ambitious. He is usually well educated and always a student of his craft. Sometimes, as is the case with Gary Snyder, he is a very learned man, and his knowledge of literature and its history is dense and extensive. Allen Ginsberg's public posture on literary matters is that of an innocent who writes from impulse, but he knows better. And one of my objections to Lawrence Ferlinghetti is that he is much too literary in tone and reference. He writes for the man in the street, but he chooses a street full of *Nation* subscribers and junior-college graduates, that is, Grant Avenue. In fact, the only untutored writer of the lot is Gregory Corso, and in his work this is neither a merit nor a handicap. His stock in trade is impertinence, and he learned that out of his own impish nature.

The reception of the beat writers, the extraordinary interest taken in the novels of Kerouac, Ginsberg's little pamphlet of poems, Ferlinghetti's *Coney Island of the Mind* (which has sold over 40,000 copies), the San Francisco issue of *Evergreen Review* (entering its seventh printing), and the publicity accorded the beat way of life by national magazines—all this has passed into not only social history but also literary history. When Meridian Books put out its anthology of *New Poets of England and America* in 1957, it included none of the beat writers and none of the writers of the San Francisco school and the Black Mountain group. Any anthology of recent poetry now appearing would practically have to include Ginsberg and Snyder, to say nothing of the nonbeat writers who have by accident been associated with them: William Everson (Brother Antoninus), Robert Creeley, Robert Duncan, Denise Levertov, Charles Olson, Kenneth Rexroth, and Jack Spicer, to name only those I take to be most distinguished.

The beat writers are not, in short, the only writers in America who live outside the universities and are not interested primarily in perpetuating the iambic line. This fact needs underlining, for one unhappy result of the publicity attendant on the rise of the beat was, simply, the tarring of all writers with experimental motives with the single brush *beat* or the further implications that the only valid experimental writers *were* beat. The terms "San Francisco Renaissance" (awakening would be more fitting) and "San Francisco writers," for instance, were cheerily applied to any writer who knew Allen Ginsberg or was published by Lawrence Ferlinghetti. As a matter of fact, only one of the writers on the City Lights list was even born in California. The writer in question is Robert Duncan, who is one of the best poets now writing in English and as nonbeat as a person can get.

The association of the beat writers with San Francisco is not entirely fortuitous. From about 1944 on, the area has been distinguished by considerable artistic activity, and during that period it was one of the strongholds of experimental poetry. There was a great deal of other literary activity, and I do not intend to depreciate the products of Stanford's writing program or of the Activist group associated with Lawrence Hart or the numerous writers who simply lived in the San Francisco Bay area because life was pleasant there or because they had jobs in the various colleges. But what especially distinguished writing in the Bay area was a group of people—mainly poets—who were interested in creating and establishing a community of literary interest. They were like coral insects building a reef that might ultimately create the calm and pleasure of a lagoon. They were interested in forming a culture rather than in shaping unimpeachable structures out of the detritus of a museum civilization. The poetry they wrote and liked was deeply religious in tone, personalist in dramaturgy, imagist in iconographic habit, and experimentalist in prosody. With this poetics was associated a loose cluster of concerns and attitudes—anarcho-pacifism in politics, relatively conservative (especially Roman Catholic) religious preoccupations, a generally receptive attitude toward Eastern art and thought that grew naturally out of the Pacific Basin orientation of the great port of San Francisco, intensive interest in the traditions of European experimentalism, and perhaps above all a very deep elegiac sense of the destruction of both the natural world and the possibilities of the American dream (its waste in the great wars and the frozen polity of the postwar period) dramatized in the brutal exploitation of California as its population swelled. Whatever was wrong with the poetry written out of these basic concerns, it was not a poetry that refused to meet squarely the challenges of great subjects.

This was accompanied by a widespread feeling of poetic community that took its center in activities organized by Robert Duncan, George Leite, and Kenneth Rexroth. George Leite's *Circle* magazine appeared first in 1944, and from then until 1950 he published ten issues of work local and international in origin. Its closest analogue in that period was the British magazine *Now*, which included many of the same contributors, and though Leite's editorial taste was far from infallible, the level of achievement was often very high. Some of his contributors—Henry Miller, Kenneth Rexroth, Josephine Miles, George P. Elliott, Robert Duncan, Brother Antoninus—have come to be well-known figures in current American letters, and a surprising number of his other contributors have been consistently productive. The attitudes that *Circle* espoused, both political and aesthetic, were hardly what could be called generally acceptable, and the magazine embodied the blithe indifference to the official culture that marked the early or postwar stages of the San Francisco Renaissance.

During the period of *Circle's* publication, Berkeley and San Francisco woke from their literary sleep of years. The chief figure in this awakening was Kenneth Rexroth. He was a poet nationally known at the time, printed by Macmillan and New Directions, and one of James Laughlin's advisors at the latter publishing house. He was interesting, well informed, friendly to the young. He gave the impression of truly patriarchal longevity. I said to him once that I had lost all my illusions about the Soviet Union at the time of the Finnish war. He said, "That just shows how young you are. I lost *my* illusions with the Kronstadt Rebellion." It was only much later that I came to realize that at the time of the rebellion he was fifteen years old, for he gave the impression that he had turned his back on Lenin with sorrow and withdrawn his counsel from the baby Soviet republics, leaving them to stumble on into disaster. He had a trick of imaginative projection that allowed him to suggest he was a contemporary of Lenin, Whitman, Tu Fu, Thoreau, Catullus, Baudelaire, John Stuart Mill—they were all so real to him. The amount of labor and confusion that he saved younger people was immense; one could be painfully working his way out of Dublin Catholicism, and he would talk of Buber or Lao-Tzu. Or with difficulty one could be moving toward understanding of his locale, and he would make some casual statement about Pacific Basin culture, adducing Morris Graves as exemplar. It would be easy to multiply instances. His recent collection of essays—*Bird in the Bush*—gives some idea of the range of his interests and talk.

Beyond his work as poet and critic, Rexroth organized discussion groups at his home, chiefly on political subjects though he conducted some literary seminars. He was certainly one of the best close readers of texts that I have ever encountered, and his technical knowledge of verse was wide, detailed, exact. I stress this because he has insisted recently on the indifference of such analysis to the study and writing of verse ("I write poetry to seduce women and overthrow the capitalist system"), and the record should be clarified. Chiefly, however, the discussions were political and religious with literary figures (Lawrence, Blake, Yeats) seen in the perspective of Schweitzer, Buber, Berdyaev, Kropotkin, Emma Goldman, Toynbee, Gill, Boehme, Thoreau, Gandhi—the list could be extended indefinitely. When poetry was discussed directly, it tended to be French poetry since Apollinaire or the most recent British poetry; he was at that time engaged in his extensive translations from Léon-Paul Fargue, Cros, Carcot, Milosz, Desnos, Reverdy and in editing his anthology of British poetry since Auden. In addition to various poets and ordinary people, the discussions were attended by many of the conscientious objectors who after the war migrated in large numbers to the Bay area and had much to do with establishing the range of intellectual interest. For example, many of the founders of the famous listener-sponsored radio station KPFA-B (with branches now in Los Angeles and New York) were among the participants, and now that the station has become more staid and respectable, it is practically forgotten that the title of its governing board—Pacifica Foundation—was not a geographical but an intellectual designation.

In Berkeley too, partly because of the sudden upsurge of enrollment at the University of California after the war, there was a great deal of extra-academic literary activity. *Circle* was published there, and Bern Porter brought out some individual books of poetry. Robert Duncan, however, was most instrumental in organizing discussions and readings of poetry, and he was the first person in the Bay area who gave large-scale public poetry readings. These readings drew on the large and relatively mature postwar student body at the university for audience. As one sour witness put it, every clique must have its claque. Very true, but the extraordinary thing about the poets was their very great variety, their degree of disagreement. Through the poetry readings in Berkeley and San Francisco and—when it began operation in 1949—over KPFA, a fairly large audience was created that accepted and took interest in poetry readings.

From about 1950 to 1953, there was a period of dispersal when this embryonic literary community developed no further, and it was with the opening of the Poetry Center at San Francisco State College that poetry in the Bay area entered its most recent phase, in which the beat writers were involved. Through the Poetry Center, Mrs. Ruth Witt-Diamant brought to the area most of the important poets of the Anglo-American world, and it was largely because of the generosity of W. H. Auden that she was able to start this always precarious enterprise. Through her hard, thankless labor, a fixed center was established for poetry readings where widely recognized poets could be heard and young poets only emerging could get an immediate audience. As the writers associated earlier with the area began drifting back from their travels, things began to quicken again, and a newly emergent group of younger writers revived the earlier excitements. There were continuities between the by-now older poets and the younger, so that Michael McClure was in some ways a disciple of Robert Duncan, and Gary Snyder and Phil Whalen took much of their poetic method from Kenneth Rexroth. Duncan, through his association with Black Mountain College and his participation (by contributing) in *Origin,* helped to bring to the attention of the writers of the area the work of Charles Olson, Robert Creeley, and Denise Levertov; and Rexroth, who remained tirelessly interested in and receptive to experimental writing of all kinds, also kept people informed of the new and as yet generally unknown.

In other words, when Lawrence Ferlinghetti came to San Francisco in 1953 and Allen Ginsberg in 1954, they were not entering a cultural void, even restricting the sense of culture to experimental writing. It seems to me fruitless to argue whether writing in the San Francisco area has been notably original, just as it is fruitless to ask whether the San Francisco painters are really separable from the main currents of recent painting. In both instances it seems more useful to consider the quality of work produced and the extent to which the producers of the art learned from each other. In both painting and poetry, it seems to me perfectly clear that there *are* San Francisco schools, that is, significant groups of artists who have learned from each other profitably and have produced work capable of competing on equal terms with work produced in other cultural centers. In painting—David Park, Elmer Bischoff, Ernie Briggs, Sam Francis, Richard Diebenkorn, Clyfford Still; in poetry—Brother Antoninus,

Robert Duncan, Michael McClure, Kenneth Rexroth, Jack Spicer, Gary Snyder, Phil Whalen. Naturally all these artists have affinities with painters or writers from other parts of the world, and it is for this reason that their names are often associated with those of artists with whom they have nothing in particular to do.

When the beat writers came to the San Francisco area, then, they found a sounding board, so that Allen Ginsberg wrote "Howl" and related poems only after moving out to the West Coast and read it first to Bay area audiences. The audience and structure of public address were there, and the literary atmosphere was receptive. Snyder, Whalen, and McClure, who were in effect a second wave of the Bay area awakening, joined forces with him, and when first Kerouac and later Corso made the trip, they also found an amiable reception. The presence of Lawrence Ferlinghetti as publisher also provided an outlet for at least Ginsberg and Corso, and so another phase in the literary life of the San Francisco area began.

In giving the historical background to the association of the beat writers with San Francisco, I am not trying to depreciate the personal role played by Allen Ginsberg in revivifying the poetic life of the Bay area. Too little stressed in all the public talk about Ginsberg are his personal sweetness and gentleness of disposition. He was a person more cohesive than disruptive in impact, and it was largely through his personal qualities, his extraordinary abilities as reader of his own verse, and his genuinely selfless dedication that the sense of literary community was again established. And he wrote well. In spite of all the miscellaneous demurs against "Howl," it still stands as a moving and important poem, and I suspect that it will hold up for a long time. And Lawrence Ferlinghetti, with his quiet easiness of manner, his very great skill as public reader, and his persistent courage, was a force of equal importance and pertinacity. It takes nothing from either of them to say they were supported by an environment that, in turn, they changed. Their great contribution was in the expression of new motives and their creation—or recognition—of a new audience. The singular force of the beat writers is manifest in the fact that they did not merely reflect the audience of American Bohemia; they substantially altered that audience, and in so doing they liberated and clarified motives until then only imperfectly realized. The intensity of reaction to their work indicates that the motives embodied in Kerouac's *On the*

*Road* and *The Subterraneans* strike some sensitive hidden nerve that is more important than, before the appearance of those works, many had cared to admit.

I have taken such historical pains because there are two confusions that I think should be unraveled. First, the best experimental poetry in the United States is not necessarily beat, any more than the beatnik pattern of conduct is the only valid response to the life of the organization man. Second, the beat writers, with the exception of McClure, Snyder, and Whalen, are all easterners whose relations with northern California are either fugitive or nonexistent. A person moving from the Left Bank to Greenwich Village to North Beach is not leaving home but is remaining in a basically constant society. The scene changes but the emotional milieu is fixed, existentialist costumes, jazz, and all. When Kerouac writes of the West Coast, he does so with a tourist's eye; it is all copy, raw material to be exploited, not substantial. No one objects to this seriously, but it is a little annoying to Californians to hear William Burroughs described as a San Francisco writer when he has not, so far as I know, ever set foot in the state. It is all the more annoying when the result is a distortion of historical fact that muddies waters.

More important than such minor pique, however, is the question of the association of all experimental writing with the beat movement. What happened in 1956 when the national news media became aware of the beat writers was a taking off of the lid. Laments had been issued because of the dullness and sameness of American poetry, and as the cold war thawed, there seemed room for a little more freewheeling treatment of experience. At the same time, there was no reason for taking such a matter too far, and the beats were suited for a surprisingly moderate role. They presented a spectacle of a romantically dark community that repelled and attracted, that satisfied and thrilled without inviting. It was possible to feel at once sympathetic, envious, and superior to the way of life they embodied. So too with the writing; if this was all that existed outside the finicky preciousness of the dandy and the plodding wholesomeness of the women's magazines, who could seek or be interested in a change of intellectual diet? In effect, it was possible to talk their work to death by considering only their odd habits, and since their contempt for the intellect preserved them from any rational critical self-defense, they could become figures of derisive fun. The fact that Gregory Corso publicly boasted that he has never combed his hair has led to the belief that he could not then have taken much care with his poetry. The quality of the work could then remain unexamined.

Of the writers represented in this casebook, several seem to me important figures, not merely as social phenomena but as literary artificers of some accomplishment. The best comments on "Howl" are probably those made by Kenneth Rexroth and Mark Schorer during the obscenity trial, and they suggest its remarkable qualities quite clearly. I have always felt that Ginsberg is the genuine article, and if he keeps on writing he will probably become a very important poet. Both he and Ferlinghetti are extremely gifted readers—entertainers— and they have been extraordinarily effective in bringing poetry to a widened audience.

A certain amount of ironic comment has been made on the importance of oral delivery and the writer's physical dramatic presence to the full impact of the poetry of Ginsberg and Ferlinghetti. Their poetry, and that of McClure and Whalen (and Snyder, to a lesser extent), attempts notation of the actual movement of mind and voice in full vernacular. It seems difficult to take this poetry off the page largely because the mode of poetic notation that fits the movement of American speech is still in the realm of the nonconventionalized. Accustomed to syllabic, stress and foot verse, the normal audience for poetry is not prepared to take into consideration intensity (loudness), pitch, and duration, and the concept of breath pause is far from being ritualized. The usual prosodic assumption is that the precise notation so readily accepted for music is not possible for poetry, that poetry will have to bumble along with concepts that more or less fit the products of another tone and tempo of speech. This seems to me predicated on a happy combination of ignorance and laziness, ignorance of the past and laziness in the face of actual problems of current experience. The primary problem of poetry is notation, through the appearance of poem on page to indicate the reality of articulation. A poem is a score.

Looked on in this way, much of the notation of this poetry ceases to seem odd or frivolous. The capital letters, the broken lines, the long long long lines, the shift from vernacular idiom to lofty rhetoric, these are attempts to shift from conventional idiom to actual, to increase the vocality of the verse. The experiments with jazz accompaniment are more dramatic instances of the stress on precision of notation.

Related to the concept of vocality that underlies much of this poetry and brings it over into the world of performance and entertainment is the concept of intimacy that affects both prose and poetry. The beat poet is best considered as a voice, the beat prose writer as an active revery. Into this revery come past and present, but the revery is chiefly preoccupied with keeping up with the process unfolding outside and inside the narrator. Hence the long sentences, endlessly attempting to include the endless, the carelessness—even negligence—with the ordinary rules of grammatical function, so that noun, adjective, and verb interchange roles; after all, if the process is endlessly unpredictable and unfixed, grammatical categories are not relevant. It is a syntax of aimlessly continuing pleasure in which all elements are "like." Release, liberation from fixed categories, hilarity—it is an ongoing prose that cannot be concerned with its origins. There are no origins and no end, and the solid page of type without discriminations is the image of life solidly continuous without discriminations in value, and yet incomplete because it is literally one damned thing after another with no salvation or cease. There are no last things in this prose whereas the very division of experience into lines compels the discrimination of element from element. Even a poetic catalogue, which is by definition one thing after another, moves in blocks which have weight, and even if each unit weighs the same, the total weight increases with each succeeding integer. Not so in prose, the only limits coming from the size of the page. The ideal book by a writer of beat prose would be written on a single string of paper, printed on a roll, and moving endlessly from right to left, like a typewriter ribbon.

Is there anything especially new about this sense of endlessness in prose or of vocal notation in poetry? *Finnegans Wake* and Molly Bloom's soliloquy at the close of *Ulysses* could also be printed on a ribbon without violating James Joyce's intention, and the classical experimental poetry of the twentieth century had as one chief aim the kind of precise notation that I have suggested as a major motive in beat poetry. There is nothing new under the sun, even the American sun, granted, but this would not disturb the beat writers. They are perfectly happy to place themselves in a tradition of experimental writing, and they are alert to the existence of writers they can claim as ancestors.

They assume that this experimental tradition should be consolidated and extended, and they do not consider it as part of the conventional work of English writers. The experimental era could be looked on as an attempt to vivify the conventions of English verse and prose, that is, as extension of the normal performances of, say, Dickens and Tennyson, corrective to it, part of the loyal opposition. In this sense, it can be assimilated into the institution of literature as generally—that is, academically—understood, just as Blake can be memorialized in Westminster Abbey.

In another sense, the experimental writers destroyed convention in order to create a completely new way of looking at experience and cannot be assimilated into the existing institution. In this view, the aim of literary creation is not to enrich the tradition but to expose its poverty and irrelevance so that it can be swept aside in favor of a literature more responsive to the realities of experience. The question raised by this aim has wide implications, for education, for politics, for human understanding. I have heard William Carlos Williams say that the poet who invented a new measure, a new line, would change the world radically. The scientists at Alamagordo certainly did change the world, as did the biochemists who produced antibiotics, and the technicians working on increased automation. Whether a literature proportionate to technological change is in the process of being shaped is certainly a question worth asking. But by the same token, one might also ask whether this literature is not merely an expression of the hopelessness and consequent frivolity that affects a world shaken to its foundations as its population, power, and problems multiply.

These are fundamental questions that may be too large for the context of beat writing. In the history of American life and letters, the phenomenon of the beat may have been a spasm rather than a "generation," and the final importance of the movement will be seen only when a larger *œuvre* is available from its several writers. The test of literature is the knowledge it realizes, using knowledge in the fullest and least exclusive sense, and literature realizes knowledge by the labor of that intelligent love we think of as art. It may be an unfair comparison, but to read Theodore Dreiser after reading Jack Kerouac—Dreiser knew so much and had so intelligent a love of life and art that he could compose an image of an entire society. He established a norm for American writers, and it is against the measure of human force represented by Cowperwood, Witla, Carrie, Jennie Gerhardt, Lester Kane, and Clyde Griffiths that any claim to embodying an image for a generation has to be placed.

The image shaped by the beat writers is partial, but without it any sense of life in these post–atom bomb years is incomplete. The solution is not, as is often absurdly suggested, to add Bohemia to suburbia and divide by two, thus achieving a golden mean or a shabby compromise. The solution is to be, where you are, what you are, with such persistence and courage as can be called to life. The best of the beat writers exemplify precisely that state of secular grace. In this world of shifting conflicts the integrity of the person might not be enough, but without it, all else is lost.

# DANIEL PINCHBECK

DANIEL PINCHBECK, the son of the novelist Joyce Johnson and the painter Peter Pinchbeck, was born several years after his mother's affair with Jack Kerouac. After attending Wesleyan University, Pinchbeck worked as a journalist, publishing articles in *The New York Times Magazine, Esquire,* and *The Village Voice;* he was also a founding editor of *Open City.* The recipient of a National Arts Journalism Fellowship at Columbia University in 1999, Pinchbeck is currently finishing a nonfiction work for Broadway Books. When "Children of the Beats" was originally published in *The New York Times Magazine* on November 5, 1995, it was introduced with the comment, "Their parents lived for art, and left them a bitter legacy," along with a nearly full-page photograph of the anguished face of Jan Kerouac, who was then in the process of suing the executor of the Jack Kerouac Estate for what she considered her fair share of her father's literary property.

## Children of the Beats

As a child, browsing through the bookshelves in my mother's apartment on Manhattan's Upper West Side, I occasionally found strange pieces of paper and scrawled notes inside the pages of old books on Zen Buddhism and magazines with names like *Big Table* and *The Evergreen Review*. The notes were from Jack Kerouac, who had been involved with my mother, Joyce Johnson, for a few years in the late 1950s, long before I was born. These accidentally unearthed scraps provided me with insight into the ghostlike fragility of an artist's physical legacy. They also introduced me to the Beat Generation's work, which I began to read even before I entered high school.

From time to time, figures from my mother's mysterious past would appear in our living room—such as Allen Ginsberg, Abbie Hoffman or Lawrence Ferlinghetti. As a teenager, I felt somewhat shy in their presence, imagining a depth of history between them and my mother that I couldn't share. I also saw a certain wariness in these poets and avatars, a certain tension, similar to what soldiers might feel after a long military campaign. It later seemed to me that decades of public attention and media scrutiny—often negative or accusatory in tone, especially in the early years—had taken a toll on them, made them somewhat inflexible, alert to invisible dangers hidden in the air like radio frequencies.

Kerouac's insidiously catchy phrase "mad to live, mad to love, mad to be saved, desirous of everything at the same moment . . ." was the message that my mother paid to have inscribed in my high school yearbook upon graduation in 1984. I saw it, even then, as both an encouragement and a reproach—a reproach because I already suspected that something lodged in my consciousness, as well as in the world that I belonged to, didn't allow for such a fervent pursuit of experience and ecstasy. The cynicism of the Reagan years had seeped into the atmosphere. When my friends and I sought parallels to the 1950s counterculture, we found ourselves unsatisfied. What we wanted no longer existed, or continued to exist only as style, parody, pastiche.

My marginal relationship to Beat history made me wonder what became of the children of the group's central figures. From the safe vantage point of my middle-class adolescence, I loved the movement's original testimonies, but I had been spared the chaos of their creators. In 1995, I went on a journey to speak to their children to see how they had been shaped by the values of that distant era—had their parents' live-for-the-moment ethos inspired them? Had it hindered or harmed them? Some of both, I discovered.

The Gramercy Park Hotel is a gloomy place that attracts traveling salesmen, rootless dowagers, tourists and low-level heavy-metal bands. A hastily assembled press conference, held in a plain, gray-carpeted suite, had been called by Jan Kerouac, the forty-three-year-old only child of Jack Kerouac, to announce litigation against her father's estate.

The meeting started late. Waiting around the coffee dispenser, lawyers in shiny gray suits smelling of cologne and hair spray chatted with frowzy-looking women journalists from the wire services, while notebook-toting writers wearing beads and T-shirts—most of them having no discernible press affiliation—drank bitter coffee from plastic cups. Jack Micheline, a "street poet" who had made something of a career based on his friendship with Kerouac in the Fifties, held court in one corner. In another, an enormously fat, brown-bearded man in a psychedelic jacket and a priest's collar gave out photocopies of his own confused manifesto. Finally, Jan appeared amid a small pack of journalists and advisers; she looked terrified and fluttery in a white linen dress. She walked to the front of the room and joined her supporters seated behind a cafeteria-style table and a microphone.

Jan's lawyer, Thomas A. Brill, a stiff-faced, blond-haired man in pinstripes, spoke first at the conference. "We hope to demonstrate," he said, "that the signature of Gabrielle Kerouac, Kerouac's mother, was forged on her last will in 1973, while she lay dying in a nursing home." That will left sole title of the state to Kerouac's last wife, Stella Sampas Kerouac, who died in 1990, and not to his daughter, whom Gabrielle Kerouac never really knew. Jan received royalty checks from her father's estate. But his physical property—manuscripts, letters, clothes—belonged to the Sampas family. The scroll on which Kerouac wrote *On the Road* during a three-week breakthrough into spontaneous prose might sell for more than one million dollars at auction, with each of his other manuscripts worth perhaps a third of that price.

Everything that Kerouac touched or wore has become sanctified with value.

In his work, Kerouac often avowed a horror of procreation, of "the wheel of the quivering meat conception" that turns in the void, "expelling human beings, pigs, turtles, frogs. . . ." He could never accept Jan as his own contribution to "that slaving meat wheel." He once showed my mother a photograph of a little girl in pigtails. Even in the snapshot, my mother could see that the girl looked like him, sharing his tan skin and solid jaw. "This isn't my daughter," said Kerouac, explaining that a former wife, Joan Haverty—Jan's mother—had been impregnated by another man while they were married.

Jan had met her father only twice before his death in 1969: when she was ten and a court ordered blood tests to determine whether Kerouac should pay child support, and when she was fifteen and had run away from home. She had published two novels, *Baby Driver* and *Trainsong,* chronicling her early life, before she became seriously ill. Alcoholism led to kidney failure, and she now had to administer dialysis to herself four times each day.

When Jan spoke, she told of her final meeting with her father. She had driven to his house in Lowell, Massachusetts, on her way to Mexico with her boyfriend, pregnant with a child that would be stillborn. In his dreary, desperate drunkenness, Kerouac said to her: "Yeah, you go to Mexico. Write a book. You can use my name." Her voice breaking and her eyes often failing so that she frequently stalled in mid-sentence, Jan also described her life on the road after she left home, living on a commune in California, then working as a stablehand and a waitress. As the audience shifted uneasily, she discussed her drinking, her years of poverty, her unhappy relationships. "For some reason," she said, "I kept being attracted to men who would abuse me."

When we met for breakfast a few days later at the Gramercy, Jan wore blue jeans and a baseball cap backward. "I hope to live for another ten years," she said to me.

Her small hands were thick and tough, like the hands of a farm laborer. Her eyes, however, were clear blue and guileless, almost childlike. "My dream is to buy my own house in New Mexico, but at the moment, I'm broke, almost completely penniless," she said. "The checks from the estate seem to arrive very erratically." (In fact, it turned out that royalty checks came regularly from Kerouac's agent, Sterling Lord.)

The huge bearded man who wore a priest's collar at the press conference hovered protectively at a nearby table.

"Who's that?" I asked.

"Oh, that's Buddha," Jan said, and waved at him.

"He calls himself Buddha?"

"Yeah. Buddha's a fan of my work. He lives in Lowell and visits my father's grave every day. He offered to act as my bodyguard while I'm in New York."

Jan said that she received about $60,000 a year from the Kerouac estate, and had another lawyer investigating to see whether she deserved more. "I didn't even know I was entitled to any royalties until 1985, and Stella fought tooth and nail to stop me from getting them. But this case is not about getting more money for me." Her dream was to have a Kerouac house "like the Hemingway house in Florida, where people can visit and scholars can go to examine my father's manuscripts, letters and books."

On the Road closed with Kerouac's alter ego Sal Paradise musing on his lost friend and hero: "I think of Dean Moriarty, I even think of old Dean Moriarty, the father we never found, I think of Dean Moriarty." For Jan, Kerouac was also "the father we never found," his absence sentencing her to a kind of permanent exile.

Speaking to her, I thought of William Burroughs Jr.—the son of Burroughs and Joan Vollmer, whom Burroughs killed in Mexico in 1951 when he drunkenly tried to shoot a glass off her head and missed—who had also endured a childhood in exile. While his father traveled the world, searching for the mystical drug yage in South America and then living in Tangier, Billy grew up with his grandparents in Florida. He followed his father into drug addiction, writing two autobiographical novels, Speed and Kentucky Ham, before a liver transplant failed. "I've always wanted to continue beyond X point," Billy wrote in Speed. "That is, I've always been kind of dumb." He died in 1981, at the age of thirty-four. Jan Kerouac would die a year after I met her of liver and kidney failure.

Unlike the Kerouac legacy, the estate of the Beat poet Bob Kaufman is not exactly a money machine. "We get a check for around $200 a year in royalties," said Parker Kaufman, the poet's thirty-six-year-old son, named after Charlie Parker. I met Parker in San Anselmo, a sunny suburban town at the foot of the mountains outside San Francisco, where he lived in a small residential hotel—what a hard-boiled writer in a previous era would have unhesitatingly called a "fleabag," with ratty carpets on the floor, bathrooms in the hallway and a laminated tree stump lodged in the dingy downstairs lobby instead of a bench.

He had a long, fine-featured face with a jagged scar running along one edge of his jaw. Tall and thin, wearing a Paula Abdul T-shirt and blue jeans, he carried a knapsack filled with schoolbooks over his slumped shoulders—he had just begun attending a small college nearby. As we shook hands, I noticed his faint grimace of reluctance. Several people, including Parker's mother, Eileen Kaufman, had warned me that he hated to talk about his father; setting up a meeting at all had been a delicate matter.

"They tell me that my dad's world-renowned and famous, but I can't see any reason to be interested in him," said Parker. "I never thought he amounted to much. Most of the times that I remember, he was totally incoherent."

Bob Kaufman was a legendary figure on the West Coast and in Europe, where he was known as the "American Rimbaud." The term "beatnik" was originally adopted to describe Kaufman after one of his spontaneous readings in the Coexistence Bagel Shop in San Francisco during the late Fifties. A street in North Beach was named after Kaufman, and his face was painted next to Baudelaire's on the mural against the wall of City Lights Books, which faces Jack Kerouac Alley. Part black, part Jewish, Kaufman was less well-known on the East Coast and in academic circles, perhaps because he had been ignored by what Lawrence Ferlinghetti, the poet and publisher of City Lights Books, has called "the East Coast Beat establishment." Other people ascribe his exclusion from the canon to racism.

It is also true that Kaufman chose to be obscure. Not long before his death in 1989, he told a scholar who sought him out in a bar around North Beach: "I don't know how you get involved with uninvolvement, but I don't want to be involved. My ambition is to be completely forgotten." Some of his poems reflect this desire, including "I Am a Camera," one of his last:

THE POET NAILED ON
THE HARD BONE OF THIS WORLD
HIS SOUL DEDICATED TO SILENCE
IS A FISH WITH FROG'S EYES,
THE BLOOD OF A POET FLOWS
OUT WITH HIS POEMS, BACK
TO THE PYRAMID OF BONES
FROM WHICH HE IS THRUST
HIS DEATH IS A SAVING GRACE
CREATION IS PERFECT.

Kaufman's life story suggests a certain chaotic helplessness. Invited to read at Harvard in 1960, he got waylaid instead in the underground world of New York City, where he became addicted to amphetamines, served time in prison and received shock therapy. When he returned to San Francisco in 1963, he began a ten-year vow of silence during which he wrote nothing. His silence lasted until the end of the Vietnam War.

"I don't really remember the silent treatment thing too well," Parker said. "The main thing I remember is when I was like fourteen, we went out to the park together and it took Dad somewhere between a half hour and forty-five minutes to hit a ball out to me. He was so wasted from all of the years of self-abuse that he couldn't swing a bat."

After his initial reluctance faded, Parker was eager to talk—his San Anselmo life, it seemed, was isolated and friendless. He led me to a coffee shop decorated in imitation of a Fifties diner, its shiny tin walls adorned with photographs of Elvis. "In San Francisco, everyone identifies me as Bob Kaufman's son," he told me. "I only want to be known for myself." Most of his early childhood was spent in North Beach where, as a toddler, he appeared with his parents and Taylor Mead in Ron Rice's experimental film *The Flower Thief*. His parents split up during Kaufman's decade of speechlessness, and Parker traveled with his white hippie mother to Mexico, Morocco and Ibiza, Spain. In Ibiza, Eileen let Parker, who was then ten, go off with a wealthy English family that was traveling around the world. She was not to hear from him again for more than two years.

"I was with my second family in the mountains of Afghanistan near Kabul when war broke out and we couldn't get across the Khyber Pass," Parker recalled. "We were trapped in this house, under two hundred feet of snow. We had to tunnel out to buy vegetables or food; we had no heat. If we were out in the streets after 5:00 p.m., starving attack dogs would chase us. This situation lasted for one and a half years."

In North Beach in the early Seventies—before Parker and his second family were rescued by a scouting party—Eileen was reunited with her husband. When Kaufman found out that Parker was missing, he broke his vow of silence only once, to say: "You lost our son." After Parker returned home, his parents were remarried in a ceremony on Mount Tamalpais, in California. But Parker found it impossible to relate to his father.

"It's frustrating when everyone's telling you, 'How dare you talk back to your dad? He's a genius,'" Parker said. "Meanwhile, it's okay for him to sleep on the sofa all day, drinking beer and smoking four packs of cigarettes."

Parker opened up a leather portfolio of his modeling and acting photographs, most of them at least a decade old. He had appeared in a few movies, including *The Right Stuff,* and in some television shows, including *Midnight Caller,* and was working on his acting career—"it was getting to the point where I was beginning to get paid"—when he was beat up and knifed at a club where he was working.

"Sometimes I just think I have bad karma," he said. He told me that he and his mother were currently destitute. "I don't know where my next meal is coming from. It's *that* bad." His elderly mother rode the bus to see him every few days, wearing a bright blue cape and bringing him lunch meat and bread. He was out of cigarettes, and I guiltily got him a couple of packs of Marlboros at a convenience store.

"Right now, I'm like this close to ending it all," he said between bites of a cheeseburger I bought him. "I was walking across the Golden Gate Bridge and I looked over and thought how easy it would be just to leap over the ledge." He sighed. "I am trying to come to terms with the possibility that I won't do anything spectacular with my life. My main goal at this point is just to be able to provide for my family someday. I want to have what we never had."

Although he never published his own creative writing, Lucien Carr was an important and original member of the Beats. He rolled the young Kerouac home in a beer barrel one drunken night, and introduced Kerouac and Ginsberg to William Burroughs. In an incident that is part of the peculiarly violent prehistory of the Beat movement, Carr stabbed David Kammerer to death in Riverside Park in New York in 1944. An older man who had fallen obsessively in love with Carr as his Boy Scout master in Missouri, Kammerer had pursued Carr to Columbia, even taking a job as a janitor at the university to be near him. Carr was found guilty of manslaughter and was sent to a state reformatory in Elmira, New York, for two years before he was pardoned by the governor. (He later became an assistant managing editor of United Press International, and is now retired.) Two of Carr's sons are Caleb Carr, the best-selling author of *The Alienist* and *Angel of Darkness,* and Simon Carr, an abstract painter.

I visited Simon Carr in his Lower East Side studio, crowded with abstract paintings of swirls rendered with a Cézanne-like palette. Slender and handsome, with brown hair going gray, Simon wore round gold-framed intellectual-style glasses, and his eyes looked gentle behind the lenses. He showed me a catalogue from his last SoHo exhibition, "Chromaticism and Joy."

Simon credited his father with giving him and his siblings "the sense that you were definitely going to do something—that you had to express it to say it. My dad was a great talker—he and his friends would talk all night." But he said he gravitated to fine art because "it's the opposite of talking: The bottom line of great painting is silence."

Simon's wife, Cristina, worked as a conservator at the Metropolitan Museum of Art; they had three children in private schools in the city. He made a living teaching at various colleges and art schools around New York; he was also running a special studio class for unwed mothers at Manhattan Community College. "I associate the Beats with the more difficult times we had as a family," he said. "There was a lot of wild drinking, a lot of people disappearing and then coming back. It was a difficult time for a ten-year-old trying to hold his world together. You might have a wild time one night and then wake up the next morning and you don't know what to eat for breakfast because there's no food around and everyone's asleep."

His brother Caleb agreed: "What's extremely romantic for adults may be disruptive and frightening for children," he said when I reached him by phone. "The Beats were so concerned with breaking molds and creating new lifestyles that they threw the baby out with the bathwater—they threw out the social framework needed to maintain a family. If any element got lost in the Beat equation, it was the idea of children."

Caleb's novel *The Alienist* was about as un-Beat a book as it is possible to imagine—as clammy as the Beats were heated—and I wondered if this was intentional. I saw personal messages in lines like this: "He probably had a troubled relationship with one or both parents early on, and eventually grew to despise everything about them—including their heritage."

"I think the Beats were extremely dysfunctional people who basically had no business raising children," said Christina Mitchell, the daughter of John Mitchell—a Beat entrepreneur who started many of the original coffeehouses in Greenwich Village, including the Fat Black Pussy Cat and the Figaro. Christina was also the daughter of Alene Lee. Part black, part Cherokee Indian, Lee appeared in Kerouac's novel *The Subterraneans* as Mardou Fox, the gorgeous dark-skinned woman that Leo Percepied loved and lost and mourned for: "No girl had ever moved me with a story of spiritual suffering and so beautifully her soul showing out radiant as an angel wandering in hell." Lee was the only woman and the only black person included in an early essay by Kerouac, defining the Beat movement by the spiritual epiphanies that the group experienced: "A.L.'s vision of everything as mysterious electricity."

During the years Christina was growing up, she and her mother lived with Lucien Carr. Her mother's relationship with Carr, Christina recalled in a voice filled with incantatory rage, was "ten years of fighting, screaming, hitting, going to the police station in the middle of the night, going to Bellevue, wandering the streets, watching Mom and Lucien beat each other to a pulp." Their narcissism was all-consuming, she thinks now. "I was basically a nonperson to them. I don't think they knew I was there."

She said she never read *The Subterraneans* or any of the other manifestoes of the group. The only Beat she really respected was Allen Ginsberg. "Most of the Beat people disappeared from our lives, but when my mother died, Allen was by her bedside. He was one of the few people to value a human being beyond their fame or status."

Christina stumbled out of her adolescence—"I was either shy or catatonic"—and joined the Reverend Sun Myung Moon's Unification Church. "I spaced out for five years. I entered the group because I wanted the stability of a family—what they talked about—one happy world. The whole time I was with them my mother never told me to come back." She finally left the Moonies and resurfaced in Denver, where she attended a community college and began to rebuild her life.

When I spoke to her, Christina was thirty-seven, living in Upstate New York and majoring in English literature. As a reaction to the horror that she feels was her own childhood, she admitted to being perhaps overly protective of her six-year-old son and infant daughter: "I am compulsive with my kids. I feel that it is a really shitty world and I want to keep the shit off of them." She accompanied her son to the first day of his first-grade class, despite the teacher's objections. "I hope my compulsion to protect them won't destroy them."

Despite her anger at her mother, Christina believed that Lee was an extraordinary person. "She went out with all of them, didn't she? Kerouac, Corso, Lucien. But she never capitalized on her involvement with the beatniks. She had no interest in having her fifteen minutes of fame. My mother was a woman who could not be typecast, stereotyped or dismissed. I think they were all a little bit in awe of her."


"I see that generation as kind of like a brilliant child," said Tara Marlowe, the twenty-seven-year-old daughter of the anarchist Beat poet Diane di Prima. "They did whatever they wanted."

Di Prima, a ferocious individualist, was the mother of five children by four different men. She reared her brood in San Francisco's rough Fillmore district. "We got chased a lot," Tara recalled the day I met her in the East Village, where our mothers had once lived. Tara's father, Alan Marlowe, was a former male model who spent his last years at the Rocky Mountain Buddhist Center. "Dad thought women were for breeding and men were for fucking." Tara didn't visit him when he was dying. "I don't regret that decision," she said. "A dying asshole is still an asshole."

Tara was short and stocky—she resembled her mother except for her long, polished fingernails and the silver chain around her neck. Frank and eloquent about her past, she said she grew up "like a kid in a potato patch. I've never met anyone poorer than we were. When I was a kid, my mother once told us that she was going on strike—she wasn't going to be the mother and cook for us anymore. She's still on strike."

"What did that mean to you?"

"It meant that no one ever taught me table manners," she said, "or how to dress or that I should clean myself, so I walked around like a filthy ragamuffin with matted hair." At thirteen, Tara left home and moved to Mendocino, where she met a seventeen-year-old coke-dealer boyfriend. "I got involved in sexual relationships that to me weren't sexual. I was basically in a rage most of the time. Now I'm sort of a born-again virgin." She lived as an "emancipated minor" in a converted chicken coop near the alternative school she was attending. Eventually, she returned home. "At our house, the drug dealers were the good guys," she recalled. "They brought Christmas presents—the whole Robin Hood thing. The poets were these icky guys with foam at the side of their mouths."

In college, Marlowe wrote poems and even published her own poetry magazine, *Dissociated Press*. She said as an adult she drinks only occasionally, noting that when she does drink, "there's not enough alcohol in the world to make me feel better." She lived in the Williamsburg section of Brooklyn, working as a freelance graphic artist. "For the first time, I'm beginning to enjoy my life," she said. "I still feel like some kind of space alien, a complete outsider from middle-class culture. It sometimes seems as if the world is this big office party and I'm the uninvited guest."

Some of my earliest memories are of visiting Hettie Jones, my mother's best friend from her blackstocking days, and her daughters, Kellie and Lisa, on the Bowery. When I was a child, Hettie's creaky, crooked and labyrinthine apartment seemed almost organic to me, as if it had grown outward from her vibrant personality to fill the space around her. I faintly recall crowded holiday parties with a cheerful mix of poets, painters and jazz musicians drinking and laughing, jammed up against each other in the narrow hallways. Growing up, I regretted that my mother put that bohemian world behind us, moving away from downtown to the more bourgeois boundaries of the Upper West Side.

"I don't know much about the Beat period," said Lisa Jones, the daughter of Hettie and the poet LeRoi Jones. "I never read the books—the writers of the Harlem Renaissance had a much greater influence on me. I guess I was trying to divorce myself from that history, from my parents' story."

A *Village Voice* columnist, Lisa had published a book of essays called *Bulletproof Diva*. She had also worked with Spike Lee and written movie and television scripts. Her older sister, Kellie, had become a curator and art historian. Lisa's father left the family early in her childhood to join the Black Nationalist movement, changing his name to Amiri Baraka. "People like my mom were already talking about a different idea of family back then," Lisa said. "We belonged to a tight community. I hate the idea that growing up with one parent automatically means you have to be dysfunctional. Though my parents weren't together, we spent time with both of them and were loved and nurtured by both of them. My grandparents were always there and they were a strong force.

"As a kid, it never struck me that we were that bohemian," Lisa said emphatically. "We had chores and curfews—although my mom might disagree. I always referred to myself as a B. A. P.—a Bohemian American Princess."

Some people found in the Beat quest for personal freedom not an excuse for nihilism or bad behavior, but a way to develop new models of commitment. For instance, the Beat poet Michael McClure's daughter, Jane McClure, followed the thread of her father's interest in naturalism to study molecular biology and eventually became a doctor. Of her life on Haight-Ashbury she recalled "nothing was scary—everything was interesting." Her father's friendships with Jim Morrison and the Hell's Angels caused no injury and seemed to leave no particular impression.

Allen Ginsberg's life demonstrated his Buddhist-Beat ethos of compassion and responsibility. Although he never had his own kids, he continued to help members of his huge community as well as their children. Many of the children I spoke to had memories of Allen's generosity. At various times, he bailed Burroughs's son, Billy, out of jail, let Jan Kerouac live at his house in Boulder, and put up Cassady's son

Curtis Hansen at his apartment in New York. Treating the Beats as an extended family, Allen nursed his friends back to health when they were sick, put them up when they ran out of money, supported their work and used his influence to help whenever possible. His empathetic behavior offers a contrast to the self-centered concerns of most artists today.

The children of Neal Cassady, the Beat Generation's most famous icon of perpetual adolescence and sexual craving, grew up as well. Cassady and his "wild yea-saying over burst of American joy" inspired some of Kerouac's and Ginsberg's best work in the Fifties. A decade later, he led the Merry Pranksters' psychedelic charge across the continent. The son of a Denver wino, Cassady wasn't much of a writer, but he played the role of Socrates to the counterculture, inspiring others by his manic example.

I met John Allen Cassady, the son of Neal and Carolyn Cassady, for several pints of beer at a bar in the North Beach section of San Francisco. John Allen told me that he found *On the Road* dull going. "A lot of that Beat stuff is so obtuse," he said. He was an expansive man with a white beard and bright blue eyes, friendly and talkative. "My friends used to call me the albino wino." He was living in San Jose, California, working for a computer company that manufactured optical scanners; he answered customers' queries about the product. Years before, he had made dulcimers and sold them at country fairs; he was also something of a Deadhead.

"Neal had such a capacity for everything," John Allen said. "I think he was a very evolved soul. I've inherited his wheel karma. Dad had eighteen cars in the back of our yard; I've got about six in mine. We must have been charioteers in ancient Rome." As John Allen spoke, I sensed that he had told some of his stories many times in other pubs, for other occasions, and I began to suspect that sadness lurked beneath his surface gregariousness.

John Allen said that his father wrote other books besides *The First Third*, an early childhood memoir published by City Lights. He added: "There was a *Second Third* and a *Third Third*, Neal told me. He wrote them on reams and reams of yellow notebook paper but, unfortunately, he had all of the papers in the backseat of this old jalopy, which he left at Ken Kesey's place. He went away for a couple of weeks, and when he came back he found that some punk kids had stolen the car. That was it—his whole life's work gone. He was really upset about that."

John Allen also told me that Billy Burroughs, the son of William, had lived with him in Santa Cruz, California, for three months in 1976, after he received a liver transplant. "That guy was hell-bent on self-destruction. His attitude was, 'Hey, I got a new one to burn.' Toward the end, he started getting pretty unintelligible." John Allen was glad when Billy moved on—he had already witnessed his own father's unraveling a decade earlier.

"By the Sixties, Dad was so burned out, so bitter," John Allen said. "He told me once that he felt like a dancing bear, that he was just performing. He was wired all the time, talking nonstop. I remember once, after a party, about 2:00 a.m., he went in the bathroom, turned on the shower and just started screaming and didn't stop. I was about fifteen then and I knew he was in deep trouble, that he was really a tortured soul. He died not too long after that."

"Maybe you can explain what all the fuss was about," said Curtis Hansen, John Allen's half-brother and Neal Cassady's other son. Curtis, forty-five when I met him, never really knew his father. Curtis's mother, Diana Hansen, was a Barnard graduate who fell in love with Cassady while working at an advertising agency in the late Forties; she ended up with a walk-on in *On the Road*. "What did those guys do that was so amazing?"

"Um, well, I suppose they offered some kind of antidote to the repression of the Cold War period," I said, hesitating at the English-lit-class banality of the phrases. "They encouraged people to find new ways of living, to rediscover America."

Curtis paused thoughtfully. "Cassady had a great public-relations department, I guess," he said, "always surrounding himself with all those phenomenal writers and so on."

A former disc jockey, Curtis was programming director for WICC-AM, a radio station in Bridgeport, Connecticut, and for WEBE-FM in Fairfield County. We drove in his Japanese compact through the city's rainy, eerily empty streets to the radio station's impersonal glass office tower. Solidly good-looking in a jungle-print tie and tan pants—he looked like a somewhat stockier version of Cassady—Hansen gave off a strong positive vibe that suggested a disposition inherited from his father. The only thing of Neal's that he owned was a sheaf of yellowing handwritten letters that Cassady wrote to Diana Hansen in the early Fifties, when he was trying to convince her to move to one town away from his wife, Carolyn, so he could continue the sexual triangulation that was one of his life's driving obsessions.

"The letters have some pretty wild stuff in them," Curtis said. "He talks about cunt hair and all the sex they're going to have when they get together. You can tell they had a real good sexual relationship."

"What did your mom tell you about Cassady?" I asked.

"Oh, she said that he was a jailbird—that I should stay away from him. I was real embarrassed when he went to prison in the late Fifties—that's why we changed my name to Hansen."

"What did you think of *On the Road?*"

"That book they wrote together?" he said. "I thought it was *boring*," he says. "I never really understood what that whole shtick was about."

Yet Hansen was inspired by the father he never knew and the book he didn't care for to go on the road himself, driving across country in 1969, after he was "invited to leave" college on suspicion of selling mescaline and for having a girl in his room. "That trip across the country is one of the things I'm proudest of in my life," he said. "Cassady had just died, I got laid for the first time, got high and took off. It was definitely a symbolic journey."

"I imagine that it must have been difficult to be Cassady's son," I offered.

"Well, I used to feel I had a lot to live up to," he said in his effusive, former-DJ voice. "I wish my dad had been around so I could have asked him about girls. I used to have a lot of trouble in that area."

In a few weeks, he and his wife, a receptionist at his office, were due to visit Salt Lake City for a creative visualization workshop. "This is definitely the dawning of the Age of Aquarius," he said. "I'm totally in favor of—what do they call it?—'popular spirituality.' Just because it's popular doesn't mean it's wrong."

At his office, Hansen excitedly showed me the computer that creates each day's playlist—it was all based on market research, studying the demographic reaction to song "burnout" and likability among baby-boomer women. "We don't want to upset our audience or they'll turn the dial," he explained, gesturing with his hands as he speaks. "We try to use only good words on the air, like 'free' and 'special offer.' "

We walked past the darkened soundstages, where insectile-looking headgear and metal protuberances dangled from the ceiling. Technicians hurried past, many of them wearing 1960s-style beards and pony-tails. "Ronald Reagan once sat here," Hansen said, pointing at a bare wooden table. "There used to be a plaque but I guess it fell off."

Listening to the drone of a Michael Bolton song in Hansen's office, where windows overlooked the gray panorama of Bridgeport, I thought about how radio once encouraged the outsider expression of someone like Alan Freed, who promoted rock & roll in its early days. In the Forties and Fifties, Symphony Sid's shows of jazz and bebop had inspired Kerouac and Cassady on their manic jaunts across the continent.

"Does it bother you that radio has become so corporate?" I asked Hansen.

"No, that's what's so great about our time," he said. "What I think has happened is that the counterculture and the mainstream have merged." He waved his hands excitedly in the air as he continued. "You don't have to listen anymore to the songs you don't like—you only listen to the songs that the *majority* of the people like. You see what I mean? The mainstream has become the new frontier." From his desk, he turned up the volume on the live feed from the soundstage down the hall, and the voice of Michael Bolton grew louder and louder until it momentarily seemed to envelop us.

---

# NORMAN PODHORETZ

NORMAN PODHORETZ, editor and critic, published "The Know-Nothing Bohemians" in *Partisan Review,* vol. XXV, No. 2 (Spring 1958). More than forty years later, in his memoir *Ex-Friends* (1999), he continued to rail at Allen Ginsberg, whose "close ness," Podhoretz explained, "consisted not in a genuine friendship but in the many years we went back and the recurrent visions and dreams he had about me." Podhoretz was a member of the informal group of New York intellectuals who journeyed from radicalism to conservatism in their careers after the Second World War. In his attack on the spontaneity, energy, and enthusiasm of the Beat writers in his 1958 article, Podhoretz appointed himself "spokesman of the rear guard," as the biographer Ted Morgan understood.

The result of Podhoretz's article was a spate of letters to the *Partisan Review* defending the Beats, including one by LeRoi Jones. In the "Correspondence" pages of the next issue of the journal, Jones wrote that Beat literature was "less a movement than a reaction. It is a reaction against, let us say to start, fifteen years of sterile, unreadable magazine poetry" by writers such as "Randall Jarrell, Robert Lowell, Karl Shapiro, Delmore Schwartz, John Berryman, Peter Viereck, George Barker, Stephen Spender, Louis Macniece, and others who were so representative of what poetry was in the 1940s, as well as [Richard] Eberhart, [Richard] Wilbur, [William] Meredith, [W. S.] Merwin, [Elizabeth] Bishop" and others who "represent the academically condoned poetry of the 1950s. But I wish to say emphatically that from this entire group of poets (which represents almost twenty years of poetry) we have about five poems of note."

Podhoretz and other critics and reviewers continued to snipe away at the Beat writers in the pages of *Partisan Review.* For example, in the Fall 1958 issue, Podhoretz wrote in "The New Nihilism and the Novel" that the "reception accorded Jack Kerouac and Allen Ginsberg, whose work combines an appearance of radicalism with a show of intense spirituality, testifies to the hunger that has grown up on all sides for something extreme, fervent, affirmative, and sweeping; five, or even three, years ago the Beat Generation would simply not have been noticed." In the same issue, the English critic Al Alvarez, reviewing Denise Levertov's small-press collection of poetry *Overland to the Islands,* began by saying, "Miss Denise Levertov is said to be the best of San Francisco's Beat poets. Since the other candidates are Allen Ginsberg, Gregory Corso, and Lawrence Ferlinghetti, no one will deny her the title." Alvarez, who had befriended the poet Sylvia Plath in London, wanted

Levertov to stop imitating William Carlos Williams and find "a language of her own." Perhaps the San Francisco scene has something to do with her timidity, for the extraordinary thing about the Beat Generation [writers] is the degree to which they are old-fashioned. They seem to feel they have to be 'modern,' and 'modern' simply means going through the ritual experiments that were already dated by the mid-'twenties. It is, after all, time someone explained to Mr. Ginsberg that Whitman and Vachel Lindsay are not so very *avant-garde*."

## The Know-Nothing Bohemians

Allen Ginsberg's little volume of poems, *Howl,* which got the San Francisco renaissance off to a screaming start a year or so ago, was dedicated to Jack Kerouac ("new Buddha of American prose, who spit forth intelligence into eleven books written in half the number of years . . . creating a spontaneous bop prosody and original classic literature"), William Seward Burroughs ("author of *Naked Lunch,* an endless novel which will drive everybody mad"), and Neal Cassady ("author of *The First Third,* an autobiography . . . which enlightened Buddha"). So far, everybody's sanity has been spared by the inability of *Naked Lunch* to find a publisher, and we may never get the chance to discover what Buddha learned from Neal Cassady's autobiography, but thanks to the Viking and Grove Presses, two of Kerouac's original classics, *On the Road* and *The Subterraneans,* have now been revealed to the world. When *On the Road* appeared last year, Gilbert Millstein commemorated the event in the New York *Times* by declaring it to be "a historic occasion" comparable to the publication of *The Sun Also Rises* in the 1920's. But even before the novel was actually published, the word got around that Kerouac was the spokesman of a new group of rebels and Bohemians who called themselves the Beat Generation, and soon his photogenic countenance (unshaven, of course, and topped by an unruly crop of rich black hair falling over his forehead) was showing up in various mass-circulation magazines, he was being interviewed earnestly on television, and he was being featured in a

Greenwich Village nightclub where, in San Francisco fashion, he read specimens of his spontaneous bop prosody against a background of jazz music.

Though the nightclub act reportedly flopped, *On the Road* sold well enough to hit the best-seller lists for several weeks, and it isn't hard to understand why. Americans love nothing so much as representative documents, and what could be more interesting in this Age of Sociology than a novel that speaks for the "young generation?" (The fact that Kerouac is thirty-five or thereabouts was generously not held against him.) Beyond that, however, I think that the unveiling of the Beat Generation was greeted with a certain relief by many people who had been disturbed by the notorious respectability and "maturity" of postwar writing. This was more like it—restless, rebellious, confused youth living it up, instead of thin, balding, buttoned-down instructors of English composing ironic verses with one hand while changing the baby's diapers with the other. Bohemianism is not particularly fashionable nowadays, but the image of Bohemia still exerts a powerful fascination—nowhere more so than in the suburbs, which are filled to overflowing with men and women who uneasily think of themselves as conformists and of Bohemianism as the heroic road. The whole point of *Marjorie Morningstar* was to assure the young marrieds of Mamaroneck that they were better off than the apparently glamorous *luftmenschen* of Greenwich Village, and the fact that Wouk had to work so hard at making this idea seem convincing is a good indication of the strength of prevailing doubt on the matter.

On the surface, at least, the Bohemianism of *On the Road* is very attractive. Here is a group of high-spirited young men running back and forth across the country (mostly hitch-hiking, sometimes in their own second-hand cars), going to "wild" parties in New York and Denver and San Francisco, living on a shoe-string (GI educational benefits, an occasional fifty bucks from a kindly aunt, an odd job as a typist, a fruit-picker, a parking-lot attendant), talking intensely about love and God and salvation, getting high on marijuana (but never heroin or cocaine), listening feverishly to jazz in crowded little joints, and sleeping freely with beautiful girls. Now and again there is a reference to gloom and melancholy, but the characteristic note struck by Kerouac is exuberance:

We stopped along the road for a bite to eat. The cowboy went off to have a spare tire patched, and Eddie and I sat down in a kind of homemade diner. I heard a great laugh, the greatest laugh in the world, and here came this rawhide oldtimes Nebraska farmer with a bunch of other boys into the diner; you could hear his raspy cries clear across the plains, across the whole gray world of them that day. Everybody else laughed with him. He didn't have a care in the world and had the hugest regard for everybody. I said to myself, Wham, listen to that man laugh. That's the West, here I am in the West. He came booming into the diner, calling Maw's name, and she made the sweetest cherry pie in Nebraska, and I had some with a mountainous scoop of ice cream on top. "Maw, rustle me up some grub afore I have to start eatin myself or some damn silly idee like that." And he threw himself on a stool and went hyaw hyaw hyaw hyaw. "And throw some beans in it." It was the spirit of the West sitting right next to me. I wished I knew his whole raw life and what the hell he'd been doing all these years besides laughing and yelling like that. Whooee, I told my soul, and the cowboy came back and off we went to Grand Island.

Kerouac's enthusiasm for the Nebraska farmer is part of his general readiness to find the source of all vitality and virtue in simple rural types and in the dispossessed urban groups (Negroes, bums, whores). His idea of life in New York is "millions and millions hustling forever for a buck among themselves . . . grabbing, taking, giving, sighing, dying, just so they could be buried in those awful cemetery cities beyond Long Island City," whereas the rest of America is populated almost exclusively by the true of heart. There are intimations here of a kind of know-nothing populist sentiment, but in other ways this attitude resembles Nelson Algren's belief that bums and whores and junkies are more interesting than white-collar workers or civil servants. The difference is that Algren hates middle-class respectability for moral and political reasons—the middle class exploits and persecutes—while Kerouac, who is thoroughly unpolitical, seems to feel that respectability is a sign not of moral corruption but of spiritual death. "The only people for me," says Sal Paradise, the narrator of *On the Road*, "are the mad ones, the ones who are mad to live, mad to talk, mad to be saved, desirous of everything at the same time, the ones who never yawn or say a commonplace thing, but burn, burn, burn like fabulous yellow roman candles exploding like spiders across the stars. . . ." This tremendous emphasis on emotional intensity, this notion that to be hopped-up is the most desirable of all human conditions, lies at the heart of the Beat Generation ethos and distinguishes it radically from the Bohemianism of the past.

The Bohemianism of the 1920's represented a repudiation of the provinciality, philistinism, and moral hypocrisy of American life—a life, incidentally, which was still essentially small-town and rural in tone. Bohemia, in other words, was a movement created in the name of civilization: its ideals were intelligence, cultivation, spiritual refine-ment. The typical literary figure of the 1920's was a midwesterner (Hemingway, Fitzgerald, Sinclair Lewis, Eliot, Pound) who had fled from his home town to New York or Paris in search of a freer, more ex-pansive, more enlightened way of life than was possible in Ohio or Minnesota or Michigan. The political radicalism that supplied the characteristic coloring of Bohemianism in the 1930's did nothing to al-ter the urban, cosmopolitan bias of the 1920's. At its best, the radical-ism of the 1930's was marked by deep intellectual seriousness and aimed at a state of society in which the fruits of civilization would be more widely available—and ultimately available to all.

The Bohemianism of the 1950's is another kettle of fish altogether. It is hostile to civilization; it worships primitivism, instinct, energy, "blood." To the extent that it has intellectual interests at all, they run to mystical doctrines, irrationalist philosophies, and left-wing Reichi-anism. The only art the new Bohemians have any use for is jazz, mainly of the cool variety. Their predilection for bop language is a way of demonstrating solidarity with the primitive vitality and spontaneity they find in jazz and of expressing contempt for coherent, rational dis-course which, being a product of the mind, is in their view a form of death. To be articulate is to admit that you have no feelings (for how can real feelings be expressed in syntactical language?), that you can't respond to anything (Kerouac responds to everything by saying "Wow!"), and that you are probably impotent.

At the one end of the spectrum, this ethos shades off into vio-lence and criminality, main-line drug addiction and madness. Allen Ginsberg's poetry, with its lurid apocalyptic celebration of "angel-headed hipsters," speaks for the darker side of the new Bohemianism.

Kerouac is milder. He shows little taste for violence, and the criminality he admires is the harmless kind. The hero of *On the Road*, Dean Moriarty, has a record: "From the age of eleven to seventeen he was usually in reform school. His specialty was stealing cars, gunning for girls coming out of high school in the afternoon, driving them out to the mountains, making them, and coming back to sleep in any available hotel bathtub in town." But Dean's criminality, we are told, "was not something that sulked and sneered; it was a wild yea-saying overburst of American joy; it was Western, the west wind, an ode from the Plains, something new, long prophesied, long a-coming (he only stole cars for joy rides)." And, in fact, the species of Bohemian that Kerouac writes about is on the whole rather law-abiding. In *The Subterraneans*, a bunch of drunken boys steal a pushcart in the middle of the night, and when they leave it in front of a friend's apartment building, he denounces them angrily for "screwing up the security of my pad." When Sal Paradise (in *On the Road*) steals some groceries from the canteen of an itinerant workers' camp in which he has taken a temporary job as a barracks guard, he comments, "I suddenly began to realize that everybody in America is a natural-born thief"—which, of course, is a way of turning his own stealing into a bit of boyish prankishness. Nevertheless, Kerouac is attracted to criminality, and that in itself is more significant than the fact that he personally feels constrained to put the brakes on his own destructive impulses.

Sex has always played a very important role in Bohemianism: sleeping around was the Bohemian's most dramatic demonstration of his freedom from conventional moral standards, and a defiant denial of the idea that sex was permissible only in marriage and then only for the sake of a family. At the same time, to be "promiscuous" was to assert the validity of sexual experience in and for itself. The "meaning" of Bohemian sex, then, was at once social and personal, a crucial element in the Bohemian's ideal of civilization. Here again the contrast with Beat Generation Bohemianism is sharp. On the one hand, there is a fair amount of sexual activity in *On the Road* and *The Subterraneans*. Dean Moriarty is a "new kind of American saint" at least partly because of his amazing sexual power: he can keep three women satisfied simultaneously and he can make love any time, anywhere (once he mounts a girl in the back seat of a car while poor Sal Paradise is trying to sleep in front). Sal, too, is always on the make, and though he isn't as successful as the great Dean, he does pretty well: offhand I can remember a girl in Denver, one on a bus, and another in New York, but a little research would certainly unearth a few more. The heroine of *The Subterraneans,* a Negro girl named Mardou Fox, seems to have switched from one to another member of the same gang and back again ("This has been an incestuous group in its time"), and we are given to understand that there is nothing unusual about such an arrangement. But the point of all this hustle and bustle is not freedom from ordinary social restrictions or defiance of convention (except in relation to homosexuality, which is Ginsberg's preserve: among "the best minds" of Ginsberg's generation who were destroyed by America are those "who let themselves be —— in the —— by saintly motorcyclists, and screamed with joy, / who blew and were blown by those human seraphim, the sailors, caresses of Atlantic and Caribbean love"). The sex in Kerouac's book goes hand in hand with a great deal of talk about forming permanent relationships ("although I have a hot feeling sexually and all that for her," says the poet Adam Moorad in *The Subterraneans,* "I really don't want to get any further into her not only for these reasons but finally, the big one, if I'm going to get involved with a girl now I want to be permanent like permanent and serious and long termed and I can't do that with her"), and a habit of getting married and then duly divorced and re-married when another girl comes along. In fact, there are as many marriages and divorces in *On the Road* as in the Hollywood movie colony (must be that California climate): "All those years I was looking for the woman I wanted to marry," Sal Paradise tells us. "I couldn't meet a girl without saying to myself, What kind of wife would she make?" Even more revealing is Kerouac's refusal to admit that any of his characters ever make love wantonly or lecherously—no matter how casual the encounter it must always entail sweet feelings toward the girl. Sal, for example, is fixed up with Rita Bettencourt in Denver, whom he has never met before. "I got her in my bedroom after a long talk in the dark of the front room. She was a nice little girl, simple and true [naturally], and tremendously frightened of sex. I told her it was beautiful. I wanted to prove this to her. She let me prove it, but I was too impatient and proved nothing. She sighed in the dark. 'What do you want out of life?' I asked, and I used to ask that all the time of girls." This is rather touching, but only because the narrator is really just as frightened of sex as that nice little girl was. He is frightened of failure and he worries about his performance. For *performance* is the point—performance and "good orgasms," which are the first duty of man and the only duty of woman. What seems to be involved here, in short, is sexual anxiety of enormous proportions—an anxiety that comes out very clearly in *The Subterraneans,* which is about a love affair between the young writer, Leo Percepied, and the Negro girl, Mardou Fox. Despite its protestations, the book is one long agony of fear and trembling over sex:

> I spend long nights and many hours making her, finally I have her, I pray for it to come, I can hear her breathing harder, I hope against hope it's time, a noise in the hall (or whoop of drunkards next door) takes her mind off and she can't make it and laughs—but when she does make it I hear her crying, whimpering, the shuddering electrical female orgasm makes her sound like a little girl crying, moaning in the night, it lasts a good twenty seconds and when it's over she moans, "O why can't it last longer," and "O when will I when you do?"—"Soon now I bet," I said, "you're getting closer and closer"—

Very primitive, very spontaneous, very elemental, very beat.

For the new Bohemians interracial friendships and love affairs apparently play the same role of social defiance that sex used to play in older Bohemian circles. Negroes and whites associate freely on a basis of complete equality and without a trace of racial hostility. But putting it that way understates the case, for not only is there no racial hostility, there is positive adulation for the "happy, true-hearted, ecstatic Negroes of America."

> At lilac evening I walked with every muscle aching among the lights of 27th and Welton in the Denver colored section, wishing I were a Negro, feeling that the best the white world had offered was not enough ecstasy for me, not enough life, joy, kicks, darkness, music, not enough night. . . . I wished I were a Denver Mexican, or even a poor overworked Jap, anything but what I was so drearily, a "white man" disillusioned. All my life I'd had white ambitions. . . . I passed the dark porches of Mexican and Negro homes; soft voices were there, occasionally the dusky knee of some mysterious sensuous gal; and

dark faces of the men behind rose arbors. Little children sat
like sages in ancient rocking chairs.

It will be news to the Negroes to learn that they are so happy and ecstatic; I doubt if a more idyllic picture of Negro life has been painted
since certain Southern ideologues tried to convince the world that
things were just as fine as fine could be for the slaves on the old plantation. Be that as it may, Kerouac's love for Negroes and other dark-
skinned groups is tied up with his worship of primitivism, not with any
radical social attitudes. Ironically enough, in fact, to see the Negro as
more elemental than the white man, as Ned Polsky has acutely remarked, is "an inverted form of keeping the nigger in his place." But
even if it were true that American Negroes, by virtue of their position
in our culture, have been able to retain a degree of primitive spontaneity, the last place you would expect to find evidence of this is
among Bohemian Negroes. Bohemianism, after all, is for the Negro a
means of entry into the world of the whites, and no Negro Bohemian
is going to cooperate in the attempt to identify him with Harlem or
Dixieland. The only major Negro character in either of Kerouac's two
novels is Mardou Fox, and she is about as primitive as Wilhelm Reich
himself.

The plain truth is that the primitivism of the Beat Generation
serves first of all as a cover for an anti-intellectualism so bitter that it
makes the ordinary American's hatred of eggheads seem positively benign. Kerouac and his friends like to think of themselves as intellectuals ("they are intellectual as hell and know all about Pound without
being pretentious or talking too much about it"), but this is only a form
of newspeak. Here is an example of what Kerouac considers intelligent discourse—"formal and shining and complete, without the tedious intellectualness":

> We passed a little kid who was throwing stones at the cars in
> the road. "Think of it," said Dean. "One day he'll put a stone
> through a man's windshield and the man will crash and die—
> all on account of that little kid. You see what I mean? God ex-
> ists without qualms. As we roll along this way I am positive
> beyond doubt that everything will be taken care of for us—
> that even you, as you drive, fearful of the wheel . . . the thing
> will go along of itself and you won't go off the road and I can

sleep. Furthermore we know America, we're at home; I can go anywhere in America and get what I want because it's the same in every corner, I know the people, I know what they do. We give and take and go in the incredibly complicated sweetness zigzagging every side."

You see what he means? Formal and shining and complete. No tedious intellectualness. Completely unpretentious. "There was nothing clear about the things he said but what he meant to say was somehow made pure and clear." *Somehow*. Of course. If what he wanted to say had been carefully thought out and precisely articulated, that would have been tedious and pretentious and, no doubt, *somehow* unclear and clearly impure. But so long as he utters these banalities with his tongue tied and with no comprehension of their meaning, so long as he makes noises that came out of his soul (since they couldn't possibly have come out of his mind), he passes the test of true intellectuality.

Which brings us to Kerouac's spontaneous bop prosody. This "prosody" is not to be confused with bop language itself, which has such a limited vocabulary (Basic English is a verbal treasure-house by comparison) that you couldn't write a note to the milk-man in it, much less a novel. Kerouac, however, manages to remain true to the spirit of hipster slang while making forays into enemy territory (i.e., the English language) by his simple inability to express anything in words. The only method he has of describing an object is to summon up the same half-dozen adjectives over and over again: "greatest," "tremendous," "crazy," "mad," "wild," and perhaps one or two others. When it's more than just mad or crazy or wild, it becomes "really mad" or "really crazy" or "really wild." (All quantities in excess of three, incidentally, are subsumed under the rubric "innumerable," a word used innumerable times in *On the Road* but not so innumerably in *The Subterraneans*.) The same poverty of resources is apparent in those passages where Kerouac tries to handle a situation involving even slightly complicated feelings. His usual tactic is to run for cover behind cliché and vague signals to the reader. For instance: "I looked at him; my eyes were watering with embarrassment and tears. Still he stared at me. Now his eyes were blank and looking through me. . . . Something clicked in both of us. In me it was suddenly concern for a man who was years younger than I, five years, and whose fate was wound with mine across the passage of the recent years; in him it was a matter that I can ascertain only from what he did afterward." If you can ascertain what this is all about, either beforehand, during, or afterward, you are surely no square.

In keeping with its populistic bias, the style of *On the Road* is folksy and lyrical. The prose of *The Subterraneans,* on the other hand, sounds like an inept parody of Faulkner at his worst, the main difference being that Faulkner usually produces bad writing out of an impulse to inflate the commonplace while Kerouac gets into trouble by pursuing "spontaneity." Strictly speaking, spontaneity is a quality of feeling, not of writing: when we call a piece of writing spontaneous, we are registering our impression that the author hit upon the right words without sweating, that no "art" and no calculation entered into the picture, that his feelings seem to have spoken themselves, seem to have sprouted a tongue at the moment of composition. Kerouac apparently thinks that spontaneity is a matter of saying whatever comes into your head, in any order you happen to feel like saying it. It isn't the *right* words he wants (even if he knows what they might be), but the first words, or at any rate the words that most obviously announce themselves as deriving from emotion rather than cerebration, as coming from "life" rather than "literature," from the guts rather than the brain. (The brain, remember, is the angel of death.) But writing that springs easily and "spontaneously" out of strong feelings is *never* vague; it always has a quality of sharpness and precision because it is in the nature of strong feelings to be aroused by specific objects. The notion that a diffuse, generalized, and unrelenting enthusiasm is the mark of great sensitivity and responsiveness is utterly fantastic, an idea that comes from taking drunkenness or drug addiction as the state of perfect emotional vigor. The effect of such enthusiasm is actually to wipe out the world altogether, for if a filling station will serve as well as the Rocky Mountains to arouse a sense of awe and wonder, then both the filling station and the mountains are robbed of their reality. Kerouac's conception of feeling is one that only a solipsist could believe in—and a solipsist, be it noted, is a man who does not relate to anything outside himself.

Solipsism is precisely what characterizes Kerouac's fiction. *On the Road* and *The Subterraneans* are so patently autobiographical in content that they become almost impossible to discuss as novels; if spontaneity were indeed a matter of destroying the distinction between life and literature, these books would unquestionably be It. "As we were going out to the car Babe slipped and fell flat on her face. Poor girl was overwrought. Her brother Tim and I helped her up. We got in the car; Major and Betty joined us. The sad ride back to Denver began." Babe is a girl who is mentioned a few times in the course of *On the Road;* we don't know why she is overwrought on this occasion, and even if we did it wouldn't matter, since there is no reason for her presence in the book at all. But Kerouac tells us that she fell flat on her face while walking toward a car. It is impossible to believe that Kerouac made this detail up, that his imagination was creating a world real enough to include wholly gratuitous elements; if that were the case, Babe would have come alive as a human being. But she is only a name; Kerouac never even describes her. She is in the book because the sister of one of Kerouac's friends was there when he took a trip to Central City, Colorado, and she slips in *On the Road* because she slipped that day on the way to the car. What is true of Babe who fell flat on her face is true of virtually every incident in *On the Road* and *The Subterraneans.* Nothing that happens has any dramatic reason for happening. Sal Paradise meets such-and-such people on the road whom he likes or (rarely) dislikes; they exchange a few words, they have a few beers together, they part. It is all very unremarkable and commonplace, but for Kerouac it is always the greatest, the wildest, the most. What you get in these two books is a man proclaiming that he is *alive* and offering every trivial experience he has ever had in evidence. Once I did this, once I did that (he is saying) and by God, it *meant* something! Because I *responded!* But if it meant something, and you responded so powerfully, why can't you explain what it meant, and why do you have to insist so?

I think it is legitimate to say, then, that the Beat Generation's worship of primitivism and spontaneity is more than a cover for hostility to intelligence; it arises from a pathetic poverty of feeling as well. The hipsters and hipster-lovers of the Beat Generation are rebels, all right, but not against anything so sociological and historical as the middle class or capitalism or even respectability. This is the revolt of the spiritually underprivileged and the crippled of soul—young men who can't think straight and so hate anyone who can; young men who can't get outside the morass of self and so construct definitions of feeling that exclude all human beings who manage to live, even miserably, in a world of objects; young men who are burdened unto death with the specially poignant sexual anxiety that America—in its eternal promise of erotic glory and its spiteful withholding of actual erotic possibility— seems bent on breeding, and who therefore dream of the unattainable perfect orgasm, which excuses all sexual failures in the real world. Not long ago, Norman Mailer suggested that the rise of the hipster may represent "the first wind of a second revolution in this century, moving not forward toward action and more rational equitable distribution, but backward toward being and the secrets of human energy." To tell the truth, whenever I hear anyone talking about instinct and being and the secrets of human energy, I get nervous; next thing you know he'll be saying that violence is just fine, and then I begin wondering whether he really thinks that kicking someone in the teeth or sticking a knife between his ribs are deeds to be admired. History, after all— and especially the history of modern times—teaches that there is a close connection between ideologies of primitivistic vitalism and a willingness to look upon cruelty and blood-letting with complacency, if not downright enthusiasm. The reason I bring this up is that the spirit of hipsterism and the Beat Generation strikes me as the same spirit which animates the young savages in leather jackets who have been running amuck in the last few years with their switch-blades and zip guns. What does Mailer think of those wretched kids, I wonder? What does he think of the gang that stoned a nine-year-old boy to death in Central Park in broad daylight a few months ago, or the one that set fire to an old man drowsing on a bench near the Brooklyn waterfront one summer's day, or the one that pounced on a crippled child and or- giastically stabbed him over and over and over again even after he was good and dead? Is that what he means by the liberation of instinct and the mysteries of being? Maybe so. At least he says somewhere in his article that two eighteen-year-old hoodlums who bash in the brains of a candy-store keeper are murdering an institution, committing an act that "violates private property"—which is one of the most morally gruesome ideas I have ever come across, and which indicates where the ideology of hipsterism can lead. I happen to believe that there is a direct connection between the flabbiness of American middle-class life and the spread of juvenile crime in the 1950's, but I also believe that juvenile crime can be explained partly in terms of the same re-sentment against normal feeling and the attempt to cope with the world through intelligence that lies behind Kerouac and Ginsberg. Even the relatively mild ethos of Kerouac's books can spill over easily into brutality, for there is a suppressed cry in those books: Kill the in-tellectuals who can talk coherently, kill the people who can sit still for five minutes at a time, kill those incomprehensible characters who are capable of getting seriously involved with a woman, a job, a cause. How can anyone in his right mind pretend that this has anything to do with private property or the middle class? No. Being for or against what the Beat Generation stands for has to do with denying that inco-herence is superior to precision; that ignorance is superior to knowl-edge; that the exercise of mind and discrimination is a form of death. It has to do with fighting the notion that sordid acts of violence are justifiable so long as they are committed in the name of "instinct." It even has to do with fighting the poisonous glorification of the adoles-cent in American popular culture. It has to do, in other words, with being for or against intelligence itself.

---

# KENNETH REXROTH

KENNETH REXROTH (1905–1982) was an early supporter and de-fender of Ginsberg and Kerouac, young writers from the East Coast who lived only briefly in the East Bay Area of San Fran-cisco and were not truly members of the resident community of poets. This talented group included Kenneth Patchen, Robert Duncan, Jack Spicer, William Everson, Mary Fabilli, Josephine Miles, Philip Lamantia, Joanne Kyger, Michael McClure, Gary Snyder, and Philip Whalen, among others, who contributed to the San Francisco Poetry Renaissance. In 1957 Rexroth pub-lished an essay, "Disengagement: The Art of the Beat Genera-tion," in number 11 of the paperback anthology *New World Writing*. In this essay, as his biographer Linda Hamilton recog-nized, Rexroth "seemed eager" to speak for the younger genera-tion of poets, "who with their youth, energy, and friendship had caught the imagination of the media in a way he had not managed to do for himself." Within a year Rexroth had rewritten the article twice after becoming hostile to Kerouac, believing that he had helped to arrange secret meetings between the poet Robert Creeley and Rexroth's wife, Marthe. When the article later appeared under the title "San Francisco's Mature Bohemians" in *The Nation,* Rexroth scoffed at Kerouac's interest in Buddhism, and described his literary style as "terrifying gibberish that sounds like a tape recording of a gang bang with everybody full of pod, juice and bennies all at once." In the article's third appearance as "San Francisco Letter" in *Evergreen Review* number 7, Rexroth cut out the references to both Kerouac and Creeley.

---

## Disengagement: The Art of the Beat Generation

Literature generally, but literary criticism in particular, has always been an area in which social forces assume symbolic guise, and work out—or at least exemplify—conflicts taking place in the contemporary, or rather, usually the just-past wider arena of society. Recognition of this does not imply the acceptance of any general theory of social or economic determinism. It is a simple, empirical fact. Because of the pervasiveness of consent in American society generally, that democratic leveling up or down so often bewailed since de Tocqueville, American literature, especially literary criticism, has usually been ruled by a "line." The fact that it was spontaneously evolved and enforced only by widespread consent has never detracted from its rigor—but rather the opposite. It is only human to kick against the prodding of an Erich Auerbach or an Andrey Zhdanov. An invisible, all-enveloping compulsion is not likely to be recognized, let alone protested against.

After World War I there was an official line for general consumption: "Back to Normalcy." Day by day in every way, we are getting better and better. This produced a literature which tirelessly pointed out that there was nothing whatsoever normal about us. The measure of decay in thirty years is the degree of acceptance of the official myth today—from the most obscure hack on a provincial newspaper to the loftiest metaphysicians of the literary quarterlies. The line goes: "The generation of experimentation and revolt is over." This is an etherealized corollary of the general line: "The bull market will never end."

I do not wish to argue about the bull market, but in the arts nothing could be less true. The youngest generation is in a state of revolt so absolute that its elders cannot even recognize it. The disaffiliation, alienation, and rejection of the young has, as far as their elders are concerned, moved out of the visible spectrum altogether. Critically invisible, modern revolt, like X-rays and radioactivity, is perceived only by its effects at more materialistic social levels, where it is called delinquency.

"Disaffiliation," by the way, is the term used by the critic and poet Lawrence Lipton, who has written several articles on this subject, the first of which, in the *Nation*, quoted as epigraph, "We disaffiliate . . ."—John L. Lewis.

Like the pillars of Hercules, like two ruined Titans guarding the entrance to one of Dante's circles, stand two great dead juvenile delinquents—the heroes of the post-war generation: the great saxophonist Charlie Parker, and Dylan Thomas. If the word deliberate means anything, both of them certainly deliberately destroyed themselves.

Both of them were overcome by the horror of the world in which they found themselves, because at last they could no longer overcome that world with the weapon of a purely lyrical art. Both of them were my friends. Living in San Francisco I saw them seldom enough to see them with a perspective which was not distorted by exasperation or fatigue. So as the years passed, I saw them each time in the light of an accelerated personal conflagration.

The last time I saw Bird, at Jimbo's Bop City, he was so gone—so blind to the world—that he literally sat down on me before he realized I was there. "What happened, man?" I said, referring to the pretentious "Jazz Concert." "Evil, man, evil," he said, and that's all he said for the rest of the night. About dawn he got up to blow. The rowdy crowd chilled into stillness and the fluent melody spiraled through it.

The last time I saw Dylan, his self-destruction had not just passed the limits of rationality. It had assumed the terrifying inertia of inanimate matter. Being with him was like being swept away by a torrent of falling stones.

Now Dylan Thomas and Charlie Parker have a great deal more in common than the same disastrous end. As artists, they were very similar. They were both very fluent. But this fluent, enchanting utterance had, compared with important artists of the past, relatively little content. Neither of them got very far beyond a sort of entranced rapture at his own creativity. The principal theme of Thomas's poetry was the ambivalence of birth and death—the pain of blood-stained creation. Music, of course, is not so explicit an art, but anybody who knew Charlie Parker knows that he felt much the same way about his own gift. Both of them did communicate one central theme: Against the ruin of the world, there is only one defense—the creative act. This, of course, is the theme of much art—perhaps most poetry. It is the theme of Horace, who certainly otherwise bears little resemblance to Parker or Thomas. The difference is that Horace accepted his theme with a kind of silken assurance. To Dylan and Bird it was an agony and terror. I do not believe that this is due to anything especially frightful about their relationship to their own creativity. I believe rather that it is due to the catastrophic world in which that creativity seemed to be the sole value. Horace's column of imperishable verse shines quietly enough in the lucid air of Augustan Rome. Art may have been for him the most enduring, orderly, and noble activity of man. But the other activities of his life partook of these values. They did not actively negate them. Dylan Thomas's verse had to find endurance in a world of burning cities and burning Jews. He was able to find meaning in his art as long as it was the answer to air raids and gas ovens. As the world began to take on the guise of an immense air raid or gas oven, I believe his art became meaningless to him. I think all this could apply to Parker just as well, although, because of the nature of music, it is not demonstrable—at least not conclusively.

Thomas and Parker have more in common than theme, attitude, life pattern. In the practice of their art, there is an obvious technical resemblance. Contrary to popular belief, they were not great technical innovators. Their effects are only superficially starting. Thomas is a regression from the technical originality and ingenuity of writers like Pierre Reverdy or Apollinaire. Similarly, the innovations of bop, and of Parker particularly, have been vastly overrated by people unfamiliar with music, especially by that ignoramus, the intellectual jitterbug, the jazz aficionado. The tonal novelties consist in the introduction of a few

chords used in classical music for centuries. And there is less rhythmic difference between progressive jazz, no matter how progressive,
and Dixieland, than there is between two movements of many conventional symphonies.

What Parker and his contemporaries—Gillespie, Davis, Monk,
Roach (Tristano is an anomaly), etc.—did was to absorb the musical
ornamentation of the older jazz into the basic structure, of which it
then became an integral part, and with which it then developed. This
is true of the melodic line which could be put together from selected
passages of almost anybody—Benny Carter, Johnny Hodges. It is true
of the rhythmic pattern in which the beat shifts continuously, or at
least is continuously sprung, so that it becomes ambiguous enough
to allow the pattern to be dominated by the long pulsations of the
phrase or strophe. This is exactly what happened in the transition
from baroque to rococo music. It is the difference between Bach and
Mozart.

It is not a farfetched analogy to say that this is what Thomas did
to poetry. The special syntactical effects of a Rimbaud or an Edith
Sitwell—actually ornaments—become the main concern. The metaphysical conceits, which fascinate the Reactionary Generation still
dominant in backwater American colleges, were embroideries. Thomas's ellipses and ambiguities are ends in themselves. The immediate
theme, if it exists, is incidental, and his main theme—the terror of
birth—is simply reiterated.

This is one difference between Bird and Dylan which should be
pointed out. Again, contrary to popular belief, there is nothing crazy or
frantic about Parker either musically or emotionally. His sinuous
melody is a sort of naïve transcendence of all experience. Emotionally
it does not resemble Berlioz or Wagner; it resembles Mozart. This is
true also of a painter like Jackson Pollock. He may have been eccen-
tric in his behavior, but his paintings are as impassive as Persian tiles.
Partly this difference is due to the nature of verbal communication.
The insistent talk-aboutiveness of the general environment obtrudes
into even the most idyllic poetry. It is much more a personal difference. Thomas certainly wanted to tell people about the ruin and disorder of the world. Parker and Pollock wanted to substitute a work of
art for the world.

Technique pure and simple, rendition, is not of major importance, but it is interesting that Parker, following Lester Young, was one of the leaders of the so-called saxophone revolution. In modern jazz, the saxophone is treated as a woodwind and played with conventional embouchure. Metrically, Thomas's verse was extremely conventional, as was, incidentally, the verse of that other tragic enragé, Hart Crane.

I want to make clear what I consider the one technical development in the first wave of significant post-war arts. Ornament is confabulation in the interstices of structure. A poem by Dylan Thomas, a saxophone solo by Charles Parker, a painting by Jackson Pollock—these are pure confabulations as ends in themselves. Confabulation has come to determine structure. Uninhibited lyricism should be distinguished from its exact opposite—the sterile, extraneous invention of the corn-belt metaphysicals, or present blight of poetic professors.

Just as Hart Crane had little influence on anyone except very reactionary writers—like Allen Tate, for instance, to whom Valéry was the last word in modern poetry and the felicities of an Apollinaire, let alone a Paul Éluard were nonsense—so Dylan Thomas's influence has been slight indeed. In fact, his only disciple—the only person to imitate his style—was W. S. Graham, who seems to have imitated him without much understanding, and who has since moved on to other methods. Thomas's principal influence lay in the communication of an attitude—that of the now extinct British romantic school of the New Apocalypse—Henry Treece, J. F. Hendry, and others—all of whom were quite conventional poets.

Parker certainly had much more of an influence. At one time it was the ambition of every saxophone player in every high school band in America to blow like Bird. Even before his death this influence had begun to ebb. In fact, the whole generation of the founding fathers of bop—Gillespie, Monk, Davis, Blakey, and the rest—are just now at a considerable discount. The main line of development today goes back to Lester Young and bypasses them.

The point is that many of the most impressive developments in the arts nowadays are aberrant, idiosyncratic. There is no longer any sense of continuing development of the sort that can be traced from Baudelaire to Éluard, or for that matter, from Hawthorne through Henry James to Gertrude Stein. The cubist generation before World War I, and, on a lower level, the surrealists of the period between the wars, both assumed an accepted universe of discourse, in which, to quote André Breton, it was possible to make definite advances, exactly as in the sciences. I doubt if anyone holds such ideas today. Continuity exits, but like the neo-swing music developed from Lester Young, it is a continuity sustained by popular demand.

In the plastic arts, a very similar situation exists. Surrealists like Hans Arp and Max Ernst might talk of creation by hazard—of composing pictures by walking on them with painted soles, or by tossing bits of paper up in the air. But it is obvious that they were self-deluded. Nothing looks anything like an Ernst or an Arp but another Ernst or Arp. Nothing looks less like their work than the happenings of random occasion. Many of the post–World War II abstract expressionists, apostles of the discipline of spontaneity and hazard, look alike, and do look like accidents. The aesthetic appeal of pure paint laid on at random may exist, but it is a very impoverished appeal. Once again what has happened is an all-consuming confabulation of the incidentals, the accidents of painting. It is curious that at its best, the work of this school of painting—Mark Rothko, Jackson Pollock, Clyfford Still, Robert Motherwell, Willem de Kooning, and the rest—resembles nothing so much as the passage painting of quite unimpressive painters: the mother-of-pearl shimmer in the background of a Henry McFee, itself a formula derived from Renoir; the splashes of light and black which fake drapery in the fashionable imitators of Hals and Sargent. Often work of this sort is presented as calligraphy—the pure utterance of the brush stroke seeking only absolute painteresque values. You have only to compare such painting with the work of, say, Sesshu, to realize that someone is using words and brushes carelessly.

At its best the abstract expressionists achieve a simple rococo decorative surface. Its poverty shows up immediately when compared with Tiepolo, where the rococo rises to painting of extraordinary profundity and power. A Tiepolo painting, however confabulated, is a universe of tensions in vast depths. A Pollock is an object of art—bijouterie—disguised only by its great size. In fact, once the size is big enough to cover a whole wall, it turns into nothing more than extremely expensive wallpaper. Now there is nothing wrong with complicated wallpaper. There is just more to Tiepolo. The great Ashikaga brush painters painted wallpapers, too—at least portable ones, screens.

A process of elimination which leaves the artist with nothing but the play of his materials themselves cannot sustain interest in either artist or public for very long. So, in the last couple of years, abstract expressionism has tended toward romantic suggestion—indications of landscape or living figures. This approaches the work of the Northwest school—Clayton Price, Mark Tobey, Kenneth Callahan, Morris Graves—who have of all recent painters come nearest to conquering a territory which painting could occupy with some degree of security. The Northwest school, of course, admittedly is influenced by the ink painters of the Far East, and by Tintoretto and Tiepolo. The dominant school of post–World War II American painting has really been a long detour into plastic nihilism. I should add that painters like Ernie Briggs seem to be opening up new areas of considerable scope within the main traditional abstract expressionism—but with remarkable convergence to Tobey or Tintoretto, as you prefer.

Today American painting is just beginning to emerge with a transvaluation of values. From the mid–nineteenth century on, all ruling standards in the plastic arts were subject to continual attack. They were attacked because each on-coming generation had new standards of their own to put in their place. Unfortunately, after one hundred years of this, there grew up a generation ignorant of the reasons for the revolt of their elders, and without any standards whatever. It has been necessary to create standards anew out of chaos. This is what modern education purports to do with finger painting in nursery schools. This is why the Northwest school has enjoyed such an advantage over the abstract expressionists. Learning by doing, by trial and error, is learning by the hardest way. If you want to overthrow the cubist tradition of architectural painting, it is much easier to seek out its opposites in the history of culture and study them carefully. At least it saves a great deal of time.

One thing can be said of painting in recent years—its revolt, its rejection of the classic modernism of the first half of the century, has been more absolute than in any other art. The only ancestor of abstract expressionism is the early Kandinsky—a style rejected even by Kandinsky himself. The only painter in a hundred years who bears the slightest resemblance to Tobey or Graves is Odilon Redon (perhaps Gustave Moreau a little), whose stock was certainly not very high with painters raised in the cubist tradition.

The ready market for prose fiction—there is almost no market at all for modern painting, and very much less for poetry—has had a decisive influence on its development. Sidemen with Kenton or Herman may make a good if somewhat hectic living, but any novelist who can write home to mother, or even spell his own name, has a chance to become another Brubeck. The deliberately and painfully intellectual fiction which appears in the literary quarterlies is a by-product of certain classrooms. The only significant fiction in America is popular fiction. Nobody realizes this better than the French. To them our late-born imitators of Henry James and E. M. Forster are just *chiens qui fument,* and arithmetical horses and bicycling seals. And there is no more perishable commodity than the middle-brow novel. No one today reads Ethel L. Voynich or Joseph Hergesheimer, just as no one in the future will read the writers' workshop pupils and teachers who fill the literary quarterlies. Very few people, except themselves, read them now.

On the other hand, the connection between the genuine highbrow writer and the genuinely popular is very close. Hemingway had hardly started to write before his style had been reduced to a formula in *Black Mask,* the first hard-boiled detective magazine. In no time at all he had produced two first-class popular writers, Raymond Chandler and Dashiell Hammett. Van Vechten, their middle-brow contemporary, is forgotten. It is from Chandler and Hammett and Hemingway that the best modern fiction derives; although most of it comes out in hard covers, it is always thought of as written for a typical pocketbook audience. Once it gets into pocketbooks it is sometimes difficult to draw the line between it and its most ephemeral imitators. Even the most *précieux* French critics, a few years ago, considered Horace McCoy America's greatest contemporary novelist. There is not only something to be said for their point of view; the only thing to be said against it is that they don't read English.

Much of the best popular fiction deals with the world of the utterly disaffiliated. Burlesque and carnival people, hipsters, handicappers and hop heads, wanted men on the lam, an expendable squad of soldiers being expended, anyone who by definition is divorced from society and cannot afford to believe even an iota of the social lie—these are the favorite characters of modern post-war fiction, from Norman Mailer to the latest ephemerid called *Caught,* or *Hung Up,* or

*The Needle*, its bright cover winking invitingly in the drugstore. The first, and still the greatest, novelist of total disengagement is not a young man at all, but an elderly former I.W.W. of German ancestry, B. Traven, the author of *The Death Ship* and *The Treasure of Sierra Madre*.

It is impossible for an artist to remain true to himself as a man, let alone an artist, and work within the context of this society. Contemporary mimics of Jane Austen or Anthony Trollope are not only beneath contempt. They are literally unreadable. It is impossible to keep your eyes focused on the page. Writers as far apart as J. F. Powers and Nelson Algren agree in one thing—their diagnosis of an absolute corruption.

The refusal to accept the mythology of press and pulpit as a medium for artistic creation, or even enjoyable reading matter, is one explanation for the popularity of escapist literature. Westerns, detective stories and science fiction are all situated beyond the pale of normal living. The slick magazines are only too well aware of this, and in these three fields especially exert steady pressure on their authors to accentuate the up-beat. The most shocking example of this forced perversion is the homey science fiction story, usually written by a woman, in which a one-to-one correlation has been made for the commodity-ridden tale of domestic whimsey, the stand-by of magazines given away in the chain groceries. In writers like Judith Merrill the space pilot and his bride bat the badinage back and forth while the robot maid makes breakfast in the jet-propelled lucite orange squeezer and the electronic bacon rotobroiler, dropping pearls of dry assembly plant wisdom (like plantation wisdom but drier), the whilst. Still, few yield to these pressures, for the obvious reason that fiction indistinguishable from the advertising columns on either side of the page defeats its own purpose, which is to get the reader to turn over the pages when he is told "continued on p. 47."

Simenon is still an incomparably better artist and psychologist than the psychological Jean Stafford. Ward Moore is a better artist than Eudora Welty, and Ernest Haycox than William Faulkner, just as, long ago, H. G. Wells was a better artist, as artist, than E. M. Forster, as well as being a lot more interesting. At its best, popular literature of this sort, coming up, meets high-brow literature coming down. It has been apparent novel by novel that Nelson Algren is rising qualitatively in this way. In his latest novel, thoroughly popular in its materials, *A Walk on the Wild Side,* he meets and absorbs influences coming down from the top, from the small handful of bona fide high-brow writers working today—Céline, Jean Genêt, Samuel Beckett, Henry Miller. In Algren's case this has been a slow growth, and he has carried his audience with him. Whatever the merits of his subject matter or his thesis—"It is better to be out than in. It is better to be on the lam than on the cover of *Time* Magazine"—his style started out as a distressing mixture of James Farrell and Kenneth Fearing. Only recently has he achieved an idiom of his own.

There is only one thing wrong with this picture, and that is that the high-brow stimulus still has to be imported. Algren, who is coming to write more and more like Céline, has no difficulty selling his fiction. On the other hand, an author like Jack Kerouac, who is in his small way the peer of Céline, Destouches or Beckett, is the most famous "unpublished" author in America. Every publisher's reader and adviser of any moment has read him and is enthusiastic about him. In other words, anybody emerging from the popular field has every advantage. It is still extremely difficult to enter American fiction from the top down.

The important point about modern fiction is that it is salable, and therefore viable in our society, and therefore successful in the best sense of the word. When a novelist has something to say, he knows people will listen. Only the jazz musician, but to a much lesser degree, shares this confidence in his audience. It is of the greatest social significance that the novelists who say, "I am proud to be delinquent" are nevertheless sold in editions of hundreds of thousands.

Nobody much buys poetry. I know. I am one of the country's most successful poets. My books actually sell out—in editions of two thousand. Many a poet, the prestige ornament of a publisher's list, has more charges against his royalty account than credits for books sold. The problem of poetry is the problem of communication itself. All art is a symbolic criticism of values, but poetry is specifically and almost exclusively that. A painting decorates the wall. A novel is a story. Music . . . soothes a savage breast. But poetry you have to take straight. In addition, the entire educational system is in a conspiracy to make poetry as unpalatable as possible. From the seventh grade teacher who rolls her eyes and chants H.D. to the seven types of ambiguity factories, grinding out little Donnes and Hopkinses with hayseeds in their hair, everybody is out to de-poetize forever the youth of the land. Again, bad and spurious painting, music, and fiction are not really well organized, except on obvious commercial levels, where they can be avoided. But in poetry Gresham's Law is supported by the full weight of the powers that be. From about 1930 on, a conspiracy of bad poetry has been as carefully organized as the Communist Party, and today controls most channels of publication except the littlest of the little magazines. In all other departments of American culture, English influence has been at a steadily declining minimum since the middle of the nineteenth century. In 1929, this was still true of American poetry. Amy Lowell, Sandburg, H.D., Pound, Marianne Moore, William Carlos Williams, Wallace Stevens—all of the major poets of the first quarter of the century owed far more to Apollinaire or Francis Jammes than they did to the whole body of the English tradition. In fact, the new poetry was essentially an anti-English, pro-French movement—a provincial but clear echo of the French revolt against the symbolists. On the other hand, Jules Laforgue and his English disciples, Ernest Dowson and Arthur Symons, were the major influence on T. S. Eliot. Unfortunately Mr. Eliot's poetic practice and his thoroughly snobbish critical essays which owed their great cogency to their assumption, usually correct, that his readers had never heard of the authors he discussed—Webster, Crashaw, or Lancelot Andrewes—lent themselves all too easily to the construction of an academy and the production of an infinite number of provincial academicians—policemen entrusted with the enforcement of Gresham's Law.

Behind the façade of this literary Potemkin village, the mainstream of American poetry, with its sources in Baudelaire, Lautréamont, Rimbaud, Apollinaire, Jammes, Reverdy, Salmon, and later Breton and Éluard, has flowed on unperturbed, though visible only at rare intervals between the interstices of the academic hoax. Today the class magazines and the quarterlies are filled with poets as alike as two bad pennies. It is my opinion that these people do not really exist. Most of them are androids designed by Ransom, Tate, and Co., and animated by Randall Jarrell. They are not just counterfeit; they are not even real counterfeits, but counterfeits of counterfeits. On these blurred and clumsy coins the lineaments of Mr. Eliot and I. A. Richards dimly can be discerned, like the barbarized Greek letters which nobody could read on Scythian money.

This is the world in which over every door is written the slogan: "The generation of experiment and revolt is over. Bohemia died in the twenties. There are no more little magazines." Actually there have never been so many little magazines. In spite of the fantastic costs of printing, more people than ever are bringing out little sheets of free verse and making up the losses out of their own pockets. This world has its own major writers, its own discoveries, its own old masters, its own tradition and continuity. Its sources are practically exclusively French, and they are all post-symbolist, even anti-symbolist. It is the Reactionary Generation who are influenced by Laforgue, the symbolists, and Valéry. Nothing is more impressive than the strength, or at least the cohesion, of this underground movement. Poets whom the quarterlies pretend never existed, like Louis Zukovsky and Jack Wheelwright, are still searched out in large libraries or obscure bookshops and copied into notebooks by young writers. I myself have a complete typewritten collection of the prereactionary verse of Yvor Winters. And I know several similar collections of "forgotten modernists" in the libraries of my younger friends. People are always turning up who say something like, "I just discovered a second-hand copy of Parker Tyler's *The Granite Butterfly* in a Village bookshop. It's great, man." On the other hand, I seriously doubt whether *The Hudson Review* would ever consider for a moment publishing a line of Parker Tyler's verse. And he is certainly not held up as an example in the Iowa Writers' Workshop. There are others who have disappeared entirely—Charles Snider, Sherry Mangan, R. E. F. Larsson, the early Winters, the last poems of Ford Madox Ford. They get back into circulation, as far as I know, only when I read them to somebody at home or on the air, and then I am always asked for a copy. Some of the old avant garde seem to have written themselves out, for instance, Mina Loy. There are a few established old masters, outstanding of whom are, of course, Ezra Pound and William Carlos Williams. I am not a passionate devotee of Pound myself. In fact, I think his influence is largely pernicious. But no one could deny its extent and power amongst young people today. As for Williams, more and more people, even some of the Reactionary Generation, have come to think of him as our greatest living poet. Even Randall Jarrell and R. P. Blackmur have good words to say for him.

Then there is a middle generation which includes Kenneth Patchen, Jean Garrigue, myself, and a few others—notably Richard Eberhart, who looks superficially as if he belonged with the Tates and Blackmurs but who is redeemed by his directness, simplicity, and honesty, and Robert Fitzgerald and Dudley Fitts. Curiously enough, in the taste of the young, Kenneth Fearing is not included in this group, possibly because his verse is too easy. It does include the major work, for example, *Ajanta,* of Muriel Rukeyser.

I should say that the most influential poets of the youngest established generation of the avant garde are Denise Levertov, Robert Creeley, Charles Olson, Robert Duncan, and Philip Lamantia. The most influential avant garde editor is perhaps Cid Corman, with his magazine *Origin.* Richard Emerson's *Golden Goose* and Robert Creeley's *Black Mountain Review* seem to have suspended publication temporarily. Jonathan Williams, himself a fine poet, publishes the Jargon Press.

All of this youngest group have a good deal in common. They are all more or less influenced by French poetry, and by Céline, Beckett, Artaud, Genêt, to varying degrees. They are also influenced by William Carlos Williams, D. H. Lawrence, Whitman, Pound. They are all interested in Far Eastern art and religion; some even call themselves Buddhists. Politically they are all strong disbelievers in the State, war, and the values of commercial civilization. Most of them would no longer call themselves anarchists, but just because adopting such a label would imply adherence to a "movement." Anything in the way of an explicit ideology is suspect. Contrary to gossip of a few years back, I have never met anybody in this circle who was a devotee of the dubious notions of the psychologist Wilhelm Reich; in fact, few of them have ever read him, and those who have consider him a charlatan.

Although there is wide diversity—Olson is very like Pound; Creeley resembles Mallarmé; Denise Levertov in England was a leading New Romantic, in America she has come under the influence of William Carlos Williams; Robert Duncan has assimilated ancestors as unlike as Gertrude Stein and Éluard, and so on—although this diversity is very marked, there is a strong bond of aesthetic unity too. No avant garde American poet accepts the I. A. Richards–Valéry thesis that a poem is an end in itself, an anonymous machine for providing aesthetic experiences. All believe in poetry as communication, statement from one person to another. So they all avoid the studied ambiguities and metaphysical word play of the Reactionary Generation and seek clarity of image and simplicity of language.

In the years since the war, it would seem as though more and more of what is left of the avant garde has migrated to Northern California. John Berryman once referred to the Lawrence cult of "mindless California," and Henry Miller and I have received other unfavorable publicity which has served only to attract people to this area. Mr. Karl Shapiro, for instance, once referred to San Francisco as "the last refuge of the Bohemian remnant"—a description he thought of as invidious. Nevertheless it is true that San Francisco is today the seat of an intense literary activity not unlike Chicago of the first quarter of the century. A whole school of poets has grown up—almost all of them migrated here from somewhere else. Some of them have national reputations, at least in limited circles. For example, Philip Lamantia among the surrealists; William Everson (Br. Antoninus, O.P.)—perhaps the best Catholic poet. Others have come up recently, like Lawrence Ferlinghetti, Allen Ginsberg, Gary Snyder, Philip Whalen, James Harmon, Michael McClure, and still have largely local reputations. But the strength of these reputations should not be underestimated. The Poetry Center of San Francisco State College, directed by Ruth Witt-Diamant, gives a reading to a large audience at least twice a month. And there are other readings equally well attended every week in various galleries and private homes.

This means that poetry has become an actual social force—something which has always sounded hitherto like a Utopian dream of the William Morris sort. It is a very thrilling experience to hear an audience of more than three hundred people stand and cheer and clap, as they invariably do at a reading by Allen Ginsberg, certainly a poet of revolt if there ever was one.

There is no question but that the San Francisco renaissance is radically different from what is going on elsewhere. There are hand presses, poetry readings, young writers elsewhere—but nowhere else is there a whole younger generation culture pattern characterized by total rejection of the official high-brow culture—where critics like John Crowe Ransom or Lionel Trilling, magazines like the *Kenyon*, *Hudson* and *Partisan* reviews, are looked on as "The Enemy"—the other side of the barricades.

There is only one trouble about the renaissance in San Francisco.

It is too far away from the literary market place. That, of course, is the reason why the Bohemian remnant, the avant garde have migrated here. It is possible to hear the story about what so-and-so said to someone else at a cocktail party twenty years ago just one too many times. You grab a plane or get on your thumb and hitchhike to the other side of the continent for good and all. Each generation, the great Latin poets came from farther and farther from Rome. Eventually, they ceased to even go there except to see the sights.

Distance from New York City does, however, make it harder to get things, if not published, at least nationally circulated. I recently formed a collection for one of the foundations of avant garde poetry printed in San Francisco. There were a great many items. The poetry was all at least readable, and the hand printing and binding were in most cases very fine indeed. None of these books were available in bookstores elsewhere in the country, and only a few of them had been reviewed in newspapers or magazines with national circulation.

Anyway, as an old war horse of the revolution of the word, things have never looked better from where I sit. The avant garde has not only not ceased to exist. It's jumping all over the place. Something's happening, man.

The disengagement of the creator, who, as creator, is necessarily judge, is one thing, but the utter nihilism of the emptied-out hipster is another. What is going to come of an attitude like this? It is impossible to go on indefinitely saying: "I am proud to be a delinquent," without destroying all civilized values. Between such persons no true enduring interpersonal relationships can be built, and of course, nothing resembling a true "culture"—an at-homeness of men with each other, their work, their loves, their environment. The end result must be the desperation of shipwreck—the despair, the orgies, ultimately the cannibalism of a lost lifeboat. I believe that most of an entire generation will go to ruin—the ruin of Céline, Artaud, Rimbaud, voluntarily, even enthusiastically. What will happen afterwards I don't know, but for the next ten years or so we are going to have to cope with the youth we, my generation, put through the atom smasher. Social disengagement, artistic integrity, voluntary poverty—these are powerful virtues and may pull them through, but they are not the virtues we tried to inculcate rather they are the exact opposite.

# ED SANDERS

ED SANDERS read "Howl" and *On the Road* as a seventeen-year-old freshman at the University of Missouri in Columbia. A few months later, in the spring of 1958, he dropped out of college and hitchhiked to New York, where he enrolled at New York University, supporting himself by a five-P.M.-to-midnight job in a Times Square cigar store. After graduating with a degree in Greek Literature in 1963, he devoted himself full time both to political activism as a militant pacifist and to literature, including the publication of *Fuck You: A Magazine of the Arts* in his East Village storefront and other activities described in his memoir, *Tales of Beatnik Glory* (1975). Sanders's collected poems, 1961–1985, *Thirsting for Peace in a Raging Century,* won an American Book Award in 1988. The title poem was also issued as a small black-and-white pamphlet by the small press BOOG in Calverton, New York, with a photograph of Sanders teaching at the Naropa Institute in Boulder, Colorado.

---

## *Thirsting for Peace in a Raging Century*

*Boulder 7-5-92*

I'm Thirsting for Peace
         in a Raging Century
Thirsting for Peace
         in a Raging Century

    I believe
    in the Feather of Justice

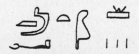

    The Egyptians
    called it the Maat Feather

It's light
  It's perfect
    It belongs to eternity

I believe
in the Feather of Justice

It measures our lives
    in the World of Forms

It calls the evil
    away from the good

   In the hieroglyph
   it's a scythe

   a loaf of bread

   an arm

   & as its visual determinative
   an ostrich feather

I believe in the Feather of Justice
It's in our cells
It's in the path of the sun
We wear it curved in our hair
I believe   I believe
    in the Feather

La Plume Égyptien.

I'm Thirsting for Peace
    in a Raging Century
Thirsting for Peace
    in a Raging Century

Kerouac
beating
    on a burgundy jug

& shouting
    Go! Go!

as Michael McClure
read
    "For the Death of 100 Whales"

at the Six Gallery
    in '55

I was
carrying it
    for so many years

It pulled
    one arm two inches
    longer than the other

Finally
I realized
it was the
    SUITCASE TO NOWHERE

& I left it
    one night on 8th Street

I'm Thirsting for Peace
    in a Raging Century
Thirsting for Peace
    in a Raging Century

John Huston
hired Jean-Paul Sartre
to write
a screen play
on the
life of Freud
    It was 1,000 pages long

Ah Lord,
at the age of 51
to be seized
with the strange
      American hunger
to own a pool table

I'm Thirsting for Peace
    in a Raging Century
Thirsting for Peace
    in a Raging Century

I hunger
to go to th'
tholos
of Agamemnon
where the
soul of Cassandra
flits
like a cecropia moth
on a
moonlit night

## At Night after the My Lai Massacre

That night
in the distance
an old woman
                    grieved & keened so
loudly and disturbingly that

one of them
lobbed a grenade
                    from an M-79 launcher

at the noise
Some others fired their M-16s, but

She continued
thru the night,
weeping & wailing

eerily, the keen of ghosts,
the lament of love
the agony
            of eternal separation

I'm Thirsting for Peace
                in a Raging Century
Thirsting for Peace
        in a Raging Century

The pools
in the wetland
garnished
with thousands
of red maple flowers

with tiny
subflowers

& everything
after all
is a subflower
of something

In the
100 years
of warming

the birch grove
hobbles
across Route 28
& up the valley

toward the
Arctic Circle

I'm Thirsting for Peace
in a Raging Century
Thirsting for Peace
in a Raging Century

Δέδυκε μὲν ἀ σέλαννα
καὶ Πληΐαδες μέσαι δὲ
νύκτες παρὰ δ᾽ ἔρχετ᾽ ὥρα
ἔγω δὲ μόνα κατεύδω

The moon
& the Pleiades
have set
in night's midst—
midnight kisses closely
& I sleep alone

—Sappho

(read from phone directory)

Cornelia Fabbie 331-2732

Gregory Squires 246-9380

James Taylor 255-64898

Cheryl Ulrich 246-8460

I'm Thirsting for Peace
        in a Raging Century
Thirsting for Peace
        in a Raging Century


        Coleridge, explaining one
        night the
        different notes of the
        nightingale
        to Dorothy Wordsworth

        In my soul
        I search
        for an
                ancient
                        flax string lyre


        to play
        by my Inner Lake

I'm Thirsting for Peace
        in a Raging Century
Thirsting for Peace
        in a Raging Century

# GARY SNYDER

GARY SNYDER, awarded the Pulitzer Prize for *Turtle Island,* his 1974 collection of poetry, said that he hoped the dust jackets for his books would finally drop the "Beat poet" label and describe him as a more honored "Pulitzer Prize–winning poet." Snyder's participation in the 6 Gallery reading in October 1955 and his close friendships with Jack Kerouac, Allen Ginsberg, Philip Whalen, and Michael McClure would have been enough to put him firmly in the Beat camp, even if he had not become famous to thousands of readers throughout the world as the inspiration for the heroic character named Japhy Ryder in *The Dharma Bums* (1958). As Kerouac described him in the second chapter of that novel,

> Japhy Ryder was a kid from eastern Oregon brought up in a log cabin deep in the woods with his father and mother and sister, from the beginning a woods boy, an axman, farmer, interested in animals and Indian lore so that when he finally got to college by hook or crook he was already well equipped for his early studies in anthropology and later in Indian myth and in the actual texts of Indian mythology. Finally he learned Chinese and Japanese and became an Oriental scholar and discovered the greatest Dharma Bums of them all, the Zen Lunatics of China and Japan.

*The Dharma Bums* concluded with Japhy Ryder's sailing from San Francisco to Japan in May 1956 to embark upon a course of study at the First Zen Institute in Kyoto. Snyder was still there the following year during the "Howl" trial and the publication of *On the Road.* Returning to the United States in 1958, he published his first book of poetry, *Riprap* (1959). Back in Japan in 1960, he published his second book, *Myths & Texts.* That year Snyder also wrote his "Notes on the Beat Generation" and "The New Wind" for the Japanese intellectual journal *Chuo-koron.* Snyder recalled,

I was living then in Kyoto. I wrote them at the urging of Hisao Kanaseki, a life-long mentor on transpacific literary matters, who wanted me to introduce the beat generation and the new American poetry to the urban intelligentsia. These folks were existentialist Marxists, with a French symbolist aesthetic—an imported mindscape, incompletely assimilated into the just-beginning Japanese industrial renaissance and rising affluence. These pieces reflect the downright joy I felt over the new American poetry. They were first published in English in *American Poetry* 2, no. 1 (Fall 1984).

## Notes on the Beat Generation

One day in September 1955, I was fixing my bicycle in the yard of a little cabin in Berkeley, California—just back from three months working on a trail crew in the Sierra Nevada—and a respectable-looking fellow in a dark business suit came around the corner and asked if I was Gary Snyder and said his name was Allen Ginsberg. It was the only time I ever saw Allen Ginsberg in a suit. We had tea together, and he said he had come from the poet Kenneth Rexroth to see me, with the idea of getting a few San Francisco poets together to hold a poetry reading in a little art gallery in the City. Two weeks later Phil Whalen came hitchhiking into town from the mountains of Washington, and at the same time Jack Kerouac arrived, riding a freight train up from Los Angeles. Ginsberg had moved to Berkeley (the site of the University of California, and only half an hour by bus from San Francisco) to enter the graduate Department of English, with the idea of settling down and having a career as a professor. He stayed with it about three weeks and quit. It was no time for any of us to worry about college degrees or what kind of work we would do in the future; it was time to write poetry. In the month of October 1955, with wine, marijuana, and jazz, Ginsberg wrote his now-famous poem "Howl," and at the end of October we gave our poetry reading. Philip Lamantia (whose new book of poems *Ekstasis* is just out), Mike McClure, Whalen, Ginsberg, and I read. Kerouac was there beating tunes on empty bottles, and Rexroth was cracking jokes about his diplomat's suit that he'd bought second-hand for a few dollars. All of us had five to ten years' worth of poems on hand, and most of them had never been heard by anyone. That night of poetry, with the wild crowd that came, was the beginning of the "San Francisco poetry renaissance"—which has since become part of the whole phenomenon known as the "beat generation." From that night on, there was a poetry reading in somebody's pad, or some bar or gallery, every week in San Francisco. We had a sudden feeling that we had finally broken through to a new freedom of expression, had shattered the stranglehold of universities on poets, and gone beyond the tedious and pointless arguments of Bolshevik versus capitalist that were (and still are) draining the imaginative life out of so many intellectuals in the world. What we had discovered, or rediscovered, was that the imagination has a free and spontaneous life of its own, that it can be trusted, that what flows from a spontaneous mind is poetry—and that this is more basic and more revolutionary than any political program based on "civilized abstractions" that end up murdering human beings in the name of historical necessity or Reason or Liberty; Russia and America are both huge witless killers of the heart of man.

Jack Kerouac, at that time, was living the hobo life—one pair of blue jeans, a pack on his back, and a notebook to write in. But even then he had the manuscripts of ten or twelve completed novels stored away. When his novel *On the Road* was published in 1957, the word *beat* became famous and overnight America became aware that it had a generation of writers and intellectuals on its hands that was breaking all the rules. This new generation was educated, but it refused to go into academic careers or business or government. It published its poems in its own little magazines, and didn't even bother to submit works to the large established highbrow journals that had held the monopoly on avant-garde writing for so long. Its members traveled easily, bumming from New York to Mexico City to San Francisco—the big triangle—and traveled light. They stayed with friends in San Francisco's North Beach or on New York's Lower East Side (the Greenwich Village of the beat, really a slum)—and made their money at almost any kind of work. Carpentry, railroad jobs, logging, farm work, dishwashing, freight handling—anything would do. A regular job ties you down and leaves you no time. Better to live simply, be poor, and have

the time to wander and write and *dig* (meaning to penetrate and absorb and enjoy) what was going on in the world. *On the Road* (translated into Japanese as *Rojo*) describes much of this life. The people
who read it were either scared or delighted. Many of the delighted
ones moved out to San Francisco (scene of Kerouac's subsequent
novel, *The Subterraneans,* which has been translated into Japanese as
*Chikagai no Hitobito*) to join in the fun. As for Ginsberg's *Howl,* after
initially being banned in San Francisco by the police, it won a court
trial and became a poetry best-seller among the younger generation,
who saw in it a poem that spoke directly to them. "Beat generation"
became a household term.

What was the reaction of the newspapers and the public to this?
They were either outraged or a little jealous. It is one of those few
times in American history that a section of the population has freely
chosen to disaffiliate itself from "the American standard of living" and
all that goes with it—in the name of freedom. And in a way, the literature of the beat generation is some of the only true proletarian literature in recent history—because actual members of the working class
are writing it, "proletarian bohemians" if you will; and it is not the sort
of thing that middle-class Communist intellectuals think proletarian
literature ought to be. There is no self-pity or accusation or politics,
simply human beings and facts. The class struggle means little to
those who have abandoned all classes in their own minds and lives.
But both the left-wing intellectuals and the newspaper editors of
America see this as heresy of the worst sort, and both sides shout "irresponsible." They point to the jazz world as decadent (whereas it is in
fact one of the most creative and profound things in America) and
write about the sexual immorality and delinquency and use of drugs by
the young writers of San Francisco and New York. To such charges,
the answers are simple: these people are interested in revolution, *real*
revolution, which starts with the individual mind and body. One of the
things that has been dragging the soul of the world down since the
end of the Bronze Age is the family system and associated notions of
sexual morality that go with patrilineal descent and the descent of
property in the male line (anybody who has read Engels's *Origins of the
Family, Private Property, and the State* knows what I am talking about).
There will be no economic revolution in this world that works, without
a sexual revolution to go with it. Any person who attempts to discover

in practice what the real values of sex are, and what marriage really means, will be called (as D. H. Lawrence was) immoral or obscene. As for delinquency, or crime, this is largely slander. Juvenile delinquents, as Lawrence Lipton points out in his book *The Holy Barbarians,* are simply teenage capitalists who want their money right away. The bohemian men and women of San Francisco's North Beach buy their clothes in secondhand stores, and none of them own radios or cars. The last charge, drugs, is a difficult point, because marijuana is classified as a dangerous narcotic in America, and hence is illegal. Marijuana (Indian hemp, *Cannabis sativa*), along with cheap red wine, is a standby of beat social life. It is either imported from Mexico or grown at home, and the penalties for possessing are very severe (at least six months in prison). But everybody smokes it—calls it "pot" or "tea" or "grass"—to enjoy the quiet sharpening of perceptions it gives, particularly to the ear, which explains why marijuana is so widely used by jazz musicians. The public is not informed of the fact that marijuana has been pronounced by doctors as non–habit forming, non–tolerance forming, and socially less dangerous than alcohol. An old and irrational prejudice against it keeps the "beat" and the "square" (square generally means any person who disapproves of jazz and/or marijuana; another opposite of "square" is "hip" from "hipster"—one who is knowledgeable around drugs and jazz) on different sides of the fence, and the beat is often on the inner side of a jail fence in this case. Now for "irresponsible." The irresponsible people in this world are the generals and politicians who test nuclear bombs; the antisocial, violent, and childish people are the ones who are running the world's governments right now. To refuse to participate in their idiocy—and this means keeping out of jobs that contribute to military preparations, staying out of the army, and saying what you think without fear of anyone—is a real responsibility and one for poets to face up to.

In a way one can see the beat generation as another aspect of the perpetual "third force" that has been moving through history with its own values of community, love, and freedom. It can be linked with the ancient Essene communities, primitive Christianity, Gnostic communities, and the free-spirit heresies of the Middle Ages; with Islamic Sufism, early Chinese Taoism, and both Zen and Shin Buddhism. The bold and moving erotic sculptures at Konorak in India, the paintings of Hieronymus Bosch, the poetry of William Blake, all belong to the same tradition. The motto in a Los Angeles beat coffeehouse is the equation "Art Is Love Is God." In America we get this through Walt Whitman and Henry David Thoreau and from our teachers of the generation above us, William Carlos Williams, Robinson Jeffers, Kenneth Rexroth, Henry Miller, and D. H. Lawrence.

What is the international significance of all this? The beat generation can be seen as an aspect of the worldwide trend for intellectuals to reconsider the nature of the human individual, existence, personal motives, the qualities of love and hatred, and the means of achieving wisdom. Existentialism, the modern pacifist-anarchist movement, the current interest of Occidentals in Zen Buddhism, are all a part of that trend. The beat generation is particularly interesting because it is not an intellectual movement, but a creative one: people who have cut their ties with respectable society in order to live an independent way of life writing poems and painting pictures, making mistakes and taking chances—but finding no reason for apathy or discouragement. They are going somewhere. It would do no harm if some of their attitudes came to liven up the poets of Japan.

## The New Wind

Everyone has heard now about the "poetry renaissance" and the "beat generation" in America (it spreads to Asia and Europe); and now, finally, a full-sized anthology of this poetry is in print: *The New American Poetry 1945–1960*, edited by Donald Allen (Grove Press). I just received this book a few days ago, and it presents the poets of my generation so well that writing this article will be in a way a review of Don Allen's book.

What is "new" about the new American poetry? First, what is new about the poets? The most striking thing is their detachment from the official literary world, be it publishing and commercial magazines or the literature departments of universities. They earn their livings in a wide variety of ways, but feel their real work to be poetry—requiring no justification. They are well educated, tough, independent, and in no way lumped into cliques. They have kept out (or been kept out) of the comfortable middle-class life in America. Many of them consider the universities to be instituted for professional liars and call them "fog factories"—and feel they are doing truth a service by staying in a position to teach and say what they like. They are gathered largely in San Francisco and New York, but a lot of them hide out in the country; some are even farmers. Places like Big Sur on the California coast (where Henry Miller has lived for over a decade) attract quite a few. They are different from their immediate predecessors in this detachment from the universities and in the fact that they have rejected the academic and neoformalist poetry of the late thirties and forties. *Poetry* magazine, which published Ezra Pound, T. S. Eliot, and a host of other now-famous modern poets in the twenties, is now considered conservative and prints almost none of the people in *The New American Poetry*.

They take poetry very seriously and have some striking views: poetry is not "beauty," not propaganda for the Bolsheviks or capitalists or whatever, not drinking sake and enjoying the moonlight, not "recollection in tranquillity" (Wordsworth), but a combination of the highest activity of trained intellect and the deepest insight of the intuitive, instinctive, or emotional mind, "all the faculties"—for Mike McClure it is "protein and fire"—it is in breath (Charles Olson) making the formal line, a sort of stylistic *ch'i*. It is sensitive awareness to things as they are (which if overstressed, takes the guts and brains out of poetry, as has too often happened in Japan), it is history, and most of all it is Magic, the power to transform by symbol and metaphor, to create a world with forms or to destroy a world with chaos. Charles Olson, in his note (at the back of the anthology) on "Projective Verse," says *form* is an extension of *content*. There is a philosophical paradigm in Buddhism that runs parallel to this and exposes the whole nature of the form/content dualism: form = emptiness, emptiness = form.

So: this poetry is in the "modern" tradition—harking back to Ezra Pound and particularly William Carlos Williams (who has been the largest single influence on the present generation of writers) but skipping over the poets of the late thirties and forties, who ran the influential poetry magazines, as being too formal and too dull. There is certainly nothing dull about the new American poetry—it is controversial, direct, topical, uninhibited, based on personal experience. The poets in this collection most closely identified with the "beat generation" are simply the most erratically imaginative, "crazy," and uninhibited. But not all the new poets would like to be described as members of the beat generation.

The nineteenth-century American poets Whitman and Herman Melville (whose fame as a poet, apart from his novels, is quite recent) have been highly appreciated. From Europe, the poetry in Spanish of Rafael Alberti and Federico García Lorca (especially!); the French poets Henri Michaux, Antonin Artaud, Guillaume Apollinaire; the German Bertolt Brecht—and Pablo Neruda of Chile—have been influential. The classical Chinese poets through the translations of Ezra Pound, Arthur Waley, and Kenneth Rexroth; the translations of Japanese haiku by R. H. Blyth, a rereading of the Greek anthology and the medieval European goliard poets have all come together to produce a poetry of irony and compassion.

The fact is there is a creative flowering in America right now the like of which we haven't seen before. Poets are everywhere, and most of them are pretty good. One is tempted to say, like Elizabethan England or the mid T'ang dynasty. It is astounding.

Don Allen, in his preface to *The New American Poetry*, divides the poets into five classes, which I will list here in case it helps anyone understand.

1. The poets who were first associated with *Origin* magazine (founded by Cid Corman, who lived quietly in Kyoto for two years ending April 1960) and *Black Mountain Review*. The most outstanding of these are Charles Olson and Robert Duncan. Others are Denise Levertov, Paul Blackburn, Robert Creeley, Paul Carroll, Larry Eigner, Edward Dorn, Jonathan Williams, and Joel Oppenheimer. These people are writing a very careful, competent, and wise poetry.

2. The San Francisco group. Kenneth Rexroth, who is too old to be included in this anthology, is in a sense the father of the San Francisco poetry renaissance, along with Robert Duncan (who somehow ended up in class I). The poets represented are Helen Adam, Brother Antoninus (William Everson), James Broughton, Madeline Gleason, Lawrence Ferlinghetti, Robin Blaser, Jack Spicer, Lew Welch, Richard Duerden, Philip Lamantia, Bruce Boyd, Kirby Doyle, and Ebbe Borregaard. Ferlinghetti is the owner of City Lights Bookshop in San Francisco, which first published Ginsberg's *Howl*.

3. The beat generation. Don Allen strictly defines it to include only Jack Kerouac, Allen Ginsberg, Gregory Corso, and Peter Orlovsky.

Kerouac is best known as a novelist, but he has a delightful book of poems in print (Grove Press) called *Mexico City Blues*—poems to a large extent concerned with Kerouac's personal interpretation of Buddhism.

4. New York poets. Those included are Barbara Guest, James Schuyler, Edward Field, Kenneth Koch, Frank O'Hara, and John Ashbery. Frank O'Hara is probably the best known.

5. The last group is a sort of miscellaneous collection of independent characters who cannot be fitted into any other class and who all have individual styles. They are Philip Whalen, Gilbert Sorrentino, Stuart Perkoff, Edward Marshall, Michael McClure, Ray Bremser, LeRoi Jones (editor of *Yugen* magazine), John Wieners, Ron Loewinsohn, David Meltzer, and myself. Actually most of these poets could be called San Francisco people, but for some reason Don Allen prefers to keep them separate.

*The New American Poetry* ends up with "Statements on Poetics" by various poets, biographical notes on everybody, and a short bibliography.

This book will become the handbook of young writers in the sixties. It is a good selection. I can only think of three poets I would like to see in it who aren't (Cid Corman, by his own choice; Theodore Enslin; and Tom Parkinson). Let us hope this fresh wind of poetry doesn't stay just in America, but blows its way about the globe.

——————

Gary Snyder first published "Buddhism and the Possibilities of a Planetary Culture" in *Earth House Hold* (1969).

——————

## Buddhism and the Possibilities of a Planetary Culture

Buddhism holds that the universe and all creatures in it are intrinsically in a state of complete wisdom, love, and compassion, acting in natural response and mutual interdependence. The personal realization of this from-the-beginning state cannot be had for and by one-"self," because it is not fully realized unless one has given the self up and away.

In the Buddhist view, what obstructs the effortless manifestation of this realization is ignorance, which projects into fear and needless craving. Historically, Buddhist philosophers have failed to analyze out the degree to which ignorance and suffering are caused or encouraged by social factors, considering fear and desire to be given facts of the human condition. Consequently the major concern of Buddhist philosophy is epistemology and "psychology," with no attention paid to historical or sociological problems. Although Mahayana Buddhism has a grand vision of universal salvation, the actual achievement of Buddhism has been the development of practical systems of meditation toward the end of liberating a few dedicated individuals from psychological hang-ups and cultural conditionings. Institutional Buddhism has been conspicuously ready to accept or ignore the inequalities and tyrannies of whatever political system it found itself under. This can be death to Buddhism, because it is death to any meaningful function of compassion. Wisdom without compassion feels no pain.

No one today can afford to be innocent, or to indulge themselves in ignorance of the nature of contemporary governments, politics, and social orders. The national polities of the modern world are "states" that maintain their existence by deliberately fostered craving and fear: monstrous protection rackets. The "free world" has become economically dependent on a fantastic system of stimulation of greed that cannot be fulfilled, sexual desire that cannot be satiated, and hatred that has no outlet except against oneself, the persons one is supposed to love, or the revolutionary aspirations of pitiful, poverty-stricken marginal societies. The conditions of the Cold War have fumed most modern societies—both communist and capitalist—into vicious distorters of true human potential. They try to create populations of *preta*—hungry ghosts, with giant appetites and throats no bigger than needles. The soil, the forests, and all animal life are being consumed by these cancerous collectivities; the air and water of the planet is being fouled by them.

There is nothing in human nature or the requirements of human social organization that requires a society to be contradictory, repressive, and productive of violent and frustrated personalities. Findings in anthropology and psychology make this more and more evident. One can prove it for oneself by taking a good look at Original Nature through meditation. Once a person has this much faith and insight, one will be led to a deep concern for the need for radical social change through a variety of nonviolent means.

The joyous and voluntary poverty of Buddhism becomes a positive force. The traditional harmlessness and avoidance of taking life in any form has nation-shaking implications. The practice of meditation, for which one needs only "the ground beneath one's feet," wipes out mountains of junk being pumped into the mind by the mass media and supermarket universities. The belief in a serene and generous fulfillment of natural loving desires destroys ideologies that blind, maim, and repress—and points the way to a kind of community which would amaze "moralists" and transform armies of men who are fighters because they cannot be lovers.

*Avatamsaka (Kegon* or *Hua-yen)* Buddhist philosophy sees the world as a vast, interrelated network in which all objects and creatures are necessary and illuminated. From one standpoint, governments, wars, or all that we consider "evil" are uncompromisingly contained in this totalistic realm. The hawk, the swoop, and the hare are one. From the "human" standpoint we cannot live in those terms unless all beings see with the same enlightened eye. The Bodhisattva lives by the sufferer's standard, and must be effective in aiding those who suffer.

The mercy of the West has been social revolution; the mercy of the East has been individual insight into the basic self/void. We need both. They are both contained in the traditional three aspects of the Dharma path: wisdom *(prajña)*, meditation *(dhyana)*, and morality *(shila)*. Wisdom is intuitive knowledge of the mind of love and clarity that lies beneath one's ego-driven anxieties and aggressions. Meditation is going into the mind to see this for yourself—over and over again, until it becomes the mind you live in. Morality is bringing it back out in the way you live, through personal example and responsible action, ultimately toward the true community *(sangha)* of "all beings." This last aspect means, for me, supporting any cultural and economic revolution that moves clearly toward a truly free world. It means using such means as civil disobedience, outspoken criticism, protest, pacifism, voluntary poverty, and even gentle violence if it comes to a matter of restraining some impetuous crazy. It means affirming the widest possible spectrum of non-harmful individual behavior—defending the right of individuals to smoke hemp, eat peyote, be polygamous, polyandrous, or homosexual. Worlds of behavior and custom long banned by the Judaeo-Capitalist-Christian-Marxist West. It means respecting intelligence and learning, but not as greed or means to personal power. Working on one's own responsibility, but willing to work with a group. "Forming the new society within the shell of the old"—the I.W.W. slogan of 70 years ago.

The traditional, vernacular, primitive, and village cultures may appear to be doomed. We must defend and support them as we would the diversity of ecosystems; they are all manifestations of Mind. Some of the elder societies accomplished a condition of Sangha, with not a little of Buddha and Dharma as well. We touch base with the deep mind of peoples of all times and places in our meditation practice, and this is an amazing revolutionary aspect of the Buddhadharma. By a "planetary culture" I mean the kind of societies that would follow on a new understanding of that relatively recent institution, the national state, an understanding that might enable us to leave it behind. The state is greed made legal, with a monopoly on violence; a natural society is familial and cautionary. A natural society is one that "follows the way," imperfectly but authentically.

Such an understanding will close the circle and link us in many ways with the most creative aspects of our archaic past. If we are lucky, we may eventually arrive at a world of relatively mutually tolerant small societies attuned to their local natural region and united overall by a profound respect and love for the mind and nature of the universe.

I can imagine further virtues in a world sponsoring societies with matrilineal descent, free-form marriage, "natural credit" economics, far less population, and much more wilderness.

---

Gary Snyder included his translations of the "Preface to the Poems of Han-shan by Lu Ch'iu-yin, Governor of T'ai Prefecture" and "Cold Mountain Poems" in *Riprap and Cold Mountain Poems*, published in 1990 by North Point Press. ("Cold Mountain Poems" originally appeared in *Evergreen Review* in 1958.) Snyder introduced the poems with a note explaining that

Kanzan, or Han-shan, "Cold Mountain," takes his name from where he lived. He is a mountain madman in an old Chinese line of ragged hermits. When he talks about Cold Mountain he means himself, his home, his state of mind. He lived in the T'ang dynasty—traditionally A.D. 627–650, although Hu Shih dates him 700–800. This makes him roughly contemporary with Tu Fu, Li Po, Wang Wei, and Po Chu-i. His poems, of which three hundred survive, are written in T'ang colloquial: rough and fresh. The ideas are Taoist, Buddhist, Zen. He and his sidekick Shih-te (Jittoku in Japanese) became great favorites with Zen painters of later days—the scroll, the broom, the wild hair and laughter. They became Immortals and you sometimes run into them today in the skidrows, orchards, hobo jungles, and logging camps of America.

### Preface to the Poems of Han-shan by Lu Ch'iu-yin, Governor of T'ai Prefecture

No one knows just what sort of man Han-shan was. There are old people who knew him: they say he was a poor man, a crazy character. He lived alone seventy li west of the T'ang-hsing district of T'ien-t'ai at a place called Cold Mountain. He often went down to the Kuo-ch'ing Temple. At the temple lived Shih-te, who ran the dining hall. He sometimes saved leftovers for Han-shan, hiding them in a bamboo tube. Han-shan would come and carry it away; walking the long veranda, calling and shouting happily, talking and laughing to himself. Once the monks followed him, caught him, and made fun of him. He stopped, clapped his hands, and laughed greatly—Ha Ha!—for a spell, then left.

He looked like a tramp. His body and face were old and beat. Yet in every word he breathed was a meaning in line with the subtle principles of things, if only you thought of it deeply. Everything he said had a feeling of the Tao in it, profound and arcane secrets. His hat was made of birch bark, his clothes were ragged and worn out, and his shoes were wood. Thus men who have made it hide their tracks: unifying categories and interpenetrating things. On that long veranda calling and singing, in his words of reply Ha Ha!—the three worlds revolve. Sometimes at the villages and farms he laughed and sang with cowherds. Sometimes intractable, sometimes agreeable, his nature was happy of itself. But how could a person without wisdom recognize him?

I once received a position as a petty official at Tan-ch'iu. The day I was to depart, I had a bad headache. I called a doctor, but he couldn't cure me and it turned worse. Then I met a Buddhist Master named Feng-kan, who said he came from the Kuo-ch'ing Temple of T'ien-t'ai especially to visit me. I asked him to rescue me from my illness. He smiled and said, "The four realms are within the body; sickness comes from illusion. If you want to do away with it, you need pure water." Someone brought water to the Master, who spat it on me. In a moment the disease was rooted out. He then said, "There are miasmas in T'ai prefecture, when you get there take care of yourself." I asked him, "Are there any wise men in your area I could look on as Master?" He replied, "When you see him you don't recognize him, when you recognize him you don't see him. If you want to see him, you can't rely on appearances. Then you can see him. Han-shan is a Manjusri hiding at Kuo-ch'ing. Shih-te is a Samantabhadra. They look like poor fellows and act like madmen. Sometimes they go and sometimes they come. They work in the kitchen of the Kuo-ch'ing dining hall, tending the fire." When he was done talking he left.

I proceeded on my journey to my job at T'ai-chou, not forgetting this affair. I arrived three days later, immediately went to a temple, and questioned an old monk. It seemed the Master had been truthful, so I gave orders to see if T'ang-hsing really contained a Han-shan and Shih-te. The District Magistrate reported to me: "In this district, seventy li west, is a mountain. People used to see a poor man heading from the cliffs to stay awhile at Kuo-ch'ing. At the temple dining hall is a similar man named Shih-te." I made a bow, and went to Kuo-ch'ing. I asked some people around the temple, "There used to be a Master named Feng-kan here. Where is his place? And where can Han-shan and Shih-te be seen?" A monk named Tao-ch'iao spoke up: "Feng-kan the Master lived in back of the library. Nowadays nobody lives there; a tiger often comes and roars. Han-shan and Shih-te are in the kitchen." The monk led me to Feng-kan's yard. Then he opened the gate: all we saw was tiger tracks. I asked the monks Tao-ch'iao and Pao-te, "When Feng-kan was here, what was his job?" The monks said, "He pounded and hulled rice. At night he sang songs to amuse himself." Then we went to the kitchen, before the stoves. Two men were facing the fire, laughing loudly. I made a bow. The two shouted HO! at me. They struck their hands together—Ha Ha!—great laughter. They shouted. Then they said, "Feng-kan—loose-tongued, loose-tongued. You don't recognize Amitabha, why be courteous to us?" The monks gathered round, surprise going through them. "Why has a big official bowed to a pair of clowns?" The two men grabbed hands and ran out of the temple. I cried, "Catch them"—but they quickly ran away. Han-shan returned to Cold Mountain. I asked the monks, "Would those two men be willing to settle down at this temple?" I ordered them to find a house, and to ask Han-shan and Shih-te to return and live at the temple.

I returned to my district and had two sets of clean clothes made, got some incense and such, and sent it to the temple—but the two men didn't return. So I had it carried up to Cold Mountain. The packer saw Han-shan, who called in a loud voice, "Thief! Thief!" and retreated into a mountain cave. He shouted, "I tell you man, strive hard!"—entered the cave and was gone. The cave closed of itself and they weren't able to follow. Shih-te's tracks disappeared completely.

I ordered Tao-ch'iao and the other monks to find out how they had lived, to hunt up the poems written on bamboo, wood, stones, and cliffs—and also to collect those written on the walls of people's houses. There were more than three hundred. On the wall of the Earth-shrine Shih-te had written some *gatha*. It was all brought together and made into a book.

I hold to the principle of the Buddha-mind. It is fortunate to meet with men of Tao. So I have made this euology.

### Cold Mountain Poems

The path to Han-shan's place is laughable,
A path, but no sign of cart or horse.

Converging gorges—hard to trace their twists
Jumbled cliffs—unbelievably rugged.
A thousand grasses bend with dew,
A hill of pines hums in the wind.
And now I've lost the shortcut home,
Body asking shadow, how do you keep up?

In a tangle of cliffs I chose a place—
Bird-paths, but no trails for men.
What's beyond the yard?
White clouds clinging to vague rocks.
Now I've lived here—how many years—
Again and again, spring and winter pass.
Go tell families with silverware and cars
"What's the use of all that noise and money?"

Men ask the way to Cold Mountain
Cold Mountain: there's no through trail.
In summer, ice doesn't melt
The rising sun blurs in swirling fog.
How did I make it?
My heart's not the same as yours.
If your heart was like mine
You'd get it and be right here.

I settled at Cold Mountain long ago,
Already it seems like years and years.
Freely drifting, I prowl the woods and streams
And linger watching things themselves.
Men don't get this far into the mountains,
White clouds gather and billow.
Thin grass does for a mattress,
The blue sky makes a good quilt.
Happy with a stone underhead
Let heaven and earth go about their changes.

I have lived at Cold Mountain
These thirty long years.
Yesterday I called on friends and family:

More than half had gone to the Yellow Springs.
Slowly consumed, like fire down a candle;
Forever flowing, like a passing river.
Now, morning, I face my lone shadow:
Suddenly my eyes are bleared with tears.

In my first thirty years of life
I roamed hundreds and thousands of miles.
Walked by rivers through deep green grass
Entered cities of boiling red dust.
Tried drugs, but couldn't make Immortal;
Read books and wrote poems on history.
Today I'm back at Cold Mountain:
I'll sleep by the creek and purify my ears.

There's a naked bug at Cold Mountain
With a white body and a black head.
His hand holds two book-scrolls,
One the Way and one its Power.
His shack's got no pots or oven,
He goes for a walk with his shirt and pants askew.
But he always carries the sword of wisdom:
He means to cut down senseless craving.

Cold Mountain is a house
Without beams or walls.
The six doors left and right are open
The hall is blue sky.
The rooms all vacant and vague
The east wall beats on the west wall
At the center nothing.

Borrowers don't bother me
In the cold I build a little fire
When I'm hungry I boil up some greens.
I've got no use for the kulak
With his big barn and pasture—
He just sets up a prison for himself.
Once in he can't get out.

Think it over—
You know it might happen to you.

Some critic tried to put me down—
"Your poems lack the Basic Truth of Tao"
And I recall the old-timers
Who were poor and didn't care.
I have to laugh at him,
He misses the point entirely,
Men like that
Ought to stick to making money.

When men see Han-shan
They all say he's crazy
And not much to look at
Dressed in rags and hides.
They don't get what I say
& I don't talk their language.
All I can say to those I meet:
"Try and make it to Cold Mountain."

---

# JACK SPICER

JACK SPICER (1925–1965), a poet who played an active role in the San Francisco Poetry Renaissance, was not a close friend of the Beat writers (he called "Howl" "the best-publicized poem in the world"). Like Robert Duncan, another leading Bay Area poet, Spicer had left San Francisco by October 1955, and he was living on the East Coast at the time of the famous reading at the 6 Gallery. As Spicer's biographers Lewis Ellingham and Kevin Killian have noted,

> While Spicer left in search of the fame and fortune he had dreamed of, this voyage east had an ironic twist, since while he was gone, the "6" Gallery, which he had helped found, could have

given him one clear shot at notoriety. Besides art
exhibitions, the Gallery was becoming well known
for poetry readings, of which perhaps the most
famous—hailed as the "birth of the Beat Generation"—was Allen Ginsberg's public reading of
*Howl*, on October 7, 1955, with Jack Kerouac
in attendance, and Kenneth Rexroth as M.C.
Michael McClure, Gary Snyder, Philip Whalen,
and Philip Lamantia also read the same evening.
McClure and Wally Hedrick, who [initially] organized the event, would have asked Spicer and
Duncan to read too, had they been in town.
"Spicer's friend John Ryan came that evening,"
McClure remembered, "and gave me a letter he'd
received from Spicer—who had left New York and
moved to Boston. It asked someone in San Francisco to help find Spicer a job and the wherewithal to come back home, because he wanted to
leave Boston. I read Jack's letter from the stage
and it got applause from his friends and fans. It
was a practical matter. 'Could anybody help Jack?'
This was a request for much needed mutual aid:
*Let's get Jack out of Boston, where he's unhappy.* It
was a letter of plaint: Help! get me out of here!
There were a lot of people there and I thought
maybe somebody could help." But no one did.
When Spicer, trapped on the East Coast, heard
how his letter had been read, he burned to return.

A year later, still living in poverty in Boston, Spicer helped
organize a poetry reading with his friends John Dunn, Robin
Blaser, John Wieners, and Steve Jonas in September 1956.
There Spicer read a new poem, "Song for Bird and Myself,"
which he had written after the anniversary of the death of the
brilliant bebop saxophonist Charlie "Bird" Parker. As Ginsberg
had advertised the 6 Gallery reading by mailing postcards in
the Bay Area, so Spicer sent out postcards in Boston stating,
"You are invited to a poetry reading where five Boston cats are
blowing their poetry REAL Hard." The Boston reading was dismally attended—only eight people came to hear the five poets.
Later, back in California, Spicer gave a well-attended reading at

the Poetry Center at San Francisco State University, which was recorded on reel-to-reel tape. He ended the program with "Song for Bird and Myself."

---

### Song for Bird and Myself

I am dissatisfied with my poetry.
I am dissatisfied with my sex life.
I am dissatisfied with the angels I believe in.
    Neo-classical like Bird,
    Distrusting the reality
    of every note.
    Half-real
    We blow the sentence pure and real
    Like chewing angels.

"Listen, Bird, why do we have to sit here dying
In a half-furnished room?
The rest of the combo
Is safe in houses
Blowing bird-brained Dixieland,
How warm and free they are. What right
Music."
    "Man,
    We
    Can't stay away from the sounds.
    *We're crazy,* Jack
    We gotta stay here 'til
    They come and get us."

Neo-classical like Bird.
Once two birds got into the Rare Book Room.
Miss Swift said,
"Don't
Call a custodian
Put crumbs on the outside of the window
Let them

Come outside."
                Neo-classical
The soft line strains
Not to be neo-classical.
But Miss Swift went to lunch. They
Called a custodian.
Four came.
Armed like Myrmidons, they
Killed the birds.
Miss Munsterberg
Who was the first
American translator of Rilke
Said
"Suppose one of them
Had been the Holy Ghost."
Miss Swift,
Who was back from lunch,
Said
"Which."
But the poem isn't over.
It keeps going
Long after everybody
Has settled down comfortably into laughter.
The bastards
on the other side of the paper
Keep laughing.
LISTEN.
STOP LAUGHING.
THE POEM ISN'T OVER. Butterflies.
I knew there would be butterflies
For Butterflies represent the lost soul
Represent the way the wind wanders
Represent the bodies
We only clasp in the middle of a poem.
See, the stars have faded.
There are only butterflies.
Listen to
The terrible sound of their wings moving.
Listen.
The poem isn't over.

Have you ever wrestled with a bird,
You idiotic reader?
Jacob wrestled with an angel.
(I remind you of the image)
or a butterfly
Have you ever wrestled with a single butterfly?
Sex is no longer important.
Colors take the form of wings. Words
Have got to be said.
A butterfly,
A bird,
Planted at the heart of being afraid of dying.
Blow,
Bird,
Blow,
Be,
Neo-classical.
Let the wings say
What the wings mean
Terrible and pure.

    The horse
    In Cocteau
    Is as neo-classical an idea as one can manage.
    Writes all our poetry for us
    Is Gertrude Stein
    Is God
    Is the needle for which
    God help us
    There is no substitute
    Or the Ace of Swords
    When you are telling a fortune
    Who tells death.
    Or the Jack of Hearts
    Whose gypsy fortune we clasp
    In the middle of a poem.

"And are we angels, Bird?"
    "That's what we're trying to tell 'em, Jack
    There aren't any angels except when
    You and me blow 'em."

So Bird and I sing
outside your window
So Bird and I die
Outside your window.
This is the wonderful world of Dixieland.
Deny
The bloody motherfucking Holy Ghost.
This is the end of the poem.
You can start laughing, you bastards. This is
The end of the poem.

*[1956]*

# ROBERT STONE

ROBERT STONE was a Stegner Fellow at Stanford University's Writing Program in 1962, along with Ken Kesey and Larry Mc-Murtry. Among Stone's many novels are *Dog Soldiers* (1975), winner of a National Book Award, and *Damascus Gate* (1998). Since 1994 Stone has taught creative writing at Yale University. He published his autobiographical essay about Melville and Kerouac in *The New York Times* on December 7, 1997.

## American Dreamers: Melville and Kerouac

In the autumn of 1957 I was 19 years old, in the Navy and also more or less permanently in the grip of romantic adolescent impulses. That year, I rashly volunteered to serve with the last of the Byrd expeditions to the Antarctic continent aboard the U.S.S. Arneb. The Arneb would depart New England in December for the bases Adm. Richard E. Byrd had established at Little America on McMurdo Sound in Antarctica. It would then proceed to circumnavigate the globe, steaming outside the shipping lanes and tracking solar storms.

Byrd would not be coming with us. He had died in February. But the operations were closely associated with him and with his schoolboy-hero mystique. The last of the explorers, he actually "discovered" places and named them—Marie Byrd Land, for example, and Mount Edsel Ford, its overmastering peak. In the tank towns and tenements from which the 50's Navy was recruited, his career evoked the essence of exotic adventure.

The journey would take almost a year. After Thanksgiving, the volunteer crew began gathering at the Seabee base in Davisville, R.I. Among them were many bookish high-school dropouts like me, along with proto-computer-nerd technicians attracted by the state-of-the-art detecting devices provided by the University of Chicago to monitor cosmic rays.

Like the Pequod from Nantucket, the Arneb departed the ice-edged New England shore at Christmastime with its complement of largely juvenile adventurers. "Yet now, federated along one keel, what a set these Isolatoes were," a 19th-century American novelist might have written of us as well. They "blindly plunged like fate into the lone Atlantic!" he might have said. In other words, I had found the ideal circumstances to read "Moby-Dick," at just the right age.

I had a second novel along, one considerably less bulky, that my mother had sent me. My mother was a free but tormented spirit, an ex-teacher who shuttled between single-room-occupancy hotels and hospitals. She'd picked it up somewhere, and thought I'd like to have a look at it. It was by a young author, one I'd never heard of. The author was Jack Kerouac and the novel was "On the Road."

I read the Melville first. Across the southern ocean, far from customary skies, I would lie in my rack each night with a pen flashlight, a force 11-plus gale screaming above decks, listening to the groaning of seams and the squealing of lockers as the ship rolled to starboard, the lockers creaking, creaking, creaking, threatening to go over. At each roll, the ship favored its congenital list, easing farther and farther toward that soft starboard side—maybe herself capsizing—while my hair stood on end at Ahab's rant when his first mate, the godly Quaker Starbuck, accuses him of blasphemy for wanting to take it all out on a dumb whale: "All visible objects, man, are but as pasteboard masks. But in each event—in the living act, the undoubted deed—there, some unknown but still reasoning thing puts forth the moldings of its features from behind the unreasoning mask. . . . That inscrutable thing is chiefly what I hate; and be the white whale agent or be the white whale principal, I will wreak that hate upon him. Talk not to me of blasphemy, man; I'd strike the sun if it insulted me."

Then I would look up into the dark compartment, because we *really* had been listing to starboard for the longest time and I had to wonder if we ever would right, and then, slowly, the big tub would find its level and begin to creak back upright toward the best it could manage by way of an even keel.

"Who's over me?" the mad captain demanded of his reasonable, humane No. 1. "Truth hath no confines."

So during gunnery practice when I found myself with frozen fingers clinging to the ladder of a sight mounting at 53 degrees south latitude while the ship fought its way, decks awash, through the swells—I could compare my condition to Tashtego's as he lashed down the Pequod's main-topsail yard amid thunder and lightning.

Then, somewhere between Montevideo and the Carolina Capes, with the Pequod settled deep beneath the Japan Ground, I picked up Kerouac's novel. After the months of half-light, the rolling ship and the blank horizon, "On the Road" floored me. Aboard the Arneb, life was a trancelike state. Each day, by design, was exactly like another except for the weather, the pattern interrupted only by drunken hallucinatory liberties in places, with people one would never see again, prostitutes and land sharks—who receded into phantoms of alcoholic memory. Here in this book with its primordially American title, by a young man with a semipronounceable name, was the World, the one I'd lost at sea while youth atrophied and my inner ear echoed with Ahab's hassles with "that unknown but still reasoning thing." In contrast, "On the Road" was the narrative of someone I imagined as not much older than myself and so like myself that—he *was* me! Me, and out occupying my rightful place in the lost World, experiencing ever new towns, new guilt-free sexual adventures, the pleasures of wonderful friends and jazz and art and bohemia.

I had a few bohemian pretensions myself, you understand. I could rejoice in the knowledge that I was certainly the only sailor aboard the Arneb with a girlfriend at the High School of Music and Art. But there was something else about the narrator, Sal Paradise, that made me identify with him, something in the sad undertone of the novel that is finally its core. That narrator was forever in search of American authenticity and it was forever somewhere else. He, like me, came from a place that seemed distressingly inauthentic. For him as for me, the road to America suggested a transcendent journey toward an ineffable reality that was somehow our lost birthright. The road to Opelousas, the road to Ogallala, the road to Truckee. Hence we must hasten, the book seemed to say in that darker key, to find ourselves no more authentic, no more at home. Because of its youthful enthusiasm, and my own, I was not so aware then of that heartbreaking subtext in "On the Road." Of course its components would years later bring the author, who brought so much wild promise to so many, into the nightmare heart of his own interior darkness.

When I'd finished the novel I started passing it along to the friends I'd made on the voyage, the underachievers and inept teen-age car thieves and feckless younger brothers of heroes of the recent war. And it turned out that they too came from hopelessly inauthentic places, they too dreamed of an infinity of willing, largehearted, well-read women and parties and big-city action, a world of jazz and girls and reefer in which they would be unwontedly at home and welcome. They too were looking for the road and they too loved Kerouac's novel. So what dreams of high times to come we projected on that endless succession of hateful, gorgeous sunsets thanks to Kerouac.

We could not know, as the author, who was then 35, would have, that in the endless formula we had already come to the Road, were already on it, that many of us would come to look back on our oceanic wanderings as the most of freedom and authenticity we would ever know.

It never occurred to me, then or since, that "On the Road" was a great book. I had just finished "Moby-Dick." For all the bright fantasies it invited, there was really nothing much in "On the Road" to ponder, to obsess over and argue about in the grave adolescent atmosphere of our nightly bull sessions. The book had very little humor. On the contrary, it had an earnestness that seemed a little much even to a pack of wised-up rubes like ourselves, the crew of the Arneb.

Yet that earnestness never seemed to bring the reader any closer to the touch of redemption through insight that finally justifies fiction. Its characters were thin and their relationship with one another consisted of unvarying admiration and affection. Situations where everybody is smart, hip and beautiful are much more satisfactory in life than in novels. It did not seem to offer the shock of recognition of the tragedy we all suspected lay at the core of things, which even the sentimentality of Thomas Wolfe, plainly Kerouac's model, provided. Even then, it seemed that when the author approached the layers of art or the emptiness of Buddha-hood there was a naïve posturing about the writing that made it seem a trifle ignorant, a self-conscious appropriation of high culture to ultimately trivial purpose.

But of course we loved the invocations of popular culture in the book, since they occupied so much of our imaginations—comic strips, B movies, all that. And it was fun to think of George Shearing as God, in whose guise he briefly appears in "On the Road," although by 1957 and 1958 he had really stopped being God and become a fairly conventional jazz pianist.

The overwhelming gratifying element in "On the Road" for its contemporary readers was the dream, the promise of life more abundant available to the young American adventurer, the intrepid traveler. Thirty or so years before, "The Sun Also Rises" had offered similar dreams, though it made them appear more difficult of access. "The Sun Also Rises" was a better book, of course, and it seems wiser, though that may be only because Hemingway was tougher and meaner and more realistic about people than Kerouac.

Years later, after our respective periods working in Vietnam, I had a conversation with Michael Herr, the author of the great war memoir "Dispatches." "There are two kinds of things guys like us do," Michael said to me. "The things we do because we read Jack Kerouac and the things we do because we read Hemingway."

As it once promised the future, "On the Road" now evokes the past, pre-Interstate America, the diners serving slabs of ice cream and fresh pie, the simple cowboys singing songs of pretty girls "sweet sixteen," the stars growing larger as Sal Paradise's ride takes him out on the High Plains. And if one thing works in a sound writerly fashion in it, that's the portrayal of Neal Cassady. The rendering of Cassady is so vivid that for years, trying to say nice things about Kerouac's novel, people who had read the book and knew Cassady would assure one another of the exactitude of that portrait.

Little did I suspect, out on the ocean, that in fewer than 10 years

I, along with various other marginal characters, would be sharing an abandoned Purina factory on the Mexican coast with the divine Cassady himself. By then a muscled-up, Popeye the Sailor-like motor-mouth speed loon, Cassady would be roaming the place with his capsules and a hypodermic full of LSD, eternally engaged in his private project of slipping psychedelics into his fellow inmates' food or drink.

When a number of us tried to elude him by buying a piglet and roasting it, Cassady ambushed us by injecting the squealing porker in vivo with about 10,000 micrograms of Owsley acid, upon which I died some kind of literary death to emerge in Book Hell. Book Hell is the place where you are compelled to wander for days, hour after garrulous hour, utterly whacked out, in the company of larger-than-life characters you once thought charming from pretty good novels you once sort of enjoyed, while they tell you absolutely everything else about themselves.

And little did I suspect that a major critic of the period, Gerald Nicosia, would decades later write:

"Both trail and superhighway, 'On the Road' led from 'Moby-Dick' . . . into the 21st century—from outer to inner space. Ahab in 'Moby-Dick' searched for the purveyors of cosmic evil. . . . By contrast, the heroes of 'On the Road,' Dean Moriarty (Neal) and Sal Paradise (Jack), no matter how far they travel in the external world, are ceaselessly penetrating deeper into their own souls. They are constantly aware that their travel, by the excitement and curiosity it generates, is a means to understanding themselves. Travel to them is a conscious philosophical method by which they test the store of hand-me-down truisms. Moreover, as a potent imaginative symbol, travel is a philosopher's stone that turns every experience into a spiritual lesson."

I wish I could agree. This is an excerpt from "On the Road," a section so typical the publishers of this year's 40th-anniversary edition (Viking, $24.95) have reproduced it on the back cover:

"So in America when the sun goes down and I sit on the old broken-down river pier watching the long, long skies over New Jersey and sense all that raw land that rolls in one unbelievable huge bulge over to the West Coast, and all that road going, all the people dreaming in the immensity of it, and in Iowa I know by now the children must be crying in the land where they let children cry, and tonight the stars'll be out, and don't you know that God is Pooh Bear? the evening star must be drooping and shedding her sparkler dims on the prairie, which is just before the coming of complete night that blesses the earth, darkens all rivers, cups the peaks and folds the final shore in, and nobody, nobody knows what's going to happen to anybody besides the forlorn rags of growing old, I think of Dean Moriarty, I even think of Old Dean Moriarty the father we never found, I think of Dean Moriarty."

Let's say that the reader must provide a good half of the genuine sentiment here from his own or other sources. And the same, I think, is true throughout "Some of the Dharma" (Viking, $32.95), a previously unpublished collection of Kerouac's Buddhist musings put out to mark the occasion of the anniversary of "On the Road." But let us, Kerouac's survivors, remember how much the work from which all this comes moved so many young people, and also remember how cruel, how brutal and heartless most of the mainstream media were to Jack Kerouac and his work during his lifetime. How in ridiculing his unarmored, vulnerable prose they broke his too tender heart and helped destroy him.

People once said that Jack Kerouac's name would be remembered when those of his contemporaries are forgotten. They may well be right, and for filial and patriotic reasons I say let it be so. But, on the whole, I think "On the Road" was more Mom's kind of book than mine.

# WARREN TALLMAN

WARREN TALLMAN, a professor of English at the University of British Columbia, was an active participant at the Vancouver Poetry Centre. His pioneering essay "Kerouac's Sound" first appeared in *The Tamarack Review* in the spring of 1959. It was reprinted in *Evergreen Review*, volume 4, number 11, and in Thomas Parkinson's *Casebook on the Beat* (1961).

## Kerouac's Sound

It is always an implicit and frequently an explicit assumption of the Beat writers that we live, if we do at all, in something like the ruins of our civilization. When the Second World War was bombed out of existence in that long-ago '45 summer, two cities were in literal fact demolished. But psychically, all cities fell. And what the eye sees as intact is a lesser truth than what the psyche knows is actually in ruins. The psyche knows that the only sensible way to enter a modern city is Gregory Corso's way, very tentatively, "two suitcases filled with despair." This assumption that the cities which live in the psyche have all gone smash is one starting point of Beat.

But if our cities are in something like ruins, there have been survivors. Those have survived who had the least to lose, those whose psychic stance in face of modern experience had already been reduced to minimum needs: the angry Negro, the pathological delinquent, the hopeless addict. These outcasts had already fought and *lost* the battle each of us makes to establish his psyche within the social continuum. The Negro who feels that integration offers worse defeats than those already suffered at the hands of the segregation to which he has long-since adjusted; the delinquent who realizes that continued irresponsibility is the only effective physician to the ills which previous irresponsibilities have brought upon him; the addict who knows that the extent to which he is hooked by his habit is as nothing alongside the extent to which he is hooked by the social purgatory he must endure in order to feed that habit—these advanced types of the social outcast have long since had to forego the psychic luxuries available to those of us who are not outcasts. Crucially, they have had to give up that main staple of psychic continuity, Ego. Here, from John Clellon Holmes's novel *Go*, is an addict evaluating the reaction of fellow passengers on a bus:

> they knew I was completely saturated with narcotics and had this disgusting skin disease and everything . . . I realize they think I'm revolting, abhorrent . . . but not only that, I know *why* they think that . . . and more important, I *accept* the fact

that they do. . . . They're disgusted because they've got to save their own egos, you see. But I haven't got one, I mean I don't care about all that anymore, so it doesn't matter to me . . . I just accept it so as not to get hung up.

The outcast knows that ego, which demands self-regard, is the enemy that can trap him into kinds of social commitment which his psyche cannot afford. Ego is for the squares. Let them be trapped. To be released from the claims of ego is to be released from the claims of others, a very necessary condition for survival if you happen to be an outcast. But the consequences can be devastating. For when ego vanishes, the continuity of one's existence is likely to vanish with it.

A most vivid instance of what can happen to a man when the continuity of his life is suddenly disrupted comes not from the Beat writers but from Conrad, in *Nostromo*. Decoud, isolated by circumstances, "dreaded the sleepless nights in which the silence, remaining unbroken in the shape of a cord to which he hung with both hands, vibrated with senseless phrases." The "senseless phrases" happen to be the names of the woman he loves, of the man with whom he is conspiring, and of the man against whom they conspire. Just because the most meaningful continuity in his life has been reduced by solitude to "senseless phrases," he begins to wish that the cord of silence to which he clings will snap; as, with his suicide, it does. The kinds of solitude from which the city-bred outcasts suffer are not as severe as Decoud's, doubtless, and the loss of continuity which follows from the abandonment of ego not as total. But what Decoud suffers in a total way is known in less intense but still devastating ways to all those outcasts who waken, without ego, to the consequent draft of their aimless day.

It is an axiom of the human spirit that whosoever wanders into purgatory will attempt to escape. With luck, with courage, with ingenuity, some succeed. The solution of the outcast who has given up a large part of his ego has been to fall back not upon the mercy of society—for society has long since been committed to the merciless proposition that only certain men are brothers—but upon, or rather into the moment. The moment becomes the outcast's island, his barricade, his citadel. Having lost his life in the social continuum, cast out and cyphered, he finds it again within the moment. But when the social outcast takes over the moment as his province, he is faced with yet another problem. He must make it habitable. How unsuccessful most such outcast efforts have been can best be seen in any skid-road district, where men come to their vacant pauses within what Ginsberg describes as "the drear light of Zoo." However, some of the animals in the skid road and slum zoos have long since rebelled. Up from the rhythms and intensities which animate the Negro, the delinquent, and the addict have risen the voices that dig and swing on the Beat streets in the North American night, a music and a language, Jazz and Hip.

First the language. Strictly speaking, a hipster is an addict and hip talk is the addict's private language. But it has become much more. Granting many exceptions in which addiction is incurred accidentally, it is almost axiomatic that the addict is an outcast first and acquires his habit in an effort to escape from the psychic ordeal of being brotherless, unable to exert claims upon anybody's love. But once hooked, he is necessarily a man living from moment to moment, from fix to fix. The intervals between become a kind of purgatorial school in which one learns to care about less and less: not surroundings, not status, not appearance, not physical condition, not even crimes, but only for the golden island ahead where one can score, then fix, then swing. To swing is to enter into full alliance with the moment and to do this is to triumph over the squares who otherwise run the world. For to enter the moment, you must yield to the moment. The square person can never get the camel caravan of his ego-commitments through the eye of the needle which opens out upon hipster heaven. Excluded from the moment and consequently seeking it out ahead in a future which never has been and never will be, all that the square person can dig is his own grave. The hip person knows that the only promised land is Now and that the only way to make the journey is to dig everything and go until you make it and can swing.

Hip talk, then, is Basic English which charts the phases, the psychology, even the philosophy of those outcasts who live for, with, and—when they can—within the moment. It is in fact less a language than a language art in which spontaneity is everything. The words are compact, mostly monosyllabic, athletic: dig, go, make it, man, cat, chick, flip, goof, cool, crazy, swing. In his very suggestive essay, "The White Negro," Norman Mailer argues that the basic words of hip form a nucleus which charts and organizes the energies of the hipster into maximum mobility for his contentions with the squares, as indeed with other hipsters, for the sweets of this world. Mailer's emphasis upon the endless battle between hip and square is true, I think, but not true enough because less vital than that is the hipster's even deeper need to establish a new continuity for his life. The most severe ordeal of his constantly emphasized isolation is not loss of the social sweets but loss of the moment. It is against this fate that he has evolved his cryptic language art. The talented hipster is as sensitive to the nuances and possibilities of his language as he necessarily is to the nuances and possibilities of his always threatened moment. Which is why the real hip cat who can dig and swing with the other cats in hipland has such close affinities with the aristocrat among such outcasts, the jazzman.

Jazz swings in and with the moment. The universal name for a good group is "a swinging group," one in which each individual is attuned to all of the others so that improvisation can answer improvisation without loss of group harmony. Baby Dodds, who drummed with Louis Armstrong in the early jazz days, describes this process very clearly:

> Louis would make something on his horn, in an afterbeat, or make it so fast that he figured I couldn't make it that fast, or he'd make it in syncopation or in Charleston time, or anything like that for a trick. And I would come back with something on the snare drums and with an afterbeat on the bass drum or a roll or something. But I had to keep the bass drum going straight for the band. I couldn't throw the band . . . at all times I heard every instrument distinctly.

Jazz played in this way can be a spontaneous, swinging poem in which the group first creates the shape, the musical metrics of the given moment. Then individuals begin to improvise in the way Dodds describes or the talented soloist to move his sound out into the possibilities of the moment. When this happens the jazzman and the hip person who can swing with him experience release into the moment that is being created, as Kerouac notes, "so he said it and sang it and blew it through to the stars and on out." Since such release is the hip person's deepest need and desire, the jazzman becomes the hipster hero who has moved among the mountains of the moment and in so doing has conquered the most vindictive of their enemies, time. In jazz the moment prevails.

But sounds die out. And are replaced by other sounds. Where jazz was factory whistles will be when Daddio Time turns on tic toc dawn to light the hipman and the jazzman home. And the square eye of morning tells both what each had been trying to forget, that when you fall out of the moment and happen to be an outcast you are back among the ruins in a world where only certain men are brothers. At which point the Beat writers appear on the scene, chanting Holy, Holy, Holy—but with a Bop beat.

BOP: In a conventional tune the melody moves along not quite like but something like an escalator, steadily and as the feet would expect, so that the good children of this world can keep their eyes fixed upward for the sign that says: TOYS. But the restless outcast children in the department store of this world know that the journey is NOW. As their jazz escalator goes at a syncopated beat from level to level, the outcast children dip into the toy shop of the moment and come up with little hops, skips, and jumps that are answered back by other hops, skips, and jumps, until, by the time the syncopated escalator reaches the top level, everybody is hopping and jumping about, together and as individuals, and this of course is improvisation—the life of jazz. However, this dual progression in which the syncopated beat of the melody escalator carries the spontaneous action of the improvisations from level to level has given way, with the advent of Bop, to a music which seems to travel from level to level on the improvisations alone. That is, the melody (the escalator) has been assimilated into the pattern of improvisations (hop, skip, jump) and the improvisations—always the life impulse of jazz—have dominated in this merger. At best Bop has freed jazz from the tedium of banal melodies. It has also given emphasis to a principle of spontaneous creative freedom which has been taken over by the Beat writers in ways likely to have a strong influence upon North American poetry and fiction.

In conventional fiction the narrative continuity is always clearly discernible. But it is impossible to create an absorbing narrative without at the same time enriching it with images, asides, themes and variations—impulses from within. It is evident that in much recent fiction—Joyce, Kafka, Virginia Woolf, and Faulkner are obvious examples—the narrative line has tended to weaken, merge with, and be dominated by the sum of variations. Each narrative step in Faulkner's work is likely to provoke many sidewinding pages before a next narrative step is taken. More, a lot of Faulkner's power is to be found in the sidewindings. In brief, what happens in jazz when the melody merges with the improvisations and the improvisations dominate, has been happening in fiction for some time now.

However, the improvisations of jazz are incomparably more fluent than have been the variations of fiction. The jazzman is free to move his sound, which is simply himself, where and as the moment prompts, "one mountain, two mountains, ten clouds, no clouds." But the fiction man has always had to move his style, which also is himself, into the present-day deviousness, the "messy imprecision" of words. The fiction man encounters deviousness and imprecision in our language because an evident fragmentation has overtaken meanings in our time. Empson's *Seven Types of Ambiguity,* the first work to *exploit* the plight of meanings in our time, may well turn out to have been the handwriting on the wall announcing the breakup of our camp, the only camp that truly signifies: the human one. For it is not, as Empson supposed, our language that is ambiguous. It is our relations with one another. Trust lacking, meanings become ambiguous. And when meanings become ambiguous language becomes imprecise, difficult, devious.

There have been a number of attempts, heroic in their single-mindedness, to confront with language the increasing ambiguity of meanings, notably those of Joyce and Eliot. But the result has been a fiction and poetry so circuitously difficult as to require years-long efforts of creation and explication—which is to communicate the slow way. The outcome for most persons has been a distinct breakdown of any vital connection with our best literature. To the fact of this breakdown the Beat writers bring a new solution.

Their solution is to be Beat. To be Beat is to let your life come tumbling down into a humpty-dumpty heap, and with it, into the same heap, the humpty-dumpty meanings which language attempts to sustain. There are fewer things beneath heaven and earth than our present-day multiple-meaning philosophers would have us believe. From the ruin of yourself pick up yourself (if you can) but let old meanings lie. Now cross on over to the outcast side of the street to where the hip folk and the jazz folk live, for the way your life is now is the way their lives have been for years. Step right in through the Open Door to where the tenor man is crouching with the bell mouth of his horn down in the basement near his feet, reaching for the waters of life that come rocking up through the debris of the day that dawned over Hiroshima everywhere long 1945 ago. The sound you hear is life, "the pit and prune juice of poor beat life itself in the god-awful streets of man." And life is Holy. And this is the meaning of words. Life is holy, and the journey is Now. Say it with a Bop beat.

## Kerouac's Sound

Kerouac's sound starts up in his first novel, *The Town and the City*, and anyone who grew up with or remembers the sentimental music of the 1930s will recognize what he is doing. The New England nights and days of his childhood and youth are orchestrated with slow violins, to which sound the children whose lives he chronicles are stirred into awareness as the stars dip down and slow breezes sweep along diminishing strings towards soft music on a farther shore. It is the considerable achievement of the novel that Kerouac is able to sustain the note of profound sentimentality his style conveys even as he is tracing, with remorseless intelligence, the downfall of the New England family, the Martins, who try to sustain their lives on this tone. The sound bodies forth their myth—soft music on a farther shore—while the action brings both myth and sound down in ruins.

The protagonist is George Martin, one version and a good one of the mythical American—big, outgoing, direct—who sustains his life, his certainties, his soul on the music Kerouac builds in around him: at the rim of all things, violins. He rises at dawn, splashing, coughing, spluttering, and plunges into the day like a playful porpoise, rolling in the life element. But his cough is cancer, and the novel concerns the downfall of this man. His career carries from the town, where he was known to every man, to New York City where he has no acquaintances at all. He ends his life on a mean Brooklyn street in a mean apartment with only a direct if ravaged love for his dispersed and tormented children to see him through disease into silence.

A main sign of Kerouac's control over the melody he projects is to be seen in the variety of fates to which he sends the Martin children. One son goes via books to success at Harvard and then on into the books and the sterility of a quasi-homosexual existence. Another son heads for adventure on the big trucks that whirr across the North American night only to discover that the whirring of trucks is a nothing song for a nowhere journey. Another son ends at Okinawa. The principal son goes via a football scholarship to Pennsylvania and early stardom. But just as he is about to become Saturday's hero and thus confirm his father's belief in the rightness of his myth, the son rebels in order to destroy the myth; and so helps destroy his father's life; and so his own. One daughter elopes with a jazzman and ends divorced in bohemian New York, singing at a second-rate bar. Another daughter disperses to Los Angeles. Another to Seattle. All of the children plunge like the playful porpoises their father had taught them to be into the swaying waters of the myth he created, soft music on a farther shore. All drown. The football-playing son who manages to break the myth, and with it his own life, swims for love of the father back to shore. He is seen at the last on a rainy roadway, hitch-hiking west and known to no man—but with no more violins.

I think it is evident that in creating this testimonial to a gone childhood, Kerouac is also breaking with the mood of that era. How decisively he does break becomes plain in his second published novel, *On the Road,* where the sounds become BIFF, BOFF, BLIP, BLEEP, BOP, BEEP, CLINCK, ZOWIE! Sounds break up. And are replaced by other sounds. The journey is NOW. The narrative is a humpty-dumpty heap. Such is the condition of NOW. The ruins extend from New York City, down to New Orleans, on down to Mexico City, back up to Denver, out to San Francisco, over to Chicago, back to New York—six cities at the end points of a cockeyed star. The hero who passed from star-point to star-point is Dean Moriarty, the mad Hamlet of the moment, shambled after by Sal Paradise, who tells the story. And all that Sal can say is, "Yes, he's mad," and "Yes, he's my brother." Moriarty is the hero-prince of all Beat people, a "madman angel and bum" out to con the North American nightmare of a chance for his soul to live. Nothing that his tormented hands reach for will come into his hands except the holiness which comes rocking up direct from the waters of life upon the jazz rhythms with which Kerouac pitches his cockeyed star of wonder about.

Moriarty is a Denver jailkid who does not have to wait for his life to come down in ruins. It begins that way. His mother "died when

Dean was a child" and his wino father is so indistinguishable from all the other winos in all the skid-road districts where Dean thinks he may find him that "I never know whether to ask." Kerouac provides only enough details about "all the bitterness and madness" of Dean's Denver childhood to make it clear that the social forms to which all good children go for their bread of life (or so they think) were made forbidden areas for Dean by reason of rejection, guilt, shame, rage, hatred—the dreadful emotions likely to orchestrate the secret lives of children who one day wake up Beat. Hence the car-stealing frenzies in which he turns himself into a car so that his thwarted energies can come "blasting out of his system like daggers." On the maddest night of the novel he climaxes one such (five-car) binge by stealing a police detective's auto (inviting punishment) which he abandons in front of the house where he then passes out in peace and calm of mind—drunk—all passion spent.

An even more definite sign of Moriarty's inability to live within existing social forms consists in the insane doubling-up of those relationships from which he does seek satisfaction, brotherhood, love. No sooner does he dig Sal Paradise the very most than he must rush into an even more intense relationship with Paradise's friend, Carlo Marx. No sooner does he set up housekeeping with his first wife, Marylou, than he must arrange an elaborate time-schedule in order to set up parallel housekeeping with his second, interchangeable wife, Camille. The Denver bohemia must be matched by bohemian San Francisco. His life on the west coast is a process of creating the complications which will be resolved by flight to the east coast. Tormented by almost complete inability to live within even the relaxed bohemian life-forms, Moriarty turns again and again to the one form in which his energies find something like release and fulfilment—the road.

In a car on the road, surrounded by darkness, the existing forms vanish and with them vanishes the distraught, guilt-tormented self. Speed, strangeness and space, dark forests, heavy-shouldered mountains and open prairies bring new transient forms, semi-forms, even formless forms, rushing into place. All of these are fleetingly familiar, for all of these are life. And because life is holy, the soul moves in behind the wheel and "every moment is precious" as the mad city Hamlet gives way to a road-going Quixote who cares only for the soul's journey, the one sweet dreadful childhood could not steal from him.

Thus "It was remarkable," Sal Paradise tells us, "how Dean could go mad and then continue with his soul . . . calmly and sanely as though nothing had happened." The mad self blends into the speeding car as the sane soul continues down the one road of life on the only journey which "must eventually lead to the whole world."

An apotheosis of sorts is achieved briefly in Mexico on the strangest yet most strangely familiar of all the roads Moriarty and Paradise take, on a womb-like jungle night, "hot as the inside of a baker's oven." Here the travellers are taken over by "billions of insects" until "the dead bugs mingled with my blood." Time, self, and history are temporarily annihilated and there is only the "rank, hot and rotten jungle" from which a prophetic white horse, "immense and phosphorescent," emerges to pace majestically, mysteriously past Moriarty's for-once sleeping head. When they waken from this dream of annihilation and rebirth it is to enter mountains where "shepherds appeared dressed as in the first time." And Moriarty "looked to heaven with red eyes," aware that he has made it out of orbit with the cockeyed star of NOW into orbit with "the golden world that Jesus came from." But if this Beat angel journeys through the jazz of the North American night finally to reach a semblance of creation day morning time in the Mexican mountains of the moment, he is much too mad to more than distractedly glimpse, and giggle, and give a wrist-watch to a Mexican creation-day child, inviting her to enter time. "Yes, he's mad," says Sal, and so Quixote gives way to Hamlet as Dean Moriarty ends with stockings down-gyv'd—"ragged in a moth-eaten overcoat"—a parking-lot attendant in New York—which is no way for a con man to live—silent—"Dean couldn't talk any more"—with only his sad Horatio, Sal, to tell his brother's story.

The jazz is in the continuity in which each episode tells a separate story—variations on the holiness theme. And it is in the remarkable flexible style as Kerouac improvises within each episode seeking to adjust his sound to the resonance of the given moment. Some moments come through tinged with the earlier *Town and City* sentimentality. Others rock and sock with Moriarty's frenzy, the sentences jerking about like muscles on an overwrought face. Still others are curiously quiescent, calm. And the melody which unifies the whole and lifts the cockeyed star up into the jazz sky is the holiness of life because this for Kerouac is the meaning of words, the inside of his sound. Dean Moriarty is sweet prince to this proposition. To read *On the Road* with attention to the variations Kerouac achieves is to realize something of his remarkable talent for meshing his sound with the strongly-felt rhythms of many and various moments. It is not possible to compare him very closely with other stylists of note because his fiction is the first in which jazz is a dominant influence.

How dominant emerges into clear focus with the third of his published novels, *The Subterraneans*. Here is a typical sentence, the fourth in the book:

> I was coming down the street with Larry O'Hara old drinking buddy of mine from all the times in San Francisco in my long and nervous and mad careers I've gotten drunk and in fact cadged drinks off friends with such "genial" regularity nobody really cared to notice or announce that I am developing or was developing, in my youth, such bad freeloading habits though of course they did notice but liked me and as Sam said "Everybody comes to you for your gasoline boy, that's some filling station you got there" or words to that effect—old Larry O'Hara always nice to me, a crazy young businessman of San Francisco with Balzacian backroom in his bookstore where they'd smoke tea and talk of the old days of the great Basie band or the days of the great Chu Berry—of whom more anon since she got involved with him too as she had to get involved with everyone because of knowing me who am nervous and many leveled and not in the least one-souled—not a piece of my pain has showed yet—or suffering—Angels, bear with me—I'm not even looking at the page but straight ahead into the sadglint of my wallroom and at a Sarah Vaughan Gerry Mulligan Radio KROW show on the desk in the form of a radio, in other words, they were sitting on the fender of a car in front of the Black Mask bar on Montgomery Street, Julien Alexander the Christ-like unshaved thin youthful quiet strange almost as you or as Adam might say apocalyptic angel or saint of the subterraneans, certainly star (now), and she, Mardou Fox, whose face when first I saw it in Dante's bar around the corner made me think, "By God, I've got to get involved with that little woman" and maybe too because she was a Negro.

I count seven shifts away from the narrative line. If these shifts are dropped, one has Leo Percepied, the narrator, walk down the street with Larry O'Hara and meet Julien Alexander and Mardou Fox as they stand beside an automobile in front of the Black Mask bar. The side-trips from this simple narrative line lead to: Percepied's drinking habits—a main variation; (2) his energies—another main variation; (3) jazz and marihuana parties in Larry O'Hara's bookshop; (4) a passage of self-analysis—a major variation; (5) circumstances under which the sentence is being written; (6) descriptions of the people Percepied is about to meet; and, repeated from a previous sentence, (7) Percepied's determination to meet Mardou, who later turns out to be part Indian as well as Negro—another major variation. Kerouac's immediate motive is the Bop motive, maximum spontaneity. The narrative melody merges with and is dominated by the improvised details. And, as Percepied emphasizes twice later, "the truth is in the details." The narrative line follows the brief love-affair between Percepied and Mardou while the improvised details move, as the title would suggest, down into the clutter of their lives among the guilts and shames which come up from subterranean depths to steal their love from them. The truth is in the improvisations.

The novel is written with the driving but hungup rhythms of a hurrying man who is also, always, alas, looking back over his shoulder. The finest scenes, I think, are those in which Mardou figures, particularly that in which she is rejected by some friends, loses control of her consciousness, and wanders out naked into nighttime San Francisco, almost insane, to be saved by the realization that she is meant for love rather than hatred and so walks about the city newly discovering and at the same time transforming the world she passes through. This self-conquest makes her able to trust others, to believe that Percepied loves her, and to love him in return. But he is unable to conquer his own guilts and shames, cannot reciprocate, and so is gradually, frantically pulled back into the clutter of his life. A failure of love by reason of deep fissuring guilts emerges from the depths on the rush but not exactly on the wings of Kerouac's spontaneous Bop style. As Percepied says, "I'm the Bop writer." As one might expect, the spontaneity falters in a good many pages. Yet I do not doubt that the method does permit Kerouac to tap his imagination in spontaneous ways. Nor do I doubt but that *The Subterraneans* is his most important novel and a very important one indeed. Of this, more in place.

The easiest way to approach *The Dharma Bums*—the truth bums—is to imagine an exceptionally talented musician trying out a new instrument in an interested but nonetheless very tentative way. The instrument is Zen Buddhism, American fashion. The novel is full of hummed songs, muttered chants, self-conversations carried on in railroad yards, on beaches, in groves of trees, in the mountains. The half-embarrassed, half-serious mutterer is Ray Smith, Zen amateur, and the style which Kerouac floats through the novel is part of an obvious attempt to adjust the practices, the flavor, the attitudes of Zen to an American sensibility.

Jazz is gone, even from the Bohemian party scenes which alternate with the Zen scenes. Moriarty's frenzy and Percepied's rush give way to a slow—and at times a too-slow—pace. It is surely significant that in the opening paragraph Smith travels past the place where the "king and founder of the Bop generation," the jazzman Charlie Parker, "went crazy and got well again." Kerouac might be hinting at the strain of writing eleven books in six years and about the need for a temporary so-long to jazz, hello to Zen. But the hello is most tentative. To put the very best construction on the novel, always advisable when considering a gifted writer, is to read it as a kind of primer of Zen experience. I spare the reader any attempts to explicate the Zen way as Kerouac relays it into the novel via Smith's friend, Japhy, the American Zen adept.[1] Suffice it to mention that the Zen emphasis upon paradoxes which will annihilate meanings is a peculiarly appropriate counterpart to the Beat writer's suspicion of meanings. Put any meaningful thought through the Zen dialectic and come out with one thought less. But if the Zen attitude is consistent with Kerouac's own, it is nonetheless apparent that the meditative world in which this attitude is best cultivated hasn't much affinity with his essentially nervous and agile sensibility. Unsustained by the driving intensities which make *On the Road* and *The Subterraneans* swing, *The Dharma Bums* frequently goes flat. There are dull scenes, mechanical passages. If there is one superb mountain-climbing episode, that is less because Zen catches hold for Kerouac, more because the mountain does. Certainly, representation of the final trip to the Northwest, where the protagonist attempts to live in the Zen way on Desolation Peak, is so sketchy as to amount to a default. And it is here that one touches upon Kerouac's limitations.

1. And just as well, for I have been informed since writing this essay that the Buddhism in *The Dharma Bums* ranges considerably beyond the Zen variety.

In *The Dharma Bums* distinctly and in his other novels in less evident ways, one becomes aware of Kerouac's receptive, his essentially feminine sensibility. Sensibility, I repeat. This receptivity is certainly his main strength as artist, accounting as it does for his capacity to assimilate the rhythms, the sounds, the life-feel of experience into his representation. When Kerouac is at his best he is able to register and project the American resonance with remarkable ease and accuracy. But on the related, weaker side of the coin, he has only a limited ability to project this sound up to heights, down to depths. Moments of climax, of revelation, of crisis, the very moments which deserve the fullest representation, frequently receive only sparse representation. The climactic Mexican journey in *On the Road* suffers from this limitation. Beginning with the madcap afternoon in the Mexican whore house, followed by the night-time sojourn in the jungle, the creation-day morning in the mountains, and subsequent arrival in Mexico City, the hipster Zion, where marihuana cascades like manna into the streets, the entire sequence is as brilliantly conceived as any in recent fiction. But representation in these scenes which show Moriarty's life sweeping up to climax, is sparse, fleeting, even sketchy. No reader will be convinced that Moriarty, the true traveller, has made it to a mountain-peak of our present moment from which creation-day is glimpsed. Nor will any reader be convinced that Ray Smith has gained access to the Zen Way in his mountain fastness.

Yet I do not think that this defect traces so much to want of creative force, though that is what it appears to be, as to Kerouac's almost animal suspicion of the meaning values toward which words tend. When his fictions converge toward meanings something vital in him flinches back. His sound is primarily a life sound, sensitive to the indwelling qualities of things, the life they bear. To be Beat is to be wary of moving such a sound into the meaning clutter. It might become lost, the life. So Kerouac draws back. Which is his limitation.

But also his strength. For in the jazz world of the Bop generation where Charlie Parker is king and founder, Jack Kerouac in a different medium is heir apparent. I do not know but would guess that a number of the six or seven books for which Kerouac can't find a publisher are Bop novels. I would also guess that it will not be until they are published and his method more generally understood than now that his likely influence will emerge. For his emphasis upon a from-under sound made spontaneous by adherence to the jazz principle of improvisation is right for our time, I think. The jazz vernacular is just that, a vernacular, and Kerouac has demonstrated that it can be transposed into fiction without serious loss of the spontaneous imaginative freedom which has made it among the most vital of the modern arts.[2]

Although Kerouac's art is limited, I am convinced that his sound is more nearly in the American grain than that of any writer since Fitzgerald. The efforts of his outcast protagonists to get life into their lives seem more closely related to our actual moment than any since Jay Gatsby, similar across worlds of difference, tried to shoot the North American moon. Gatsby failed and finished like a sad swan, floating dead on the surface of a pool. And Kerouac's protagonists fail too. Dean Moriarty does not make it to creation-day as was his mad desire. Ray Smith fumbles the Zen football. Leo Percepied cannot enter guilt-forbidden realms of Mardou's Negro love. Fitzgerald's efforts got lost in the personal, national, and international chaos from which he summoned Gatsby into presence. But it was only after his energies lost coherence that Fitzgerald woke up in the ruins of that dark midnight of the soul where it is always three o'clock in the morning. Kerouac starts in with the dark midnight and it is his effort to bring his protagonists through the jazz of that night, naked, into something like a new day. He fails too. The moment, NOW, which is the only promised land, shrugs off Moriarty, Percepied, and Smith, shrugs off

2. Since this essay was written, *Doctor Sax* and portions of *Old Angel Midnight* have appeared. Both indicate a far more ambitious attempt than I have suggested to develop a writing style which will spontaneously represent the nuance of Kerouac's deep-reaching awareness. I say deep-reaching because both works suggest possession of an almost photographic sensibility; he evidently projects his sound from a matrix of directly registered impressions reaching back to early childhood even as they reach down to deep levels of consciousness. These works provide more than a few signs that with the appearance of his yet unpublished works Kerouac will emerge not simply as an important innovator, as I have tried to suggest, but as a major writer. A word more about Bop. University of British Columbia English professor Elliott Gose has pointed out how closely Percepied, the "Bop writer" of *The Subterraneans*, is identified with Baudelaire—both writers, both with Negro mistresses, both with compelling mother attachments. And Kerouac elsewhere styles himself "an artful story teller, A WRITER in the great French narrative tradition." To stress these is to stress the obvious implication that although Kerouac's Bop writing style stems from jazz it is doubtlessly heavily influenced by his literary affinities. I do so only in order to counterstress that it is the Bop influence rather than the literary which has been the shaping spirit of his imagination.

Kerouac too. Outcasts they began and end as outcasts. But very distinctly Kerouac's protagonists press more sharply close to the truth about our present moment than have fictional protagonists for many years. And that's a help. And very distinctly he has created new ground of possibility for fiction to stand upon with renewed life. And that's a help.

*November, 1958*
*Vancouver, B.C.*

---

# DIANA TRILLING

DIANA TRILLING was the wife of Lionel Trilling, a distinguished literary critic and one of Ginsberg's professors at Columbia University, when she set off on the evening of February 5, 1959, with other Columbia faculty wives to hear the three Beat poets Ginsberg, Orlovsky, and Corso read their poetry by invitation of the John Dewey Society at McMillin Theater on Broadway, a few blocks from her home. The last poet to read there the previous year had been T. S. Eliot. Trilling was surprised to find hundreds of people being turned away at the door of McMillin, and more than a thousand listeners in the audience. Among them was Louis Ginsberg, Allen's father, who was moved to tears when for the first time he heard his son read "Kaddish," an elegy for Naomi Ginsberg, Allen's mother. Emotionally involved in the poetry reading almost despite herself, Trilling described her experience in "The Other Night at Columbia: A Report from the Academy." The article was accepted by editor William Phillips for publication in the Spring 1959 *Partisan Review*. Trilling also included it in her collection *Claremont Essays* (1964). There Trilling wrote a foreword calling attention to her belief "that even in an unsatisfactory society the individual is best defined by his social geography." Trilling also published a second essay collection, *We Must March My Darlings: A Critical Decade* (1977).

## The Other Night at Columbia:
## A Report from the Academy

The "beats" were to read their poetry at Columbia on Thursday evening and on the spur of the moment three wives from the English department had decided to go to hear them. But for me, one of the three, the spur of the moment was not where the story had begun. It had begun much farther back, some twelve or fourteen years ago, when Allen Ginsberg had been a student at Columbia and I had heard about him much more than I usually hear of students for the simple reason that he got into a great deal of trouble which involved his instructors, and had to be rescued and revived and restored; eventually he had even to be kept out of jail. Of course there was always the question, should this young man be rescued, should he be restored? There was even the question, shouldn't he go to jail? We argued about it some at home but the discussion, I'm afraid, was academic, despite my old resistance to the idea that people like Ginsberg had the right to ask and receive preferential treatment just because they read Rimbaud and Gide and undertook to put words on paper themselves. Nor was my principle (if one may call it that) of equal responsibility for poets and shoe clerks so firm that I didn't need to protect it by refusing to confront Ginsberg as an individual or potential acquaintance. I don't mean that I was aware, at the time, of this motive for disappearing on the two or three occasions when he came to the house to deliver a new batch of poems and report on his latest adventures in sensation-seeking. If I'd been asked to explain, then, my wish not to meet and talk with this troublesome young man who had managed to break through the barrier of student anonymity, I suppose I'd have rested with the proposition that I don't like mess, and I'd have been ready to defend myself against the charge, made in the name of art, of a strictness of judgment which was intolerant of this much deviation from respectable standards of behavior. Ten, twelve, fourteen years ago, there was still something of a challenge in the "conventional" position; I still enjoyed defending the properties and proprieties of the middle class against friends who persisted in scorning them. Of course, once upon a time—but that was in the '30's—one had had to defend even having a comfortable chair to sit in, or a rug on the floor. But by the '40's things had changed; one's most intransigent literary friends had capitulated by then, everybody had a well-upholstered sofa and I was reduced to such marginal causes as the Metropolitan Museum, after-dinner coffee cups, and the expectation that visitors would go home by 2 A.M. and put their ashes in the ashtrays. Then why should I not also defend the expectation that a student at Columbia, even a poet, would do his work, submit it to his teachers through the normal channels of classroom communication, stay out of jail, and then, if things went right, graduate, start publishing, be reviewed, and see what developed, whether he was a success or failure?

Well, for Ginsberg, things didn't go right for quite a while. The time came when he was graduated from Columbia and published his poems, but first he got into considerable difficulty, beginning with his suspension from college and the requirement that he submit to psychiatric treatment, and terminating—but this was quite a few years later—in an encounter with the police from which he was extricated by some of his old teachers who thought he needed a hospital more than a prison. The suspension had been for a year, when Ginsberg had been a Senior; the situation was not without its grim humor. It seems that Ginsberg had traced an obscenity in the dusty windows of Hartley Hall; the words were too shocking for the Dean of Students to speak, he had written them on a piece of paper which he pushed across the desk: "F--- the Jews." Even the part of Lionel that wanted to laugh couldn't, it was too hard for the Dean to have to transmit this message to a Jewish professor—this was still in the '40's when being a Jew in the university was not yet what it is today. "But he's a Jew himself," said the Dean. "Can you understand his writing a thing like that?" Yes, Lionel could understand; but he couldn't explain it to the Dean. And anyway he knew that the legend in the dust of Hartley Hall required more than an understanding of Jewish self-hatred and also that it was not the sole cause for administrative uneasiness about Ginsberg and his cronies. It was ordinary good sense for the college to take therapeutic measures with Ginsberg.

I now realize that even at this early point in his career, I had already accumulated a fund of information about young Ginsberg which accurately forecast his present talent for self-promotion although it was surely disproportionate to the place he commanded in his teacher's mind and quite contradicted the uncertain physical impression I had caught in opening the door to him when he came to the apartment. He was middling tall, slight, dark, sallow; his dress suggested shabby gentility, poor brown tweed gone threadbare and yellow. The description would have fitted any number of undergraduates of his or any Columbia generation; it was the personal story that set him acutely apart. He came from New Jersey where his father was a school teacher, or perhaps a principal, who himself wrote poetry too—I think for *The New York Times,* which would be as good a way as any of defining the separation between father and son. His mother was in a mental institution, and, off and on, she had been there for a long time. This was the central and utterly persuasive fact of this young man's life; I knew this before I was told it in poetry at Columbia the other night, and doubtless it was this knowledge that underlay the nervous irritability with which I responded to so much as the mention of Ginsberg's name. Here was a boy to whom an outrageous injustice had been done: his mother had gone mad on him, and now whoever crossed his path became somehow responsible, guilty, caught in the impossibility of rectifying what she had done. It was an unfair burden to put on those who were only the later accidents of his history and it made me more defensive than charitable with this poor object of her failure. No boy, after all, could ask anyone to help him build a career on the terrible but gratuitous circumstance of a mad mother; it was a justification for neither poetry nor prose nor yet for "philosophy" of the kind young Ginsberg liked to expound to his teacher. In the question period which followed the poetry-reading the other night at Columbia, this matter of a rationale for the behavior of Ginsberg and his friends came up: someone asked Ginsberg to state his philosophy. It was a moment I had been awaiting and I thought: "Here we go; he'll tell us how he's crazy like a daisy and how his friend Orlovsky is crazy like a butterfly." I had been reading *Time* magazine; who hadn't? But, instead, Ginsberg answered that he had no philosophy; he spoke of inspiration, or perhaps it was illumination, ecstatic illumination, as the source of his poetry and I was more than surprised, I was curiously pleased for him because I took it as a considerable advance in self-control that he could operate with this much shrewdness and leave it, at least for this occasion, to his audience to abstract a "position" from his and his friends' antics while he himself moved wild, mild, and innocent through the jungle of speculation. Back in the older days, it had always been my feeling that so far as his relationship with his teacher was concerned, this trying to formulate a philosophy must reveal its falseness even to himself, so that his recourse to it insulted his intelligence. Two motives, it seemed to me, impelled him then: the wish to shock his teacher, and the wish to meet the teacher on equal ground. The first of these motives was complicated enough, involving as it did the gratifications of self-incrimination and disapproval, and then forgiveness; but the second was more tangled still. To talk with one's English professor who was also a writer, a critic, and one who made no bones about his solid connection with literary tradition, about one's descent from Rimbaud, Baudelaire or Dostoevsky was clearly to demonstrate a good-sized rationality and order in what was apparently an otherwise undisciplined life. Even more, or so I fancied, it was to propose an alliance between the views of the academic and the poet-rebel, the unity of a deep discriminating commitment to literature which must certainly one day wipe out the fortuitous distance between boy and man, pupil and teacher. Thus, Ginsberg standing on the platform at Columbia and refusing the philosophy gambit might well be taken as an impulse toward manhood, or at least manliness, for which one might be grateful.

But I remind myself: Ginsberg at Columbia on Thursday night was not Ginsberg at Chicago—according to *Time,* at any rate—or Ginsberg at Hunter either, where Kerouac ran the show and a dismal show it must have been, with Kerouac drinking on the platform and clapping James Wechsler's hat on his head in a grand parade of contempt—they were two of four panelists gathered to discuss, "Is there such a thing as a beat generation?"—and leading Ginsberg out from the wings like a circus donkey. For whatever reason—rumor had it he was in a personal crisis—Kerouac didn't appear on Thursday night, and Ginsberg at Columbia was Ginsberg his own man, dealing with his own history, and intent, it seemed to me, on showing up the past for the poor inaccurate thing it so often is: it's a chance we all dream of but mostly it works the other way around, like the long-ago story of Jed Harris coming back to Yale and sitting on the fence weeping for a youth he could never re-write no matter how many plays of Chekhov he brought to Broadway, no matter how much money he made. I suppose I have no right to say now, and on such early and little evidence, that Ginsberg had always desperately wanted to be respectable, or respected, like his instructors at Columbia, it is so likely that this is a hindsight which suits my needs. It struck me, though, that this was the most unmistakable and touching message from platform to audience the other night, and as I received it, I felt I had known something like it all along. Not that Ginsberg had ever shown himself as a potential future colleague in the university; anything but that. Even the implied literary comradeship had had reference, not to any possibility of Ginsberg's assimilation into the community of professors, but to the professor's capacity for association in the community of rebellious young poets. Still, it was not just anyone on the campus to whom Ginsberg had come with his lurid boasts which were also his confession; it was Lionel, it was Mark Van Doren; if there was anyone else he would very likely be of the same respectable species, and I remember saying, "He wants you to forbid him to behave like that. He wants you to take him out of it, else why does he choose people like you and Mark to tell these stories to?" To which I received always the same answer, "I'm not his father," with which there could of course be no argument.

And yet, even granting the accuracy of this reconstruction of the past, it would be wrong to conclude that any consideration of motive on Ginsberg's part was sufficiently strong to alter one's first and most forceful image of Ginsberg as a "case"—a gifted and sad case, a guilt-provoking and nuisance case but, above all, a case. Nor was it a help that Lionel had recently published a story about a crazy student and a supposedly normal student in which the author's affection was so plainly directed to the former; we never became used to the calls, often in the middle of the night, asking whether it wasn't the crazy character who was really sane. Ginsberg, with his poems in which there was never quite enough talent or hard work, and with his ambiguous need to tell his teacher exactly what new flagrancy he was now exploring with his Gide-talking friends at the West End Café had at any rate the distinction of being more crudely justified in his emotional disturbance than most; he also had the distinction of carrying mental unbalance in the direction of criminality, a territory one preferred to leave unclaimed by student or friend.

Gide and the West End Café in all its upper-Broadway dreariness:

what could the two conceivably have in common except those lost boys of the '40's? How different it might have been for Ginsberg and his friends if they had come of age ten or fifteen years sooner was one of the particular sadnesses of the other evening, it virtually stood on the platform with them as the poets read their poems whose chief virtue, it seemed to me, was their "racial-minority" funniness, their "depressed-classes" funniness of a kind which has never had so sure and live a place as it did in the '30's, the embittered fond funniness which has to do with one's own awful family, funniness plain and po- etical, always aware of itself, of a kind which would seem now to have all but disappeared among intellectuals except as an eclecticism or a device of self-pity. It's a real loss; I hadn't quite realized how much I missed it until Thursday night when Ginsberg read his poem, "The Ignu," and Corso read his poem, "Marriage" (a compulsive poem, he called it, about a compulsive subject) and they were still funny in that old racial depressed way but not nearly as funny and authentic as they would have been had they been written before the Jews and the Ital- ians and the Negroes, but especially the Jews, had been crammed down their own and everyone else's throat as Americans-like-everyone- else instead of outsiders raised in the Bronx or on Ninth Avenue or even in Georgia. The Jew in particular is a loss to literature and life— I mean the Jew out of which was bred the Jewish intellectual of the '30's. For a few short years in the '30's, as not before or since, the Jew was at his funniest, wisest best; he perfectly well knew the advantage he could count on in the Gentile world, and that there was no ascen- dancy or pride the Gentile comrades could muster against a roomful of Jewish sympathizers singing at the tops of their voices, "A SOCial- ist union is a NO good union, is a COM-pan-y union of the bosses," or against Michael Gold's mother who wanted to know did her boy have to write books the whole world should know she had bedbugs. If Gins- berg had been born in an earlier generation it would surely have been the Stewart Cafeteria in the Village that he and his friends would have hung out at instead of the West End, that dim waystation of under- graduate debauchery on Morningside Heights—and the Stewart Cafe- teria was a well-lighted place and one of the funniest places in New York; at least, at every other table it was funny, and where it was deca- dent or even conspiratorial, this had its humor too, or at least its ro- bustness. As for Gide—the Gide of the '30's was the "betrayer of the

Revolution," not the Gide of the *acte gratuite* and homosexuality in North Africa. One didn't use pathology in those days to explain or excuse or exhibit oneself and one never had to be lonely; there was never a less lonely time for intellectuals than the Depression, or a less depressed time—unless, of course, one was recalcitrant, like Fitzgerald, and simply refused to be radicalized, in which stubborn case it couldn't have been lonelier. Intellectuals talk now about how, in the '30's, there was an "idea" in life, not the emptiness we live in. Actually, it was a time of generally weak intellection—so many of us who put our faith in Marx and Lenin had read neither of them—but of very strong feeling. Everyone judged everyone else, it was a time of incessant cruel moral judgment; today's friend was tomorrow's enemy; whoever disagreed with oneself had sold out, God knows to or for what, maybe for $10 more a week; there was little of the generosity among intellectuals which nowadays dictates the automatic, "Gee, that's great" at any news of someone else's good fortune. But it was surely a time of quicker, truer feeling than is now conjured up with marijuana or the infantile camaraderie of *On the Road*. And there was paradox but no contradiction in this double truth, just as there was no contradiction in the fact that it was a time in which the neurotic determination of the intellectual was being so universally acted out and yet a time in which, whatever his dedication to historical or economic determinism, personally he had a unique sense of free will. In the '30's one's clinical vocabulary was limited to two words—escapism and subjectivism—and both of them applied only to other people's wrong political choices.

Well, the "beats" weren't lucky enough to be born except when they were born. Ginsberg says he lives in Harlem, but it's not the Harlem of the Scottsboro boys and W. C. Handy and the benign insanity of trying to proletarianize Striver's Row; their comrades are not the comrades of the Stewart Cafeteria nor yet of the road, as Kerouac would disingenuously have it, but pick-ups on dark morning streets. But they have their connection with us who were young in the '30's, their intimate political connection, which we deny at risk of missing what it is that makes the "beat" phenomenon something to think about. As they used to say on 14th Street, it is no accident, comrades, it is decidedly no accident that today in the '50's our single overt manifestation of protest takes the wholly nonpolitical form of a bunch of panic-stricken kids in blue jeans, many of them publicly homosexual, talking about or taking drugs, assuring us that they are out of their minds, not responsible, while the liberal intellectual is convinced that he has no power to control the political future, the future of the free world, and that therefore he must submit to what he defines as political necessity. Though of course the various aspects of a culture must be granted their own autonomous source and character, the connection between "beat" and respectable liberal intellectual exists and is not hard to locate: the common need to deny free will, divest oneself of responsibility and yet stay alive. The typical liberal intellectual of the '50's, whether he be a writer for *Partisan Review* or a law school professor or a magazine or newspaper editor, explains his evolution over the last two decades—specifically, his present attitude toward "co-existence"—by telling us that he has been forced to accept the unhappy reality of Soviet strength in an atomic world, and that there is no alternative to capitulation—not that he calls it that—except the extinction of nuclear war. Even the diplomacy he invokes is not so much flexible, which he would like to think it is, as disarmed and, hopefully, disarming, an instrument of his impulse to surrender rather than of any wish to dominate or even of his professed wish to hold the line. Similarly docile to culture, the "beat" also contrives a fate by predicating a fate. Like the respectable established intellectual—or the organization man, or the suburban matron—against whom he makes his play of protest, he conceives of himself as incapable of exerting any substantive influence against the forces that condition him. He is made by society, he cannot make society. He can only stay alive as best he can for as long as is permitted him. Is it any wonder, then, that *Time* and *Life* write as they do about the "beats"—with such a conspicuous show of superiority, and no hint of fear? These periodicals know what genuine, dangerous protest looks like, and it doesn't look like Ginsberg and Kerouac. Clearly, there is no more menace in *Howl* or *On the Road* than there is in the Scarsdale PTA. In the common assumption of effectlessness, in the apparent will to rest with a social determination over which the individual spirit and intelligence cannot and perhaps even should not try to triumph, there merge any number of the disparate elements of our present culture—from the liberal intellectual journals to Luce to the Harvard Law School, from Ginsberg to the suburban matron.

But then why, one ponders, do one's most relaxed and nonsquare friends, alongside of whom one can oneself be made to look like the original object with four sides of equal length; why do one's most politically "flexible" friends, alongside of whom one's own divergence from dominant liberal opinion is regularly made to look so ungraceful, so like a latter-day sectarianism, even a fanaticism, feel constrained to dispute Columbia's judgment in giving the "beats" a hearing on the campus and my own wish to attend their poetry-reading? Why, for instance, the dissent of Dwight Macdonald, whom I happened to see that afternoon; or of W. H. Auden, who, when I said I had been moved by the performance, gently chided me, "I'm ashamed of you"; or of William Phillips who, although he tells me yes, I may go ahead with this article, can't hide his puzzlement, even worry, because I want to give the "beats" this kind of attention? In strict logic, it would seem to me that things should go in quite the other direction and that I, who insist upon at least the assumption of free will in our political dealings with Russia, who insist upon what I call political responsibility, should be the one to protest a university forum for the irresponsibles whereas my friends whose politics are what I think of as finally a politics of victimization, of passivity and fatedness, should be able to shrug off the "beats" as merely another inevitable, if tasteless, expression of a *Zeitgeist* with which I believe them to be far more in tune than I am. I do not mean, of course, to rule out taste, or style, as a valid criterion of moral judgment. A sense of social overwhelmment which announces itself in terms of disreputableness or even criminality asks for a different kind of moral assessment than the same emotion kept within the bounds of acceptable social expression. But I would simply point to the similarities which are masked by these genuine moral differences between the "beats" and my friends who would caution us against them. Taste or style dictates that most intellectuals behave decorously, earn a regular living, disguise instead of flaunt whatever may be their private digressions from the conduct society considers desirable; when they seek support for the poetical impulse or ask for light on their self-doubt and fears, they don't make the naked boast that they are crazy like daisies but they elaborate a new belief in the indispensability of neurosis to art, or beat the bushes for some new deviant psychoanalysis which will generalize their despair without curing it. And these differences of style are of course important, at least for the moment. It is from the long-range, and no doubt absolute, view of our immediate cultural situation, which bears so closely upon our continuing national crisis, that the moral difference between a respectable and a disreputable acceptance of defeat seems to me to constitute little more than a cultural footnote to history.

But perhaps I wander too far from the other night at Columbia. There was enough in the evening that was humanly immediate to divert one from this kind of ultimate concern. . . .

It was not an official university occasion. The "beats" appeared at Columbia on the invitation of a student club—interestingly enough, the John Dewey Society. Whether the club first approached Ginsberg or Ginsberg initiated the proceedings, I don't know, but what had happened was that Ginsberg in his undergraduate days had taken a loan from the university—$200? $250?—and recently the Bursar's office had caught up with him in his new incarnation of successful literary itinerant, to demand repayment. Nothing if not ingenious, Ginsberg now proposed to pay off his debt by reading his poetry at Columbia without fee. It was at this point that various members of the English department, solicited as sponsors for the operation, had announced their rejection of the whole deal, literary as well as financial, and the performance was arranged without financial benefit to Ginsberg and without official cover; we three wives, however, decided to attend on our own. We would meet at 7:45 at the door of the theater; no, we would meet at 7:40 at the door of the theater; no, we would meet no later than 7:30 across the street from the theater: the telephoning back and forth among the three women was stupendous as word spread of vast barbarian hordes converging on poor dull McMillin Theater from all the dark recesses of the city, howling for their leader. The advance warnings turned out to be exaggerated; it was nevertheless disconcerting to be associated with such goings-on, and the fact that Fred Dupee, at the request of the John Dewey Society, had consented to be moderator, chairman, introducer of Ginsberg and his fellow-poets, while it provided the wives of his colleagues with the assurance of seats in a section of the hall reserved for faculty, was not without its uncomfortable reminder that Ginsberg had, in a sense, got his way; he was appearing on the same Columbia platform from which T. S. Eliot had last year read his poetry; he was being presented by, and was thus bound to be thought under the sponsorship of, an important person in the academic and literary community who was also one's long-time friend. And indeed it was as Dupee's friend that one took a first canvass of the scene: the line of policemen before the entrance to the theater; the air of suppressed excitement in the lobbies and one's own rather contemptible self-consciousness about being seen in such a crowd; the shoddiness of an audience in which it was virtually impossible to distinguish between student and camp-follower; the always-new shock of so many young girls, so few of them pretty, and so many dreadful black stockings; so many young men, so few of them—despite the many black beards—with any promise of masculinity. It was distressing to think that Dupee was going to be "faculty" to this rabble, that at this moment he was backstage with Ginsberg & Co., formulating a deportment which would check the excess of which one knew them to be capable, even or especially in public, without doing violence to his own large tolerance.

For me, it was of some note that the auditorium smelled fresh. The place was already full when we arrived; I took one look at the crowd and was certain that it would smell bad. But I was mistaken. These people may think they're dirty inside and dress up to it. Nevertheless, they smell all right. The audience was clean and Ginsberg was clean and Corso was clean and Orlovsky was clean. Maybe Ginsberg says he doesn't bathe or shave; Corso, I know, declares that he has never combed his hair; Orlovsky has a line in one of the two poems he read—he's not yet written his third, the chairman explained—"If I should shave, I know the bugs would go away." But for this occasion, at any rate, Ginsberg, Corso and Orlovsky were all clean and shaven; Kerouac, in crisis, didn't appear, but if he had come he would have been clean and shaven too—he was at Hunter, I've inquired about that. And anyway, there's nothing dirty about a checked shirt or a lumberjacket and blue jeans, they're standard uniform in the best nursery schools. Ginsberg has his pride, as do his friends.

And how do I look to the "beats," I ask myself after that experience with the seats, and not only I but the other wives I was with? We had pulled aside the tattered old velvet rope which marked off the section held for faculty, actually it was trailing on the floor, and moved into the seats Dupee's wife Andy had saved for us by strewing coats on them; there was a big grey overcoat she couldn't identify: she stood holding it up in the air murmuring wistfully, "Whose is this?"—until the young people in the row in back of us took account of us and answered sternly, "*Those* seats are reserved for faculty." If I have trouble unraveling undergraduates from "beats," neither do the wives of the Columbia English department wear their distinction with any certainty.

But Dupee's distinction, that's something else again: what could I have been worrying about, when had Dupee ever failed to meet the occasion, or missed a right style? I don't suppose one could witness a better performance than his on Thursday evening; its rightness was apparent the moment he walked onto the stage, his troupe in tow and himself just close enough and just enough removed to indicate the balance in which he held the situation. Had there been a hint of betrayal in his deportment, of either himself or his guests—naturally, he had made them his guests—the whole evening might have been different: for instance, a few minutes later when the overflow attendance outside the door began to bang and shout for admission, might not the audience have caught the contagion and become unruly too? Or would Ginsberg have stayed with his picture of himself as poet serious and triumphant instead of succumbing to what must have been the greatest temptation to spoil his opportunity? "The last time I was in this theater," Dupee began quietly, "it was also to hear a poet read his works. That was T. S. Eliot." A slight alteration of inflection, from irony to mockery, from condescension to contempt, and it might well have been a signal for near-riot, boos and catcalls and whistlings; the evening would have been lost to the "beats," Dupee and Columbia would have been defeated. Dupee transformed a circus into a classroom. He himself, he said, welcomed the chance to hear these poets read their works—he never once in his remarks gave them their name of "beats" nor alluded even to San Francisco—because in all poetry it was important to study the spoken accent; he himself didn't happen especially to admire those of their works that he knew; still, he would draw our attention to their skillful use of a certain kind of American imagery which, deriving from Whitman, yet passed Whitman's use of it or even Hart Crane's. . . . It was Dupee speaking for the Academy, claiming for it its place in life, and the performers were inevitably captive to his dignity and self-assurance. Rather than Ginsberg and his friends, it was a photographer from *Life,* exploding his flashbulbs in everybody's face, mounting a ladder at the back of the stage the more effectively to shoot his angles, who came to represent vulgarity and disruption and disrespect; when a student in the audience disconnected a wire which had something to do with the picture-taking, one guessed that Ginsberg was none too happy but it was the photographer's face that became ugly, the only real ugliness of the evening. One could feel nothing but pity for Ginsberg and his friends that their front of disreputableness and rebellion should be this transparent, this vulnerable to the seductions of a clever host. With Dupee's introduction, the whole of their defense had been penetrated at the very outset.

Pity is not the easiest of our emotions today; now it's understanding that is easy, and more and more—or so I find it for myself—real pity moves hand-in-hand with real terror; it's an emotion one avoids because it's so hard; one understands the cripple, the delinquent, the unhappy so as not to have to pity them. But Thursday night was an occasion of pity so direct and inescapable that it left little to the understanding that wasn't mere afterthought—and pity not only for the observed, the performers, but for us who had come to observe them and reassure ourselves that we were not implicated. One might as readily persuade oneself one was not implicated in one's children! For this was it: these *were* children, miserable children trying desperately to manage, asking desperately to be taken out of it all; there was nothing one could imagine except to bundle them home and feed them warm milk, promise them they need no longer call for mama and papa. I kept asking myself, where had I had just such an experience before, and later it came to me: I had gone to see O'Neill's *Long Day's Journey into Night* and the play had echoed with just such a child's cry for help; at intermission time all the mothers in the audience were so tormented and anxious that they rushed in a body to phone home: was the baby really all right, was he really well and warm in his bed; one couldn't get near the telephone booths. A dozen years ago, when Ginsberg had been a student and I had taxed Lionel with the duty to forbid him to misbehave, he had answered me that he wasn't the boy's father, and of course he was right. Neither was Mark Van Doren the boy's father; a teacher is not a father to his students and he must never try to be. Besides, Ginsberg had a father of his own who couldn't be replaced at will: he was in the audience the other night. One of the things Ginsberg read was part of a long poem to his mother who, he told us, had died three years ago, and as he read it, he choked and cried; but no one in the audience tittered or showed embarrassment at this public display of emotion, and I doubt whether anyone thought, "See, he has existence: he can cry, he can feel." Nor did anyone seem very curious when he went on to explain, later in the evening, that the reason he had cried was because his father was in the theater. I have no way of knowing what Ginsberg's father felt the other night about his son being up there on the stage at Columbia (it rather obsesses me), but I should guess he was proud; it's what I'd conclude from his expression at the end of the performance when Ginsberg beat through the admirers who surrounded him, to get to his father as quickly as he could: surely that's nice for a father. And I should suppose a father was bound to be pleased that his son was reading his poems in a university auditorium: it would mean the boy's success, and this would be better than a vulgarity, it would necessarily include the chairman's critical gravity and the fact, however bizarre, that T. S. Eliot had been the last poet in this place before him. In a sense, Orlovsky and Corso were more orphans than Ginsberg the other night, but this was not necessarily because they were without fathers of their own in the audience; I should think it would go back much farther than this, to whatever it was that made them look so much more armored, less openly eager for approval; although they were essentially as innocent and childlike as Ginsberg, they couldn't begin to match his appeal; it was on Ginsberg that one's eye rested, it was to the sweetness in his face and to his sweet smile that one responded; it was to him that one gave one's pity and for him one felt one's own fullest terror. Clearly, I am no judge of his poem, "Lion in the Room," which he announced was dedicated to Lionel Trilling; I heard it through too much sympathy, and also self-consciousness. The poem was addressed as well as dedicated to Lionel; it was about a lion in the room with the poet, a lion who was hungry but refused to eat him; I heard it as a passionate love poem, I really can't say whether it was a good or bad poem, but I was much moved by it, in some part unaccountably. It was also a decent poem, it now strikes me; I mean, there were no obscenities in it as there had been in much of the poetry the "beats" read. Here was something else that was remarkable about the other evening: most of the audience was very young, and Ginsberg must have realized this because when he read the poem about his mother and came to the place where he referred to the YPSLs of her girlhood, he interposed his only textual exegesis of the evening: in an aside he explained, "Young People's Socialist League"—he was very earnest about wanting his poetry to be understood. And it wasn't only his gentility that distinguished Ginsberg's father from the rest of the audience; as far as I could see, he was the only man in the hall who looked old enough to be the father of a grown son; the audience was crazily young, there were virtually no faculty present, I suppose they didn't want to give this much sanction to the "beats." For this young audience the obscenities read from the stage seemed to have no force whatsoever; there was not even the shock of silence, and when Ginsberg forgot himself in the question period and said that something or other was bull-shit, I think he was more upset than his listeners; I can't imagine anything more detached and scientific outside a psychoanalyst's office, or perhaps a nursery school, than this young audience at Columbia. Of Corso, in particular, one had the sense that he mouthed the bad words only with considerable personal difficulty: this hurts me more than it hurts you.

Obviously, the whole performance had been carefully devised as to who would read first and what, then who next, and just how much an audience could take without becoming bored and overcritical: it would be my opinion we could have taken a bit more before the question period which must have been an anti-climax for anyone who had come, not as a tourist, but as a fellow-traveller. I've already reported how Ginsberg dealt with the philosophy question. There remains, of the question period, only to report his views on verse forms.

I don't remember how the question was put to Ginsberg—but I'm sure it was put neutrally: no one was inclined to embarrass the guests—which led him into a discussion of prosody; perhaps it was the question about what Ginsberg as a poet had learned at Columbia; but anyway, here, at last, Ginsberg had a real classroom subject: he could be a teacher who wed outrageousness to authority in the time-honored way of the young and lively, no-pedant-he performer of the classroom, and suddenly Ginsberg heard himself announcing that no one at Columbia knew anything about prosody; the English department was stuck in the nineteenth century, sensible of no meter other than the old iambic pentameter, whereas the thing about him and his friends was their concern with a poetic line which moved in the rhythm of ordinary speech; they were poetic innovators, carrying things forward the logical next step from William Carlos Williams. And now all at once the thing about Ginsberg and his friends was not their social protest and existentialism, their whackiness and beat-upness: suddenly it had become their energy of poetic impulse that earned them their right to be heard in the university, their studious devotion to their art: Ginsberg was seeing to that. Orlovsky had made his contribution to the evening; he had read his two whacky uproarious poems, the entire canon of his work, and had won his acclaim. Corso had similarly given his best, and been approved. The question period, the period of instruction, belonged to Ginsberg alone, and his friends might be slightly puzzled by the turn the evening had taken, the decorousness of which they suddenly found themselves a part—Corso, for instance, began to look like a chastened small boy who was still determined, though his heart was no longer in it, to bully his way through against all these damned grown-ups—but they had no choice except to permit their companion his deviation into high-mindedness. (Rightist opportunism?) Thus did one measure, finally, the full tug of something close to respectability in Ginsberg's life, by this division in the ranks; and thus, too, was the soundness of Dupee's reminder, that there is always something to learn from hearing a poet read his poems aloud, borne in on one. For the fact was that Ginsberg, reading his verse, had naturally given it the iambic beat: after all, it is the traditional beat of English poetry where it deals with serious subjects as Ginsberg's poems so often do. A poet, one thought—and it was a poignant thought because it came so immediately and humanly rather than as an abstraction—may choose to walk whatever zany path in his life as a man; but when it comes to mourning and mothers and such, he will be drawn into the line of tradition; at least in this far he has a hard time avoiding respectability.

The evening was over, we were dismissed to return to our homes. A crowd formed around Ginsberg; he extricated himself and came to his father a few rows ahead of us. I resisted the temptation to overhear their greeting. In some part of me I wanted to speak to Ginsberg, tell him I had liked the poem he had written to my husband, but I didn't do it: I couldn't be sure that Ginsberg wouldn't take my meaning wrong; after all, his social behavior is not fantasy. Outside, it had blown up a bit—or was it just the chill of unreality against which we hurried to find shelter?

There was a meeting going on at home of the pleasant professional sort which, like the comfortable living-room in which it usually takes place, at a certain point in a successful modern literary career confirms the writer in his sense of disciplined achievement and well-earned reward. I had found myself hurrying as if I were needed, but there was really no reason for my haste; my entrance was an interruption, even a disturbance of the attractive scene. Auden, alone of the eight men in the room not dressed in a proper suit but wearing his battered old brown leather jacket, was first to inquire about my experience. I told him I had been moved; he answered that he was ashamed of me. I said, "It's different when it's a sociological phenomenon and when it's human beings," and he of course knew and accepted what I said. Yet as I prepared to get out of the room so that the men could sit down again with their drinks, I felt there was something more I had to add—it was not enough to leave the "beats" only as human beings—and so I said, "Allen Ginsberg read a love poem to you, Lionel. I liked it very much." It was a strange thing to say in the circumstances, perhaps even a little foolish. But I'm sure that Ginsberg's old teacher knew what I was saying, and why I was impelled to say it.

# DAVID L. ULIN

DAVID L. ULIN is the author of *Cape Cod Blues* (1992), a collection of poems. His essay "The Disappearing Bohemian" was included in the Winter 1998–1999 issue of *Hungry Mind Review*.

## The Disappearing Bohemian

I'm not a great believer in nostalgia. Nor do I generally wish I'd lived in some other age. Every now and then, though, I find myself longing for bohemia, for a movement that might have the power to reconfigure the way we think. It's an odd sort of yearning, since I have never been a joiner; I've walked away from nearly every group with which I've ever been affiliated, wary of having my own identity subsumed by theirs. But there's something about the idea that continues to move me, usually at odd instants—late at night, or in the car at twilight, when a certain cast of sun and shadow makes me feel unbound. Sitting there, as darkness descends and the sky goes flat with indistinctness, the pavement takes on a sepia cast and I lose sight of where I am. And in that moment, I can't help wondering about a time when all this might have mattered, when it was still possible to believe in bohemia and the avant-garde.

These days, it feels naive even to *talk* about bohemia, or to invoke the discredited notion of the avant-garde. Living, as we do, in a culture where the twin spheres of business and information have become so all-encompassing, interconnected, the idea of someone actually working in opposition to the machinery seems like a fantasy, a willful projection of some long-lost world. Everywhere you look, mainstream culture has co-opted the fringes, or maybe it's the fringes that have co-opted themselves. Either way, the very notion of bohemia has been reduced to nothing more than another label, a self-congratulatory catchphrase that gets thrown around as an instant badge of credibility, even as it's being offered up for sale. In his 1995 essay "Why Johnny Can't Dissent," Thomas Frank maps out the territory, noting that as "our businessmen imagine themselves rebels, and our rebels sound more and more like ideologists of business," bohemia has fallen prey to the fallacy of the countercultural idea. "The problem with cultural dissent in America," Frank writes, "isn't that it's been co-opted, absorbed, or ripped off. Of course it's been all of these things. But it has proven so hopelessly susceptible to such assaults for the same reason it has become so harmless in the first place . . . : It is no longer any different from the official culture it's supposed to be subverting." As much as I agree with Frank's argument, it does beg one important question: Given the reach of corporate culture, is there still a place for the bohemian ideal?

On the face of it, such an issue seems simple enough to resolve, but it's complicated by the amorphous state of American bohemia, whose confusion predates the rise of contemporary corporate society and has even contributed to the development of so-called hip capitalism in many ways. Adding to the paradox is the fact that this dichotomy goes back to those original rebel angels, the Beats, who, in the fifty-plus years since Jack Kerouac, Allen Ginsberg, and William S. Burroughs first began to articulate their own mythologies, have been institutionalized as the quintessential postwar bohemian movement, influencing everything from literature to advertising, and, in the process, helping to turn the countercultural aesthetic from one of ideas, of art, to one of style. In some sense, the Beats embody the equivocal nature of American bohemianism, which has always seemed to straddle the cultural divide, with one foot in the avant-garde and the other firmly in the middle class. Certainly, that was true of Kerouac, who, in 1952, outlined the split in his journal: "This mere thought of it disgusts me—The Beat Generation, my relationships with Solomon & Allen & Holmes, Giroux's repudiation of my dedicatory poem ('This isn't a poetic age'), the brutality of football, the shame of literature, the whole arbitrary mess of my mother's disapproval of the generation and all its modern activities & the generation's arbitrary disapproval of doting mothers, my whole room cluttered with manuscripts, the disgust of quitting just when I'm underway."

Kerouac, of course, was a special case who spent the bulk of his adult life running back and forth between the opposing poles of his mother and his friends, looking for security, or meaning, in each one, yet unable to integrate the two into a coherent vision of himself. On a less personal level, however, a similar conflict was played out in the way the Beats presented themselves through the defining lens of American mass culture, which they simultaneously embraced and rejected. As early as 1955, Ginsberg was promoting himself and several other key figures (Kerouac, Gregory Corso, Gary Snyder, Michael McClure) as representing the heart and soul of the San Francisco Poetry Renaissance, even going so far as to help set up a 1956 photo shoot for *Mademoiselle* magazine that Steven Watson describes in his book *The Birth of the Beat Generation* as "the beginning of unlikely connections between the literary movement and popular culture." But whereas for preceding generations, such a confluence might have led to arguments about authenticity—or at the very least, intention—for the Beats, it was just another method of getting their message across. Because of that, they can be interpreted as the first truly modern (or postmodern) bohemia, the first avant-garde movement explicitly to sell itself.

Where the legacy of all this became most apparent was as the Beats moved into the mainstream, reconfiguring the pantheon they had once sought to dissolve. By the time of their deaths, Ginsberg and Burroughs had both been inducted into the American Academy of Arts and Letters, and Ginsberg had received a National Book Award. In the past, such honors might have come at a cost (the loss of bohemian credibility, the sense that one's work had grown safe enough to be recognized by society at large), but the Beats may be more remarkable for managing to maintain the image of outsiders even as they infiltrated the inside—in other words, to have it both ways. If you compare their position in official culture with the underground stature they continue to possess, you begin to see a whole new paradigm of bohemia, in which it is possible to be part of the mainstream *and* the counterculture. It's an idea that even carries over into the commercial world, as in the series of television advertisements Burroughs did for Nike in the late 1980s, or the *Beat Culture and the New America* exhibition that opened in 1995 at New York's Whitney Museum of American Art—underwritten, with Ginsberg's blessings, by those noted bohemians at AT&T—in which artifacts like Kerouac's scroll manuscript of *On the Road* were displayed with the solemnity of religious icons, while the gift shop offered thirty-dollar sets of bongo-shaped salt and pepper shakers and twenty-five-dollar boxes of pencils imprinted with Kerouac's "Essentials of Spontaneous Prose." In that sense, the Beats may not have been the first avant-garde movement to embrace mainstream credibility, but they *were* the first to claim it didn't matter, that such a move was subversive in its own right.

On a certain level, there's something admirable about this, a kind of willful self-invention, as if one might maintain an edge of iconoclasm merely by proclaiming that all one's acts cut against the grain. But the same notion speaks volumes about contemporary culture, where even our so-called revolutionaries seem to have lost their sense of history, and the power of image, rather than action, motivates our souls. In such a context, if the Beats' tendency to self-commercialize had any impact on bohemia, it was by setting a bad example—or, more accurately, by changing the rules. The evidence of this is everywhere, from Max Blagg, the "underground" New York poet who wrote and performed an original poem for a Gap commercial (shot in a smoky jazz club, with a neo-bop combo providing the sound track, the clip appropriated the most recognizable images of Beat culture), to Laurie Anderson, once the doyenne of mixed-media performance art, who recently had dinner at the White House with her live-in lover, Lou Reed. Not long ago, *The New York Times Magazine* even showcased not one but two print ads featuring the pitchman's smile of performance artist Spalding Gray. The interesting thing about all this is that, as with the Burroughs/Nike collaboration, there's an absolute lack of anything resembling shame. In each case, rather, the presentation— the clothes, the atmosphere, the overwhelming sense of hip—seems entirely consistent with the way these artists carry themselves within the world. It's as if, in our commodified culture, the specter of selling out has yielded to the purer concept of *selling,* which makes bohemia just another product, as easy to slip on as a pair of Gap jeans. At the same time, though, it blurs the boundaries of what compromises are acceptable, until it's no longer clear where anything begins or ends.

What's troubling about this is that, by allowing themselves to be usurped so unquestioningly by the mainstream, artists like Gray and Burroughs have contributed to the illusion that bohemia is little more than a matter of lifestyle, defined by the clothes you wear or the products you buy, rather than a fundamental philosophical stance. More to the point, they've helped the dominant culture seem, somehow, anti-authoritarian, less about corporate manipulation than creative self-fulfillment, in which the passive algebra of consumption becomes its own subversive pose. Again, there's a certain self-justifying logic to all this, for if hawking products is now a hip, iconoclastic act of cultural insurrection, then we no longer need to wrestle with any fundamental notion of consequence. But the truth is that there *is* a consequence, for if bohemia is to mean anything, it must do so in opposition to the mainstream, offering a real alternative that has its roots in the attitudes we bring to our lives. That kind of intention doesn't come packaged at Starbucks, and it can't be found at Borders or Barnes & Noble, nor in the pages of your local alternative weekly, which is most likely owned by a conglomerate like Stern Publishing or New Times. No, those places, like the corporate culture that supports them, are *anti-*progressive; they use the trappings of bohemia—the cool jazz and alternative rock, the coffeehouse atmosphere, the illusion of independence—to encourage us to feel like rebels, even as they support the status quo. For proof of that, just walk into any Borders and look for material that challenges the party line. Sure, they'll have plenty of books by Gray and Burroughs, but you won't find much in the way of, say, zines or odd small presses—unless, of course, you mean *The Factsheet Five Zine Reader*, published by Three Rivers Press, a division of Random House.

This is not to say there's no bohemian undercurrent in corporate culture, no legitimate avant-garde sentiment to critique the mainstream on its own terms. What seems undeniable, however, is that, as things grow increasingly commodified, increasingly chain-driven and homogeneous, outlets have become more difficult to come by, giving such endeavors less opportunity to slip between the cracks. That's why the crisis in independent publishing and bookselling—hell, the crisis in independent *anything*—is so significant, because these venues have traditionally been sympathetic to dissenting points of view. Yet equally important is the predominance of the money culture, which has come to influence nearly every aspect of our lives. Bohemias, after all, have always flourished in environments where artists could live inexpensively, from Paris in the 1950s to Manhattan's Lower East Side, which during the late 1970s and early 1980s became the fulcrum for an astonishing variety of talents, all drawn to the area by its cheap rents and history of cultural foment. Today, it's more than most people can manage just to pay their bills, which doesn't leave much room for anything else. One friend of mine, only recently out of college, reports that when she and her former classmates get together, the main subject of discussion is how much money they need to come up with simply to survive. This image is one I find hard to get away from because it seems so totemic, so indicative of the direction we as a society have gone. It also goes a long way toward explaining our willingness to settle for a manufactured model of bohemia, a simulacrum, since in a culture where money has, of necessity, become the lingua franca even of the young and iconoclastic, this may be the only thing allowing us to maintain the illusion that there's something idiosyncratic about the way we face the world.

Where all this comes together is in the area of community, which has always been part of the bohemian ideal. Every great bohemia goes hand in hand with a physical nexus, from Paris and the Lower East Side to fin de siècle Vienna and San Francisco's North Beach, where the Beat movement continued to flower after spreading west from

New York. That's a matter not just of superficial coincidence but of necessity, since a countercultural movement must have a landscape where it can develop. This gets back to the issue of venues and outlets: of clubs, bookstores, and even coffeehouses, where work can be shared and elaborated upon with others of sympathetic mind. On the most basic level, it's how a buzz gets started, the way subversive thoughts begin to filter up through the strata of society and change the way we think about the world. If the Beats, for instance, had not been part of a community, their efforts might never have reached the critical mass required to explode. Yet even more essential is the notion that such communities are organic: in them ideas emerge from the participants, and not the other way around. When writers and artists began gathering on the Lower East Side in the late 1970s, it wasn't because the neighborhood had been labeled cutting edge by the denizens of official culture, but because there was something real, something creative, going on. Twenty years later, however, the only community that matters is the community of consumers, which is determined by demographics rather than ideas. With this as a defining ethos, community itself has become manufactured, another lifestyle choice to be put on or discarded according to the prevailing mood.

Faced with that, what still passes for bohemia has been increasingly pushed to the edges, among its terminal locations the Internet and the universities, which makes sense, since cyberspace has room for everything, and academia is nothing if not a museum for obsolete culture, a shadow box of the mind. While these destinations may marginalize bohemia even further, making it seem esoteric, disembodied, unconnected to the movements of the world, it might ultimately be a different edge that recontextualizes it—the edge of interior vision, existing in what Ginsberg once called "the vast empty quiet space of our own Consciousness," where the only arbiters are ourselves. This was the stance of another 1950s bohemian, the artist Wallace Berman, who spent time with the Beats but eventually went his own way. In his book *Utopia and Dissent: Art, Poetry, and Politics in California*, Richard Cándida Smith draws a vivid portrait of Berman's life in Venice, California, presenting it as a wholly autonomous alternative to the accepted model of bohemia: "Berman positioned himself in society through the relationships he developed with his wife and son. Family rather than profession structured his life, and domesticity became the focal point for defining both himself and the art that he created. . . . There can be no mistaking the ethos of domesticity running through Berman's work. . . . His home became the sole focus of his relationship to the world."

Berman's stance seems at first almost antithetical, an attempt to balance two apparently incompatible forces—bohemia and family—and make them cohere by sheer force of will. The more you think about it, however, the more it makes sense as a variation on the bohemian idea. If family as an institution is often seen as antibohemian, promoting conformity and social stability as a condition of the status quo, there's something almost transgressive about the idea that, in times like these, it might actually be the last refuge of resistance, a representation of community in its rawest, most organic form. When you consider how successfully bohemia has been absorbed into the mainstream, the most subversive act available to us may be to co-opt the family—to take it back, as it were. It was this vision that Berman pursued throughout his lifetime, creating collages featuring family images and producing a journal, *Semina,* that, in its use of found objects, personal texts, and photographs, makes a compelling case for the avant-garde as a source of integration, in which the components of one's life (art, work, family, love) can come together in a lasting way. The irony is that, in a society where such ideas now seem like their own form of nostalgia, it should be bohemia that brings them back to us, while in the process, renewing its own sense of purpose in the world. But in an age in which individual expression has become little more than just another product, there may be no more fitting framework for insurgence, no more overtly bohemian sentiment, than the idea that revolution begins at home.

# JOHN UPDIKE

JOHN UPDIKE, the prolific American novelist, short-story writer, and literary critic, wrote his parody "On the Sidewalk" of Kerouac's *On the Road* for *The New Yorker* as an up-and-coming young staff writer, still in his twenties. At the time, between 1956 and 1961, Updike's literary idols were the magazine's humorists James Thurber, Robert Benchley, and Walcott Gibbs. Updike later confessed in his foreword to *Assorted Prose* (1965), that he had an "ambition to emulate them . . . when I was young at heart. I leave it to the percipient reader to deduce, where appropriate, that Eisenhower was still President and that Robert Frost was still alive." In 1959, not long after writing his Kerouac parody, Updike published both his first collection of short fiction, *The Same Door,* and his first novel, *The Poorhouse Fair.*

## On the Sidewalk

### (After Reading, at Long Last, *On the Road*, by Jack Kerouac)

I was just thinking around in my sad backyard, looking at those little drab careless starshaped clumps of crabgrass and beautiful chunks of some old bicycle crying out without words of the American Noon and half a newspaper with an ad about a lotion for people with dry skins and dry souls, when my mother opened our frantic banging screendoor and shouted, "Gogi Himmelman's here." She might have shouted the Archangel Gabriel was here, or Captain Easy or Baron Charlus in Proust's great book: Gogi Himmelman of the tattered old greenasgrass knickers and wild teeth and the vastiest, most vortical, most insatiable wonderfilled eyes I have ever known. "Let's go, Lee," he sang out, and I could see he looked sadder than ever, his nose all rubbed raw by a cheap handkerchief and a dreary Bandaid unravelling off his thumb. "I know the WAY!" That was Gogi's inimitable unintellectual method of putting it that he was on fire with the esoteric paradoxical Tao and there was no holding him when he was in that mood. I said, "I'm going, Mom," and she said, "O.K." and when I looked back at her hesitant in the pearly mystical UnitedStateshome light I felt absolutely sad, thinking of all the times she had vacuumed the same carpets.

His scooter was out front, the selfsame, the nonpareil, with its paint scabbing off intricately and its scratchedon dirty words and its nuts and bolts chattering with fear, and I got my tricycle out of the garage, and he was off, his left foot kicking with that same insuperable energy or even better. I said, "Hey wait," and wondered if I could keep up and probably couldn't have if my beltbuckle hadn't got involved with his rear fender. This was IT. We scuttered down our drive and right over Mrs. Cacciatore's rock garden with the tiny castles made out of plaster that always made me sad when I looked at them alone. With Gogi it was different; he just kept right on going, his foot kicking with that delirious thirtyrevolutionsasecond frenzy, right over the top of the biggest, a Blenheim six feet tall at the turrets; and suddenly I saw it the way he saw it, embracing everything with his unfluctuating generosity, imbecile saint of our fudging age, a mad desperado in our Twentieth Century Northern Hemisphere Nirvana deserts.

We rattled on down through her iris bed and broke into the wide shimmering pavement. "Contemplate those holy hydrants," he shouted back at me through the wind. "Get a load of those petulant operable latches; catch the magic of those pickets standing up proud and sequential like the arguments in Immanuel Kant; boom, boom, bitty-boom BOOM!" and it was true.

"What happens when we're dead?" I asked.

"The infinite never-to-be-defiled subtlety of the late Big Sid Catlett on the hushed trap drums," he continued, mad with his own dreams, imitating the whisks, "Swish, swish, swishy-swish SWOOSH!"

The sun was breaking over the tops of Mr. Linderman's privet hedge, little rows of leaves set in there delicate and justso like mints in a Howard Johnson's roadside eatery. Mitzi Leggett came out of the house, and Gogi stopped the scooter, and put his hands on her. "The virginal starchblue fabric; printed with stylized kittens and puppies," Gogi explained in his curiously beseechingly transcendent accents. "The searing incredible *innocence!* Oh! Oh! Oh!" His eyes poured water down his face like broken blisters.

"Take me along," Mitzi said openly to me, right with Gogi there and hearing every word, alive to every meaning, his nervous essence making his freckles tremble like a field of Iowa windblown nochaff barley.

"I want to," I told her, and tried to, but I couldn't, not there. I didn't have the stomach for it. She pretended to care. She was a lovely beauty. I felt my spokes snap under me; Gogi was going again, his eyes tightshut in ecstasy, his foot kicking so the hole in his shoesole showed every time, a tiny chronic rent in the iridescent miasmal veil that Intrinsic Mind tries to hide behind.

Wow! Dr. Fairweather's house came up on the left, delicious stucco like piecrust in the type of joints that attract truckers, and then the place of the beautiful Mrs. Mertz, with her *canny* deeprooted husband bringing up glorious heartbreaking tabourets and knickknacks from his workshop in the basement, a betooled woodshavingsmelling fantasy worthy of Bruegel or Hegel or a seagull. Vistas! Old Miss Hooper raced into her yard and made a grab for us, and Gogi Himmelman, the excruciating superbo, shifted to the other foot and laughed in her careworn face. Then the breathless agape green space of the Princeling mansion, with its rich calm and potted Tropic of Cancer plants. Then it was over.

Gogi and I went limp at the corner under a sign saying ELM STREET with irony because all the elms had been cut down so they wouldn't get the blight, sad stumps diminishing down the American perspective whisperingly.

"My spokes are gone," I told him.

"Friend—ahem—*zip, zip*—parting a relative concept—Bergson's invaluable marvelchocked work—tch, tch." He stood there, desperately wanting to do the right thing, yet always lacking with an indistinguishable grandeur that petty ability.

"Go," I told him. He was already halfway back, a flurrying spark, to where Mitzi waited with irrepressible womanwarmth.

Well. In landsend despair I stood there stranded. Across the asphalt that was sufficiently semifluid to receive and embalm millions of starsharp stones and bravely gay candywrappers a drugstore twinkled artificial enticement. But I was not allowed to cross the street. I stood on the gray curb thinking, They said I could cross it when I grew up, but what do they mean grown up? I'm thirty-nine now, and felt sad.

# ANNE WALDMAN

ANNE WALDMAN described the experience of being the co-founder with Allen Ginsberg and Diane di Prima of the Jack Kerouac School of Disembodied Poetics at the Naropa Institute in Boulder, Colorado, in her essay "Lineages & Legacies." A decade earlier, after graduating from Bennington College, she lived on the Lower East Side in Manhattan, where she was also instrumental in developing the Poetry Project at St. Marks Church in the late 1960s. Waldman analyzed the effect of reading Kerouac's work in "Influence: Language, Voice, Beat and Energy of Kerouac's Poetry." One of Ginsberg's closest associates, Waldman wrote the poems "Notes on Sitting Beside a Noble Corpse" and "One Inch of Love Is An Inch of Ashes" in response to his death. Her lecture on William S. Burroughs, "Hurry up. It's time," was delivered as a talk at the Jack Kerouac School of Disembodied Poetics in August 1997. As editor and author of over thirty books, Waldman possesses a seemingly tireless energy that sustains her on her busy schedule as Distinguished Professor of Poetics at Naropa University and as a reader of poetry on her frequent whirlwind, worldwide tours. She has on occasion expressed her exasperation with her responsibilities, as in her poem "The Little Red Hen" from *No Hassles* (1971):

> I am the little red hen
> I work my ass off
> for all the poets
>
> And what do I get?
> A pat on the butt
> when the sun goes down
> Who will help me put out this magazine?
> "I won't," says Ted Bear.
> "Not I," says Ron Giraffe.
> "Who me?" says Mike The Whale.
> "Fat chance," says Jim The Lion.

"Very well then, I shall do it myself,"
Says the little red hen,
And she does.

---

## Lineages & Legacies

"A hundred-year project, at least!" the Buddhist meditation teacher Chogyam Trungpa had slyly suggested as we founded the Naropa Institute (now "University") and the Jack Kerouac School of Disembodied Poetics in Boulder, Colorado. Allen Ginsberg and Diane di Prima and I had been invited to Boulder, summer 1974, to help develop this "crazy wisdom school." Allen and I roomed together, staying up many nights to bandy about ideas for an "academy of the future" (John Ashbery's line: "the academy of the future is opening its doors to us"). We argued about a name for our poetics institute. I thought the Gertrude Stein School might be apt. She was outrageous, experimental, sexually provocative. But we finally and happily settled on The Jack Kerouac School of Disembodied Poetics as a banner for our poetic project. Allen wanted to honor his comrade and Kerouac was certainly a major inspiration for writers of my generation—poets particularly. Jack Kerouac had also realized the First Buddhist Noble Truth of suffering. I suggested the "disembodied" as a tantric twist. We had no budget, no building, no office, no telephone, no desk, no stationery, et cetera. We were also honoring ancient poetries and lineages, modernists, and all measure of unsung heroes and heroines of the poetic craft who were no longer bodily present. Of course it is a "body" poetics. How could we rage and sing without physical instrument? And yet, the name sounded right. Allen and I, also imagined honorary "chairs" for our department: The Emily Dickinson Chair of Silent Scribbling. The Frank O'Hara Chair of Deep Gossip, and others. We thought we'd give An Arabic Poetic Chair to a deserving Israeli writer and the like. . . .

What could lure us away from New York to found a school on the spine of the continent? The idea was an "outrider" program outside the official verse culture mainstream that could weather the slings and arrows of outrageous fortune and be a challenge to the mono-culture and its attendent mediocrities. Also a Buddhist-inspired project as well with emphases on meditative awareness and noncompetitive education.

After twenty-six years, we have the Allen Ginsberg Library, an Environmental Studies Program, a World Wisdom Chair that is held by Rabbi Zalman Shacter, Study Abroad programs in Nepal, Bali, Thailand, India. Also Project Outreach, where writing students work with victims of AIDS, teach workshops at nursing homes, grade schools, homeless shelters. Everyone has a story or poem to tell, everyone is interested in reading something besides newspapers or waiting to turn off the set. Refine the senses through colorful vivid language. Use the imagination. The hell realms of planet earth are versions of egomaniacal power mad hungry ghosts! It's bad poetry! It's land grabs, fossil fuel driven, genocides of all kinds that need our limber-witted poetic attention and muscle. Jump in, turn it around. So we've got an activist agenda. And hundreds of graduates are out there spawning their own projects, schools, publications, bookstores, manifestos, "To Keep The World Sane For Poetry," as our motto goes. In Seattle, in Prague, in New York City. The spirit of Beat maverick writers lives on.

## Influence: Language, Voice, Beat and Energy of Kerouac's Poetry

*Dedicated to the memory of Allen Ginsberg, this "talk" is generated by notes for a panel I participated in & Allen chaired at New York University in 1995.*

What spoke to me initially (first read *Mexico City Blues*) was passionate cry & heartbreak, sensitive, goofy—energetic lines popping open, all antennae raw & in the wind, and the constantly shifting exchange of earth & sky. Down to earth, down to his own rhythm, then out with the spin of an infinite mind riff. And up, way up, to revelation like "The Victor is not Self" or "(ripping of paper indicates/helplessness anyway")" or "We die with same/unconcern we lie." Philosophical. And *stoned.* And details. And naming things. And naming people. And naming heroes, writers, musicians, Buddhist saints & Boddhisattvas & deities. So *everybody's included.* People's names are pure sound & sacred because they exist & are therefore holy. It's like the "sacred conversation" you see in Italian paintings where all the saints are smiling beatifically and conversing in gentle tones on profound subjects. Nothing's excluded, and yet *Mexico City Blues* is a very discriminating serial poem. It has an amazing clarity, honesty, aspiration. Nothing is unnecessary inside it. And friendly, too. A real experiment in original mind living in conditioned mind wanting to "blow" free. Pop through on other side which is sound, energy, shape on page of ear & eye. If you can't sustain the images, if you don't "get" his *logopoeia* right off, try staying with the sound and the persona and sheer energy. I also appreciate in here the idea of choruses. Reminiscent of Gertrude Stein's *Four Saints.* You thinking of angels & saints singing, of choirs of kids in church, of resounding classical pieces singing out the sufferings of Christ or man. And in a particular vernacular mode. And the exhilaration too of salvation, redemption, life, life, life! It's always pounding like that. See, I'm *alive* I'm *thinking!* And everything around me has got life too. And these are sounds also made in heaven. *And I write because it's all fleeting & we're all going to die & my poetic duty is to make this experiment holy.* This is certainly the sense you get when you hear Kerouac's voice reading aloud on the discs & tapes.

> Punk! says Iron Pot Lid
> Tup! says finger toilet
> Tuck! says dime on Ice
> Ferwut says Beard Bird.

And improvising on a thought, a word, an increment of a word, a phone or phoneme and responding. So fast. A "perfect explication of mind" said the Tibetan meditation teacher Chogyam Trungpa after Allen Ginsberg read parts of the poem to him. Allen & I named a poetics school after Jack Kerouac at the Buddhist-inspired Naropa Institute in Colorado because he had the most spontaneously lucid sound. And he'd also realized the first Buddhist Noble Truth which is the Truth of Suffering that wafts through all his work, deep pain & empathy. And sometimes it's as if he's just whistling in the dark in *Mexico City Blues.* And so *hip* for a white guy. And mixed-breed American being interesting ethnic Quebecois origin, and macho even, but a secret scaredy cat. But this funny Buddhist twist keeps coming around into everything. Because, I think, he was always thinking, following his mind, checking things out & reading sacred scripture (see his explicit massive

journal/poetics collage *Some of the Dharma*, Penguin 1997) which are subtle & spontaneous & illuminating insights into the very nature of mind. So
what you have is the literal *practice* inherent in his mind-work. Each
chorus is an examination & delight in language-mind. This in lines like:

> Starspangled Kingdoms bedecked
>     in dewy joint
> DON'T IGNORE OTHER PARTS
>     OF YOUR MIND, I think,
> And my clever brain sends
>     ripples of amusement
> Through my leg nerve halls
>
> And I remember the Zigzag
>                     Original
>                     Mind
>
> of Babyhood
> when you'd let the faces
>         crack & mock
>         & yak & change
>         & go mad utterly
>         in your night
>         firstmind
>         reveries
> talking about the mind
>
> The endless Not Invisible
>     Madness Rioting
> Everywhere

*(from 17th Chorus)*

You've got here a "mental" sound as in

> A bubble pop, a foam snit
> Time on a Bat—growl of truck.

which also has terrific consonant mantra properties.

The glories of simultaneity explode all over the text. How can

Lester Young in eternity, Cleopatra's knot, Rabelais, Marco Polo & his Venetian genitals, Charlie Chaplin, Joe McCarthy, Charlie Parker, various friends & family, and Buddha co-exist? *They do so in the mind of the poet.*

What I appreciated as young teen girl growing up on Macdougal Street in Manhattan's West Village was this poem's particular accessibility. Its obvious relationship to jazz, to dharma (I was seriously starting to read Buddhist texts at my Quaker high school Friends Seminary), to smoking pot (a hot topic at the time!). And how it was delineated by small notebook page. Perfect form/content marriage. I was writing shapely (goofy?) poems which had a look of e.e. cummings. But I wanted to be as romantic as Keats and Yeats with the cosmic consciousness of Whitman. But these very tangible "Beat" literary poets were now walking my streets (Gregory Corso—quintessential poete maudit—lived just several blocks away on Bleecker Street), alive & in the world I too inhabited doing things I was doing. My friend Martin Hersey, son of the novelist John Hersey, was wandering around with a well-worn copy of *Naked Lunch* in his guitar case. I traveled to Greece & Egypt by the time I was eighteen, hitching around, sleeping on freighters. Twenty years old I caught a ride to the West Coast to the Berkeley Poetry Conference and then Lewis Warsh & I hitched to Mexico under false IDs (being underage) later that summer after founding our magazine Angel Hair at a Robert Duncan reading. One thinks of *influence. The work? The life? I took a vow at Berkeley to dedicate my life to poetry & the sangha (spiritual community) of poets.*

Kerouac was in stride poetically with many of the writers—the consociates—of his own time, not just his particular buddies. Certainly his companions were conducting some extremely outrageous experiments themselves. Burroughs's jump cuts, Ginsberg's cosmic consciousness—wanting to get all the details in—Gregory Corso's subtle autodidactic troubadour finesse, Gary Snyder's Buddhist thinking & content. And the idea of capturing the sound of the physical world (like Gertrude Stein wanting to get the rhythms of her dog lapping milk). Synethesia. Kinesthesia. Mix of senses. A saw, a hammer—rip rap. But think, also, of Frank O'Hara's poetics statement *Personism,* as a comparable poetics. The poem as a phone call. Think of endless rapping with Friends. How he wanted Neal Cassady's vocal rhythms down, Lucien Carr's, etc. And also as in Frank O'Hara poems a jaunty persona, who also, like Kerouac, names his world. Places, people, things. Duncan & Olson's composition by field. Projective verse. Even Williams's "No ideas but in things." All this was in the air. And the example of Gertrude Stein (who is mentioned in *Mexico City Blues*) who also followed the *grammar of her own mind*.

Technically, aside from the phenomenal legacy of the prose, we have Poems as Poems—*San Francisco Blues, Mexico City Blues, Book of Haikus, Poems All Sizes,* and the poetry of & inside the entire opus. The poems *as* poems. That look feel are defined as such. Pome: *If I don't use the cork/I may spill the wine/But if I do?* The insistent pitch of the Blues poems.

> Mexico City Bop
> I got the huck bop
> I got the floogle mock
> I got the thiri chiribim
>     bitchy bitchy bitchy
>     batch batch
> Chippely bop
>         Noise like that
>         Like fallin off porches
>             Of Tenement Petersburg
>         Russia Chicago O Yay.

> Mr Beggar & Mrs Davy—
> Looney and CRUNEY,
> I made a poem out of it,
> Haven't smoked Luney
>         & Cruney
> In a Long Time.

> Dem egges & dem dem
> Dere bacons, baby,
> If you only lay that
>     down on a trumpet
>     Lay that down
>         solid brother

> Bout all dem
>         bacon & eggs

Ya gotta be able
to lay it down
solid—
All that luney
& fruney

As active reader of classic novels, I always identified with the (mostly male) protagonists. I've talked to other women writers of my generation about this. Yes, we went with the hero. We were classic "puer" types—wanting the picaresque freedom the youths had. A kind of artistic bi-sexuality? You could say something about Kerouac's stance as American male born 1922 & how that tugged on the particular heartstrings of understanding (maternal) women, the fruition of his generation's identity problems around being soldiers (warriors) & all the attendant strands of his karmic stream adding up to the solid man, poet, writer, battling the expectation of whatever that could be in some eyes. Heroic? Certainly. So that was a lure. And he looked like a movie star! Normal, athletic, well-built, handsome, smart. And from such & such a family that he loved so deeply, loyally, the underdog class thing had sentimental appeal. His language was Quebecois & working Massachusetts, and all the types & personalities around him fed into that sound. But don't forget he devoured literature he was true intellectual, thinking, thinking. He was extremely well read as an early letter to Elbert Lenrow indicates. Also the dominant *outrider* culture of the time: black jazz, scat singing. He was empathetic, symbiotic. But more than that Kerouac came through as a witness, a cosmic common denominator, one who would take the whole ride and then survive and tell you what it was like. And loving every minute of the telling. Propelled by an unnatural gift & original poetic idea to follow the grammar of his own mind & minds of others, a son of Gertrude Stein! Like the Tibetan "delog" who dies, travels & comes back to life to tell you what he or she "saw." The shaman's or poet's call & duty. Because he took a lot "on," Kerouac did.

He loved "scatting." With a nod toward black improvisational music, he made amateur recordings of himself scatting with Neal Cassady & John Clellon Holmes. Holmes had a record-making machine where you could record your voice directly onto vinyl. He wrote his improvisations down as "Blues." He read poems to Frank Sinatra crooning on the radio. He was drawn to this form for a number of reasons—he liked the spontaneous approach. He intended these blues poems to be heard, preferably with a jazz background, and made recordings for Verve & Hanover in 1958 & 1959. He performed with Zoot Sims & Al Cohn on one recording, with Steve Allen at piano on another. These now seem remarkable & unique auditory adventures. I could feel my own yearning toward performance back then. Composer/musician David Amram, who worked with Kerouac & Allen, others, became a close friend in 1962 (I was still in high school) & he'd take me around to some of the clubs. I met painter Larry Rivers at the Five Spot, another hipster linked to the poets. My former sister-in-law married Steve Lacy & I used to see Thelonius Monk at their loft. My mother was a nut for Mingus & Lacy.

In "The Origins of Joy in Poetry" Kerouac conjures the new Zen-Lunacy. He speaks of the ORAL, of the exciting new poets like Lamantia and Whalen: They SING They SWING. "It is diametrically opposed to the Eliot shot, who so dismally advises his dreary negative rules like the objective correlative, etc., which is just a lot of constipation and ultimately emasculation of the pure masculine urge to freely sing."

He speaks of the "mental discipline typified by the haiku . . . , that is, the discipline of pointing things out directly, purely, concretely, no abstractions or explanations, wham wham the true blue song of man."

So his poetics so sensible in my own sensibility is clear and traceable in his own letters, exchanges, explications, responses. You only have to read him aloud to get the brilliant oral torque & command. Although I never met the man he was everywhere in my immediate surroundings, and still haunts the premises like a holy ghost.

### Notes on Sitting Beside a Noble Corpse—
### Light Breeze Stirring the Curtains, Blue—
### Faint Tremor of His Blue Shroud

Allen Ginsberg will never raise this body up, go out board a shiny air-
                                                            plane travel
  a thousand miles—Denver?—thousands—Milano?
  to pump the harmonium—how ecstatically he does this!—chant
                        OM NAMO SHIVAYA
"all ashes, all ashes again"

Allen Ginsberg will never sit across the street hunched over Chinese
                                        noodle bowl,
   the old professor stayed up late reading the young poet's poems

Allen Ginsberg will never meditate this body, spine straight to
                                heaven, holding up the roof
   of the world on the bright orange cushion

Allen Ginsberg's eyes will never water again—of tear gas, Bell's palsy,
                                    or flow on the
   death of a guru, read Blake Shelley lines to freeze your soul & you
                                    weep you weep
   & the whole Naropa Disembodied Kerouac tent is weeping

Allen Ginsberg will never tell awkward teen boy he's known since
                                    birth he's sexy again
   from hospital bed, the boy stood at the window while his mother
                                        sobbed
   because Allen Ginsberg said he's dying today

Allen Ginsberg will never brush this corpse's thin hair, get groomed,
                                oil feet, brush teeth
   (he's so conscientious!) mix mushroom leeks & winter squash
                                breakfast again

The telephone rings, Allen Ginsberg will never answer it again

Allen Ginsberg will never embarrass China, Russia, the White House,
                                    dead corrupt
   presidents, Cuba, the C.I.A. Universe again

But Allen Ginsberg will ever ease the pain of living with human story
                                    & song
   that's borne on wings of perpetual prophecy—life & death's a spiral!
   He's mounting the stairs now with Vajra Yogini

Full Century's brilliant Allen's gone, in other myriad forms live on
See through this palpable skull's tender eye, kind mind kind mind
                                    don't die!

Written by the poet's bed, at home in his own loft,
his body in repose after
death, Gelek Rinpoche & monks chanting
Chakrasamvara sadhana
April 5, 1997, New York City

### One Inch of Love Is An Inch of Ashes

Allen Ginsberg came to me in a dream:

it's goofy here,
all the conversations are in my head
the gods & goddesses get busy communing
    with the world, day in day out
they're distracted
I have no body! No notebooks
I'm scribing my good looks & dangerous poetry
    on heaven
Heaven's so BIG too, & they're lots of rogues
 around
I'm just a No-body

You know what the Chinese poet said, Anne,
"one inch of love is an inch of ashes."

### Burroughs: "Hurry up. It's time."

"I have constrained myself to escape death"

I remember a class William S. Burroughs taught at City College in
New York in the early '70s wherein he constructed a beast—the ideal
"alien"—that would have the radar of a bat, the gift of reptiles to grow
back limbs, the capability of shedding skin like the renewing serpent,
the sharp hearing of whales through miles of ocean, and so on. A sci-fi
"exquisite corpse," or biological cut-up, and certainly we have movie
versions of the remarkable beast or variants thereof—(human mixed
with fly gene, etc). But his beast was a metaphor for what might be
possible with language, just as he proposed taking childbearing away

from women at one point, seeing a scientific way that men could reproduce through their anuses! (Some of us women forgave him such interesting fantasies, others confined him mentally to a kind of misogynist's hell where men have menstrual periods, change diapers . . .)

Yet these cut-up ideas, not so alien in science, allowed Burroughs as writer to break with narrative linear Aristotelian realities, as well as play with image, time & permutations of phrase. Take the bit players, scatter & mix them in a variety of combinations. Take the words or phrases, do the same: "The American trailing cross the wounded galaxies con su medicina, William." / "Light verse of wounded galaxies at the dog I did"/"Suburban galaxies on the nod"/"Fade out muttering: "There's a lover on every corner cross the wounded galaxies—"

Burroughs could break further the sentimental myths of god, country, woman, as well as indulge some rather outrageous, freakish fantasies. His work with Konstantin Raudive's texts based on his experiments (behind the then–Iron Curtain) *Breakthrough—Voices from the Dead,* was, for Burroughs, a natural excursion. He was working with these texts extensively during his early years at the Naropa Institute. Raudive investigates the phenomena of intelligible phrases spoken in different languages by humans, appearing on blank tape run through a machine at high record level in an otherwise silent environment. In other words, with no apparent input. "The theory of a prerecorded universe is venerable, and many people have believed in it; especially those on the way up believe in their 'destiny' as they call it. The Arab conception of fate: *Mektoub,* it is written. It goes back to the Mayan control calendar; it is written. And what is it written on? No doubt some material similar to magnetic tape, but infinitely more sophisticated. This attempt to predict by controlling and control by predicting is very old. It can now be computerized."

The basic theme in *Soft Machine* and *Nova Express,* quintessential cut-up texts, is that the planet earth has been invaded by Venusians who want to impose conditions fatal to earth ("like the White man arriving in the New World") yet the book ends with the dissolution of both space and time. The invaders because they are spiritually empty use the gods of the white man, attempting to destroy the good guys ("Just as we destroyed the Indians by destroying their spiritual life . . . If you want to destroy people, destroy their gods. . . ."). Silence is a desirable state in *Nova Express.* Words, Burroughs has said, stand in the way of the nonbody experience. They are killer viruses. "It's time we thought about leaving the body behind."

William Seward Burroughs left his body behind August 2, 1997, in Lawrence, Kansas. The undertaker did a fine job for the open casket ceremony held the evening of the 6th at the Liberty Hall in Lawrence. William looked luminous, peaceful, his forehead somehow lifting toward the future, if such a thing is possible. He wore a tawny-colored velvet Moroccan vest dear old friend Brion Gysin, departed some years back now, had given him. His honorific florets from the French & American academies were pinned to his left jacket (an elegant one) lapel. His hat and signature cane rested on the fine cherry-wood coffin. Schubert's "Fantasie" from Sonata Opus no. 78 played as over a hundred folk—mostly friends from William's sixteen years in Lawrence—entered the Hall. The ceremony began as James Grauerholz's (Grauerholz: Burroughs's companion & secretary of many years) mother, Selda, sang "For All the Saints Who from Their Labours Rest" to piano accompaniment. David Ohle read aloud "Ulysses" by Alfred Lord Tennyson, one of William's favorite poems, and Tim Miller of the University of Kansas's religion department officiated, reminding us all that we too had to "pick up the torch" since the passing of William and Allen Ginsberg to maintain our basic human (& artistic) freedoms of lifestyle, independence, self-expression, and how precious they are and how precious these men were and their examples still are. Joujouka music, Ry Cooder's "Paris, Texas," Louis Armstrong's "St. Louis Blues" (with Bessie Smith), & other recordings were piped in. Various personal items—including a gun and a joint—were added into the casket before it was closed, presumed accoutrements for the difficult journey into the Western Lands—the place of the dead in Egyptian mythology that held such fascination for William (see his book *The Western Lands*, which describes this afterlife). The next morning close friends accompanied the elegant white hearse in a motorcade five hours to Belle Florette cemetary in St. Louis, Missouri, to the Burroughs's family plot presided over by a monument to William Seward Bur-roughs Senior of Adding Machine fame, a monument erected to "his genius" by his loyal workers & colleagues. Friends said farewell, making little speechs & personal statements at the gravesite. John Giorno gave a rousing invocation, James Grauerholz a humble, respectful eulogy. Patti Smith sang "Oh Dear What Can the Matter Be (Johnny's So Long at the Fair)". I read the last lines from *The Western Lands:*

The old writer couldn't write anymore because he had reached the end of words, the end of what can be done with words. And then? "British we are, British we stay." How long can one hang on in Gibraltar, with the tapestries where mustached riders with scimitars hunt tigers, the ivory balls one inside the other, bare seams showing, the long tearoom with mirrors on both sides and the tired fuchsia and rubber plants, the shops selling English marmalade and Fortnum & Mason's tea . . . clinging to their Rock like the rock apes, clinging always to less and less.

In Tangier the Parade Bar is closed. Shadows are falling on the Mountain.

"Hurry up, please. It's time."

The casket was placed in large metal outercasing by efficient men in hard hats, earth moving machines standing by, and was lowered into the good Missouri sod. But looking at the imposing box we knew he'd already escaped. Steven Lowe (friend and assistant to Burroughs) had said it a few moments before, paraphrasing William, "the point is not to live but to travel."

---

# WILLIAM CARLOS WILLIAMS

WILLIAM CARLOS WILLIAMS (1883–1963), physician and influential avant-garde American writer, was of two minds about the Beat writers. Practicing medicine in New Jersey, he met and corresponded with the young Allen Ginsberg in the 1940s, even including one of Ginsberg's letters to him in his epic poem *Paterson*. But Williams primarily thought of Allen as the son of Louis Ginsberg, a dedicated high school English teacher and respected local poet who published his polished traditional verses frequently in *The New York Times* and other periodicals. In the early 1950s, Williams was willing to write a letter of recommendation for Allen to present to Kenneth Rexroth when young Ginsberg moved from New York City to San Francisco, and a few years later Williams also agreed to write a now-famous introduction to the City Lights volume of *Howl and*

*Other Poems.* In his private correspondence, Williams wavered in his appreciation of Beat poetry, as in his letter to Joseph Renard on March 24, 1958. Perhaps Williams was baffled by the storm of publicity aroused by the publication of Ginsberg's and Kerouac's books. They attracted much wider attention than either his own writing or the work of his respected old friends such as the poets Wallace Stevens and Marianne Moore.

## Howl for Carl Solomon

When he was younger, and I was younger, I used to know Allen Ginsberg, a young poet living in Paterson, New Jersey, where he, son of a well-known poet, had been born and grew up. He was physically slight of build and mentally much disturbed by the life which he had encountered about him during those first years after the first world war as it was exhibited to him in and about New York City. He was always on the point of "going away," where it didn't seem to matter; he disturbed me, I never thought he'd live to grow up and write a book of poems. His ability to survive, travel, and go on writing astonishes me. That he has gone on developing and perfecting his art is no less amazing to me.

Now he turns up fifteen or twenty years later with an arresting poem. Literally he has, from all the evidence, been through hell. On the way he met a man named Carl Solomon with whom he shared among the teeth and excrement of this life something that cannot be described but in the words he has used to describe it. It is a howl of defeat. Not defeat at all for he has gone through defeat as if it were an ordinary experience, a trivial experience. Everyone in this life is defeated but a man, if he be a man, is not defeated.

It is the poet, Allen Ginsberg, who has gone, in his own body, through the horrifying experiences described from life in these pages. The wonder of the thing is not that he has survived but that he, from the very depths, has found a fellow whom he can love, a love he celebrates without looking aside in these poems. Say what you will, he proves to us, in spite of the most debasing experiences that life can offer a man, the spirit of love survives to ennoble our lives if we have the wit and the courage and the faith—and the art! to persist.

It is the belief in the art of poetry that has gone hand in hand with this man into his Golgotha, from that charnel house, similar in every way, to that of the Jews in the past war. But this is in our own country, our own fondest purlieus. We are blind and live our blind lives out in blindness. Poets are damned but they are not blind, they see with the eyes of the angels. This poet sees through and all around the horrors he partakes of in the very intimate details of his poem. He avoids nothing but experiences it to the hilt. He contains it. Claims it as his own—and, we believe, laughs at it and has the time and affrontery to love a fellow of his choice and record that love in a well-made poem.

Hold back the edges of your gowns, Ladies, we are going through hell.

## Letter to Joseph Renard, March 24, 1958

WILLIAM C. WILLIAMS M. D.
9 RIDGE ROAD
RUTHERFORD, N. J.

Mar. 24/58

Dear Joseph Renard:

Do you know any of the San Francisco gang who are making a name for themselves in the papers now-a-days? Your own poems are not an off shoot from that impetus - which is really illiterate though I should be strung up it were known.

You seem to have some feeling for the older disciplines of composition, of English compsition. Your poems are devoted to a cleanly and respectful address to the word. The individual word and a choice among the words for le mot juste or at least the well chosen word rather than an overall feeling possibly a jazzy refrain makes me pay attention to what you are doing.

You have a strong feeling for that kind of composition - which is perhaps somewhat old fashioned. It attracts me. Carry it on, it is #####
perhaps the future. I like it. God help you.

Sincerely yours

# TOM WOLFE

TOM WOLFE emerged as a practitioner of the New Journalism, a form of reportage applying novelistic techniques to factual material, with his first book, *The Kandy-Kolored Tangerine-Flake Streamline Baby* in 1965. Three years later, he published *The Electric Kool-Aid Acid Test,* a novelistic account of the writer Ken Kesey and his group of Merry Pranksters, dramatizing the prominent role they played in defining the new drug culture and the "hippie" movement in the United States. In his book, Wolfe said that "all the events, details, and dialogue I have recorded are either what I saw or heard myself or were told to me by people who were there themselves or were recorded on tapes or film or in writing." "What Do You Think of My Buddha?" is Wolfe's account of Kesey's first meeting at the end of the summer of 1962, in the front yard of his student bungalow on Perry Lane in Palo Alto, California, with the legendary Neal Cassady, who became the driver of the Merry Pranksters' bus "Further" on its cross-country odyssey and subsequent flight to Mexico. This chapter appears in the early pages of *The Electric Kool-Aid Acid Test.*

## What Do You Think of My Buddha?

Right after he finished *One Flew Over the Cuckoo's Nest,* Kesey sublet his cottage on Perry Lane and he and Faye went back up to Oregon. This was in June, 1961. He spent the summer working in his brother Chuck's creamery in Springfield to accumulate some money. Then he and Faye moved into a little house in Florence, Oregon, about 50 miles west of Springfield, near the ocean, in logging country. Kesey started gathering material for his second novel, *Sometimes a Great Notion,* which was about a logging family. He took to riding early in the morning and at night in the "crummies." These were pickup trucks that served as buses taking the loggers to and from the camps. At night he would hang around the bars where the loggers went. He was Low

Rent enough himself to talk to them. After about four months of that, they headed back to Perry Lane, where he was going to do the writing.

*One Flew Over the Cuckoo's Nest* was published in February, 1962, and it made his literary reputation immediately:

"A smashing achievement"—*Mark Schorer*

"A great new American novelist"—*Jack Kerouac*

"Powerful poetic realism"—*Life*

"An amazing first novel"—Boston *Traveler*

"This is a first novel of special worth"—New York *Herald Tribune*

"His storytelling is so effective, his style so impetuous, his grasp of characters so certain, that the reader is swept along . . . His is a large, robust talent, and he has written a large, robust book"—*Saturday Review*

And on the Lane—all this was a confirmation of everything they and Kesey had been doing. For one thing there was the old Drug Paranoia—the fear that this wild uncharted drug thing they were into would gradually . . . *rot your brain*. Well, here was the answer. Chief Broom!

And McMurphy . . . but of course. The current fantasy . . . he was a McMurphy figure who was trying to get them to move off their own snug-harbor dead center, out of the plump little game of being ersatz daring and ersatz alive, the middle-class intellectual's game, and move out to . . . Edge City . . . where it was scary, but people were whole people. And if drugs were what unlocked the doors and enabled you to do this thing and realize all this that was in you, then so let it be . . .

Not even on Perry Lane did people really seem to catch the thrust of the new book he was working on, *Sometimes a Great Notion*. It was about the head of a logging clan, Hank Stamper, who defies a labor union and thereby the whole community he lives in by continuing his logging operation through a strike. It was an unusual book. It was a novel in which the strikers are the villains and the strikebreaker is the hero. The style was experimental and sometimes difficult. And the main source of "mythic" reference was not Sophocles or even Sir James Frazer but . . . yes, Captain Marvel. The union leaders, the strikers, and the townspeople were the tarantulas, all joyfully taking their vow: "We shall wreak vengeance and abuse on all whose equals we are not . . . and 'will to equality' shall henceforth be the name for virtue; and against all that has power we want to raise our clamor!" Hank Stamper was, quite intentionally, Captain Marvel. Once known as . . . *Übermensch.* The current fantasy . . .

. . . on Perry Lane. Nighttime, the night he and Faye and the kids came back to Perry Lane from Oregon, and they pull up to the old cottage and there is a funny figure in the front yard, smiling and rolling his shoulders this way and that and jerking his hands out to this side and the other side as if there's a different drummer somewhere, different drummer, you understand, corked out of his gourd, in fact . . . and, well, Hi, Ken, yes, uh, well, you weren't *around,* exactly, you understand, doubledy-clutch, doubledy-clutch, and they told me you wouldn't mind, generosity knoweth no—ahem—yes, I had a '47 Pontiac myself once, held the road like a prehistoric bird, you understand . . . and, yes, Neal Cassady had turned up in the old cottage, like he had just run out of the pages of *On the Road,* and . . . what's next, Chief? Ah . . . many Day-Glo freaking curlicues—

All sorts of people began gathering around Perry Lane. Quite an . . . *underground* sensation it was, in Hip California. Kesey, Cassady, Larry McMurtry; two young writers, Ed McClanahan and Bob Stone; Chloe Scott the dancer, Roy Seburn the artist, Carl Lehmann-Haupt, Vic Lovell . . . and Richard Alpert himself . . . all sorts of people were in and out of there all the time, because they had heard about it, like the local beats—that term was still used—a bunch of kids from a pad called the Chateau, a wild-haired kid named Jerry Garcia and the Cadaverous Cowboy, Page Browning. Everybody was attracted by the strange high times they had heard about . . . the Lane's fabled Venison Chili, a Kesey dish made of venison stew laced with LSD, which you could consume and then go sprawl on the mattress in the fork of the great oak in the middle of the Lane at night and play pinball with the light show in the sky . . . Perry Lane.

And many puzzled souls looking in . . . At first they were captivated. The Lane was too good to be true. It was Walden Pond, only without any Thoreau misanthropes around. Instead, a community of

intelligent, very open, out-front people—out front was a term everybody was using—out-front people who cared deeply for one another,
and *shared* . . . in incredible ways, even, and were embarked on some
kind of . . . *well,* adventure in living. Christ, you could see them trying
to put their finger on it and . . . then . . . gradually figuring out there
was something here they weren't *in on* . . . Like the girl that afternoon
in somebody's cottage when Alpert came by. This was a year after he
started working with Timothy Leary. She had met Alpert a couple of
years before and he had been 100 percent the serious young clinical
psychologist—legions of rats and cats in cages with their brainstems,
corpora callosa and optic chiasmas sliced, spliced, diced, iced in the
name of the Scientific Method. Now Alpert was sitting on the floor in
Perry Lane in the old boho Lotus hunkerdown and exegeting very seriously about a baby crawling blindly about the room. Blindly? What do
you mean, blindly? That baby is a very sentient creature . . . That baby
sees the world with a completeness that you and I will never know
again. His doors of perception have not yet been closed. He still experiences the moment he lives in. The inevitable bullshit hasn't constipated his cerebral cortex yet. He still sees the world as it really is,
while we sit here, left with only a dim historical version of it manufactured for us by words and official bullshit, and so forth and so on, and
Alpert soars in Ouspenskyian loop-the-loops for baby while, as far as
this girl can make out, baby just bobbles, dribbles, lists and rocks
across the floor . . . But she was learning . . . that the world is sheerly
divided into those who have had *the experience* and those who have
not—those who have been through that door and—

It was a strange feeling for all these good souls to suddenly realize
that right here on woody thatchy little Perry Lane, amid the honey-
suckle and dragonflies and boughs and leaves and a thousand little
places where the sun peeped through, while straight plodding souls
from out of the Stanford eucalyptus tunnel plodded by straight down
the fairways on the golf course across the way—this amazing experiment in consciousness was going on, out on a frontier neither they nor
anybody else ever heard of before.

PALO ALTO, CALIF., July 21, 1963—and then one day the end of an era,
as the papers liked to put it. A developer bought most of Perry Lane

and was going to tear down the cottages and put up modern houses and the bulldozers were coming.

The papers turned up to write about the last night on Perry Lane, noble old Perry Lane, and had the old cliché at the ready, End of an Era, expecting to find some deep-thinking latter-day Thorstein Veblen intellectuals on hand with sonorous bitter statements about this machine civilization devouring its own past.

Instead, there were some kind of *nuts* out here. They were up in a tree lying on a mattress, all high as coons, and they kept offering everybody, all the reporters and photographers, some kind of venison chili, but there was something about the whole *setup*—

and when it came time for the sentimental bitter statement, well, instead, this big guy Kesey dragged a piano out of his house and they all set about axing the hell out of it and burning it up, calling it "the oldest living thing on Perry Lane," only they were giggling and yahooing about it,

high as coons, in some weird way, all of them, hard-grabbing off the stars, and it was hard as hell to make the End of an Era story come out right in the papers, with nothing but this kind of freaking Olsen & Johnson material to work with,

but they managed to go back with the story they came with, End of an Era, the cliché intact, if they could only blot out the cries in their ears of *Ve-ni-son Chi-li*—

—and none of them would have understood it, anyway, even if someone had told them what was happening. Kesey had already bought a new place in La Honda, California. He had already proposed to a dozen people on the Lane that they come with him, move the whole scene, the whole raggedymanic Era, off to . . .

Versailles, his Low Rent Versailles, over the mountain and through the woods, in La Honda, Calif. Where—where—in the lime :::::: light :::::: and the neon dust—

". . . a considerable new message . . . the blissful counterstroke . . ."

# PART TWO

# Panel Discussion with Women Writers

# of the Beat Generation (1996)

Were the women caught in the orbit of the Beat writers in the 1950s forced into the role of minor characters as the hapless victims of male chauvinism? Recent feminist critics of Beat Generation literature have argued as much, insisting that the relatively minor status of women writers in the Beat pantheon—the spotlight is usually on Kerouac, Ginsberg, and Burroughs instead of on di Prima, Johnson, and Waldman, for example—is an indication of the men's insensitivity to feminist concerns. Certainly the women writers cannot be charged with insensitivity or indifference to the men. Take, for example, Jack Kerouac: six of the women in his life have written books about him, including his first two wives, Edie Parker and Joan Haverty; his daughter, Jan Kerouac; his lovers Carolyn Cassady and Joyce Johnson; and his bibliographer, biographer, and editor Ann Charters.

Exposing the social hypocrisy rampant in the 1950s (what Burroughs called "punching a hole in the big lie"), the male Beat writers targeted their society's discriminatory treatment of homosexuals and African Americans, and railed against the destructive effects of capitalism and consumerism in everyday life. But in Beat literature, was the empowerment of women a burning issue? Not in the 1950s. Kerouac, Ginsberg, and Burroughs's heady endorsement of choice and change, and their headlong flight from domesticity and conventional heterosexual commitment, did not mean that they understood or supported women's feelings of entrapment in traditional gender roles. Rather, as feminist historian Barbara Ehrenreich understood in *The Hearts of Men: American Dreams and the Flight from Commitment* (1983), "In the Beats, the two strands of male protest—one directed against the white-collar work world and the other against the suburbanized family life that work was supposed to support—came together into the first all-out critique of American consumer culture."

If Kerouac, Ginsberg, and Burroughs were no more supportive of contemporary feminist movements than any other men of their generation, does it follow that their attitudes *resulted* in the relatively minor status of women Beat writers? I don't think so. In the 1950s, many American women were expressing their dissatisfaction with their traditional domestic roles and the consumer culture. The beginning of the second wave of feminism in the United States dates back to 1963, with the publication of Betty Friedan's *The Feminine Mystique,* the most influential book in radicalizing American women readers. Yet the 1950s should be seen as transitional years, when gifted women writers began to break away from their conventional backgrounds to enter an unprecedented period of artistic fulfillment.

Although none of the women writers associated with the Beats achieved a major literary career, many of them wrote books that continue to be relevant to contemporary readers because they anticipated the changes to come for women in our society. In the 1950s and 1960s a new generation of women writers came of age. They included Elizabeth Bishop, Sylvia Plath, and Anne Sexton, who created poetry that revealed astonishing details about their emotional lives. In 1953 Adrienne Rich won the Yale Younger Poets award, and she went on in her later books to become our foremost feminist poet. In this period American fiction writers and playwrights expressed their sense of social injustice in such enduring works as Tillie Olsen's *Tell Me a Riddle* (written in the 1950s, published in 1961), Grace Paley's *The Little Disturbances of Man* (1959), and Lorraine Hansberry's *A Raisin in the Sun* (1959). Rachel Carson sparked the conservationist movement with her best-selling books *The Sea Around Us* (1951), *The Edge of the Sea* (1955), and *Silent Spring* (1961).

Fifty years ago, most American women like myself were raised in traditional two-parent families, with fathers who considered themselves breadwinners, and mothers and grandmothers who defined themselves primarily as homemakers. It is hardly surprising that most of us who fell in love with Beat writers were conditioned to accept a traditional caretaking role, even if we chose to break away from home before marriage and rebel against our parents' ideas of what was good for us. When Joan Burroughs, Joyce Johnson, Eileen Kaufman, and I made the decision to live independently, we took jobs and paid the rent on our own apartments, but we also found it natural to offer support to writers such as William S. Burroughs, Jack Kerouac, Bob Kaufman, and fledging writers like Samuel Charters. It was in our nature to nurture. We knew that by providing a place for our lovers to stay, we often enabled them to create their poetry and fiction. We wouldn't accept the alternative—living at home and losing our independence. Why should they?

But we women wanted marriage too. Our sexual freedom came at a high price in the 1950s, when most men respected a woman only if she was somebody's wife. We knew the score. Although we were in rebellion against what we considered our second-class status in American society, we still respected marriage. Ironically, at the time we thought it was the final proof of our independence. A wedding ring was a visible sign to an uncaring world that we weren't immature or irresponsible or unstable, that we had accomplished something of value on our own.

There were countless educated women like us throughout the United States in the 1950s, each of us a rebel with her own personal cause against conventional gender roles. On November 27, 1957, the staff writer "Flavia" in a "Voice Feminine" column in *The Village Voice* described the typical young Greenwich Village "chick," the backbone of the new Bohemia:

> The present "chick" is keeper of the Pad. By definition, she has her own apartment, a job or income of some sort, and is ready to feed and house her males on short notice. The intellectual variety comes equipped with some college background and a rigid set of rules: she will have no truck with professional men; finds sensitive manual workers O.K., and saves her soul for the creative crew who are beating their brains out "because everything's so beautiful, wild, mad, and gone."
>
> Though her manner of living gives no clues, this "chick" is a girl with marriage on her mind. . . . Like many other Villagers, the "chick" works in fields connected with the arts—preferably ones in which she can meet itinerant actors, artists, or writers whose marital suitability depends on the amount of success, notoriety, or potential talent they have to offer. In return, the "chick" accepts the role of housekeeper, mistress, and nurse. While her "hip" lad is around, she will be a faithful drudge, an earnest listener, and often his sole economic support. From the moment she gets back to the Pad until she leaves for work the following day, she's demonstrating what a great wife she'd be. She understands all—and

what's more, she's younger, prettier, and stronger than his mother. Accordingly, where could he find a better mate, she thinks. . . .

Flavia concluded that "until economic fatigue or psychoanalysis sets in, the 'chick' in her Pad will remain 'nowhere.' But save your sympathy—she's just where she wants to be."

The *Voice* columnist was being facetious, but the poet Denise Levertov, whose book *Here and Now* (1957) was number six in the City Lights Pocket Poets series (after Ginsberg's *Howl* and Marie Ponsot's *True Minds*), was in basic agreement. Levertov observed that in the 1950s "women were, by and large, either muses or servants" to the men in their lives. We women understood the irony implicit in our roles as so-called minor characters. Our traditional backgrounds prepared us for the compliant silence expected of us; it was not "put up or shut up" so much as "put out *and* shut up." As Diane di Prima understood in *Dinners and Nightmares* (1961), her account of her early years as a Bohemian, it was "so fucking uncool to talk about" her private grievance that the men who moved into her apartment always took for granted that, in addition to her writing, she was the only one responsible for the "women's work" of cooking, cleaning, and caring for the children.

Focusing on the darker, destructive impulses in the human psyche, Kerouac (in *Maggie Cassidy, The Subterraneans,* and *Tristessa*) and Ginsberg (in "Kaddish") portrayed women as irresistible, inconstant temptresses or the fragile, unstable victims of society. Those women of independent spirit in the Beat Generation who became writers were survivors, experiencing firsthand the huge personal cost of gender biases, and dramatizing their difficult, complex journeys to self-discovery in their poetry, novels, and memoirs. At their best, their works "extend and enliven the language," to use the criteria of literary excellence formulated in 1958 by LeRoi Jones in his response to Norman Podhoretz's attack on Beat writing in *Partisan Review.* Disregarding the achievement of women writers was so endemic at the time that when Jones reeled off a list of the poets whom the Beats were rebelling against in his letter to *Partisan Review,* he named thirteen men and only one woman (Elizabeth Bishop). The Beat women shared the men's sense of rebellion against mainstream culture, but most women buried their feelings about gender issues under what they considered their more pressing grievances against society. As Joyce Johnson understood,

> In the bland and sinister 1950s there were thousands like me—women as well as men—young people with longings we couldn't yet articulate bottled up inside us. Ginsberg and Kerouac would give powerful, irresistible voices to these subversive longings; they'd release us from our weirdness, our isolation, tell us we were not alone.

In the 1950s the women Beat writers might not have shared the spotlight with the men in the glare of publicity on the front lines of the battle, but behind the scenes they were an integral part of the Beat Generation and—as girlfriends, wives, and mothers—its primary support. The critic Amy L. Friedman pointed out that the women writers' "extensive publishing and educational work has put into practice much of what was best about Beat ideas. In their sustained literary careers, which grew out of their participation in the Beat movement, the women writers also undermine the celebrated Beat myth of the self-destructive artist."

On November 2, 1996, a panel of so-called Beat chicks assembled at the San Francisco Book Festival to celebrate the publication of Brenda Knight's anthology *Women of the Beat Generation*, issued by the Conari Press in Berkeley. The participants included Carolyn Cassady, Joyce Johnson, Hettie Jones, Eileen Kaufman, Joanna McClure, and me, serving as moderator. (The poet Lenore Kandel was also on the panel, but, describing herself as "willful," she has withheld her remarks. This is regrettable, since Kandel was one of the few women Beat writers who found herself, like Ginsberg, Kerouac, and Burroughs, in a storm of controversy in 1967 after her small-press pamphlet of poems *The Love Book* was challenged in a San Francisco court as obscene and pornographic.) In the course of an hour and a half, we women writers of the Beat Generation gave our opinions about several controversial topics, including those introduced by members of the sizable standing-room-only audience drawn to the event.

## Women of the Beat Generation Panel
## San Francisco Book Festival
## November 2, 1996

Moderator: Ann Charters
Participants: Carolyn Cassady
Joyce Johnson
Hettie Jones
Eileen Kaufman
Joanna McClure

ANN CHARTERS: My first question is suggested by yesterday's review of Brenda Knight's anthology *Women of the Beat Generation* in the *San Francisco Chronicle*. It was a very favorable review, but it left me feeling disconcerted in its assumption that the women writers of the Beat Generation had been silenced, presumably until now; that they were victims, and that only now are we getting to hear their stories. So what I would like to know, from each of the members of the panel, is if you consider yourselves a victim as described in the *Chronicle* article in Friday's paper?

JOYCE JOHNSON: No, I Don't consider myself a victim. I consider my years with the Beat Generation the really formative experience of my life, my real education. I was very young. The men whom I knew who were my friends, people like Allen and Jack, were considerably older. I was just beginning to write myself, they had ten or fifteen years ahead of me. I learned a lot, I listened, I looked. It gave me great material for the memoir I would later write. And I would also like to say it was a very, very different time and the attitudes towards women throughout the whole culture were absolutely terrible. I wanted the life of an outlaw rather than the kind of life my mother had had. In intellectual circles, literary circles, there was tremendous actually hatred of what Elizabeth Hardwick called, in an essay she wrote at the time, "hatred of the culture hungry women." I don't know if any of you read Anatole Broyard's [Greenwich Village] memoir [*Kafka Was the Rage* (1993)], but the contempt for women at the time just permeates that book. He talks about sensitive girls who wouldn't take off their intellects like negligees they refused to remove. That was the attitude and in a sense the Beats were more generous than that. Kerouac was always very interested in my writing, very encouraging, gave me a lot of advice. He felt I should go on the road. He wanted to take me on the road with him to Mexico but it never happened, which is one of the great regrets of my life. But no, I don't consider myself a victim.

ANN CHARTERS: Thank you. Carolyn, would you?

CAROLYN CASSADY: No, I don't either. I always felt I had a choice. If I didn't like it I could leave it. I think everyone has a choice.

HETTIE JONES: Not only do I not consider myself a victim, but I *never* considered myself a victim from the time I was conscious, so I grew up knowing that I was going to leave home, knowing that I was going to leave the fate that was intended for me and I just had to figure out how to get out of it. That wasn't until I landed downtown in Greenwich Village and found myself in what I thought was adequate company. As I've mentioned in speeches I've made, I think it was a question that strong women require strong men or at least noisy ones. It wasn't until I found myself there among these people that I could make as much noise as I wanted, and no one gave a shit.

EILEEN KAUFMAN: No, I never considered myself a victim. I considered myself quite fortunate to sit at a poet's feet that was a genius that Bob Kaufman was.

JOANNA MCCLURE: I concur with the different things that have been said here. There was never a feeling of being a victim—and there was this sense of actually waiting to get out of where I was and what I saw around me. Nobody told me there was more to the world than Tucson, Arizona, but something in me sensed more and was waiting, so when Michael came and brought me that larger world—Bartok, Yeats, Ezra Pound—I thought "this is just where I belong." I fit very well into your category of strong women choosing men who spoke out. At one time someone said of Fidel Castro— had the United States not existed, he would have created it to rebel against. Michael was what I needed, and I always felt that if he had not come along I would have invented him in order to liberate me from Tucson.

ANN CHARTERS: I think we have an answer to the question of victimization. It could very well be that the *Chronicle* reviewer hadn't read the anthology thoroughly and had just bundled it into the currently fashionable category of women's survivor literature. My next question is whether or not the members of our panel feel comfortable being identified as a Beat writer. Remember the title of the anthology is *Women of the Beat Generation*. But before we proceed, let me say that I am very sorry that the celebration of this book today does not include the presence of the other women who are included in it. I'm thinking, of course, of Jan Kerouac, whose recent death saddens us all, and who definitely would be here today, talking as well as reading from her work. Others who could not come today are Mary Fabilli (just a few names), Mary Norbert Korte, and Brenda Frazer, among many others. And they also are identified in this book as Beat Generation writers. So my question to the women here today is: Do you feel comfortable being identified as a Beat Generation writer, or would you like to get rid of the tag altogether?

JOYCE JOHNSON: I don't feel comfortable being categorized in that way. Although I have written about the Beat Generation, I don't consider myself a Beat Generation writer. I have my own aesthetic. I've done very different kinds of writing, and I'm *my* kind of writer.

CAROLYN CASSADY: I don't even know what the Beat Generation is. But I've always been against putting people in boxes and cubbyholes and becoming stereotyped. The individual qualities of each person are lost, I find, and I certainly don't fit in whatever it is.

HETTIE JONES: I used to complain that the Beat Generation was really a misnomer because at one point everyone identified with it could fit into my living room and I didn't think a whole generation could fit into my living room. I think no matter how much you resist labeling you are going to be somehow, just for purposes of literary history, put somewhere at some time. I don't care particularly how people want to remember me as long as the truth of my existence on this planet is somehow adhered to in some fashion. I've dealt so much more—rather than with the issues that define the Beat Generation I think, whatever those issues are—but I've dealt so much more with the issues of race in America and multiplicity of our races and ideas that I somehow find myself more identified as that. These days I'm identified as my children's mother. It's not bad: the better they get, the better I feel. Even though I have resisted "Beat," I feel it's somewhat inevitable and now that there's a book out I don't know what we're going to do to deny it.

EILEEN KAUFMAN: Well, I felt at home with the Beat Generation; I felt at home with it. I felt at home in Paris with the Bohemians, I felt at home.

JOANNA McCLURE: I don't mind being of the Beat Generation because I really thought everything they were searching for was interesting, vital, and a springboard to new freedoms. Then it wasn't a generation, it was my friends in the living room with whom I strongly identified. Once I remember going to a houseboat party in Sausalito, and as I was climbing up the ladder somebody at the top said, "What are you beatniks doing here with us old Bohemians?" So there were generational titles I became familiar with. I didn't mind being associated with the Beats in the fifties, or the hippies in the sixties. When we moved into the Haight from New York, it was because it had a good school for our daughter and was a quiet neighborhood with a fair amount of open space with trees. It even had a "dry goods" store on the corner of Haight and Ashbury. Quite an old-fashioned neighborhood. Then suddenly the hippie generation erupted around us. Michael always had a taste for where new things were happening and I thought it was interesting. I loved the hippie generation. I also loved being part of the ecology movement in the seventies. All those years are part of who I am, so I don't mind labels at all.

ANN CHARTERS: Good, because that's the next question. What do each of the panelists think of when she thinks of the term "Beat Generation"? How do you define it? I know that in my own case, it pretty much depends on what I am interested in writing about, and where I happen to be when I am talking to people about the Beat writers. If I'm lecturing to a group in Italy, for example, I've found that they are primarily interested in Kerouac because his books about his road experience give them the possibility of participating in something that they regard as quintessentially American—going on the road. Italian readers tell me that they wouldn't have known what it felt like without Jack's writing. Others, for example, in France, say that Allen Ginsberg is the most representative Beat writer, and that the epitome of Beat is Allen Ginsberg. The Czechs and Japanese tell me this too. They say that the freedom, the political freedom, that Ginsberg writes about, is how they define Beat. Readers of Beat literature in France tell me something else. They feel that it is Ginsberg's idea of expanding consciousness that is Beat; they are more philosophical and less political. Gary Snyder and the ecology movement is the topic that many of the students at my campus, the University of Connecticut in Storrs, want to talk about when we talk about the Beats. So I'm curious—what do the women who were *there* feel is the essence of Beat?

JOYCE JOHNSON: I think categories are dangerous and once you begin to look at people in terms of categories you lose a lot of nuance. Any good writer, any *really* good writer knows that human nature is infinitely varied and that categories don't mean very much. When I hear "Beat Generation" I actually think of it rather narrowly. I think of Jack and Allen and Gregory Corso and William Burroughs and Herbert Hunke, who invented the term in the first place, and John Clellon Holmes, who wrote about it in that famous article. It began as a code word among friends and then it got very, very widely disseminated with the publication of *On the Road* and progressively lost a lot of its specific meaning; it became debased into "Beatnik," which was almost a contemptuous term. I witnessed that change and it was very distressing. It was certainly terribly distressing to Kerouac.

CAROLYN CASSADY: I agree, but also I agree with Lawrence Ferlinghetti, who said Allen Ginsberg invented the Beat Generation and when I think of it I mainly think of Allen's interests, but I never recognized it in either Neal or Jack, who couldn't care less. I think Jack was forced into it by Allen, dragged into it, but he was never really sympathetic, certainly not with the political action. Neither Neal nor Jack was an activist. They were apolitical, so that part of the whole picture was alien to them. Again I don't know what it is really.

HETTIE JONES: Thinking about it now seems to me a very different thing from thinking about it then. I remember how I thought about it then; I refused to be labeled. Life was much messier than that, and what I liked about what came to me as Beat was the messiness of it. It was just the anithesis of the life of order, the American order at that time, that really belied its own existence. I thought being part of something that was going to erupt, that was going to change people's minds, no matter what you called it, was going to eventually work out in a way that [resulted] in a better life for all of us women. I think I always took the part of women. I'm called Mother Jones in this book.

EILEEN KAUFMAN: The way I see Beat is as it pertains to Beatitude and I have certain feelings about Beatitude.

JOANNA McCLURE: Well, it's true, I guess it depends whether you are thinking of Beatitude or "Beatnik." "Beatnik" was often pejorative, and there was a great deal of unpleasant press around "Beatnik" when it first began. There was an article in *Life* magazine ["Beats: Sad but Noisy Rebels" or "The Only Rebellion Around," by Paul O'Neil, *Life,* November 30, 1959] that pictured Michael and Philip Whalen and Philip Lamantia and Allen Ginsberg as really low-life sycophants, taking drugs and living off their mothers, wives or whomever—the worst imaginable people. It was so defamatory that I couldn't believe it. Michael thought we might be rounded up and put in prison camps for being Beatniks. It was the McCarthy era, and we had reason to fear the paranoia taking over the country. We almost went to live in Mexico. On the other hand my feeling about the movement was that it was Beatific. Those artists and poets are now honored in the show of "The Beat Generation," at the DeYoung museum. Back then they were friends who lived around us on Fillmore Street. Fillmore Street between California and Jackson had low-rent flats where artists and medical interns lived. It was the buffer zone between the blacks on Lower Fillmore and the very rich on upper Fillmore. Billy and Joan Jahrmarkt opened the Batman Gallery, which was a center for all of us—Jay DeFeo, Bruce Conner, Wally Berman, and others—the place where Michael's first play, "The Feast," was acted out by all his friends. It was Shirley Berman and I trading baby sitting, Jay DeFeo painting the Rose downstairs and baby-sitting our daughter Jane an hour a day. It was Bob LaVigne making Michael up for his book photograph, Kirby Doyle reading us snatches of his novel, Lawrence Jordan showing us Eisenstein movies on a sheet in our Fillmore street flat—a rich mix of artists, women, and children. We were a lively group of creators until the *Life* magazine article labeled us and we had to live through some unpleasant months of feeling uncomfortable with that label and its implications. I enjoyed the new art, the new ideas, and forging my own separate existence as a new mother, wife, and student who was fascinated by early childhood development.

ANN CHARTERS: Okay, more questions then, and this one is a personal one. It took a long time for Brenda Knight to compile a book called

*Women of the Beat Generation*. Fifty years to be exact, since Jack and Allen and Neal and Bill Burroughs were gathering in Joan Vollmer's apartment near Columbia University. Could you please respond to the question: How does it feel to be associated with a generation primarily defined by male authors?

JOYCE JOHNSON: I feel that I have had a life as a writer. My real life as a writer began many years after the Beat Generation. As I said before, at the time that I was just beginning to write I was aged twenty-one years old. Jack and Allen were men in their thirties who had been writing for years and years, so of course they were way ahead of me then. As I said before, I do not consider myself a Beat Generation writer.

CAROLYN CASSADY: I don't relate to that question.

HETTIE JONES: I think I have to agree with that entirely, because my life as writer also began after that particular time and I think it's very funny, the first conference at NYU on the Beats, the panel that I was on with Joyce was titled "Women *and* the Beats," so that we weren't part of it at all, but [since] then this metamorphosis has happened, so by the time I got the letter from Conari Press asking to be a part of this book, the letter was addressed to: "Dear Beat Woman." But never, I don't think women are *ever* going to be identified as the Beats, we're all going to be qualified, we're just not going to be considered a Beat writer. So just give up, right now.

EILEEN KAUFMAN: Well, the thing is, I didn't begin to write about my experiences at that time. I began to write it in 1973 *after* the experiences at that time. I had quite a little leeway at that point and I never thought my book might be published as a book but as a talking book from 1973 on.

JOANNA McCLURE: I still don't think of myself as a Beat woman. I think it's amusing and interesting and am pleased with the association I had in the past, but the writing I did then is the same as the writing I've continued to do all through the years and it hasn't changed greatly. So although I'm pleased with past associations, I don't feel defined by them.

ANN CHARTERS: Before I ask if there are any questions from the members of the audience, is there anything that anyone on the panel would like to say, any comment, any prepared speech, any polemic, whatever. Here's your chance before the questions.

HETTIE JONES: I just want to talk about my mother's response to that *Life* magazine article. My mother saved a letter that I wrote to her, because—obviously, I can't remember this, but she must have called up and said, "Oh, my God, what are you doing?"—and I wrote her this irate letter saying that I was entirely clean, that I kept my child entirely clean. I reread the letter about a month ago and I just laughed and laughed at my response, thinking, "Boy, I was really overreacting." But I think we were all, just to make a comment on what Joanna said, we were all so *offended* by the idea that we were portrayed as animals, that I was . . .

JOANNA McCLURE: Drug addicted animals.

HETTIE JONES: Drug addicted animals.

JOYCE JOHNSON: With cockroaches.

HETTIE JONES: Well, it was partly true. But I think we were so appalled at the idea that we had been labeled, when we were really a *literary* movement in a lot of ways, and the talk centered around—in all those parties where the Beat Generation fit in my living room—the talk centered around how to change, how to wake up the American consciousness through a new arts and letters. The magazine that I published with my then husband, LeRoi Jones, was called "a new consciousness." Its subtitle was "a new consciousness in arts and letters," and that's what we were trying to do. I think that suddenly we got on, I think it was Jack, got on television, and we were seen as subversive; "nik" on "Beatnik" came from *Sputnik*, so that we were just put square with the enemy. I think America was looking for a subversive culture at the time, or young Americans were, because pretty soon the parties got so big that the whole generation couldn't fit in my living room.

CAROLYN CASSADY: I was going to add to the *Life* magazine article, what it did for me. I had kept the fact that Neal was in San Quentin prison both from my parents and my children, and good old *Life* magazine came out and announced it, and my father read every word in *Life* magazine. They didn't actually tell me they had read it or knew, until my sister told me they had, and so I asked my mother if she'd like to know any more and all she wanted to know was: is it true? And then she told me it would have been far better if Neal had killed every one of his children rather than disgrace them. If you want to get a period thing here, "death before dishonor" was still very, very with it. So it wasn't always the best thing, that article.

JOANNA McCLURE: That was actually the attitude of my family to the article too. It was the exact mindset I had left behind. The country at that time had many false fears, fears that said the enemy was out there. Anyone who was not mainstream was dangerous. When my family finally talked to me about the article around a month later, I said, "Yes, wasn't it upsetting?" And my mother said, "What do you mean upsetting? Your aunt Leta said they couldn't publish it unless it was true."

JOYCE JOHNSON: I think there were terrible, terrible rifts between the women who got involved with the Beats and their parents. The older generation just didn't understand. My parents, for example, were very gentle, very timid people. They had sort of been zapped by the Depression, they didn't want . . . they were afraid of change, they were afraid of being different, and so anything like the Beats was just horrific as far as they were concerned. I would see them once in a while, but I had very little relationship with them during that period. I think that's true that a lot of us just did go through these terrible rifts, and many of these rifts never really got repaired.

CAROLYN CASSADY: Well, my brother too, he had . . . well, I was subsequently disowned from the family after my parents found out about it. My brother had several children and I think one of them got busted for marijuana and the other one got a girl pregnant or something and he said it was all my fault. And my niece said, "Well, how well do your children know Aunt Carolyn?" and he said, "Oh, they never met."

ANN CHARTERS: Now let's open the discussion up for questions from the audience.

QUESTIONER 1: Could you define, without making any category, the word "Beatitude"?

ANN CHARTERS: I'll repeat the question. I think you mean it for Eileen Kaufman. Could you define "Beatitude," please?

EILEEN KAUFMAN: I define it the way it is in the Bible. You have to. Poetry.

QUESTIONER 2: It appears in the writing of the men Beats that drugs, acid, played a very major role in their creativity and camaraderie. Could you comment on that, any or all of you?

ANN CHARTERS: Okay, what part do you feel acid, the drug LSD, played in the creativity . . . or drugs, can we just say drugs or do you want it to be acid? Okay, drugs. There is a difference, a powerful one. What effect do you think drugs played in the creativity and camaraderie of the males in the movement?

JOYCE JOHNSON: I think the main drug was alcohol.

CAROLYN CASSADY: Well, I think they were all destructive, actually. The people I knew before and after, there was a definite decline, at least it seems to me.

HETTIE JONES: I think it was mostly experimental, and I think you have to understand that there is a difference between drug taking now as when you find it as a way of life, and it certainly wasn't like that. If you're talking about creativity, as people simply wanting to expand their consciousness, this wasn't particularly a Beat Generation thing. Aldous Huxley, other people, had done this before, a lot of writers, nineteenth-century writers. You can go way, way back; you can go back to the Greeks. People were always trying to expand their consciousness and write it down or do something about it.

EILEEN KAUFMAN: I don't know what to tell you. If I only stopped . . . I can't . . .

JOANNA McCLURE: A little too much to tell?

EILEEN KAUFMAN: I think if you could drop acid, when it was legal . . . had to be legal. I think if you had those trips and you came down the mountain on the other side, I think it was okay. But some people had the worst acid trips because they didn't know how often it burnt—or how to use it for creativity.

JOANNA McCLURE: I was interested in the people around me who were taking drugs for mind expansion and soul exploration purposes. It was not party time when they took hallucinogenic drugs. Whether it helped or hindered their creativity I have no idea. I was curious and always thought that I would like drugs. But I tried each one in turn, and sadly found out I just didn't like any. I had read a book about drugs by Aleister Crowley—all about the beauties and excitements of cocaine—and decided that surely that would be my drug of choice. When I first tried it, and the two following times, I was disappointed to find it made my nose raw, my throat sore, and everything around me too bright and too loud. I gave up then. Later I saw something on a bathroom wall that said: "Reality is a crutch for people who can't take drugs." And I laughed and knew it described me.

ANN CHARTERS: Another question. Yes?

QUESTIONER 3: When people think of the family of the men of the Beats, it's usually each other as buddies. About a year ago, *The New York Times* ran a photo essay of the children of Beats, so I was wondering if any of you could comment on being artists and mothers and what your children may have learned coming from this particular generation. Some of you may have children who are middle-aged now, so it's very interesting to find out if you have particular reflections.

ANN CHARTERS: I think you are referring to the *New York Times* article written by Daniel Pinchbeck, who is Joyce's son, on the children of the Beats. How do the women on the panel respond to the Beat experience as giving something to their children? Is that a way to phrase it?

QUESTIONER 3: You probably can't do the subject justice here.

ANN CHARTERS: We'll do our best. Joyce?

JOYCE JOHNSON: Daniel was always very, very, very interested in stories, stories of the old days. He started reading everything that I had in the house written by Beats. When he was in his teens he started a literary magazine of his own when he was in high school. He and some friends have another literary magazine called *Open City* now that they are working on. He always had this idea that writers should know each other, be involved with each other, publish each other's work. That whole idea has really energized his career. He himself writes fiction and nonfiction and poetry, so it sort of started him on a literary life.

CAROLYN CASSADY: All three of my children and one of my grandchildren are here today, so maybe you'd like to ask them.

HETTIE JONES: Do they want to answer?

CAROLYN CASSADY: Some journalist said that John's name, John Allen Cassady, there's the Beat Generation in one phrase. He's named for Jack and Allen.

JOHN CASSADY: Joyce, I wanted to say how much I enjoyed meeting your son when he interviewed me for that *New York Times* article. He was very charming. I think it came out a little negative though. I think it was probably the editors.

JOYCE JOHNSON: A lot of it was the editing.

JOHN CASSADY: I figured as much because he was very nice. He took down all the funny stories and stuff, at least that I said, but none of *those* showed up. It was just like, how it came out is like everybody picked it over. It sounded to me like it was the worst thing in the world to be brought up by these people. I think they just edited all the good stuff out.

JOYCE JOHNSON: They cut it radically, by about fifty percent, unfortunately. [The original article is in this anthology.]

JOHN CASSADY: I was disappointed when I read it, because I think he did a good job. A lot of it was negative, but it was interesting that it was even in there at all, because nobody followed the families after that. So that was kind of a score to get into the paper. Other than that, it was a pleasure meeting your son. It was a very nice time. That's about all I've got to say. Do any of you? Jami? Cathy? I had a great time. It wasn't negative at all.

CATHY CASSADY: I would say that it was not a childhood that I would recommend to everybody, but it was definitely interesting. It's not true that you're doomed to drugs and crime to be brought up by Beat people. There is life after Beat.

HETTIE JONES: One of my daughters was in that article, the other said she just didn't want to be identified this way. My children are black and, brought up at that time, they felt that their influences were far more the civil rights revolution that was going on at the time, and that their political purpose was defined for them more by what was going on in a wider political sense. I think Lisa said, "We didn't have a bad time." I don't know whether she said she wasn't dirty or not. She also didn't have a negative attitude about it, you know, there is life afterward. A friend of mine who was also raising children at the time, Martha King, who is not mentioned here, said that the way the article was edited really put a bad light on "permissive" child rearing. That is, if you bring a child into a situation where there is a kind of looseness, what are you dooming them to? Look at this failure, this, that, and the other thing. Again it was the tightening of the reins of the establishment on a way to live with openness, just the same kind of reaction we see in a lot of things now.

EILEEN KAUFMAN: One good thing came out of that article. My son found the people who had taken him around the world, whom we knew overseas. They had been looking for him for years, so thank you for that. I think that since I traveled a lot and Bob wasn't with us at the time, that I did as best a job as I could raising Parker, our son. Travel broadens one, they say. I think twenty-three countries was enough for him and we found people, extended family really, and it was just a good time to do these things. I think our timing was pretty good.

JOANNA McCLURE: Actually, I was torn as a mother, but it was partly because I was shaken and unsure of my mothering ability. I went into parent education because I got busy reading all of the early childhood books. I was interested in the permissive ideas of A. S. Neal and Summerhill because "freedom" was threaded through everything I wanted in *my* life, so of course I wanted it for my daughter also—so she was raised permissively, at least until adolescence. We're a little embarrassed now that she's a successful pediatrician married to a family practice doctor with two fine boys. But she does speak fondly of her childhood and honors her odd and sometimes outrageous upbringing.

ANN CHARTERS: Another question? Yes?

QUESTIONER 4: I think if someone finds a way or a group to break free from the predominant, robotic conditioning we experience, it is a beautiful process of liberation. I think that you had a remarkable experience and I wish I was there with you. Once the dam breaks, it's like a sense of freedom, and you become a teacher teaching how to be more free in a society or culture that has become very unfree.

QUESTIONER 5: But is that how you really felt, free, with this group of men? Did you really feel like you were partaking in what they were experiencing, this freedom of movement and freedom of being able to do the drugs? Everything I've read has made me feel like the women were really confined. There was a lot of, especially with Carolyn, it just seemed like the readings were Neal doing this and Neal doing that and Carolyn not getting really what she needed as far as love and a husband.

ANN CHARTERS: Good question, I'll repeat it for those on this side who didn't hear it. Was there a shared sense of freedom within the relationships or were the women on this panel not free as women of the fifties while their husbands did experience the breaking of the dam, the freedom of the new lifestyle? Shall we just start with the person you asked, Carolyn?

CAROLYN CASSADY: I'm all for freedom but not when it becomes license and then chaos. As I said, I always felt I had a choice and I was doing what I wanted to do. I would have liked it better if Neal's job on the railroad had been all year round so I could have saved money and done more painting and gardening and things. I always thought my mother had it really right. My father [a doctor] loved what he was doing and he loved his job. She got this wonderful house she could decorate; she could do anything she wanted all day. You know, I thought, "That's heaven." So I figured her life was not quite like mine. Anyway, I didn't have to stay with it if I didn't like it. It was fine. Who gets everything they want? You're certainly not going to get it from somebody else. You're going to have to find it in yourself.

HETTIE JONES: I want to respond to that too, because I just wanted to do everything and I felt that even though I was having children and doing the things that my mother was doing, I had completely, in a way, reversed the context. Unlike Carolyn, I didn't care what my house looked like. I had a job. I was the first woman I had ever known who was completely independent. I was always self-supporting even when I was married. I did all the things I wanted. In my twenties I burned the candle at both ends. I felt I had gone as far as a woman could go at that time, other than casting off my sex, which I didn't want to do.

JOYCE JOHNSON: I think what a lot of younger women don't understand is that at that time, in the late fifties, it was an enormous thing for a young woman who wasn't married to leave home, support herself, have her own apartment, have a sex life. This was before the pill, when having sex was like Russian roulette, really. It wasn't the moment *then* to try to transform relationships with men. Just to get your foot out the door into the world as an independent person was just such an enormous thing. I'm sorry I never got to go down to Mexico with Jack. It wasn't a time when women really could go on the road, in the sense that Jack and Neal went on the road as male travelers. We women could not do that then. Our experience for most of the women of my generation was quite limited. I went to a college reunion of my Barnard College class, class of 1955, and there were all these women who had become matrons. And we were saying, "What do you do?" The women said, "I live in Scarsdale." "Well, what do you do?" "I have a son in Harvard." I really felt that I had escaped all that. I had had my own life, whatever it was.

I didn't do everything; I didn't travel around the world, but I had made my own decisions, and my own choices and taken my own risks.

JOANNA McCLURE: I also made my own decisions and choices and took my own risks. The men then did talk and act like chauvinists, but we were strong independent women. As a matter of fact I once moderated a panel of "women in Kerouac's life." I introduced myself and said that since all moderators have a viewpoint, I would like to announce mine upfront. It was "just because you were married to a male chauvinist didn't mean you needed to be downtrodden." Carolyn Cassady said at that conference, "Oh, I had the best of all worlds—two men I really liked." I did feel Michael and I were equal partners, and that I did battle for that equality. We changed our relationship many times during the thirty-three years we were together. I didn't join the women's movement, but I did my personal part in creating freedom for myself.

ANN CHARTERS: Time for one more question. . . .

QUESTIONER 6: A change of pace, I wanted to ask about the influence of Buddhism and spirituality in the period. In particular, I remember *The Dharma Bums*, about how everybody went traipsing over to the houseboat in Sausalito to see what's his face . . . Alan Watts. Of course Ginsberg became more or less of a Hindu and Snyder became a very good Buddhist, but I think how sad it was was for Kerouac in *The Dharma Bums*, that he didn't really have a teacher, didn't really find a way of life. The good teachers didn't come until the sixties. Can you tell us anyway, anything, especially you, Joyce, about what that influence was?

ANN CHARTERS: This was a question, I'll repeat it briefly, about Buddhism and the influence of Buddhism.

QUESTIONER 6: . . . and spirituality . . .

ANN CHARTERS: And spirituality—who will speak to this topic, our last topic?

JOYCE JOHNSON: Well, Jack was a man who was deeply troubled in his relationships with women. The trouble had begun in his early childhood when his brother Gerard died and that overintense relationship developed with his mother. That was a really tough one to get past. She was the big woman in his life. He had a horror of the idea of bringing life into the world because he had seen a child die, that child being his brother. With Buddhism, he was very eloquent on the subject of Buddhism. My own feeling is that he sort of misused Buddhism as a way of rationalizing his deepest hang-ups rather than trying to overcome them, rather than trying to work toward finding a way to have a really strong relationship with a woman apart from his mother, to overcome his horror of bringing children into the world. Buddhism was used to justify all that. I think it sort of added to his confusion. I know that point of view may make me very unpopular, but that's the way I feel.

CAROLYN CASSADY: I would agree with that too. He was pretty escapist in most of his attitudes. I think one of the things he liked about Buddhism was because when he got into sticky situations you could say, "Oh, it's all an illusion." That's how he sort of resolved things. Instead of, as Joyce said, really trying to analyze the problem and overcome it, he just said, "It's not really there." He wasn't very Buddhist about it. He only followed the practices that appealed to him anyhow.

HETTIE JONES: I think in a general way the whole Beat idea and its relationship to Buddhism and its whole place in American society at that time was really an antimaterialist point of view. Buddhism was very attractive to those of us who were disaffected with the organized religion that we were brought up in and wanted to use this little bit of knowledge that we acquired at that time, in a way, to see a more peaceable kingdom. Because we were in the middle of the Cold War, don't forget, and people were setting off nuclear blasts in Nevada. You have to put all this in a context, and so I think that no matter how watered down we approached it, we still made use of the tenets of Buddhism as far as we could.

EILEEN KAUFMAN: There's still a tree in North Beach and we called it our Zen tree and we used to go there, Bob and I. Bob had a different kind of family religion. He was a grandson of a woman who was brought over on a slave ship from the Gold Coast of Africa who practiced lute voodoo. He was the son of a Martinique woman who was a high Catholic and took him to mass on Sunday. The father was then an orthodox Jew, so of course Bob became Zen Buddhist. He had no choice. I mean he's a black Jew, as he says, with Negro stripes. When he took a ten-year vow of silence, he went into it wholeheartedly after some very bad times in New York City. He went into it in 1963 while we were watching Kennedy being assassinated on the tube, and it stayed that way. I would come back from one of the trips I was on, and I ask Bob if he wanted to speak again, and he just shook his head. In 1973 at the end of the Vietnam war, we were at a friend's exhibition in Palo Alto, and that's when he began to speak again. It was forty-five minutes of [T. S. Eliot's] *Murder in the Cathedral* and a poem he had written titled "All of the Ships That Never Sail," and that was his way.

JOANNA McCLURE: Actually I think we were more concerned with new consciousness than with spirituality. The Zen Center was very much around and in our minds and Buddhism was a part of our milieu. It's just that spiritually our concerns were more individual. The people around us of course were bringing in Buddhism, were bringing in Zen. I think mainly there was a dislike of becoming part of any body or group. Having broken away from the conformity of the times, there was not a push to go toward any spiritual practice that had a body around it that would insist on some sort of conformity. So actually it was very individual, a spiritual striving that I still go through, and still haven't made into any one spiritual practice.

ANN CHARTERS: That's my experience also. Women who were attracted, as my husband says, fatally attracted, to Bohemians, as I was also in the 1950s, were not usually attracted to organized religion. We were more interested in a state of consciousness, rather than a sense of spirituality—or we felt that they were one and the same. We felt that consciousness and spirituality were equally sacred.

This panel has run out of time, but if the members of this audience want to hear more on the subject, I invite you to stay for the poetry reading, which will follow in a few minutes. Anne Waldman, associated with the Buddhist practice at the Naropa Institute in Boulder, Colorado, and Diane di Prima, who is also very knowledgeable about Buddhism, will be speaking very shortly. Thank you for coming.

# PART THREE

## Chronology of Selected Books, Magazines, Films, and Recordings Relating to Beat Generation Authors

### (1950–2000)

**1950**
Kerouac, Jack. *The Town and the City*. New York: Harcourt, Brace.
Legman, Gershon, and Jay Landesman, eds. *Neurotica* magazine.

**1951**
Buckley, Richard. "Royal Holiness of the Far Out and Prophet of the Hip,"
    records hipster monologues, including "The Nazz" and "The Hip Gahn"
    to be released as "The Best of Lord Buckley." New York: Elektra long-
    playing record.

**1952**
Holmes, John Clellon. *Go*. New York: Ace Books.
Martin, Peter, and others, eds. *City Lights*. San Francisco: 1952–1955.

**1953**
Burroughs, William S. *Junkie*. New York: Ace Books.

**1954**
Creeley, Robert, ed. *The Black Mountain Review*. Black Mountain, North
    Carolina: 1954–1957.
Williams, William Carlos. *The Desert Music*. New York: Random House.

**1955**
Brossard, Chandler, ed. *The Scene Before You: A New Approach to American
    Culture*. New York: Rinehart & Co.
Corso, Gregory. *The Vestal Lady on Brattle*. Cambridge, Mass.: Richard
    Brukenfeld.
Ferlinghetti, Lawrence. *Pictures of the Gone World*. San Francisco: City
    Lights Books.
Patchen, Kenneth. *Poems of Humor and Protest*. San Francisco: City Lights
    Books.

**1956**
Ginsberg, Allen. *Howl and Other Poems*. San Francisco: City Lights Books.
McClure, Michael. *Passage*. Big Sur, Calif.: Jonathan Williams.

Rexroth, Kenneth. *In Defense of the Earth*. New York: New Directions.
Wilson, Colin. *The Outsider*. Boston: Houghton Mifflin.

**1957**
Kerouac, Jack. *On the Road*. New York: Viking.
Mailer, Norman. *The White Negro: Superficial Reflections on the Hipster*. San Francisco: City Lights Books.

**1958**
Corso, Gregory. *Bomb*. San Francisco: City Lights Books.
———. *Gasoline*. San Francisco: City Lights Books.
di Prima, Diane. *This Kind of Bird Flies Backwards*. New York: Totem Press.
Feldman, Gene, and Max Gartenburg, eds. *The Beat Generation and the Angry Young Men*. New York: Citadel.
Ferlinghetti, Lawrence. *A Coney Island of the Mind*. New York: New Directions.
———. *Tentative Description of a Dinner Given to Promote the Impeachment of President Eisenhower*. San Francisco: Golden Mountain Press.
Frank, Robert, and A. Leslie, directors. *Pull My Daisy*. Narrated by Jack Kerouac, with Gregory Corso, Peter Orlovsky, Larry Rivers, and David Amram. Houston: Houston Museum of Art.
Holmes, John Clellon. *The Horn*. New York: Random House.
Jones, LeRoi, and Hettie Cohen, eds. *Yugen*. New York: 1958–1962.
Kerouac, Jack. *The Dharma Bums*. New York: Viking.
———. *The Subterraneans*. New York: Grove Press.
Micheline, Jack. *River of Red Wine*. New York: Troubadour Press.
Wieners, John. *The Hotel Wentley Poems*. San Francisco: Auerhahn Press.

**1959**
Antoninus, Brother, and Josephine Miles, Michael McClure, Jack Spicer, James Broughton, Robert Duncan, Lawrence Ferlinghetti, Kenneth Rexroth, Philip Whalen, Allen Ginsberg. *San Francisco Poets*. New York: Hanover Records LP.
Burroughs, William S. *Naked Lunch*. Paris: Olympia Press.
Frank, Robert. *The Americans*. Introduction by Jack Kerouac. New York: Grove Press.
Ginsberg, Allen. *Howl and Other Poems*. Notes by Allen Ginsberg. Berkeley, Calif.: Fantasy LP.
Joans, Ted. *Jazz Poems*. New York: Rhino Review.
Kaufman, Bob. *Abomunist Manifesto*. San Francisco: City Lights Books.
Kerouac, Jack. *Doctor Sax: Faust Part Three*. New York: Grove Press.
———. *Maggie Cassidy*. New York: Avon Books.
———. *Mexico City Blues*. New York: Grove Weidenfeld.
———. *Visions of Cody*. New York: New Directions.

———. *Readings on the Beat Generation*. Notes by Bill Randle. New York: Verve Records LP.

———. *Blues and Haikus*. Featuring Al Cohn and Zoot Sims. Notes by Gilbert Millstein. New York: Hanover Records LP.

Kerouac, Jack, and Steve Allen (pianist). *Poetry for the Beat Generation*. Notes by Gilbert Millstein. New York: Hanover Records LP.

Lamantia, Philip. *Ekstasis*. San Francisco: Auerhahn Press.

———. *Narcotica*. San Francisco: Auerhahn Press.

Lipton, Lawrence. *The Holy Barbarians*. New York: Julian Messner.

McClure, Michael. *Hymns to St. Geryon*. San Francisco: Auerhahn Press.

Patchen, Kenneth. *Kenneth Patchen Reads with Jazz in Canada*. Notes by Alan Neil. New York: Folkways Records LP.

Snyder, Gary. *Riprap*. Kyoto: Origin.

Whalen, Philip. *Self-Portrait from Another Direction*. San Francisco: Auerhahn Press.

## 1960

Allen, Donald, ed. *The New American Poetry: 1945–1960*. New York: Grove Press.

*Beatnik: The Magazine for Hipsters*. Includes "Like Special: 18 New Ways to Rebel Against Society" and "Like Extra Special: 100 Crazy New Kicks You Can Get On." *Mad* magazine parody, July 1960.

Blackburn, Paul. *Brooklyn-Manhattan Transit*. New York: Totem Press.

Corso, Gregory. *The Happy Birthday of Death*. New York: New Directions.

Duncan, Robert. *The Opening of the Field*. New York: Grove Press.

Ferlinghetti, Lawrence, ed. *Beatitude Anthology*. San Francisco: City Lights Books.

Fisher, Stanley, ed. *Beat Coast East: An Anthology of Rebellion*. New York: Excelsior Press.

Goodman, Paul. *Growing Up Absurd: Problems of Youth in the Organized Society*. New York: Random House.

Gysin, Brion (with William S. Burroughs, Gregory Corso, and Sinclair Belles). *Minutes to Go*. Paris: Two Cities Editions.

Kerouac, Jack. *Lonesome Traveler*. New York: McGraw-Hill.

———. *The Scripture of the Golden Eternity*. New York: Corinth Books.

———. *Tristessa*. New York: Avon Books.

Krim, Seymour, ed. *The Beats*. Greenwich, Conn.: Fawcett Publications.

McDarrah, Fred W., photographer, Elias Wilentz, ed. *The Beat Scene*. New York: Corinth Books.

O'Hara, Frank. *Second Avenue*. New York: Totem Press.

Snyder, Gary. *Myths and Texts*. New York: Totem Press/Corinth Books.

Trocchi, Alexander. *Cain's Book*. New York: Evergreen Original Novel.

Welch, Lew. *Wobbly Rock*. San Francisco: Auerhahn Press.

Whalen, Philip. *Like I Say*. New York: Totem Press.

————. *Self-Portrait from Another Direction*. San Francisco: Auerhahn Press.

Wilentz, Elias, ed. *The Beat Scene*. New York: Corinth Books.

## 1961

Baro, Gene, ed. *"Beat" Poets*. London: Vista Books.

Burroughs, William. *The Soft Machine*. Paris: Olympia Press.

Corso, Gregory. *The American Express*. Paris: Olympia Press.

di Prima, Diane. *Dinners and Nightmares*. New York: Corinth Books.

di Prima, Diane, and LeRoi Jones, eds. *The Floating Bear*. New York: 1961–1971.

Ehrlich, J. W., ed. *Howl of the Censor*. San Carlos, Calif.: Nourse Publishing Co.

Ferlinghetti, Lawrence. *Starting from San Francisco*. Norfolk, Conn.: New Directions.

Ginsberg, Allen. *Kaddish and Other Poems: 1958–1960*. San Francisco: City Lights Books.

Joans, Ted. *All of Ted Joans and No More: Poems and Collages*. New York: Excelsior Press.

————. *The Hipsters*. New York: Corinth Books.

Jones, LeRoi. *Preface to a Twenty Volume Suicide Note*. New York: Corinth Books.

Kerouac, Jack. *Book of Dreams*. San Francisco: City Lights Books.

————. *Pull My Daisy*. New York: Grove Press.

Krim, Seymour. *Views of a Nearsighted Cannoneer*. New York: Excelsior.

Kupferberg, Tuli. *1001 Ways to Live Without Working*. New York: Birth Press.

Lamantia, Philip. *Destroyed Works*. San Francisco: Auerhahn Press.

McClure, Michael. *Dark Brown*. London: Auerhahn Press.

McClure, Michael, Lawrence Ferlinghetti, David Meltzer, and Gary Snyder, eds. *Journal for the Protection of All Beings*. San Francisco: 1961–1978.

Parkinson, Thomas, ed. *A Casebook on the Beat*. New York: Thomas Y. Crowell Co.

## 1962

Burroughs, William S. *The Ticket That Exploded*. Paris: Olympia Press.

Corso, Gregory. *Long Live Man*. New York: New Directions.

Creeley, Robert. *For Love: Poems 1950–1960*. New York: Scribner.

Kerouac, Jack. *Big Sur*. New York: Farrar, Straus and Cudahy.

Kesey, Ken. *One Flew Over the Cuckoo's Nest*. New York: Viking.

Meltzer, David. *We All Have Something to Say to Each Other*. San Francisco: Auerhahn Press.

## 1963

Burroughs, William S., and Allen Ginsberg. *The Yage Letters*. San Francisco: City Lights Books.

Ginsberg, Allen. *Reality Sandwiches*. San Francisco: City Lights Books.
Jones, LeRoi, ed. *The Moderns: An Anthology of New Writing in America*. New York: Corinth Books.
Kerouac, Jack. *Visions of Gerard*. New York: Farrar, Straus and Cudahy.
McClure, Michael. *Meat Science Essays*. San Francisco: City Lights Books.
Sanders, Ed. *Poem from Jail*. San Francisco: City Lights Books.
Williams, William Carlos. *Paterson*. New York: New Directions.

### 1964
Berrigan, Ted. *The Sonnets*. New York: Lorenz & Ellen Gude.
Burroughs, William S. *Nova Express*. New York: Grove Press.
Holmes, John Clellon. *Get Home Free*. New York: Dutton.
Leary, Timothy, et al. *The Psychedelic Experience*. New York: University Books.
Sanders, Ed. *The Toe Queen Poems*. New York: Fuck You Press.
Whalen, Philip. *On Bear's Head*. New York: Harcourt, Brace, and World.

### 1965
Ferlinghetti, Lawrence. *Where Is Vietnam?* San Francisco: City Lights Books.
Huncke, Herbert. *Huncke's Journal*. New York: Poets Press.
Kaufman, Bob. *Solitudes Crowded with Loneliness*. New York: New Directions.
Kerouac, Jack. *Desolation Angels*. New York: Coward-McCann.
Kupferberg, Tuli. *Kill for Peace*. New York: Birth Press.
Kyger, Joanne. *The Tapestry and the Web*. San Francisco: Four Seasons Foundation.
McClure, Michael. *The Beard*. San Francisco.
Welch, Lew. *Hermit Poems*. San Francisco: Four Seasons Foundation.
———. *On Out*. Berkeley: Oyez.
*Wholly Communion. International Poetry Reading at the Royal Albert Hall*. With poems by Gregory Corso, Lawrence Ferlinghetti, Allen Ginsberg, Andrei Voznesensky, and others. New York: Grove Press.

### 1966
Ginsberg, Allen. *Allen Ginsberg Reads Kaddish: A 20th Century American Ecstatic Narrative Poem*. Notes by Allen Ginsberg. New York: Atlantic Verbum Series LP.
Kandel, Lenore. *The Love Book*. San Francisco: Stolen Paper Review Editions.
Kerouac, Jack. *Satori in Paris*. New York: Grove Press.
Kupferberg, Tuli. *1001 Ways to Beat the Draft*. New York: Birth Press.
Lamantia, Philip. *Touch of the Marvelous*. Berkeley: Oyez.
Leary, Timothy. *Psychedelic Prayers*. New York: Poets Press.
McClure, Michael. *Love Lion Book*. San Francisco: Four Seasons Foundation.
Rexroth, Kenneth. *The Collected Shorter Poems*. New York: New Directions.

Roy, Gregor. *Beat Literature*. New York: Monarch Press.

Snyder, Gary. *A Range of Poems*. London: Fulcrum Press.

Solomon, Carl. *Mishaps, Perhaps*. Edited by Mary Beach. San Francisco: City Lights Books.

### 1967

Charters, Ann. *A Bibliography of Works by Jack Kerouac*. New York: Phoenix Bookshop.

Duncan, Robert. *The Truth and Life of Myth*. New York: House of Books.

Holmes, John Clellon. *Nothing More to Declare*. New York: E. P. Dutton.

Kandel, Lenore. *Word Alchemy*. New York: Grove Press.

Kaufman, Bob. *Golden Sardine*. San Francisco: City Lights Books.

Lamantia, Philip. *Selected Poems*. San Francisco: City Lights Books.

### 1968

Everson, William. *The Residual Years*. New York: New Directions.

Ginsberg, Allen. *Planet News: 1961–1967*. San Francisco: City Lights Books.

Kerouac, Jack. *Vanity of Duluoz*. New York: Coward-McCann.

Pommy Vega, Janine. *Poems to Fernando*. San Francisco: City Lights Books.

Rexroth, Kenneth. *The Collected Longer Poems*. New York: New Directions.

Snyder, Gary. *The Back Country*. New York: New Directions.

Solomon, Carl. *More Mishaps*. San Francisco: City Lights.

### 1969

Bremser, Bonnie. *Troia: Mexican Memoirs*. New York: Croton Press.

di Prima, Diane. *Memoirs of a Beatnik*. New York: Olympia Press.

Ferlinghetti, Lawrence. *Tyrannus Nix?* New York: New Directions.

Joans, Ted. *Black Pow Wow: Jazz Poems*. New York: Hill & Wang.

Kherdian, David. *Six San Francisco Poets*. Fresno, Calif.: Giligia.

McClure, Michael. *Ghost Tantras*. San Francisco: Four Seasons.

*Penguin Modern Poets 13: Charles Bukowski, Philip Lamantia, Harold Norse*. London: Penguin Books.

Snyder, Gary. *Earth House Hold: Technical Notes & Queries to Fellow Dharma Revolutionaries*. New York: New Directions.

Welch, Lew. *The Song Mt. Tamalpais Sings*. San Francisco: Maya.

### 1970

Burroughs, William Jr. *Speed*. London: Olympia Press.

Charters, Ann. *Scenes Along the Road: Photographs of the Desolation Angels 1944–1960*. New York: Portents/Gotham Book Mart.

Corso, Gregory. *Elegiac Feelings American*. New York: New Directions.

Ginsberg, Allen. *Allen Ginsberg/William Blake Songs of Innocence and of Experience by William Blake, tuned by Allen Ginsberg*. Notes by Allen Ginsberg. New York: Verve Forecast, MGM LP.

————. *Indian Journals.* San Francisco: City Lights Books.

Krim, Seymour. *Shake It for the World, Smartass.* New York: Dial Press.

Kyger, Joanne. *Places To Go.* Los Angeles: Black Sparrow.

Odier, Daniel. *The Job: Interviews with W. S. Burroughs.* New York: Grove Press.

Snyder, Gary. *Regarding Wave.* New York: New Directions.

## 1971

Baraka, Amiri. *Dutchman and the Slave.* New York: William Morrow.

Cassady, Neal. *The First Third.* San Francisco: City Lights Books.

Charters, Samuel. *Some Poems/Poets: Studies in American Underground Poetry Since 1945.* Berkeley: Oyez.

Cook, Bruce. *The Beat Generation: The Tumultuous '50s Movement and Its Impact on Today.* New York: Quill/William Morrow.

di Prima, Diane. *Revolutionary Letters.* San Francisco: City Lights Books.

Kerouac, Jack. *Pic.* New York: Grove Press.

————. *Scattered Poems.* San Francisco: City Lights Books.

Meltzer, David, ed. *The San Francisco Poets.* New York: Ballantine Books.

O'Hara, Frank. *Collected Poems.* New York: Alfred Knopf.

Plymell, Charles. *The Last of the Moccasins.* San Francisco: City Lights Books.

Rexroth, Kenneth. *American Poetry in the Twentieth Century.* New York: Herder and Herder.

## 1972

Ginsberg, Allen. *The Fall of America.* San Francisco: City Lights Books.

Wieners, John. *Selected Poems.* London & New York: Cape Goliard/ Grossman.

## 1973

Burroughs, William Jr. *Kentucky Ham.* New York: E. P. Dutton.

Charters, Ann. *Kerouac: A Biography.* San Francisco: Straight Arrow Books.

di Prima, Diane. *Loba: Part I.* Santa Barbara, Calif.: Capra.

di Prima, Diane, and LeRoi Jones, eds. *Floating Bear: A newsletter 1961–1969.* La Jolla, Calif.: Lawrence McGilvery.

Gifford, Barry. *Kerouac's Town.* Santa Barbara, Calif.: Capra.

Kerouac, Jack. *Visions of Cody.* New York: McGraw-Hill Book Co.

Kesey, Ken. *Kesey's Garage Sale.* New York: Viking.

Welch, Lew. *How I Work as a Poet and Other Essays.* San Francisco: Grey Fox.

————. *Ring of Bone.* Bolinas, Calif: Grey Fox.

## 1974

Ferlinghetti, Lawrence. *City Lights Anthology.* San Francisco: City Lights Books.

Ginsberg, Allen. *Allen Verbatim: Lectures on Poetry, Politics, Consciousness.* New York: McGraw-Hill.

Knight, Arthur Winfield, and Glee Knight, eds. *The Beat Book*. California, Pa.: Unspeakable Visions of the Individual.

McClure, Joanna. *Wolf Eyes*. San Francisco: Bearthm Press.

McClure, Michael. *September Blackberries*. New York: New Directions.

Snyder, Gary. *Turtle Island*. New York: New Directions.

### 1975

di Prima, Diane. *Selected Poems: 1956–1975*. Plainfield, Vt.: Atlantic Books.

Green, Martin, ed. *A Kind of Beatness: Photographs of a North Beach Area 1950–1965*. San Francisco: Focus Gallery.

Kyger, Joanne. *All This Every Day*. Berkeley, Calif.: Big Sky.

Le Pellec, Yves, ed. *Beat Generation*. Paris: Edition Subervie.

Perkoff, Stuart. *Love Is the Silence: Poems 1948–1974*. Los Angeles: Red Hill Press.

Sanders, Ed. *Tales of Beatnik Glory*. New York: Stonehill Publishing.

Waldman, Anne. *Fast Talking Woman*. San Francisco: City Lights Books.

### 1976

Cassady, Carolyn. *Heart Beat: My Life with Jack and Neal*. Berkeley, Calif.: Creative Arts Book Co.

Micheline, Jack. *North of Manhattan: Collected Poems, Ballads, and Songs, 1954–1975*. South San Francisco, Calif.: ManRoot.

Tytell, John. *Naked Angels: The Lives & Literature of the Beat Generation*. New York: McGraw-Hill.

Waldman, Anne. *Journals & Dreams*. New York: Stonehill Publishing.

### 1977

Ball, Gordon, ed. *Allen Ginsberg: Journals, Early Fifties, Early Sixties*. New York: Grove Press.

Ginsberg, Allen. *As Ever: The Collected Correspondence of Allen Ginsberg & Neal Cassady*. Berkeley: Creative Arts Books.

Knight, Arthur Winfield, and Kit Knight, eds. *The Beat Diary*. California, Pa.: Unspeakable Visions of the Individual.

Mottram, Eric. *William Burroughs: The Algebra of Need*. London: Marion Boyars.

Snyder, Gary. *Mountains and Rivers Without End*. Washington, D.C.: Counterpoint.

Welch, Lew. *I, Leo: An Unfinished Novel*. San Francisco: Grey Fox.

———. *How I Work as a Poet*. Bolinas, Calif.: Grey Fox Press.

### 1978

Allen, Donald, ed. *Off the Wall: Interviews with Philip Whalen*. Bolinas, Calif.: Four Seasons Foundation.

Bremser, Ray. *Blowing Mouth/The Jazz Poems: 1958–1970*. Cherry Valley, New York: Cherry Valley Editions.

di Prima, Diane. *Loba: Parts I–VII.* Berkeley: Wingbone.

Gifford, Barry, and Lawrence Lee. *Jack's Book.* New York: St. Martin's Press.

Ginsberg, Allen. *Mind Breaths.* San Francisco: City Lights Books.

Knight, Arthur Winfield, and Kit Knight, eds. *The Beat Journey.* California, Pa.: Unspeakable Visions of the Individual.

McClure, Michael. *Antechamber and Other Poems.* New York: New Directions.

Orlovsky, Peter. *Clean Asshole Poems and Smiling Vegetable Songs: Poems 1957–1977.* San Francisco: City Lights Books.

Waldman, Anne, and Marilyn Webb, eds. *Talking Poetics from Naropa Institute, Annals of the Jack Kerouac School of Disembodied Poetics.* 2 vols. Boulder and London: Shambhala Publications.


### 1979

Cherkovski, Neeli. *Ferlinghetti: A Biography.* Garden City, New York: Doubleday and Company.

Ginsberg, Allen. *Two Evenings with Allen Ginsberg, Peter Orlovsky, Gregory Corso, Steven Taylor.* Frankfurt, Germany: Loft LP.

Marshall, Edward. *Leave the Word Alone.* New York: Pequod Press.

McNally, Denis. *Desolate Angel: Jack Kerouac, the Beat Generation, and America.* New York: Dell Publishing.

Saroyan, Aram. *Genesis Angels: The Saga of Lew Welch and the Beat Generation.* New York: William Morrow and Company.

Welch, Lew. *Ring of Bone: Collected Poems 1950–1971.* San Francisco: Grey Fox Press.


### 1980

Burroughs, William S., Kathy Acker, John Ashbery, John Cage, Allen Ginsberg, Patti Smith, Gary Snyder, Andrei Vosnesensky, Anne Waldman, et al. *Sugar, Alcohol, & Meat: The Dial-A-Poem Poets.* New York: Giorno Poetry Systems LP.

Ferlinghetti, Lawrence, and Nancy J. Peters. *Literary San Francisco: A Pictorial History from Its Beginnings to Present Day.* San Francisco: City Lights Books and Harper and Row.

Ginsberg, Allen. *Composed on the Tongue.* Bolinas, Calif.: Grey Fox Press.

Ginsberg, Allen, and Peter Orlovsky. *Straight Heart's Delight: Love Poems and Selected Letters.* San Francisco: Gay Sunshine.

Huncke, Herbert. *The Evening Sun Turned Crimson.* New York: Cherry Valley Editions.

Kesey, Ken. "The Day After Superman Died." *Spit in the Ocean,* no. 6.

Knight, Arthur Winfield, and Kit Knight, eds. *The Unspeakable Visions of the Individual.* California, Pa.: Unspeakable Visions of the Individual.

Kyger, Joanne. *The Wonderful Focus of You.* Calais, Vt.: Z Press.

Snyder, Gary. *The Real Work: Interviews & Talks 1964–1979.* New York: New Directions.

Welch, Lew. *I Remain: The Letters of Lew Welch and the Correspondence of His Friends.* 2 vols. San Francisco: Grey Fox Press.

Whalen, Philip. *The Diamond Noodle.* Berkeley, Calif.: Poltroon.

## 1981

Bartlett, Lee, ed. *The Beats: Essays in Criticism.* Jefferson, N.C.: McFarland.

Corso, Gregory. *Herald of the Autochthonous Spirit.* New York: New Directions.

Ferlinghetti, Lawrence. *Endless Life: Selected Poems.* New York: New Directions.

Ginsberg, Allen. *First Blues, Rags, Ballads and Harmonium Songs.* Recorded by Harry Smith. Notes by Ann Charters. New York: Folkways LP.

Hunt, Tim. *Kerouac's Crooked Road.* Hamden, Conn.: Archon Books.

Kaufman, Bob. *The Ancient Rain: Poems 1956–1978.* Raymond Foye, ed. New York: New Directions.

Kerouac, Jan. *Baby Driver.* New York: St. Martin's Press.

Kyger, Joanne. *Up My Coast.* Pt. Reyes, Calif.: Floating Island.

———. *The Japan and India Journals 1960–1964.* Bolinas, Calif.: Tombouctou.

Landesman, Jay, ed. *Neurotica: The Authentic Voice of the Beat Generation.* London: Jay Landesman, Ltd.

Plummer, William. *The Holy Goof: A Biography of Neal Cassady.* Englewood Cliffs, N.J.: Prentice-Hall.

## 1982

Burroughs, William S. *Letters to Allen Ginsberg: 1953–1957.* New York: Full Court Press.

Ginsberg, Allen. *Plutonian Ode.* San Francisco: City Lights Books.

Knight, Arthur Winfield, and Kit Knight, eds. *Beat Angels.* California, Pa.: Unspeakable Visions of the Individual.

McClure, Michael. *Scratching the Beat Surface.* San Francisco: North Point Press.

Orlovsky, Peter. *Leper's Cry.* New York: Phoenix Bookshop.

Rexroth, Kenneth. *Between Two Wars: Selected Poems Written Prior to the Second World War.* San Francisco: Iris Press.

Snyder, Gary. *Axe Handles.* New York: Farrar, Straus & Giroux.

## 1983

Charters, Ann, ed. *The Beats: Literary Bohemians in Postwar America* (Dictionary of Literary Biography, 16). Detroit: Gale Research Company.

Johnson, Joyce. *Minor Characters.* Boston: Houghton Mifflin Company.

Nicosia, Gerald. *Memory Babe: A Critical Biography of Jack Kerouac.* New York: Grove Press.

Norse, Harold. *Beat Hotel*. San Diego: Atticus.

Olson, Charles. *The Maximus Poems*. George F. Butterick, ed. Berkeley, Calif.: University of California Press.

Smith, Larry, *Lawrence Ferlinghetti: Poet-at-Large*. Carbondale, Ill.: Southern Illinois University Press.

## 1984

Baraka, Amiri. *The Autobiography of LeRoi Jones/Amiri Baraka*. New York: Freundlich Books.

Burroughs, William S., with Daniel Odier. *The Job: Writings and Interviews*. London: Calder.

Chapman, Harold. *The Beat Hotel*. Paris: Gris Banal, Editeur.

Hyde, Lewis, ed. *On the Poetry of Allen Ginsberg*. Ann Arbor: University of Michigan Press.

Knight, Arthur Winfield, and Kit Knight. *The Beat Road*. California, Pa.: Unspeakable Visions of the Individual.

Sanders, Ed, Tuli Kupferberg, Steve Taylor, et al. *The Fugs: Refuse to Be Burnt-out*. Copenhagen, Denmark: Olufsen Records LP.

Snyder, Gary. *Passage Through India*. San Francisco: Grey Fox Press.

## 1985

Antonelli, John, director. *Kerouac*. Beverly Hills, Calif.: Active Home Video.

Brookner, Howard. *Burroughs*. New York: Giorno Video.

Ginsberg, Allen. *Collected Poems 1947–1980*. New York: Harper & Row.

Holmes, John Clellon. *Gone in October: Last Reflections on Jack Kerouac*. Hailey, Idaho: Limberlost Press.

Horemans, Rudi, ed. *Beat Indeed!* Antwerp: Exa Publishers.

McDarrah, Fred W. *Kerouac and Friends: A Beat Generation Album*. New York: William Morrow and Company.

Skerl, Jennie. *William S. Burroughs*. Boston: Twayne.

## 1986

Charters, Ann. *Beats & Company: A Portrait of a Literary Generation*. Garden City, New York: Doubleday and Company.

French, Warren. *Jack Kerouac: Novelist of the Beat Generation*. Boston: Twayne.

Ginsberg, Allen. *Howl: Original Draft Facsimile, Transcript and Variant Versions*. Barry Miles, ed. New York: Harper & Row.

Kerouac, Jack. *Sea*. East Buffalo, New York: East Buffalo Media Association LP.

McClure, Michael. *Selected Poems*. New York: New Directions.

Montgomery, John, ed. *Kerouac at the "Wild Boar" & Other Skirmishes*. San Anselmo, Calif.: Fels & Firn Press.

Sanders, Edward. *Star Peace: A Musical Drama in Three Acts.* Performed by a special, expanded version of The Fugs. Woodstock, New York: P.C.C. Productions, two LPs.

Snyder, Gary. *Left out in the Rain.* Berkeley, Calif.: North Point.

Weinburg, Jeffery H., ed. *Writers Outside the Margin.* Sudbury, Mass.: Water Row Press.

Wieners, John. *Selected Poems: 1958–1984.* Santa Barbara, Calif.: Black Sparrow.

## 1987

Gysin, Brion. *The Third Mind,* with William Burroughs. New York: Seaver.

Holmes, John Clellon. *Displaced Person: The Travel Essays.* Fayetteville: The University of Arkansas Press.

Honan, Park, ed. *The Beats: An Anthology of Beat Writing.* London: J. M. Dent & Sons, Ltd.

Huncke, Herbert. *Guilty of Everything.* Madras and New York: Hanuman Books.

Knight, Arthur Winfield, and Kit Knight, eds. *The Beat Vision: A Primary Sourcebook.* New York: Paragon House Publishers.

Rexroth, Kenneth. *World Outside the Window: Selected Essays.* New York: New Directions.

Weinrich, Regina. *The Spontaneous Prose of Jack Kerouac: A Study of the Fiction.* Carbondale, Ill.: Southern Illinois University Press.

## 1988

Burroughs, William S. *The Western Lands.* New York: Viking Penguin.

Holmes, John Clellon. *Passionate Opinions: The Cultural Essays.* Fayetteville: The University of Arkansas Press.

———. *Representative Men: The Biographical Essays.* Fayetteville: The University of Arkansas Press.

Knight, Arthur Winfield, and Kit Knight, eds. *Kerouac and the Beats: A Primary Sourcebook.* New York: Paragon House Publishers.

Morgan, Ted. *Literary Outlaw: The Life and Times of William S. Burroughs.* New York: Henry Holt and Company.

Wieners, John. *Cultural Affairs in Boston.* Santa Rosa, Calif.: Black Sparrow.

## 1989

Corso, Gregory. *Mindfield: New and Selected Poems.* New York: Thunder's Mouth.

Davidson, Michael. *The San Francisco Renaissance: Poetics and Community at Mid-Century.* New York: Cambridge University Press.

Hickey, Morgen. *The Bohemian Register. An Annotated Bibliography of the Beat Literary Movement.* Metuchen, N.J., and London: The Scarecrow Press.

Koehler, Bradley, and Christopher Hartman-Manapsar. *Queer: A Soundtrack to the Novel by William S. Burroughs*. Brussels, Belgium: Sub Rosa LP.

Kyger, Joanne. *Phenomenological*. Canton, New York: Institute of Further Studies.

Miles, Barry. *Ginsberg: A Biography*. New York: Simon and Schuster.

Sanders, Ed, et al. *The Fugs: Songs from a Portable Forest 1984–1989*. Mansfield Center, Conn.: Gazell Productions CD.

Stephenson, Gregory. *The Daybreak Boys: Essays on the Literature of the Beat Generation*. Carbondale, Ill.: Southern Illinois University Press.

———. *Exiled Angel: A Study of the Work of Gregory Corso*. London: Hearing Eye.

## 1990

Burroughs, William S. *Dead City Radio*. New York: Island CD.

Cassady, Carolyn. *Off the Road: My Years with Cassady, Kerouac, and Ginsberg*. New York: William Morrow and Company.

Chiasson, Hermenegilde, director. *Jack Kerouac's Road*. Quebec: National Film Board of Canada video.

di Prima, Diane. *Pieces of a Song: Selected Poems*. San Francisco: City Lights Books.

French, Warren. *The San Francisco Poetry Renaissance: 1955–1960*. Boston: Twayne Publishers.

Ginsberg, Allen. *Allen Ginsberg: Photographs*. Altadena, Calif.: Twelvetrees Press.

———. *Howl, U.S.A.* Read by Allen Ginsberg and performed by the Kronos Quartet. New York: Nonsuch Records CD.

*The Jack Kerouac Collection*. Produced by James Austin. Santa Monica, Calif.: Rhino Records.

Jones, Hettie. *How I Became Hettie Jones*. New York: E. P. Dutton & Company.

Maynard, John Arthur. *Venice West: The Beat Generation in Southern California*. New Brunswick, N.J., and London: Rutgers University Press.

Sanders, Ed. *Tales of Beatnik Glory*. New York: Carol Publishing.

Silesky, Barry. *Ferlinghetti: The Artist in His Time*. New York: Warner Books.

Snyder, Gary. *The Practice of the Wild*. New York: Farrar, Straus & Giroux.

Solnit, Rebecca. *Secret Exhibition: Six California Artists of the Cold War Era*. San Francisco: City Lights Books.

## 1991

Baraka, Amiri. *The LeRoi Jones/Amiri Baraka Reader*. William J. Harris, ed. New York: Thunder's Mouth.

Bartlett, Lee, ed. *Kenneth Rexroth and James Laughlin: Selected Letters*. New York: W. W. Norton & Co.

Burroughs, William S. *Naked Scientology, Ali's Smile*. New York: Left Bank.

Charters, Ann, ed. *The Portable Beat Reader.* New York: Viking.

Cook, Ralph T. *City Lights Books: A Descriptive Bibliography.* Metuchen, N.J., and London: The Scarecrow Press.

Foster, Edward Halsey. *Understanding the Beats.* Columbia: University of South Carolina Press.

Halper, Jon, ed. *Gary Snyder: Dimensions of a Life.* San Francisco: Sierra Club Books.

Hamalian, Linda. *A Life of Kenneth Rexroth.* New York: W. W. Norton & Co.

Kyger, Joanne. *Just Space: Poems 1979–1989.* Santa Rosa, Calif.: Black Sparrow Press.

McClure, Michael. *Rebel Lions.* New York: New Directions.

Skerl, Jennie, and Robin Lydenberg. *William S. Burroughs at the Front.* Carbondale, Ill.: Southern Illinois University Press.

**1992**

*The Beat Generation* (cassette). Produced by James Austin. Santa Monica, Calif.: Rhino Records.

Berman, Wallace. *Support the Revolution.* Amsterdam: Institute of Contemporary Art.

Burroughs, William S. *Nova Express.* New York: Grove-Atlantic.

———. *Port of Saints.* Berkeley: Blue Wind.

———. *The Wild Boys: A Book of the Dead.* New York: Grove-Atlantic.

Charters, Ann. *The Portable Beat Reader.* New York: Penguin Books.

Jones, James T. *A Map of Mexico City Blues: Jack Kerouac as Poet.* Carbondale, Ill.: Southern Illinois University Press.

Kerouac, Jack. *Pomes All Sizes.* San Francisco: City Lights Books.

Miles, Barry. *William Burroughs: El Hombre Invisible: A Portrait.* New York: Hyperion.

Murphy, Patrick D. *Understanding Gary Snyder.* Columbia: University of South Carolina Press.

Schumacher, Michael. *Dharma Lion: A Critical Biography of Allen Ginsberg.* New York: St. Martin's Press.

Snyder, Gary. *No Nature: New and Selected Poems.* New York: Pantheon Books.

Waldman, Anne, ed. *Out of This World: An Anthology of Writing from the St. Marks Poetry Project 1966–1991.* New York: Crown.

**1993**

Broyard, Anatole. *Kafka Was the Rage: A Greenwich Village Memoir.* New York: Crown Publishers.

Burroughs, William S. *Letters 1945–1959.* Oliver Harris, ed. New York: Viking.

Cassady, Neal. *Grace Beats Karma: Letters from Prison 1958–60.* Foreword and Notes by Carolyn Cassady. New York: Blast Books.

Ferlinghetti, Lawrence. *These Are My Rivers: New and Selected Poems 1955–1993*. New York: New Directions.

Ginsberg, Allen. *Snapshot Poetics: Allen Ginsberg's Photographic Memoir of the Beat Era*. San Francisco: Chronicle Books.

Gooch, Brad. *City Poet: The Life and Times of Frank O'Hara*. New York: Alfred A. Knopf.

Harris, Oliver, ed. *The Letters of William Burroughs 1945–1959*. New York: Viking Penguin.

*Howls, Raps & Roars: Recording from the San Francisco Poetry Renaissance* (CD). Compiled by Ann Charters. Berkeley, Calif.: Fantasy Records.

Kerouac, Jack. *Good Blonde & Others*. San Francisco: Grey Fox Press.

———. *Old Angel Midnight*. San Francisco: Grey Fox Press.

McClure, Michael. *Lighting the Corners: On Art, Nature, and the Visionary: Essays and Interviews*. Albuquerque: University of New Mexico College of Arts and Sciences.

Sanders, Edward. *Hymn to the Rebel Cafe*. Santa Rosa, Calif.: Black Sparrow Press.

Snyder, Gary, and the Paul Winter Consort (cassette). *Turtle Island*. Litchfield, Conn.: Earth Music Productions.

Waits, Tom, and William S. Burroughs. *The Black Rider*. New York: Island CD.


## 1994

Ginsberg, Allen. *Cosmopolitan Greetings: Poems 1986–1992*. New York: HarperCollins Publishers.

———. *Holy Soul Jelly Roll: Poems and Songs 1949–1993* (CD). Produced by Hal Willner. Santa Monica, Calif.: Rhino Records.

McClure, Michael. *Scratching the Beat Surface: Essays on New Vision from Blake to Kerouac*. New York: Penguin Books.

Sheehan, Aurelie. *Jack Kerouac Is Pregnant: Stories*. Normal, Ill.: Dalkey Archive.

Waldman, Anne. *Kill or Cure*. New York: Penguin Books.

Waldman, Anne, and Andrew Schelling, eds. *Disembodied Poetics: Annals of the Jack Kerouac School*. Albuquerque: University of New Mexico Press.

Weissner, Carl. *Burroughs: Eine Bild-Biographie*. Berlin: NiSHEN.


## 1995

Baraka, Amiri. *Transbluescency: Selected Poems 1961–1995*. New York: Marsilio.

Burroughs, William S. *My Education: A Book of Dreams*. New York: Viking.

Charters, Ann. *The Portable Jack Kerouac*. New York: Penguin Books.

———, ed. *Jack Kerouac: Selected Letters 1940–1956*. New York: Viking Penguin.

Ginsberg, Allen. *Journals Mid-Fifties: 1954–1958.* New York: HarperCollins Publishers.

Kerouac, Jack. *San Francisco Blues.* New York: Penguin Books.

Lombreglia, Ralph, and Kate Bernhardt. *A Jack Kerouac ROMnibus.* Chapel Hill, N.C.: Mind in Motion, and New York: Penguin Books.

Morgan, Bill. *The Works of Allen Ginsberg 1941–1994: A Descriptive Bibliography.* Westport, Conn.: Greenwood Press.

Snyder, Gary. *A Place in Space.* Washington, D.C.: Counterpoint.

Tonkinson, Carole, ed. *Big Sky Mind: Buddhism and the Beat Generation.* New York: Riverhead Books.

Watson, Steven. *The Birth of the Beat Generation: Visionaries, Rebels, and Hipsters.* New York: Pantheon Books.

## 1996

Cherkovski, Neeli. *Elegy for Bob Kaufman.* Northville, Mich.: Sun Dog Press.

Ginsberg, Allen. *Selected Poems 1947–1995.* New York: HarperCollins Publishers.

Ginsberg, Allen, Paul McCartney, Philip Glass, and Lenny Kaye. *The Ballad of the Skeletons.* New York: Mercury Records CD.

Kaufman, Bob. *Cranial Guitar.* Minneapolis: Coffee House.

Knight, Brenda, ed. *Women of the Beat Generation.* Berkeley, Calif.: Conari Press.

Lee, A. Robert, ed. *The Beat Generation Writers.* East Haven, Conn.: Pluto Press.

McDarrah, Fred W., and Gloria S. McDarrah. *Beat Generation: Glory Days in Greenwich Village.* New York: Schirmer Books.

Morgan, Bill. *The Response to Allen Ginsberg 1926–1994: A Bibliography of Secondary Sources.* Westport, Conn.: Greenwood Press.

Natsoulas, John, et al. *The Beat Generation Galleries and Beyond.* Davis, Calif.: John Natsoulas Press.

Pacifico, Massimo, and Silvestro Serra. *Lowell, Massachusetts: Where Jack Kerouac's Road Begins/The Origin of an American Myth.* Florence, Italy: Fos.

Phillips, Lisa, ed. *Beat Culture and the New America: 1950–1965.* New York: Whitney Museum of American Art.

Snyder, Gary. *Mountains and Rivers Without End.* Washington, D.C.: Counterpoint.

Sobieszek, Robert A. *Ports of Entry: William S. Burroughs and the Arts.* Los Angeles: Los Angeles County Museum of Art.

Talbot, Ashleigh. *Beat Speak: An Illustrated Beat Glossary Circa 1956–1959.* Sudbury, Mass.: Water Row Press.

Turner, Steve. *Jack Kerouac: Angelheaded Hipster.* New York: Viking.

Waldman, Anne, ed. *The Beat Book: Writings from the Beat Generation.* Boston: Shambhala Publications.

Welch, Lew. *How I Read Gertrude Stein.* San Francisco: Grey Fox Press.

Whalen, Philip. *Canoeing Up Carbarga Creek: Buddhist Poems 1955–1986.* Berkeley, Calif.: Parallax Press.

Workman, Chuck, director. *The Source.* With performance sequences by Johnny Depp, Dennis Hopper, and John Turturro. New York: Calliope video.

## 1997

Cregg, Magda, ed. *Hey Lew: Homage to Lew Welch.* Bolinas, Calif.

Ferlinghetti, Lawrence. *A Far Rockaway of the Heart.* New York: New Directions.

Kerouac, Jack. *Some of the Dharma.* New York: Viking.

Morgan, Bill. *The Beat Generation in New York: A Walking Tour of Jack Kerouac's City.* San Francisco: City Lights Books.

Murphy, Timothy S. *Wising Up the Marks: The Amodern William Burroughs.* Berkeley: University of California Press.

Peabody, Richard. *A Different Beat: Writings by Women of the Beat Generation.* London: Serpent's Tail.

Sanders, Edward. *1968: A History in Verse.* Santa Rosa, Calif.: Black Sparrow Press.

Sargeant, Jack. *The Naked Lens: An Illustrated History of Beat Cinema.* London: Creation Books.

Schafer, Ben, ed. *The Herbert Huncke Reader.* New York: William Morrow and Co.

Vazakas, Laki, director. *Huncke and Louis.* Pittsfield, Mass.: Video.

## 1998

Burroughs, William S. *Word Virus.* James Grauerholz and Ira Silverberg, eds. New York: Grove Press.

Caveney, Graham. *Gentleman Junkie: The Life and Legacy of William S. Burroughs.* Boston: Little, Brown.

Christy, Jim. *The Long Slow Death of Jack Kerouac.* Toronto: ECW Press.

Clay, Steven, and Rodney Phillips. *A Secret Location on the Lower East Side.* New York: The New York Public Library and Granary Books.

di Prima, Diane. *Loba.* New York: Penguin Books.

Ellingham, Lewis, and Kevin Killian. *Poet Be Like God: Jack Spicer and the San Francisco Renaissance.* Hanover, N.H.: University Press of New England.

Forman, Janet, film director and producer. *The Beat Generation.* New York: Fox Lorber Video.

Lawlor, William. *The Beat Generation: A Bibliographical Teaching Guide.* Lanham, Md.: The Scarecrow Press.

*The Silent Beat. Discourse: Theoretical Studies in Media and Culture.* No. 20.1 & 2 (Winter and Spring, 1998).

Sterritt, David. *Mad to Be Saved: The Beats, the '50s, and Film*. Carbondale, Ill.: Southern Illinois University Press.

The Unbearables. *Crimes of the Beats*. Brooklyn, New York: Autonomedia.

1999

Briggs, Robert. *Poetry and the 1950s: Homage to the Beat Generation*. Sky Society CD.

Campbell, James. *This Is the Beat Generation: New York—San Francisco—Paris*. London: Secker & Warburg.

Caveney, Graham. *Screaming with Joy: The Life of Allen Ginsberg*. London: Bloomsbury.

Charters, Ann, ed. *Jack Kerouac Selected Letters 1957–1969*. New York: Viking.

Cherkovski, Neeli. *Whitman's Wild Children: Portraits of Twelve Poets*. South Royalton, Vt.: Steerforth Press.

Coolidge, Clark. *Now It's Jazz: Writings on Kerouac and the Sounds*. Albuquerque: Living Batch Press.

Edington, Stephen D. *Kerouac's Nashua Connection*. Nashua, N.H.

Forte, Robert, ed. *Timothy Leary: Outside Looking In*. Rochester, Vt: Park Street Press.

George-Warren, Holly, ed. *The Rolling Stone Book of the Beats*. New York: Hyperion.

Ginsberg, Allen. *Death & Fame: Poems 1993–1997*. New York: HarperFlamingo.

Joans, Ted. *Teducation: Selected Poems 1949–1999*. Minneapolis, Minn: Coffee House Press.

Jones, James T. *Jack Kerouac's Duluoz Legend: The Mythic Form of an Autobiographical Fiction*. Carbondale, Ill.: Southern Illinois University Press.

Jones, Jim. *Use My Name: Jack Kerouac's Forgotten Families*. Toronto: ECW Press.

Kaufman, Alan, ed. *The Outlaw Bible of American Poetry*. New York: Thunder's Mouth Press.

Kerouac, Jack. *Atop an Underwood: Early Stories and Other Writings*. Paul Marion, ed. New York: Viking.

McClure, Michael. *Huge Dreams: San Francisco and Beat Poems*. New York: Penguin.

———. *Rain Mirror: New Poems*. New York: New Directions.

———. *Touching the Edge: Dharma Devotions from the Hummingbird Sangha*. Boston: Shambhala.

Plimpton, George, ed. *Beat Writers at Work: The* Paris Review *Interviews*. New York: The Modern Library.

Sandison, David. *Jack Kerouac: An Illustrated Biography*. Chicago: Chicago Review Press.

Skau, Michael. *A Clown in a Grave: Complexities and Tensions in the Works of Gregory Corso*. Carbondale, Ill.: Southern Illinois University Press.

Snyder, Gary. *The Gary Snyder Reader: Prose, Poetry, and Translations*. Washington, D.C.: Counterpoint.

Swartz, Omar. *The View from On the Road: The Rhetorical Vision of Jack Kerouac*. Carbondale, Ill.: Southern Illinois University Press.

Tytell, John. *Paradise Outlaws: Remembering the Beats*. New York: William Morrow and Co.

Whalen, Philip. *Overtime: Selected Poems*. New York: Penguin.


2000

Ginsberg, Allen. *Deliberate Prose: Selected Essays 1952–1995*. Bill Morgan, ed. New York: HarperCollins Publishers.

Ginsberg, Allen, ed., with Andy Clausen and Eliot Katz. *Poems for the Nation: A Collection of Contemporary Political Poems*. New York: Seven Stories Press.

Grauerholz, James, ed. *Last Words: The Final Journals of William S. Burroughs*. New York: Grove Press.

Johnson, Joyce. *Door Wide Open: Jack Kerouac and Joyce Johnson: A Beat Love Affair in Letters, 1957–1958*. New York: Viking.

Kerouac, Joan. *Nobody's Wife*. Berkeley, Calif.: Creative Arts Book Co.

Lardas, John. *The Bop Apocalypse: The Religious Visions of Kerouac, Ginsberg, and Burroughs*. Carbondale, Ill.: University of Illinois Press.

Sanders, Edward. *America: A History in Verse. Volume 1 1900–1939*. Santa Rosa, Calif.: Black Sparrow Press.

————. *The Poetry and Life of Allen Ginsberg: A Narrative Poem*. Woodstock, N.Y.: Overlook Press.

*Teaching Beat Literature. College Literature*. Special Issue 27.1 (Winter 2000).

Theado, Matt. *Understanding Jack Kerouac*. Columbia: University of South Carolina Press.

Waldman, Anne. *Marriage: A Sentence*. New York: Penguin.

# SELECTED BIBLIOGRAPHY

*Beatitude Anthology.* San Francisco: City Lights Books, 1960.

Bergé, Carol. "Picketing the Zeitgeist: A Dissenting Opinion." *American Book Review.* July–August 2000.

Breslin, James E. B. *From Modern to Contemporary: American Poetry 1945–1965.* Chicago: University of Chicago Press, 1984.

Brossard, Chandler, ed. *The Scene Before You: A New Approach to American Culture.* New York: Rinehart & Co., 1955.

Burroughs, William S. *Word Virus.* Edited by James Grauerholz and Ira Silverberg. New York: Grove Press, 1998.

Charters, Ann, ed. *The Beats: Literary Bohemians in Postwar America.* Dictionary of Literary Biography, vol. 16. Detroit: Gale Research Co., 1983.

————, ed. *The Portable Beat Reader.* New York: Penguin, 1992.

————, ed. *The Portable Jack Kerouac.* New York: Penguin, 1995.

Clay, Steven, and Rodney Phillips. *A Secret Location on the Lower East Side: Adventures in Writing, 1960–1980.* New York: The New York Public Library and Granary Books, 1998.

Davidson, Michael. *The San Francisco Renaissance.* Cambridge: Cambridge University Press, 1989.

Ellingham, Lewis, and Kevin Killian. *Poet Be Like God: Jack Spicer and the San Francisco Renaissance.* Hanover, N.H.: University Press of New England, 1998.

Everson, William. *Earth Poetry: Selected Essays and Interviews.* Edited by Lee Bartlett. Berkeley, Calif.: Oyez, 1980.

Feldman, Gene, and Max Gartenberg, eds. *The Beat Generation and the Angry Young Men.* New York: Citadel Press, 1958.

Ferlinghetti, Lawrence. "It's Time for a Populist Laureate." *San Francisco Chronicle Book Review,* October 22–28, 2000.

Foley, Jack. "Beat." *Discourse* 20.1 & 2 (Winter and Spring, 1998).

Friedman, Amy L. " 'Being There as Hard as I Could': Beat Generation Women Writers." *Discourse* 20.1 & 2 (Winter and Spring, 1998).

George-Warren, Holly, ed. *The Rolling Stone Book of the Beats: The Beat Generation and American Culture.* New York: Hyperion, 1999.

Ginsberg, Allen. *Deliberate Prose: Selected Essays 1952–1995.* Edited by Bill Morgan. New York: HarperCollins, 2000. (Contains "The 6 Gallery Reading.")

Goodman, Paul. *Growing Up Absurd: Problems of Youth in the Organized Society.* New York: Random House, 1960.

Hamalian, Linda. *A Life of Kenneth Rexroth.* New York: Norton, 1991.

Johnson, Joyce. "Letters from Jack." *Vanity Fair.* June 2000.

Kaufman, Alan, ed. *The Outlaw Bible of American Poetry.* New York: Thunder's Mouth Press, 1999.

Knight, Brenda, ed. *Women of the Beat Generation.* Berkeley, Calif.: Conari Press, 1996.

Krim, Seymour. *The Beats.* Greenwich, Conn.: Fawcett Publications, 1960.

Lawlor, William. *The Beat Generation: A Bibliographical Teaching Guide.* Lanham, Md.: Scarecrow Press, 1998.

Lee, A. Robert, ed. *The Beat Generation Writers.* London: Pluto Press, 1996.

Meltzer, David, ed. *Reading Jazz.* San Francisco: Mercury House, 1993.

———, ed. *The San Francisco Poets.* New York: Ballantine Books, 1971.

Miller, Douglas T., and Marion Nowak. *The Fifties: The Way We Really Were.* Garden City, New York: Doubleday, 1977.

Morgan, Ted. *Literary Outlaw: The Life and Times of William S. Burroughs.* 1988; reprint, New York: Avon Books, 1990.

Murphy, Patrick D. *Understanding Gary Snyder.* Columbia: University of South Carolina Press, 1992.

Natsoulas, John, et al. *The Beat Generation Galleries and Beyond.* Davis, Calif.: John Natsoulas Press, 1996.

Odier, Daniel. *The Job: Interviews with William S. Burroughs.* New York: Grove Press, 1970.

Paley, Grace. "A Conversation with Ann Charters." *The American Short Story and Its Writer,* edited by Ann Charters. Boston: Bedford/St. Martin's, 2000.

Parkinson, Thomas, ed. *A Casebook on the Beat.* New York: Thomas Y. Crowell, 1961.

———. *Poets, Poems, Movements.* Ann Arbor, Mich.: University of Michigan Research Press, 1987.

Passaro, Vince. "The Forgotten Killer: William S. Burroughs." *Harper's Magazine.* April 1998.

Peabody, Richard, ed. *A Different Beat: Writings by Women of the Beat Generation.* London: Serpent's Tail, 1997.

Plimpton, George, ed. *Beat Writers at Work: "The Paris Review" Interviews.* New York: The Modern Library, 1999.

Pynchon, Thomas. *Slow Learner.* Boston: Little, Brown, 1984.

Schumacher, Michael. *Dharma Lion: A Critical Biography of Allen Ginsberg.* New York: St. Martin's Press, 1992.

Skerl, Jennie, and Robin Lydenberg, eds. *William S. Burroughs at the Front: Critical Reception 1959–1989.* Carbondale, Ill.: Southern Illinois University Press, 1991.

Smith, Richard Candida. *Utopia and Dissent: Art, Poetry, and Politics in California.* Berkeley: University of California Press, 1995.

Snyder, Gary. *The Gary Snyder Reader: Prose, Poetry, and Translations 1952–1998.* Washington, D.C.: Counterpoint, 1999.

Solnit, Rebecca. *Secret Exhibition: Six California Artists of the Cold War Era.* San Francisco: City Lights Books, 1990.

Tytell, John. *Paradise Outlaws: Remembering the Beats.* New York: William Morrow, 1999.

Waldman, Anne, ed. *The Beat Book.* Boston: Shambhala Publications, 1996.

Watson, Steven. *The Birth of the Beat Generation: Visionaries, Rebels, and Hipsters, 1944–1960.* New York: Pantheon Books, 1995.

Wilentz, Elias, ed. *The Beat Scene.* New York: Corinth Books, 1960.

Wolf, Daniel, and Edwin Fancher. *The Village Voice Reader: A Mixed Bag from the Greenwich Village Newspaper.* New York: Grove Press, 1962.

*Eileen Kaufman:* From *Who Wouldn't Walk with Tigers?* © 1983 by Eileen Kaufman. Reprinted by permission of the author.

*Alfred Kazin:* "He's Just Wild About Writing" © 1971 by The New York Times Co. Reprinted by permission of The New York Times News Services Division.

*Joan Haverty Kerouac:* Chapter 17 from *Nobody's Wife* © 2000 by Joan Haverty Kerouac. Used by permission of Creative Arts Book Company.

*Ken Kesey:* I Ching forecast for Ann Charters used by permission of Ken Kesey.

*Joanne Kyger:* "Tapestry," "It Is lonely," and "My Father Died This Spring" were published in *The Tapestry and the Web* (1965) by the Four Seasons Foundation Press. Copyright © 1965 by Joanne Kyger. Used by permission of the author.

*Wayne Lawson:* "The Beats" in the *Encyclopedia Americana 1958 Annual.* Copyright © 1958 by the Encyclopedia Americana. Used by permission of Grolier Educational.

*A. Robert Lee:* "Black Beats" © 1996 by A. Robert Lee. Used by permission of the author.

*Norman Mailer:* "Hipster and Beatnik" © 1959 by Norman Mailer. Used by permission of the author.

*Edward Marshall:* "Leave the Word Alone" © 1957 by Edward Marshall. Used by permission of the author.

*Ian Marshall:* "Where the Open Road Meets Howl" from *Story Line: Exploring the Literature of the Appalachian Trail* © 1998 by the Rector and Visitors of the University of Virginia. Used by permission of the University Press of Virginia, Charlottesville, VA.

*Mary McCarthy:* "Review of Burroughs' *Naked Lunch*" from *The Writing on the Wall and Other Literary Essays*" © 1963 by Harcourt, Inc. and renewed 1991 by James Raymond West. Reprinted by permission of the publisher.

*Joanna McClure:* "1957," "A Letter to My Daughter Who Will Be Four Years Old," "The Hunt," and "Piece" © 2001 Joanna McClure. Used by permission of the author.

*Michael McClure:* "Poetry of the 6" originally published in *The Beat Generation Galleries and Beyond* (Davis, CA: John Natsoulas, 1996). Copyright © 1996 by Michael McClure. Used by permission of the author.

*Fred McDarrah:* "Anatomy of a Beatnik" © 1960 by Fred McDarrah. Used by permission of the author.

*David Meltzer:* From *Beat Thing* and "Poetry and Jazz" © 2001 by David Meltzer. Used by permission of the author.

*Henry Miller:* Preface to Kerouac's *The Subterraneans* © 1959 by Henry Miller. Used by permission of Valentine Miller and the Henry Miller estate.

*Gilbert Millstein:* Review of Kerouac's *On the Road* © 1957 by The New York

Times. Used by permission of The New York Times News Services Division.

*Czelaw Milosz:* "To Allen Ginsberg" from *Facing the River: New Poems* by Czelaw Milosz. Copyright © 1995 by Czelaw Milosz. Reprinted by permission of HarperCollins Publishers, Inc.

*Joyce Carol Oates:* "Down the Road" originally published in *The New Yorker* on March 27, 1995, and collected in *Where I've Been and Where I'm Going: Collected Essays* by Joyce Carol Oates. Copyright © 1999, The Ontario Review, Inc. Used by permission of the author.

*Paul O'Neil:* "The Only Rebellion Around" appeared in *Life* magazine on November 30, 1959. Copyright © Time Inc. Reprinted by permission.

*Peter Orlovsky:* "Collaboration: Letter to Charlie Chaplin" is reprinted by permission of the author.

*Grace Paley:* "A Conversation with My Father" from *Enormous Changes at the Last Minute* (1974). Reprinted by permission of Farrar, Straus, and Giroux.

*Thomas Parkinson:* "The Beat Writers: Phenomenon or Generation" from *A Casebook on the Beat* (1961). Copyright © 1961 by Thomas Parkinson. Reprinted by permission of the author's estate.

*Daniel Pinchbeck:* "Children of the Beats" © 1995 by Daniel Pinchbeck. Reprinted by permission of the author.

*Norman Podhoretz:* "The Know-Nothing Bohemians" © 1958 by Norman Podhoretz. Reprinted by permission of Norman Podhoretz and Writers' Representatives Inc. First published in *Partisan Review,* Spring 1958.

*Kenneth Rexroth:* "Disengagement: The Art of the Beat Generation" © 1957 by Kenneth Rexroth. Used by permission of the Kenneth Rexroth Trust.

*Edward Sanders:* "Thirsting for Peace in a Raging Century" used by permission of the author.

*Gary Snyder:* "Notes on the Beat Generation" and "The New Wind" from *A Place in Space* by Gary Snyder. Copyright © 1995 by Gary Snyder. Reprinted by permission of Counterpoint Press, a member of Perseus Books, LLC.

*Gary Snyder:* "Buddhism and the Possibilities of a Planetary Culture" from *Earth House Hold* by Gary Snyder. Copyright © 1969 by Gary Snyder. Reprinted by permission of New Directions Publishing Corp.

*Gary Snyder:* "Preface to the Poems of Han-Shan" and selections from "Cold Mountain Poems" from *Riprap and Cold Mountain Poems* by Gary Snyder. Copyright © 1990 by Gary Snyder. Reprinted by permission of North Point Press, a division of Farrar, Straus and Giroux, LLC.

*Jack Spicer:* "Song for Bird and Myself" copyright © 1975 by the Estate of Jack Spicer. Reprinted from *The Collected Books of Jack Spicer* with the permission of Black Sparrow Press.

*Robert Stone:* "American Dreamers: Melville and Kerouac" © 1997 by The New York Times Co. Reprinted by permission.

# FOR THE BEST IN PAPERBACKS, LOOK FOR THE

In every corner of the world, on every subject under the sun, Penguin represents quality and variety—the very best in publishing today.

For complete information about books available from Penguin—including Puffins, Penguin Classics, and Compass—and how to order them, write to us at the appropriate address below. Please note that for copyright reasons the selection of books varies from country to country.

**In the United Kingdom:** Please write to *Dept. EP, Penguin Books Ltd, Bath Road, Harmondsworth, West Drayton, Middlesex UB7 0DA.*

**In the United States:** Please write to *Penguin Putnam Inc., P.O. Box 12289 Dept. B, Newark, New Jersey 07101-5289* or call *1-800-788-6262.*

**In Canada:** Please write to *Penguin Books Canada Ltd, 10 Alcorn Avenue, Suite 300, Toronto, Ontario M4V 3B2.*

**In Australia:** Please write to *Penguin Books Australia Ltd, P.O. Box 257, Ringwood, Victoria 3134.*

**In New Zealand:** Please write to *Penguin Books (NZ) Ltd, Private Bag 102902, North Shore Mail Centre, Auckland 10.*

**In India:** Please write to *Penguin Books India Pvt Ltd, 11 Panchsheel Shopping Centre, Panchsheel Park, New Delhi 110 017.*

**In the Netherlands:** Please write to *Penguin Books Netherlands bv, Postbus 3507, NL-1001 AH Amsterdam.*

**In Germany:** Please write to *Penguin Books Deutschland GmbH, Metzlerstrasse 26, 60594 Frankfurt am Main.*

**In Spain:** Please write to *Penguin Books S. A., Bravo Murillo 19, 1° B, 28015 Madrid.*

**In Italy:** Please write to *Penguin Italia s.r.l., Via Benedetto Croce 2, 20094 Corsico, Milano.*

**In France:** Please write to *Penguin France, Le Carré Wilson, 62 rue Benjamin Baillaud, 31500 Toulouse.*

**In Japan:** Please write to *Penguin Books Japan Ltd, Kaneko Building, 2-3-25 Koraku, Bunkyo-Ku, Tokyo 112.*

**In South Africa:** Please write to *Penguin Books South Africa (Pty) Ltd, Private Bag X14, Parkview, 2122 Johannesburg.*